A TEXT BOOK OF
GEOTECHNICAL ENGINEERING

FOR
SEMESTER - I

SECOND YEAR DEGREE COURSE IN CIVIL ENGINEERING

**Strictly According to New Revised Credit System Syllabus
of Savitribai Phule Pune University**
(w.e.f June 2016)

V. R. PHADKE
M.E. (Civil)
Formerly Professor Civil Engg. Deptt.,
Rajashri Shahu College of Engineering,
Tathawade, Pune .

Dr. R. K. JAIN
M.E. (Civil), Ph.D.
Principal,
Rajashri Shahu College of Engineering,
Tathawade, Pune.

Mrs. S. S. JAIN
M.E. (Civil)
Asst. Prof., Civil Engg. Deptt.
Sinhgad College of Engineering,
Vadgaon (Bk), Pune

Dr. R. R. SORATE
M.Tech (Geotech.) P.h.D.
Asso. Prof. & Head, Civil Engg. Deptt.,
Sinhgad Academy of Engineering
Kondhawa, Pune.

N3529

GEOTECHNICAL ENGINEERING (SE CIVIL)   **ISBN 978-93-86084-03-3**

Second Edition   :   June 2017

©   :   **Authors**

Published By :   **Polyplate**

NIRALI PRAKASHAN

Abhyudaya Pragati, 1312, Shivaji Nagar,
Off J.M. Road, Pune – 411005
Tel - (020) 25512336/37/39, Fax - (020) 25511379
Email : niralipune@pragationline.com

☞ **DISTRIBUTION CENTRES**

PUNE

Nirali Prakashan : 119, Budhwar Peth, Jogeshwari Mandir Lane, Pune 411002, Maharashtra
Tel : (020) 2445 2044, 66022708, Fax : (020) 2445 1538
Email : bookorder@pragationline.com, niralilocal@pragationline.com

Nirali Prakashan : S. No. 28/27, Dhyari, Near Pari Company, Pune 411041
Tel : (020) 24690204 Fax : (020) 24690316
Email : dhyari@pragationline.com, bookorder@pragationline.com

MUMBAI

Nirali Prakashan : 385, S.V.P. Road, Rasdhara Co-op. Hsg. Society Ltd.,
Girgaum, Mumbai 400004, Maharashtra
Tel : (022) 2385 6339 / 2386 9976, Fax : (022) 2386 9976
Email : niralimumbai@pragationline.com

☞ **DISTRIBUTION BRANCHES**

JALGAON

Nirali Prakashan : 34, V. V. Golani Market, Navi Peth, Jalgaon 425001,
Maharashtra, Tel : (0257) 222 0395, Mob : 94234 91860

KOLHAPUR

Nirali Prakashan : New Mahadvar Road, Kedar Plaza, 1st Floor Opp. IDBI Bank
Kolhapur 416 012, Maharashtra. Mob : 9850046155

NAGPUR

Pratibha Book Distributors : Above Maratha Mandir, Shop No. 3, First Floor,
Rani Jhanshi Square, Sitabuldi, Nagpur 440012, Maharashtra
Tel : (0712) 254 7129

DELHI

Nirali Prakashan : 4593/21, Basement, Aggarwal Lane 15, Ansari Road, Daryaganj
Near Times of India Building, New Delhi 110002
Mob : 08505972553

BENGALURU

Pragati Book House : House No. 1, Sanjeevappa Lane, Avenue Road Cross,
Opp. Rice Church, Bengaluru – 560002.
Tel : (080) 64513344, 64513355,Mob : 9880582331, 9845021552
Email:bharatsavla@yahoo.com

CHENNAI

Pragati Books : 9/1, Montieth Road, Behind Taas Mahal, Egmore,
Chennai 600008 Tamil Nadu, Tel : (044) 6518 3535,
Mob : 94440 01782 / 98450 21552 / 98805 82331,
Email : bharatsavla@yahoo.com

niralipune@pragationline.com | www.pragationline.com

Also find us on 🅕 www.facebook.com/niralibooks

PREFACE TO THE SECOND EDITION

We are glad and excited to announce that the First Edition of this book received an overwhelming response from the engineering student community, compelling us to release its **Second Edition** within a very short period of time.

This thoroughly revised **Second Edition** has been updated with additional matter, including **All Solved University Examination Papers December 2013 to May 2017**.

Special care has been taken to maintain high degree of accuracy in the theory and numericals throughout the book.

We take this opportunity to express our sincere thanks to Dineshbhai Furia of Nirali Prakashan, a reputed pioneer in the publication field. Our special thanks to Jignesh Furia and Mrs. Nirali Verma for their effective cooperation and great care in bringing out this revised edition. We also appreciate the efforts of M. P. Munde and the entire staff of Engineering Books Deptt. of Nirali Prakashan namely Mrs. Deepali Lachake (Co-ordinator) and Mrs. Shilpa Kale for bringing this book to the students in a timely manner.

We sincerely hope that this **"Second Edition"** will also be warmly received by all concerned as in the past.

Valuable suggestions from our esteemed readers to improve the book are most welcome and highly appreciated.

Pune –   **Authors**

PREFACE TO THE FIRST EDITION

It gives us great pleasure in publishing this text book on **"Geotechnical Engineering"** for the students of Second Year Degree Course in Civil Engineering. This book is strictly written according to **New Revised Credit System Syllabus** of Savitribai Phule Pune University (2015 Pattern).

As per the policy of the University, Engineering Syllabi is revised every five years. Last revision was in the year 2012. New revision is coming little earlier, as university has introduced **Online System of Examination** from year 2012.

As per the **New Credit System**, the **In Sem (Online) Examinations** (Phase-I and Phase-II) will be conducted based on first, second, third and fourth units. The **Online** examinations will have objective types of questions with multiple choices. End Semester Examination will be based on all the six units and that will be conducted in traditional way.

New text book is written, taking in to account all the new features that have been introduced. All the entrants to the engineering field will definitely find this book, complete in all respect. Students will find the subject matter presentation quite lucid. There are large number of illustrative examples and well graded exercises.

We have given Free Separate book of Multiple Choice Questions (MCQ's), which will be very useful to the students, especially for Online Examinations.

We take this opportunity to express our sincere thanks to Shri. Dineshbhai Furia, Shri. Jignesh Furia, Mrs. Nirali Verma and Shri. M. P. Munde and entire team of Nirali Prakashan namely Mrs. Deepali Lachake (Co-ordinator), Mr. Gopal Shitole and Baliram Varvate who really have taken keen interest and untiring efforts in publishing this text.

We have no doubt that like our earlier texts, student's community will respond favourably to this new venture.

The advice and suggestions of our esteemed readers to improve the text are most welcomed, and will be highly appreciated.

16th June 2016
Pune

Authors

SYLLABUS

Unit I : Introduction and Index Properties   **(08 Hrs)**

(a) Introduction to Geotechnical Engineering and its applications to Civil Engineering, Types of soil structure, major soil deposits of India, Field identification of soils. Introduction to soil exploration: objective and purpose.

(b) Three Phase Soil System, Weight– volume relationships, Index properties of soil: Methods of determination and their significance. IS and Unified Soil classification systems.

Unit II: Permeability and Seepage   **(08 Hrs)**

(a)   Soil water, permeability definition and necessity of its study, Darcy's law, factors affecting permeability. Laboratory measurement of permeability: Constant head method and Falling head method as per IS 2720. Field test for determination of permeability- Pumping in test and Pumping out test as per IS 5529 Part-I. Permeability of stratified soil deposits.

(b) Seepage and Seepage Pressure, quick sand phenomenon, critical hydraulic gradient, General flow equation for 2-D flow (Laplace equation), Flow Net, properties and application, Flow Net construction for flow under sheet pile and earthen dam.

Unit III: Compaction and Stress Distribution   **(08 Hrs)**

(a) Compaction – Introduction, Comparison between compaction and consolidation, compaction tests- Standard Proctor test, Modified Proctor test, Zero air void line. Factors affecting compaction. Effect of compaction on soil properties.

Field compaction methods and compaction equipment for different types of soil, Placement water content, Field compaction control- use of compaction test result, Proctor needle in field compaction control.

(b) Stress Distribution in Soils – Geostatic stress, Boussinesq's theory with assumptions for point load and circular load (with numerical), Pressure Distribution diagram on a horizontal and vertical plane, Pressure bulb and its significance. Westergaard's theory, equivalent point load method, Approximate stress distribution method.

Unit IV: Shear Strength of Soil   **(08 Hrs)**

(a) Introduction – Shear strength an Engineering Property. Mohr's stress circle, Mohr-Coulomb failure theory. The effective stress principle- Total stress, effective stress and neutral stress / pore water pressure. Peak and Residual shear strength, factors affecting shear strength. Stress-strain behavior of sands and clays.

(b) Measurement of Shear Strength – Direct Shear test, Triaxial Compression test, Unconfined Compression test, Vane Shear test. Their suitability for different types of soils, advantages and disadvantages. Different drainage conditions for shear tests. Sensitivity and thixotropy of cohesive soils.

Unit V: Earth Pressure   **(08 Hrs)**

(a) Earth Pressure – Introduction, Rankine's state of Plastic Equilibrium in soils- Active and Passive states due to wall movement, Earth Pressure at rest. Rankine's Theory : Earth pressure on Retaining wall due to submerged backfill.

(b) Backfill with uniform surcharge, backfill with sloping surface, layered backfill. Coulomb's Wedge theory. Rebhann's and Culmann's graphical method of determination of earth pressure.

Unit VI: Stability of Slopes and Introduction to Geo-environmental Engineering   **(08Hrs)**

(a) Stability of Slopes – Classification of slopes and their modes of failure, Taylor's stability number, Infinite Slopes in cohesive and cohesion less soil, Landslides- Causes and remedial measures.

(b) Introduction to Geo-environmental engineering, subsurface contamination, contaminant transport, effects of subsurface contamination, Control and remediation, Soil- A geochemical trap, detection of polluted zones, Monitoring effectiveness of designed facilities.

CONTENTS

Unit II : Permeability and Seepage

Unit III : Compaction and Stress Distribution

Unit IV : Shear Strength of Soil

Unit V : Earth Pressure

Chapter 1
INTRODUCTION

1.1 SOIL

People from different disciplines have different ideas about the term 'soil'. The definition of soil by an agriculturist or a geologist is different from the one used by a civil engineer. To a geologist, soil is thin outer layer of loose sediments within which plant roots are present. A geologist considers the rest of the earth's crust as rock, irrespective of the intensity of bonding forces of sediments.

To an agriculturist soil means only top layer of the earth which supports plants. For a civil engineer, *"soil means all naturally occurring relatively unconsolidated earth material, organic or inorganic in character, that lies above the bed rock. It includes different materials like boulders, sands, gravels, clays and silts"*. The particle sizes in a soil varies from 10^{-4} micron in diameter up to large size boulders.

According to Dr. Terzaghi [who is known as Father of Soil Mechanics], soils can be divided into their constituent particles relatively easily, such as by agitation in water. On the other hand, rocks are an agglomeration of mineral particles which are bonded together by strong molecular forces. But the distinction between soils and rocks is not very clear. Many hard soils can be termed as soft rock or vice versa.

1.2 SOIL MECHANICS

Soil Mechanics or Geotechnique is a branch of civil engineering that concerns the application of principles of mechanics, hydraulics, chemistry to engineering problems related to the soils. According to Dr. Terzaghi [1948], 'Soil Mechanics or Geotechnique' is the application of laws of mechanics and hydraulics to engineering problems dealing with sediments and other unconsolidated accumulations of solid particles produced by the mechanical and chemical disintegration of rocks regardless of whether or not they contain an admixture of organic constituents. The study of the science of soil mechanics equips a civil engineer with the basic scientific tools needed to understand soil behaviour.

1.3 SOIL ENGINEERING OR GEOTECHNICAL ENGINEERING

Soil engineering is a broader term which encompasses not only soil mechanics or geotechnique but also soil dynamics, part of structural engineering and many other disciplines which are frequently essential to obtain practical solution to problems of soils. Geotechnical Engineering is a new term and includes soil mechanics, soil engineering, rock mechanics and rock engineering. Rock mechanics is defined as *'a science dealing with the application of the principles of mechanics to understand the behaviour of rock masses'.*

The scope of the present volume is restricted to the study of the engineering of the soil mass and an introduction to "Rock Mechanics".

1.4 COMPLEXITY OF SOIL

Soil is a naturally occurring loose or soft deposit forming part of earth's crust, produced as a result of weathering, disintegration or decomposition of rock formation, or decay of vegetation, intermingled together. The top layer of ground that supports vegetation is termed as 'top soil' or soil and undisturbed strata lying immediately below the natural top soil is termed as 'subsoil'.

A natural deposit is quite unlike any other material of construction known to man. Among all available common construction materials, one can select the material which best meets the prevailing conditions and then determine the allowable stresses for that material. The material can be expected to behave in a reasonably predictable manner. On the other hand, no choice of soil is normally available to an engineer. Most of the suitable sites for construction have already been used up and often one has to compromise with a site having unsatisfactory subsoil conditions. Occasionally, it may be possible to improve the soil conditions by some suitable treatment, but more often the soil has to be accepted in its natural state.

The natural deposits are complex to deal with for the following reasons :

- The *stress - strain* relationship for soil deposit is non-linear; hence there is difficulty in using easily determinable parameters to describe its behaviour.

- Soil deposits have a memory for stress undergone in their geological history. Their *behaviour is vastly influenced by their stress history.* Time and environment are other factors which may alter their behaviour.

- Soil deposits being far from homogeneous, exhibit properties which *vary from location to location.*

- As soil layers are buried and hidden from view, one has to rely on tests carried out on small samples obtained from selected depths and locations. Since, there is a constraint on the number of samples that can be taken, there is *no guarantee that the soil parameters are truly representative* of the field strata.

- No sample is truly undisturbed. In a soil which is sensitive to disturbance, the test results obtained from the laboratory and performance of the same sample in the field is normally different for most of the cases.

It must now be clear why it is essential for a soil engineer in search of practical solutions, to possess the knowledge of the principles of soil mechanics.

He needs to have geology as his ally. The knowledge of various processes that determine the composition of natural soil mass is important since these have a direct bearing on soil behaviour. He must also draw upon *experience of others*.

He must also continually evaluate his own designs in the light of data obtained from field measurements. The basis of observational method in soil mechanics is the comparison of the predicted performance with the actual measured performance. One then tries to fill the gaps in the original reasoning.

With all this, a soil engineer is a practitioner of an art, rather than a science. Thus, soil engineering is an intuitive science where intuition comes from combination of the knowledge of theory, experience and skill.

1.5 COMPARISON OF SOIL WITH OTHER MATERIALS

Soil is a highly complex material. It differs from conventional structural materials such as steel, concrete, plastic etc. Terzaghi has rightly said that, **"Unfortunately soil is not a man made material and all products of nature are complex"**. Behaviour and properties of man made material can be predicted fairly accurately, whereas, it is difficult in case of natural product such as soil.

A comparison of soil with such materials is shown in Table 1.1.

Table 1.1 : Comparison of Soil with Other Structural Materials

Soil [and rocks]	Other structural materials
1. It is a material which has been subjected to vagaries of nature without any control.	These are manufactured materials, the properties of which are accurately controlled.

…Conti.

2. Universally available abundant and cheap material.	Restricted supply, expensive materials, availability depends on raw materials.
3. Complex, variable and changeable properties with little scope for improvement.	Uniform with more or less constant properties, which may be altered if desired.
4. Non-inelastic, non-homogeneous, non-plastic, 3-phase particulate system.	Can be treated as isotropic, linearly elastic and homogeneous system.
5. Relatively weak and highly compressible material. Resist only compression and shear.	Relatively strong and unyielding materials, resist compression, shear, tension and bending.
6. Soil strength depends on rate of loading and drainage condition.	Material strength is a constant property.

EXERCISE

1. What is complicity of soil.
2. Write a short note on: Soil engineering.
3. Distinguish between soil and other materials.
4. Define soil. Explain the concept of soil Mechanics.

Chapter 2
SOIL AS ENGINEERING MATERIAL

2.1 ORIGIN OF SOIL

Soils are formed due to mechanical disintegration or chemical decomposition of rocks. When a rock surface gets exposed to atmosphere for an appreciable time, it disintegrates or decomposes into small particles and thus soils are formed.

Soil may be considered as an incidental material obtained from the geological cycle which goes on continuously in nature. The geological cycle consists of erosion, transportation, deposition and upheaval of soil.

2.2 TYPES OF ROCKS AND GEOLOGICAL CYCLE

The geologists describe three principal types of rocks :

1. Igneous or Primary Rocks.

2. Sedimentary or Secondary Rocks.

3. Metamorphic Rocks.

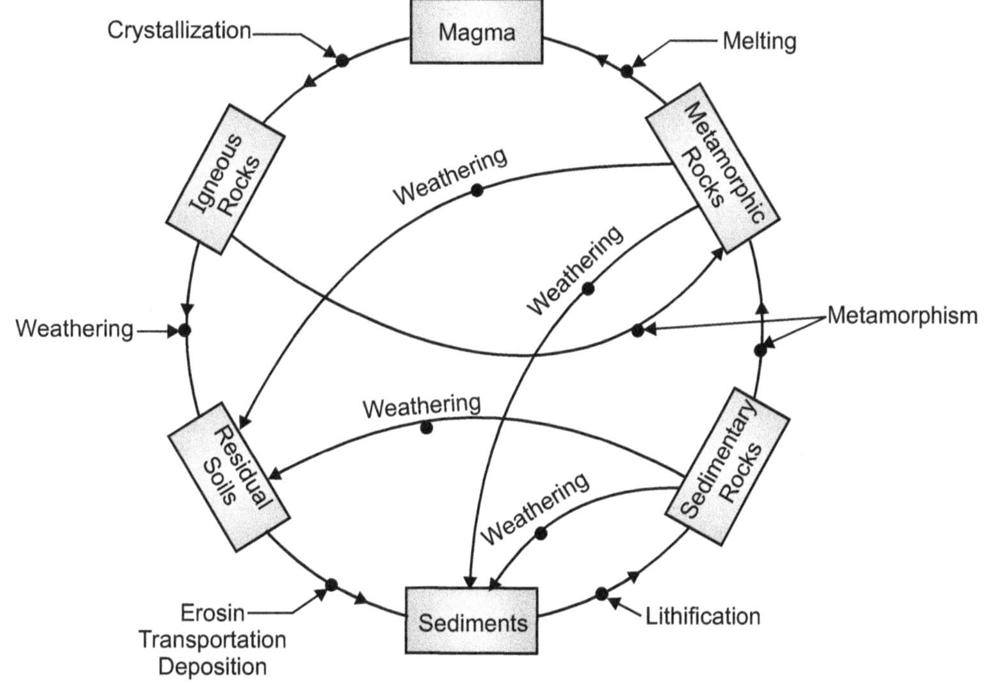

Fig. 2.1 : Geological cycle

Igneous rocks are formed by cooling of molten magma either exposed at the earth's surface or located deep under the surface cover. The surface rocks are subjected to the geological processes of denudation [surface wear], weathering [mechanical and chemical destruction] and transportation. A sedimentary soil deposit is formed when a transported sediment is deposited. A sediment deposit is consolidated or cemented into a sedimentary rock. Under heavy pressures and high temperatures, rock mass transforms into metamorphic rocks. Later, crustal movement exposes rocks to further weathering or returns them to molten magma, to start the entire cycle fresh [Fig. 2.1]. It consists of four main operations : (1) Denudation, (2) Deposition, (3) Sedimentation, (4) Crustal movement.

2.3 PRINCIPAL SOIL TYPES [May 17]

On the basis of the geological origin of their constituent sediments, soils can be divided into two main groups :

1. Those which owe their origin to the physical and chemical weathering of the parent rocks and

2. Those which are chiefly of organic origin.

The latter type are extremely compressible and their use as foundation material is best avoided. Of the former group, soils which are a product of *physical weathering* or *mechanical disintegration*, retain the minerals that were present in the parent rocks are called as coarse grained. Gravels and sands fall into this category. The physical agencies responsible for weathering are the impact and grinding action of flowing water, ice, wind and the splitting actions of ice, plants and animals. As against this, *chemical weathering* or *decomposition of rocks* is caused mainly by oxidation, hydration, carbonation and leaching by organic acids and water. Clays and to some extent, silts are formed by chemical weathering.

2.3.1 Residual and Transported Soils [Dec. 13, 14]

On the basis of the formation, soils can be divided into two large groups:

[1] Residual soils   [2]   Transported soils.

1.   Residual Soils : If the products of rock weathering are still located at the place where they originated, they are called residual soils. These soils lie directly over the bed rock. Igneous rocks such as granite or basalt and sedimentary rocks such as sandstone, shale or limestone are the parent material for residual soils. Lateritic soils and black cotton soils are examples of residual soils.

2.   Transported Soils : Any soil that has been transported from its place of origin by wind, water, ice or any other agent and has been redeposited, is called as *transported soil.*

Characteristics of soil such as the size of the particles, their shape and roundness, surface texture and the degree of sorting that takes place in a soil deposit are influenced by the method of transportation. Table 2.1 summarizes these effects. Transported soils are further classified according to the transporting agency and method of deposition.

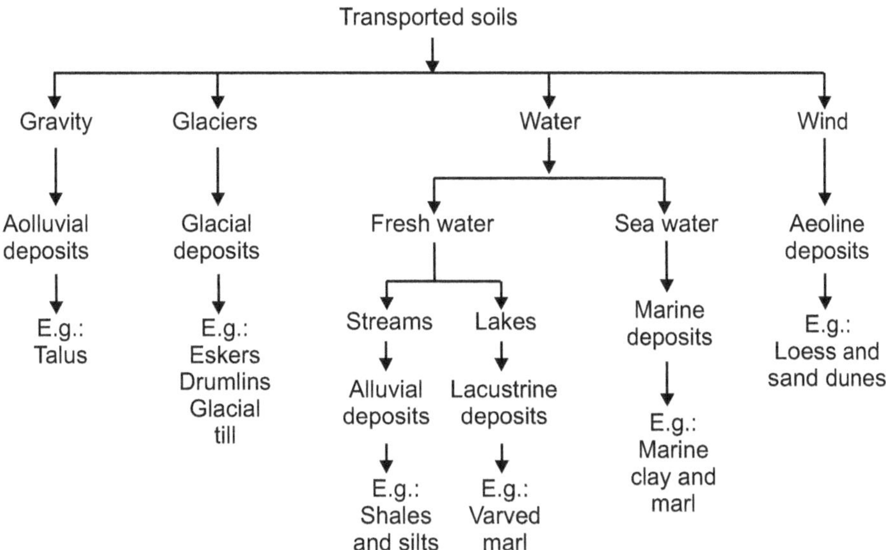

(a) Alluvial deposit : Soils that have been deposited from suspension in running water.

(b) Lacustrine deposit : Soils that have been deposited from suspension in still fresh water of lakes.

(c) Marine deposit : Soils that have been deposited from suspension in sea water.

(d) Aeoline deposit : Soils that have been transported by wind.

(e) Glacial deposit : Deposits that have been transported by ice.

Table 2.1 : Effects of Transportation on Sediments

	Water	Air	Ice	Gravity	Organisms
Size	Reduction through solution, little abrasion in suspended load, some abrasion and impact in traction load	Considerable reduction	Considerable grinding and impact	Considerable impact	Minor abrasions effects from direct organic transportation
Shape and roundness	Rounding of sand and gravel	High degree of rounding	Angular particles	Angular, non-spherical	
Surface texture	Sand : smooth, polished, shiny	Impact produces frosted surfaces	Striated surfaces	Striated surfaces	
Sorting	Considerable sorting	Very considerable sorting [progressive]	Very little sorting	No sorting	Limited sorting

Names of some of the soils that have been formed by various methods of transportation and deposition are given and explained below.

1. Loess : A loose deposit of wind-blown silt that has been weakly cemented with calcium carbonate and montmorillonite. Loess is formed in arid and semi-arid regions and stands in nearly vertical banks.

2. **Tuff :** A small-grained slightly cemented volcanic ash that has been transported by wind or water.

3. **Bentonite :** A chemically weathered volcanic ash.

4. **Glacial fill [boulder clay] :** Typically, a mixture of boulders, gravel, sand, silt and clay, deposited by glaciers and not transported or segregated by water.

5. **Varved clay :** Alternate thin layers of silt and clay deposited in fresh water glacial lakes by outwash from glaciers. The silt is deposited in warm weather during heavy run off and clay is deposited in cold weather during small run off. Generally, one band of silt and clay is deposited each year.

6. **Marl :** A very fine-grained calcium-carbonated soil of marine origin.

7. **Gumbo :** A sticky, plastic, dark coloured clay.

8. **Peat :** A highly organic soil, consisting almost entirely of vegetative matter in varying states of decomposition, brown to black in colour, possessing an organic odour. Peat is fibrous and highly compressible.

9. **Muck :** A mixture of fine particles, inorganic soil and black decomposed organic matter. It is usually found accumulated in conditions of imperfect drainage as in swamps or is deposited by overflowing rivers.

   Peat and muck are also called *cumulose soils.*

10. **Humus :** A dark brown, organic, amorphous earth of top soil, consisting of partly decomposed vegetative matter.

11. **Hard pan :** A layer of extremely hard, cohesive soil that can hardly be drilled with ordinary, earth boring tools.

12. **Colluvial soil :** The accumulation of rock debris or talus at the base of a steep cliff or a rock escarpment. Its position results mainly from the effect of the force of gravity acting on the rock fragments broken from above rocks.

13. **Mine tailings :** These are silt-sized materials resulting as waste after extraction of minerals from natural rock and are usually deposited by hydraulic fill.

14. **Fill :** Transported soils and residual soils are formed by agencies of nature. A man-made deposit is called a *fill* and the process of forming the deposits is called filling. A fill is actually a transported soil where human being is a transporting agency. A blasting may be used to form a soil from rock. Trucks, scrappers or bulldozers are used to transport the soil.

15. **Inorganic soil and organic soil :** If a soil consists of organic matter, the soil may be termed as organic soil, otherwise it is an inorganic soil. Organic matter consists of the more or less decomposed remains of plants and animals organisms. Such soils undergo considerable volume changes under load. In general, dark colours of grey, brown or black, indicate organic soils. Inorganic soils are having brighter colours. Organic soils have distinctive smell. They are not good soils from an engineering point of view.

2.4 SOIL STRUCTURE

The geometrical arrangement of soil particles with respect to each other is known as *soil structure*. Soil structure is an important factor which influences many soil properties such as permeability, compressibility and shear strength etc. The following types of soil structure are generally recognized.

2.4.1 Single Grained Structure

This type of structure is observed in coarse-grained soils like sands, gravels etc. (Fig. 2.2). Each particle of this type of soil settles out of suspension separately and independently. This settlement of particles is due to the gravitational forces acting on the particles. The specific surface of all particles is comparatively less and hence the effective surface forces are negligible. These surface forces are neglected for all practical purpose in case of coarse grained soils [Diameter > 0.02 mm].

2.4.2 Honeycomb Structure

This type of structure is observed in silts i.e. soil particles having diameter between 0.0002-0.02 mm. Both gravitational forces and surface forces play an important role in case of such soils. The soil grains settle down due to gravitational forces and the surface forces at contact areas, are large enough as compared to the submerged weight to prevent the grains from immediate rolling. The grains in contact are held together until miniature arches are formed. These arches are joined over relatively large void spaces which is termed as *honeycomb structure* (Fig. 2.3). Comparatively large amount of water is enclosed within the voids. This structure has high void ratio.

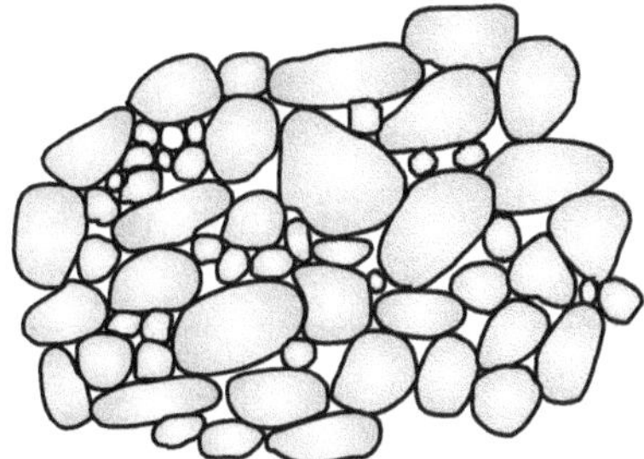

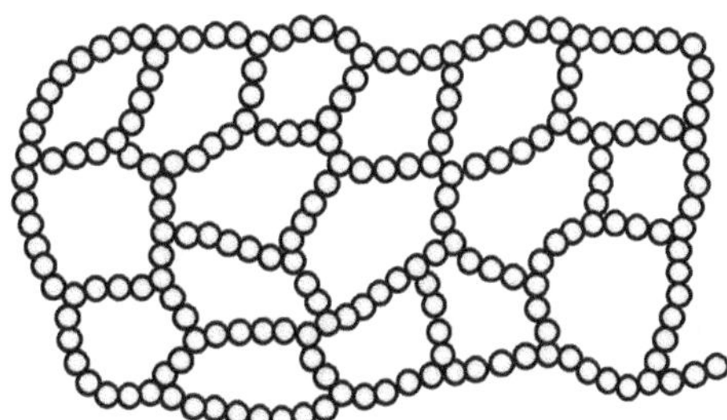

Fig. 2.2 : Single grained structure   **Fig. 2.3 : Terzaghi Casagrande concept of honeycomb structure**

2.4.3 Flocculent Structure

This type of structure is observed in clays with fine particles. When there is an edge contact between the clay platelets such structure form. The basic reason for the formation of this type of structure is the electrical forces between adjacent soil particles at the time of deposition being attraction forces. The tendency of flocculation can be increased when there is concentration of dissolved minerals in the water.

2.4.4 Dispersed Structure

Clays with fine particles are also seen in the form of dispersed structures when there is face to face contact between more or less parallel array. The formation of dispersed or oriented structure takes place when the net electrical forces between adjacent soil particles at the time of deposition are repulsion.

Fig. 2.4 : Flocculated structure   **Fig. 2.5 : Dispersed structure**

The clays having flocculent structure are subjected to heavy load, the clay particles are subjected to bending, slipping along contact surfaces, producing denser arrangement finally resulting in dispersed or oriented structure. Thus, remoulding, compacting and consolidation tend to orient particles to form dispersed arrangement.

2.4.5 Composite Soil Structures

Two types of structures can be possible in composite soils depending upon the relative proportions of fine grained particles and coarse grained particles.

(a) Coarse grain skeleton

(b) Cohesive matrix.

In first case, the voids are filled with clay particles. Here, void means empty space in the single grained structure. The bulky particles form continuous framework.

In cohesive matrix, the clay content is more as compared to coarse particles and hence bulky particles are not capable of having particle to particle contact.

2.5 SOIL DEPOSITS OF INDIA   [May 14]

The soils of India can be broadly divided into the following groups, based on the climatic conditions, topography and geology of their formation.

(a) Marine deposits

(b) Black cotton soils

(c) Laterites and lateritic soils

(d) Desert soils

(e) Boulder deposits

(f) Alluvial soil deposits

Fig. 2.6 shows the general areas of occurrence of different types of soils in India.

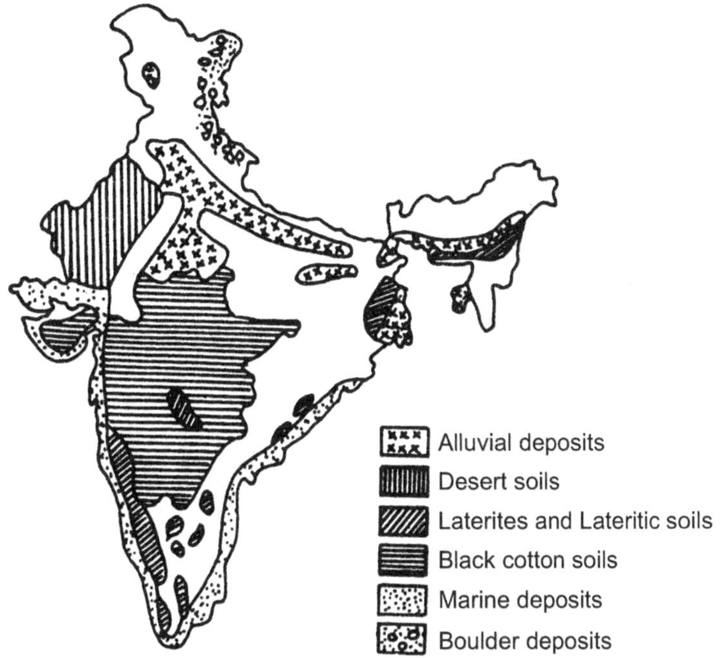

Fig. 2.6 : Regional soil deposits of India

(a) Marine Deposits : These deposits are found all along the coast in narrow tidal plains. The marine clays are very soft and may contain organic matter. They possess low shear strength and high compressibility and hence pose problems as a foundation material or as a material of construction.

(b) Black Cotton Soil : This is the Indian name given to expansive soil deposits in the central part of the country. They cover an area of approximately 3,00,500 sq. km which extends over the states of Maharashtra, Madhya Pradesh, Karnataka, Andhra Pradesh, Tamil Nadu and Uttar Pradesh. These soils have been formed from basalt or trap and contain the clay mineral montmorillonite, which is responsible for the excessive swelling and shrinkage characteristics of the soil. Lightly loaded structures are most susceptible to damage as a result of the volume changes in the soil. Under-reamed piles are considered most suitable as foundations for houses and other light structures. These piles are taken to depths below the zone of seasonal variation in moisture content.

(c) Laterites and Lateritic Soils : Lateritic soils cover an area of about 100,000 sq. km and extend over Kerala, Karnataka, Maharashtra, Orissa and West Bengal. Laterites are formed by the decomposition of rock, removal of the bases and silica and formation of oxides of iron and aluminium at the top of the soil profile. In Kerala, the laterites are soft when wet but hardened with age.

There are two types of laterites, namely, the primary and the secondary. Primary laterite is found in-situ. The original rock structures, joints and quartz material are intact and the laterite deposit overlies the bedrock. Primary laterite is found at high altitudes near hills.

Secondary laterites are found in the coastal belt. These are formed from sedimentary deposits such as gravels and pebbles by sesquioxide impregnation and cementation. They are pellet type and are quite different from the underlying soil or bed rock. This may create problems in foundations, if a thin laterite layer overlies a soft material. Laterites are reddish in colour and are hard in the dry state. But not all soils which show these characteristics are laterites. If the grain size increases upon alternate wetting and drying cycles, the soil is a laterite. Lateritic soils do not show this characteristic. Generally, laterites pose no difficulties as foundation material and retain their slopes well. However, there is a continuous softening effect with depth and in some cases, the presence of worm holes in laterites need to be examined carefully. Like all residual soils, laterites show variability in their properties, depending upon the stage of weathering.

(d) Alluvial Deposits : Large parts of Northern India lying North of Vindhya-Satpura range in the Indo-Gangetic and Brahmaputra flood plains are covered by the alluvial deposits. The thickness of the deposit is sometimes over 100 m. The deposits have alternating layers of sand, silt and clay. There is a great deal of variation in the thickness of these layers and their horizontal development. The alluvial deposits extend from Assam in the East to Punjab in the West.

The fine silty sand deposits in this area are loose and prone to liquefaction under earthquake shocks.

(e) Desert Soils : Large part of Rajasthan, covering about 500,000 sq. km consists of desert soils which are wind-blown deposits of sand. The sand dunes have an average height of about 15 m but can at times be considerably higher. They are formed under highly arid conditions. Dune sand is a non-plastic uniformly graded, fine sand. Some of the problems associated with this soil are of soil stabilization for roads and runways, reducing settlement under static and dynamic loads and reducing its perviousness to make it suitable for storage and transport of water.

(f) Boulder Deposits : Rivers flowing in hilly terrains and near foot-hills carry large boulders downstream. The deposits that such flows make may contain large quantities of boulders. Such deposits are often found in the sub-Himalayan regions of Himachal Pradesh and Uttar Pradesh. The properties of these deposits depends on the relative proportions of the boulders and the soil matrix. The boulder to boulder contact may result in large friction resulting in higher angles of shearing resistance.

2.6 FIELD IDENTIFICATION TEST OF SOIL   [May 15, 16]

Field identification of soil is of great importance for civil engineering. It requires a considerable amount of experience. The soils to be identified in field may be Coarse grained soil or Fine grained soil.

2.6.1 Coarse Grained Soil

Coarse grained soils are easily identified by visual inspection on the basis of particle size. Rounded to angular, bulky, hard rock fragments of average diameter more than 20 cm are described as boulders. Stones of sizes between 20 cm and 6 cm are termed as cobbles. Soil fraction between the sizes of 60 mm and 2 mm is known as the gravel fraction. Soil with particle size visible to the naked eye but less than 2 mm is classified as sand. Sand is further divided into coarse, medium and fine fractions for which a sieve analysis is usually required. Mixtures of gravel and sand are given in dual designations in the following Table 2.2.

Table 2.2 : Description of Gravel and Sand Mixtures

Main content	Descriptive term	Subsidiary constituent per cent
Gravel	Gravel and sand	About 50
	Gravel with some sand or sandy gravel	25 to 40
	Gravel with a little sand	10 to 25
	Gravel with a trace sand	Upto 1

If sand is the main constituent, gravel and sand will interchange in the above descriptive terms, for example, sand with some gravel or gravelly sand will represent sand having 25 to 40 per cent of gravel. Very fine, uniform sand is difficult to be distinguished visually from silt. However, when dry, it does not hold together (no cohesion) and feel gritty in contrast to the very slight cohesion and smooth feel of the dried silt.

The description of coarse grained soils should describe grading, grain-shape, colour, in-situ strength and structural features and presence of fines, if any.

Grading : The grading or particle size distribution as judged by visual inspection is expressed by the terms well-graded, poorly graded or uniformly graded.

Grain Shape : The terms used to describe the grain shape are angular, sub-angular and rounded. Angular particles have sharp edges and relatively plane sides with unpolished surfaces. Sub-angular particles are similar to angular but have rounded edges. Rounded particles have smooth curvy sides and no edges.

Colour : The colour of the soil is expressed as brown, white, yellow, red-brown etc.

Strength and Structure : The in-situ strength of a deposit of coarse-grained soil is expressed as compact or loose. If a pick is required for excavation, it is compact and if it can be done with a spade, it is loose.

The arrangement and the state of aggregation of soil particles in a soil mass is known as *soil structure*. The structure of coarse grained soils recognized in the field can be described as homogeneous or stratified. When a soil mass is essentially one type, it is said to be homogeneous. If it is arranged in strata or layers, e.g. stratified alluvium, it is said to have stratified structure.

Presence of Fines : If the soil contains some fines (particle size not individually visible to the naked eye), but not sufficient to cause cohesion this should be noted. Presence of organic matter, if any, should also be indicated.

2.6.2 Fine Grained Soil

Fine grained soils are identified by performing the following simple tests on the minus 425 micron IS sieve size particles. In the field, use of the sieve is not intended. The coarser particles that interfere with the tests may be simply removed by hand.

1. **Dilatancy or Shaking Test :** When a wet pat of soil is shaken vigorously in the palm of one hand which may also be struck several times with the other hand, the surface may become glossy and show free water. If the pat of the soil is then sqeezed between fingers, the free water disappears and the surface becomes dull i.e. dilates. This phenomenon is clearly evident with silt and sand unlike clay where no such reaction is observed.

2. **Dry Strength Test :** If a small piece of dry fine grained soil is broken or crushed with fingers, the breaking strength is an indication of the relative amounts of silt or clay. If the soil can be powdered easily with the fingers, it is said to have slight dry strength and indicates silt or sandy silt. If considerable strength is required, but the soil can still be broken into small pieces without great difficulty, it is said to have medium dry strength, and is indicative of silty clays and clays of low plasticity. When the pat of dry soil cannot be broken with fingers, it has high dry strength and represents a highly plastic clay. The presence of water soluble cementing materials, such as calcium carbonate or iron oxides, may also cause high dry strength. Soil with high strength is treated with a little dilute hydrochloric acid. A strong reaction indicates that the strength may be due to calcium carbonate as cementing agent, rather than colloidal clay.

3. **Toughness Test :** The consistency or the resistance to moulding at the plastic limit is called the toughness. The water content of a wet soil sample is gradually reduced by working and moulding until it reaches the plastic limit when soil threads should crumble at about 3 mm diameter. The time required to dry the pat is an indication of its plasticity. After the threads crumble, the pieces are lumped together and a slight kneading action continued until the lump also crumbles. If the lump can still be moulded slightly drier than the plastic limit and the threads can still be rolled with considerable pressure, the soil is of high toughness which represents clays of high plasticity or fat clays. Medium toughness represents soils of medium plasticity whose threads are medium tough and a lump formed of the threads slightly below the plastic limit crumbles. Weak threads that break easily and cannot be lumped together, when drier than the plastic limit indicate slight toughness representing soils of low plasticity. The number of times the procedure can be repeated is an indication of the plasticity index of the soil. Non-plastic soils cannot be rolled into 3 mm diameter threads at any water content.

4. **Other Identification Tests :** If a dry or slightly moist lump of soil when cut or rubbed with considerable pressure with a knife blade produces a shiny surface, high plasticity is indicated. A dull surface indicates silt or clay of low plasticity. Wet clay sticks to the fingers, gives a greasy feel and does not wash off readily, whereas, silt will wash away easily or brush off, if dry. In a soil suspension of water of about 10 cm depth, sand will settle within half a

minute, most of the silt in about 5 to 60 minutes, whereas, clay-size particles will remain in suspension for several hours or may even remain for several days.

5. Organic silt or clay : Finely divided organic matter present in combination with mineral soil materials is not easily recognized, particularly if the amount of organic matter is small. However, if the soil has a dark-brown, dark-gray or black colour, presence of organic matter may be suspected. Organic soils usually have a distinctive organic odour, specially when fresh and wet. Sometimes the organic odour can be made more noticeable by heating the wet sample. Highly organic clays have a very weak and strong feel at the plastic limit. Fibrous organic soils, such as peat or muck, are usually dark brown to black in colour with a characteristic odour and have organic matter in various stages of decomposition.

2.7 INTRODUCTION TO SOIL EXPLORATION

2.7.1 Soil Exploration and Site Investigation

The basic aim of sub-surface exploration or site investigation is to obtain the information about the surface conditions at the site of proposed construction. For every big or major engineering project site investigation is essential, since it is beneficial for the design of structures and for planning construction techniques.

Purpose of Soil Exploration Program :

Site investigation for one or more of the following purposes is carried out :

- Determination of the bearing capacity of the soil.
- Selection of type and depth of foundation for a given structure.
- Investigation of the safety of the existing structures and for necessary remedial measures.
- Selection of suitable construction technique.
- Calculation of the lateral earth pressure against retaining walls and abutments.
- Estimation of probable maximum and differential settlements.
- Prediction and solving of potential foundation problems.
- Establishing the ground water table level and determination of the properties of water.
- Determining the suitability of the soil as a construction material.

2.7.2 Steps in Soil Exploration

Soil exploration broadly involves the following :

- Planning of a programme for soil exploration.
- Collection of disturbed and undisturbed soil or rock samples from the holes drilled in the field. The number and depths of holes depend upon the project.
- Conducting all the necessary in-situ tests for obtaining the strength and compressibility characteristics of the soil or rock directly or indirectly.
- Study of ground-water conditions and collection of water samples for chemical analysis.
- Geophysical exploration, if required.

- Conducting all the necessary tests on the samples of soil/rock and water collected.
- Preparation of drawings, charts etc.
- Analysis of the data collected.
- Preparation of report.

2.7.3 Planning the Ground Investigation Program

Basically in a ground investigation, one is interested in finding the details of sub-surface strata and their engineering properties such as strength, deformation and hydraulic characteristics. The program should aim at obtaining the maximum information.

The ground investigation, irrespective of the magnitude of the projects, consists of four phases :

1. **Available Information :** This is the first phase in which collection of published geological and topographical information of the area, hydrological data, details of existing or historic development, local regulations for construction activity etc. are made.

2. **Reconnaissance :** This is the phase during which an engineer along with other specialists, such as the geologist, land surveyer, geotechnical engineer, etc. visits the area for first examination. At this stage a thorough study on the existing structures for the type of construction and defects such as cracks and settlement, soil profiles in highway or railroad cuts and quarries, erosion in existing cuts, high water marks on bridge abutments, rock, outcrops is performed. A history of flood and scour levels etc. is also collected from the local people around the site.

3. **Preliminary Investigation :** This is an important phase of the entire program. In this stage the engineer plans the investigation program. The first step towards a ground investigation is a thorough understanding of the geology of the site, which enables an efficient working out of the investigation program. The second step is to obtain more details of the subsoil strata (e.g. thickness of individual strata) from one or two exploratory drill holes. All further steps depend on the magnitude of the job and the character of the soil profile.

During this stage, the possible location of the ground water is also found. For small jobs this preliminary investigation itself may be sufficient. It is a common practice to limit the number of quality samples recovered except the one obtained from penetration tests. The strength and settlement are estimated from standard correlations using index properties and supplemented by the results from samples obtained from penetration tests. Further, this is the stage which practically decides the feasibility of the project.

4. **Detailed Investigation :** Additional borings are planned from the data obtained from the preliminary borings. If the subsoil is uniform in stratification, an orderly spacing may be planned. Many a times additional borings are made to locate weak soil or rock zones, outcrops etc. which may influence the design and construction of the project. Necessary in-situ tests should also be performed. Sufficient samples should be procurred to obtain relevant parameters for design and construction. Certain additional samples should be recorded to redefine the design or construction procedure.

2.7.4 Methods of Obtaining Soil Samples

Following methods are used to obtain soil samples to identify/classify the type of strata, and to send the same for testing :

(1) Auger boring

(2) Wash boring

(3) Rotary drilling

(4) Percussion drilling

(5) Core drilling

(6) Trial pits

(1) Auger Boring

It is quite useful in cohesive and other soft soils above water table.

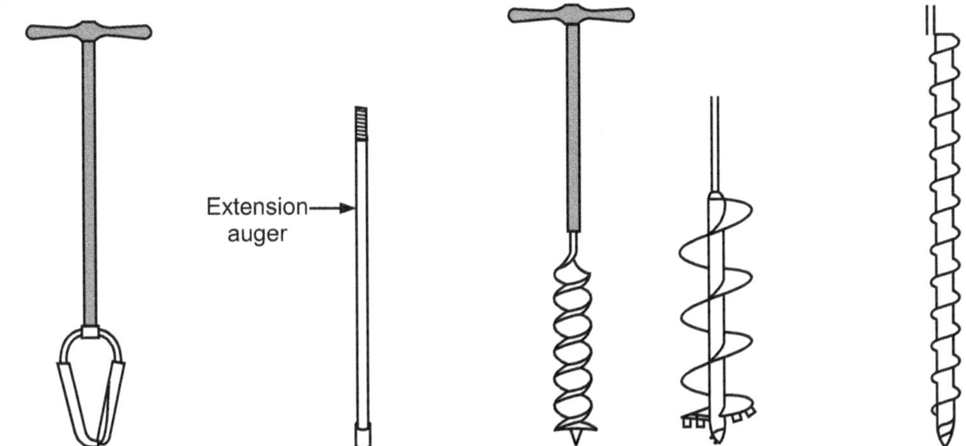

(a) Post-hole auger   (b) Helical auger (c) Short-flight auger (d) Continuous flight auger

Fig. 2.7 : Types of augers

Hand operated auger methods are suitable for identifying various types of soils with depth and also for getting information about the depth to the ground water table. For deeper boring, solid or hollow-stem, continuous-flight augers (rotary augers) are frequently used. As the drill advances, additional auger flights are added and soil is brought to the surface in a disturbed form.

In auger boring, it is possible to identify even disturbed soils. Since, the borehole is kept dry, it is particularly suitable for advancing borings above water table to obtain undisturbed partially saturated samples. It further facilitates the determination of free water level.

Augers can be operated mechanically or manually (Fig. 2.7). Hand augers are used for depths upto about 6 m whereas mechanically operated augers are used for greater depth and they can also be used for gravely soils.

The hand augers used in boring are about 15 to 20 cm in diameter. The lower end of hand auger is attached to a pipe of 18 mm diameter.

For taking samples from readily driven hole, an auger known as 'Post-Hole Auger' is used.

Mechanical augers are driven by power. If depth of bore hole increases above 12 m, then mechanical augers become inconvenient and other boring methods are used.

Auger boring becomes troublesome, when there are large boulders or cobbles.

The site investigation is done quite rapidly and economically by using auger boring.

(2) Wash Boring

Wash boring (Fig. 2.8) is commonly used for boring in difficult soil. To start with, the hole is advanced a short depth by auger and then a casing pipe is pushed to prevent the sides from caving in. The hole is then continued by the use of a chopping bit fixed at the end of a string of hollow drill rods. A stream of water under pressure is forced through the rod and the bit into the hole, which loosens the soil as the water flows up around the pipe. The loosened soil in suspension in water is discharged into a tub. The soil in suspension settles down in the tub and the clean water flows into a sump which is reused for circulation. The power for wash boring is either mechanical or man power drawn.

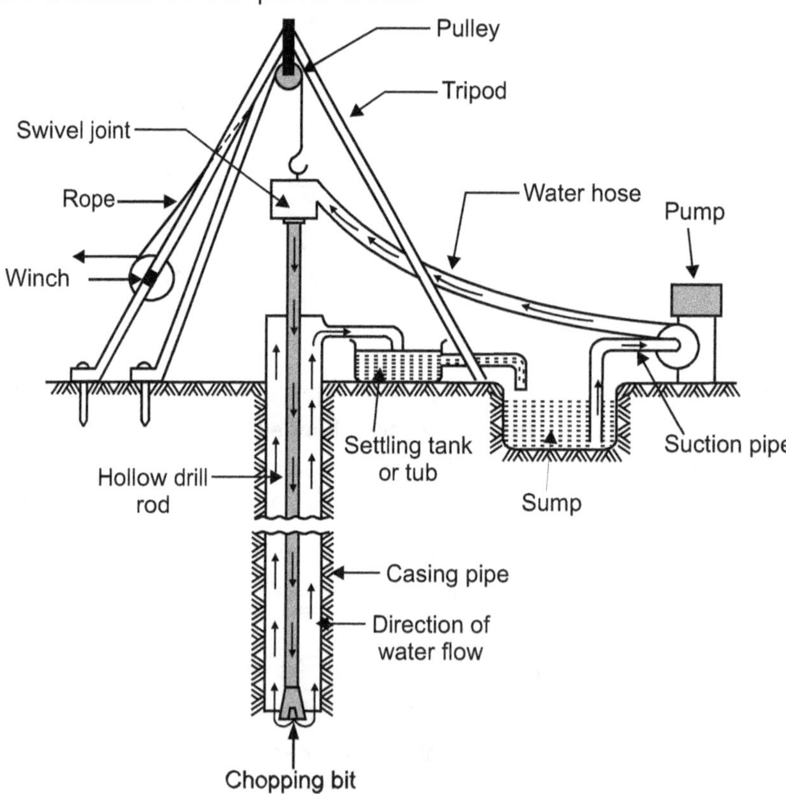

Fig. 2.8 : Wash boring

Mainly wash boring is used for drilling holes in the ground. Once hole is drilled, a sampler is inserted to obtain soil samples for laboratory testing.

Advantages :

- Instrument used is relatively light in weight.
- Inexpensive method of boring.
- Fast and simple method.

Disadvantages :

- It is slow in stiff and coarse grained soils.
- Cannot be used in rocky strata.
- Good quality undisturbed samples cannot be obtained.
- Not suitable in areas where ground water table is very near to ground.

(3) Rotary Drilling (Core Boring or Core Drilling)

Rotary boring or rotary drilling is a very fast method of advancing hole in the rocks and soils. In this method, hole is drilled by rotating a hollow drill rod which has a cutting bit at its lower end (Fig. 2.9). At the top of drill rod, drill head is provided. It comprises of a rotary mechanism and an arrangement for applying pressure.

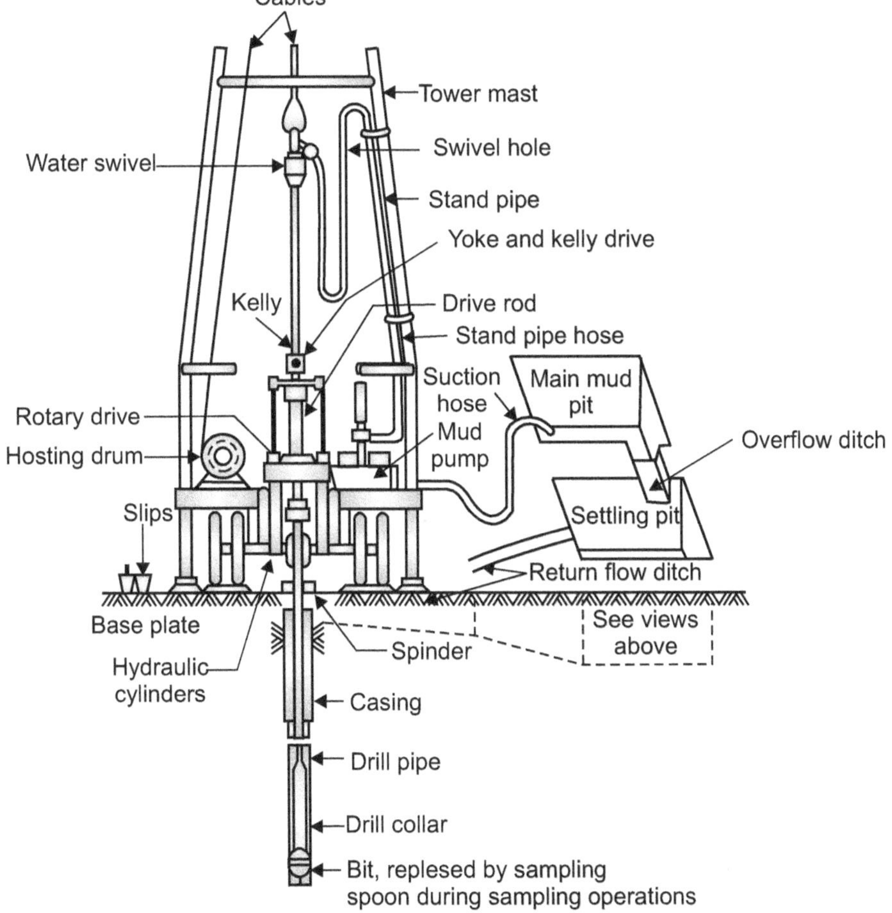

Fig. 2.9 : Rotary drilling rig (After Hvorslev, 1948)

When the drilling rod is rotated, the cutting bit shears off chips of the material penetrated. A drilling fluid is introduced under pressure through the drilling rod to the bottom of the hole. The cuttings of the material penetrated are carried to the ground by the fluid through the annular space between the drilling rod and the walls of the hole. Another function of fluid is to cool the drilling bit. The drilling fluid also supports the walls of the hole, in case of un-cased hole.

The drilling bit is replaced by a sampler, when soil sample is required to be taken.

Advantages :
- Rotary drilling can be used in clay, sand and rocks.
- Bore holes of diameter 50 mm to 200 mm can be easily drilled by this method.

Disadvantage :
If soil is containing a large percentage of particles of gravel size and larger, this method is not well adapted because, the particles of this size start rotating below the drill rod and it becomes difficult to drill the hole.

(4) Percussion Drilling

Percussion drilling is another method of drilling hole in which a heavy drilling bit is alternately raised and dropped in such a manner that it powders the underlying material and forms into a slurry in water. This slurry is removed out of the hole by means of bailers or sand pumps.

In all types of drilling the sides of the holes may be stabilized, if required, by the use of drilling mud or casing pipes. A drilling mud is nothing but bentonite clay mixed in water.

The machinery used to advance holes and take sample is called a *drill rig*.

Percussion drilling method is specially used for making holes in rocks, boulders and other hard strata. Percussion drilling consists of lifting and dropping of a very heavy chisel in a vertical hole. The material gets pulverised. Water is added to the hole, if the chisel strikes above water table. The water forms a slurry of the disintegrated material, which is removed by sand pump or a boiler at intervals. Casing may be required for this method. For drilling tube well also, percussion drilling is used.

Advantages :
- Percussion drilling can be used in all types of soils.
- It is very much useful for boring deeper holes like that for tube well through rock or boulders.

Disadvantages :
- Because of heavy blows by the chisel, the material at the bottom is in disturbed state.
- More expensive as compared to other methods.
- Difficult to detect minor changes in the properties of the strata penetrated.

(5) Core Drilling

This method is used for advancing holes and for obtaining rock cores. It consists of a core barrel fitted with a drilling bit and is fixed to a hollow drilling rod. The bit advances and cuts an annular hole around an intact core, as the drilling bit is rotated. Then the core is removed from its bottom and is retained by a core lifter and brought to ground surface. To keep the drilling bit cool and to carry the disintegrated material to the ground surface, water is pumped continuously into the drilling rod.

Drilling may be done by a diamond studded bit or a cutting edge having chilled shot. The diamond drilling is costlier, but is superior to the other type of drilling. If double tube core barrel is used, it gives good quality of the rock sample.

(6) Test Pits

This is one of the most dependable and informative method of soil exploration, however, it is limited to a depth of 4 to 5 m only. Trial pits are suitable for all types of soils and permit most detailed visual examination of soil formation for the entire depth. Another advantage of this method lies in getting relatively undisturbed soil sample, from the walls or bottom of pit, by pushing a thin walled steel tube in the soil strata, Deeper pits have to be supported by sheeting and bracing [Fig. 2.10 (a)] or by cribbing [Fig. 2.10 (b)] to prevent collapse (IS : 4453, 1980). Ventilation of deep test pits is necessary to prevent accumulation of dead air. This is done by providing pipes starting slightly above the floor and extending about one metre above the top of the pit. Special precautions have to be exercised if presence of obnoxious gases is anticipated (IS : 3764, 1966). A dewatering system has to be used if pits are to extend below the water table.

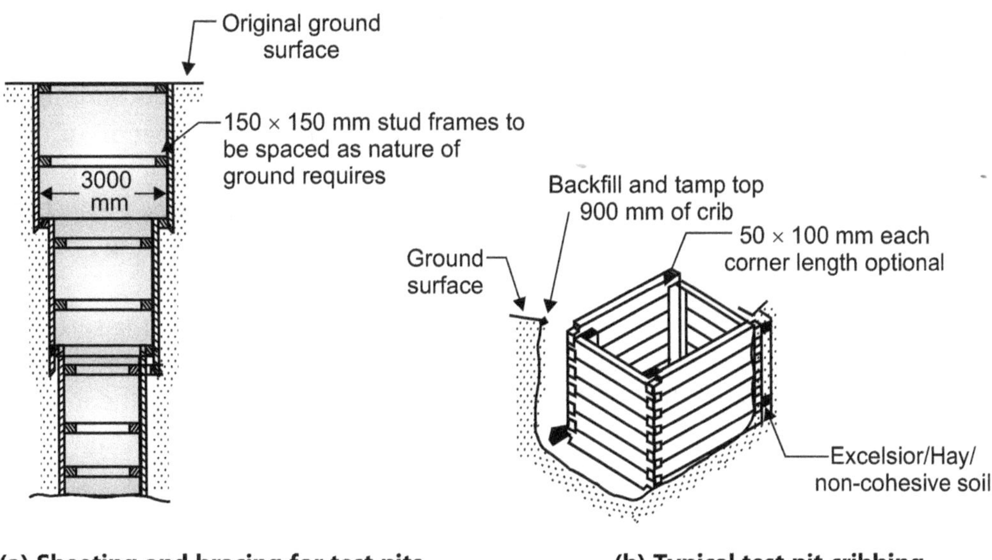

(a) Sheeting and bracing for test pits   **(b) Typical test pit cribbing**

Fig. 2.10 : Arrangement for protecting test pits

(From IS : 4453, 1980. Reproduced with permission of Bureau of Indian Standards)

Trenches : These are similar to test pits. They provide a long continuous exposure of the surface of the ground along a desired line or section. They are best suited for exploration on slopes. Necessary safety precautions have to be taken as in deep test pits.

2.8 GEOTECHNICAL PROBLEMS

A civil engineer has many diverse and important encounters with soil. Every civil engineering structure whether it be a building, a bridge, a tower, an embankment, a road pavement, tunnel, dam or a railway line has to be constructed on foundation soil or rock depending upon site conditions. Soil is therefore, ultimate foundation material which supports the structure. The proper functioning of the structure will therefore depend critically on the success of the foundation element resting on the subsoil. Soil is also the most abundantly available construction material. From ancient times, man has used soil for the construction of tombs, monuments, dwelling and barrages for storing water.

Some of soil related problems are as follows :

1. **Soil Under Road Pavements :** A pavement can be flexible or rigid and its performance depends upon the subsoil on which it rests. Certain characteristics of the subsoil need to be determined before the design of various components of pavement are made. On pavements with high traffic intensity, the effect of repetition of loading and the consequent fatigue failure has to be taken into account. Apart from this, problems related to pavement design are : [1] Frost, heave and thaw, [2] Problems of pumping of clay subsoils and suitability of soil as a construction material for constructing highways, railways, earthfills or cuts.

2. **Soil for Earth Dams :** Soil is used as the only construction material in an earth dam. Hence, the construction of earth dam requires a thorough knowledge of soil mechanics. Since, the soil available can either be homogeneous or of composite section, its design requires the determination of all physical properties of soil. The determination of optimum water content at which maximum density would be obtained after compaction is the most essential aspect of the design. Characteristics regarding stability of slopes, consolidation, reduction in pore pressure and possible effects of vibrations during an earthquake are also required to be taken into account.

3. **Soil Under the Foundations :** Every structure is to be founded in or on the surface of the earth. It is therefore, necessary to know the bearing capacity of the soil, the pattern of stress distribution in the soil beneath the loaded area, the probable settlement of the foundations, effect of vibrations and ground of water etc. A knowledge of swelling and shrinkage characteristics of soil beneath the foundation is also very essential.

In design and construction of underground structures such as tunnels, conduits, power houses, bracing for excavations and earth retaining structures, the role of soil is again very crucial. Since, the soil is in direct contact with the structures, it acts as a medium of load transfer and hence for any analysis of forces acting on the structures, one has to consider the aspect of the stress distribution through the soil. This however, cannot be done by considering the behaviour of the structure in isolation of the soil or by treating the soil independently of the structure. The structure too, causes stresses and strains to the soil, while the stability of the structure itself is affected by soil behaviour. The class of problems where the structure and soil mutually interact, are known as *soil structure interaction problems.*

For designing foundations for machines such as turbines, compressors, forges, lathes etc., which transmit vibrations to the soil, one has to understand the behaviour of soils under vibratory loads. The effect of quarry blasts, earthquakes and nuclear explosions on structures is greatly influenced by the soil medium through which the shock waves traverse. The regions which experience freezing temperatures, problems arise because the soils expand upon freezing and exert a force on the structures in contact with them. Thawing of the soil results in a loss of strength in the soil. Structures resting on these soils will perform satisfactorily only if measures are taken to prevent frost, heave or designed to withstand the effects of freezing and thawing. Thawing occurs due to melting of ice.

2.9 THREE PHASE SYSTEM OF SOIL   [May 14]

The soil mass in general, is a three phase system composed of solid, liquid and gaseous matter. The solid particles are called as *soil grains*. The void between the solid particles is filled partially with water and partially with air. The liquid phase is generally water that fills the voids partly or wholly. The gaseous phase is usually air that occupies the voids not filled by water. These three constituents of soil mass are blended together forming a complex material. They do not occupy separate spaces. The properties of soil mass depend upon the relative percentage of these constituents and their arrangements. Hence, the relative volumetric and gravimetric proportions of the solids, water and air in a soil mass are required to be studied.

Though the different phases present in the soil mass cannot be separated as shown in Fig. 2.11 (a), but for a better understanding of soil behaviour, it is helpful to separate them and study the phase diagram. The diagrammatic representation of the different phases present in the soil mass is termed as a phase diagram. Fig. 2.11 (b) shows three phase system, combination of solids, air and water. When soil mass is not saturated, the voids present in the soil mass are filled by liquid (water) or air.

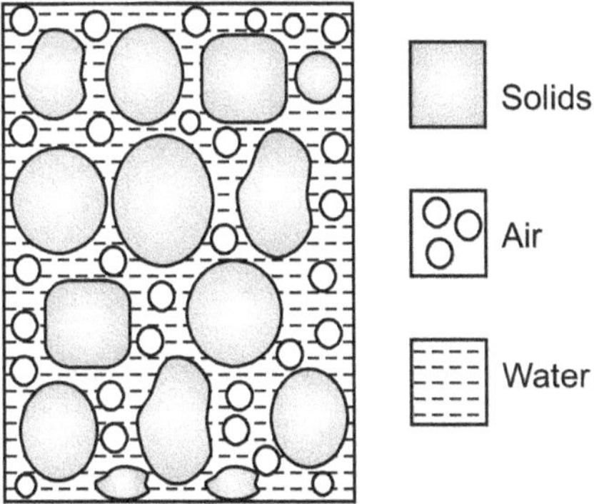

Fig. 2.11 (a) : Natural soil

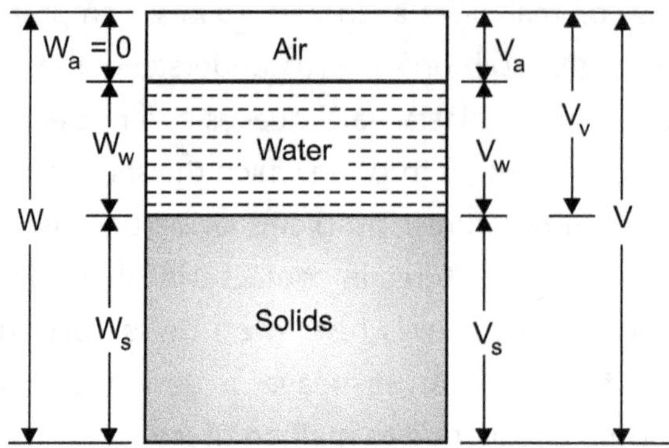

Fig. 2.11 (b) : Partially saturated condition

Three phase system of soil mass

W = Total weight of soil mass

W_a = Weight of air = 0

W_w = Weight of water

W_s = Weight of solids

V = Total volume of soil mass

V_a = Volume of air

V_w = Volume of water

V_v = Volume of voids

V_s = Volume of solids

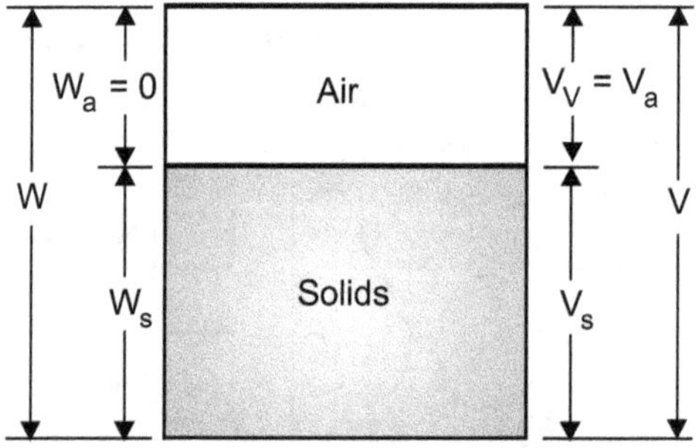

Fig. 2.11 (c) : Dry condition

Fig. 2.11 (c) shows the combination of air and solid particles forming 2-phase system. When soil mass is completely dry, the voids present in the soil mass are completely filled only with air [gaseous phase]. The liquid phase [water] remains absent in such case and hence $V_a = V_v$.

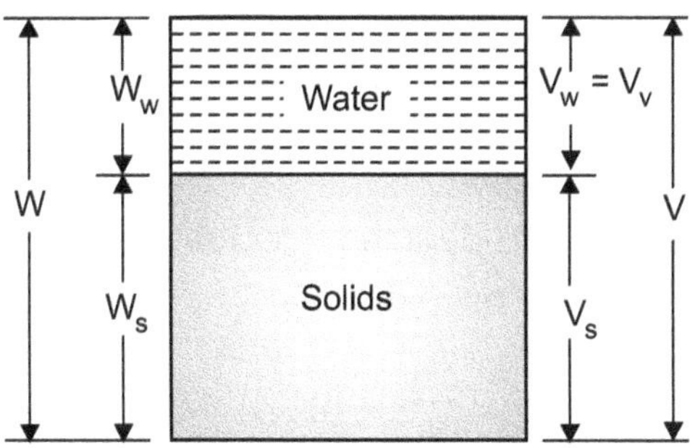

Fig. 2.11 (d) : Saturated condition

Fig. 2.11 (d) shows 2-phase system of saturated soil. Since, soil is saturated, the voids are fully filled only with water and hence $V_v = V_w$.

From Fig. 2.11 (b),

$$\text{Total weight, } W = W_s + W_w$$

The weight of air is negligible and hence for all practical purposes, it can be assumed to be zero.

$$\text{Total volume, } V = V_s + V_v = V_s + V_a + V_w \text{ (3-phase system)}$$

From Fig. 2.11 (c) for dry soil :

$$W = W_s$$

$$V = V_s + V_a \text{ (2-phase system)}$$

From Fig. 2.11 (d) for fully saturated soil :

$$W = W_s + W_w$$

$$V = V_s + V_w \text{ (2-phase system)}$$

2.10 BASIC DEFINITIONS   [May 17]

(a) Water Content : The water content [w] of a soil mass is defined as 'the ratio of mass of water [M_w] in voids to the mass of solids [M_s]'.

$$w = \frac{M_w}{M_s} \times 100\% \qquad\qquad [0 \leq w < \infty]$$

It is expressed as percentage.

(b) Void Ratio : The ratio of volume of voids [$V_v = V_a + V_w$], to the volume of solids [V_s] is defined as void ratio (e).

$$e = \frac{V_v}{V_s} \qquad\qquad [0 < e < \infty]$$

It is expressed as decimal [fraction].

(c) Porosity : It is the ratio of volume of voids [V_v] to the total volume of soil [V]. It is denoted by (n).

$$n = \frac{V_v}{V} \times 100\% \qquad\qquad [0 < n < 100\%]$$

It is expressed as percentage.

(d) The Degree of Saturation : The degree of saturation $[S_r]$ is a ratio of the volume of water $[V_w]$ in the voids to the volume of voids $[V_v]$.

$$S_r = \frac{V_w}{V_v} \times 100\% \qquad\qquad [0 \leq S_r \leq 100\%]$$

It is expressed as percentage.

(e) Density : Density $[\rho]$ of a soil mass is defined as 'the mass of unit volume of a soil'.

$$\rho = \frac{M}{V}$$

where,

M = Mass of soil

V = Total volume of soil

It is expressed as kg/cubic metre or gram/cubic centimeters.

(f) Unit Weight : Unit weight $[\gamma]$ of a soil is defined as 'the weight of unit volume of a soil'.

$$\gamma = \frac{W}{V}$$

where,

W = Weight of soil

V = Total volume of soil

It is expressed as a kN/cubic metre.

$$\gamma = \frac{W}{V} = \frac{M \times g}{V} = \frac{M}{V} \times g$$

$$\gamma = \rho \times g$$

This is also known as *'bulk unit weight'* of a soil.

(g) Unit Weight of Water : The unit weight of water at a given temperature is expressed as the ratio of the weight of water to the volume of water at same temperature and is designated as $[\gamma_w]$. The notation $[\gamma_o]$ is normally used for unit weight of water at reference temperature 4°C.

$$\gamma_w = \frac{W_w}{V_w} \text{ kNm}^3 \text{ at certain temperature.}$$

(h) Dry Unit Weight : The dry unit weight $[\gamma_d]$ of a soil mass is expressed as the ratio of the weights of solids $[W_s]$ to the total volume $[V]$.

$$\gamma_d = \frac{W_s}{V} \text{ kN/m}^3$$

(i) Saturated Unit Weight : The saturated unit weight $[\gamma_{sat}]$ of a soil mass is the ratio of the saturated weight $[W_{sat}]$ of the mass [i.e. $S_r = 100\%$] to the total volume [V].

$$\gamma_{sat} = \frac{W_{sat}}{V} \ kN/m^3$$

(j) Unit Weight of Solids : The unit weight of solids $[\gamma_s]$ is defined as 'the ratio of the weight of solids $[W_s]$ to the volume of solids $[V_s]$'.

$$\gamma_s = \frac{W_s}{V_s} \ kN/m^3$$

Note : Similar expressions can be written for density also.

(k) Specific Gravity : The specific gravity of any substance is the ratio of its weight in air to the weight of an equal volume of water at reference temperature 4°C. The specific gravity of a soil mass including air, water and solids is termed as mass specific gravity $[G_m]$.

$$G_m = \frac{\gamma_t}{\gamma_o} = \frac{W}{V} \times \frac{1}{\gamma_o} = \frac{W}{V\,\gamma_o}$$

where,

γ_t = Unit weight of soil in air

γ_o = Unit weight of water at reference temperature 4°C

W = Total weight of soil

V = Total volume of soil

The specific gravity of only soil solids, excluding water and air is expressed by

$$G = \frac{\gamma_s}{\gamma_o} = \frac{W}{V_s\,\gamma_o}$$

(*l*) Percentage Air Voids, n_a : It is percentage of air in the voids. It is defined as 'the ratio of the volume of air $[V_a]$ to the volume of voids $[V_v]$'.

$$n_a = \frac{V_a}{V_v} \times 100\% \qquad\qquad [0 \le n_a \le 100]$$

It is expressed as percentage.

If $n_a = 0\%$, normally soil sample is saturated.

If $n_a = 100\%$, soil sample is dry, i.e. all the voids are filled only with air, and no water is present in the voids.

(m) Air Content, a_c : It is the ratio of the volume of air (V_a) to the total volume of the soil.

$$a_c = \frac{V_a}{V}$$

$$a_c = n\,(1 - S_r)$$

(n) Absolute Specific Gravity : It is the ratio of weight of absolute solids to the weight of equal volume of water.

The soil solids are not perfect solids. They contain some voids or pores or small holes on the surface of the solids. Some of these voids are permeable through which water can enter, whereas others are impermeable. Since, the permeable voids get filled with water when the soil is wet, they are in reality a part of void space and not part of solids. If both these permeable and impermeable voids are excluded from the volume of solids, the remaining is the correct volume of solids.

$$G_a = \frac{[\gamma_s]_a}{\gamma_w}$$

$$G_a = \text{Absolute specific gravity}$$

where, $[\gamma_s]_a = \text{Unit weight of the absolute solids}$

$$\gamma_w = \text{Unit weight of equal volume of water.}$$

The absolute specific gravity is not of much practical use, as it is difficult to differentiate the permeable and impermeable voids. In most of the cases, the impermeable voids are taken as part of solids.

2.11 INTER-RELATIONSHIPS   [May 14, 15, Nov. 15]

(a) Relation between Void Ratio [e] and Porosity [n] :

By definition,

$$e = \frac{V_v}{V_s} = \frac{V_v}{V - V_v} = \frac{\dfrac{V_v}{V}}{1 - \dfrac{V_v}{V}}$$

$$\boxed{e = \frac{n}{1 - n}}$$

Also,

$$n = \frac{V_v}{V} = \frac{V_v}{V_s + V_v} = \frac{\dfrac{V_v}{V_s}}{1 + \dfrac{V_v}{V_s}}$$

$$\boxed{n = \frac{e}{1 + e}}$$

(b) Relation between Void Ratio (e) and the Water Content (w) :

$$\text{Water content} = w = \frac{M_w}{M_s} = \frac{W_w}{W_s} \qquad \qquad ... (2.1)$$

But　　　　　　　　　$W_w = V_w \times \gamma_w$　and　$W_s = V_s \times \gamma_s$

Hence,　　　　　　　$w = \dfrac{V_w \times \gamma_w}{V_s \times \gamma_s} = \dfrac{V_w}{V_s} \times \dfrac{\gamma_w}{\gamma_s}$

But　　　　　　　　　$\dfrac{\gamma_s}{\gamma_w} = G$

Hence,　　　　　　　$w = \dfrac{V_w}{V_s} \times \dfrac{1}{G}$　　　　　　　... (2.2)

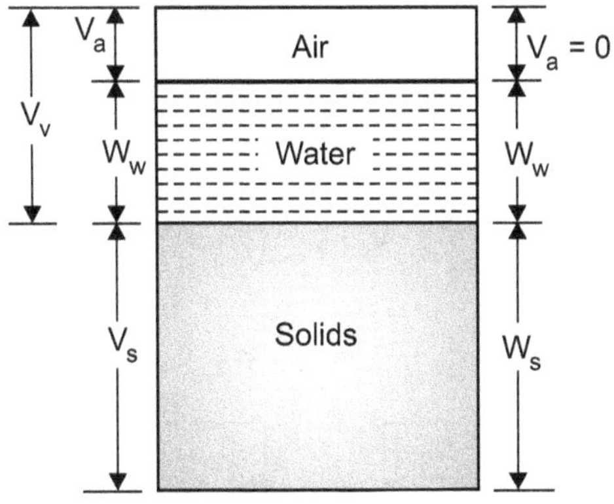

Fig. 2.12

We know that saturation,　　$S_r = \dfrac{V_w}{V_v}$　or　$V_w = S_r \cdot V_v$

Using in (2.2),　　　　　　$w = \dfrac{S_r \cdot V_v}{V_s} \times \dfrac{1}{G}$

But　　　　　void ratio (e) $= \dfrac{V_v}{V_s}$

　　　　　　　　$w = \dfrac{S_r \times e}{G}$;　$e = \dfrac{w\,G}{S_r}$

i.e.　　　　　　$\boxed{e \cdot S_r = wG}$

For $S_r = 1$ (fully saturated soil), $e = wG$

Alternative Method :

　　　　　　$S_r \cdot e = \dfrac{V_w}{V_v} \times \dfrac{V_v}{V_s} = \dfrac{V_w}{V_s}$　　　　　　... (2.3)

But,　　　　　$\gamma_w = \dfrac{W_w}{V_w}$　$\therefore$　$V_w = \dfrac{W_w}{\gamma_w}$　　　　　... (2.4)

and　　　　　$\gamma_s = \dfrac{W_s}{V_s}$　$\therefore$　$V_s = \dfrac{W_s}{\gamma_s}$　　　　　... (2.5)

$\therefore$ From equations (2.3), (2.4) and (2.5),

$$S_r \cdot e = \frac{V_w}{V_s} = \frac{W_w}{\gamma_w} \cdot \frac{\gamma_s}{W_s}$$

$$= \left(\frac{W_w}{W_s}\right) \cdot \left(\frac{\gamma_s}{\gamma_w}\right) = w \cdot G$$

(c) Relation between G, e, w and γ :

$$\text{Bulk unit weight} = \gamma = \frac{W}{V} = \frac{W_s + W_w}{V_s + V_v}$$

$$= \frac{W_s\left(1 + \dfrac{W_w}{W_s}\right)}{V_s\left(1 + \dfrac{V_v}{V_s}\right)}$$

Since, $\dfrac{W_w}{W_s} = w, \quad \dfrac{V_v}{V_s} = e \quad$ and $\quad \dfrac{W_s}{V_s} = \gamma_s = G\gamma_w$

$$\boxed{\gamma = \frac{G\,\gamma_w\,[1 + w]}{1 + e}} \quad \text{and} \quad \boxed{\rho = \frac{G\rho_w\,(1 + w)}{1 + e}} \qquad \dots (2.6)$$

We know that $\qquad S_r \cdot e = w \cdot G \quad$ or $\quad w = \dfrac{S_r \cdot e}{G}$

Using in (2.6), $\qquad \boxed{\gamma = \left(\frac{G + S_r \cdot e}{1 + e}\right)\gamma_w} \quad \text{and} \quad \boxed{\rho = \left(\frac{G + S_r \cdot e}{1 + e}\right)\rho_w}$

If $S_r = 1$ (saturated soil), $\boxed{\gamma_{sat} = \left(\frac{G + e}{1 + e}\right)\gamma_w} \quad \text{and} \quad \boxed{\rho_{sat} = \left(\frac{G + e}{1 + e}\right)\rho_w}$

If $w = 0$ (dry soil), $\qquad \boxed{\gamma_d = \frac{G \cdot \gamma_w}{1 + e}} \quad \text{and} \quad \boxed{\rho_d = \frac{G \cdot \rho_w}{1 + e}}$

$$\therefore \qquad \frac{1}{\gamma_d} = \frac{1 + e}{G \cdot \gamma_w}$$

or, $\qquad e = \dfrac{G \cdot \gamma_w}{\gamma_d} - 1 \quad \text{and} \quad e = \dfrac{G\,\rho_w}{\rho_d} - 1$

(d) Relation between γ' (submerged unit weight), G, e :

γ', submerged unit weight $= \gamma_{sat} - \gamma_w$

$$= \left(\frac{G + e}{1 + e}\right)\gamma_w - \gamma_w$$

$$\boxed{\gamma' = \left(\frac{G-1}{1+e}\right)\gamma_w} \quad \text{and} \quad \boxed{\rho' = \left(\frac{G-1}{1+e}\right)\rho_w}$$

(e) Relation between γ, γ_d and w :

$$w = \frac{M_w}{M_s} = \frac{W_w}{W_s}$$

$$1 + w = \frac{W_w + W_s}{W_s} = \frac{W}{W_s}$$

$$W_s = \frac{W}{1+w}$$

$$\gamma_d = \frac{W_s}{V} = \frac{W}{V[1+w]}$$

$$\boxed{\gamma_d = \frac{\gamma}{1+w}} \quad \text{and} \quad \boxed{\rho_d = \frac{\rho}{1+w}}$$

(f) Relation between ρ_d, n_a, S_r, w and G :

$$V = V_a + V_w + V_s$$

$$1 = \frac{V_a}{V} + \frac{wM_s}{V\,\gamma_w} + \frac{M_s}{V\,\gamma_s}$$

$$1 - n_a = \frac{w\,\gamma_d}{\gamma_w} + \frac{\gamma_d}{G\,\gamma_w}$$

$$\boxed{\gamma_d = \frac{G\,[1-n_a]\,\gamma_w}{1+wG}} \quad \text{and} \quad \boxed{\rho_d = \frac{G\,(1-n_a)\,\rho_w}{1+wG}}$$

If $n_a = 0$ (saturated soil, $w = w_{sat}$) :

$$\gamma_d = \left(\frac{G}{1 + w_{sat}\cdot G}\right)\gamma_w$$

If soil is not fully saturated, $e = \dfrac{wG}{S_r}$

$$\gamma_d = \frac{G\cdot\rho_w}{1+e} = \frac{G\cdot\gamma_w}{1 + \dfrac{wG}{S_r}}$$

(g) Density index or Relative density, R_d :

The density index (I_d) for coarse grained soils is defined as

$$I_d = \frac{e_{max} - e}{e_{max} - e_{min}} = \frac{V_{max} - V}{V_{max} - V_{min}}$$

or

$$I_d = \frac{1/\gamma_{d\ min} - 1/\gamma_d}{1/\gamma_{d\ min} - 1/\gamma_{d\ max}}$$

where,

e_{max} = Maximum void ratio [loosest state]

e_{min} = Minimum void ratio [densest state]

e = Natural void ratio of soil

V = Natural volume

V_{max} = Maximum volume

V_{min} = Minimum volume

$\gamma_{d\ max}$ = Maximum dry density

$\gamma_{d\ min}$ = Minimum dry density

γ_d = Dry density in natural state

The density index varies from 0 to 100%.

Qualitatively, it is described as :

Density Index	Compaction state
0 - 15	Very loose
15 - 35	Loose
35 - 65	Medium dense [compact]
65 - 85	Dense
85 - 100	Very dense

The concept of relative density is purely arbitrary and is not based on density of any physical body. The concept applies only to sand and not silt or clay.

The relation between void ratio and I_d can be represented by a graph shown below; and the mathematical equation can be derived from the same.

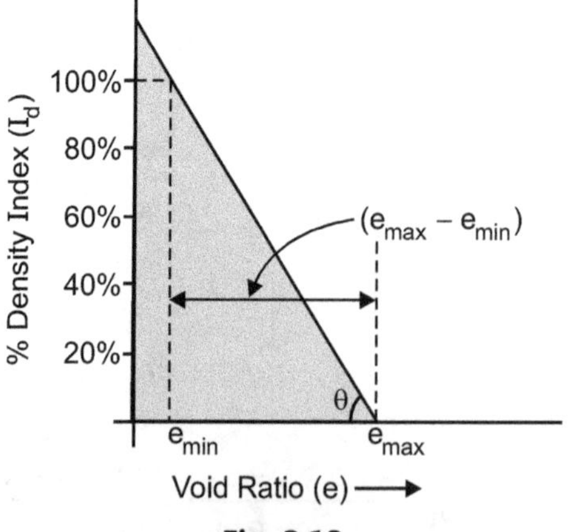

Fig. 2.13

From Fig. 2.13,

$$\tan \theta \;=\; \frac{I_d \;[100\%]}{e_{max} - e_{min}}$$

i.e.
$$\frac{e_{max} - e_{min}}{100} \;=\; \cot \theta$$

Any intermediate value of I_d can be expressed as,

$$e_{max} \;=\; e + I_d \cdot \cot \theta$$
$$=\; e + I_d\,[e_{max} - e_{min}]$$

$\therefore$
$$I_d \;=\; \frac{e_{max} - e}{[e_{max} - e_{min}]}$$

Expression for I_d in terms of dry density can be derived as under :

$$\gamma_d \;=\; \frac{G \cdot \gamma_w}{1 + e}$$

$\therefore$
$$e \;=\; \left(\frac{G \cdot \gamma_w}{\gamma_d} - 1\right)$$

$$e_{max} \;=\; \left(\frac{G \cdot \gamma_w}{\gamma_{d\,min}} - 1\right) \;\text{and}\; e_{min} \;=\; \left(\frac{G \cdot \gamma_w}{\gamma_{d\,max}} - 1\right)$$

It may be noted that, when void ratio is e_{max}, dry density will be $\gamma_{d\,min}$ and when void ratio is minimum, i.e. e_{min}, dry density will be maximum [i.e. $\gamma_{d\,max}$].

$\therefore$
$$I_d \;=\; \frac{e_{max} - e}{e_{max} - e_{min}}$$

$$=\; \frac{\left(\dfrac{G \cdot \gamma_w}{\gamma_{d\,min}} - 1\right) - \left(\dfrac{G \cdot \gamma_w}{\gamma_d} - 1\right)}{\left(\dfrac{G \cdot \gamma_w}{\gamma_{d\,min}} - 1\right) - \left(\dfrac{G \cdot \gamma_w}{\gamma_{d\,max}} - 1\right)}$$

$$=\; \left(\frac{\dfrac{1}{\gamma_{d\,min}} - \dfrac{1}{\gamma_d}}{\dfrac{1}{\gamma_{d\,min}} - \dfrac{1}{\gamma_{d\,max}}}\right)$$

$$=\; \frac{\gamma_d - \gamma_{d\,min}}{\gamma_d \cdot \gamma_{d\,min}} \times \frac{\gamma_{d\,min} \times \gamma_{d\,max}}{\gamma_{d\,max} - \gamma_{d\,min}}$$

$\therefore$
$$I_d \;=\; \left(\frac{\gamma_{d\,max}}{\gamma_d}\right)\left(\frac{\gamma_d - \gamma_{d\,min}}{\gamma_{d\,max} - \gamma_{d\,min}}\right)$$

For very dense gravelly sand sometimes density index can be more than 100%. This would mean that the natural packing does not permit itself to be repeated in the laboratory. The application of the relative density test to sand is to check the achieved density and the compactness of fills made of granular material. Loose sand can best be densities by vibration. In evaluating sandy soils, their natural and relative densities are of paramount importance for the evaluation of their properties as a material upon which to found structures.

From the change in the volume of voids in a soil, for example on compaction, it is possible to evaluate the changes in density of a soil medium, and thus to judge the achieved degree of compaction.

Depending upon the properties of the particles of the sand and the texture of the latter, two kinds of sands of the same volume of voids [porosity] may possess totally different abilities of densification [compaction]. Hence, the coefficient of relative density of a given sand usually gives us a clearer idea of the density than the value of the void ratio itself.

SOLVED EXAMPLES

Example 2.1 : The moisture content of saturated soil is 30% and specific gravity is 2.7. Find void ratio [e] and porosity [n]. What will be the degree of saturation [S_r] and the air content [a_c] if moisture content gets reduced to 5% on drying ?

Solution :

$$e \times S_r = wG$$

But for full saturation, $S_r = 1$

$$e = wG$$
$$= 0.30 \times 2.7 = 0.810$$

$$n = \frac{e}{1 + e}$$
$$= \frac{0.810}{1.810} = 0.45 = 45\%$$

$$S_r = \frac{wG}{e}$$
$$= \frac{0.05 \times 2.7}{0.810} = 0.167 = \mathbf{16.7\%}$$

$$a_c = n [1 - S_r]$$
$$= 0.45 [1 - 0.167] = 0.375 = \mathbf{37.5\%}$$

Example 2.2 : The dry density [ρ_d] of a soil is 1.75 g/cm³. What is its dry unit weight γ_d ? Find the bulk density [ρ] if the unit weight is 19.8 kN/m³.

Solution :

$$\gamma_d = \rho_d \times g = 1.75 \times 9.81 = \mathbf{17.17 \ kN/m^2}$$

$$\rho = \frac{\gamma}{g} = \frac{19.80}{9.81} = \mathbf{2.02 \ g/cm^3}$$

Example 2.3 : The dry unit weight $[\gamma_d]$ of a soil having 12% water content is 18.2 kN/m³. Find bulk unit weight $[\gamma]$, saturated unit weight $[\gamma_{sat}]$, and submerged unit weight $[\gamma]$. Assume G = 2.65.

Solution :

$$\gamma = \rho_d [1 + w]$$
$$= 18.2 [1 + 0.12] = \mathbf{20.38 \ kN/m^3}$$
$$e = \frac{G \gamma_w}{\gamma_d} - 1 = \left(\frac{2.65 \times 9.81}{18.2} - 1\right) = 0.43$$
$$\gamma_{sat} = \frac{[G + e] \gamma_w}{1 + e}$$
$$= \frac{[2.6 + 0.43] \times 9.81}{1.43} = \mathbf{21.13 \ kN/m^3}$$
$$\gamma' = \frac{[G - 1] \gamma_w}{1 + e}$$

$\therefore \qquad$
$$\gamma' = \frac{[2.65 - 1] \times 9.81}{1.43} = 11.32 \ kN/m^3$$

or
$$\gamma' = \gamma_{sat} - \gamma_w$$
$$= 21.13 - 9.81 = \mathbf{11.32 \ kN/m^3}$$

Example 2.4 : The bulk unit weight $[\gamma]$ of a soil is 19.5 kN/m³, water content is 20% and degree of saturation $[S_r]$ is 75%. What will be the moisture content and unit weight on full saturation ?

Solution :

$$S_r = \frac{e_w}{e} = \frac{wG}{w_{sat} \, G} = \frac{w}{w_{sat}}$$
$$w_{sat} = \frac{w}{S_r}$$
$$= \frac{20}{0.75} = \mathbf{26.67\%}$$
$$\gamma_{sat} = \gamma \left(\frac{1 + w_{sat}}{1 + w}\right)$$
$$= 19.5 \left(\frac{1 + 26.67}{1 + 20}\right) = \mathbf{25.69 \ kN/m^3}$$

Example 2.5 : The bulk density of soil sample is 18 kN/m³. The specific gravity of soil solids is 2.70 and moisture content 15%. Calculate void ratio, porosity, degree of saturation and dry unit weight.

Solution : Given :

$$\gamma = 18 \ kN/m^3 \qquad\qquad \text{Take } \gamma_w = 9.81 \ kN/m^3$$
$$G = 2.70$$
$$w = 15\% = 0.15$$

(i) Dry unit weight,

$$\gamma_d = \frac{\gamma}{1 + w}$$

$$= \frac{18}{1 + 0.15} = \mathbf{15.65 \ kN/m^3}$$

(ii) Void ratio,

$$e = \frac{G \cdot \gamma_w}{\gamma_d} - 1$$

$$= \frac{2.7 \times 9.81}{15.65} - 1 = 0.692 = \mathbf{69.2\%}$$

Porosity,

$$n = \frac{e}{1 + e}$$

$$= \frac{0.692}{1 + 0.692} = \mathbf{40.9\%}$$

(iii) Degree of saturation, S_r :

Since,

$$e \cdot S_r = w \cdot G$$

$\therefore$

$$0.692 \times S_r = 0.15 \times 2.7$$

$\therefore$

$$S_r = 0.585 = \mathbf{58.5\%}$$

Example 2.6 : If specific gravity of soil sample is 2.67, find the ratio of submerged density of its soil mass to its dry density.

Solution :

$$\rho_{sub} = \left(\frac{G - 1}{1 + e}\right) \rho_w$$

$$\rho_d = \left(\frac{G}{1 + e}\right) \rho_w$$

$\therefore$

$$\frac{\rho_{sub}}{\rho_d} = \left(\frac{G - 1}{1 + e}\right) \times \left(\frac{1 + e}{G}\right)$$

$$= \frac{G - 1}{G} = \frac{2.67 - 1}{2.67} = 0.625$$

$\therefore$

$$\frac{\rho_{sub}}{\rho_d} = \mathbf{0.625}$$

Example 2.7 : A soil sample weighing 310 N has a volume of 0.0183 m³. When dried out in oven its weight reduces to 270 N. The specific gravity of soil solid is 2.65. Determine γ_d, n and S_r. **(Nov. 16 [6 M])**

Solution : Given :

$$V = 0.0183 \ m^3$$

$$W = 310 \ N$$

$$W_d = 270 \ N = W_s$$

$$G = 2.65$$

(i)
$$\gamma_d = \frac{W_s}{V}$$

$$= \frac{270}{0.0183} = 14754.098 \text{ N/m}^3 = 14.75 \text{ kN/m}^3$$

$$e = \frac{G \cdot \gamma_w}{\gamma_d} - 1 = \frac{2.65 \times 9.81}{14.75} - 1 = \mathbf{0.762}$$

(ii)
$$n = \frac{e}{1 + e}$$

$$= \frac{0.762}{1 + 0.762} = 0.4325 = \mathbf{43.25\%}$$

(iii) Since,
$$e \cdot S_r = w \cdot G$$

$$\therefore \quad 0.762 \times S_r = \left(\frac{310 - 270}{270}\right) \times 2.65$$

$$\therefore \quad S_r = 0.515 = \mathbf{51.5\%}$$

Example 2.8 : A natural deposit of soil has bulk unit weight of 16.8 kN/m^3 and water content 15%. How many litres of water will have to be added to 5 m^3 of this soil to raise its water content to 25% ?

Solution :
$$w = \frac{M_w}{M_s} = \frac{W_w}{W_s}$$

Given : $W_{w1} = 0.15 \, W_s$, $W_{w2} = 0.25 \, W_s$, $\gamma = 16.8$ kN/m^3

$\therefore$ Quantity of water added,

$$= 0.25 \, W_s - 0.15 \, W_s$$

$$= \mathbf{0.10 \, W_s}$$

Since,
$$\gamma_d = \frac{\gamma}{1 + w} = \frac{16.8}{1 + 0.15} = 14.61 \text{ kN/m}^3$$

$\therefore$
$$W_s = \gamma_d \cdot V = 14.61 \times 5$$

$$= \mathbf{73.05}$$

$\therefore$ Quantity of water added,

$$W_w = 0.1 \, W_s$$

$$= 0.1 \times 73.95 = \mathbf{7.305 \ kN}$$

$\therefore$ Volume of water added to raise w to 25%

$$V_w = \frac{W_w}{\gamma_w}$$

$$= \frac{7.305}{9.81} = 0.74466 \text{ m}^3 = \mathbf{744.65 \ litres}$$

Example 2.9 : A soil sample has a bulk density of 2.1 gm/cm³ when w = 15%. Calculate the water content [w] if the soil partially dries to the bulk density of 1.96 gm/cm³, e is unaltered.

Solution :

$$\rho = \left(\frac{G + wG}{1 + e}\right) \rho_w$$

$$\rho = \frac{G \cdot \rho_w}{1 + e} [1 + w]$$

$\therefore \qquad 2.1 = \dfrac{G \cdot \rho_w}{1 + e} [1 + 0.15]$

$\therefore \qquad \dfrac{G \cdot \rho_w}{1 + e} = \mathbf{1.826}$

Similarly,

$$1.96 = \frac{G \cdot \rho_w}{1 + e} [1 + w]$$

$\therefore \qquad 1.96 = 1.826\ [1 + w]$

$\therefore \qquad w = 0.0734 = \mathbf{7.34\%}$

Example 2.10 : 2,20,000 m³ of soil is removed from a site. This dry soil has in site voids ratio of 1.20. (i) How many m³ of a fill having voids ratio [e] 0.72 could be constructed from this soil ? (ii) With 2.7 specific gravity of soil particles what would be the weight of soil mass moved ?

Solution : (i) Total volume of soil,

$$V = V_S + V_V \qquad\qquad \text{... (i)}$$

$\therefore \qquad 2,20,000 = V_S + V_V$

Since $\qquad\qquad e = 1.2 = \dfrac{V_V}{V_S}$

$\therefore \qquad\qquad V_V = \mathbf{1.2\ V_S}$

Putting this value in (i)

$\therefore \qquad 2,20,000 = 1.2\ V_S + V_S$

$\therefore \qquad\qquad V_S = 1,00,000 \text{ m}^3$

Now, $\qquad$ filling has voids ratio $= 0.72 = \dfrac{V_{VF}}{V_{SF}}$

$\therefore \qquad\qquad V_{VF} = 0.72\ V_{SF}$

$\qquad$ Total volume for filling $= V_{VF} + V_{SF}$

$\qquad\qquad V_F = 0.72\ V_{SF} + V_{SF}$

$\therefore \qquad\qquad V_F = 1.72\ V_{SF}$

Since, volume of solids does not change,

$\therefore$ $\qquad V_F = 1.72 \times 1,00,000 = \mathbf{1,72,000 \ m^3}$

(ii)   Weight of soil mass moved = Weight of solids moved = $[W_s]$

Since $\qquad G = \dfrac{\gamma_s}{\gamma_w}$

$\therefore$ $\qquad \gamma_s = 2.7 \times 9.81 = 26.487 \ kN/m^3$

Since, $\qquad \gamma_s = \dfrac{W_s}{V_s}$

$\therefore$ $\qquad W_s = \gamma_s \cdot V_s$

$\qquad = 26.587 \times 1,00,000 = \mathbf{26,48,700 \ kN}$

Ans. 1,72,000 m^3 of a fill having voids ratio of 0.72 could be constructed from the given soil. The weight of soil mass moved is 26,48,700 kN.

Example 2.11 : Moisture content of a moist soil sample was found to be 20% and its bulk density 2000 kg/m³. Determine (i) S_r, (ii) e and (iii) n, if G = 2.70.

Solution :

$$\rho_d = \frac{\rho}{1 + w} = \frac{2000}{1 + 0.20} = 1666.6 \ kg/m^3$$

$$e = \frac{G \times \rho_w}{\rho_d} - 1 = \frac{2.7 \times 1000}{1666.6} - 1 = \mathbf{0.62}$$

$$n = \frac{e}{1 + e}$$

$$= \mathbf{38.2\%}$$

$$S_r \cdot e = w \cdot G$$

$$S_r = \frac{0.2 \times 2.7}{0.62} = \mathbf{87.0\%}$$

Example 2.12 : Assuming cubical packing of spherical grains of uniform size, determine (i) void ratio, (ii) porosity.

Solution : Consider a cube d $\times$ d $\times$ d enclosing a sphere of diameter d.

Volume of sphere, $\qquad V_s = \dfrac{\pi}{6} d^3$

Volume of cube, $\qquad V = d^3$

Volume of voids, $\qquad V_v = V - V_s = d^3 - \dfrac{\pi}{6} d^3$

Void ratio, $\qquad e = \dfrac{V_v}{V_s} = \dfrac{d^3 - \dfrac{\pi}{6} d^3}{\dfrac{\pi}{6} d^3} = \mathbf{0.910}$

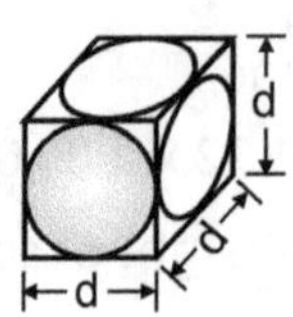

Fig. 2.14

Porosity,
$$n = \frac{V_v}{V} = \frac{d^3 - \frac{\pi}{6} d^3}{d^3} \times 100 = \mathbf{47.6\%}$$

Example 2.13 : Prove that maximum dry density of soil is 1.4 times the minimum for value of G = 2.6, e = 0.4 and 1.0 respectively.

Solution : Dry density (maximum) :

$$\rho_{d\,[max]} = \frac{G \cdot \rho_w}{1 + e_{min}}$$

$$\rho_{d\,[min]} = \frac{G \cdot \rho_w}{1 + e_{max}}$$

$$\therefore \quad \rho_{d\,[max]} = \frac{2.6 \times 1.0}{1 + 0.4} = 1.85 \text{ gm/cc}$$

$$\rho_{d\,[min]} = \frac{2.6 \times 1.0}{1 + 1.0} = \mathbf{1.3 \text{ gm/cc}}$$

Hence, $\quad \rho_{d\,[max]} = b$

Example 2.14 : The total unit weight of a soil sample is 18.5 kN/m^2. Calculate the Dry unit weight, porosity, void ratio, degree of saturation if the same soil sample has water content 17% and specific gravity 2.65. **[May 14, 4 M]**

Solution :

$$\gamma_s = 18.5 \text{ w/m}^2$$
$$w = 177$$
$$G = 2.65$$

- Dry unit weight = $\gamma_d = \dfrac{\gamma_s}{1 + w} = \dfrac{18.5}{1 + 17} = \dfrac{18/5}{1.17} = 15.81 \text{ kN/m}^3$

- Void ratio = $e = \dfrac{G \cdot g_w}{g_q} - 1 = \dfrac{2.65 \times 9.81}{15.81} - 1 = 64.43\%$

- Porosity = $n = \dfrac{e}{1 + e} = \dfrac{0.6443}{1 + 0.6443} = 39.18\%$

- Degree of solution $= e.S_r = w.G$

$$0.6443 \times S_r = 0.17 \times 2.65$$

$$\therefore \quad S_r = 69.92\%$$

Example 2.15 :A partially saturated soil from an earth fill has a natural water content of 19% and bulk unit weight of 19.33 kN/m^3. Assuming the specific gravity of soil solids as 2.6, calculate the degree of saturation, void ratio and porosity.   **[Nov. 15, 6 M]**

Solution

$$\gamma = 19.33 \text{ kN/m}^3$$
$$G = 2.6$$
$$W = 19\% = 0.19$$

(i) Dry unit weight,

$$\gamma = \frac{v}{1 + w} = \frac{19.33}{1 + 0.19} = 16.24 \text{ kN/m}^3$$

(ii) Void ration,

$$e = \frac{G. v_w}{v_d} - 1 = 0.570 = 57\%$$

Porosity

$$n = \frac{e}{1 + e} = \frac{0.570}{1 + 0.570} = 0.3630 = 36.3\%$$

(iii) Degree of saturation Sr,

$$e.Sr = WG$$
$$0.570 \times Sr = 0.19 \times 2.6$$
$$Sr = 0.8666 = 86.66\%$$

SUMMARY

1. Soil forms due to mechanical disintegration or chemical decomposition of rocks when it gets exposed to atmosphere for an appreciable time.

2. There are three principle types of rocks.

    (a) Igneous or primary rocks (b) Sedimentary rocks (c) Metamorphic rocks.

3. Soils can be divided in to two main group.

    (a) Residual soils   (b) Transported soils

4. The geometrical arrangement of soil particles to each other is known as soil structure.

5. The soil structure are generally classified as,

    (a) Single grained structure   (b) Honey comb structure

6. Field identification of soil is of great importance for civil engineering.

7. The basic aim of soil exploration is to obtain the information about the surface conditions at the site of proposed construction.

8. These are six methods to obtain soil samples.

    (a) Auger boring   (b) Wash boring
    (c) Rotary drilling   (d) Percussion drilling
    (e) Core drilling   (f) Trial pits

EXERCISE

1. Distinguish between :
   (a) Residual soil and transported soil.
   (b) Inorganic soil and organic soil.
   (c) Coarse grained soils and fine grained soils.
   (d) Mechanical weathering and chemical weathering of soil.
   (e) Alluvial and colluvial soils.
   (f) Honeycomb structure and flocculent structure.

2. Explain how (i) grain size (ii) gradation (iii) grain shape (iv) mineralogical composition (v) state of compaction (vi) moisture content are used to identify coarsed grained soil.

3. Prepare a tree type chart giving the details of four natural transportation agents for formation of soils and give one example of each category.

4. Describe the various stages of soil formation.

5. Sketch the geological cycle, explaining the processes of denudation, deposition and sedimentation.

6. Explain the role of weathering in the formation of soils.

7. Write notes on : Loess, Bentonite, Marl, Gumbo, Alluvial and Peat.

8. Define the terms : Void ratio, Water content, Degree of saturation and Dry density with the help of three phase system.

9. The natural water content of a sand sample is 20 per cent, the bulk density weight being 1.8 g/cc. Assuming specific gravity of soils as 2.65 and the sand sample to be partially saturated, calculate the degree of saturation and void ratio of the sample.

   (**Ans.** S_r = 69.7%, e = 0.76)

10. A sample of saturated clay weighs 15.45 and its moisture content is 38.0 per cent. If the particle specific gravity is 2.70, find the void ratio, porosity, dry and bulk unit weights of the soil.

    (**Ans.** e = 1.026, n = 50.6%, γ_d = 13.07 kN/m^3, γ = 18.04 kN/m^3)

11. The weight of an undried specimen of clay was 34.629. The oven-dry weight of same specimen was 28.369. Before drying, the specimen was immersed in mercury and its volume found to be 20.26. Calculate the water content, void ratio and the degree of saturation of the soil. Assume specific gravity of solids as 2.68.

    (**Ans.** w = 22.06%,   e = 0.91, S_r = 64.9%)

12. A sample of sand with the specific gravity of solids as 2.65 has a porosity of 40 per cent. Find out the dry unit weight, saturated unit weight of the sample when fully saturated, submerged unit weight and bulk weight when the degree of saturation is 50 per cent.

    (**Ans.** (i) γ_d = 15.66 kN/m^3, γ_{sat} = 19.56 kN/m^3, (ii) γ' = 9.75 kN/m^3, γ = 17.61 kN/m^3)

13. A partially saturated sample of a soil from an embankment has a natural moisture content of 20 per cent and bulk density of 2.0 g/cc and specific gravity of solids as 2.7. Compute its degree of saturation and void ratio.   (**Ans.** $S_r = 87\%$, $e = 0.62$)

14. Why is soil known as a three phase system ?

SOLVED UNIVERSITY QUESTIONS AND NUMERICALS

December 2013

1. Explain residual soil and transported soils with types and examples of each.   **[6]**
   [**Ans.:** Refer Article 2.3.1]

May 2014

1. Discuss the various types of soil deposits in India with their significant soil property.   **[4]**
   [**Ans.:** Refer Article 2.5]

2. Explain three phase soil system and derive the equation w. $G = e. S_r$ **[4]**
   [**Ans.:** Refer Article 2.9, 2.11 (6)(b)]

3. The total unit weight of a soil sample is 18.5 kN/m^2. Calculate the Dry unit weight, porosity, void ratio, degree of saturation if the same soil sample has water content 17% and specific gravity 2.65.   **[4]**
   [**Ans.:** Refer Example 2.14]

December 2014

1. State details of all natural transportation agents for formation of soils and give one example of each category.   **[6]**
   [**Ans.:** Refer Article 2.3.1]

May 2015

1. Starting from first principles derive the following equations with usual nomenclature : $\gamma = \dfrac{(G + eSr)\, Y\omega}{(1 + e)}$ **[6]**
   [**Ans.:** Refer Article 2.11 (c)]

2. On a single graph paper, draw neat labelled graphs for :   **[6]**
   (i)   Uniformly graded soil
   (ii) Well graded soil
   (iii) Gap graded soil
   (iv) Show on the same graph, zones of clay size, silt size, sand and gravel clearly.

November 2015

1. Derive with usual notation : $\rho = \dfrac{(1 + \omega)\, G\, \rho_\omega}{(1 + e)}$ **[6]**
   [**Ans.:** Refer Article 2.11 (c)]

2. A partially saturated soil from an earth fill has a natural water content of 19% and bulk unit weight of 19.33 kN/m^3. Assuming the specific gravity of soil solids as 2.6, calculate the degree of saturation, void ratio and porosity. **[6]**

[**Ans.:** Refer Example 2.15]

May 2016

1. Explain any one method to determine the field density of soil with a neat sketch. **[6]**

[**Ans.:** Refer Article 2.6]

November 2016

1. A sample weighing 310 N has a volume of 0.0183 m^3. When dried out in oven its weight reduction is 270 N. If specific gravity is 2.65, determine γ_d, porosity, η degree of saturation, S_r. **[6]**

[**Ans.:** Refer Example 2.7]

May 2017

1. Explain weathering and distinguish between mechanical and chemical weathering giving examples. **[6]**

[**Ans.:** Refer Article 2.3]

2. Define and mention the formulae for the following terms :

Void ratio, Porosity. Degree of saturation. Percentage air voids, Water content, Specific gravity. **[6]**

[**Ans.:** Refer Article 2.10]

◈ ◈ ◈

Chapter 3
GEOTECHNICAL PROPERTIES

3.1 NATURE OF SOIL

1. **Cohesion (C) :** Cohesion is the internal molecular attraction which resists the rupture or shear of material. Cohesion is derived in fine grained soils from the water films which bind together the individual particles in the soil mass. Cohesion is characteristic of the fine materials with particle size below about 0.002 mm (clay). Cohesion of a soil decreases as the moisture content increases. Cohesion is greater in well compacted clays than in badly compacted soils and is independent of the external loads applied.

2. **Internal Friction :** Internal friction is due to the resistance of grains to slide over each other and is the characteristic of the coarse materials of particle size larger than about 0.075 mm. The magnitude of the internal fraction of a granular mass depends on the grading, shape and surface texture of the particles, the degree of compaction, moisture content of the soil mass, and load to which it is subjected. Frictional resistance is highest with angular particles having a rough surface of varied size and shape and increases with increasing load. It reduces in the presence of a lubricant such as water, present in excessive proportions. For the coarse material it is usually assumed that the particle size distribution giving the greatest dry density has the greatest internal friction. The strength of a non-cohesive soil depends entirely on internal friction.

3. **Angle of Internal Friction (ϕ) :** The resistance to sliding of grain particles of a soil mass depends upon the angle of internal friction. It is usually considered that the value of the angle of internal friction is almost dependent on the normal pressure, but varies with the degree of packing of the particles, i.e. with the density. The soils subjected to the higher normal stresses will have lower moisture contents and higher bulk densities at failure than those subjected to lower normal stresses and the angle of internal friction may thus change.

The true angle of internal friction of clay is seldom zero and may be as much as 26°. For further discussions about the angle of internal friction for granular soils, please refer chapter on "Shear Strength of Soils".

Note : C and ϕ are known as shear parameters of soil.

4. **Capillarity :** Capillarity is the ability of the soil to transmit moisture in all directions regardless of any gravitational force. Soils possess capillary action similar to a dry cloth with one end immersed in water. Water rises up through soil pores due to capillary action. The maximum theoretical height of capillary rise depends upon the pressure which tends to force

the water into the soil and this force increases as the size of the soil particles decreases. The capillary rise in a soil when wet, may equal as much as 4 to 5 times the height of capillary rise in the same soil, when dry.

Coarse gravel has no capillary rise; whereas for coarse sand it is upto 30 cm. Fine sands and silts have capillary rise upto 1.2 m but dry sands have very little capillarity. Clays may have capillary rise upto 0.9 to 1.2 m.

5. Permeability : Permeability of a soil is the rate at which water flows through it under the action of [unit] hydraulic gradient. The passage of moisture through the inter spaces or pores of the soil is called *"percolation"*. Soils through which water percolates easily are termed as *"pervious"* or *"permeable"* while those soils which do not permit the passage of water easily are termed as *"impervious"* or *"impermeable"*. In the majority of the soil, the rate of flow is directly proportional to the head of water, and the permeability is therefore a constant for a particular soil. Permeability is the property of the soil mass and not of individual particles, and varies as the square of the diameter of the grains of the soil. It also depends upon the percentage of the fine material and with the arrangement of the grain particles of the soil mass. The permeability of cohesive soils, in general, is very small. Sands drain readily whilst silts and clays are difficult or impossible to drain. A knowledge of permeability is required not only for seepage, drainage and ground water problems, but also for the rate of settlement of structures on saturated soils. Soils yield under pressure when moisture content is increased. Ground water level depends upon a combination of the permeability of the strata and the pressure head causing the water to flow.

6. Elasticity : A soil is said to be elastic when it suffers a reduction in volume [or is changed in shape and bulk] while the load is applied, but recovers its initial volume immediately after the load is removed. The most important characteristic of the elastic behaviour of soil is that no matter how many repetitions of load are applied to it, provided that the stresses set up in the soil do not exceed the "yield stresses", the soil does not become permanently deformed. This elastic behaviour is characteristic of peat.

7. Resiliency : Resiliency of a body is regarded as the extreme limit to which it can repeatedly be strained without fracture or permanent change of shape.

8. Compressibility : Gravels, sands and silts are incompressible, i.e. if a moist mass of these soils is subjected to compression, they do not suffer significant volume change. Clays are compressible, i.e. if a moist mass of clay is subjected to compression, moisture and/or air may be expelled, resulting in a reduction in volume which is not immediately recovered when the compression load is withdrawn. The decrease in volume per unit increase of pressure is defined as the *"compressibility"* of the soil, and a measure of the rate at which consolidation proceeds is given by the *"coefficient of consolidation"* of the soil.

Compressibility of sand and silt varies with density. Compressibility of clay varies directly with water content and inversely with cohesive strength. Clays and other highly compressible soils are known to swell when overburden pressure is removed.

9. Density : The density or true weight of a soil is equal to the specific gravity of soil materials × 1000 [weight of density of water per cu. m.]. A soil consists of solids, pores or voids and the moisture. The overall weight of the soil [including soil particles and the effect of voids whether filled with air or water per unit volume, i.e. total weight of soil + total volume of soil, is termed *"bulk density"*. Bulk density varies with the type of the soil, moisture content and its compaction. The weight of the dry soil matters contained in a unit volume of soil i.e. weight of solid particles + total volume of soil [determined after the water has been dried without bulk volume change] is termed as *dry density*.

The usual method of measuring compaction in the field is to determine the dry density of the soil in-situ. The maximum dry density of a soil is obtained by a specified amount of compaction at the optimum moisture content by the Proctor Compaction Test. For each compaction method, there is an optimum moisture content at which a given soil can be compacted to maximum density, and different soils have different maximum densities and optimum moisture contents. Dry density varies from about 2.00 grams/cu.m. for coarse grained well graded gravels and sands to about 1.45 g/cu.m. for heavy clays, the corresponding moisture contents being about 4 per cent for the gravel and 26 per cent for the clay. The density of the solids alone is sometimes termed absolute density.

3.2 PROPERTIES OF SOILS

The properties of soil can be divided into engineering properties and index properties.

3.2.1 Engineering Properties

The main engineering properties are permeability, compressibility and shear strength.

- Permeability indicates the ease with which the water can flow through soils.

- Compressibility is related with the deformations which soil undergoes when subjected to compressive loads.

- The shear strength helps in determining stability of slopes, bearing capacity of soils and the earth pressures on retaining structures. The engineering properties of soils are discussed in later chapters.

3.2.2 Index Properties

The physical properties of soil aggregates which are useful to identify and distinguish soils from one another are known as index properties.

The tests required for determination of engineering properties are normally elaborate and time-consuming. For most of the cases, the geotechnical engineer requires some rough assessment without conducting elaborate tests. These tests or properties which are not of primary interest to the geotechnical engineer but which are indicative of the engineering properties are termed as index properties. The simple tests which are required to determine the index properties are known as 'classification tests'.

The main index properties are :
- Particle size distribution,
- Density index or Relative density,
- Consistency.

First two index properties are related to coarse grained soils and third property is related to fine grained soils.

The index properties are sometimes divided into two categories :

(a) Properties of soil mass (aggregate properties).

(b) The properties of individual particle size and

(a) Aggregate Properties : The properties of soil mass depend upon the mode of soil formation, soil history and soil structure. These properties are required to be determined from undistributed samples or preferably from in-situ tests.

(b) Individual Properties : The properties of individual particles can be determined for a remoulded, disturbed sample. These properties depend upon the individual grains and are independent of the manner of soil formation.

The index property give some information about the engineering properties. Generally, it is assumed that the soils with similar index properties have identical engineering properties. However, the correlation between the index properties and engineering properties is not perfect. A sufficient factor of safety should be provided if design is based only on index properties. Design of important structures should be made only after the determination of engineering properties.

3.3 SPECIFIC GRAVITY DETERMINATION

The laboratory specific gravity determination is carried out by the following methods :

1. Density bottle method
2. Pycnometer method
3. Gas jar method
4. Measuring flask method.

1. Density Bottle Method : This method is used to find the specific gravity of preferably fine grained soils. A density bottle of 50 ml capacity is used for this purpose.

$$G = \frac{\gamma_s}{\gamma_w}$$

or

$$G = \frac{\dfrac{M_d}{V_s}}{\dfrac{M_w}{V_w}}$$

If $V_s = V_w$, then, $G = \dfrac{M_d}{M_w}$

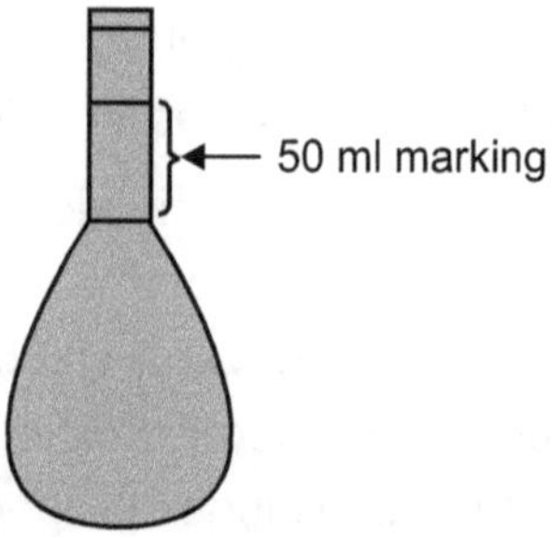

Fig. 3.1

Hence, we know that specific gravity is the ratio of weight of dry soil to the weight of equal volume of water.

Procedure :

- Find mass of empty density bottle (M_1).

- Put some overdried soil sample in the density bottle, weigh it (M_2).

- Fill the density bottle in stage (ii) completely with distilled water and take its mass (M_3).

- Fill empty density bottle completely with distilled water and weigh it (M_4).

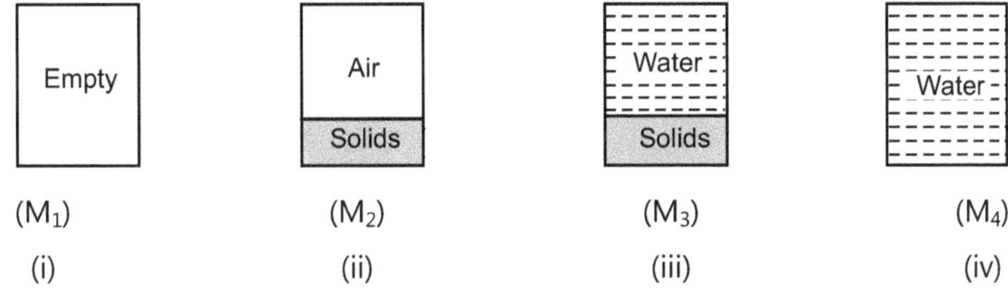

Fig. 3.2 (a)

(I)　　　　Mass of dry soil, $M_d = M_2 - M_1$

Mass of water in stage (iii) $= M_3 - M_2$

Mass of water in stage (iv) $= M_4 - M_1$

(II)　Mass of equal volume of water

$$M_w = \text{Mass of water in stage (iv)} - \text{Mass of water in stage (iii)}$$
$$= (M_4 - M_1) - (M_3 - M_2) = (M_2 - M_1) + M_4 - M_3$$
$$= M_d + M_4 - M_3 = M_d - (M_3 - M_4)$$

Now, specific gravity,　　$G = \dfrac{M_2 - M_1}{M_2 - M_1 + M_4 - M_3}$

$$= \dfrac{M_d}{M_d + M_4 - M_3} = \dfrac{M_d}{M_d - (M_3 - M_4)} \qquad \ldots (3.1)$$

Dividing numerator and denomenator by M_d, we get

$$G = \dfrac{1}{1 - \left(\dfrac{M_3 - M_4}{M_d}\right)} \qquad \ldots (3.2)$$

2. Pycnometer Method : This method is similar to the density bottle method. This method can be used for all types of soils but it is more suitable for coarse grained soils. The rest of the procedure is same as that of density bottle method.

The specific gravity is reported at 27°C (IS 2720 - II) or at 4°C. The specific gravity at 27°C and 4°C are determined as follows :

$$G_{27} = G_t \times \frac{\text{Specific gravity of water at t°C}}{\text{Specific gravity of water at 27°C}}$$

$$G_4 = G_t \times \text{Specific graviy of water at t°C}$$

where,

$$G_{27} = \text{Specific gravity at 27°C (soil)}$$

$$G_4 = \text{Specific gravity at 4°C (soil)}$$

$$G_t = \text{Specific gravity at t°C (soil)}$$

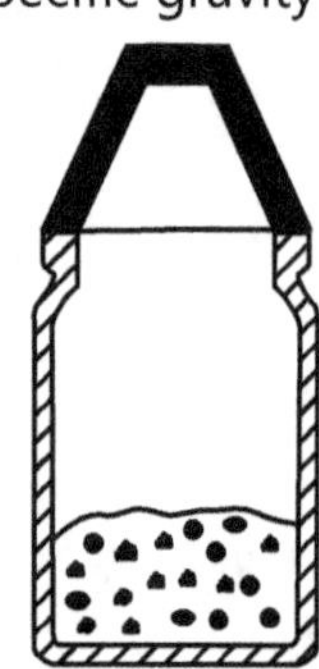

Fig. 3.2 (b) : Pycnometer

Entrapped and dissolved air is great source of error which results in a lower calculated value of specific gravity. For certain soils, kerosene, in place of water gives better results. If G_k is specific gravity of kerosene, then,

$$G = \frac{M_d \times G_k}{M_d + M_4 - M_3} = \left(\frac{G_k}{1 - \dfrac{M_3 - M_4}{M_d}} \right) \qquad \dots (3.3)$$

Above equation is used only when kerosene is used as better wetting agent, in place of water.

3. Gas Jar Method : A gas jar of about 1 litre capacity is used. The jar is fitted with rubber bung. The gas jar serves as a pycnometer. The method is similar to the pycnometer method.

4. Measuring Flask Method : A measuring flask of 250 ml or 500 ml capacity, with graduated mark at that level is used. The entrapped air is removed. The procedure is similar to the density bottle method. This method is suitable for fine grained and medium grained soils.

3.4 WATER CONTENT DETERMINATION

Most of the properties of a soil are governed by the water content of a soil sample. It controls the behaviour of a soil. It is a quantitative measure of wetness of a soil mass. The water content can be determined to a high degree of precision, as it involves only weights (which can be determined more accurately than volumes). Following methods are used to find the water content.

1. Oven drying method

2. Infrared torsion balance method

3. Calcium carbide method

4. Sand bath method

5. Alcohol method

6. Radiation method

7. Pycnometer method

1. Oven Drying Method : This is a standard and most accurate laboratory method to find the water content. A small, non-corrodable, airtight container is taken. Its empty mass is taken (M_1). The soil sample is taken in the container. The mass of sample with container is obtained (M_2).

The soil sample in the container is then dried in an oven at a temperature of 110°C ± 5°C for 24 hours. This temperature range is suitable for most of the soils. The temperature lower than 110°C ± 5°C may not cause complete evaporation of water and temperature higher than this may cause breaking down of crystalline structure of the soil particles due to loss of chemically bound structural water. However, this temperature is not suitable for soils with sufficient amount of organic matter. For such soils the temperature of 60°C to 80°C is recommended.

The drying period of 24 hours is suitable for most of the soils to cause complete evaporation of water. The soil may be deemed to be dry when the difference in successive weighing of the cooled sample does not exceed about 0.1% of the original weight. The soil containing organic matter may require drying period more than 24 hours. Mass of sample after drying is taken [M_3].

$$w = \frac{M_w}{M_s} \times 100$$

$$M_s = M_3 - M_1$$

$$M_w = M_2 - M_3$$

$$w = \frac{M_2 - M_3}{M_3 - M_1} \times 100$$

where, M_1 = Mass of container with lid

M_2 = Mass of container with wet soil

M_3 = Mass of container with dry soil

2. Infrared Torsion Balance Method : This is a rapid method to find the water content. The equipment has two main parts :

* The infrared lamp.

* The torsion balance.

The infrared radiation is provided by a 250 W lamp built in the balance for use with an alternating current 230 V, 50 cycles single phase main supply (IS : 2720, Part II, 1973).

The sample is kept in suitable container so that its water content is not affected by ambient conditions. The torque is applied to one end of the torsion wire by means of a calibrated drum to balance the loss of weight of water as sample dries out under infrared lamp. A thermometer is provided for recording the drying temperature which is kept at 110°C ± 5°C. The provision is made to adjust the input voltage to the infrared lamp to control the heat for drying of the sample.

The balance scale is divided in terms of moisture content (m) based on wet weight. It is also termed as water content on wet basis.

$$M = \frac{M_w}{M}$$

$$\frac{1}{m} = \frac{M}{M_w} = \frac{M_s + M_w}{M_w}$$

But

$$w = \frac{M_w}{M_s}$$

Hence,

$$\frac{1}{m} = \frac{1}{w} + 1$$

$$\therefore \quad \frac{1}{w} = \frac{1}{m} - 1 = \frac{1-m}{m}$$

$$\therefore \quad w = \text{Water content on dry basis} = \frac{m}{1-m}$$

If (m) and (w) are expressed as percentages, then,

$$w = \left(\frac{m}{100-m}\right) \times 100$$

The time required for complete drying depends upon the type of soil and quantity of water content in the sample. This method is suitable for soils which quickly absorb moisture from the air after drying, since drying and weighing occurs simultaneously.

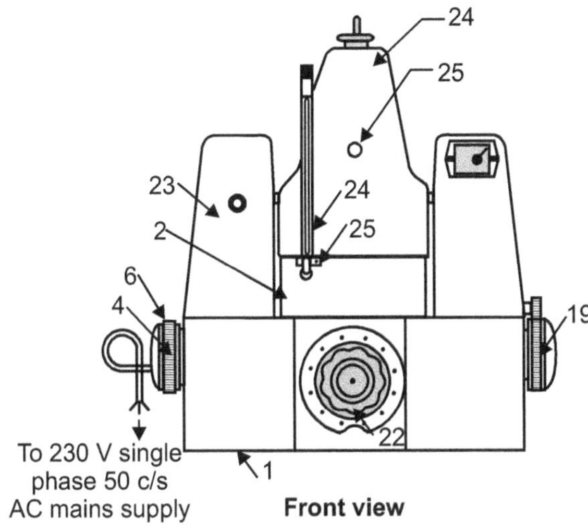

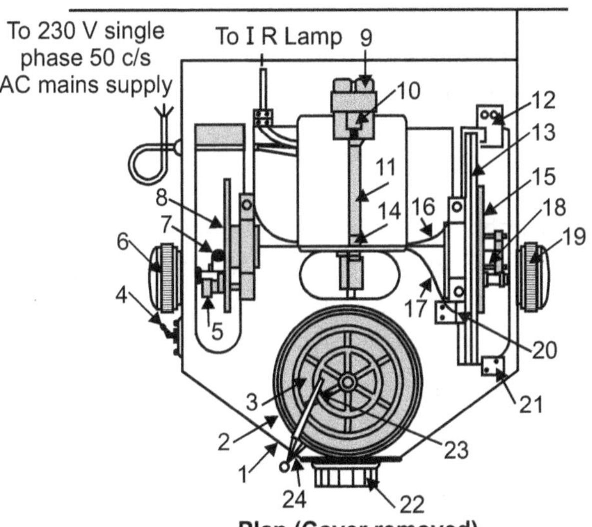

Description

1.   Base
2.   Pan housing
3.   Pan
4.   On-off switch
5.   Wire tensioner
6.   Initial adjustment knob
7.   Left-hand wire grip
8.   Gear
9.   Damping magnet
10. Damping vane
11. Balance arm
12. Stopper
13. Calibrated drum
14. Wire grip for balance
15. Gear
16. Torsion wire
17. Pointer
18. Right-hand wire grip
19. Drum drive knob
20. Index mark
21. Lock
22. Variac knob (for heat control)
23. Lock
24. Thermometer
25. Thermometer bracket

Fig. 3.3 : Torsion balance moisture method (0 – 100%)

3.   Calcium Carbide Method : This method can be used in the field and in the laboratory too. The instrument used is known as *rapid moisture tester*. The method makes use of fact that when water reacts with calcium carbide (CaC_2), acetylene gas (C_2H_2) is generated.

$$CaC_2 + 2H_2O = C_2H_2 + Ca(OH)_2$$

The acetylene gas produced exerts pressure and it is recorded in the dial gauge attached to the moisture tester. The soil sample of 6 grams is taken in the test cylinder (moisture tester) containing calcium carbide. The soil sample is required to be ground and pulverized. The steel balls (charges) are also used to serve the purpose in case of cohesive and plastic soils.

The quantity of gas produced is indicated on the dial gauge in terms of pressure. From the calibrated scale of pressure gauge the moisture content (m) based on total mass is determined. The water content (w) based on dry mass is calculated as

$$w = \frac{m}{1-m}$$

or

$$w = \left(\frac{m}{100-m}\right) \times 100\%$$

4. Sand Bath Method : This is a field method for determination of water content. It is rapid but not very accurate. A sand bath is large open vessel containing sand filled to a depth of 5 cm or more.

The soil is taken in a tray. It is crumbled. A few pieces of white paper are also kept on the sample. Mass of wet sample is obtained by weighing the tray.

The tray is then placed on sand bath. The sand bath is heated over a stove. During heating, the sample is turned with a palette knife. Overheating of soil should be avoided. The white paper turns brown when overheating occurs. When drying is complete, the tray is removed, cooled and weighed. The water content is determined by

$$W = \frac{M_w}{M_s} \times 100\%$$

5. Alcohol Method : The sample is broken, crumbled and taken in an evaporating dish. The mass of wet sample is taken. The sample is then mixed with alcohol. About one millilitre of alcohol is added for every gram of soil. Mixing of alcohol and soil is done properly.

The alcohol is then ignited. The mixture is turned with spatula when ignition is taking place. After the alcohol is burnt away completely, the dish is allowed to cool and mass of dry soil is obtained. Water content is found out as usual.

Care should be taken to prevent fire since alcohol is extremely volatile. This method is quite rapid, but not very accurate and cannot be used if the soil contains large proportion of organic matter, gypsum and any other calcareous material.

6. Radiation Method : In this method, radioactive isotopes are used for the determination of water content of soils. A radioactive isotope material like cobalt-60 is placed in a capsule. It is then lowered in a steel casing A, in a bore hole.

A steel casing has small opening on its one side through which rays can come out. A detector is placed inside another steel casing B, which also has an opening facing that in casing A.

Neutrons are emitted by radioactive material. The hydrogen atoms in the water from the soil sample cause scattering of neutrons. As these neutrons strike with the hydrogen atoms, they lose energy. The loss of energy is proportional to the quantity of water present in the soil. The detector is calibrated to give directly the water content. This method may lead to radiation problems if proper shielding precautions are not taken.

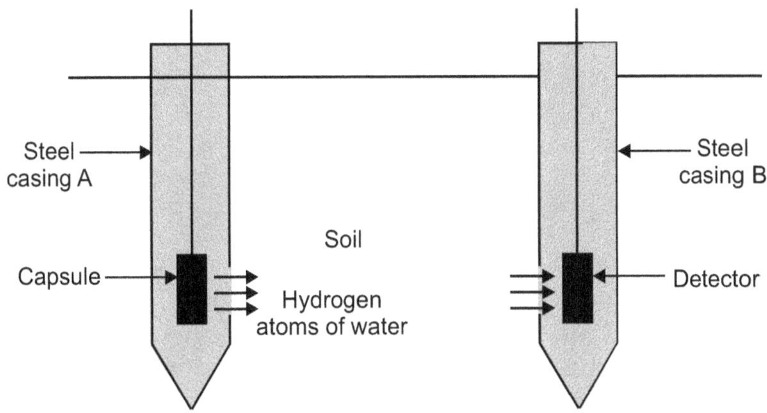

Fig. 3.4

7. Pycnometer Method : To use this method to find the water content, it is necessary to know the specific gravity of the soil.

A sample of wet soil, about 300 g is taken in the pycnometer and weighed (M_2). Distilled water is then added to the soil in the pycnometer to make it about half full. The contents are thoroughly mixed and entrapped air is removed. Pycnometer is filled with water flush with hole in the conical cap. The pycnometer is wiped dry and weighed (M_3). Then pycnometer is filled completely with water only and weighed (M_4).

Let

$$M_1 = \text{Mass of pycnometer}$$

$$M_2 = \text{Mass of pycnometer with wet soil}$$

$$M_3 = \text{Mass of pycnometer + wet soil + water}$$

$$M_4 = \text{Mass of pycnometer filled with water}$$

Obviously,

$$M_4 = M_3 - M_s + \frac{M_s}{[G\gamma_w]} \times \gamma_w$$

$$M_4 = M_3 - M_s + \frac{M_s}{G}$$

$$\therefore \quad M_3 - M_4 = M_s\left(1 - \frac{1}{G}\right)$$

Mass (M_4) equals to mass (M_3) minus the mass of solids (M_s), plus the mass of equal volume of water.

$$M_s = (M_3 - M_4) \cdot \frac{G}{G-1}$$

$$\text{Mass of wet soil} = M_2 - M_1$$

Therefore,

$$\text{mass of water} = M_w$$

$$M_w = (M_2 - M_1) - (M_3 - M_4)\left(\frac{G}{G-1}\right)$$

$$w = \frac{M_w}{M_s} \times 100$$

$$w = \left[\frac{(M_2 - M_1) - (M_3 - M_4)\left(\frac{G}{G-1}\right)}{(M_3 - M_4)\left(\frac{G}{G-1}\right)} \right] \times 100$$

$$w = \left[\frac{(M_2 - M_1)}{(M_3 - M_4)} \times \left(\frac{G-1}{G}\right) - 1 \right] \times 100$$

This method is suitable for coarse grained soils, from which the entrapped air can easily be removed.

Let G_{app} be apparent specific gravity of a moist soil sample of mass $M_{d'}$

Then substituting for G_{app} and $M_{d'}$ in the equation $G = \dfrac{M_d}{M_d + M_4 - M_3}$,

$$G_{app} = \frac{M_{d'}}{M_{d'} - (M_3 - M_4)}$$

$$\therefore \quad G_{app} \times M_{d'} - G_{ap}(M_3 - M_4) = M_{d'}$$

$$\therefore \quad M_{d'}(G_{app} - 1) = G_{app}(M_3 - M_4)$$

$$\therefore \quad M_{d'} = \frac{G_{app}}{G_{app} - 1} \times (M_3 - M_4)$$

$$\therefore \quad w = \left[\frac{M_{d'}}{M_3 - M_4} \times \frac{G-1}{G} - 1 \right] \times 100$$

$$= \left[\frac{G_{app}}{G_{app} - 1} \times \frac{M_3 - M_4}{M_3 - M_4} \times \frac{G-1}{G} - 1 \right] \times 100$$

$$= \left[\left(\frac{G_{app}}{G_{app} - 1}\right) \times \frac{G-1}{G} - 1 \right] \times 100 \quad \text{... (3.4)}$$

It may be noted that G_{app} is always less than correct value of G of soil sample.

3.5 FIELD DENSITY (UNIT WEIGHT) DETERMINATION

The bulk density of a soil is the ratio of mass of soil sample to its volume. Following methods are generally used to determine the field density of soils.

1. Water displacement method.
2. Core cutter method.
3. Sand replacement method.

1. Water Displacement Method : The volume of a sample is determined by water displacement. As soil mass disintegrates when it comes in contact with water, it is coated with a paraffin wax to make it impervious.

A test sample is trimmed to more or less a regular shape and weighed (M). It is then coated with thin layer of paraffin by dipping in molten wax. The specimen is allowed to cool and weighed (M_1). Difference between the two weights viz. M and M_1 will be the weights of wax.

The waxed sample is then immersed in a water displacement container. The volume of water displaced by the specimen equals the volume of the waxed sample. The actual volume of the sample is less than the water of waxed sample. If unit weight of wax is known, the volume of wax can be determined.

$$\text{Total volume of soil, } V = V_1 - \left(\frac{M_1 - M}{\gamma_p}\right)$$

where,

$$V_1 = \text{Volume of waxed sample}$$
$$V = \text{Volume of sample}$$
$$M_1 = \text{Mass of waxed sample}$$
$$M = \text{Mass of sample}$$
$$\gamma_p = \text{Unit weight of paraffin wax (approximately 0.95 gm/ml)}$$

$$\text{Bulk density of soil, } \rho = \frac{M}{V}$$

$$\text{Dry density, } \rho_d = \frac{\rho}{1 + w}$$

$$\text{Unit weight, } \gamma = \frac{W}{V} = \frac{M \times g}{V}$$

Water content (w) is determined by taking soil from middle of the sample.

Dry unit weight of soil,

$$\gamma_d = \frac{\gamma}{1 + w}$$

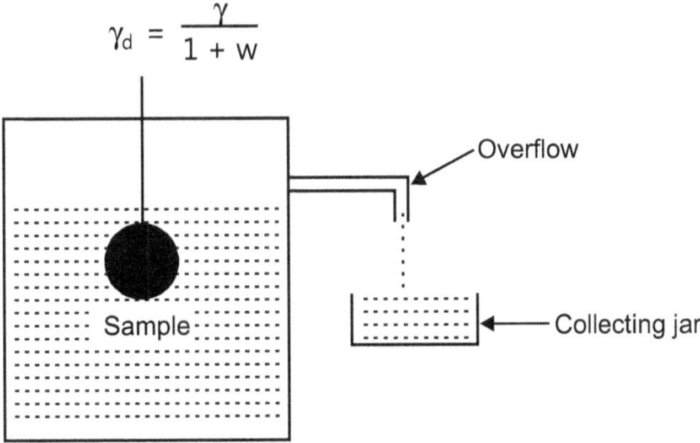

Fig. 3.5 : Water displacement method

2. Core Cutter Method : A core cutter consists of an open, cylindrical section, with a hardened, sharp cutting edge. A core cutter is hammered into the soil. In order to prevent the damage of top edge of the core cutter, it is provided with dolly. After removing the surrounding soil, a core cutter with soil is removed from the ground. The weight of core cutter filled with soil is taken. The weight of soil in the core cutter is calculated by deducting weight of empty core cutter from total weight. The dimensions of core cutter are measured to calculate volume of core cutter which is 1000 ml.

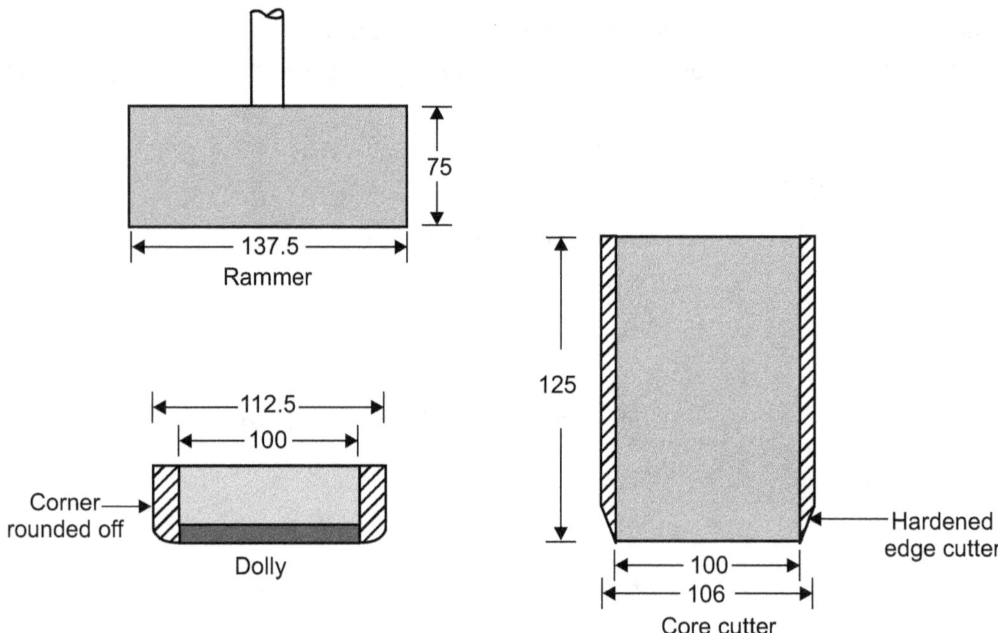

Fig. 3.6 : Core cutter method

Then, Bulk density, $\rho = \dfrac{M}{V}$

Dry density, $\rho_d = \dfrac{\rho}{1 + w}$

The water content (w) is determined by taking representative sample from the middle portion of sample.

where,   M = Mass of soil

V = Volume of core cutter (soil)

w = Water content

3. Sand Replacement Method : This method includes two steps :

(a) Determination of density of sand,

(b) Determination of density of soil.

It consists of calibrating cylinder, pouring cylinder and tray.

(a) Determination of Density of Sand : The density of sand is determined by using calibrating cylinder. The sand to be used should be standard sand passing through 600 microns and retained on 300 microns. The diameter and length of calibrating cylinder is measured to find volume of the calibrating cylinder. The weight of empty calibrating cylinder is taken, the calibrating cylinder is then filled with sand and weighed. The weight of sand filled in the calibrating cylinder is obtained and then density of sand is calculated as follows :

$$\rho_{sand} = \frac{M}{V}$$

where,

$$\rho_{sand} = \text{Density of sand}$$

$$M = \text{Mass of sand in the cylinder}$$

$$V = \text{Volume of sand (cylinder)}$$

(b) Determination of Density of Soil : A pouring cylinder consists of conical portion at the bottom and a opening which allows flow of sand from cylinder to the cone. Arrangement of closing and opening is also available. The steps to find density of soil are as follows :

- Close the opening and fill the pouring cylinder with sand. Take its mass (M_1).

- Place the sand pouring cylinder on a glass plate. Open the opening and allow the sand to fill in the core. Close the opening and take its mass (M_2).

- The mass of sand in the cone, $M = M_1 - M_2$.

- Refill the pouring cylinder with sand which weighs (M_1).

- Clear and level the ground and make a hole of approximately 10 cm ϕ and about 15 cm to 20 cm deep. Take out soil from the hole. Take its mass (M_3) and find water content (w) of the soil.

- Place the pouring cylinder over the hole and allow the sand to fill in the hole. Then close the openings and take mass of pouring cylinder with sand (M_4).

- Find the mass of sand required to fill the hole.

$$M_5 = M_1 - M_4 - M$$

- Find the volume of hole (V).

$$V = \frac{M_5}{\rho_{sand} \times g}$$

This volume (V) equals the volume of soil taken out from the hole.

$$\text{Unit weight of soil, } \gamma = M_5 \times g$$

$$\text{Bulk density, } \rho = \frac{M_5}{V}$$

$$\text{Dry density, } \rho_d = \frac{\rho}{1 + w}$$

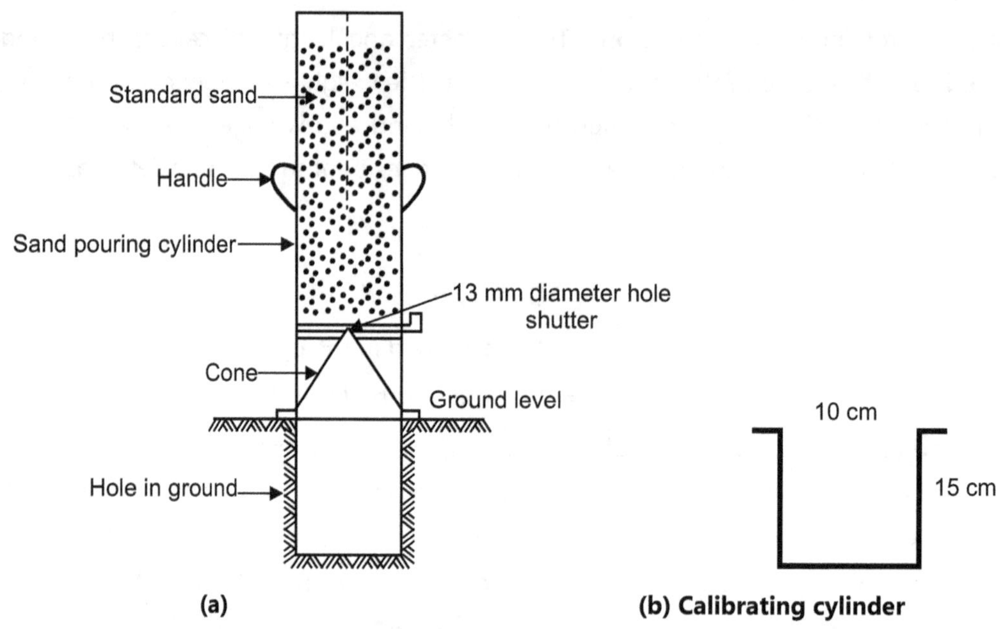

Fig. 3.7 : Determination of density of soil by sand replacement method

3.6 CONSISTENCY AND CONSISTENCY LIMITS   [Dec. 14]

Consistency is the property of material which shows its resistance to flow. When referred to soil, it means, the degree of resistance offered by fine grained soil to deformation. To certain extent, it denotes firmness of a soil.

Cohesion is the binding together of like substances by intramolecular forces and in soils through medium of moisture as well. Due to cohesion, various soil particles stick together and hold the soil mass intact. The cohesion of soil is that part of its shear strength, which does not depend upon inter particle friction. Consistency pertains to cohesive soils only. It is described by such terms as stiff, sticky, plastic, soft etc. and is influenced by moisture content.

A Swedish agricultural engineer, Atterberg, introduced that a fine grained soil can exist in four states, namely, liquid, plastic, semisolid and solid state. The water content at which the soil changes from one state to another state are termed as **consistency limits** or **Atterberg's limits.**

A soil containing high water content is in liquid state. It offers no shearing resistance and flows like liquids. It has shear strength equal to zero. As water content is reduced, soil starts developing resistance to shear deformations.

The water content at which the soil changes from liquid state to the plastic state is known as liquid limit (W_l). Thus, liquid limit is a water content at which the soil ceases to be liquid or it is the water content at which soil is on the verge of becoming liquid.

The water content at which the soil becomes semisolid is known as plastic limit (W_p). Thus, the plastic limit is the water content at which the soil just fails to behave plastically.

The difference between the liquid limit and plastic limit is known as Plasticity Index (P.I.).

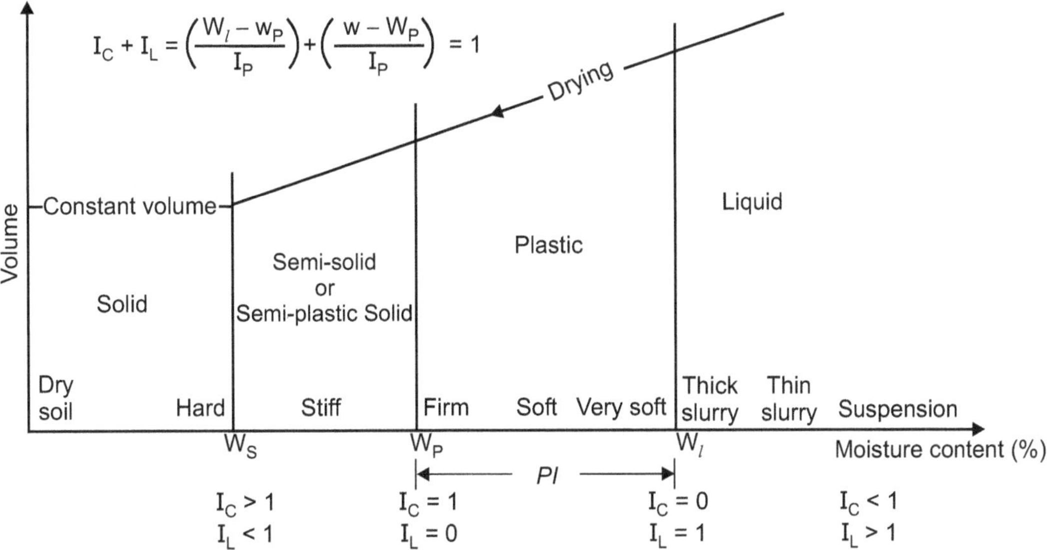

Fig. 3.8 : Different states of soil

As water content is reduced, the soil gradually transfers from liquid to plastic state. As water content is further reduced, the plasticity of soil decreases. When water content is reduced below the plastic limit, the soil attains semisolid state. In this situation, soil cracks when moulded. The volume of soil decreases with decrease in water content till a stage is reached when further reduction of water content does not cause any reduction in the volume of the soil. The soil is said to have reached a solid state. The water content at which the soil changes from semisolid state to solid state is known as the shrinkage limit. With further reduction in the water content below the shrinkage limit, there is no decrease in the volume of soil. This is due to the capillary tension developed. The air enters the voids emptied by the water.

Thus, the shrinkage limit is the water content at which the soil stops shrinking further and attains a constant volume. The shrinkage limit can also be defined as the lowest water content at which the soil is fully saturated.

3.6.1 Determination of Consistency Limits

1. Liquid Limit : As defined earlier, the liquid limit is the water content at which soil changes from liquid state to plastic state. The liquid limit of soil depends upon clay materials. At the liquid limit, the clay is practically like slurry (liquid), but possesses a small shearing strength. The thinner the particle and stronger the surface charge, the greater will be the amount of absorbed water and therefore, higher will be the liquid limit.

Following are the two methods used for the determination of limit in the laboratory :

(a) By Casagrande's method

(b) By Cone penetrometer

(a) Casagrande's Method : The device used in this method consists of a brass cup which drops through a height of 1 cm on a hard base when operated by a handle. The height of drop is adjusted with the help of adjusting screws.

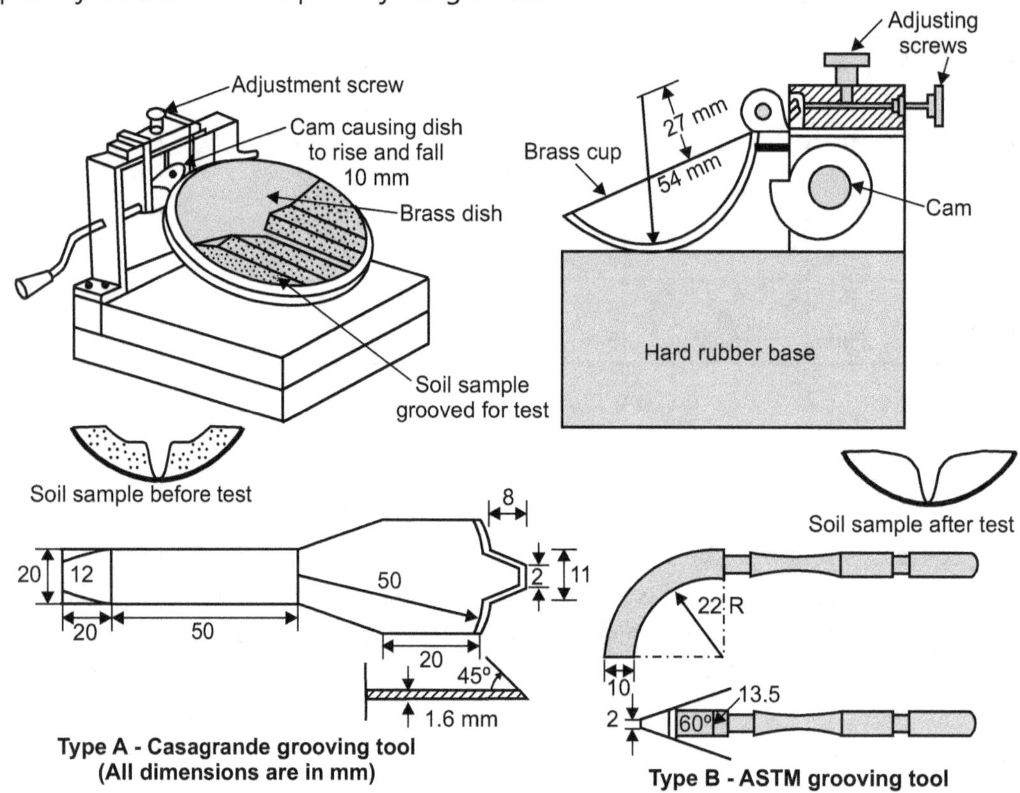

Casagrande apparatus

Fig. 3.9 (a) : Liquid limit apparatus

Procedure : About 120 g to 150 g of air-dried soil sample passing through 425 μ IS sieve is taken and mixed with distilled water to make uniform paste. In case of clayey soils, the soil paste shall be left to stand for 24 hours so as to ensure uniform distribution of moisture, throughout the soil mass. Some portion of this paste is placed in the cup of liquid limit device. The surface is levelled with a spatula to a maximum depth of 1 cm.

IS 2720 part V recommends two types of grooving tools : (1) Casagrande tool, (2) ASTM tool. The Casagrande tool cuts a groove of width 2 mm at the bottom, 11 mm at the top and 8 mm deep. The ASTM tool cuts a groove of width 2 mm at the bottom, 13.6 mm at the top and 10 mm deep. The Casagrande tool is recommended for clayey fine grained soils. The ASTM tool is recommended for silty fine grained soil i.e. soils having low plasticity indices, in which Casagrande tool tends to tear the soil in the groove.

After levelling the surface, a groove is cut through the sample along the symmetrical axis of the cup, in one stroke, using one of the above tools, depending upon type of soil. The handle is turned at a rate of 2 revolutions per second until the two parts of the soil sample come to close at the bottom of the groove for a distance of 10 mm. The groove should close by a flow of soil and not by slippage between the soil and the cup. Soils having low plasticity indices, tend to slide on the surface of cup instead of soil flowing. In such case results should be discarded and test repeated, until flowing does occur. The number of blows required to close the groove are noted. The soil near the closed groove is taken for water content determination.

The test is repeated by changing the water content of the sample. Every time water content of sample and number of blows required to close the groove are noted. The water content of the sample is adjusted such that number of blows come in the range of 10 to 40. The liquid limit is the water content at which the soil is sufficiently fluid to flow so as to close the groove by 25 blows.

Using semi-log papers, graph is plotted with % water content as ordinate and number of blows on log scale as abscissa. The plot is approximately a straight line. This plot is known as *flow curve*. The water content corresponding to 25 number of blows is the liquid limit. Thus, the liquid limit is arbitrarily taken as the water content at which the soil has shear strength sufficient to withstand the shearing stresses induced in 25 blows. Normally, the shear strength of soil at liquid limit is about 2.7 kN/m^2.

One-Point Method : Above method requires 5 - 6 repetitions for plotting the graph. Thus, procedure becomes inconvenient and consumes lot of time. It is possible to obtain an approximate value of liquid limit by conducting only one test provided the number of blows is in the limited range. This method is based on assumption that the flow curve is a straight line.

$$\text{Liquid limit } (W_l) \ = \ \frac{w_n}{1.3215 - 0.23 \log_{10} N}$$

where, $w_n =$ Water content of sample when groove closes in (N) blows

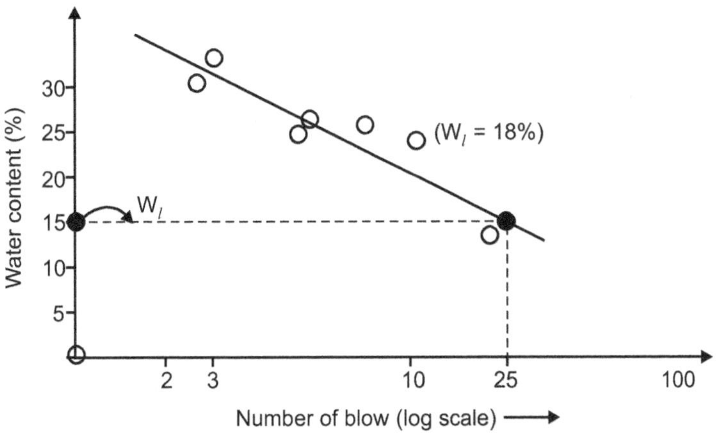

Fig. 3.9 (b) : Flow curve

(b) Cone Penetrometer Method : This method consists of a stainless steel cone having an apex angle $30° \pm 1/2°$ and length of 35 mm. The cone is fixed at the lower end of the sliding rod, fitted with disc at its top. The total weight of the cone, sliding rod and disc is 148 gm.

A paste is prepared and placed in a cup of 50 mm internal diameter and 50 mm height. The cup is fitted with sample. The surface of the soil is levelled.

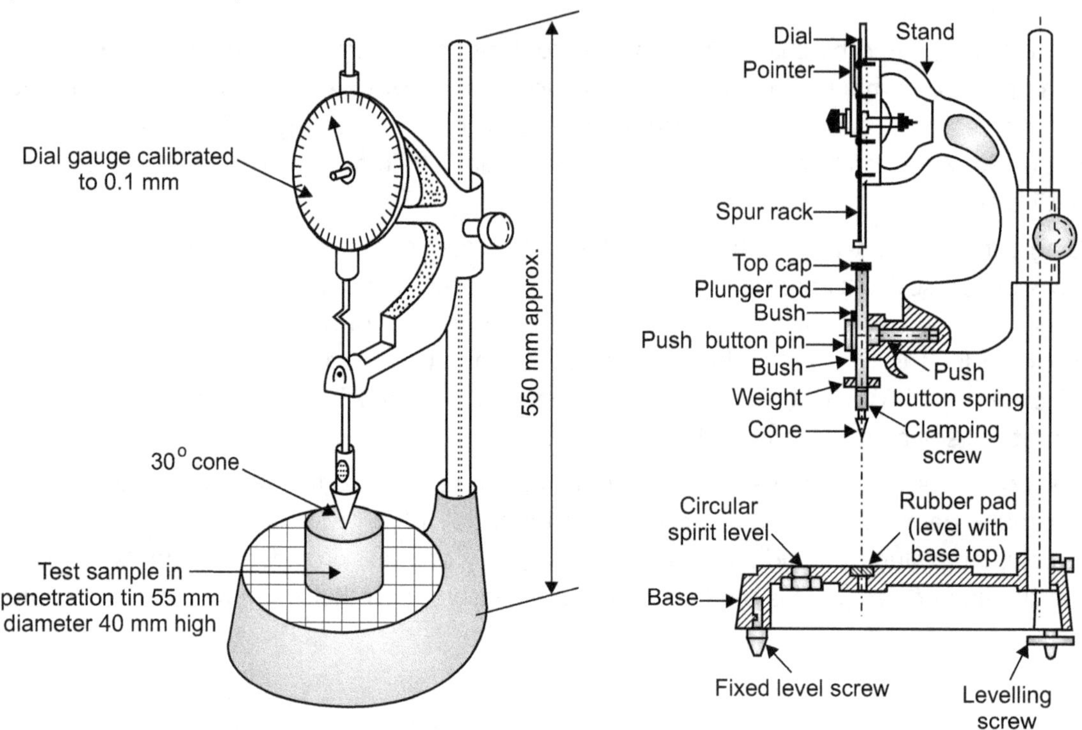

Fig. 3.10 : Liquid limit apparatus : Cone penetrometer method

(i) The cup is placed below the cone and cone is gradually lowered so as to just touch the surface of the soil in the cup. The graduated scale is adjusted to zero. The cone is released and allowed to penetrate the soil for 5 seconds. The water content at which the penetration is 20 mm is the liquid limit. For other penetration values following formulae may be used.

$$\text{Liquid limit, } W_l = \frac{w_x}{0.77 \log_{10} x} \text{ or } \frac{w_x}{0.65 + 0.0175\, x}$$

where, w_x = Water content corresponding to penetration x [mm]

Above equation is applicable when penetration (x) lies between 14 to 28 mm.

The shear strength of the soil at liquid limit obtained by this method is about 1.76 kN/m^2.

This method is easy, applicable for wide range of soils, reliable and is specified in IS 2720 part V - 1985. It may be emphasized that, there is drastic change in the method specified in the I.S. 2720 part V - 1985 than that specified in I.S. 2720 part V - 1970.

(ii) Liquid limit can also be calculated by the formula

$$W_l = w_x + 0.01 (25 - x) (w_x + 15)$$

where w_x is water content corresponding to penetration x between (20 to 30 mm) and cone is calibrated to read penetration of 25 mm at the liquid limit.

2.　Plastic Limit : Plastic limit is the water content below which the soil stops behaving as a plastic material. At this stage, soil begins to crumble when rolled to 3 mm diameter thread.

An air-dried soil passing through 425 μ IS sieve is taken. It is mixed with distilled water, till it becomes plastic. Some plastic soil mass is taken and ball is prepared. The ball is rolled with fingers on a glass plate to form a soil thread of uniform diameter of 3 mm. If soil mass does not crumble, it shows that the water content is more than the plastic limit. The soil is kneaded further. The soil is then re-rolled to 3 mm diameter and if it crumbles, then corresponding water content is the plastic limit. The test is repeated and average value of three readings is taken as the plastic limit.

Note : A brass rod of 3 mm diameter is used to compare the diameter of soil thread.

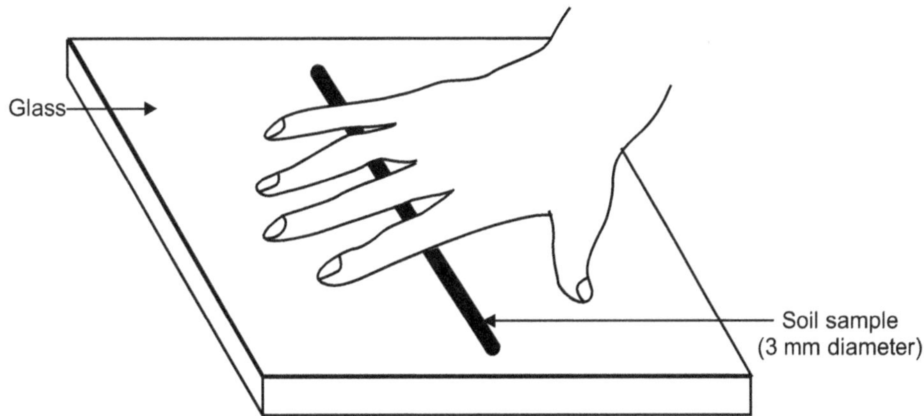

Fig. 3.11 : Plastic limit determination

3.　Shrinkage Limit : Shrinkage limit is the water content at which soil mass stops shrinking. It is a maximum water content at which a reduction of water content will not cause a decrease in the volume of the soil mass.

In Fig. 3.12 (a), the soil sample is fully saturated.

The mass of water in (a) $= M_1 - M_d$

where,　　　　　$M_1 =$ Mass of saturated soil sample with volume V_1

　　　　　　　$M_d =$ Mass of dry soil solids

The water content of saturated soil is gradually reduced and sample is brought at shrinkage limit. Let V_2 be the volume at this stage.

Consider Fig. 3.12 (b). The sample is at shrinkage limit. Hence, further reduction in the water content will not reduce the volume of soil sample.

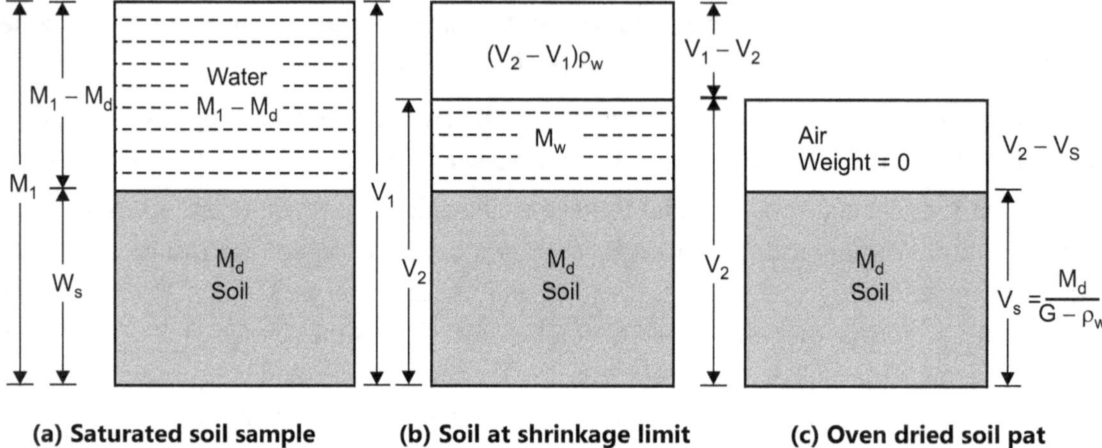

(a) Saturated soil sample   (b) Soil at shrinkage limit   (c) Oven dried soil pat

Fig. 3.12 : Determination of volume of dry pat in shrinkage limit test

Loss of water from stage (a) to stage (b) $= (V_1 - V_2)\, \rho_w$

Mass of water in (b) $= (M_1 - M_d) - (V_1 - V_2)\, \rho_w$

But shrinkage limit is the water content in stage (b).

$$W_s = \frac{(M_1 - M_d) - (V_1 - V_2)\, \rho_w}{M_d} \times 100$$

In Fig. 3.12 (c), since there is no reduction in the volume with further reduction in water content, $(V_2 = V_d)$ where (V_d) is volume of sample in dry state and M_d is dry weight of sample.

$$W_s = \frac{(M_1 - M_d) - (V_1 - V_d)\, \rho_w}{M_d} \times 100$$

Laboratory Procedure :

About 50 gm of soil passing through 425 μ is taken and mixed with distilled water to form a saturated soil mass.

A circular shrinkage dish of diameter 30 to 40 mm and a height of 15 mm is taken. The capacity (volume) of shrinkage dish is determined by filling it with mercury. A dish is placed in the large porcelain evaporating dish and filled with mercury. Excess mercury is removed by pressing a plain glass plate firmly over the top of the shrinkage dish. The mass of mercury in the shrinkage dish is obtained. The volume of shrinkage dish (V_1) in ml is equal to the mass of mercury in grams divided by the density of mercury (usually 13.6 gm/cm³). The inside surface of dish is coated with grease. The mass of empty dish is obtained.

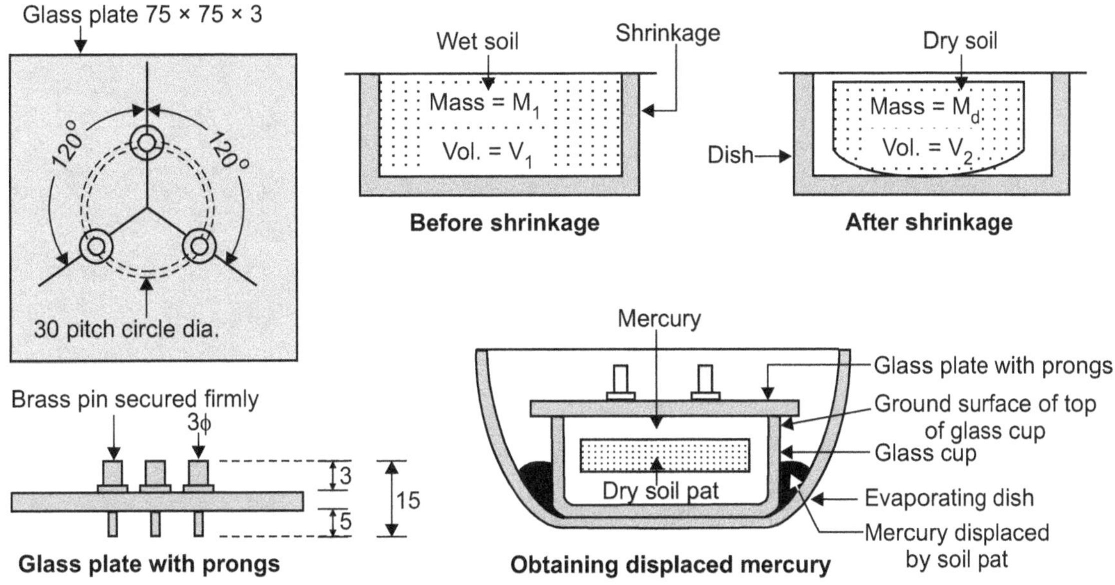

Fig. 3.13 : Determination of volume of dry pat in shrinkage limit test

The saturated soil sample is then filled in the shrinkage dish. Top surface is levelled. Air entrapped is removed. The mass of dish with sample is taken.

The soil is then dried. Drying is initially at room temperature and then it is oven dried. The mass of dish with dry soil is obtained. The mass of dry soil in the dish can be calculated. To determine the volume of dry soil pat, a glass cup of 50 mm diameter and 25 mm height is taken and placed in the large dish. The cup is filled with mercury. The dry soil pat is removed from the dish and placed on the surface of the mercury in the cup and pressed with glass plate having prongs, the volume of mercury displaced is determined from its mass and density. The volume of dry soil pat (V_d) is equal to the volume of mercury displaced by it. The shrinkage limit is then determined by the following formula :

$$W_s \; = \; \frac{(M_1 - M_d) - (V_1 - V_d)\,\rho_w}{M_d}$$

where,

M = Mass of shrinkage dish filled with saturated soil sample

M_d = Mass of soil solids = Mass of dry soil pat

V_1 = Volume of saturated sample

V_d = Volume of dry soil pat

ρ_w = Density of water

Determination of W_s when G is known : Shrinkage limit can be determined only with the observation of final volume V_2 (V_d) and mass m_2 if the specific gravity of the soil G is determined previously. Thus,

Shrinkage limit, $W_s \; = \; \dfrac{M_w}{M_d}$ (in final state)

Refer Fig. 3.12 (b).

But,
$$M_w = (V_d - V_s) \cdot \rho_w$$

$$= \left(V_d - \frac{M_d}{G \cdot \rho_w}\right) \cdot \rho_w \quad \text{since, } G = \frac{M_d}{V_s \cdot \rho_w}$$

Therefore,
$$W_s = \frac{\left(V_d - \dfrac{M_d}{G \cdot \rho_w}\right) \rho_w}{M_d}$$

$$= \frac{V_d \cdot \rho_w}{M_d} - \frac{1}{G}$$

$\therefore$
$$\boxed{W_s = \frac{\rho_w}{\rho_d} - \frac{1}{G}} = \frac{V_d}{M_d} - \frac{1}{G} \quad \ldots (3.6)$$

i.e. knowing the volume and mass of oven dried pat, $\left(\rho_d = \dfrac{M_d}{V_d}\right)$ and G, W_s can be determined.

Determination of specific gravity of solids from shrinkage limit : The data available while carrying out shrinkage limit test, can as well be used to determine specific gravity of the soil.

$$V_s = \frac{M_d}{G\rho_w}$$

$$= V_1 - \text{Volume of water present at the start of test}$$

$\therefore$
$$\frac{M_d}{G\rho_w} = V_1 - \frac{M_1 - M_d}{\rho_w}$$

$\therefore$
$$\frac{M_d}{G} = V_1 \rho_w - M_1 - M_d$$

$\therefore$
$$G = \frac{M_d}{V_1 \rho_w - (M_1 - M_d)} \quad \ldots (3.7)$$

$\therefore$
$$G = \frac{1}{1 - \left[\dfrac{M_1 - V_1 \rho_w}{M_d}\right]} \quad \ldots (3.8)$$

Shrinkage Characteristics :

- **Shrinkage index (I_s) :** It is defined as 'the difference of water content between plastic limit and shrinkage limit'.

i.e.
$$I_s = W_p - W_s$$

Shrinkage index is directly proportional to the percentage of clay size fraction present in the soil.

- **Shrinkage ratio (S.R.) :**

$$\text{Shrinkage ratio} = \frac{\left(\dfrac{V_1 - V_2}{V_d}\right) \times 100}{W_1 - W_2} = \frac{M_d}{V_d\,\rho_w}$$

$$= \frac{\text{Mass of the dry soil}}{\text{Volume of dry soil}} \times \frac{1}{\rho_w} \qquad \ldots (3.9)$$

$$= \frac{\rho_d}{\rho_w} \quad \text{where,} \quad \rho_d = \frac{M_d}{V_d}$$

- **Volumetric shrinkage (V.S.) :**

$$\text{V.S.} = \text{S.R.} \, (W_l - W_s) \times 100$$

where, W_l is liquid limit of soil.

- **Linear shrinkage (L.S.) :**

$$\text{L.S.} = \left(1 - \frac{1}{V_s + 1}\right)^{1/3} \times 100\%$$

The linear shrinkage is related with plasticity index (I_p) as under :

$$I_p = 2.13 \times \text{L.S.}$$

- **Degree of shrinkage (D.S.) :**

$$\text{D.S.} = \frac{V - V_d}{V} \times 100\%$$

On the basis of the degree of shrinkage, the soils can be classified as follows :

D.S. %	Quality of soil
< 5	
5 - 10	Medium good
10 - 15	Poor
> 15	Very poor

The soils that belong to the montmorillonite group shrink more than the kaolinite and illite groups. Due to shrinkage of soils, cracks develop on the surface, which may extend to great depths. The soils that shrink and swell more are called expansive soils. Black cotton soils belong to this category.

3.6.2 Consistency Indices

Plasticity Index : It is the range of water content over which the soil remains in plastic state. Its magnitude equals to the difference between the liquid limit (W_l) and plastic limit (W_p).

$$I_p \text{ or } PI = W_l - W_p \qquad \ldots (3.10)$$

If (W_l) and (W_p) cannot be determined, the soil is non-plastic. The plasticity index cannot be negative. In such case, it is expressed as zero.

1. **Liquidity Index :** It indicates the nearness of its water content to its liquid limit. It is defined as :

$$I_l = \left(\frac{w - W_p}{I_p}\right) \qquad \ldots (3.11)$$

where, I_l = Liquidity index

w = Water content of soil in natural condition

W_p = Plastic limit

I_p = Plasticity index

The liquidity index is also known as water-plasticity ratio.

When liquidity index of a soil at liquid limit is 1 the soil is in liquid state. The liquidity index becomes zero at plastic limit state. The negative liquidity indicates the water content is smaller than plastic limit.

2. **Consistency Index :** It shows the nearness of the water content of soil to its plastic limit. It is defined as :

$$I_c = \frac{W_l - w}{I_p} \qquad \ldots (3.12)$$

The consistency index indicates the consistency (firmness) of a soil. It is also known as relative consistency. The consistency index becomes zero at liquid limit and 100% at a water content equal to the plastic limit of soil. The consistency index greater than 100% shows semisolid state of soil and negative value of consistency index indicates that the water content is greater than the liquid limit.

It can be proved that, sum total of consistency index I_c and liquidity index I_l is always one.

$$I_c + I_l = \frac{W_l - w}{I_p} + \frac{w - W_p}{I_p} = \frac{W_l - W_p}{I_p} = \frac{I_p}{I_p} = 1 \qquad \ldots (3.13)$$

Both consistency index and liquidity index can have 0, +ve or −ve value.

Fig. 3.14 and Table 3.1 given below shows variation in consistency index and liquidity index due to variation in moisture content. As per Kezdi, knowing consistency index of a soil sample, approximate value of unconfined compressive strength of the cohesive sample can be estimated.

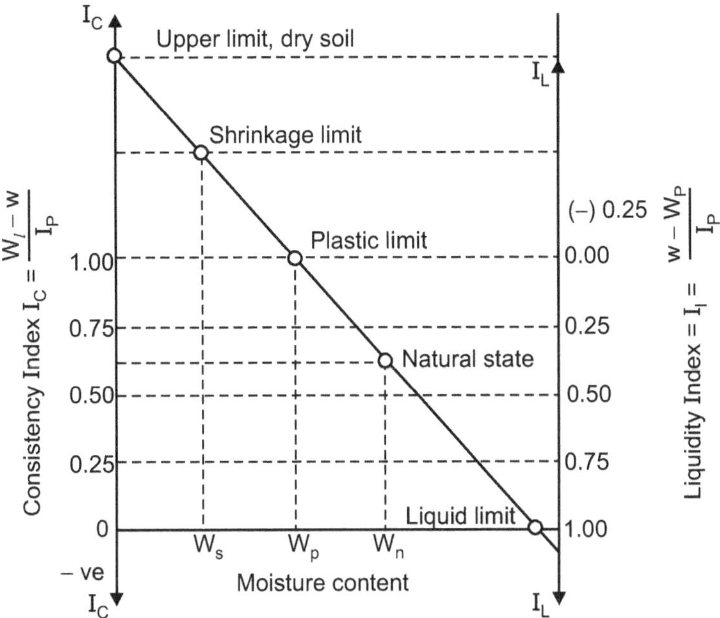

Fig. 3.14 : Variation of consistency index and liquidity index with moisture content etc.

Table 3.1

Consistency	Field identification	Unconfined compressive strength ... kN/m³
Hard	Can be indented with difficulty by thumb nail.	> 400
Medium hard	Can be readily indented with thumb nail.	200 to 400
Stiff	The thumb leaves imprint but can be pressed with great effort only.	100 to 200
Deformable	The thumb can be pressed with light pressure.	50 to 100
Soft	Thumb can be pressed easily.	25 to 50
Very soft	The fist can be pressed easily.	< 25

Numerous other methods have been suggested, and are, in fact, in use for characterising soil consistency. Among these, Polshin's squeeze test, Ball penetration test and Swedish cone penetration test are worth mentioning. The plasticity of clays depends on the manner in which the determination is made. Organic soils show a considerable reduction in the liquid limit of the soils if dried before determination of the liquid limit. If the plasticity index drops by more than 30%, it is an indication of the organic nature (Terzaghi and Peck, 1967). Finely deposited sediments also show a significant reduction in L.L. on air drying and if values of consistency ratio have to be used, it is necessary to determine L.L. and P.L. using undried soil from the remoulded wet state.

3. Flow Index : It is a slope of flow curve obtained between water content and number of blows in Casagrande's method of determination of liquid limit. It is given as follows :

$$\text{Flow index } (I_f) \;=\; \frac{w_1 - w_2}{\log_{10} \dfrac{N_2}{N_1}} \qquad \text{... (3.14)}$$

where,

N_1 = Number of blows at water content (w_1)

N_2 = Number of blows at water content (w_2)

Flow index indicates the rate at which a soil mass looses its shear strength with increase in the water content.

4. Toughness Index : It is a measure of shearing strength of soil at its plastic limit. It is defined as :

$$\text{Toughness index,} \qquad I_t \;=\; \frac{I_p}{I_f} \qquad \text{... (3.15)}$$

where,

I_p = Plasticity index

I_f = Flow index

The value of toughness index less than one indicates the soil is friable at the plastic limit. The value of (I_f) lies between zero to three. It is clear that, lesser the value of flow index I_f, higher will be the toughness and toughness index of the soil. Toughness index less than one indicates that soil will crumble easily at plastic limit.

5. Activity Number : It is defined as 'the ratio of plasticity index to percentage of clay $(2\,\mu$ fraction)'.

$$\therefore \qquad A \;=\; \frac{I_p}{\% \text{ fines} < 0.002 \text{ mm}} \qquad \text{... (3.16)}$$

It is a measure of physio-chemical behaviour of soil. On the basis of activity of soil, it is classified as inactive when $A < 0.75$, normal when $A = 0.75$ to 1.25 and active when $A > 1.25$. It also depends on the mineral composition as shown below.

Mineral	Activity number
Kaolinite	0.4 to 0.5
Illite	0.5 to 1.0
Montmorillonite	1.0 to 7.0

6. Sensitivity : A cohesive soil in its natural state of occurrence has a certain structure. When the soil is remoulded, its structure is disturbed, and its engineering properties change considerably. Sensitivity (S_t) of a soil indicates its weakening due to remoulding.

$$S_t \;=\; \frac{(q_u)_u}{(q_u)_r} \qquad \text{... (3.17)}$$

where, $(q_u)_u$ = Unconfined compressive strength of undisturbed clay

$(q_u)_r$ = Unconfined compressive strength of remoulded clay

Following is the soil classification based on (S_t).

Table 3.2

Sr. No.	Sensitivity	Soil type
1.	< 1.00	Insensitive / Non-sensitive
2.	1.0 to 2.0	Little sensitive
3.	2.0 to 4.0	Moderately sensitive
4.	4.0 to 8.0	Sensitive
5.	8.4 to 16.0	Extra sensitive
6.	> 16	Quick

7. Use of Consistency Limits : The engineering properties of such soils can be related to index properties as under :

- The plasticity index of a soil is a measure of the amount of clay in soil.
- As the particle size decreases, both the liquid limit and plastic limit increase, but liquid limit increases at a greater rate. Thus, plasticity index increases at a rapid rate and it is a measure of the fineness of the particles.
- Plasticity chart, (Ip) gives idea about the type of clay.
- Soils with liquid limit less than 20% are normally sands. They possess no plasticity and are called as non-plastic (NP).
- The soils with high organic matter have low plasticity index.
- The compressibility of a soil normally increases with an increase in liquid limit.
- A high value of toughness index indicates high percentage of colloidal clay.

3.7 MECHANICAL ANALYSIS (SIZE GRADATION ANALYSIS)

[Nov. 16]

The particle size analysis is known as mechanical analysis. It expresses quantitatively the proportions by weight of various sizes of particles present in a soil. It is represented graphically on a particle size distribution curve. The mechanical analysis is done in two stages.

(i) Sieve analysis.

(ii) Sedimentation analysis.

Sieve analysis is meant for coarse-grained soils (particle size greater than 75 micron). Sedimentation is meant for fine grained soils (particle size smaller than 75 micron). Sedimentation analysis is also known as wet mechanical analysis. Particle size smaller than 0.2 micron cannot be determined by the sedimentation method. These can be determined by an electron microscope or by X-ray diffraction techniques.

3.7.1 Sieve Analysis

The soil is sieved through a set of sieves. Sieves are made up of spun brass and phosphor bronze or stainless steel sieve cloth. According to IS : 149 - 1970, the sieves are designed by the size of square opening, in millimetres or microns.

The coarse grained soils can be further subdivided into gravel fraction (particle size greater than 4.75 mm) and sand fraction (particle size greater than 75 micron but less than 4.75 mm). For gravels, the set of sieves used is 80 mm, 40 mm, 20 mm, 10 mm and 4.75 mm. For sands, the set of sieves used is 2.36 mm, 2 mm, 1.7 mm, 1.18 mm, 600 μ, 425 μ, 300 μ and 75 μ. However, all the sieves may not be required for a particular soil. The selection of required number of sieves is done to obtain good particle size distribution curve. The sieves are arranged one over the other, with decreasing size from the top to the bottom. A lid or cover is placed at the top of largest sieve. A receiver known as pan, which has no opening, is placed at the bottom of the smallest sieve.

(a) Dry Sieve Analysis : The soil sample is taken in suitable quantity. The larger the particle size, the more is the quantity of soil required. The soil should be oven dry. It should be pulverised. It should not contain any lump. If it contains organic matters, it can be used air dry, instead of oven dry.

The sample is sieved through the set of sieves arranged in descending order of their sieves. The portion retained on 4.75 mm sieve is gravel fraction. The portion passed through 4.75 mm and retained on 75 micron sieve is sand fraction. These fractions are expressed by weight of original sample to give gravel content and sand content in percentage.

The weight of the soil portion retained on each sieve and pan is obtained to the nearest 0.1 gm. The weight of the retained soil is checked against the original weight.

Dry sieve analysis is suitable for cohesionless soils, with little or no fine particles. If sand is sieved in wet conditions, the surface tension may cause erroneous results.

(b) Wet Sieve Analysis : If the soil contains substantial quantity (about more than 5%) of fine particles, a wet sieve analysis is done. All lumps are broken into individual particles. A representative sample is taken using riffler and dried in an oven. The dried sample is taken in a tray and soaked in the water. If necessary, deflocculating agents like sodium hexametaphosphate at the rate 2 gm per litre of water may be added. The sample is stirred and left soaking for period of at least one hour.

The slurry is sieved through 4.75 mm sieve. The portion retained on 4.75 mm sieve is gravel fraction. The material passing through 4.75 mm sieve is sieved through a 75 micron sieve. The material is washed until the wash water becomes clear. The material retained on 75 μ sieve is collected and dried in an oven. It is then sieved through the set of sieves of sizes 2.36 mm, 2 mm, 1.7 mm, 1.18 mm, 600 μ, 300 μ and 75 μ. The material retained on each sieve is weighed and analysed as illustrated in the following table of observations.

Table 3.3 : Table of Observations - Sieve Analysis

Total mass of sample = 1000 gm (oven dried)

Sieve size in mm	Retained mass (gm)	Retained per cent	Cumulative retained per cent	Per cent finer	Remark
(1)	(2)	(3)	(4)	(5)	(6)
10	80	8.0	8.0	92.0	
4.75	113	11.3	19.3	80.7	
2.36	152	15.2	34.5	65.5	
1.18	115	11.5	46.0	54.0	
0.60	116	11.6	57.6	42.4	
0.30	202	20.2	77.8	22.2	
0.15	144	14.4	92.2	7.8	
0.075	048	4.8	97.0	3.0	
Passing 0.075	30	3.0	100.00	0.0	

The results of the mechanical analysis are plotted to get a particle distribution curve, with % finer (N) as ordinate and the particle size diameter as the abscissa (See article 3.8).

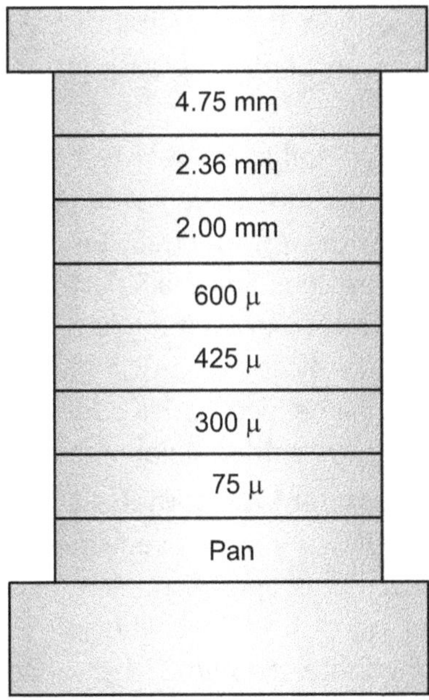

Fig. 3.15 : Arrangement of sieves

3.7.2 Sedimentation Analysis

The particles of soil finer than 75 micron cannot be sieved. The particle size distribution of such soils is determined by sedimentation analysis which is based upon Stoke's law. Pipette method and hydrometer method are the two sedimentation methods in use.

Stoke's Law : Stoke's law states that the terminal velocity of settling of spherical particle in suspension, varies with square of the diameter of the sphere, density and viscosity of the fluid and the density of the sphere, i.e.

$$\upsilon \;=\; \frac{g\,(\rho_s - \rho_w)}{18\,\eta} \cdot D^2 \;=\; \frac{(G-1)\cdot \rho_w \cdot g \cdot D^2}{18\,\eta} \qquad \text{... (3.18)}$$

or
$$D \;=\; \left[\frac{\dfrac{18\,\eta}{g}}{(G-1)\,\rho_w} \cdot \frac{H}{t} \right]^{1/2} \qquad \text{... (3.19)}$$

where,
$$\rho_s \;=\; G \cdot \rho_w \text{ is the density of solid sphere of diameter D}$$

$$\rho_w,\ \eta \;=\; \text{Density and viscosity of fluid respectively}$$

$$\upsilon \;=\; \text{Terminal velocity} \;=\; \frac{H}{t}\text{ , where H is distance from surface}$$

Using $G = 2.67$, $\rho_w = 0.9963$ g/ml, $\eta = 8.36 \times 10^{-3}$ poise at temperature $T = 28{}^{\circ}C$, equation (3.19) can be simplified as :

$$D \text{ (in mm)} \;=\; 0.030 \sqrt{\frac{H}{t}}$$

Thus, at a given depth H in a suspension, the diameter of the largest settling size D after time t, can be determined. Also, at a given depth, the suspension containing particles with sizes smaller than D can be determined.

Theory of Sedimentation : During initial stage of sedimentation, the soil particles are uniformly dispersed throughout the suspension and the concentration of particles of different sizes is the same at all depths. After certain time, at a particular depth, only those particles remain which have not settled. Since all particles of same size have the same velocity, the particles of given size, if they exist at any level, are in the same concentration as at the beginning of sedimentation. In short, all particles smaller than a particular size (D) will be present at a depth (H) in the same degree of concentration as at the beginning. All particles larger than size (D) would have settled below that depth.

Preparation of Suspension for Sedimentation Analysis : Soil sample passing through 75 μ is analysed by this method. About 50 gm of oven-dried soil is weighed accurately and transferred to an evaporating dish. For proper dispersion of soil, about 100 ml of dispersing solution is added to the evaporating dish to cover the soil. IS 2720 part IV recommends the use of dispersing solution obtained after adding 33 gm of sodium hexametaphosphate and 7 gm of sodium carbonate to distilled water to make one litre of solution. After adding dispersing solution to soil, the mixture is warmed gently for about 10 minutes.

The material from evaporating dish is transferred to the cup of mechanical stirrer. The distilled water is added to make the cup about three-fourths full. The suspension is stirred for about 10 to 15 minutes. The stirring period may be more for clay soils.

The suspension is then washed through 75 µ sieve using jet of distilled water. The part of the suspension which has passed through the sieve is used for sedimentation analysis. The specimen is taken into the jar and enough water is added to make 1000 ml of suspension.

If the soil contains calcium compounds and organic matters, it should be pretreated before adding the dispersion agents. If M_d is the mass of particles per ml of suspension at depth (H) after time (t) and M_s is the mass of particle per ml of suspension at the beginning of sedimentation, the per cent finer for the size (D), denoted by Stoke's law is given by :

$$\% \ N = \frac{M_d}{M_s} \times 100$$

(A) Pipette Method : 500 ml of soil suspension is required in this method. All the quantities required for 1000 ml suspension are halved to get a 500 ml suspension. The suspension is taken in the sedimentation tube. A 10 ml capacity pipette is used for extraction of sample. The pipette is fitted with suction inlet.

The sedimentation tube is placed in a constant temperature bath at 27°C for one hour. The suspension is thoroughly mixed in the sedimentation tube, after taking out of constant temperature bath. After thoroughly mixing, the tube is again kept in the constant temperature bath. The instant when the tube is placed in the bath is taken as the beginning of the sedimentation. The stop watch is started to record the time. The constant temperature bath is kept just below the tip of the pipette.

The pipette is gradually lowered into the suspension in the sedimentation tube. The samples are taken from a depth of 100 mm below the surface. The first sample is taken after two minutes of the start of sedimentation. More samples are taken out after 4, 8, 15 and 30 minutes, and 1, 2, 4, 8, 12 and 24 hours. Exact time at which sample is taken is noted.

The samples taken out are dried in an oven at 100°C to 110°C for 24 hours to obtain the mass of solids per ml.

Calculations : % finer and diameter of particle is calculated as shown below :

At time t = 0 : 10 ml contains mass $(M_d)_0$

(Initial uniform suspension)

At time $t = t_1$ at depth H : 10 ml contains $(M_d)_{t_1}$

At time $t = t_2$ at depth H : 10 ml contains $(M_d)_{t_2}$

$$\text{Hence,} \qquad \% \text{ finer } (N_1) = \frac{(M_d)_{t_1}}{(M_d)_0} \times 100\%$$

$$N_1 = \frac{(M_d)_{t_2}}{(M_d)_0} \times 100\%$$

and diameter : $$D_1 = 0.030\sqrt{\frac{H}{t_1}}$$

$$D_2 = 0.030\sqrt{\frac{H}{t_2}} \ , \ \ldots\ldots \ \text{etc.}$$

The pipette is calibrated before use. For calibration, the nozzle of the pipette is immersed in distilled water. The stop cock (T_1) is closed. The three-way stop cock (T_2) is opened and water is sucked up into the pipette until it rises in safety bulb. T_2 is closed and pipette is taken out. T_2 is now connected to wash outlet to drain the excess water from the safety bulb. T_2 is then turned other way round to discharge the water contained in the pipette into a glass weighing bottle. The mass of water in the bottle in grams is equal to the volume of the pipette in (ml).

The pipette method is a very accurate laboratory method for the particle size distribution. But the apparatus is quite delicate and expensive. It requires a very sensitive weighing balance.

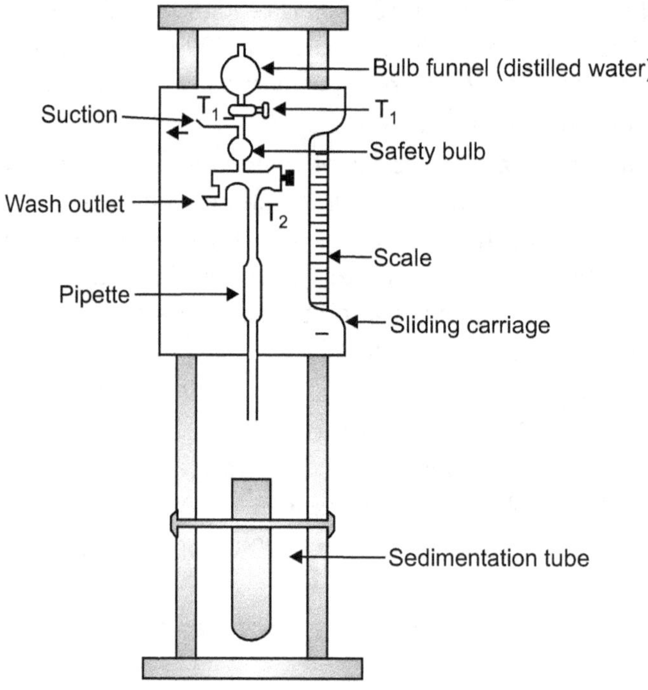

Fig. 3.16 : Pipette method

(B) Hydrometer Method : The hydrometer method is more convenient for quick particle size distribution. A hydrometer is an instrument used for determination of specific gravity of liquids. A special type of hydrometer with long neck is used for this purpose. The stem is marked from top to the bottom.

At the time of commencement of the sedimentation, the specific gravity of suspension is uniform at all the depths. When sedimentation takes place, the larger particles settle more deeper than the smaller particles. This results in greater specific gravity for lower layers of suspension than that of the upper layers.

The hydrometer measures the specific gravity of suspension, at a point where the centre of the immersed volume is the same as the centre of the bulb. Thus, the hydrometer gives the specific gravity of the suspension at the centre of the bulb.

1000 ml suspension is prepared as explained earlier. The suspension is taken in a jar. It is stirred properly. The jar is placed on the table and stop watch is started. The hydrometer is inserted in the suspension and the first reading is taken after half minute of the commencement of the sedimentation. Further readings are taken after one minute, two minutes, four minutes and six minutes of the sedimentation. The hydrometer is then removed from the jar and rinsed with distilled water and floated in a cylinder containing distilled water with the dispersing agent of same concentration as that of soil suspension.

Further readings are taken after 8, 15, 30 minutes, one hour, 2, 4, 8 and 24 hours. The time is measured from the beginning of sedimentation. For each of these readings, the hydrometer is inserted about 20 seconds before the reading. The hydrometer is taken out after the reading and floated in the cylinder containing distilled water with dispersing agent of same concentration as that of soil suspension.

Before using the hydrometer, its calibration is necessary. The volume of hydrometer is determined either by immersing it in a graduated cylinder partly filled with water and noting the rise in water level or by taking the weight of hydrometer. The volume of hydrometer is approximately equal to the weight of hydrometer in grams, assuming that the specific gravity of hydrometer is unity. This volume is measured in (ml).

The depth of any layer (A - B) form the free surface. (P - Q) is the depth at which the specific gravity is measured by the hydrometer. As soon as the hydrometer is inserted in the jar, the layers of suspension which are at level (A - B) rise to (A' - B') and those at level (P - Q) rise to level (P' - Q'). Therefore, the effective depth (H_e) is

$$H_e = \left(H + \frac{h}{2}\right) - \frac{V_H}{A} + \frac{V_H}{2A} \qquad \text{... (3.20)}$$

where, V_H = Volume of hydrometer

h = Height of bulb

A = Cross-sectional area of the jar

H = Depth from the free surface (P' - Q') to the lowest mark on the stem.

In above equation, it is assumed that the rise in suspension level from (A - B) to (A' - B') at the centre of the bulb is equal to half the total rise due to the volume of the hydrometer.

Thus, $$H_e = H + \frac{1}{2}\left(h - \frac{V_H}{A}\right) \qquad \text{... (3.21)}$$

The marking on the hydrometer stem gives the specific gravity of the suspension at the centre of the bulb. The hydrometer readings are recorded after subtracting unity from the value of specific gravity and multiplying remaining quantity by 1000. Thus, specific gravity of 1.018 is represented by a hydrometer reading (R_h) of $(1.018 - 1.00) \times 1000 = 18$, the graduations on the right side of the stem directly give the reading (R_h). A calibration chart can be prepared between the hydrometer reading (R_h) and effective depth (H_e). As the sedimentation progresses, the specific gravity of the suspension decreases hydrometer goes deeper and deeper, resulting in increase in the effective depth and decrease in hydrometer reading (R_h).

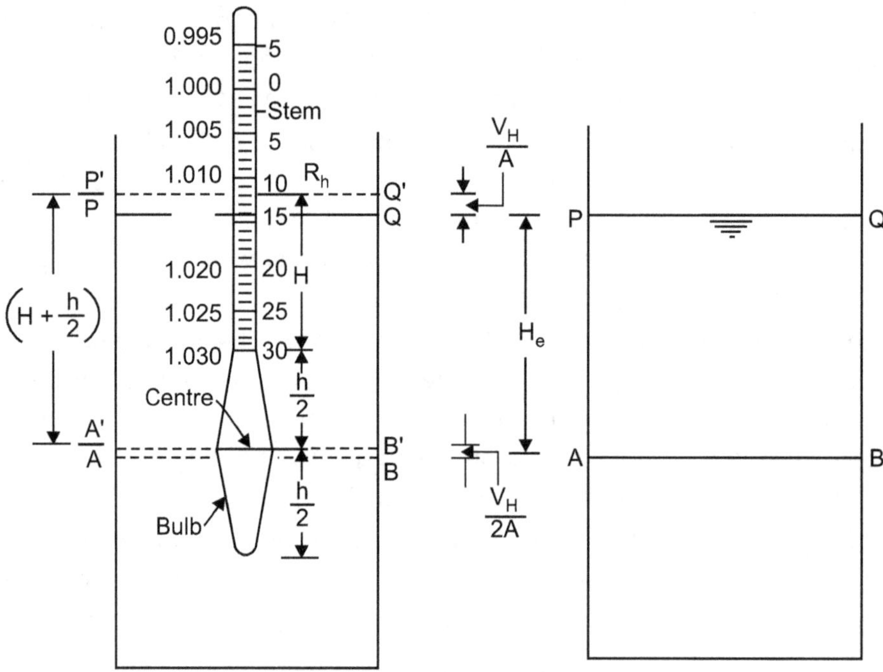

Fig. 3.17 : Hydrometer method

Corrections Applied to the Hydrometer Reading :

(i) Meniscus Correction : Since, the soil suspension is opaque, the hydrometer reading is taken at the top of the meniscus. Actual reading is to be taken at the bottom of the meniscus. Since, reading increases in downward direction, this correction is positive. The meniscus correction (C_m) can be found out by immersing the hydrometer in a jar containing clear water and finding the difference between the readings corresponding to the top and bottom of the meniscus.

(ii) Temperature Correction : The hydrometers are normally calibrated at 27°C. If the temperature of the soil suspension is not 27°C, a temperature correction (C_t) should be applied to observed hydrometer reading. If the temperature is more than 27°C, the suspension becomes lighter and the actual reading will be less than corrected reading. Hence, temperature correction will be positive. On the other hand, if the temperature is less than 27°C, the temperature correction will be negative.

(iii) Dispersing Agent Correction : Addition of dispersing agent to soil specimen increases the specific gravity of the suspension. Correction C_d due to the dispersing agent can be determined by taking the hydrometer reading in clear water and again in same water after adding the dispersing agent. This correction is always negative.

(iv) Composite Correction : Instead of finding the corrections individually, it is convenient to find one composite correction. The composite correction is algebraic sum of all the corrections. The composite correction (C) can be positive or negative.

Thus, $$R = R_h' \pm C = R_h' \pm C_t + C_m - C_d$$

where,

R = Corrected hydrometer reading

R_h' = Observed hydrometer reading

C = Composite correction

To find the composite correction (C), an identical cylinder is filled with distilled water and same quantity of dispersing agents is used as in case of preparation of suspension. The temperature of water with and without dispersing agent in both the cases must be same. The hydrometer is immersed in the cylinder (called as comparison cylinder) containing distilled water and dispersing agent. The reading is taken at the top of the meniscus. The negative of the hydrometer reading so obtained gives the composite correction. The composite correction is found before the start of the test and at every 30 minute interval.

As hydrometer has been calibrated at 27°C to give specific gravity equal to 1000, the difference between the reading taken at the top of the meniscus and 1000 is in magnitude equal to the composite correction. If reading is more than 1000, then plus sign is given to the difference. For example, if the hydrometer reading is 1003, then the difference will be (+ 3). Then the composite correction will be negative of (+ 3), hence (– 3).

If the reading is less than 1000, then minus sign is given to the difference. For example, if the hydrometer reading is 0.995, the difference will be (– 5). Then composite correction will be negative of (– 5), hence (+ 5).

After getting corrected by hydrometer reading (R), the percentage finer than (D) given by Stoke's law is computed as,

$$\% N = \left(\frac{G}{G-1}\right)\left(\frac{R}{W_s}\right) \times 100$$

where,

G = Average specific gravity of solids

R = Corrected hydrometer reading

N = % finer than (D)

W_s = Shrinkage limit

Limitations of Sedimentation Analysis :

- The Stoke's law is applicable when liquid is infinite. The presence of walls of jar affects the results.
- In Stoke's law, it has been assumed that only one sphere settles and there is no interference from the other spheres. In the sedimentation analysis, as many particles settle simultaneously, there is some interference.
- The sedimentation analysis cannot be used for the particles large than 0.2 mm as the turbulent condition invalids the Stoke's law.
- Specific gravity of solids differ from particle to particle. Therefore, use of average value of (G) is likely to introduce source of error.
- The sedimentation analysis is not applicable for particles smaller than 0.2 micron because Brownian movements takes place and the particles do not settle as per Stoke's law.
- This method cannot be used for chalky soils.
- The sedimentation analysis gives the particle size in terms of equivalent diameter which is less than the particle size given by sieve analysis, since the soil particles are not perfectly spherical. (The equivalent diameter is the diameter of sphere which falls with the same velocity as the actual particle.)

3.8 GRADING OF SOIL   [Nov. 16]

The results of the mechanical analysis are plotted to get a particle size distribution curve with % finer (N) as the ordinate and the particle size diameter as the abscissa, the diameter being plotted on a logarithmic scale. It gives an idea about the gradation of soil. A curve situated towards left top corner represents relatively fine grained soils and curve situated to the right represents a coarse grained soil.

A soil is said to be well graded when it has good representation of particles of all sizes. A soil is said to be poorly graded if it has an excess of particles of certain sizes and deficiency of other sizes or if it has most of the particles of about the same size in which case it is known as uniformly graded soil. A flat S curve represents well graded soil.

Uniformity Coefficient (C_u) : The uniformity of a soil is expressed quantitatively by a term known as coefficient (C_u) given by

$$(C_u) \;=\; \frac{D_{60}}{D_{10}} \qquad\qquad ...(3.22)$$

where, D_{60} = Particle size such that 60% of the soil is finer than this size.

           D_{10} = Particle size such that 10% of the soil is finer than this size.

Sometimes D_{10} is called as the effective size or effective diameter because knowing D_{10}, size of a sandy sample, its coefficient of permeability can be approximately determined using Allen Hazen formula :

$$K \;=\; 100\, D_{10}^{2} \;\text{cm/sec, where D is the effective grain size in cm}$$

For purely gravels C_u must be greater than 4 and for purely sand C_u must be greater than 6.

Coefficient of Curvature (C_c) : The general shape of the particle size distribution curve is described by coefficient of curvature (C_c), given by

$$(C_c) = \frac{(D_{30})^2}{D_{60} \times D_{10}} \qquad \qquad \dots (3.23)$$

where D_{30} = Particle size such that 30% of the soil is finer than the size.

For a well graded soil, (C_c) lies between 1 to 3. Otherwise, it is poorly graded.

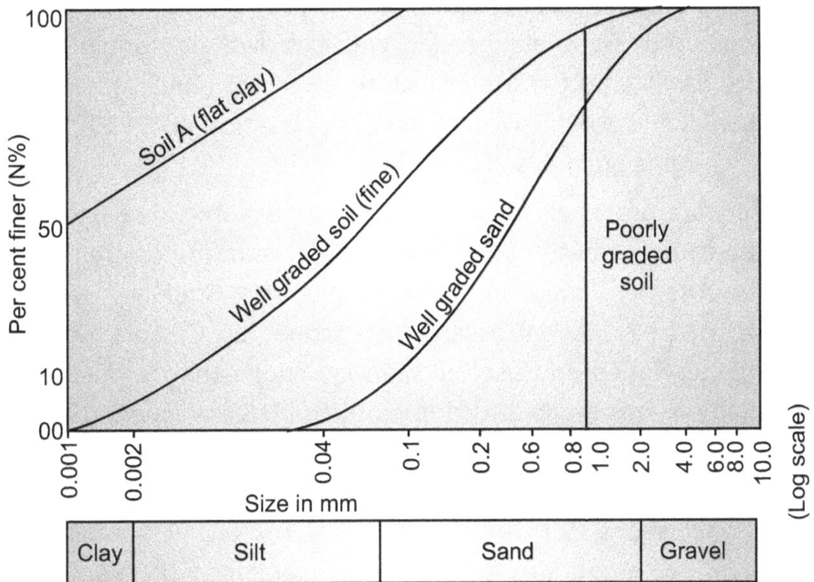

Fig. 3.18 : Particle distribution curve

Uses of Particle Size Distribution Curve :

- It can be used for coarse grained soils.
- It is used to know the susceptibility of a soil to frost action.
- The particle size distribution curve is required for the design of drainage filters.
- The particle size distribution provides an index to the shear strength of the soil. Generally, a well graded, compacted sand has high strength.
- The compressibility of a soil should also be judged from its particle size distribution curve. A uniform soil is more compressible than a well graded soil.
- The particle size distribution curve is useful in soil stabilization and for the design of pavements.
- The coefficient of permeability of a coarse grained soil depends to a large extent on the size of the particles. An approximate value of the coefficient of permeability can be determined from the particle size.
- The particle size distribution curve of a residual soil may indicate the age of the soil deposit.
- The particle size distribution curve may indicate the mode of deposition of a soil. For example, a gap-graded soil indicates deposition by two different agencies.

3.9 SOIL IDENTIFICATION AND CLASSIFICATION

A soil classification system is meant essentially to facilitate communication between different groups of engineers, widely separated and may thus be considered as a language of communication. However, the use of classification system does not eliminate the need for detailed soil investigations and testing for engineering purpose.

Various classification systems are prevalent in different organisations/countries. Most classification systems used in civil engineering practices owe their origin to agricultural soil science and thus are based on grain size or texture. Atterberg (1905) was the first to suggest properties other than grain size which can be used for classification. In 1911, he proposed the limits of consistency for fine grained soils.

At that time, these were proposed for agricultural purpose but were later accepted in soil engineering. U.S. Bureau of Public Roads developed a classification system of soil which was based practically on Atterberg limits and other simple tests. Gradually, several classification systems were developed by different organizations/countries. Casagrande, (1948) describes the several systems developed and used in highway engineering, airfield construction etc. The two classification systems which are adopted by the U.S. engineering agencies and state departments are the Unified Soil Classification System (USCS) and American Association of State Highway and Transport Officials (AASHTO) system. Other countries have adopted the USCS with minor modifications.

For general engineering purposes, soils may be classified by the following systems :

1. Particle size classification.

2. Unified soil classification and I.S. classification system.

3.9.1 Particle Size Classification

In this system, soils are arranged according to the grain size. Terms, such as gravel, sand, silt and clay are used to indicate grain sizes. These terms are used only as designation of particle size, and do not signify the naturally occurring soil types. It is preferable to use the word 'silt size' and 'clay size' in place of simply silt or clay in this system.

Following are the most widely used grain size classifications :

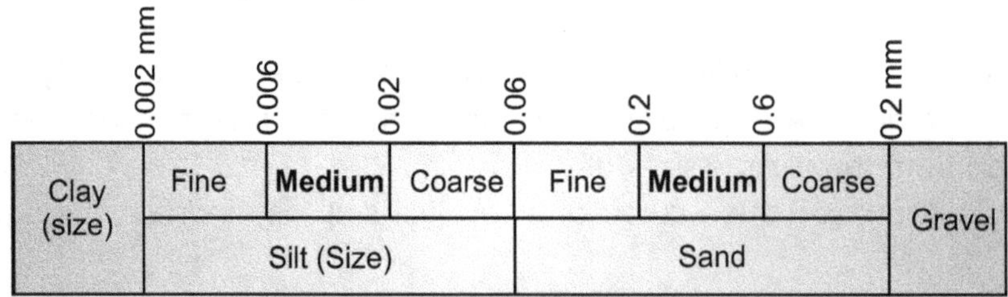

(a) M.I.T. system

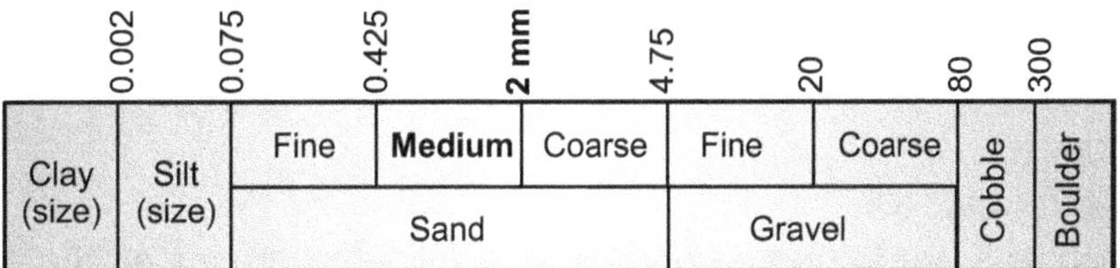

(b) Indian standard classification
Fig. 3.19

3.9.2 Unified Soil Classification and Indian Standard Classification

The Unified Classification is based on the airfield classification system that was developed by A. Casagrande. The system is based on both grain size and plasticity properties of the soil, and is therefore, applicable to any use.

The Indian Standard Institution (now Bureau of Indian Standards) adopted the unified classified system in 1954. The soil classification system IS 1498 : 1970 is generally in conformity with U.S. classification system, except for some minor modifications. Hence, the salient features of Indian Standards on the classification of soils are described below :

Classification : According to this system, soils are broadly divided into three divisions :

1.   Coarse Grained Soils : In these soils, more than half the total material by mass is larger than 75 micron IS sieve size.

2.   Fine Grained Soils : In these soils, more than half the total mass of material is smaller than 75 micron sieve size.

3.   Highly Organic Soils and other Miscellaneous Soil Materials : These soils contain large percentages of fibrous organic matter such as peat, and the particles of decomposed vegetation. In addition, certain soils containing shells, concretions, cinders and other non-soil material in sufficient quantities are also grouped in this division.

1.   Coarse Grained Soils : These are further divided into two sub-divisions :

(a) Gravels (G) : In these soils, more than half the coarse fraction (+ 75 μ) **is larger than** 4.75 IS sieve size.

(b) Sand (S) : In these soils, more than half the coarse fraction (+ 75 μ) **is smaller than** 4.75 IS sieve size.

Each of the above sub-divisions are further sub-divided into four groups :

*   Well graded, clean (W).
*   Well graded with excellent clay binder (C).
*   Poorly graded, fairly clean (P).
*   Not covered in other groups (M).

These symbols are used in combination and designate the type of coarse grained soils. For example, GC means clayey gravels.

2. Fine Grained Soils : These are further divided into three sub-divisions.

* Inorganic silt and very fine sands (M).
* Inorganic clay (C).
* Organic silt and clays (O).

The fine grained soils are further divided into the following groups on the basis of liquid limit, which is a good index of compressibility.

* Silts and clays of low compressibility, having a liquid limit less than 35% (L).
* Silts and clays of medium compressibility having a liquid limit greater than 35 and less than 50% (I).
* Silts and clays of high compressibility having a liquid limit greater than 50% (H).

Combination of these symbols indicate the types of fine grained soil. For example, ML means inorganic silt with low to medium compressibility.

Laboratory classification of fine grained soil is done with the help of plasticity chart shown in Fig. 3.20.

Plasticity Chart : A. Casagrande devised a chart useful for identifying and classifying fine grained soils. The basis of classification is the relationship between liquid limit (W_l) and the plasticity index (I_p). A line called 'A-line' is drawn diagonally across the chart. The area above the A-line represents inorganic clay and that below A-line represents silt and organic soils. The equation of A-line is

$$I_p = 0.73 (W_l - 20) \qquad\qquad \ldots (3.24)$$

Majority of Indian black cotton soils lie along a band above the A-line. The plot of some of the black cotton soils is also found to lie below the A-line. Care should be taken in classification of such soils.

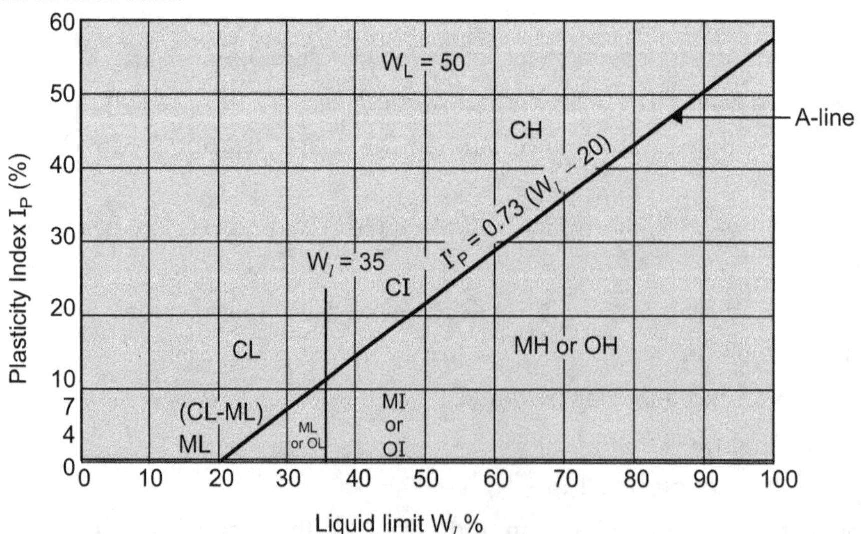

Fig. 3.20 : Plasticity chart

3.9.3 Boundary Classification

There are no rigid boundaries between soil groups, and the boundary cases can be designated by dual symbols such as GW-SW or CL-ML. The common boundary classification for fine grained soils are : GW-GP, GM-GC, GW-GM, GW-GC, SW-SP, SM-SC, SW-SM, SW-SC, GW-SW, GP-SP, GM-SM and GC-SC. The common boundary classification for the fine grained soils are : ML-MI, CL-CI, OL-OI, OI-MH, CI-CH, OI-OH, CL-ML, ML-OL, CL-OL, CI-ML, MI-OI, CI-OI, MH-CH, MH-OH and CH-OH. The boundary classification between coarse fine grained soils are : SM-ML and SC-CL. The fine grained soils whose plot on the chart falls on

(i) A-line,   (ii)   Wl= 35% line and (iii) Wl = 50% line, shall be assigned the proper boundary classification.

3.9.4 Field Tests for Soil Classification

The soil can be identified in the field using the following simple tests :

1.   Visual examination

2.   Dilatency test

3.   Toughness

4.   Dry strength

5.   Organic and colour

6.   Other identification tests.

1.   Visual Examination : The visual examination is carried out by naked eyes after taking a representative sample of soil and spreading it on a flat surface on palm of the hand. The visual examination is carried out with respect to size, angularity, touch and grading.

For fine grained soils, the following tests are carried out on the fraction finer than 425 micron IS sieve.

2.   Dilatency (Reaction of Shaking) : About 5 cc of soil sample is taken and enough water is added to nearly saturate it. The part of soil is placed in the open palm of the hand and shaken horizontally, striking rigorously against the other hand several times. The pat is then squeezed between the fingers. The appearance and disappearance of water with shaking and squeezing is referred to as a positive reaction. The reaction is called quick, if water appears and disappears rapidly. It is called slow, if water appears and disappears slowly and no reaction if the water does not appear. The type of reaction is observed and recorded. Inorganic soils exhibit a quick reaction whereas clays exhibit none to slow.

3.   Toughness (Consistency Near Plastic Limit) : The soil sample used in the dilatency test is dried by working and moulding until it reaches the consistency of putty. The time required to dry the sample is indicative of its plasticity. Further, the moisture content is reduced by rolling and re-rolling into 3 mm diameter thread till it reaches the plastic limit. The resistance to moulding at the plastic limit is called "toughness". After the thread crumbles, lump also crumbles. If the lump can still be moulded slightly drier than the plastic limit and if high pressure is required to roll the thread between the palms of the hand, the soil is said to have high toughness. Medium toughness is indicated by a medium thread. A lump formed of the threads slightly below the plastic limit will crumble. Low toughness is indicated by a weak thread that breaks easily and cannot be lumped when drier than plastic limit.

Non-plastic soils cannot be rolled into threads of 3 mm diameter at any moisture content.

4. Dry Strength (Crushing Resistance) : The prepared soil sample is completely dried in the sun or by air drying. Its strength is tested by breaking between fingers. Dry strength or resistance to breaking, is a measure of plasticity and is considerably induced by the colloidal fraction content of the soil. If the dry sample can be easily powdered, it is said to have low dry strength, whereas, if considerable finger pressure is required to break the lump, it is said to have a medium dry strength and if it cannot be powdered at all, it is said to have a high dry strength.

Dry strength is characteristic of clays of high plasticity. Typical inorganic silts have only a slight dry strength. Silty fine sands and silts have practically the same low dry strength but can be distinguished from each other by their feel during powdering of the dry sample.

5. Organic Content and Colour : Fresh, wet organic soils have the characteristic odour of organic matter. Organic soils have usually dark colouration.

6. Other Identification Tests :

(i) Acid Test : Reaction to hydrochloric acid. The test is to assess the presence of calcium carbonate. In case of solids with high dry strength, a strong reaction indicates that the strength may be due to calcium carbonate as a cementing agent rather than colloidal clay.

(ii) Shine Test : The test is performed by cutting a lump of dry or slightly dry soil with a knife. A shiny surface of the soil indicates highly plastic clay whereas a dull surface indicates a silt or clay of low plasticity.

(iii) Miscellaneous Tests : Other tests which may be developed by an individual on the basis of experience, e.g. the feel of soils in fingers, sticking of soils to fingers etc.

Both the Unified Soil Classification System and the Indian Standard Soil Classification System are based on particle size and the plasticity characteristics. The division of coarse grained soils in the two systems is practically identical. However, for the fine grained soils, the Indian Standard divides the soils into three broad groups namely soils of high, medium and low plasticity, whereas USCS puts these into two groups only, i.e. of low and high plasticity. Both the systems suggest methods of classifying boundary soils which possess characteristics of two groups.

3.9.5 Difference Between Sand and Clay

The main difference between sand and clay is the size and shape of their particles; which determine physical properties of soils and their behaviour under load, water and temperature; and their differences are summerized in the following table.

Table 3.4 : Physical Differences between Sand and Clay

	Properties	Sand	Clay
1.	Particle size	Large : 0.05 to 1.00 mm, mostly distinguishable by eye.	Minute, less than 0.005 mm, not visible to the naked eye.
2.	Appearance of particles	Bulky and rigid	Flexible
3.	Particle shape	Angular and rounded	Scaly-like
4.	Texture	Coarse	Fine
5.	Uniformity	Uniform	Less uniform
6.	Internal friction	High	Small, or negligible
7.	Size of pores	Large	Very minute
8.	Volume of voids	Relatively small, about 50% at a maximum of the total volume.	Very high, as high as approx. 98% of the total volume.
9.	Void ratio	Low	High
10.	Specific surface	Small	Large
11.	Plasticity	Non-plastic	Plastic
12.	Cohesion	Negligible	Marked
13.	Surface	Low	Immense surface tension forces
14.	Capillarity	Not appreciable	Very high
15.	Capillary pressure	Low	Great
16.	Shrinkage upon drying	Negligible	Very high
17.	Swelling	None	Considerable
18.	Expansion	Practically none	Most expansive
19.	Compressibility	Slight	Very compressible
20.	Compression when load applied to surface	Immediate	Slow
21.	Elasticity	Low	High
22.	Permeability	High degree, drains readily	Low degree, drains slowly

Table 3.5 : Classification of Coarse-Grained Soils(As per IS 1498 - 1970)

Division	Subdivision		Group symbol	Typical names	Laboratory Criteria		Remark
(1) Coarse grained soils (More than half of material is larger than 75-micron IS sieve size)	Gravel (G) (More than half of coarse fraction of larger than 4.75 mm IS sieve)	Clean gravels (Fines less than 5%)	(1) GW (2) GP	Well graded gravels Poorly graded gravels	C_u greater than 4, C_c between 1 and 3 Not meeting all gradation requirements for GW		When fines are between 5% to 12% border line cases requiring dual symbols as GP-GM, SW-SC etc.
		Gravels with appreciable amount of fines (Fines more than 12%)	(3) GM	Silty gravels	Atterberg limits below A-line or Ip less than 4.	Atterberg limits plotting above A-line with Ip between 4 and 7 are border line cases requiring use of dual symbol GM-GC	
			(4) GC	Clayey gravels	Atterberg limits above A-line and Ip greater than 7		
	Sand (S) (More than half of coarse fraction is smaller than 4.75 mm IS sieve)	Clean sands (Fines less than 5%)	(5) SW (6) SP	Well graded sands Poorly graded sands	C_u greater than 6, C_c between 1 and 3 Not meeting all gradation requirements for SW		
		Sands with appreciable amount of fines (Fines more than 12%)	(7) SM (8) SC	Silty sands Clayey sands	Atterberg limits below A-line or Ip less than 4 Atterberg limits above A-line with Ip greater than 7	Atterberg limits plotting above A-line with Ip between 4 and 7 are border line cases requiring use of double symbols SM-SC	

Table 3.6 : Classification of Fine-Grained Soils
(As per IS 1498 - 1970)

Division	Sub-division	Group symbols	Typical names	Laboratory criteria (See Fig. 3.20)		Remarks
(2) Fine grained soils (More than 50% pass 75 micron, IS sieve)	Low compressibility (L) (Liquid Limit less than 35%).	(1) ML	Inorganic silts with none to low plasticity	Atterberg limits plot below A-line or I_p less than 7	Atterberg limits plotting above A-line with I_p between 4 to 7 (hatched zone) ML-CL	
		(2) CL	Inorganic clays of low plasticity	Atterberg limits plot above A-line and I_p greater than 7		
		(3) OL	Organic silts of low plasticity	Atterberg limits plot below A-line		
	Intermediate compressibility (I) (Liquid limit greater than 35% but less than 50%)	(4) MI	Inorganic silts of medium plasticity	Atterberg limits plot below A-line		
		(5) CI	Inorganic clays of medium plasticity	Atterberg limits plot above A-line		
		(6) OI	Organic silts of medium plasticity	Atterberg limits plot below A-line		
	High compressibility (H) (Liquid limit greater than 50%)	(7) MH	Inorganic silts of high compressibility	Atterberg limits plot below A-line		Black cotton soils of India lie along a band partly above the A-line and partly below the A-line. See, plasticity chart
		(8) CH	Inorganic clays of high plasticity	Atterberg limits plot above A-line		
		(9)	Organic clays of medium to high plasticity	Atterberg limits plot below A-line		
(3) Highly organic soil		Pt	Peat and other highly organic soils	Readily identified by colour, odour, spongy feel and fibrous texture.		

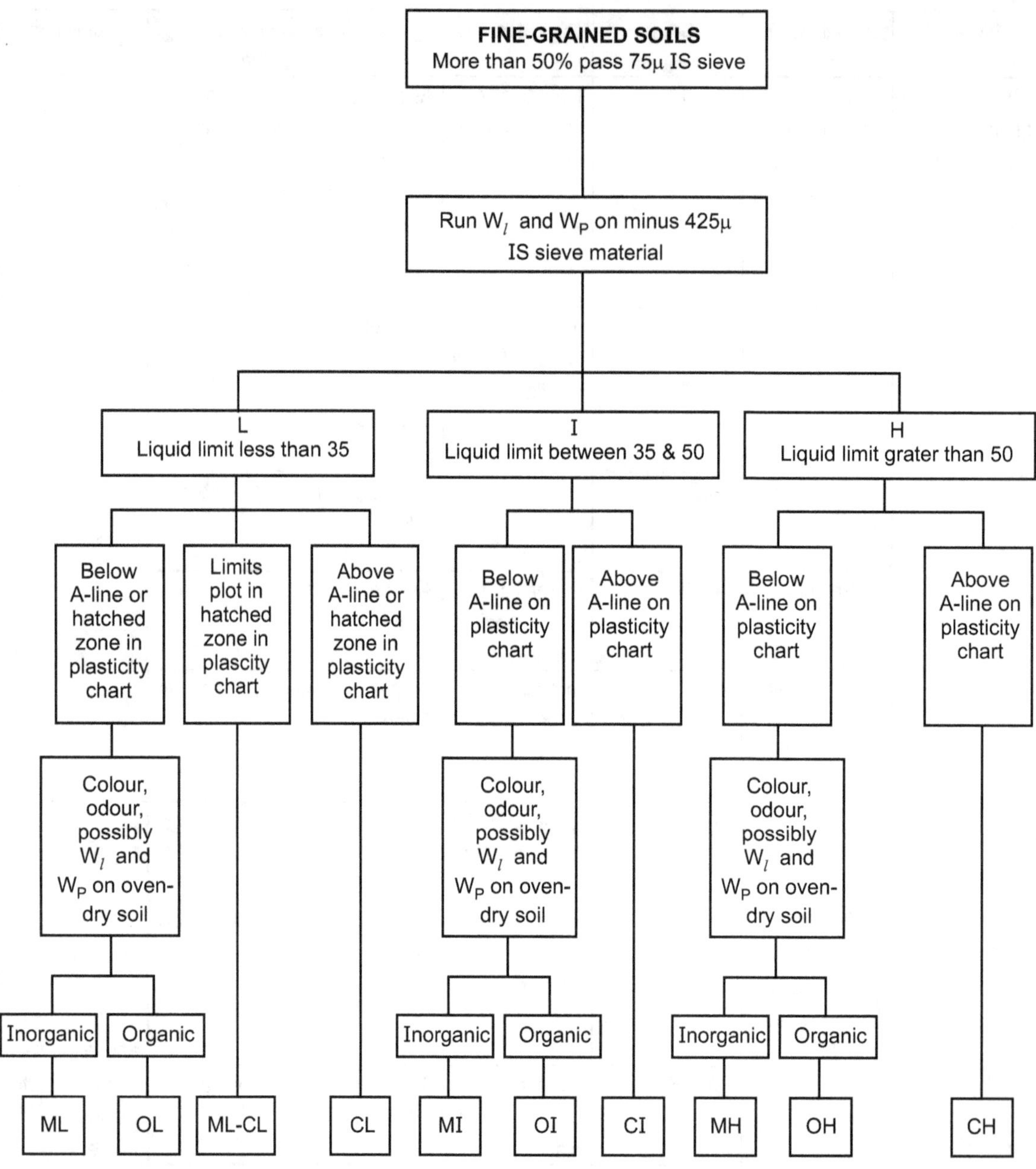

FINE-GRAINED SOILS
More than 50% pass 75µ IS sieve
Run W_l and W_P on minus 425µ IS sieve material
L
Liquid limit less than 35
I
Liquid limit between 35 & 50
H
Liquid limit grater than 50
Below A-line or hatched zone in plasticity chart
Limits plot in hatched zone in plascity chart
Above A-line or hatched zone in plasticity chart
Below A-line on plasticity chart
Above A-line on plasticity chart
Below A-line on plasticity chart
Above A-line on plasticity chart
Colour, odour, possibly W_l and W_P on oven-dry soil
Colour, odour, possibly W_l and W_P on oven-dry soil
Colour, odour, possibly W_l and W_P on oven-dry soil
Inorganic
Organic
Inorganic
Organic
Inorganic
Organic
ML
OL
ML-CL
CL
MI
OI
CI
MH
OH
CH

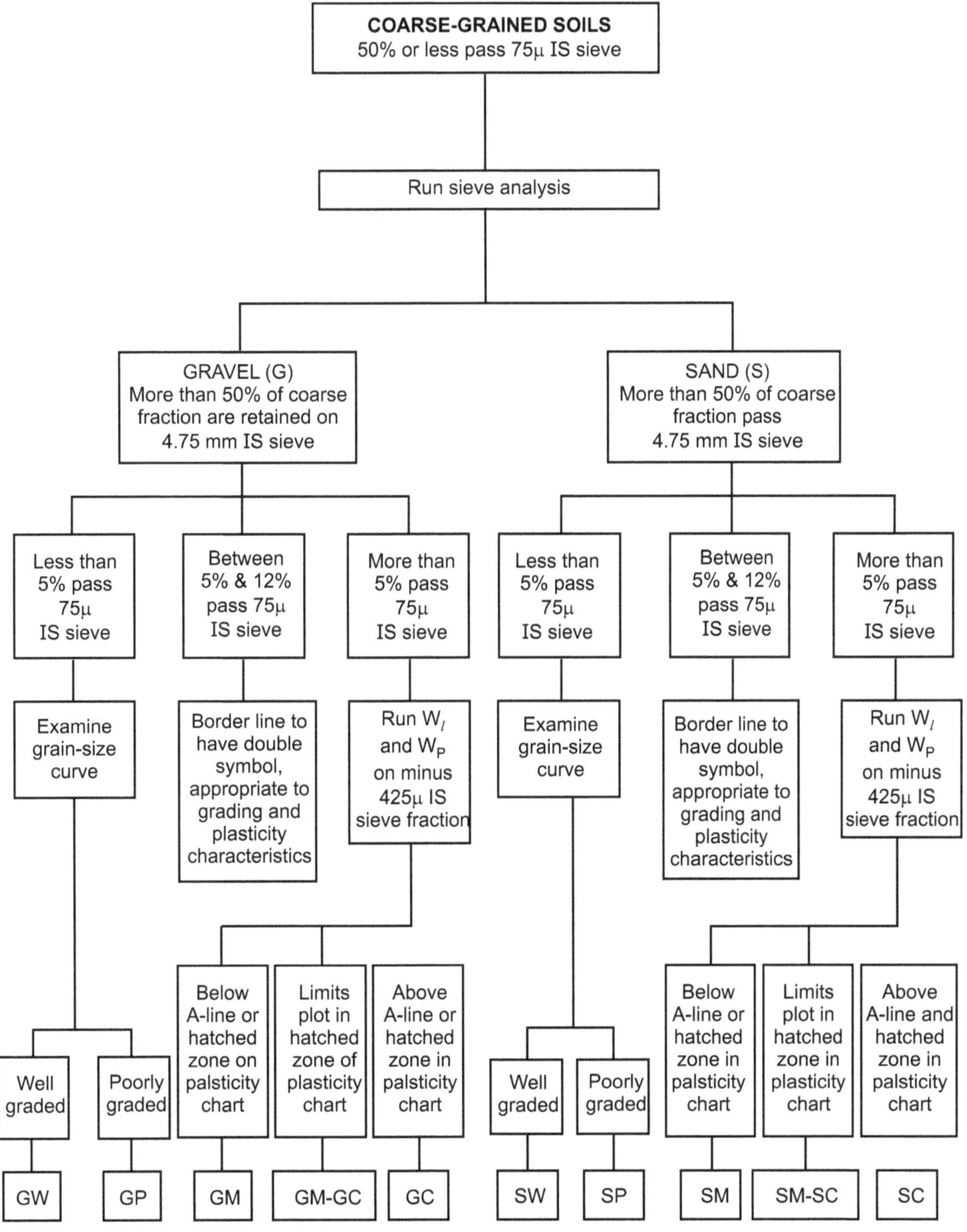
COARSE-GRAINED SOILS
50% or less pass 75μ IS sieve
Run sieve analysis
GRAVEL (G)
More than 50% of coarse fraction are retained on 4.75 mm IS sieve
SAND (S)
More than 50% of coarse fraction pass 4.75 mm IS sieve
Less than 5% pass 75μ IS sieve
Between 5% & 12% pass 75μ IS sieve
More than 5% pass 75μ IS sieve
Less than 5% pass 75μ IS sieve
Between 5% & 12% pass 75μ IS sieve
More than 5% pass 75μ IS sieve
Examine grain-size curve
Border line to have double symbol, appropriate to grading and plasticity characteristics
Run W_l and W_P on minus 425μ IS sieve fraction
Examine grain-size curve
Border line to have double symbol, appropriate to grading and plasticity characteristics
Run W_l and W_P on minus 425μ IS sieve fraction
Below A-line or hatched zone on palsticity chart
Limits plot in hatched zone of plasticity chart
Above A-line or hatched zone in palsticity chart
Below A-line or hatched zone in palsticity chart
Limits plot in hatched zone in plasticity chart
Above A-line and hatched zone in palsticity chart
Well graded
Poorly graded
Well graded
Poorly graded
GW
GP
GM
GM-GC
GC
SW
SP
SM
SM-SC
SC

Table 3.7 : Soil Classification Procedure

1. **Fine Percentage (P_f) :**
    (a) Less than 5% - clean gravel or clean sand, (G-, S-) GO TO 3 ......
    (b) More than 50% - silts or clays - (C-, M-, O-) - GO TO 2 ......
    (c) Fines less than 50% more than 12% - GO TO 2
    (d) Fines between 5% and 12% - GO TO 2 and 3.
         Double symbols, GW-GM, SP-SG etc.

2. **Plasticity Chart (W_l, I_p) :**
    (a) Plot below A-line (M and O) - GO TO 4, 5 ......
    (b) Plot above A-line, (C) - GO TO 4 ......
    (c) For gravels and sands with fines, (G-, S-) - GO TO 6 ......

3. **Uniformity Coefficient and Coefficient of Curvature :**
    (a) For gravel C_u more than 4, (C_c - 1 to 3) - GW, (otherwise) GP
    (b) For sand C_u more than 6, (C_c - 1 to 3) - SW, (otherwise) - SP

4. **Liquid Limit (W_l) :**
    (a) W_l between 20 and 35 - L - CL, ML, OL
    (b) W_l between 35 and 50 - I - CI, MI, OI
    (c) W_l more than 50 - H - CH, MH, OH
    (d) W_l less than 20 and I_p - 4 to 7, - fine, silty sands, - non-plastic silts, CL, ML

5. **Organic Soils :**
    Identify by feel, touch, odour, organic content.
    (a) Gritty feel, no odour, - silts - (M-group)
    (b) Soapy, smooth feel, strong odour - organic soils - (O-group)

6. **Gravels and Sands with Appreciable Fines (P_f > 12 p.c.) :**
    (a) Combine (1) with (2) and (4) as GCL, GML, SCL, SML, GCH.
    (b) Drop L, I, H as GCH $\rightarrow$ GC, SMI $\rightarrow$ SM etc.

SOLVED EXAMPLES

Example 3.1 : The following observations are obtained for determining the specific gravity of soil. Find the value of G.

Mass of empty density bottle (M_1) = 500 g

Mass of bottle + soil (M_2) = 729 g

Mass of bottle + soil + water (M_3) = 1670 g

Mass of bottle + water (M_4) = 1513 g

Solution :

$$G = \frac{M_2 - M_1}{(M_4 - M_1) - (M_3 - M_2)}$$

$$= \frac{729 - 500}{(1513 - 500) - (1670 - 729)} = \mathbf{3.18}$$

Example 3.2 : The following observations were taken during a pipette analysis for the determination of particle size distribution of a soil sample :

(i)   Depth below the water at which sample was taken = 100 mm

(ii) Capacity of pipette = 10 ml

(iii) Mass of sample when dried = 0.5 gm

(iv) Time of taking sample = 16 minutes

(v) Volume of soil suspension in the sedimentation tube = 500 ml

(vi) Dry weight of soil used in making suspension = 25 gm

Take G = 2.65 and η = 11.00 millipoise

Determine % finer and comment.

Solution :

$$D = \sqrt{\frac{0.30\, \eta H}{(G-1)\, t}} = \sqrt{\frac{0.30 \times 11 \times 1.02 \times 10^{-6} \times 10}{(2.65 - 1) \times 16}}$$

$$= 0.00113 \text{ cm} = \mathbf{0.0113 \text{ mm}}$$

$$\text{\% finer,} \quad n = \frac{M_d}{M_s} \times 100 = \frac{\dfrac{0.5}{10}}{\dfrac{25}{100}} \times 100 = \mathbf{100\%}$$

Thus, given samples contain all particles having size smaller than 0.0113 mm.

Example 3.3 : A dry sample of weight 50 gm is mixed with distilled water to prepare a suspension of 1000 ml for hydrometer analysis. The reading of the hydrometer taken after 5 minutes was 20 and the depth of the centre of the bulb below the water surface when the hydrometer was in the jar was 140 mm. The volume of hydrometer was 62 ml and area of cross-section of the jar was 50 cm^2. Find % finer. Assume G = 2.65 and η = 1.02 $\times$ 10^{-5} gm-sec/cm^2.

Solution : The depth between (P' - A') and (A' - B') is given as 140 mm.

The effective depth between (P - Q) and (A - B) is given by

$$H_e = 14.0 - \frac{V_H}{A} + \frac{V_H}{2A} = 14.0 - \frac{V_H}{2A}$$

$$H_e = 14.0 - \frac{62}{2 \times 50} = 13.38 \text{ cm}$$

$$D = \sqrt{\frac{0.3 \times \eta \times H_e}{(G-1) \times 1}} = \sqrt{\frac{0.3 \times 1.02 \times 10^{-5} \times 13.38}{(2.65 - 1) \times 5}}$$

$$D = 0.0022 \text{ cm} = 0.022 \text{ mm}$$

$$\text{\% finer (N)} = \left(\frac{G}{G-1}\right) \times \frac{R}{M_d} \times 100 = \frac{2.65}{1.65} \times \frac{20}{50} \times 100 = \mathbf{64.24\%}$$

Example 3.4 : 500 gm of dry soil was used for sieve analysis. The weights of soil retained on each sieve are given below :

I.S. Sieve	Weight in gm
2.00 mm	10
1.40 mm	18
1.00 mm	60
500 µ	135
250 µ	145
125 µ	56
75 µ	45

Plot a grain size distribution curve and compute the following :

(a) Percentages of gravel, coarse sand, medium sand, fine sand and silt, as per IS : 1498 - 199.

(b) Uniformity of coefficient.

(c) Coefficient of curvature.

Comment on the type of soil.

Solution : (a)   Percentage gravel $= 100 - 98 = 2$ per cent

Percentage of coarse sand $= 98 - 61.5 = 36.5$ per cent

Percentage of medium sand $= 61.5 - 22.0 = 39.5$ per cent

Percentage of fine sand $= 22.0 - 3.0 = 19.0$ per cent

Percentage of silt $= 3$ per cent

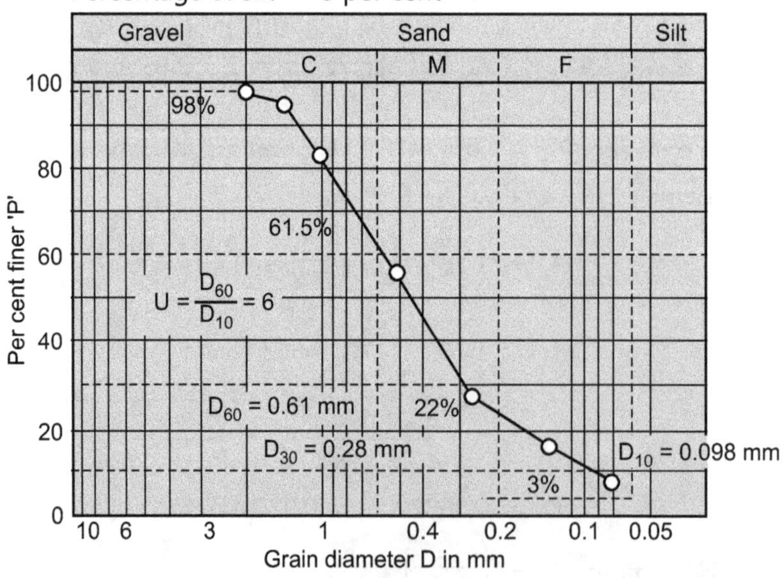

Fig. 3.21

I.S. sieve	Diameter (D) of grains	Weight retained (gm)	% retained	Cumulative % retained	% finer (N)
2.00 mm	2.00 mm	10	2.0	2.0	98.0
1.40 mm	1.40 mm	18	3.6	5.6	94.4
1.00 mm	1.00 mm	60	12.0	17.6	82.4
500 μ	0.500 mm	135	27.0	44.6	55.4
250 μ	0.250 mm	145	29.0	73.6	26.4
125 μ	0.125 mm	56	11.2	84.8	15.2
75 μ	0.075 mm	45	9.0	93.8	6.2

(b) Uniformity coefficient (C_u),

$$\frac{D_{60}}{D_{10}} = \frac{0.61}{0.098} = \mathbf{6.22}$$

(c) Coefficient of curvature (C_c) $= \frac{(D_{30})^2}{D_{10} \times D_{60}} = \frac{(0.28)^2}{0.098 \times 0.61} = \mathbf{1.3}$

As per the value of uniformity coefficient, the soil is sand and as per the value of C_c, the soil is said to be well graded since the value lies between 1 and 3. Hence, soil is SW.

Example 3.5 : What time a spherical particle of 2 micron size will take to settle through a depth of 100 mm through a water suspension ?

(Use the relation $V = 10850\ D^2$)

Solution : Given equation :

$$V = 10850\ D^2$$
$$D = 2\,\mu = 0.002\ \text{mm}$$
$$H = 100\ \text{mm}$$

Now,

$$V = \frac{H}{t} = 10850\ D^2$$

or

$$t = \frac{H}{10850\ D^2}$$

$$= \frac{100}{10850\ (0.002)^2} = \mathbf{2304\ seconds}$$

Example 3.6 : The grading curve of a soil gives the effective size as 0.16 mm, $D_{30} = 0.40$ mm and $D_{60} = 0.80$ mm. Find C_u and C_c . Classify the soil.

Solution : We know,

$$C_u = \frac{D_{60}}{D_{10}} = \frac{0.8}{0.16} = 5$$

and

$$C_c = \frac{(D_{30})^2}{D_{60} \times D_{10}}$$

$$= \frac{(0.4)^2}{(0.8)^2 \times (0.16)^2} = \mathbf{1.25}$$

As $C_u > 4$, soil is gravel and since C_c is between 1 and 3 it is well graded. Therefore, soil is (GW).

Example 3.7 : The following are the details of laboratory test on a sample of soil :

Bulk density by core cutter = 2000 kg/m³

G = 2.7 and water content = 25%

Determine ρ_d, n and S_r.

Solution : Using equation

$$\rho = \frac{G(1+w)}{1+e} \times \rho_w$$

$\therefore \qquad 2000 = \frac{2.7(1+0.25)}{1+e} \times 1000$

$\therefore \qquad e = 0.68 \qquad\qquad \text{... (i)}$

Now, $\qquad n = \dfrac{e}{1+e}$

$$= \frac{0.68}{1+0.68} = \mathbf{40.7\%} \qquad\qquad \text{... (ii)}$$

Also, $\qquad \rho_d = \dfrac{\rho}{1+w}$

$$= \frac{2000}{1+0.25} = \mathbf{1600\ kg/m^3}$$

and $\qquad S_r = \dfrac{w \cdot G}{e} = \dfrac{0.25 \times 2.7}{0.68}$

$$= \mathbf{99.26\%}$$

Example 3.8 : In a liquid limit test using penetration device 23.9 mm of penetration was recorded corresponding to water content of 66%. Determine the liquid limit.

Solution :

$$W_l = w_x + 0.01(25 - x)(w_x + 15)$$
$$= 66 + 0.01(25 - 23.9)(66 + 15)$$
$$= \mathbf{66.9\%}$$

Example 3.9 : A liquid limit test by the Casagrande apparatus gave the following results :

No. of blows	15	21	38	51	62
Moisture content %	74.6	68.4	66.67	52.60	48.10

Plot the flow curve and find the liquid limit and the flow index.

Solution : From Fig. 3.22, the liquid limit W_l = 65.6%. Fig. 3.22 is a flow curve. Flow index $I_F = W_{10} - W_{100}$, W_{10} = 83%, W_{100} = 40%. The curve is extrapolated on both sides to get W_{10} and W_{100}.

$$\therefore \qquad I_F = (83 - 40) = \mathbf{43\%}$$

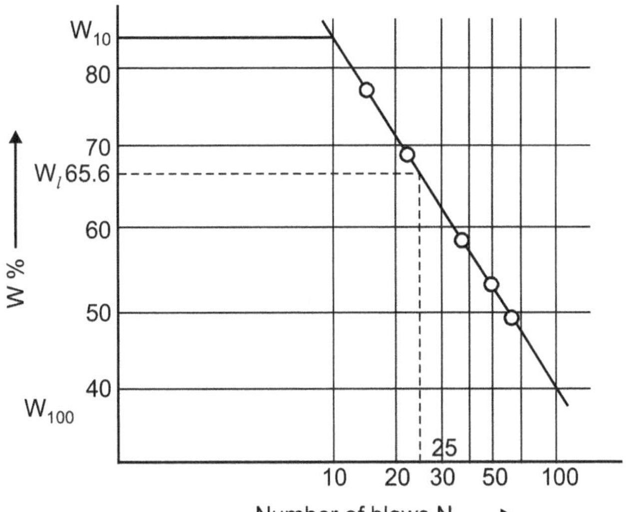

Fig. 3.22 : Flow curve

Example 3.10 : Find the liquid limit by one point method if the water content at 29 blows is 54.5%.

Solution : As per Lambe formula,

$$W_l = w \left(\frac{N}{25}\right)^{0.12}$$

$$\therefore \quad W_l = 0.545 \left(\frac{29}{25}\right)^{0.12} = \mathbf{55.47\%}$$

Example 3.11 : Determine flow index, liquidity index and consistency index, given $W_l = 65\%$, $W_p = 38\%$, $W_n = 45\%$ and number of jerks is 48 at W = 31%.

Solution : (1) Flow index,

$$I_f = \frac{W_l - W_p}{\log N_2 - \log N_1}$$

$$= \frac{0.65 - 0.38}{\log 32 - \log 25} = 1.586$$

(As liquid limit is for N = 25)

(2) Toughness index,

$$I_t = \frac{I_p}{I_f} = \frac{W_l - W_p}{I_f}$$

$$= \frac{0.65 - 0.38}{1.586} = 0.17$$

(3) Liquidity index,

$$I_l = \frac{W_n - W_p}{I_p}$$

$$= \frac{0.45 - 0.38}{0.65 - 0.38} = \frac{0.07}{0.27} = 0.2593$$

(4) Consistency index, $I_c = \dfrac{W_l - W_n}{I_p}$

$$= \dfrac{0.65 - 0.45}{0.27} = 0.74$$

$$I_p = W_l - W_p = 0.65 - 0.38 = \mathbf{0.27}$$

Alternatively, $I_l + I_c = 1$

$\therefore$ $I_c = 1 - 0.26$

$$= 0.74$$

Example 3.12 : If for a soil % finer passing 0.002 mm is 95% and W_l = 70%, W_p = 24%, find activity number.

Solution : Activity number, $A = \dfrac{I_p}{\% \text{ fines } < 0.002 \text{ mm}}$

$$= \dfrac{0.70 - 0.24}{0.95} = \mathbf{0.48}$$

Example 3.13 : A shrinkage limit test gave the following observations. Determine the shrinkage limit.

$$\begin{aligned}
\text{Volume of dry pat} &= 29.30 \text{ ml} \\
\text{Mass of dry pat} &= 48.32 \text{ gm} \\
\text{Initial volume (wet)} &= 43.50 \text{ ml} \\
\text{Initial mass (wet)} &= 66.66 \text{ gm} \\
\text{If } G &= 2.68, \text{ find the shrinkage limit.}
\end{aligned}$$

Solution : (1) $W_s = \dfrac{M_1 - M_2 - \rho_w (V_1 - V_2)}{M_2}$

$$= \dfrac{(66.66 - 48.32) - 1 \times (43.50 - 29.30)}{48.32} \times 100 = 8.7\%$$

(2)   When G = 2.68, $\rho_d = \dfrac{M_d \cdot \rho_w}{V_d} - \dfrac{1}{G}$

$$= \dfrac{1}{\left(\dfrac{48.32}{29.30}\right)} - \dfrac{1}{2.68}$$

$\therefore$ $\rho_d = \dfrac{1}{1.649} - \dfrac{1}{2.68} = \mathbf{22\%}$

Example 3.14 : The field density of a non-cohesive backfill was found to be 1647 kg/m³ at a water content of 8.4%. If void ratio in the loosest and densest states were found out as 0.859 and 0.462, determine the density index.

Solution :

$$\rho_{dry} = \frac{\rho}{1 + w} = \frac{1647}{1 + 0.084} = 1544 \text{ kg/m}^3$$

$$e = \frac{G \cdot \rho_w}{\gamma_{dry}} - 1 = \frac{2.7 \times 1000}{1544} - 1 = 0.748$$

Now, density index,

$$I_d = \frac{e_{max} - e}{e_{max} - e_{min}} \times 100$$

$$= \frac{0.859 - 0.748}{0.859 - 0.462} \times 100 = \textbf{27.70\%}$$

Example 3.15 : On oven drying of 35 gm of saturated soil having a volume of 21 cc, mass reduced to 22.5 gm and volume reduced to 10 cc.

Determine shrinkage limit, specific gravity, void ratio and shrinkage ratio.

Solution :

$$\text{Mass of water in soil} = 35 - 22.5 = 12.5 \text{ gm}$$

$$\therefore \quad \text{Volume occupied by water} = 12.5 \text{ cc}$$

$$\therefore \quad \text{Volume occupied by solids} = 21 - 12.5 = 8.5 \text{ cc}$$

$$w = \text{Initial water content}$$

$$= \frac{35 - 22.5}{22.5} = \frac{12.5}{22.5} = 55.55\%$$

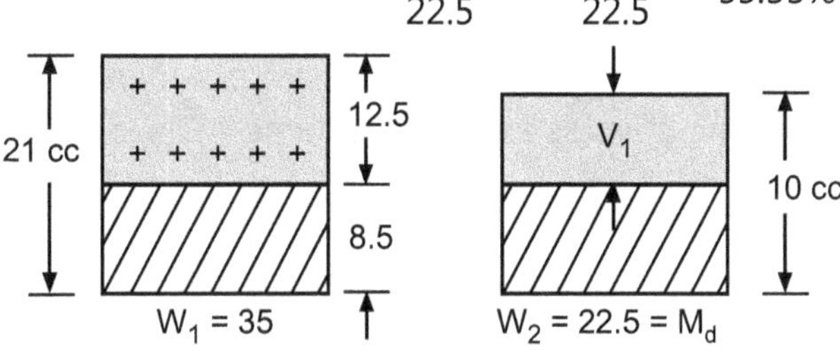

Fig. 3.23

$$S_r \cdot e = w \cdot G$$

$$S_r = 1$$

$$w = 0.5555$$

$$e = 0.5555 \, G$$

From figure,

$$G = \frac{\gamma_s}{\gamma_w} = \frac{W_s/V_s}{\gamma_w} = \frac{22.5/8.5}{1} = 2.647$$

At final stage,

$$V_w = 10 - 8.5 = 1.5 \text{ cc}$$

$$M_w = V_w \cdot \rho_w = 1.5 \text{ g}$$

$$W_s = \frac{M_w}{M_d} = \frac{1.5}{22.5} \times 100 = \mathbf{6.66\%}$$

$$e = 0.5555 \times G = 0.5555 \times 2.647 = 1.47$$

$$S.R. = \frac{\left(\dfrac{V_1 - V_2}{V_2}\right) \times 100}{W_1 - W_2}$$

$$= \frac{\left(\dfrac{21 - 10}{10}\right) \times 100}{55.55 - 6.66} = \frac{\left(\dfrac{11}{10}\right) 100}{48.89} = 2.250$$

Determine, whether it is economical to transport from borrow pit A or borrow pit B.

Location	Unit weight in kN/m³	% Moisture content = m	Lead in kM from embankment
A	16.00	8%	8 km
B	17.00	12%	12 km
Embankment	19.50	15%	–

Solution :
$$\gamma_{bulk} = \frac{G \cdot \gamma_w (1 + m)}{1 + e}$$

Let suffix a, b and x relate to borrow pits A, B and embankment respectively. If volume of solids is taken as 1 and volume of voids as e, total volume = 1 + e.

$$V_a = \text{Volume of soil from borrow pit A} = 1 + e_a = \frac{G \cdot \gamma_w (1 + m_a)}{\gamma_a}$$

Similarly,
$$V_b = \frac{G \cdot \gamma_w (1 + m_b)}{\gamma_b}$$

$$V_x = \frac{G \cdot \gamma_w (1 + m_x)}{\gamma_x}$$

Assuming G, γ_w as 2.7 and 10 kN/m³ respectively,

$$V_a = \frac{2.7 \times 10 \times 1.08}{10} = 1.8225$$

$$V_b = \frac{2.7 \times 10 \times 1.12}{17} = 1.7788$$

$$V_x = \frac{2.7 \times 10 \times 1.15}{19.5} = 1.592$$

$$\frac{V_a}{V_x} = \frac{1.8225}{1.592} = 1.4478$$

$\therefore$ For borrow pit A,

$$(V_a \times \text{Lead}) = (1.4478 \times 8)\, V_x = \mathbf{9.1583\ V_x} \qquad \dots \text{(i)}$$

For borrow pit B, $(V_b \times \text{Lead}) = (1.7788 \times 12)\, V_x = \mathbf{13.408\ V_x}$ ... (ii)

From (i) and (ii), it is clear that, it is economical to obtain soil from borrow pit A.

Example 3.17 : An embankment is to be constructed with dry density of 18.5 kN/m³ with 15% moisture content. The soil is to be obtained from borrow pit with unit weight of 17 kN/m³ and has moisture content of 8%. Determine :

(i)   Quantity of soil to be excavated from borrow pit per cu. m. of embankment.

(ii) Mass of water to be added per cu. m. of soil excavated from borrow pit.

Solution :

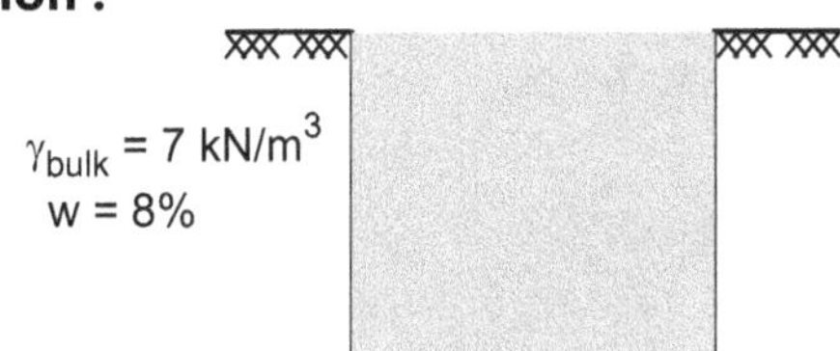
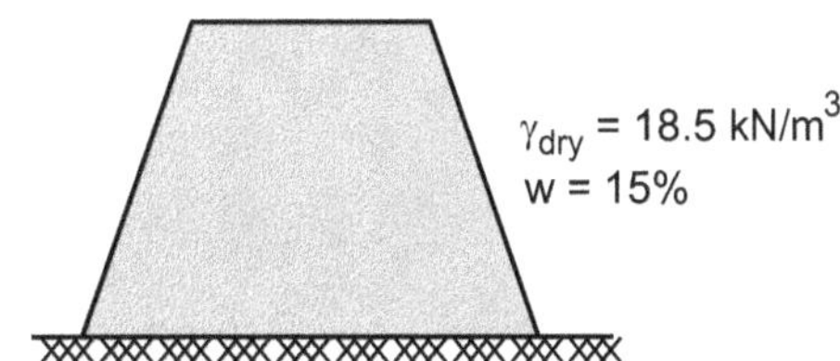

Fig. 3.24

$$\gamma_b = \frac{G \cdot \gamma_w (1 + w)}{1 + e_b}$$

$G = 2.7, \quad \gamma_w = 10, \quad \gamma_b = 17, \quad w = 8\%$

$$1 + e_b = \frac{2.7 \times 10\, (1 + 0.08)}{17} = 1.7153$$

Similarly, for embankment, $\gamma_{dry} = \dfrac{G \cdot \gamma_w}{1 + e_{embank}}$

$\therefore$ $$1 + e_{embank} = \frac{G \cdot \gamma_w}{\gamma_{dry}} = \frac{2.7 \times 10}{18.5} = 1.4595$$

$$\frac{V_{borrow}}{V_{embankment}} = \frac{1 + e_b}{1 + e_{embank}} = \frac{1.7153}{1.4595} = 1.1753$$

$\therefore$ $\begin{bmatrix} \text{Volume of soil from borrow pit} \\ \text{to be excavated/cm of embankment} \end{bmatrix} = 1.1753\ \text{cu.m.}$ ... (i)

$$\gamma_{dry}\ \text{borrow pit} = \left(\frac{17}{1 + 0.08}\right) = 15.7407\ \text{kN}$$

Wt. of water/unit wt. $= 17 - 15.7407 = 1.2593$ ... (ii)

Quantity of embankment achieved per cu. m. of borrow pit soil $= \dfrac{1}{1.1753} = \mathbf{0.8508\ cu.m}$

Wt. of water/cm of embankment,   w $= 15\%$

$$= \frac{\text{Wt. of water}}{\gamma_d \text{ of soil}} = 18.50 \times 15\% = \textbf{2.775 kN}$$

$\therefore$ Quantity of water for 0.8508 cu.m. of embankment

$$= (0.8508) \times 2.775$$
$$= 2.3610 \text{ kN} \qquad\qquad ... \text{(iii)}$$

$\therefore$ Weight of water to be added per cu.m of soil from borrow pit

$$= \text{(iii)} - \text{(ii)} = 2.3610 - 1.2593 = \textbf{1.1017 kN}$$

Example 3.18 : A fully saturated clay sample has volume of 186 cc and mass of 337 gm. If G = 2.67, find e, n, w and ρ.

Solution :

$$\rho_{sat} = \frac{337}{186} = \textbf{1.81 gm/cc}$$

$$\rho_{sat} = \frac{(G + e)\,\rho_w}{1 + e} \quad (\text{Assume } \rho_w = 1 \text{ gm/cc})$$

$$\therefore \quad 1.81 = \frac{2.67 + e}{1 + e}$$

$$\therefore \quad 1.81 + (1.81) \times e = 2.67 + e$$

$$\therefore \quad e = \frac{2.67 - 1.81}{0.81} = \textbf{1.062}$$

$$S_r \cdot e = w \cdot G$$

$$\therefore \quad w = \frac{1.062}{2.67} = 0.3976 \text{ or } \textbf{39.76\%}$$

$$n = \frac{e}{1 + e} = \frac{1.062}{2.062} = 0.515 = \textbf{51.5\%}$$

Example 3.19 : From particle size distribution curve of a sandy sample, following data is obtained. Determine C_u, C_c and classify sand.

Particle size	% Finer than
0.425 mm	60%
0.200 mm	30%
0.05 mm	10%

Solution :

$$C_u = \frac{D_{60}}{D_{10}} = \frac{0.425}{0.05} = 8.5 \ (> 6)$$

$$C_c = \frac{(D_{20})^2}{D_{10} \times D_{60}} = \frac{0.2 \times 0.2}{0.425 \times 0.05}$$

$$= \textbf{1.8825} \ (\text{between 1 and 3})$$

For well graded sand $C_u > 6$ and C_c should be between 1 to 3.

$\therefore$ It is well graded sand (SW).

Example 3.20 : A soil sample has e = 0.8, S_r = 45%, G = 2.7. Find w, n, γ_{bulk} and γ_{dry}. By how much quantity water content can be increased without changing e ?

Solution :
$$S_r \cdot e = w \cdot G$$

$\therefore$
$$w = \frac{S_r \cdot e}{G} = \frac{0.45 \times 0.8}{2.7} = 0.1333 = 13.33\%$$

If $S_r = 1,$
$$w = \frac{0.8}{2.7} = \mathbf{29.63\%}$$

$\therefore$ Water content can be increased from 13.33 to 29.63 or by (29.63 − 13.33 = 16.30%)

$$n = \frac{e}{1 + e} = \frac{0.8}{1.8} = \mathbf{44.44\%}$$

$$\gamma_{bulk} = \frac{G \cdot \gamma_w}{1 + e} = \frac{2.7 \times 9.81}{1 + 0.8} = \mathbf{14.72\ kN/m^3}$$

$$\gamma_{dry} = \frac{\gamma_{bulk}}{1 + w} = \frac{14.72}{1 + 1.333} = \mathbf{12.98\ kN/m^3}$$

Example 3.21 : Natural dry density of sand is 18 kN/m³. Find relative density, if maximum and minimum dry densities are 18.75 and 15.5 kN/m³ respectively.

$$\text{Take } G = 2.65.$$

Solution :
$$I_d = \frac{e_{max} - e}{e_{max} - e_{min}} = \left(\frac{\gamma_{max}}{\gamma_d}\right) \times \left(\frac{\gamma_d - \gamma_{min}}{\gamma_{max} - \gamma_{min}}\right) \times 100$$

By substituting for γ_{max}, γ_d and γ_{min} values 18.75 kN/m³, 18 kN/m³ and 15.5 kN/m³, we can find I_d.

$$I_d = \left(\frac{18 - 15.5}{18.75 - 15.5}\right) \frac{18.75}{18} \times 100 = \mathbf{80.128\%}$$

Alternatively,
$$\gamma_{dry} = \frac{G \cdot \gamma_w}{1 + e}$$

$\therefore$
$$e = \left(\frac{G \cdot \gamma_w}{\gamma_{dry}} - 1\right)$$

$\therefore$
$$e_{natural} = \left(\frac{2.65 \times 9.81}{18} - 1\right) = 0.4442$$

$$e_{max} = \frac{2.65 \times 9.81}{15.5} - 1 = 0.6772$$

$$e_{min} = \frac{2.65 \times 9.81}{18.75} - 1 = 0.38645$$

$\therefore$
$$I_d = \frac{0.6772 - 0.4442}{0.6772 - 0.3864} \times 100 = \frac{0.233}{0.2908} = \mathbf{80.12\%}$$

Example 3.22 : A soil sample weigh 520 gm in wet condition and 400 gm in dry condition. If its volume is 270 ml, find e, n, S_r, γ_{bulk}, γ_{dry} . (G = 2.7)

Solution :

$$\gamma_b = \frac{520 \times 9.81}{270} = \textbf{18.893 kN/m}^3$$

$$\gamma_{dry} = \frac{400 \times 9.81}{270} = \textbf{14.533 kN/m}^3$$

$$= \frac{\gamma_b}{1 + w} = \frac{G \cdot \gamma_w}{1 + e}$$

$\therefore$

$$w = \frac{18.893}{14.533} - 1 = 0.3 = 30\%$$

$$e = \frac{2.7 \times 9.81}{14.533} - 1 = \textbf{0.8225}$$

$$n = \frac{e}{1 + e} = \frac{0.8225}{1 + 0.8225} = \textbf{45.13\%}$$

$$S_r = \frac{w \cdot G}{e} = \frac{0.3 \times 2.7}{0.8225} = 0.985 = \textbf{98.5\%}$$

Example 3.23 : Natural water content, liquid limit and plastic limit of a soil sample was found to be 40%, 50% and 30% respectively. The graph plotted on semi-log paper to determine liquid limit made an angle of 30° to the horizontal.

Find : (i) Flow index, (ii) toughness index, (iii) liquidity index, (iv) consistency index, (v) classify soil, (vi) find e. (Take G = 2.7).

Solution :

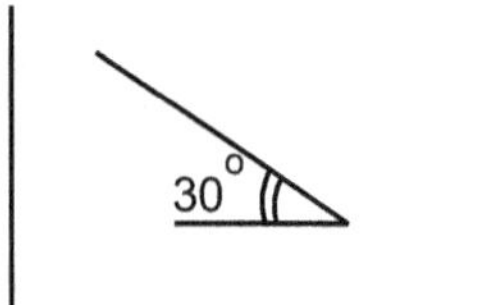

Fig. 3.25

$$I_f = \tan 30 = 0.577$$

$$I_p = W_l - W_p = 50 - 30 = \textbf{20}$$

Toughness index,
$$I_t = \frac{I_p}{I_f} = \frac{0.20}{0.577} = \textbf{0.3466}$$

$$I_l = \frac{w - W_p}{I_p} = \frac{40 - 30}{20} = \frac{10}{20} = \textbf{0.5}$$

$$I_c = 1 - I_l = 1 - 0.5 = \textbf{0.5}$$

At liquid limit, soil will be saturated and its moisture content = 50% i.e. S_r = 1

$\therefore$
$$S_r \cdot e = e \cdot 1 = wG = 0.5 \times 2.7 = \textbf{1.35}$$

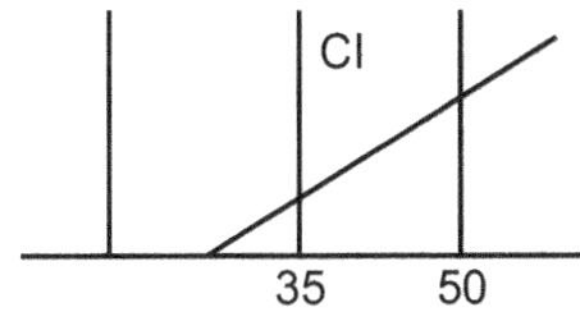

Fig. 3.26

I_p for point to be on A-line $= 0.73 (W_l - 20) = 0.73 (50 - 20) = 21.9\% > 20$

∴   Point is below A-line.

∴   Silty soil with intermediate plasticity i.e. MI.

Example 3.24 : If $W_p = 25\%$, $I_p = 30$, $W_{natural} = 34\%$, find I_c, I_l .

Solution :
$$I_l = \frac{w - W_p}{I_p} = \frac{34 - 25}{30} = \frac{9}{30} = \textbf{0.3}$$

$$I_c = 1 - I_l = 1 - 0.3 = \textbf{0.7}$$

or
$$I_c = \frac{W_l - w}{I_p} = \frac{(25 + 30) - 34}{30} = \frac{21}{30} = \textbf{0.7}$$

Example 3.25 : Plot on semi-log paper, particle size distribution curve showing % finer than on Y-axis and particle size in mm on X-axis. Using semi-log scale for (i) well graded sand, (ii) uniformly graded sand and tabulate results as under :

	For well graded sand	For uniformly graded sand
D_{10} size		
D_{30} size		
D_{60} size		
C_u		
C_c		

Solution :

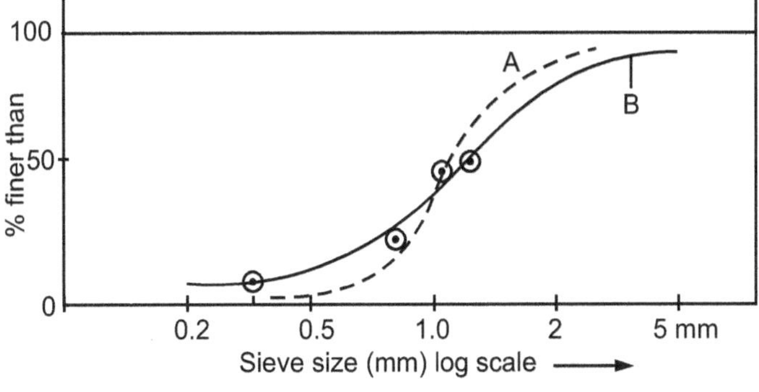

Fig. 3.27

	For well graded sand (Curve A)	For uniformly graded sand (Curve B)
D_{10}	0.65 mm	0.20
D_{30}	0.90	0.72
D_{60}	1.00	1.20
C_u	$D_{60} \div D_{10} = 1.53$	6.00
C_c	$(D_{30})^2 \div D_{60} \times D_{10} = 1.38$	2.16

Example 3.26 : Gradation curve of a soil gives effective grain size as 0.16 mm. D_{30} and D_{60} as 0.4 mm and 0.8 mm respectively. Find C_u, C_c and classify soil.

Solution :

$$C_u = \frac{0.80}{0.16} = \mathbf{5 < 6}$$

$$C_c = \frac{0.4 \times 0.4}{0.8 \times 0.16} = \mathbf{1.25}$$

$\therefore$　　Does not meet requirements of SW.

$\therefore$　　　　　　SP = Poorly graded sand.

Example 3.27 : If $\dfrac{C_u}{C_c} = 4$ and $C_u \cdot C_c = 9$, find C_u, C_c, D_{60}, D_{30}.

　Assume　　　　　$D_{10} = 0.1$ mm

Solution :　　　$\dfrac{C_u}{C_c} \times C_u \cdot C_c = 4 \times 9 = 36$

$\therefore$　　　　　　$(C_u)^2 = 36$

$\therefore$　　　　　　$C_u = \mathbf{6}$

$\therefore$　　　　　　$C_c = \dfrac{9}{C_u} = \dfrac{9}{6} = \mathbf{1.5}$

　　　　　　$C_u = 6 = \dfrac{D_{60}}{D_{10}}$

$\therefore$　　　　$D_{60} = 0.1 \times 6 = \mathbf{0.6\ mm}$

　　　$(D_{30})^2 = D_{60} \times D_{10} \times C_c = 0.6 \times 0.1 \times 1.5 = 0.09\ mm^2$

$\therefore$　　　　$D_{30} = \mathbf{0.3\ mm}$

Example 3.28 : (a) In a shrinkage limit test, 18 gm of oven dried soil displaced 136 gm of mercury. If G = 2.7, find W_s.

　(b) If liquidity index is 1.2, determine its consistency index.

Solution :

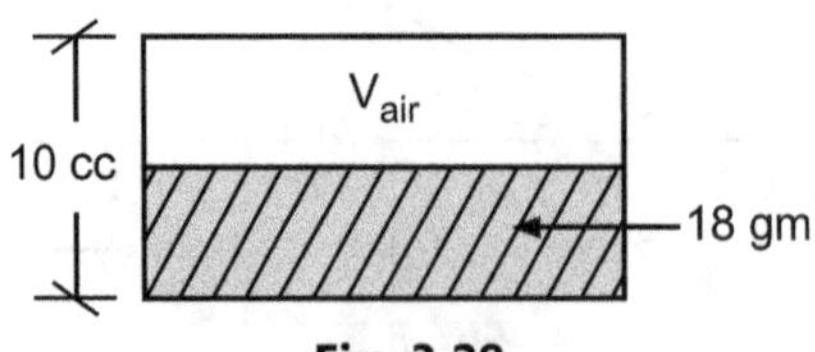

Fig. 3.28

$$V_s = \frac{18}{2.7} = 6.6667 \text{ cc}$$

$$V_{voids} = 10 - 6.6667 = 3.3333 \text{ cc} = 3.3333 \text{ gm of water at } W_s$$

$$W_s = \frac{M_w}{\text{Dry mass}} = \frac{3.3333}{18} = \textbf{18.52\%}$$

$$I_c = I - I_l = 1 - 1.2 = \textbf{(–) 0.2}$$

Example 3.29 : γ_b = 19.1 kN/m³, w = 12.5%, G = 2.67. Find γ_{dry} , e, n, S_r.

Solution :
$$\gamma_b = \frac{G \cdot \gamma_w (1 + w)}{1 + e}$$

$\therefore$
$$e = \left[\frac{G \cdot \gamma_w (1 + w)}{\gamma_b} - 1 \right]$$

$$= \left[\frac{2.67 \times 9.81}{19.1} (1 + 0.125) - 1 \right] = \textbf{0.5427}$$

$$\gamma_{dry} = \frac{\gamma_b}{1 + w} = \frac{19.1}{1 + 0.125} = \textbf{16.978 kN/m}^3$$

$$n = \frac{e}{1 + e} = \frac{0.5427}{1.5427} = \textbf{0.3518}$$

$$S_r \cdot e = wG$$

$\therefore$
$$S_r = \frac{0.125 \times 2.67}{0.5427} = \textbf{0.615 or 61.5\%}$$

Example 3.30 : If W_l = 65% W_p = 35%, natural water constant = 45%, determine flow index, liquidity index, consistency index, toughness index. Assume number of jerks for determination of liquid limit by Casagrande's method, as 48 when water content was 32%.

Solution :

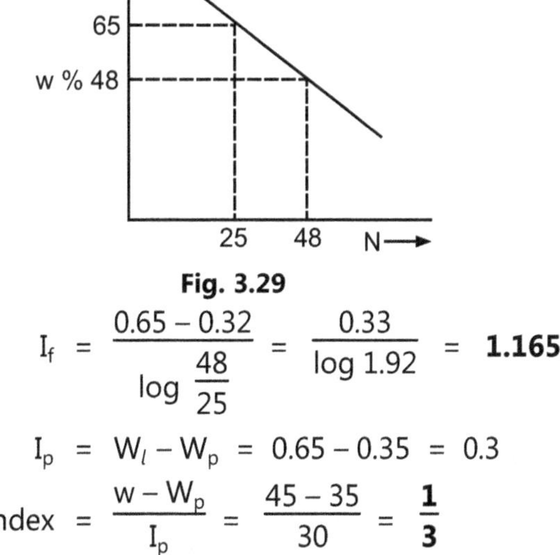

Fig. 3.29

$$I_f = \frac{0.65 - 0.32}{\log \dfrac{48}{25}} = \frac{0.33}{\log 1.92} = \textbf{1.165}$$

$$I_p = W_l - W_p = 0.65 - 0.35 = 0.3$$

$$\text{Liquidity index} = \frac{w - W_p}{I_p} = \frac{45 - 35}{30} = \frac{1}{3}$$

$$I_c = \text{Consistency index} = 1 - \frac{1}{3} = \frac{2}{3}$$

$$\text{Toughness index} = \frac{I_p}{I_f} = \frac{0.3}{I_f} = \frac{0.3}{1.165}$$

$$= \mathbf{0.26}$$

Example 3.31 : A soil has w = 12% and n = 36%. Find mass of water required to be added to 100 m³ of soil for full saturation.
Assume G = 2.67.

Solution :

$$e = \frac{n}{1-n} = \frac{0.36}{1-0.36}$$

$$\therefore \quad e = \frac{0.36}{0.64} = 0.5624$$

$$\rho_d = \frac{G \cdot \rho_w}{1+e} = \frac{2.67 \times 1000}{1.56} = 1709 \text{ kg/m}^3$$

$$0.12 = \frac{\text{Mass of water}}{\text{Mass of dry soil}}$$

$$\therefore \quad \text{Mass of water} = 0.12 \times 1709 = 205 \text{ kg} \qquad \qquad \dots \text{(i)}$$

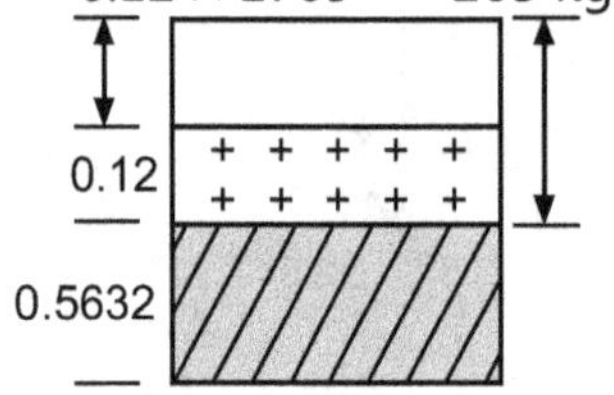

Fig. 3.30

$$\text{Volume of solids,} \quad V_s = \frac{1709 - 205}{2670} = 0.5632 \text{ cu.m}$$

$$V_{air} = 1 - 0.5632 - 0.12 = 0.3167 \text{ cu.m}$$

∴ Additional quantity of water per cu.m to make it saturated

$$= (0.3167 \times 100) = 316.7 \text{ kg/cu.m.}$$

∴ For 100 cu.m., quantity of water = **31670 kg**

Example 3.32 : A soil specimen shrinks from volume of 42.5 cc at W_l to 26.8 cc of shrinkage limit. If W_l = 51 %, W_p = 32% and W_s = 19% determine specific gravity.

Solution :

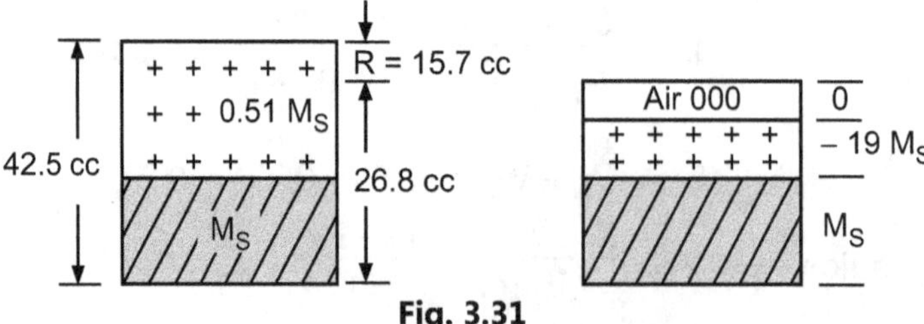

Fig. 3.31

Reduction in volume, $\qquad$ $R = 42.5 - 26.8$

$\qquad = 15.7 \text{ cc} = 15.7 \text{ gm}$

% reduction in water content $= 51 \text{ to } 19 = 32\%$

$$w = \frac{M_w}{M_s} = 0.32$$

$\therefore \qquad M_s = \dfrac{M_w}{0.32} = \dfrac{15.7}{0.32} = 49.06 \text{ gm} \qquad \ldots \text{(i)}$

Initial M_w in soil sample $= 0.51\, M_s = 0.51 \times 49.06 = 25.02 \text{ gm}$

$\therefore \qquad$ Volume of water (initially) $= 25.02 \text{ cc}$

$\therefore \qquad V_s = $ Volume of solids $= 42.5 - 25.02 = 17.478 \text{ cc} \qquad \ldots \text{(ii)}$

$$G = \frac{M_s}{V_s \times \rho_w} = \frac{\text{(i)}}{\text{(ii)}} = \frac{49.06}{17.478 \times 1} = \mathbf{2.806}$$

Example 3.33 : If $W_l = 53\%$, $W_p = 30\%$, classify soil according to plasticity chart.

Solution : $\qquad I_p = 53 - 30 = 23$

As per A-line equation,

$$I_p = 0.73\,(W_l - 20) = 0.073 \times 33 = 24.09 > \text{Actual } I_p \text{ of } 23$$

$\therefore \qquad$ Point is below A-line, and liquid limit > 50.

$\therefore \qquad$ Soil will be classified as MH.

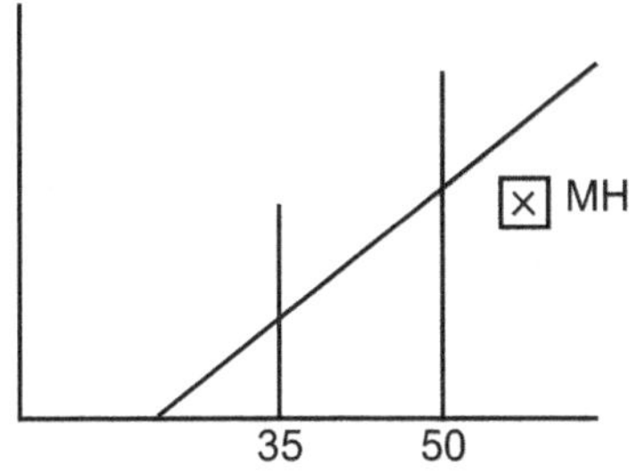

Fig. 3.32

Example 3.34 : Prove that for $G = 2.6$ and $e = 0.4$ and 1, maximum dry density is 1.4 times the minimum.

Solution : $\qquad (\rho_d)_{max} = \dfrac{G \cdot \rho_w}{1 + e} = \dfrac{G \times 1}{1 + 0.4} = \dfrac{G}{1.4} \quad (\rho_w = 1 \text{ g/cc})$

$$(\rho_d)_{min} = \frac{G}{1 + 1} = \frac{G}{2}$$

$$\frac{(\rho_d)_{max}}{(\rho_d)_{min}} = \frac{G}{1.4} \times \frac{2}{G} = \mathbf{1.428}$$

Example 3.35 : A sand sample has porosity of 30%. Find (a) Dry unit weight, (b) Unit weight of sand if degree of saturation is 60%. Assume $G = 2.65$.

Solution : (a)

$$n = \frac{e}{1 + e} = 0.3$$

$\therefore$

$$e = 0.3 + 0.3\,e$$

$\therefore$

$$e = \frac{0.3}{0.7} = \frac{3}{7}$$

$$\rho_d = \frac{\rho_w \cdot G}{1 + e}$$

$$= \frac{2.65}{1 + \dfrac{3}{7}}$$

$$= 0.7 \times 2.65 = \mathbf{1.855\ gm/cc}$$

(b)

$$S_r \cdot e = wG = 0.6\,e$$

$\therefore$

$$w = \frac{S_r \cdot e}{G}$$

$$= \frac{0.6 \times 3}{7 \times 4} = 9.7\%$$

$$\rho_b = \frac{G \cdot \rho_w\,(1 + w)}{1 + e}$$

$$= \frac{2.65\,(1 + 0.97)}{1 + 3/7} = \mathbf{2.034\ gm/cc}$$

Example 3.36 : $\rho_b = 2000\ \text{kg/m}^3$, $G = 2.7$, natural water content $= 25\%$, find ρ_d, e, n, S_r.

Solution :

$$\rho_d = \frac{\rho_b}{1 + w}$$

$$= \frac{2000}{1 + 0.25} = 1600\ \text{kg/m}^3$$

$$\rho_d = \frac{G \cdot \rho_w}{1 + e}$$

$\therefore$

$$e = \left(\frac{G \cdot \rho_w}{\rho_d} - 1\right)$$

$$= \left(\frac{2.7 \times 1}{1600} - 1\right) = \mathbf{0.6554}$$

$$n = \frac{e}{1 + e}$$

$$= 0.3963$$

$$S_r = \frac{wG}{e}$$

$$= \frac{0.25 \times 2.7}{0.6554}$$

$$= \mathbf{1.0299}$$

Example 3.37 : Calculate the relative density of saturated sand deposit having moisture content of 25%, if maximum and minimum void ratios of sand are 0.95 and 0.45 respectively and specific gravity of sand particles is 2.6. **[Dec. 13, 6 M]**

Solution :

$W = 25\%$, $\qquad\qquad S = 1$ As saturated soil

$$e_{max} = 0.95$$
$$e_{min} = 0.45$$
$$G = 2.6$$
$$I_D = ?$$
$$Se = WG$$
$$1 \times e = 0.25 \times 2.6$$
$$e = 0.65$$

$$\text{Relative Density } (I_D) = \frac{e_{max} - e}{e_{max} - e_{min}} = \frac{0.95 - 0.65}{0.95 - 0.45} = \frac{0.3}{0.5} = 0.6$$

$$\boxed{I_D = 60\%}$$

Example 3.38 : A sand deposit with specific gravity of 2.65, has bulk density of 19.20 kN/m^3 on the field. Its natural moisture content is 9%. Determine the critical hydraulic gradient of the sand deposit. Take $\gamma w = 9.81$ kN/m^3. **[Dec. 14, 6 M]**

Solution :

$$ic = \left(\frac{G-1}{1+e}\right)\frac{1}{gw}$$

$$\gamma b = 19.2 = \frac{G(1+w)}{1+e}$$

$$= \frac{2.65(1.09).gw}{1+e}$$

$$\therefore \quad \frac{1}{1+e} = \frac{19.2}{2.65 \times 1.09}$$

$$i_c = \frac{2.65-1}{9.81} \times \frac{19.2}{2.65 \times 1.09} = 1.118$$

SUMMARY

1. The ratio of the volume of voids in the sample to the total volume of the soil mass is called as porosity, n, whereas the ratio of the volume of voids to that of the soil solids, is called as void ratio. Porosity n is always less than 1, but void ratio can be more than 1. The inter-relation between e and n is :

$$n = \frac{e}{1 + e}, \ e = \frac{n}{1 - n}$$

2. Degree of saturation of a solid mass is defined as the ratio of the volume of water in the voids to the volume of voids. $s = (v_w \div v_v)$. Also $s \cdot e = wa$.

3. (a) Bulk unit weight of a soil mass weight per unit volume of the soil

   $$mass = \gamma = \frac{(G + se) \ \gamma_w}{1 + e}.$$

   (b) Saturated unit weight is unit weight of the soil mass in the saturated condition.

   $$\gamma_{sat} = \frac{(G + e) \ \gamma_w}{1 + e}$$

   (c) Dry unit weight is the weight of soil solids per unit of total volume.

   $$\gamma_{dry} = \frac{G \cdot \gamma_w}{1 + e}$$

   (d) Sumberged unit weight is the difference between saturated unit weight and the unit weight of water. $\gamma' = \frac{(G - 1) \ \gamma_w}{1 + e}.$

4. Grain specific gravity is more commonly used than mass or apparent specific gravity of the soil in many calculations in soil mechanics because it has relatively constant value.

5. The moisture content obtained by a rapid moisture tester is expressed as a percentage of total or wet weight of the soil.

6. When the soil voids are completely filled with water, the gaseous phase being absent, it is said to be fully saturated.

7. Particle size distribution, also known as mechanical analysis, gives the percentage of various sizes of soil grains present in a given dry soil sample, is an important soil grain property. The sieve analysis is done for coarse-grained soils, which can be further sub-divided into gravel fraction and sand fraction.

8. A gap-graded soil is the one in which some of the particle sizes are missing, whereas in uniformly graded soil, particals of various sizes and in uniform proportion are present.

9. Grain size analysis is a useful index for textural classification, it consists of sieve analysis applicable to coarse fraction and wet analysis applicable to fine fraction.

10. Stokes' law is the basis for wet analysis and gives terminal velocity of spherical particle. Falling freely in an infinite liquid medium.

11. The sedimentation analysis most convenient for determining the grain size distribution of the soil fraction finer than 75 μ in size.

12. The pipette method is a standard laboratory method for the particle size analysis of fine-grained soils. It is a very accurate method.

13. A hydrometer is an instrument used for the determination of the specific gravity of liquids. As the specific gravity of the soil suspension depends upon the particle size a hydrometer can be used the particle size analysis.

14. Consistency limits or Atterberg limits provide the main basis for the classification of cohesive soils, plasticity index indicating the range of water content over which the soil exhibits plasticity, is the most important index. The plasticity of a soil is its ability to undergo deformation without cracking or fracturing.

    The water content at which the soil :

    (a) changes from the liquid state to the plastic state is known as liquid limit

    (b) becomes semi-solid is known as the plastic limit

    (c) changes from the semi-solid state to the solid state is known as the shrinkage limit

    (d) the shrinkage index = (Plastic limit) – (Shrinkage limit).

15. Flow index is the slope of the flow curve obtained between the number of blows and the water content in Casagrande's method of determination of the liquid limit.

16. Toughness index = (Plasticity index) – (Flow index).

17. Fine grained soil can be classified using plasticity chart. Equation of A line on plasticity chart is PI = 0.73 (W_{LL} – 20). If a point lies above A line then it is clayey soil, but if it lies below A line it is silty soil.

18. If more than 50% of soil

    (a) is retained on 75 μ sieve then the soil is classified as coarse grained soil and

    (b) passes through 75 μ sieve, then it will be classified as fine grained soil.

EXERCISE

1. Define the following terms:

    (a) Cohesion   (b) Internal friction

    (c) Capillarity   (d) Permeability

    (e) Elasticity   (f) Resiliency

    (g) Compressibility   (h) Density.

2. Write the classification of soils.

3. Explain following specific gravity determination method in detail.

    (a) Density bottle method

    (b) Gas jar method.

4. List the methods of water content determination of soil.

5. Write short note on determination of density of soil.

6. State various consistency indices.

7. Write a note on grading of soil.

8. Differentiate between sand and clay.

9. What is Stoke's low.

10. State various tests for soil classification and explain in brief.

11. What time a spherical particle of 3 micron size will take to settle through a depth of 90 mm through a water suspension ?

12. The field density of a non-cohesive backfill was found to be 1650 kg/m^3 at a water content of 9%. If void ratio in the loosest and densest states were found out as 0.759 and 0.562, calculate the density index.

13. The liquid limit and plastic limit of sample are 55% and 30% respectively. The percentage of the soil fraction with grain size finer than 0.002 mm is 24. Calculate The activity ratio of the soil sample.

SOLVED UNIVERSITY QUESTIONS AND NUMERICALS

December 2013

1. Calculate the relative density of saturated sand deposit having moisture content of 25%, if maximum and minimum void ratios of sand are 0.95 and 0.45 respectively and specific gravity of sand particles is 2.6. **[6]**

[**Ans.:** Refer Example 3.37]

December 2014

1. A sand deposit with specific gravity of 2.65, has bulk density of 19.20 kN/m^3 on the field. Its natural moisture content is 9%. Determine the critical hydraulic gradient of the sand deposit. Take γ_w = 9.81 kN/m^3. **[6]**

[**Ans.:** Refer Example 3.38]

2. Define consistency of soils and show the four states of consistency graphically with appropriate consistency limits. **[6]**

[**Ans.:** Refer Article 3.6]

November 2016

1. Explain a method of determining the grain size distribution of cohesion less soils. Discuss the significance of the values of uniformity coefficient and coefficient of curvature. **[6]**

[**Ans.:** Refer Article 3.7, 3.8]

Chapter 4
PERMEABILITY AND SEEPAGE

Water is the second important constituent of soil. Its interaction with the solid constituent influences soil behaviour to a very large degree because of its dipole character.

4.1 SOIL WATER

The water present in the voids of a soil mass is called *Soil Water.* It can be classified in two categories :

- Held water and
- Free water

The *held water* is independent of the gravitational force. It is retained in the mass of the soil and cannot move under the influence of gravity. The free water moves in the pores of soil under the influence of the gravitational force.

The *free water* is discussed in the permeability article. Held water is further divided into three types :

(1) Capillary water

(2) Structural water

(3) Absorbed water

The structural water is chemically combined water in the crystalline structure of the soil particles. The removal of this water breaks the structure of soil minerals. A temperature of $300^{\circ}C$ is required for complete removal of structural water. For most of the soil the removal of structural water starts from a temperature of 110° C. The structural water is considered as an integral part of soil solids.

The water retained by electrochemical forces existing on the soil surface is known as absorbed water. It is important only for clayey soils. The quantity of absorbed water depends upon colloidal fraction, chemical composition and environmental surrounding of the clay particle.

The water held in the interstices of soil due to capillary forces is called as *capillary water*. The capillary water is always under tension (negative pressure). But the properties of capillary water are same as that of normal free water. Capillary water exists in the soils so long as there is an air-water interface. As soon as the soil is submerged under water, the interface is destroyed and capillary water becomes normal free water.

Normal air drying removes capillary water and free water, the remaining water is approximately equal to absorbed water. In this case it is known as 'hygroscopic water'. Hygroscopic water is found as a microscopic film of water surrounding soil particles. It is tightly bound to the soil by molecular attraction which is so strong that it cannot be removed by natural forces.

4.2 SURFACE TENSION

Consider a molecule of water surrounded by other molecules in a body of water. The molecule is in equilibrium, since forces due to the molecular attraction act all round.

But for a molecule at the free surface, the force exerted by the water molecules below it exceeds that of the air molecules above it and the equilibrium is disturbed. The surface assumes a curved shape to maintain the equilibrium. Thus, surface tension exists at the interface. It acts in the direction normal to the line drawn on the surface and is defined as 'the force per unit length at that line'. Surface tension decreases with increase in temperature. It is only due to surface tension a small needle can float on water and insects can walk on it.

4.3 CAPILLARY WATER

The rain water which falls on the ground percolates through the soil to a level is known as ground water table. The ground water table level is nothing but ground phreatic surface. Ground water is an underground stream which flows under gravity. It is a form of free water. The ground water table takes the shape of the topography. The water is drawn above the water table by capillary action.

The interconnected interstices of a soil mass act as capillary tubes of varying diameter. The channels formed in a soil mass are not necessarily vertical and may be inclined in any direction.

The capillary rise is inversely proportional to the diameter of the tube. Hence, the capillary rise is small in coarse grained soils and more in fine grained soils. Capillary rise depends upon the size and grading of the particles. The diameter of the channel in a pore passage is generally taken as one fifth of the effective diameter (D_{10}) in case of coarsed grained soils.

The space above the water table is divided into two regions :

1. Zone of fully saturated soil which is the capillary saturation zone.

2. Zone of partially saturated soil which is the aeration zone.

The height to which the capillary water rises in the soil is known as *Capillary Fringe*. It includes the zone of saturation and part of the zone of aeration. The relation between the maximum height of capillary fringe and the effective diameter is :

$$(h_c)_{max} = \frac{C}{e \times D_{10}} \ (mm)$$

where, C = Constant which depends upon the impurities and the shape of the particle (varies between 10 to 50 mm^2).

$$e = \text{Void ratio}$$

$$D_{10} = \text{Effective diameter in mm}$$

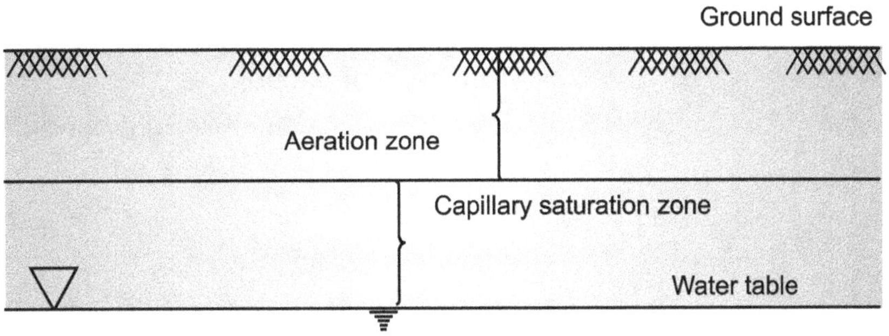

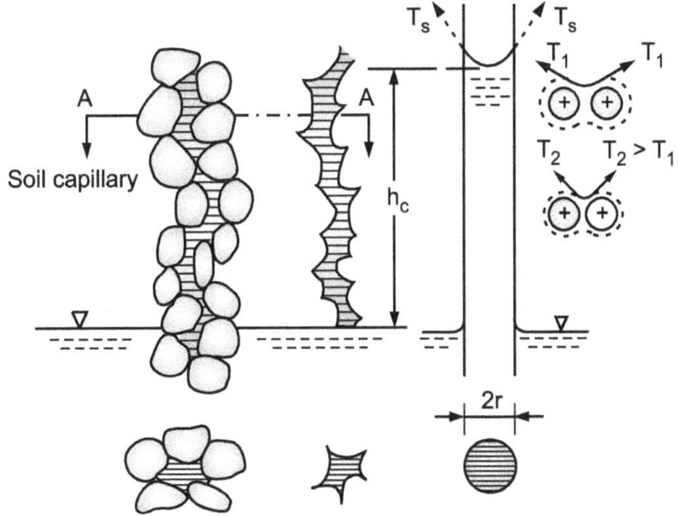

Fig. 4.1 : Space above water table

The soil above the capillary fringe may contain water in the form of contact water. Here water forms a meniscus around the point of contact and is held with the soil due to surface tension. Due to the tension in the capillary, water contact pressure is developed and it presses the particles together. The contact pressure depends upon the water content and particle size.

4.4 CAPILLARY RISE IN SOILS

In the case of a glass capillary, the capillary rise can be determined by equating the weight of the water column in the capillary to the force in the meniscus exerting a upward pull. Thus, in Fig. 4.2, at point A,

Upward force of surface tension in the meniscus = Downward force of weight of water.

Fig. 4.2 : Capillary rise in soils

If the meniscus makes an angle θ with the wall of the glass tube, the tensile surface tension, T_s acts at an angle θ with the vertical and its vertical component $T_S . \cos\theta$, acts on the periphery of the meniscus. Hence,

$$F_u = \text{Upward pull due to surface tension}$$

$$= (T_S \cos\theta)\ \pi d$$

where, T_s = Surface tension

d = Diameter of the tube

F_d = Downward force due to weight of water in the tube

$$= \gamma_w \left(\frac{\pi}{4} \times d^2 \right) \times h_c$$

where, h_c = Height of capillary rise

T_w = Density of water

For equilibrium, $F_u = F_d$

or $$(T_s \cos \theta) \, \pi \, d = \gamma_w \left(\frac{\pi}{4} d^2 \right) h_c$$

or $$h_c = \frac{4 \, T_s \cos \theta}{\gamma_w \cdot d}$$

For a clean glass tube and pure water, the meniscus is approximately hemispherical, i.e. $\theta = 0$.

Therefore, $$h_c = \frac{4 \, T_s}{\gamma_w \cdot d} \qquad \qquad \text{... (4.1)}$$

Taking, T_s = 0.076 gm/cm, $(75.0 \times 10^{-6}$ kN/m$)$

and γ_w = 1 gm/cm^3 (10 kN/m^2)

$$\therefore \quad h_c = \frac{4 \times 0.076}{1.0 \times d} = \frac{0.304}{d} \text{ cm}$$

where, d is in cm.

This theory which is applicable to a glass capillary may be roughly extended to the soil capillary. Voids in soils, having irregular shapes and different sizes, are interconnected to form an irregular capillary tube, for which a single radius cannot be defined. An equivalent radius, however, may be empirically determined, as being a function of the grain size, and void ratio, as given below :

Capillary rise, $$d \simeq D_{10} \sqrt[3]{e}$$

or $$d \simeq 0.2 \, D_{10} \qquad \qquad \text{... (4.2)}$$

where D_{10} is effective size and e is void ratio.

Thus, the size of the capillary tube in gravels will be too large to cause any appreciable capillary rise. Capillary rise is significant in fine sands and silts. In clays, it could be high, but the capillary flow is slow in clayey soils.

4.5 FROST HEAVE

The water flowing upward, from the water table to the capillary fringe may freeze if the temperature falls to freezing point. When water is converted into ice, its volume increases by about 9%. This results in an increase in the volume of the soil. Due to this frost heave, the soil at the ground surface is lifted. This may cause the lifting of light structures on the ground. The basic conditions for the formation of a frost heave is listed as follows :

- The temperature in the soil should be below freezing point.
- The soil is saturated during the freezing period.
- The soil has good permeability to move water quickly through it.
- The soil has sufficiently high capillary potential.

4.6 FROST BOIL

Thawing process starts after occurrence of frost heave, when the temperature rises. The frozen soil thaws and free water is liberated. This thawing process moves from the upper layer to the lowest layer. The process of softening of soil occurs due to liberation of angle of contact and density. Contact pressure decreases with increase in the water content. At a certain stage contact pressure becomes zero and the soil becomes fully saturated.

Water during thawing is known as frost boil. It affects the structures resting on the ground surface. Coarse grained soils are not affected much by frost boil. Silty soils are most prone to this effect. The effect of frost boil is more pronounced on highway pavements.

Prevention of Frost Action : Following measures can be taken to reduce the ill effects of the frost action :

- To replace the frost susceptible soil by coarse grained soils.
- To provide an insulating blanket between the water table and ground surface.
- To provide good drainage system.
- To use additives like dispersing agents.

4.7 SOIL SUCTION

The water in the soil mass above the water table has a negative pressure. This state of reduced pressure is known as *soil suction*. It depends upon many factors such as water content, particle size, soil structure, temperature, density, angle of contact, dissolved salts etc.

Even though the soil suction represents the negative pressure, it is usual practice to omit the negative sign. The soil suction is measured in terms of the height of the water column suspended in the soil. It is expressed in logarithm to the base ten of height in centimetres.

4.8 BULKING OF SAND   [Nov. 16]

The process of increase in volume of sand due to dampness is known as *bulking of sand*. If damp sand is loosely deposited, its volume is much more than that when the same is deposited in loose, dry state. The increase in volume due to bulking is between 20 to 30% for most of the sands.

4.9 SLAKING OF CLAY

When clay is dried below its shrinkage limit and suddenly immersed in water it disintegrates into a soft, wet mass. This process is known as *slaking of clay*.

4.10 SHRINKAGE AND SWELLING

The effect occurs in clayey soils. When water is added to these soils, these soils swell, when the water evaporates, they shrink. Shrinkage is due to the tension in the soil water. Swelling occurs due to attraction of dipolar molecules of water to the negatively charged soil particles. Coarse grained soils have very little effect of swelling and shrinkage.

Following are the effects of swelling and shrinkage.

- Increase in maintenance cost of the highway pavements.
- May cause the deformations and stresses in the structures.
- May cause the failure of retaining walls due to cracks.
- May lead to differential settlement.

4.11 PERMEABILITY

Permeability is defined as 'the property of a porous material which permits the passage or seepage of water (or other fluids) through its interconnecting voids'. A soil is highly pervious when water flows through it very easily. A soil is termed impervious when the permeability is extremely low.. However, such soil does not exist in nature. In general, all soils are permeable. The flow of free water depends upon the permeability of soil and the head causing the flow. The total head of any point is equal to the sum of the elevation head, pressure head and the velocity head. The elevation head is equal to the vertical level difference between the point under consideration and datum. The pressure head is the level of water in the piezometer tube. The velocity head is equal to $\dfrac{V^2}{2g}$. However, the velocity head for flow through soil is extremely small and therefore, neglected.

4.12 DARCY'S LAW   [May 14]

The velocity of laminar flow through homogeneous soil mass is given by Darcy's law, which states that the rate of flow or the discharge per unit time is proportional to the hydraulic gradient.

i.e $\qquad\qquad\qquad\qquad v \propto i \quad \text{OR} \quad v = ki$ $\qquad\qquad\qquad\qquad$ ... (4.3)

where, $\qquad\qquad\qquad\qquad$ k = Coefficient of permeability

$\qquad\qquad\qquad\qquad\qquad\quad$ i = Hydraulic gradient

$\qquad\qquad\qquad\qquad\qquad\quad$ v = Velocity of flow

The loss of head per unit length of flow through the soil is equal to the hydraulic gradient (i)

$$i = \frac{h}{L}$$

where, $\qquad\qquad\qquad\qquad$ h = Hydraulic head

$\qquad\qquad\qquad\qquad\qquad\quad$ L = Length of specimen

The velocity given by Darcy's law is known as superficial velocity or discharge velocity. The discharge through the total cross-sectional area normal to the direction of flow is given by

$$q = vA$$
$$= kiA$$

where, q = Total discharge

              A = Cross-sectional area

In equation 4.3, when $i = 1$, k is equal to v.

Thus, the coefficient by permeability is defined as 'the velocity of flow which would occur under unit hydraulic gradient'. It has units and dimensions of velocity.

According to USBR soils having the coefficient of permeability greater than 10^{-3} mm/sec, are termed as pervious and those with value less than 10^{-5} are termed as impervious. The soils with inbetween values are classified as semi-previous soils.

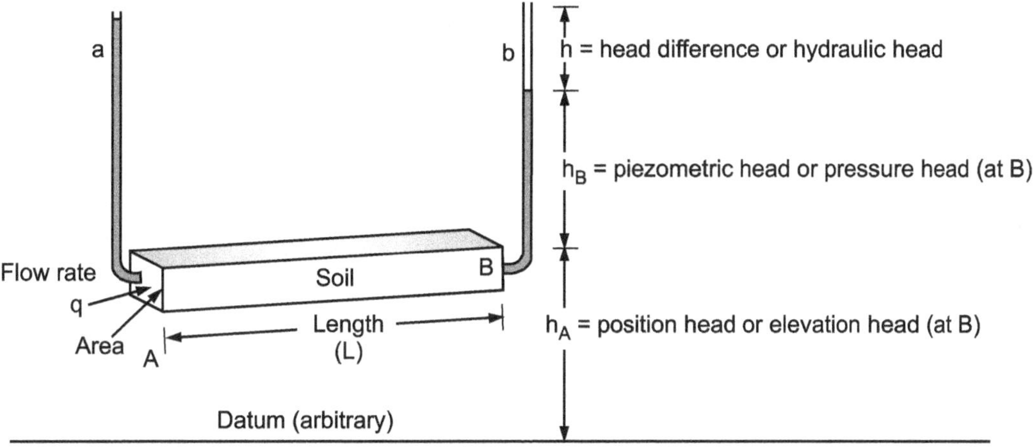

Fig. 4.3 : Flow of water through soil

4.13 VALIDITY OF DARCY'S LAW   [May 14, 17]

The Darcy's law is valid if the flow through the soil is laminar. In fine grained soils, the flow remains necessarily laminar. But in coarse grained soils like coarse gravels, the flow may be turbulent. For flow of water through pipe, the flow remains laminar when Reynolds number is less than 2000. For flow through soils the flow is laminar if the Reynolds number is less than unity. It has been found that the maximum diameter of the particle for the flow to be laminar is about 0.50 mm. Thus, Darcy's law valids for flow through clays, silts and fine sands. It may not be valid for flow through coarse sand, gravels and boulders.

Hough gave the following equation for the velocity when the flow is turbulent.

$$v = k\,(i)^n$$

where n = Exponent, with value of 0.65

For ground water flow, the law is generally valid. In extremely fine grained soils such as a colloidal clay, the interstices are very small and hence the velocity is very small. In such soils, this law is not valid.

4.14 DETERMINATION OF COEFFICIENT OF PERMEABILITY

[Nov. 16, May 15, 17]

The coefficient of permeability can be determined by many methods :

(a) Laboratory Methods :
1. Constant head method
2. Variable head method or Falling head method

(b) Field Methods :
1. Pumping out method
2. Pumping in method

The laboratory methods are discussed here.

1. Constant Head Method : This method is suitable for *coarse grained soils* and is conducted with a constant head permeater. It is a metallic mould, having 100 mm internal diameter, 127.3 mm effective height and 1000 m*l* capacity. The mould is provided with the detachable extension collar and drainage base plate.

The soil sample is placed inside the mould between two porous discs. The porous plates should be ten times more permeable than the soil. The porous plates, mould and water pipes are first de-aired.

The soil is then poured into the permeater and tamped to obtain the required density and it is fully saturated.

After sample has been saturated, it is connected to the constant head reservoir and water is allowed to flow till a steady state is established. The water level in the constant head chamber is kept constant throughout the experiment. The head causing the flow equals to the difference in the water levels between the constant head reservoir and the constant head chamber.

The discharge is given by

$$q = \frac{Q}{t} = kiA$$

$$q = k\,\frac{h}{L}\,A = \frac{khA}{L}\,, \text{ where } i = \frac{h}{L}$$

$$\therefore \qquad k = \frac{qL}{Ah} \qquad \qquad \dots (4.4)$$

where,
Q = total quantity of flow in time 't'
q = discharge through cross-sectional area A
L = length of the specimen
h = head causing flow

For more reliable results, it would be advisable to measure the loss of head (h') over a middle length (L') to determine the hydraulic gradient (i). The density of the specimen should be equal to that in the field.

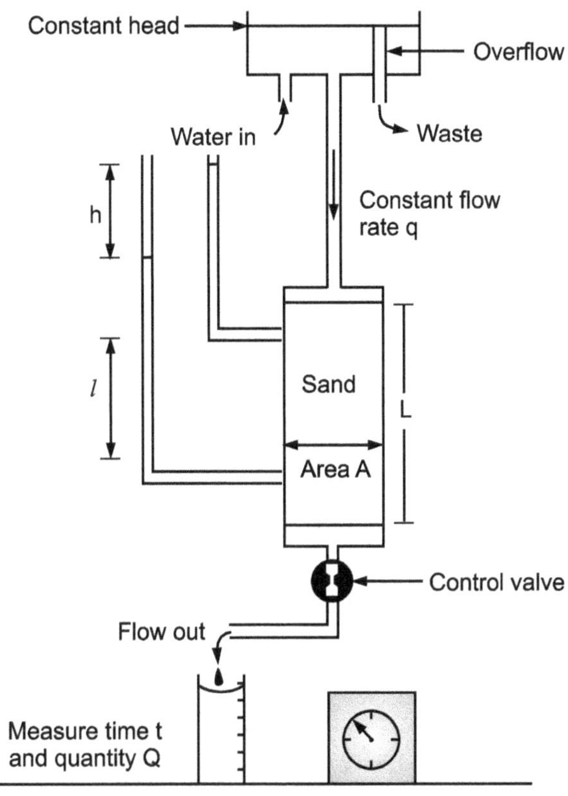

Fig. 4.4 : Constant head parameter

Table 4.1 : Table of Observations

Constant Head Method

Temp. (T) = ...   Specimen diameter (D) = ...

Length (L) = ...   Constant Head (h) = ...

Sr. No.	Particulars	Test 1	Test 2	Test 3
1.	Time (t)			
2.	Quantity, (Q)			
3.	Cross-section area (A)			
4.	Length of Specimen (L)			
5.	Permeability (k)			
6.	Correction for temp. (k_{28})			
	Average : k ...... m/s.			

2. Variable Head Method : The constant head cannot be used for fine grained soils, since quantity of water collected through the soil mass is very less and cannot be measured accurately. Hence, the variable head method is used to determine the coefficient of permeability for the grained soil. In this case, too the same mould is used. The experimental setup is as shown in Fig. 4.5.

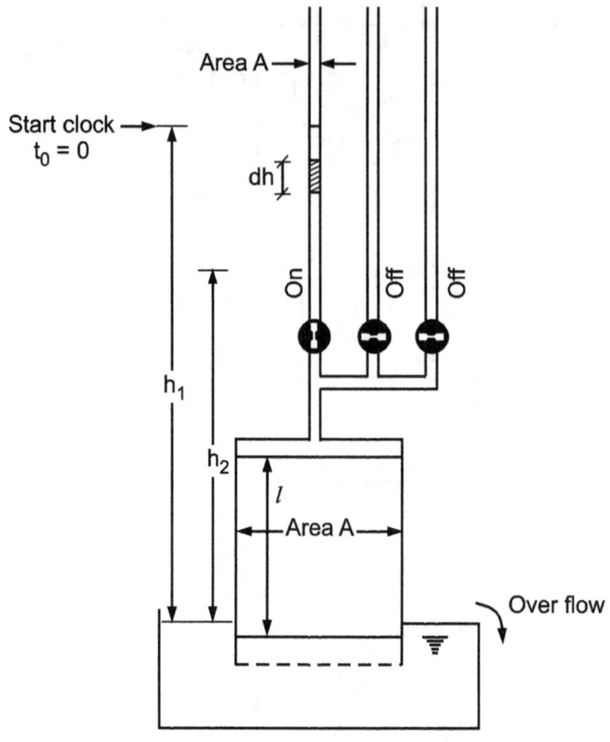

Fig. 4.5 : Variable head method

A stand pipe is attached to the mould. The water is allowed to flow from the stand pipe through the sample. As the water flows, the water level in the stand pipe falls. The time required for the water level to fall from a known initial head (h_1) to known final head (h_2) is determined.

Let us consider any instant when head is (h). For an infinitely small time (dt), the head falls by (dh). Let q be the discharge through the sample. From continuity of flow, we have :

$$adh = - \ qdt \ \text{(minus sign indicates fall of head)}$$

where (a) is cross-sectional area of the flow through standpipe :

But $q = A \times k \times i$

Then, $adh = - Akidt$

$$Adh = - A \frac{h}{L} kdt$$

$$\frac{Akdt}{aL} = - \frac{dh}{h}$$

Integrating $\frac{Ak}{aL} \int_{t_1}^{t_2} dt = - \int_{h_1}^{h_2} \frac{dh}{h}$

$$\frac{Ak}{aL}\,(t_2 - t_1) \;=\; +\,\log_e \left(\frac{h_1}{h_2}\right)$$

$$k \;=\; \frac{aL}{At}\,\log_e \left(\frac{h_1}{h_2}\right)$$

where, $t = t_2 - t_1 =$ time interval during which head reduces from h_1 to h_2.

$$k \;=\; \frac{2.30\,aL}{At}\,\log_{10}\left(\frac{h_1}{h_2}\right) \qquad\qquad \text{... (4.5)}$$

Normally coefficient of permeability is determined at 27° C. The smaller diameter pipes are used for less pervious soils. The test is useful for soils with permeability in the range, $k = 10^{-2}$ m/s to 10^{-9} m/s.

Table 4.2 : Table of Observations

Falling Head Method

Temp. (T) = ...   Specimen dia. (D) = ...

Length (L) = ...   Standpipe area (a) = ...

Sr. No.	Particulars	Test 1	Test 2	Test 3
1.	Zero time at start			
2.	Time t, $(t_2 - t_1)$			
3.	Head (h_1)			
4.	Head (h_2)			
5.	Permeability (k)			
6.	Correction for temperature (k_{28})			

Average : k ...... m/s.

4.15 SEEPAGE VELOCITY AND DISCHARGE VELOCITY

The total cross-sectional area of soil mass consists of not only the voids but also the solids. Hence the discharge velocity (V) is not the actual velocity through the soil mass. It is a fictitious velocity obtained by dividing the total discharge (q) by total cross-sectional area (A). As flow takes place only through the voids, the actual velocity through voids is much greater than the discharge velocity. This actual velocity on a microscopic scale is known as the seepage velocity (V_s).

From continuity of flow,

$$q \;=\; V \times A \;=\; V_s \times A_v$$

where,

q = Total discharge through total cross-sectional (A)

V_1 = Total volume of soil mass

V_v = Volume of voids

A_v = Area of voids

$$V \times A \;=\; V_s \times A_v$$

$$V_s = \frac{V \times A}{A_v} = V \times \frac{A}{A_v}$$

Multiplying and dividing by (L),

$$V_s = V \times \frac{AL}{A_v \times L} = V \times \frac{V_1}{V_v}$$

But $\qquad\qquad \dfrac{V_v}{V_1} = \eta = $ Porosity

$\therefore \qquad\qquad V_s = \dfrac{V}{n} = \dfrac{ki}{n}$

where, $\qquad\qquad V = $ Discharge velocity

$\qquad\qquad\qquad V_s = $ Seepage velocity

Putting $\qquad\qquad k_p = \dfrac{k}{n}$

$$V_s = k_p \times i \qquad\qquad\qquad \dots (4.6)$$

The coefficient k_p is known as the coefficient of percolation.

Strictly speaking, the seepage velocity is not absolute velocity through soil mass. The voids in the soil mass are tortuous and irregular in cross-section. The absolute velocity varies from point to point. Its direction may also change. In fact, the problem itself is so complex that the analysis has to be done on a macroscopic scale as described above.

The total discharge is computed either from discharge velocity (V) or the seepage velocity (V_s). The discharge velocity is more convenient to use.

4.16 FACTORS AFFECTING THE PERMEABILITY [Nov. 15, May 17]

The coefficient of permeability of a soil depends basically on the characteristics of both the soil medium and the pore fluid. Lambe and Whitman have grouped particle size, void ratio, composition and degree of saturation as major soil characteristics, and viscosity, unit weight and polarity as major pore fluid characteristics. For a civil engineer dealing with soils, the permeant is water, whose variation in property may be presumed to be very less. Thus, soil characteristics may have to be given more importance.

Based on Poiseuille's law for flow through a bundle of capillary tubes, Taylor has given a theoretical expression for flow through soil medium as :

$$k = D_s^2 \cdot \frac{\gamma_w}{\eta_w} \cdot \frac{e^3}{1 + e} \cdot C_s \qquad\qquad \dots (4.7)$$

where, $\qquad\qquad D_s = $ Effective particle diameter

$\qquad\qquad\qquad C_s = $ Composite shape factor

Thus, the factors affecting permeability are :

1. Shape of particles
2. Voids ratio of soil

3. Particle size

4. Structure of soil mass

5. Degree of saturation

6. Impurities in the water

7. Properties of water.

1. Shape of Particles : Angular particles have greater specific surface area as compared to rounded particles. The permeability is inversely proportional to the specific surface. Hence for the same void ratio, the soils with angular particles are less permeable than those with rounded particles.

2. Void Ratio : The coefficient of permeability varies as $\dfrac{e^3}{(1 + e)}$. Thus, greater the void ratio, the higher is the coefficient of permeability.

3. Particle Size : The coefficient of permeability of a soil is proportional to the square of the particle size. Thus, the permeability of coarse grained soil is more than that of fine grained soil.

$$k = CD_{10}^{2} \qquad \qquad \dots (4.8)$$

If D_{10} is in mm and k in ms^{-1}, the value of $C = \dfrac{1}{100}$.

4. Structure of Soil Mass : For the same void ratio, the permeability is more for flocculant structure as compared to that of a dispersed structure.

5. Degree of Saturation : The permeability of partially saturated soil is smaller than that of a fully saturated soil. This is due to the air pockets formed in the partially saturated soil.

6. Impurities in the Water : The permeability may get *reduced* due to the presence of foreign impurities in the water flowing through the soil mass.

7. Properties of Water : The coefficient of permeability is proportional to the unit weight of water (γ_w) and inversely proportional to the viscosity (η). There is not much variation in the unit weight but there is a large variation in the viscosity (η) with the variation in the temperature. The coefficient of permeability decreases with an increase in temperature due to reduction in the viscosity.

The permeability (k) measured at temperature 'T' in the laboratory can be corrected for a standard temperature of 28°C as follows :

$$k_{(28)} = \frac{k\left(\dfrac{\gamma_w}{\eta}\right)_{28}}{\left(\dfrac{\gamma_w}{\eta}\right)_T} \cong k \cdot \frac{\eta_T}{\eta_{28}} \qquad \qquad \dots (4.9)$$

Table 4.3 : Typical Values of k

k (m/s)	Soil type		Drainage characteristics
10 1	Coarse gravel, cobbles, boulders flow may become turbulent $\therefore$ Darcy's Law may not be valid		Very good
10^{-1}	Clean gravels		
10^{-2} 10^{-3}	Clean sands Clean sand-gravel mixtures		Good
10^{-4}		Impervious soils modified by	
10^{-5} 10^{-6}	Very fine sands Silty sands		Poor
10^{-7}		Silts	
10^{-8}	Stratified clay/silt deposits		Practically impervious
10^{-9}	Unweathered, unfissured, homogeneous clays (Clay content > 20%)		

4.17 SEEPAGE PRESSURE

There is an energy transfer between the water and the soil due to the viscous friction exerted on water flowing through the soil pores. The pressure exerted by water on the soil through which it percolates, is known as seepage pressure (P_s). It is given by

$$P_s = h\gamma_w$$

$$P_s = \frac{h}{L} \times L\gamma_w = iL\gamma_w$$

where,

h = Hydraulic head

L = Length over which the head (h) is lost

i = Hydraulic gradient

γ_w = Unit weight of water

Seepage force (F_s) is given by

$$F_s = P_s \cdot A = i \cdot L \cdot \gamma_w \cdot A$$

where

A = Total cross-sectional area of the soil mass

The seepage force per unit volume is given by :

$$F_s = \frac{i \cdot L \cdot A \cdot \gamma_w}{L \cdot A} = i\gamma_w$$

This seepage pressure always acts in the direction of the flow.

The effective pressure (P_e) in the soil mass is given by

$$P_e = L\gamma' \pm P_s$$

$$P_e = L\gamma' \pm iL\gamma_w \qquad \text{... (4.10)}$$

For downward flow,

i.e.
$$P_e = L\gamma' + iL\gamma_w$$

For upward flow,

i.e.
$$P_e = L\gamma' - iL\gamma_w$$

4.18 QUICK SAND CONDITION OR CRITICAL HYDRAULIC GRADIENT
[Dec. 13, May 14, 16]

The seepage is responsible for the phenomenon of quick sand. This condition occurs when the flow takes place in the upward direction.

When flow takes place in an upward direction, the effective pressure gets reduced since the seepage pressure also acts in the upward direction. When the seepage pressure becomes exactly equal to the submerged weight of the soil, through which the flow is taking place, the effective pressure becomes zero. In this case, the soil with less cohesion loses all its shear strength and soil particles move up in the direction of flow. This lifting of soil particles is known as quick sand, boiling condition or quick condition. During this condition the effective pressure reduces to zero.

$$P_e = L\gamma' - P_s = 0$$

$$P_s = L\gamma'$$

or
$$iL\,\gamma_w = L\gamma'$$

$$i\gamma_w = \gamma'$$

$$i = \frac{\gamma'}{\gamma_w}$$

But
$$\gamma' = \frac{(G-1)\,\gamma_w}{1+e}$$

Thus,
$$i = i_c$$

$$= \frac{G-1}{1+e} \qquad \text{... (4.11)}$$

The hydraulic gradient of the quick sand condition is known as the critical hydraulic gradient (i_c). Thus, quick sand condition is the particular flow condition which occurs when effective pressure reduces to zero during upward flow.

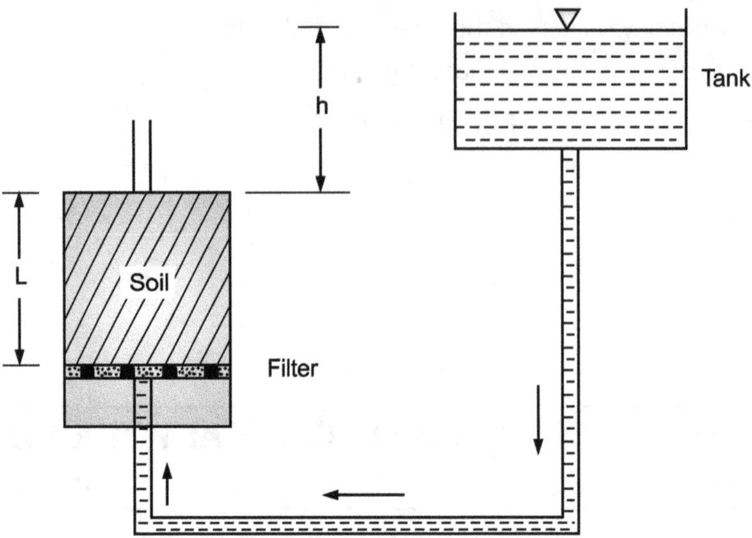

Fig. 4.6 : Quick sand condition

In the above Fig. 4.6, (h) can be adjusted to depict the quick sand condition.

4.19 LAPLACE'S EQUATION

The flow through soils is generally two-dimensional. Hence the simple method of construction of flow net cannot be used in such cases. The Laplace's equation is used.

Following assumptions are made to derive Laplace's equation :

- Darcy's law is valid.
- The soil is fully saturated.
- Soil is isotropic and homogeneous.
- The flow is steady.
- The flow is two-dimensional.
- Water and soil are incompressible.

Let us consider an element of soil dx, dz through which the flow is taking place. The third dimension of the element is taken as unity.

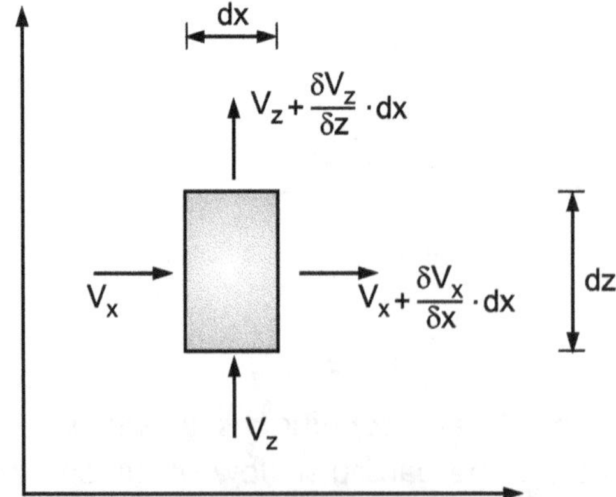

Fig. 4.7 : Two-dimensional flow

Let the velocity at the inlet and outlet faces be V_x and $\left(V_x + \dfrac{\partial V_x}{\partial x}\,dx\right)$ in the x direction and V_z

and $\left(V_z + \dfrac{\partial V_z}{\partial z}\cdot dz\right)$ in the z direction.

As the flow is steady and the soil is incompressible, the discharge entering the element equal to that leaving the element.

Thus,
$$V_x\,dz + V_z\,dx = \left(V_x + \frac{\partial V_x}{\partial x}\,dx\right)dz + \left(V_z + \frac{\partial V_z}{\partial z}\cdot dz\right)dx$$

or
$$\left(\frac{\partial V_x}{\partial x} + \frac{\partial V_z}{\partial z}\right)dx\cdot dz = 0$$

or
$$\frac{\partial V_x}{\partial x} + \frac{\partial V_z}{\partial z} = 0 \qquad\qquad \dots (4.12)$$

Equation (4.2) is the continuity equation for a two-dimensional flow.

Let (h) be the total head at any point. The horizontal and vertical components of hydraulic gradient (i) are respectively :

$$i_x = -\frac{\partial h}{\partial x} \quad \text{and} \quad i_z = -\frac{\partial h}{\partial z}$$

Negative sign indicates that the head decreases in the direction of flow.

From Darcy's law :

$$V_x = -k_x\,\frac{\partial h}{\partial x}$$

$$V_z = -k_z\,\frac{\partial h}{\partial x}$$

Substituting in (4.2),

$$-k_x\,\frac{\partial^2 h}{\partial x^2} - k_z\,\frac{\partial^2 h}{\partial z^2} = 0$$

$$k_x\,\frac{\partial^2 h}{\partial x^2} + k_z\,\frac{\partial^2 h}{\partial z^2} = 0$$

Since, the soil is assumed to be isotropic,

$$k_x = k_z$$

$$\frac{\partial^2 h}{\partial x^2} + \frac{\partial^2 h}{\partial z^2} = 0 \qquad\qquad \dots (4.13)$$

Equation (4.13) is the Laplace equation in terms of head (h).

If the velocity potential $\phi = -kh$

$$\frac{\partial \phi}{\partial x} = V_x = -k\,\frac{\partial h}{\partial x} \quad \text{and} \quad \frac{\partial \phi}{\partial z} = V_z = -k\,\frac{\partial h}{\partial z}$$

Substituting in equation (4.12),

$$\frac{\partial^2 \phi}{\partial x^2} + \frac{\partial^2 \phi}{\partial z^2} = 0 \qquad \qquad \text{... (4.14)}$$

Equation (4.14) is Laplace's equation in terms of velocity potential (ϕ).

4.20 SOLUTION OF LAPLACE EQUATION – FLOW NET

Laplace equation expresses the fundamental relationship for a steady state potential flow in isotropic soils. For the two-dimensional case, the solution of this equation represents two families of orthogonal curves known as streamlines or flow lines (ψ lines) and potential lines (ϕ lines). When drawn on a sheet of paper, these curves form a pattern appearing like a *net*. Because this net represents flow, it is known as *flow net.* (Fig. 4.8).

Thus, flow net is a graphical representation of the solution of Laplace equation for two-dimensional flow. Flow lines (f_1, f_2, f_3, ...) trace the flow of a particle of water and equipotential lines (p_1, p_2, p_3, ...) are the lines joining points a equal potentials.

The space between adjacent flow lines is known as flow path or flow channel and difference between potentials of adjacent equipotential lines is known as *potential drop*, which is equal for any two adjacent potential lines. The space between two successive flow lines and successive equipotential lines is called a field.

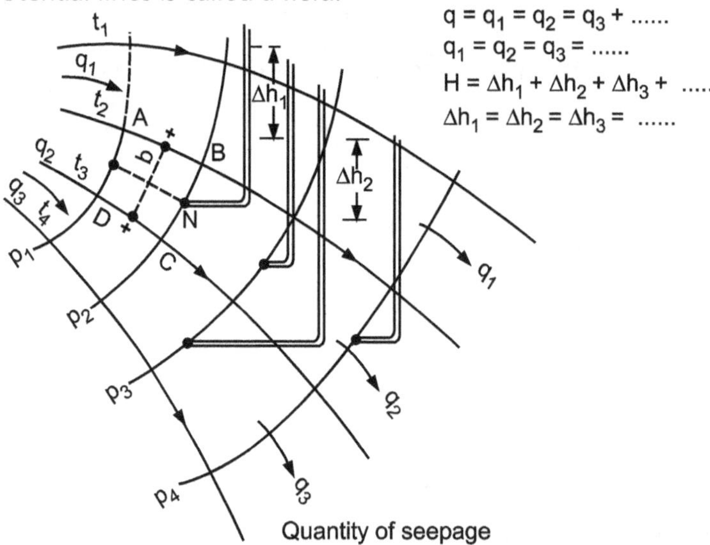

Fig. 4.8 : Properties of flow net

4.20.1 Properties of Flow Net

- Discharge q_1, q_2, q_3, ... through each flow path are equal and total discharge, $q = q_1 + q_2 + q_3 + ...$
- Potential drops h_1, h_2, h_3 ... between any two adjacent equipotential lines are equal and total drop, $h = h_1 + h_2 + h_3 + ...$
- Flow lines and equipotential lines are orthogonal, i.e. they intersect each other at right angles.

- Flow lines and equipotential lines form "square figures", i.e. their corners are at right angles and the median distances are equal.
- Flow lines do not intersect. Similarly potential lines do not intersect except at boundaries.
- Convergence of flow lines means concentration of flow and consequently increasing hydraulic gradient, and divergence of flow lines indicates decreasing hydraulic gradients.

4.20.2 Construction of Flow Net

The flow net can be obtained by any one of the following methods :

- Solution of Laplace's equation (Analytical method).
- Electrical analogy method (Experimental method).
- Graphical method.

  Since graphical method is widely used, it is explained here.

4.21 GRAPHICAL METHOD

The most common procedure for obtaining flow nets is a graphical, trial and error sketching method, for seepage problems with well defined boundary conditions. Reasonably good flow nets can be obtained by practice and by adhering to the correct boundary conditions and use of square figures. The following points may be observed to obtain a reasonably good flow net.

(i)   Right Angles : Flow lines and equipotential lines must cross at right angles.

(ii)   Square Blocks : The areas formed by intersecting flow lines and equipotential lines must be as near a square as possible i.e. the central dimensions should be equal. A useful test is to visualise whether a circle can be placed inside the block and touch all four sides.

(iii) Boundary Conditions :

(a) Permeable Boundaries : A – B, D – E, P – Q and S – T are permeable boundaries. There surfaces have constant head and hence are equipotential lines [Fig. 4.9 (b)].

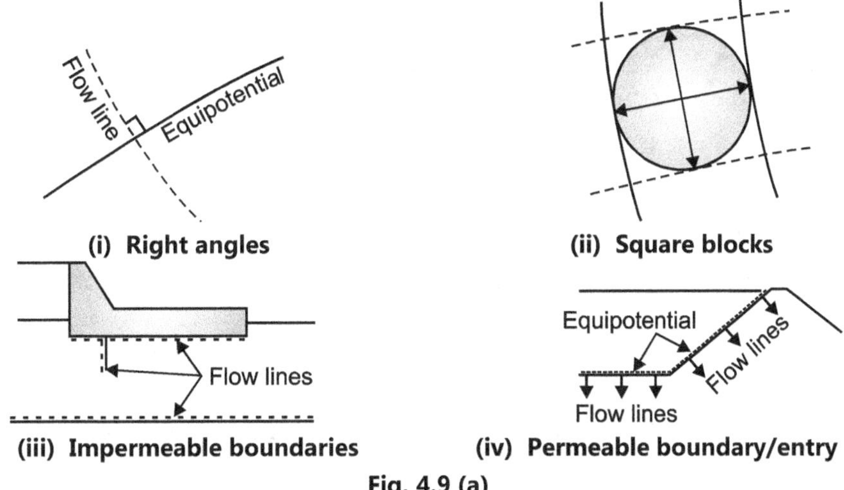

Fig. 4.9 (a)

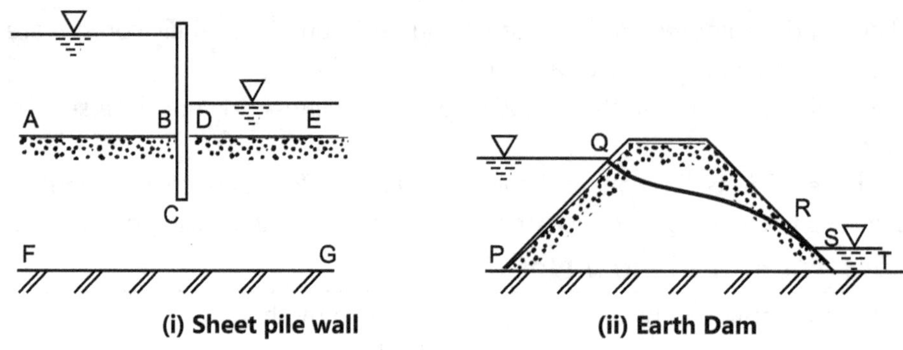

Fig. 4.9 (b)

(b) **Impermeable Boundaries :** F – G, B – C – D and P – T are impermeable boundaries. There is no flow across these boundaries, and ψ is constant. Thus, there are flow lines. Fig. 4.9 (b).

(iv) Normally 4 to five flow channels are sufficient.

(v) The entire flow net should be observed.

(vi) The curves should be roughly parabolic or elliptical in shape.

(vii) The flow lines (stream lines) and equipotential lines should be *orthogonal* and form approximate *squares*.

(viii) All transitions should be smooth.

(ix) The size of the squares in a *flow channel should change* gradually from the *upstream* to the *downstream*.

(x) The *quantity of water* flowing through each channel is the *same*.

(xi) Same potential drop occurs between two successive equipotential lines.

(xii) Smaller the dimension of field, greater will be the hydraulic gradient and velocity of flow through it.

(xiii) The hydraulic boundary conditions have a great effect on the shape of the flow net.

4.22 EXAMPLES OF CONSTRUCTING FLOW NETS

Following two examples of constructing flow nets are illustrated below :

(i)   Sheet pile

(ii) Earthen dam

4.22.1 Sheet Pile

PQR is a sheet pile driven in a pervious layer of depth d, the depth of embedment QR being d'. [Fig. 4.10 (a), (b), (c)].

UQ and TV are potential boundaries with known heads. QRST and XY are flow line boundaries because these are impervious surfaces across which water cannot pass. Flow lines will emerge at right angles from UQ and end at right angles at TV. Because of symmetry flow net will be symmetrical, about vertical axis.

Steps :

- Make, a scale drawing showing the structure, soil mass, the pervious boundaries and the impervious boundaries.
- Sketch the first trial flow line as f_1f_1, emerging at right angles at UQ running round the sheet pile and meeting TV at right angles.
- Sketch the first equipotential line p_1p_1 so as to make a square figure with the flow line f_1f_1 and the boundary QR and ending at right angles to the boundary flow line XY.

Now sketch the second flow line f_2f_2, again emerging at right angles with UQ, making square figures with p_1p_1 going round the sheet pile parallel to the first line f_1f_1 and ending at right angles to TV.

- Then sketch the next trial potential line, emerging at right angles from QR, making square figures with neighbouring flow lines and meeting XY at right angles. Continue sketching to complete the flow net.
- Now, check (by drawing circles touching all the sides of the square) the square figures and orthogonality every where in the flow net. The first attempt can hardly produce a good flow net. Make a second, third and if required more attempts, till a reasonably good flow net has been sketched.

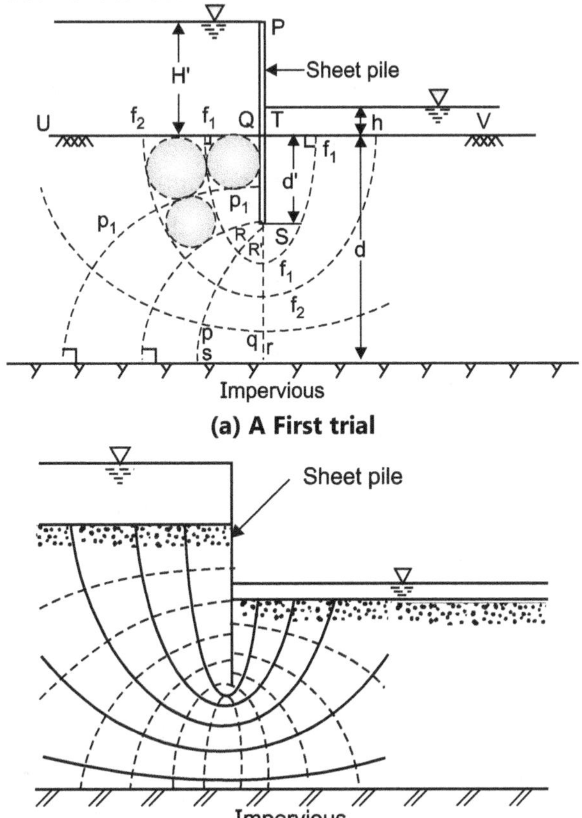

(a) A First trial

(b) Flow net for sheet pile with varied ground surface

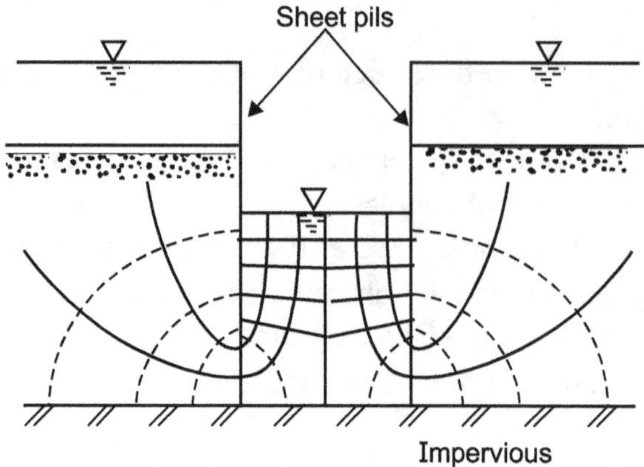

(c) Flow net for double sheet piles

Fig. 4.10

4.22.2 Homogeneous Earthen Dam   [Dec. 14]

Fig. 4.11 shows the dam selection ABCD, has FC as blanket filter and ENJ as top seepage line (also called phreatic line (method of drawing top seepage line is outlined in sec. 4.23) BC represents the rock line.

Steps :

- Boundaries : EB and FC are potential boundaries and ENJ and BF are bound flow lines.
- Sketch the first trial flow line f_1f_1 that emerges from EB at right angles, runs keeping the distance from top seepage line and ends at filter boundary at right angles.
- Sketch equipotential lines p_1p_1 , p_2p_2 , ... so that they emerge and meet the boundary flow lines at right angles and form square figures.
- Check the orthogonality and square figures. In Fig. 4.11 pqrs is a non-square. If many figures are found to be "non–squares" adjust the trial flow line and sketch new equipotential lines. Three or more such trials will yield a reasonably good flow net.

In case of earthen dam even one flow line (f_1f_1) may even be adequate as shown in Fig. 4.11 (a).

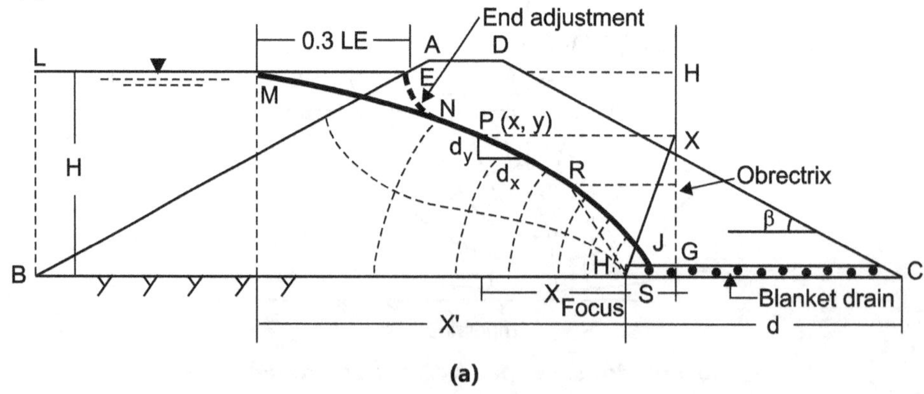

(a)

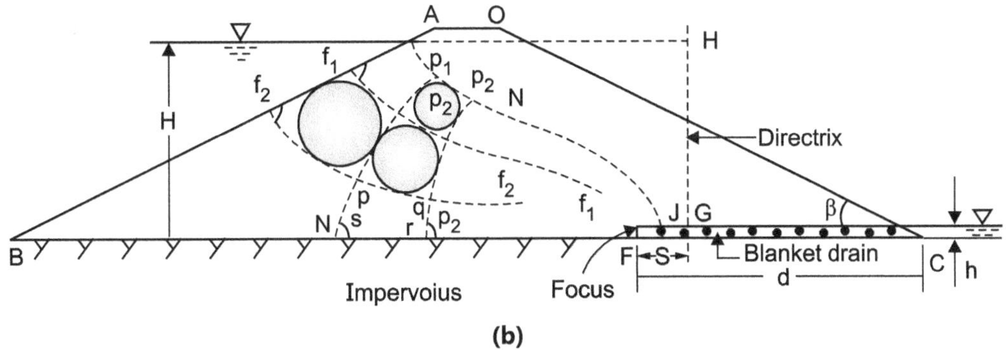

(b)

Fig. 4.11 : Flow net for earthen dam

4.23 CONSTRUCTION OF TOP SEEPAGE LINE OF EARTH DAM

The phreatic line or seepage line is defined as 'the line within a dam section below which there are positive hydrostatic pressures in the dam'. The hydrostatic pressure on the phreatic line is atmospheric. The following is the procedure for locating the phreatic line graphically.

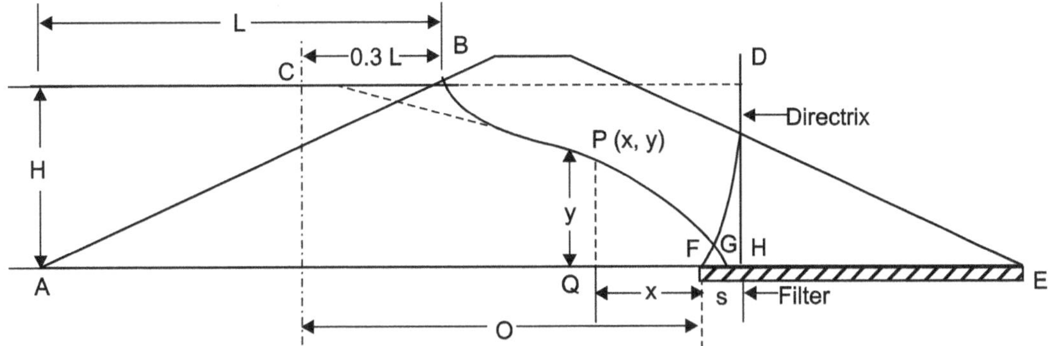

Fig. 4.12 : Casagrande's method of determining phreatic line in a dam with horizontal drainage filter

- AB is the upstream face. Let its horizontal projection be L. On the water surface, measure a distance BC = 0.3 L. Then the point C is the starting point of the base parabola.

- The directrix of the parabola is located by utilising the principle that any point on the parabola is equidistant from the focus as well as from the directrix. Hence with point C as the centre and CF as radius, draw an arc to cut the horizontal line through CB in D. Draw a vertical tangent to the curve FD at D. Since CD = CF, the vertical line DH is the directrix.

- The last point G of the parabola will lie between F and H.

- To locate the intermediate points on the parabola, the principle that its distances from the focus and directrix must be equal will be used. For example, to locate any point P, draw a vertical line QP at any distance x from F. Measure QH with F as the centre and QH as the radius draw an arc to cut the vertical line through Q at point P.

- Join all these points (C, P, G) to get the box parabola.

- Entry point correction : The phreatic line is a flow line, it must start from B and not from C and it should be perpendicular to the upstream face AB, which is a 100% equipotential line. Therefore, a portion of the phreatic line at B is sketched free hand in such a way that it starts perpendicularly to AB. The base parabola should also meet the downstream filter perpendicularly at G.

4.24 USES OF FLOW NET   [May 15]

A flow net chart can be used for the following purposes :

1. Determination of discharge.
2. Determination of total head.
3, Determination of pressure head.
4. Determination of exit hydraulic gradient.

1. Determination of Discharge :

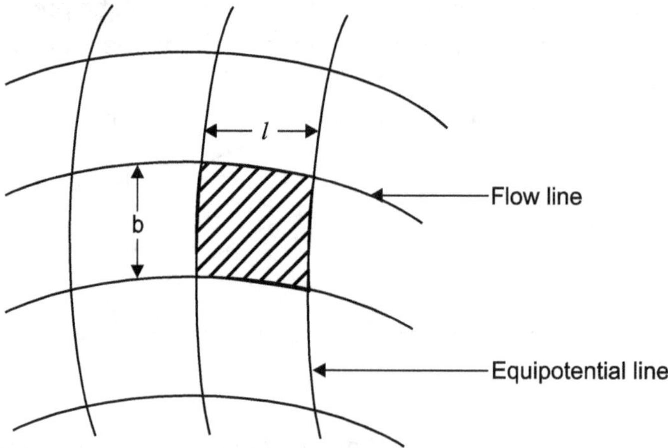

Fig. 4.13 : Flow net

Flow Channel : The portion between any two successive flow lines.

Field : The portion between two successive flow lines and successive equipotential lines (hatched portion).

Let

l = Length of the field

b = Width of the field

Δh = Head drop through the field

Δq = Discharge passing through the flow channel

H = Total hydraulic head

From Darcy's law :

$$\Delta q = k \cdot \frac{\Delta h}{l} \cdot (b \times 1)$$

Assuming the thickness of field as unity.

If N_d = Total number of potential drops in a complete flow net,

Then,
$$\Delta h = \frac{H}{N_d}$$

Hence
$$\Delta q = k \cdot \frac{H}{N_d} \left(\frac{b}{l}\right)$$

The total discharge through complete flow net

$$q = \Sigma \, \Delta q = k \frac{H}{N_d} \left(\frac{b}{l}\right) \times N_f$$

where, N_f = Total number of flow channels in the flow net.

$$q = kH \frac{N_f}{N_d} \cdot \frac{b}{l}$$

Since, the field is square ($b = l$), hence

$$q = kH \frac{N_f}{N_d} \qquad \qquad \ldots (4.15)$$

This equation is valid for isotropic soils ($k_x = k_y = k$).

2. **Determination of Total Head :** The loss of head from one equipotential line to the next equipotential line is $\dfrac{H}{N_d}$. The total head (H_t) at any point can be determined as :

$$H_t = H - \left(n \times \frac{H}{N_d}\right)$$

where, $\qquad\qquad\qquad\qquad$ n = The number of equipotential drops.

3. **Determination of Pressure Head :** The pressure at any point equals to the head minus the elevation head. The downstream water level is taken as datum.

$$H_p = H_t - (- H_e)$$
$$H_p = H_t + H_e$$

where,
$$H_p = \text{Pressure head}$$
$$H_t = \text{Total head}$$
$$H_e = \text{Elevation head}$$

Thus, the pressure head at any point is the height of water column in the piezometer at that particular point.

4. **Determination of Hydraulic Gradient :** The average value of the hydraulic gradient for any flow field is given by :

$$i_{exit} = \frac{\Delta h}{l}$$

where,
$$\Delta h = \text{Equipotential drop in the last field}$$
$$i = \text{Length of last field}$$

The hydraulic gradient and hence the velocity at exit is maximum where length (l) is minimum.

4.25 PIPING

When movement of soil particles by percolating water takes place leading to the formation of a hole or pipe, the phenomenon of piping is said to have occurred. Heave-piping and backward-erosion piping are the two types of piping observed in practice.

Heave Piping : When the upward seepage pressure becomes equal to downward pressure due to submerged weight of soil at a certain level, the soil above this level becomes quick. This may cause the entire soil above the level of instability to heave up and be blown out by the flowing water. This phenomenon is known as heave piping. The mechanics of heave piping was first analysed by Terzaghi. According to Terzaghi, if, D is the depth of soil above the level of instability, heave piping generally occurs within a distance of about D/2 from the sheet piling. For a single row of sheet piles the critical section passes through the lower edge of sheet pile.

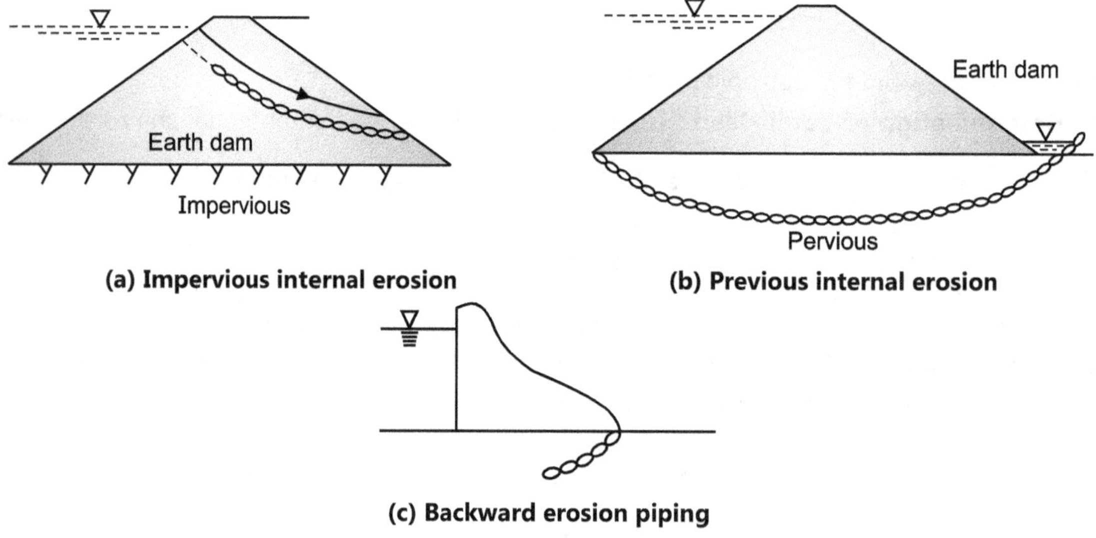

(a) Impervious internal erosion   **(b) Previous internal erosion**

(c) Backward erosion piping

Fig. 4.14 : Piping

Backward-erosion Piping : This is illustrated in Fig. 4.14 (c). The maximum exit gradient occurs at the downstream toe of the weir. If this exit gradient exceeds the critical hydraulic gradient, the soil at this point becomes quick and may be removed by the flowing water. With the removal of soil, there will be further concentration of flow lines into the resulting depression and some more soil will be removed. The process continues slowly with the erosion progressing towards the upstream bed level. One can visualize the pipe like formation becoming larger and longer as the erosion approaches the upstream bed level. Finally, it can lead to a large volume of water rushing through the pipe with subsequent failure of dam. Unlike in the case of the heave piping, it has not been possible to develop a theoretical analysis for backward erosion piping.

Measures to prevent piping attempt to increase the path of percolation of water by providing sheet pile walls below a structure and reduce seepage in the body of dam by providing impervious core walls. The provision of upstream blanked reduces the exist gradient. Provision of filters will protect the downstream face of dam by preventing piping in the body of dam.

4.26 DESIGN OF FILTERS

Filter or drain materials used for preventing piping should satisfy two requirements apart from adding weight, viz.

- The gradation of filter material should be capable of forming small size pores such that the migration of adjacent particles through the pores is prevented.

- The gradation of filter material should be such that it allows a rapid drainage without developing large seepage forces.

To meet these requirements, the filter material should satisfy the following criteria :

    (i)   Ensure fineness to prevent piping :

$$\frac{(D_{15})_f}{(D_{85})_s} < 4 \text{ to } 5 \qquad \qquad \dots (4.16)$$

    (ii)   Ensure drainage requirements :

$$R_{15} = \frac{(D_{15})_f}{(D_{15})_s} > 20 \qquad \qquad \dots (4.17)$$

$$R_{50} = \frac{(D_{50})_f}{(D_{50})_s} \leq 25 \qquad \qquad \dots (4.18)$$

$$k_f < 20\, k_s \qquad \qquad (4.19)$$

subscript - f denotes the filter material and subscript - s denotes the base material or soil to be protected and R denotes the size ratio.

To increase the stability of the filter, the protective filter may be surcharged with the weight of stone uniformly distributed on the surface. The thickness of graded filter ranges from $\frac{H}{5}$ to $\frac{H}{40}$ depending on the relative permeabilities of the filter and soil, where H is the head to be dissipated through the filter.

4.27 FIELD PERMEABILITY

Like all in-situ testing, field determination of permeability is more reliable than laboratory testings, especially when good undisturbed soil specimens cannot be procured for testing. The field tests may be in the form of pumping out test, wherein the water is pumped out from the wells drilled for this purpose. The other type of the field tests are pumping-in tests, wherein the water is pumped into the drilled holes.

4.27.1 Some Definitions

1. Aquifer : *Aquifers* are permeable formations having structures which permit appreciable quantity of water to move through them under ordinary field conditions. These are the geological formations in which the ground water occurs. Aquifers are mainly of two types : (i) unconfined aquifer, and (ii) confined aquifer. When the impervious layer exists only at the bottom, it is known as unconfined and when an aquifer is sandwitched between two impervious strata, it is known as confined.

2. Acquicludes and Aquifuge : *Aquicludes* are the impermeable formations which contain water but are not capable of transmitting or supplying a significant quantity. *Acquifuge* is an impermeable formation which neither contains water nor transmits any water.

3. Storage Coefficient : The water yielding capacity of a confined acquifer can be expressed in terms of its *storage coefficient.* Storage coefficient is defined as the volume of water that an aquifer releases, per unit surface area of acquifer per unit change in the component of head normal to that surface. In most of the confined aquifers, the values of storage coefficient ranges between 0.00005 to 0.005. Its value can be determined from pumping tests on wells penetrating fully into the confined aquifer. The storage coefficient for an unconfined aquifer corresponds to its specific yield.

4. Coefficient of Permeability and Transmissibility : The *coefficient of permeability 'k'* is defined as 'the velocity of flow which will occur through the total cross-sectional area of the soil (or aquifer) under a unit hydraulic gradient'. The *coefficient of transmissibility 'T'* is defined as 'the rate of flow of water (in m³/day) through a vertical strip of acquifer of unit width (1.0 m) and extending the full saturation height under unit hydraulic gradient'. Thus, the coefficient of transmissibility 'T' equals the field coefficient of permeability multiplied by the aquifer thickness b :

$$T = bk$$

4.28 FIELD DETERMINATION OF 'K'

In field, k can be determined by :

- Pumping out test, and
- Pumping in test.

4.28.1 Pumping Out Test

(a) Unconfined aquifer (Fig. 4.15) : For carrying out a pumping out test, a test well is drilled through the aquifer to reach the underlying impervious layer. Two additional perforated casings of small diameter are sunk at some distance from the test well. Water is pumped from the main well at a constant rate. The draw-down of water table takes place and the steady-state water table in each of the nearby observation wells is recorded. The steady state is established when the water level in the main well and the observation wells become constant.

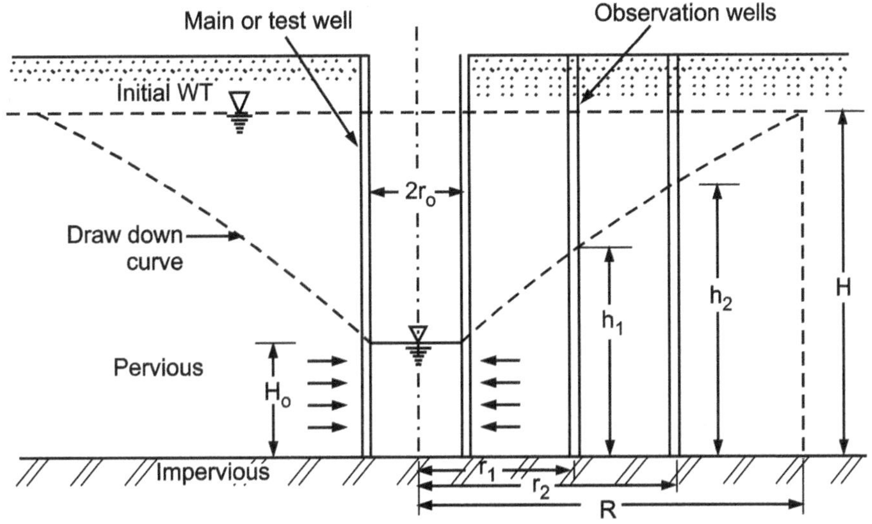

Fig. 4.15 : Pumping test from unconfined aquifer

Assume the water is flowing into a well in a horizontal, radial direction. Consider an elementary cylinder of soil having radius r, thickness dr and height h. Let the water level fall in the observation wells at the rate of dh. At the steady state, the rate of discharge 'q' due to pumping is given by Darcy's law :

$$Q = kiA$$

where,

$$i \simeq \frac{dh}{dr} \text{ (Dupit's assumption)}$$

and

$$A = 2\pi rh$$

$\therefore$

$$Q = k\frac{dh}{dr} \cdot 2\pi rh$$

Rearranging and integrating

$$\int_{r_1}^{r_2} \frac{dr}{r} = \frac{2\pi k}{Q} \int_{h_1}^{h_2} h\, dh$$

$$k = \frac{2.303\, Q \log_{10}\left(\frac{r_2}{r_1}\right)}{\pi \left(h_2^2 - h_1^2\right)} \qquad \dots (4.20)$$

(b) Confined aquifer (Fig. 4.16) : In case of a confined aquifer the incoming flow is restricted only to the thickness H_c of the confined aquifer.

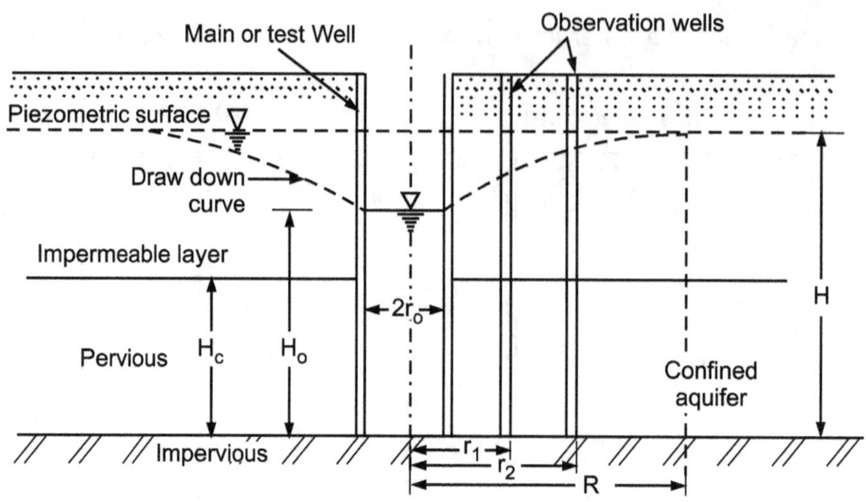

Fig. 4.16 : Pumping test from confined aquifer

The quantity Q in this case is written as :

$$Q = k\,i\,A = k.\frac{dh}{dr} \cdot 2\pi r H_c$$

where, H_c is the depth of the confined aquifer. Thus, integrating between limit of r and h and simplifying.

$$\int_{r_1}^{r_2} \frac{dr}{r} = \int_{h_1}^{h_2} \frac{2\pi r H_c \cdot dh}{Q} \cdot k$$

or

$$k = \frac{2.303\, Q\, \log_{10}\left(\dfrac{r_2}{r_1}\right)}{2\pi\, H_c\, (h_2 - h_1)} \qquad \ldots (4.21)$$

4.28.2 Pumping-in Tests

Pumping-in tests are conducted to determine the coefficient of permeability of an individual stratum through which a hole is drilled. These tests are more economical than the pumping-out test. However, the pumping-out tests give more reliable values than that given by pumping-in tests. The pumping-in tests give the value of coefficient of permeability of stratum just close to the hole, whereas the pumping-out tests give the value for a large area around the hole. There are basically two types of pumping-in tests :

1. Open-end tests and

2. Packer tests.

In an open-end tests, the water flows out of the test hole through its bottom end, whereas in packer tests, the water flows out through the sides of the section of a hole enclosed between packers. The value of the coefficient of permeability is obtained from the quantity of water accepted by the hole. The water pumped-in should be clean, as the impurities, such as silt, clay or any other foreign matter, may cause plugging of the flow passages. If the water available is turbid, it should be clarified in a settling tank or by using a filter. The temperature of the water pumped in should be slightly higher than the temperature of the ground water to preclude the formation of air bubbles in stratum.

1. Open-end Tests : A pipe casing is inserted into the bore hole to the desired depth and it is cleaned out. The hole is kept filled with water during cleaning if it extends below the water table. This is necessary to avoid squeezing of the soil into the bottom of the pipe casing when the driving tool is withdrawn.

After the hole has been cleaned out, water is added to the hole through a metering system. The constant rate of flow (q) is determined at which the steady conditions are established. The coefficient of permeability is determined by the following equation :

$$k = \frac{q}{5.5r\,H} \qquad\qquad \text{... (4.22)}$$

where,   r = Inside radius of the casing

H = Difference of levels between the inlet to the casing and the water table as shown in Fig. 4.17 (a)

q = Discharge

If required, the discharge can be increased by pumping-in water under a pressure P as shown in Fig. 4.17 (b). In this case, the value of H becomes equal to $\left(H + \dfrac{P}{\gamma_w}\right)$.

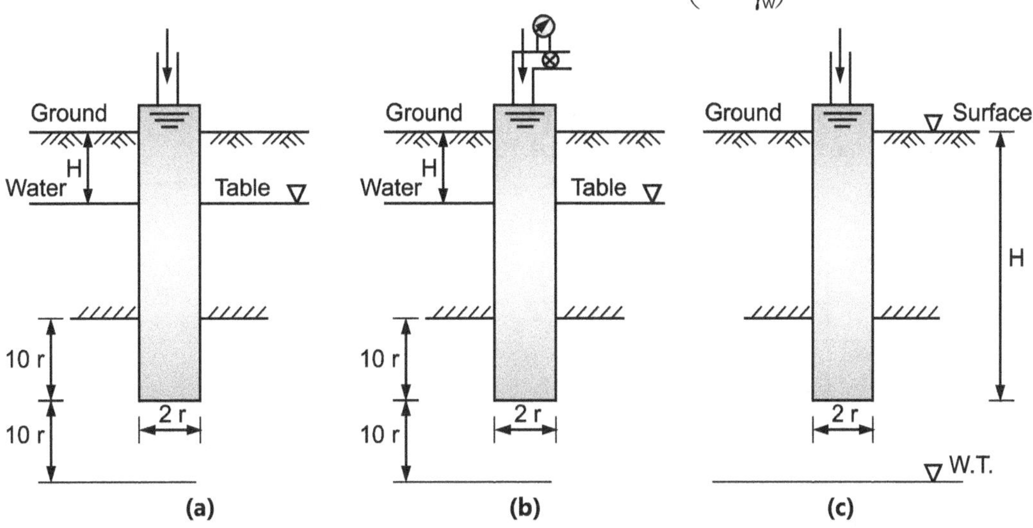

Fig. 4.17 : Open end tests

For accurate results, the lower end of the pipe should be at a distance of not less than 10r from the top as well as from the bottom of the stratum.

The open-end test can also be conducted above the water table as shown in Fig. 4.17 (c). In this case, however, it is difficult to maintain a constant water level in the casing and some surging of this level has to be tolerated.

Equation (4.22) can also be used in this case. However, in this case H is equal to the difference of inlet level and the bottom end of the pipe. If required, the rate of flow (q) can be increased by pumping-in water under a pressure p, with a total head of $\left(H + \dfrac{P}{\gamma_w}\right)$.

2. Packer Tests : The packer tests are performed in an uncased portion of the pipe casing. The packer tests are more commonly used for testing of rocks. The tests are occasionally used for testing of soils if the bore hole can stay open without any casing.

(a) Single Packer Tests : If the hole cannot stand without a casing, single-packer test is used. The packer is placed as shown in Fig. 4.18 (a). Water is pumped into the hole. It comes out the sides of uncased portion of the hole below the packet. If the casing is used for the full depth, it should have perforations in the portion of the stratum being tested. The lower end of the casing is plugged.

When the steady conditions are attained, the constant rate of flow (q) is determined. The value of the coefficient of permeability is found by the following equation

$$k = \frac{q}{2\pi\,LH}\,\log_e (L/r) \quad \text{if } L \geq 10r \qquad\qquad \text{... (4.23)}$$

or

$$k = \frac{q}{2\pi\,LH}\,\sinh^{-1} (L/2r) \ \text{if } 10r > L \geq r \qquad\qquad \text{... (4.24)}$$

where,
r = inside radius of hole,
L = length of the hole tested,
H = difference of water levels at the entry and the ground water table for the hole tested below the water table
$\sinh^{-1}$ = hyperbolic sine

For the holes tested above the water table, H is equal to the difference of levels of water at the entry and middle of the test section [Fig. 4.18 (b)].

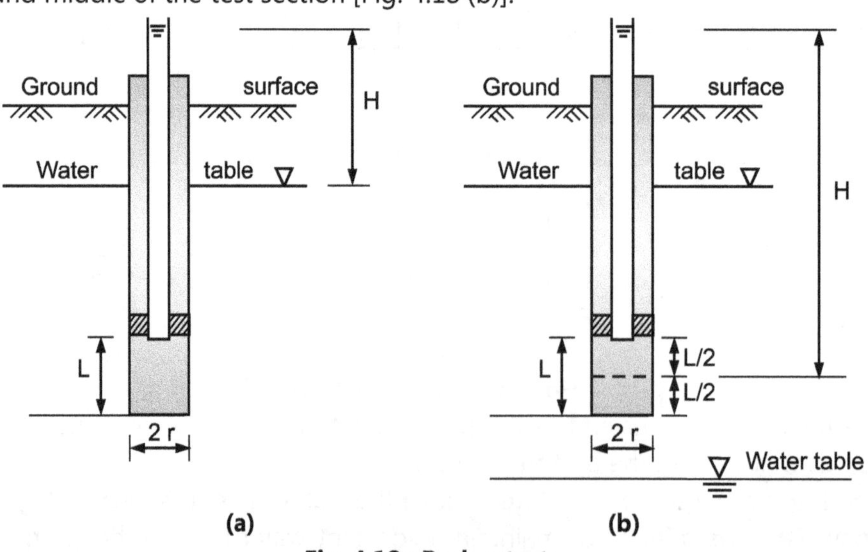

Fig. 4.18 : Packer tests

If the water is applied under pressure (P), the value of H becomes $\left(H + \dfrac{P}{\gamma_w}\right)$, as in the case of open-end tests. After the tests is complete, the packer is removed. If required, the hole is made deeper and again a packer is placed and the procedure is repeated for that portion.

(b) Double-Packer Test : If the hole can stand without a casing double-packer test can be used. The hole is drilled to the final depth. It is filled with water, surged and bailed out. Two packers are fitted to a small diameter pipe, as shown in Fig. 4.19. The bottom of the pipe fitted with packers is plugged. Fig. 4.19 (a) shows the conditions when the test section is below the ground water table and Fig. 4.19 (b), when above the ground water table. The value of the coefficient of permeability is determined using equation (4.23) or equation (4.24) depending upon the value of L and r as specified.

The double-packer test is conducted first in the lowest portion near the bottom of the hole and later repeated for the upper layers.

The packer tests give better result when conducted below the water table than when above the water table. For reliable results, the thickness of the stratum should be at least five times the length (L) of the hole tested.

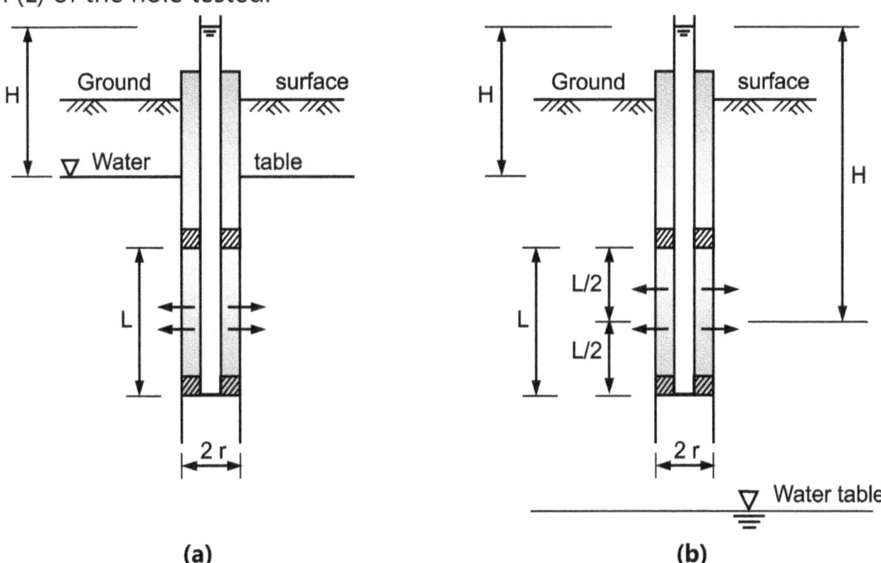

Fig. 4.19 : Double-packer test

SOLVED EXAMPLES

Example 4.1 : A constant head permeability test was carried out on a cylindrical sample of sand 10 cm diameter and 15 cm height. 160 cm³ of water was collected in 1.75 minutes under a head to 30 cm. Compute the coefficient of permeability in m/year and the velocity of flow in m/sec.

Solution : k can be calculated as :

$$k = \frac{q}{iA} = \frac{Q}{i \cdot A \cdot t}$$

where,

q = Total discharge

Q = Discharge per unit time = 160 m³

$$A = 3.14 \times \frac{10^2}{4} = 78.5 \text{ cm}^2$$

$$i = \frac{h}{L} = \frac{30}{15} = 2$$

t = 105 seconds

$$k = \frac{160}{78.5 \times 2 \times 105} = 0.97 \times 10^{-3} \text{ cm/sec.}$$

$$k = 9.7 \times 10^{-5} \text{ m/sec} = \textbf{3060 m/year}$$

Velocity of flow, $v = ki$

$$= 9.7 \times 10^{-5} \times 2 = \textbf{1.94} \times \textbf{10}^{\textbf{-4}} \textbf{ m/sec.}$$

Example 4.2 : In a falling head permeability test on a sample 12.2 cm height and 44.41 cm² in cross-sectional area, the water level in the stand pipe of 6.25 mm internal diameter dropped from a height of 75 cm to 24.7 cm in 15 minutes. Find the coefficient of permeability.

Solution :

$$k = \frac{al}{At} \log_e \frac{h_1}{h_2}$$

$$k = \frac{2.303 \, al}{At} \log_{10} \frac{h_1}{h_2},$$

a = c/s area of flow, A = area, l = length of sample

$$a = \frac{\pi \times (0.625)^2}{4} = 0.307 \text{ cm}^2$$

t = 15 × 60 = 900 seconds

$$k = \frac{2.303 \times 0.307 \times 12.2}{44.41 \times 900} \log_{10} \left(\frac{25}{24.7}\right)$$

$$= \textbf{1.04} \times \textbf{10}^{-4} \textbf{ cm/sec.}$$

Example 4.3 : If soil P has permeability of 4 × 10⁻³ cm/sec, and the heat lost in soil Q is 9 times the head lost in soil P.

(a) What is permeability of flow per hour ?

(b) What is the quantity of flow per hour ?

(c) To what elevation would water rise when a piezometer is inserted in soil Q at elevation 5 cm ?

Solution :

$$h_Q = 9 \, h_P$$

Total head lost during flow = 10 cm (From Fig. 4.20)

$$h_Q + h_P = 10$$

$$10\,h_P \;=\; 10 \quad OR \quad h_P \;=\; 1\ cm$$

$$h_Q \;=\; 9\ cm$$

(a) For vertical flow, velocity of flow is constant in soil (P) and (Q).

$$V_P \;=\; V_Q \;=\; V$$

$$V_Q \;=\; k_Q\, i_Q \;=\; k_P\, i_P$$

$$k_Q \times \frac{9}{10} \;=\; 4 \times 10^{-3} \times \frac{1}{10}$$

$$\therefore \qquad k_Q \;=\; \mathbf{4.4 \times 10^{-4}\ cm/sec.}$$

(b)

$$q \;=\; K_P \cdot i_P \cdot A = 4 \times 10^{-3} \times \frac{1}{10} \times 10$$

$$=\; 4 \times 10^{-3}\ cm^3/sec.$$

$$q \;=\; \mathbf{14.4\ cm^3/hour}$$

(c) Elevation of water in piezometer at elevation zero in soil (Q) = 40 cm. Elevation of water in piezometer inserted at elevation 5 cm = 36.5 cm.

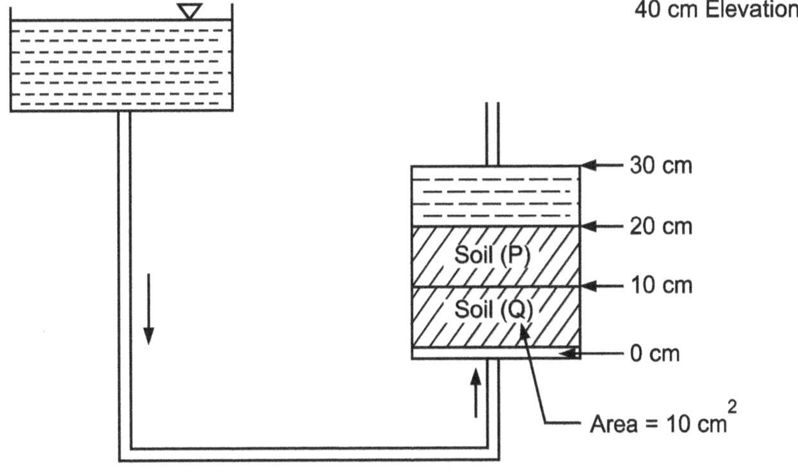

Fig. 4.20

Example 4.4 : The depth of water on the upstream side of a zoned earth dam is 20 cm. The coefficient of permeabilities of upstream and downstream zones are 1.5×10^{-7} m/s and 6.0×10^{-7} m/s respectively. Determine the quantity of seepage per unit length through the dam. $N_f = 3.5$, $N_d = 8$.

Solution :

$$q \;=\; kH\ \frac{N_f}{N_d} \times \frac{b}{l}$$

Assuming square field,

$$b \;=\; l$$

$$q \;=\; kH\ \frac{N_f}{N_d} \;=\; 1.5 \times 10^{-7} \times 20 \times \frac{3.5}{8}$$

$$=\; \mathbf{13.1 \times 10^{-7}\ m^3/sec.}$$

Example 4.5 : The void ratio for sand deposit varies from 0.4 to 0.85. The specific gravity of sand is 2.67. What is the range of critical hydraulic gradient ?

Solution :
$$i_c = \frac{G-1}{1+e}$$

For
$$e = 0.4$$

$$i_c = \frac{2.67-1}{1+0.4} = 1.19$$

For
$$e = 0.85$$

$$i_c = \frac{2.67-1}{1+0.85} = 0.90$$

Example 4.6 : For a weir on pervious foundation, the exit gradient does not exceed 75% of the gradient causing quick condition. Determine maximum exit gradient if porosity $n = 40\%$.

Solution :
$$e = \frac{n}{1-n} = \frac{0.4}{1-0.4} = 0.67$$

$$i_c = \frac{G-1}{1+e} = \frac{2.7-1}{1+0.67} = 1.02$$

But i_c should not exceed 75%.

Thus,
$$\text{max. } i_c = 0.75 \times 1.02 = \mathbf{0.76}$$

Example 4.7 : Excavation with dewatering is carried out in a submerged sandy layer, using sheet pile, reaching a depth of 10 cm below the ground surface. Normal water table is 3 m below the ground surface.What will be the maximum depth of excavation if one metre depth of water is always maintained above the depth of excavation, to avoid quick sand.

Solution :

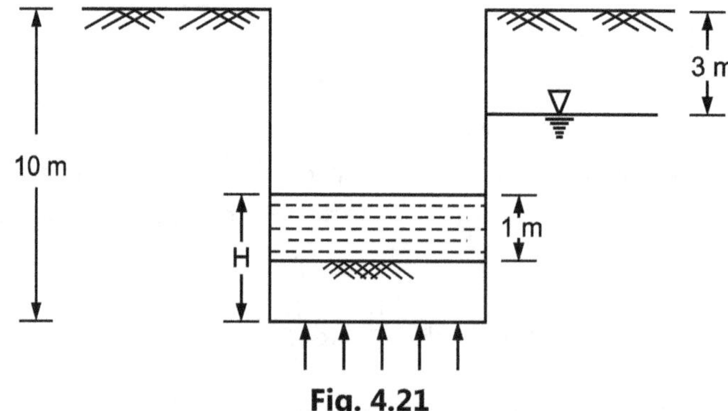

Fig. 4.21

Let H be depth of water above the bottom of the sheet pile.

$$\text{Upward force} = \text{Downward force}$$

$$\therefore \qquad h_w\, \gamma_w = h\gamma_{soil}$$

$\therefore$ $\qquad (10 - 3)\ 10\ =\ 10 \times 1\ (H - 1)\ 20$ [where, $\gamma_w\ =\ 10\ kN/m^3$

$\therefore$ $\qquad\qquad\qquad H\ =\ 4\ m \qquad\qquad \gamma_{soil}\ =\ 20\ kN/m^3$]

Hence, depth of excavation $=\ 6\ m$

Example 4.8 : The flow net for a sheet pile gave 3 flow channels and 7 equipotential drops. Determine the quantity of seepage per metre length of the sheet pile per day, if coefficient of permeability k = 0.7 $\times$ 10^{-5} m/sec and head loss is 5 m.

Solution : $\qquad\qquad q\ =\ kH\ \dfrac{N_f}{N_d}$

$$=\ 0.7 \times 10^{-5}\ (5)\ \frac{3}{7}$$

$q\ =\ 15 \times 10^{-6}$ litres per sec./m length

$q\ =\ 15 \times 10^{-6} \times 24 \times 3600$

$=\ $ **1296 litres per sec/m length in one day**

Example 4.9 : In a falling head permeability test, soil sample of 75 mm diameter and length 150 mm indicated a fall of head from 600 mm to 300 mm in 193 seconds. If the stand pipe has a diameter equal to 12 mm, determine k.

Solution : $\qquad\qquad k\ =\ 2.303\ \dfrac{aL}{At}\ \log_{10} \left(\dfrac{h_1}{h_2} \right)$

$$=\ 2.303 \times \frac{\frac{\pi}{4}\ (12)^2 \times 150}{\frac{\pi}{4}\ (75)^2 \times 193}\ \log_{10} \left(\frac{600}{300} \right)$$

$$=\ \textbf{0.013 mm/sec.}$$

Example 4.10 : Calculate k for a sample of sand given the following data :

$\qquad$ Diameter of permeameter $=\ 15\ mm$

$\qquad$ Loss of head on 200 mm length $=\ 83.2\ mm$

$\qquad$ Water collected in 1 min $=\ 66.8\ lit.$

Solution : $\qquad\qquad Q\ =\ Aik\ =\ A \cdot \dfrac{h}{L}\ k$

$\therefore \qquad\qquad \dfrac{66.8 \times 10^{-3}}{60}\ =\ \dfrac{\pi}{4}\ (75)^2 \times \dfrac{83.2}{200} \times k$

$\therefore \qquad\qquad k\ =\ \textbf{6.057} \times \textbf{10}^{-7}\ \textbf{mm/sec.}$

Example 4.11 : What is the critical hydraulic gradient for a sandy soil with a submerged unit weight of 9 kN/m^3 ?

Solution : We know that $\quad i_c\ =\ \dfrac{\gamma_{sub}}{\gamma_w}\ =\ \dfrac{9.0}{9.81}\ =\ \textbf{0.9174}$

Example 4.12 : During preparations for a pumping test, a test well was driven to the bottom of a sandy stratum which overlies a horizontal impervious shale. Observation bore holes were drilled at distances 18 and 36 m from the centre of the test well. Water was pumped from the test well at a rate of 180 litres/mm until the water level became steady. The water level in the two bore holes was then found to be 4.5 and 6.8 m above the impermeable bed. Determine the coefficient of permeability of the sandy soil in mm/sec.

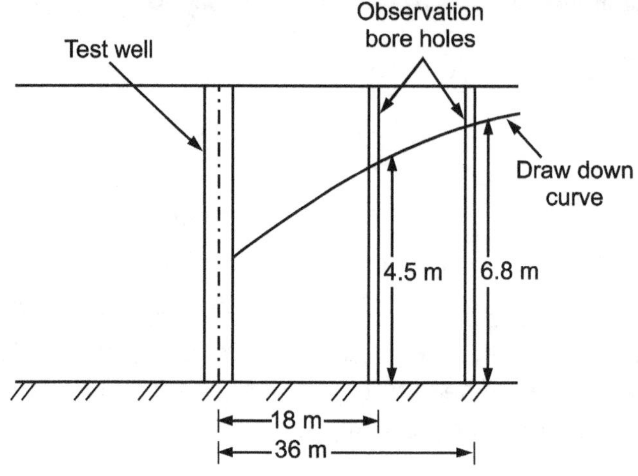

Fig. 4.22

Solution : From equation,

$$k = \frac{2.303 \, q \, \log_{10}\left(\dfrac{r_2}{r_1}\right)}{\pi \left(h_2^2 - h_1^2\right)}$$

Here $r_1 = 18$ m, $r_2 = 36$ m, $h_1 = 4.5$ m, $h_2 = 6.8$ m and $q = 180$ litres/min.

$$\therefore \quad k = \frac{\left[2.303 \times \dfrac{(180 \times 1000 \times 1000)}{60}\right] \log_{10}\dfrac{36}{18}}{\pi \, (6.8^2 - 4.5^2) \, 1000^2}$$

or $\qquad k = 0.0255$ mm/sec.

Example 4.13 : At the foot of a dam, the foundation soil has a void ratio of 0.72. The specific gravity of the soil solids is 2.65. To ensure safety against piping, the upward gradient must not exceed 30% of the critical gradient at which quick sand condition occurs. Estimate the maximum permissible upward gradient.

Solution : Gradient, $\qquad i_c = \dfrac{G-1}{1+e} = \dfrac{2.65-1}{1+0.72} = 0.959$

The permissible upward gradient is 30% of critical gradient.

$\therefore \quad$ Maximum permissible upward gradient $= 0.959 \times \dfrac{30}{100} = 0.288$

Example 4.14 : For the dam of Fig. 4.22, draw the flownet and determine the following :

(i)   the quantity of flow ;

(ii)   the seepage pressure in the middle of square B

(iii)   the upward pressure at the point B.

(iv)   the exit gradient at point A.

The coefficient of permeability is 4.0×10^{-2} m/s.

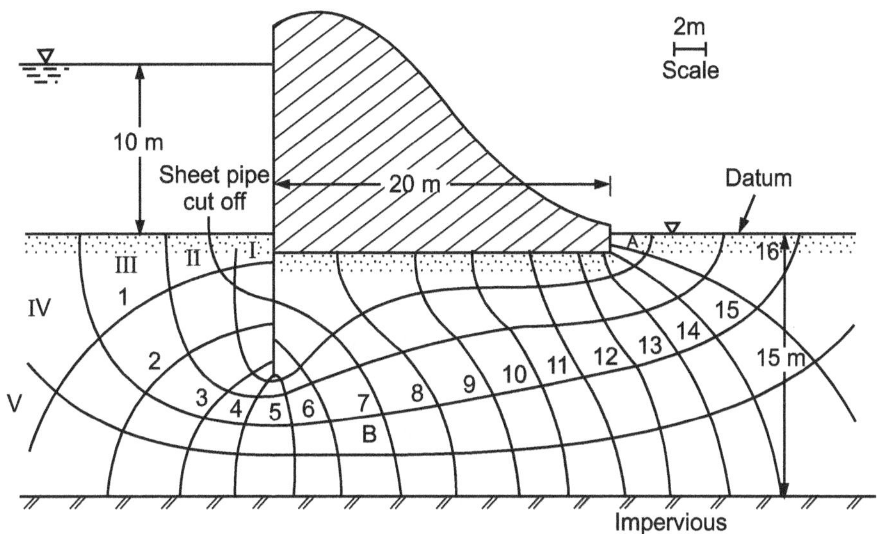

Fig. 4.23

Solution : The flow net is drawn as in Fig. 4.23.

Number of flow channels, $N_f = 5$

Number of potential drops, $N_d = 16$

Head loss = 10 m

Potential drop, $\Delta h = \dfrac{H}{N_d} = \dfrac{10}{16} = 0.625$

(i)   The quantity of flow

$$q = KH \frac{N_f}{N_d}$$

or

$$q = \frac{4.0 \times 10^{-2}}{1000} \times 10 \times \frac{5}{16}$$

$$= \mathbf{1.25 \times 10^{-4} \ m^3/sec./m \ length}$$

(ii) The potential head at B is

$$h_i = H - N_d \ \Delta h$$

$$= 10 - 6.5 \times 0.625 = 5.94 \ m$$

Seepage   Pressure, $P_s = h_i \ \gamma_w = 5.94 \times 9.81 = \mathbf{58.27 \ kN/m^2}$

(iii) The uplift pressure head, $h_w = h_i - Z$. Consider the downstream water level as datum.

$$h_w = 5.94 + 11.6 = \mathbf{17.54\ m}$$

and uplift pressure,

$$u_w = 17.54 \times 9.81 = \mathbf{172.07\ kN/m^2}$$

(iv) Exit gradient,

$$i_c = \frac{\Delta h}{l} = \frac{0.625}{0.60} = \mathbf{1.04}$$

Example 4.15 : Derive an equation for critical hydraulic gradient. Draw flow net for a sheet pile driven below the ground. State the properties of the flow net. While determining permeability of a soil sample using variable head method, the water head is dropped from 100 cm to 80 cm in 5 minutes.

(a) How much time will be required to drop the head from 80 cm to 60 cm.

(b) How much head will drop between 5 minutes to 10 minutes.

Solution :

$$k = 2.3\frac{aL}{At}\log\frac{h_1}{h_2} \qquad \text{...(i)}$$

(a) $\therefore$

$$\frac{2.3 \cdot aL}{A \cdot 5}\log\frac{100}{80} = \frac{2.3\ aL}{A \cdot t}\log\frac{80}{60}$$

$\therefore$

$$t = 5 \times \frac{\log\dfrac{80}{60}}{\log\dfrac{100}{80}} = 5 \times \frac{0.1249387}{0.09691}$$

$$= \mathbf{6.446\ min.}$$

(b) From equation (i), other parameters being equal,

$$\frac{\log\dfrac{100}{80}}{5} = \frac{\log\dfrac{80}{h_2}}{10}$$

by

$$\frac{80}{h_3} = 2\log\frac{100}{80} = 0.19382$$

$$= \log 1.5625$$

$\therefore$

$$h_3 = \frac{80}{1.5125} = \mathbf{51.2\ cm}$$

Example 4.16 : A sand deposit with specific gravity of 2.65, has bulk density of 19.20 kN/m^3 on the field. Its natural moisture content is 9%. Determine the critical hydraulic gradient of the sand deposit. Take $\gamma_w = 9.81$ kN/m^3.

Solution :

$$i_c = \left(\frac{G-1}{1+e}\right)\frac{1}{\gamma_w}$$

$$\gamma_b = 19.2 = \frac{G\,(1+w)}{1+e}$$

$$= \frac{2.65 \,(1.09) \cdot \gamma_w}{1 + e}$$

$$\therefore \quad \frac{1}{1 + e} = \frac{19.2}{2.65 \times 1.09}$$

$$i_c = \frac{2.65 - 1}{9.81} \times \frac{19.2}{2.65 \times 1.09}$$

$$= \mathbf{1.118}$$

Example 4.17 : At the toe of a dam, the foundation soil has a void ratio of 0.72. The specific gravity of the soil solids is 2.65. To ensure safety against piping, the upward gradient must not exceed 30% of the critical gradient at which quick sand condition occurs. Estimate the maximum permissible upward gradient.

Solution :
$$i_{max} = 0.3 \, i_c = 0.3 \left(\frac{G - 1}{1 + e}\right) \cdot \frac{1}{\gamma_w}$$

$$\text{Permissible gradient} = 0.3 \left(\frac{2.65 - 1}{1 + 0.72}\right) = \frac{0.3 \times 1.65}{1.72} = \mathbf{0.2878}$$

Example 4.18 : Estimate the quantity of flow of water through soil mass in 300 seconds, when a constant head of 1 m is maintained. The length of the sample is 150 mm and the cross-sectional area is 100 × 100 mm. The coefficient of permeability of the soil sample is 1×10^{-1} mm/s.

Solution :
$$Q = \left[k \cdot A \cdot \frac{h}{l}\right] \times t = \frac{1}{10} \times 100 \times \frac{100 \times 1000}{150} \times 300$$

$$= 20 \times 1000 \times 1000 \text{ mm}^3$$

But,
$$1 \text{cm}^3 = 1000 \text{ mm}^3 \text{ and } 1000 \text{ cm}^3 = 1 \text{ litres}$$

$$\therefore \quad Q \text{ in } 300 \text{ sec.} = 20 \times \frac{1000}{1000} \times \frac{1000}{1000} = \mathbf{20 \text{ litres}}$$

Example 4.19 : A drainage pipe beneath a dam is clogged with sand. Its coefficient of permeability is found to be 10 m/day. The difference between the head water and the tail water is 25 m. It has been observed that there is flow of 175 litres of water every day through the pipe. The pipe is 80 m long and has a cross-sectional area of 200 sq. cm. Find the length of the pipe, filled with sand.

Solution : Let, L be logged length of the pipe.

$$k = \frac{QL}{h \cdot A}$$

$$Q = 175 \text{ lit/day}; \, k = 10 \text{ m/day} = 0.175 \text{ m}^3/\text{day}$$

$$A = 200 \text{ cm}^2 = \frac{200}{100 \times 100} \text{ m}^2, \, h = 25 \text{ m}$$

$$\therefore \quad L = \frac{K \cdot h \cdot A}{Q} = \frac{80 \times 25 \times 200}{100 \times 100 \times 0.175}$$

$$= \frac{200 \times 200}{100 \times 200} \times \frac{40}{7} = \frac{160}{7} \text{ m}$$

$$= 22.86 \text{ m}$$

$$\therefore \quad \text{Length of pipe clogged} = \frac{160}{7 \times 80}$$

$$= \frac{2^{th}}{7} \text{ of the pipe}$$

Example 4.20 : A variable head permeameter test give the following observations.

(i)   Cross-sectional area of specimen $= 15$ cm^2

(ii)   Cross-sectional area of standpipe $= 0.075$ cm^2

(iii)   Length of the specimen $= 10$ cm

(iv)   Initial head above datum $= 27.5$ cm

(v)   Head after 5 minutes $= 20.0$ cm

Determine the coefficient of permeability.

Solution :
$$k = 2.3 \frac{a}{A} \cdot \frac{L}{t} \log \frac{h_1}{h_2} = 2.3 \times \frac{0.075}{15} \times \frac{10}{300} \log \frac{27.5}{20}$$

$$= \mathbf{5.3016 \times 10^{-5} \text{ cm/sec.}}$$

Example 4.21 : While determining the permeability of a soil sample using variable head permeameter, the water head is dropped from 100 cm to 60 cm in 10 minutes :

(a) How much will it further drop in the next 10 minutes ?

(b) How much time will be required to drop the head from 60 cm to 20 cm ?

Solution :
$$k = 2.3 \frac{a}{A} \cdot \frac{l}{t_1} \log \frac{h_1}{h_2} = 2.3 \frac{a}{A} \cdot \frac{l}{t_2} \log \frac{h_2}{h_3}$$

(a) $\therefore$
$$\frac{1}{10 \text{ minutes}} \times \log \frac{100}{60} = \frac{1}{10} \log \frac{60}{h_3}$$

$\therefore$
$$\frac{100}{60} = \frac{60}{h_3}$$

$\therefore$
$$h_3 = \frac{60 \times 60}{100} = \mathbf{36 \text{ cm}}$$

(b)
$$\log \frac{100}{60} = \frac{l}{t_2} \log \frac{60}{20}$$

$\therefore$
$$t_2 = \frac{10 \log 3}{\log 10/6} = \mathbf{21.5066 \text{ min.}}$$

Example 4.22 : A permeameter of 80 mm diameter with a sample length of 300 mm has been used for constant head tests. While conducting a constant head test the loss of head was 1150 mm for a length of 250 mm and the rate of flow was 2700 mm³/sec. Find the coefficient of permeability in mm/sec.

If a falling head test was performed on the same sample at the same void ratio, find the time taken for head to fall from 900 to 450 mm. The diameter of stand pipe is 25 mm in the falling head test.   **[May 16, 6 M]**

Solution :

$$Q = k \cdot i \cdot A$$

$$\frac{2700 \text{ mm}^3}{\text{sec}} = k \cdot \frac{1150}{290} \times \frac{\pi}{4} \, 80^2$$

$$\therefore \quad k = \frac{2700 \times 250}{1150} \times \frac{4}{\pi \times 80^2}$$

$$= 0.11677 \text{ mm/sec.}$$

$$k = 2.3 \frac{a}{A} \cdot \frac{l}{t} \, \log \frac{900}{450}$$

$$\therefore \quad t = \frac{2.3 \times 25^2 \times \frac{\pi}{4}}{80^2 \times \frac{\pi}{4}} \times \frac{300 \log 2}{0.11677}$$

$$= \frac{2.3 \times 625}{6400} \times \frac{300 \log 2}{0.11677} = \textbf{173.709 sec.}$$

Example 4.23 : Derive the expression for the capillary rise in soils. The water content of a coarse grained soil is 9% and the degree of saturation value is 27%. Determine the critical gradient at which the quicksand condition will occur if the specific gravity of the soil is 2.65.

In a falling head permeability test the time interval for the fall between h_1 to h_2 and h_2 to h_3 is same. Prove that :

$$h_2 = \sqrt{h_1 \cdot h_3}$$

Solution :

$$S_\gamma \cdot e = w \cdot G$$

$$\therefore \quad e = \frac{0.09 \times 2.65}{0.27}$$

$$= 0.883$$

$$i_c = \left(\frac{G-1}{1+e}\right) \cdot \gamma_w$$

$$= \frac{2.65 - 1}{1 + 0.883} = \frac{1.65}{1.883}$$

$$= 0.8763$$

$$k = \frac{2.3\,a}{A} \cdot \frac{l}{t_1}\, \log \frac{h_1}{h_2} = \frac{2.3\,a}{A} \cdot \frac{l}{t_1} \cdot \log \frac{h_2}{h_3}$$

$$\therefore \qquad \frac{\log \dfrac{h_1}{h_2}}{t_1} = \frac{\log \left(\dfrac{h_2}{h_3}\right)}{t_1}$$

$$\therefore \qquad \frac{h_1}{h_2} = \frac{h_2}{h_3}$$

$$\therefore \qquad h_2^2 = h_1 \cdot h_3$$

$$\therefore \qquad h_2 = \sqrt{h_1 \cdot h_3}$$

Hence, the proof.

Example 4.24 : In a falling head permeability test the following observations were recorded :

Diameter of soil sample	= 100 mm
Size of soil sample	= 125 mm
Diameter of stand pipe	= 20 mm
Final head	= 1.25 m
Initial head	= 1.80 m
Time	= 30 min
a	= Cross-sectional area of stand pipe
A	= Cross-sectional area of sample

Calculate the permeability of soil sample.

Solution :

$$k = 2.303\, \frac{aL}{At}\, \log_{10} \frac{h_1}{h_2}$$

Here,

$$a = \frac{\pi}{4}\,(20)^2 = 314.159 \text{ mm}^2$$

$$L = 125 \text{ mm}$$

$$A = \frac{\pi}{4}\,(100) = 7853.98 \text{ mm}^2$$

$$h_1 = 1.8 \times 10^3 \text{ mm}$$

$$h_2 = 1.25 \times 10^3 \text{ mm}$$

$$t = 30 \times 60 \text{ sec.}$$

$$\therefore \qquad k = 2.303 \times \frac{314.159 \times 125}{7853.98 \times 30 \times 60}\, \log_{10} \left(\frac{1.8 \times 10^3}{1.25 \times 10^3}\right)$$

$$= 1.013 \times 10^{-3} \text{ mm/sec.}$$

Example 4.25 : A sample representing sand has been tested in constant head test for 'k'. The inside diameter holding the sand is 102 mm. The head loss 'h' over a distance L = 125 mm between two piezometers is 860 mm. The amount of water collected during the time of 2 minutes is 733 ml. Calculate k.

Solution : Given : d = 102 mm, h = 860 mm, Q = 733 ml, L = 125 mm, t = 2 minutes.

k can be calculated as :

$$k = \frac{q}{iA} = \frac{Q}{iAt} = \frac{Q \times L}{hAt}$$

$$k = \frac{733 \times 12.5}{860 \times \dfrac{\pi(10.2)^2}{4} \times 2 \times 60} \text{ cm/sec.}$$

$$= \mathbf{1.08 \ m/sec.}$$

Example 4.26 : The following data pertains to the conditions on the downstream side of an impervious dam on previous foundation :

Potential drop, Δh = 0.2 m

Average length for drop, ΔL = 0.2 m

G = 2.67 , e = 0.65

The flow is vertically upwards.

Find whether quick sand condition can occur.

Solution :

1.   Hydraulic gradient (i) $= \dfrac{\Delta h}{\Delta L}$

$$= \frac{0.2}{0.2} = 1$$

2. Critical hydraulic gradient (i_c) $= \dfrac{G-1}{1+e} = \dfrac{2.67-1}{1+0.65} = 1.012$

As $i \cong i_c$, quick sand will occur.

Example 4.27 : In a falling head permeameter the initial head h_1 drops down to h_2 in the same time as required for a drop from h_2 to h_3. Show that $h_2^2 = h_1 \cdot h_3$.

Solution : For variable head permeability test :

$$k = \frac{aL}{AT} \log_e \frac{h_1}{h_2}$$

Now, for head h_1 and h_2 $k_1 = \dfrac{aL}{AT} \log_e \dfrac{h_1}{h_2}$

and for head h_2 and h_3 $k_2 = \dfrac{aL}{AT} \log_e \dfrac{h_2}{h_3}$

Since sample is the same, hence $k_1 = k_2$

$\therefore \qquad \dfrac{aL}{AT} \log_e \dfrac{h_1}{h_2} = \dfrac{aL}{AT} \log_e \dfrac{h_2}{h_3}$

or $\qquad \dfrac{h_1}{h_2} = \dfrac{h_2}{h_3}$

$\therefore \qquad h_2^2 = h_1 \cdot h_3$

Example 4.28 : If the saturated density of a soil is 1.9 g/ml , what is the value of the critical hydraulic gradient ?

Solution :

$\rho_{sat} = 1.9 \text{ gm/m}l = 1900 \text{ kg/m}^3$

$\therefore \qquad \gamma_{sat} = 1900 \times 9.81 \times 10^{-3} \text{ kN/m}^3 = 18.639 \text{ kN/m}^3$

and $\qquad \gamma_{sub} = \gamma_{sat} - \gamma_w = 18.639 - 9.81 = 8.829 \text{ kN/m}^3$

$\therefore \qquad i_c = \dfrac{\gamma_{sub}}{\gamma_w} = \dfrac{8.829}{9.81} = 0.90$

Example 4.29 : The flow net sheet pile gave 5 flow channels and 8 equipotential channels. Determine the quantity of seepage per m length or sheet pile per day if coefficient of permeability k is 0.8×10^3 m/sec and head loss of 6 m. **[Dec. 13, 6 M]**

Solution:

$K = 0.8 \times 10^{-3} \text{ m/sec}$

$H_L = 6\text{m}$

$N_F = 5$

$N_D = 8$

$q = KH_L \dfrac{N_F}{N_D}$

$\qquad = 0.8 \times 10^{-3} \times 6 \times \dfrac{5}{8}$

$\qquad = 3 \times 10^{-3} \text{ m}^3/\text{sec/m}$

$q = 3 \times 10^{-3} \times 24 \times 60 \times 60 \text{ m}^3/\text{day/m}$

$\qquad = 259.2 \text{ m}^3/\text{day/m}$

Example 4.30 : In a falling head permeability test on a silty-clay sample, the following results were obtained : sample length 120 mm, sample diameter 80 mm, initial head = 1150 mm, final head = 420 mm, time for fall in head = 8 minutes, stand pipe diameter being 10 mm. Find the coefficient of permeability of the soil. **[May. 14, 4 M]**

Solution:

$L = 120 \text{ mm}$

$D = 80 \text{ mm}$

$h_1 = 1150 \text{ mm}$

$h_2 = 420 \text{ mm}$

$t = 8 \text{ min} = 8 \times 60 = 480 \text{ sec}$

$$d = 10 \text{ mm}$$

$$a = \frac{\pi}{4} \times d^2 = 78.13 \text{ mm}^2$$

$$A = \frac{\pi}{4} \times 80^2 = 5026.54 \text{ mm}^2$$

$$k = \frac{2.303 \text{ aL}}{At} \log_{10} \frac{h_1}{h_2}$$

$$= \frac{2.303 \times 78.53 \times 120}{5026.54 \times 480} \log_{10} \left(\frac{1150}{420}\right)$$

$$= 8.99 \times 10^{-3} \times 0.43 = 3.86 \times 10^{-3} \text{ mm/sec.}$$

Example 4.31 : In a falling head permeameter a soil sample with 75 mm in diameter and 55 mm in length was tested. At the commencement of the test, the initial head was 80 cm and after one hour, the head was 40 cm. Find the coefficient of permeability if the diameter of stand pipe is 1 cm. **[Dec.15, 6 M]**

Solution:

$$K = 2.303 \frac{aL}{At} \log_{10} \frac{h_1}{h_2}$$

$$a = \frac{p}{4} \times (10)^2 = 78.53 \text{ mm}^2$$

$$L = 55 \text{mm}$$

$$A = \frac{\pi}{4} \times (75)^2 = 4417.31 \text{ mm}^2$$

$$h_1 = 800 \text{ mm}$$
$$h_2 = 400 \text{ mm}$$
$$t = 60 \times 60 \text{ sec} = 3600 \text{ sec}$$

$$k = \frac{2.303 \times 78.53 \times 55}{4417.31 \times 3600} \log_{10} \left(\frac{800}{400}\right)$$

$$= 1.88 \times 10^{-4} \text{mm/sec.}$$

Example 4.32 : A permeameter of 80 mm diameter with a sample length of 300 mm has been used for constant head test. While conducting a constant head test the loss of head was 1150 mm for a length of 250 mm and the rate of flow was 2700 mm^3/sec. Find the coefficient of permeability in mm/sec.

If a falling head test was performed on the same sample at the same void ratio, find the time taken for head to fall from 900 to 450 mm. The diameter of stand pipe is 25 mm in the falling head test. **[May 16, 6 M]**

Solution: For constant head test :

$$a = \frac{\pi}{4} \times (80)^2 = 5026.54 \text{ mm}^2$$

$$h = 1150 \text{ mm}$$

For L

$$= 250 \text{ mm}$$

$$q = 2700 \text{ mm}^3/ \text{sec. i}$$

$$i = \frac{h}{L} = \frac{1150}{250} = 4.6$$

$$K = \frac{q}{iA} = \frac{2700}{4.6 \times 5026.54}$$

$$K = 0.116 \text{ mm/sec}$$

For falling Head Test

$$a = \frac{\pi}{4} \times (25)^2 = 490.81$$

$$L = 300 \text{ mm,}$$

$$h_1 = 900 \text{ mm}$$

$$h_2 = 450 \text{ mm,}$$

$$t = ?$$

$$K = 2.303 \frac{aL}{At} \log_{10}\left(\frac{h_1}{h_2}\right)$$

$$0.116 = \frac{2.303 \times 490.81 \times 300}{5026.54 \times t} \log_{10}\left(\frac{900}{450}\right)$$

$$t = 175.09 \text{ sec}$$

Example 4.33 : If W_L = 65%, W_P = 35%, natural water constant = 45%, determine flow index, liquidity index, consistency index, toughness index. Assume number of jerks for the determination of liquid limit by Casagrande's method, as 48 when water content was 32%.

[May 16, 6 M]

Solution :

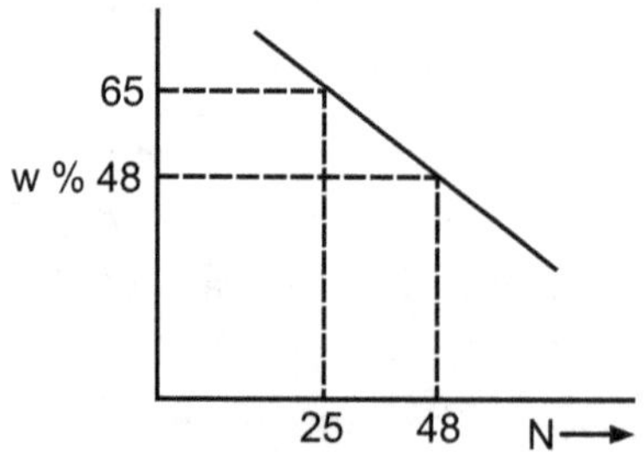

Fig. 2

$$I_f = \frac{0.65 - 0.32}{\log \dfrac{48}{25}} = \frac{0.33}{\log 1.92} = 1.165$$

$$I_p = W_l - W_p = 0.65 - 0.35 = 0.3$$

$$\text{Liquidity index} = \frac{w - W_p}{I_p} = \frac{45 - 35}{30} = \frac{1}{3}$$

$$I_c = \text{Consistency index} = 1 - \frac{1}{3} = \frac{2}{3}$$

$$\text{Toughness index} = \frac{I_p}{I_f} = \frac{0.3}{I_f} = \frac{0.3}{1.165} = 0.26$$

Example 4.34 : What do you mean by sand boiling? A masonry dam has previous sand as foundation. Determine the maximum upward gradient for factor of safety = 4 against sand boiling. Assume porosity, $\eta = 45\%$, G = 2.65. **[Nov. 16, 6 M]**

Solution :

$$i_{max} = 0.3 \, i_c = 0.3 \left(\frac{G - 1}{1 + e}\right) \frac{1}{r_w}$$

$$= 0.3 \left(\frac{2.65 - 1}{1 + 0.45}\right) \times \frac{1}{1} = 0.341$$

SUMMARY

1. The water present in the void, of soil mass is called soil water. It has two types:

    (a) Held water   (b) Free water.

2. Soil suction is negative pressure of the water in the soil mass above the water table.

3. Permeability is defined as property of porous materials which permits the passage of water through it's interconnecting voids.

4. The rate of flow per unit time is proportional to the hydraulic gradient

    i.e. $V \propto i$ or $V = ki$

    Where, K = Coefficient of permeability

    i = Hydraulic gradient

    V = velocity of flow

5. When flow take place in an upward direction the effective pressure gets reduced due to seepage pressure also acts in upward direction.

6. Field determination carried away by

    (a) Pumping out test   (b) Pumping in test.

7. **Formula :**

    (i) Confined Aquifer : $A = 2\pi \, rz = $ Area of flow

    (ii) $$\int \frac{dr}{r} = \frac{2\pi \, kz \int dh}{Q}$$

    (iii) $$k = \frac{2.3 \, Q \cdot \log_{10} \frac{r_2}{r_1}}{2\pi z \, (h_2 - h_1)}$$

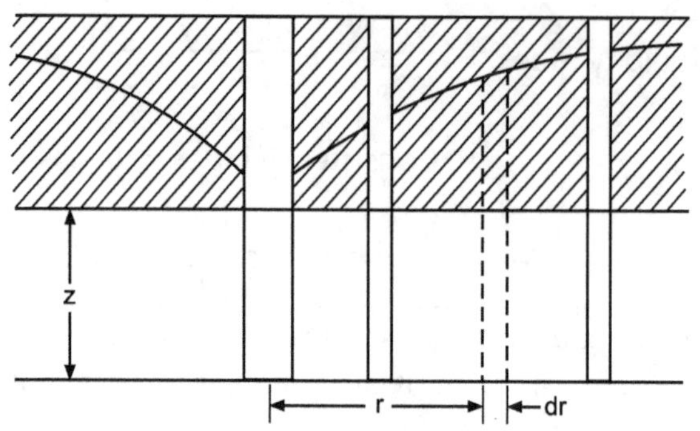

Fig. 4.26

(iv)
$$Q = ki \cdot A$$

(v)
$$k = \frac{2.3\, a \cdot L}{A}\, \log_{10} \frac{h_1}{h_2}$$

(vi)
$$k = \frac{QL}{h \cdot A}$$

(vii)
$$Q = \left\{ C_k\, D_{10}^2 \cdot \frac{\gamma_w}{\mu} \cdot \frac{e^3}{1+e} \right\} i \cdot A$$

(viii)
$$Q = k_i \cdot A = k \cdot \frac{dh}{dr} \cdot 2\pi\, rh$$

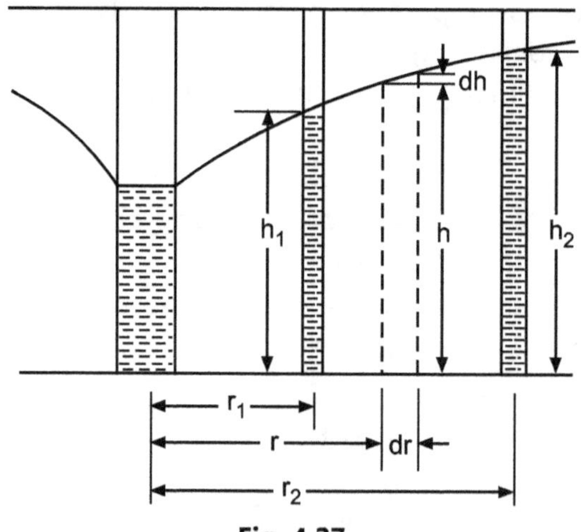

Fig. 4.27

(ix)
$$\frac{dr}{r} = \frac{2\pi\, Kh\, dh}{Q}$$

(x)
$$k = \frac{Q \log_e \dfrac{r_2}{r_1}}{\pi \left(h_2^2 - h_1^2 \right)} = \frac{2.3\, Q \log_{10} \dfrac{r_2}{r_1}}{\pi \left(h_2^2 - h_1^2 \right)}$$

(xi) $\quad \sigma$ = Effective pressure = $\sigma - u = \gamma_{sat} \cdot h - \gamma_{wh}$

$$= \left(\frac{G + e}{1 + e}\right) \gamma_{wh} - \gamma_{wh} = \left(\frac{G - 1}{1 + e}\right) \gamma_{wh}$$

(xii) $\quad i_c$ = Critical hydraulic gradient = $\dfrac{h}{L} = \left(\dfrac{G - 1}{1 + e}\right) = \dfrac{\gamma_{sat}}{\gamma_w}$

(xiii) $\quad h_c$ = Capillary rise in soil = $\dfrac{c}{eD_{10}}$

EXERCISE

1. Explain capillary rise in soils.
2. Define the following terms.
   - (a) Soil suction
   - (b) Bulking of sand
   - (c) Slaking of clay
   - (d) Shrinkage
   - (e) Swelling
   - (f) Permeability
3. What is the Darcy's law? State validity of law.
4. What are the methods of determination of coefficient of permeability? Explain any one in detail.
5. Define seepage velocity and discharge velocity.
6. Write a note on factors affecting the permeability.
7. State assumptions in laplace equation.
8. Describe in detail, used of flow net.
9. Write a short note on piping?
10. Define the following terms.
    - (a) Aquifer
    - (b) Acquicludes and aquifuge
    - (c) Storage coefficient
    - (d) Coefficient of permeability and transmissibility.
11. Explain
    - (i) Pumping out test
    - (ii) Pumping in test.
12. A constant head permeability test was carried out on a cylindrical sample of sand 12 cm diameter and 16 cm height. 150 cm^3 of water was collected in 1.50 minutes under a head to 25 cm. Calculate the coefficient of permeability in m/year and the velocity of flow in m/sec.

13. If soil P has permeability of 5×10^{-3} cm/sec, and the heat lost in soil Q is 8 times the head lost in soil P.

    (a) What is permeability of flow per hour ?

    (b) What is the quantity of flow per hour ?

14. A flownet for an earth dam on impervious foundation consists of 4 flow channels and 15 equipotential drops. The full reservoir level is 15 m above the downstream horizontal filter. Given that horizontal permeability is 9×10^{-6} m/s and vertical permeability is 1×10^{-6} m/s, calculate the quantity of seepage through the dam.

15. A 20 mm diameter well fully penetrates a confined aquifer of 30 m depth. For a pump–age of 35 litres/second the steady drawdowns at 100 m and 300 m distances from the well are observed as 3.2 m and 2.5 m respectively. Estimate the coefficient of permeability in m/day and transmissibility of the aquifer in m^2 per day. Estimate also the drawdown at the well.

SOLVED UNIVERSITY QUESTIONS AND NUMERICALS

December 2013

1. The flow net sheet pile gave 5 flow channels and 8 equipotential channels. Determine the quantity of seepage per m length or sheet pile per day if coefficient of permeability k is 0.8×10^3 m/sec and head loss of 6 m.   **[6]**

   [**Ans.:** Refer Example 4. 29]

2. Explain quick sand phenomenon with a nest sketch and state the equation of critical hydraulic gradient.   **[6]**

   [**Ans.:** Refer Article 4. 18]

May 2014

1. State Darcy's Law. Discuss the validity of Darcy's Law for flow of water through soils.   **[4]**

   [**Ans.:** Refer Articles 4.12, 4.13]

2. With help of neat sketch explain the quick sand phenomenon.   **[4]**

   [**Ans.:** Refer Article 4.18]

3. In a falling head permeability test on a silty-clay sample, the following results were obtained : sample length 120 mm, sample diameter 80 mm, initial head = 1150 mm, final head = 420 mm, time for fall in head = 8 minutes, stand pipe diameter being 10 mm. Find the coefficient of permeability of the soil.   **[4]**

   [**Ans.:** Refer Example 4.30]

December 2014

1. With neat sketch explain the procedure of construction of flownet for seepage through earthen dam. **[6]**

   [**Ans.:** Refer Article 4.22.2]

May 2015

1. State the applications of flownet and explain how seepage through a dam can be determined using flow net. (State the equation and terms involved in it). **[6]**

   [**Ans.:** Refer Articles 4.24]

1. Explain with diagram a method for determining coefficient of permeability 'K' for clayey soils in the laboratory. **[6]**

   [**Ans.:** Refer Article 4.14 (a)]

November 2015

1. In a falling head permeameter a soil sample with 75 mm in diameter and 55 mm in length was tested. At the commencement of the test, the initial head was 80 cm and after one hour, the head was 40 cm. Find the coefficient of permeability if the diameter of stand pipe is 1 cm. **[6]**

   [**Ans.:** Refer Example 4.31]

2. Discuss the factors that influence permeability of soils with relation. **[6]**

   [**Ans.:** Refer Articles 4.16]

May 2016

1. A permeameter of 80 mm diameter with a sample length of 300 mm has been used for constant head test. While conducting a constant head test the loss of head was 1150 mm for a length of 250 mm and the rate of flow was 2700 mm^3/sec. Find the coefficient of permeability in mm/sec.

   [**Ans.:** Refer Example 4.32]

2. If a falling head test was performed on the same sample at the same void ratio, find the time taken for head to fall from 900 to 450 mm. The diameter of stand pipe is 25 mm in the falling head test. **[6]**

   [**Ans.:** Refer Example 4.22]

3. If W_L = 65%, W_P = 35%, natural water constant = 45%, determine flow index, liquidity index, consistency index, toughness index. Assume number of jerks for the determination of liquid limit by Casagrande's method, as 48 when water content was 32%. **[6]**

   [**Ans.:** Refer Example 4.33]

November 2016

1. What do you mean by sand boiling? A masonry dam has previous sand as foundation. Determine the maximum upward gradient for factor of safety = 4 against sand boiling. Assume porosity, η = 45%, G = 2.65. **[6]**

   [**Ans.:** Refer Article 4.8 and Example 4.34]

2. Explain the variable head permeameter experiment for determination of coefficient of permeability. **[6]**

   [**Ans.:** Refer Article 4.14 (a) (2)]

May 2017

1. Explain in brief six factors affecting permeability of soils. **[6]**

   [**Ans.:** Refer Article 4.16)]

2. State Darcy's law. Define coefficient of permeability and derive equation for coefficient of permeability used in constant head method. **[6]**

   [**Ans.:** Refer Article 4.13, 4.14]

Chapter 5
COMPACTION

5.1 COMPACTION – DEFINITION [May 14]

Compaction is a process of stabilizing loose soil by densification, using either static or dynamic effort. The process involves permanent reduction in the volume of air voids, at constant water content. Compaction is the most common and cheapest method of soil improvement. It generally increases the shear strength of the soil and hence the stability and bearing capacity.

5.2 MECHANICS OF COMPACTION

When a network of soil particles is subjected to an external effort, the particles slide over one another and rearrange to occupy more stable positions, resulting in a denser packing. The process basically involves the following three mechanics Fig. 5.1.

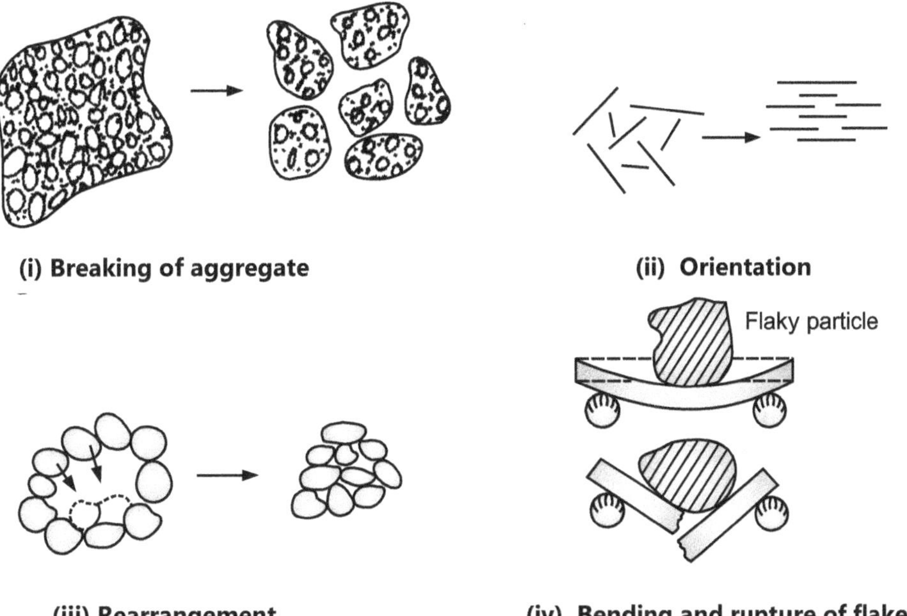

Fig. 5.1 : Mechanics of compaction

- Breaking or crushing of large aggregates into smaller ones.
- Dislocation and rearrangement of particles causing the structure to collapse or reorientation of flaky particles.

- Bending and rupture to flaky particles.

A combination of these mechanisms under an external effort leads to volume reduction which is due to one or more of the following :

- Compression of air.

- Expulsion of air.

- Solution of air in soil water.

There is no removal of water from the soil.

Compaction of Sand :

The compaction characteristics of cohesionless and freely draining sands are somewhat different from those of cohesive soils.

A typical pattern of the moisture-density relationship for a cohesionless, freely-draining sand from a laboratory test will be somewhat as shown in Fig. 5.2.

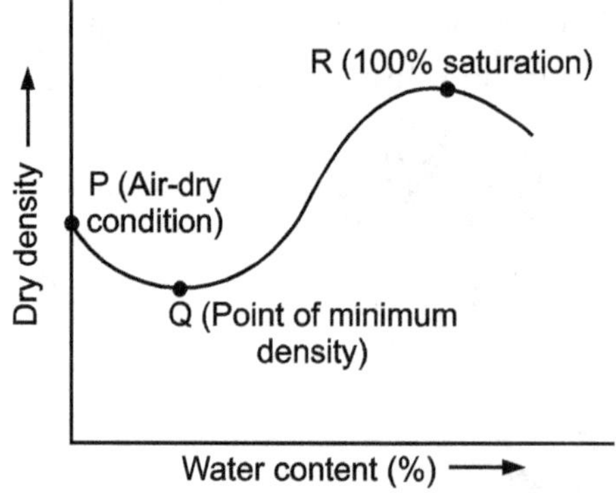

Fig. 5.2 : Typical moisture - density relationship for sand

Small moisture films around the grains tend to keep them apart and can decrease the density upto a certain water content. The point Q on the curve indicates the minimum density. Later on, the apparent cohesion gets reduced as the water content increases and is destroyed ultimately at 100% saturation of sand. Thus, the point R on the curve indicates maximum density. Thereafter, once again, the density decreases with increase in water content. Increase of compactive effort has much less effect in the case of cohesionless soils than on cohesive soils. Vibration is considered to be the best method suitable for densifying cohesionless soils, which are either fully dry or fully saturated. This is because the stresses at the soil water menisci tend to prevent full densification. Also, relative density or density index is invariably used to indicate relative compaction or densification of sand.

5.3 DIFFERENCE BETWEEN COMPACTION AND CONSOLIDATION

[May 14]

Compaction is an entirely different process than consolidation, even though both the processes cause a reduction in the volume. In compaction some dynamic load is applied for a small interval of time and compaction is achieved by the expulsion of air from the soil mass. In consolidation, steady load is applied for a long time and in the process water is expelled from the saturated soil (Fig. 5.3).

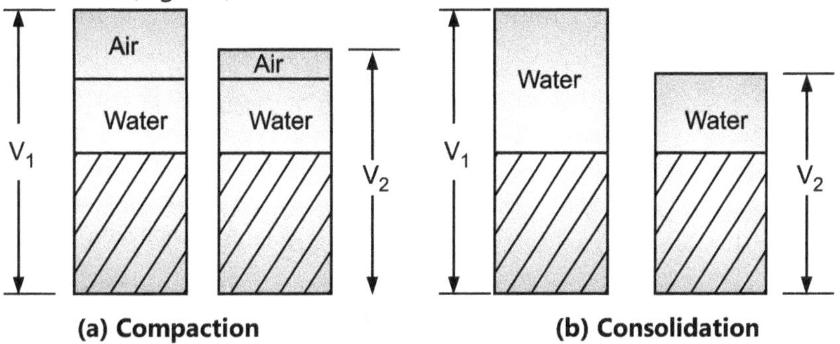

Fig. 5.3

The difference between consolidation and compaction is tabulated below :

		Compaction	**Consolidation**
1.	Air	Air is expelled .	No air is present.
2.	Water	Water is not expelled.	Water is expelled.
3.	Load and Time	Dynamic load is applied. It is applied for a short duration. Load application is by artificial or human agency.	Static load is applied. It is required to be applied for a long time to attain 100% consolidation. Load application can be by natural or artificial agencies.
4.	Saturation	Soil is partially saturated.	Soil is fully saturated.
5.	Soil type	Applies to cohesive and cohesionless soils.	Applies to cohesive soils only.

5.4 FACTORS AFFECTING COMPACTION

[May 14]

1. Water Content of Soil : At low water content, the soil is stiff and offers more resistance to compaction. As the water content is increased, the soil particles get lubricated. The soil mass becomes more workable and the particles have closer packing. The dry density of the soil increases with an increase in the water content till the optimum water content is reached. At that stage, the air voids attain approximately a constant volume. With further increase in water content, the air voids do not decrease, but the total voids (air plus water) increase and the dry density decreases. Thus, the higher dry density is achieved upto an optimum water content by forcing air out from the soil voids. After the optimum water content is reached, it becomes more difficult to force air out and to further reduce the air voids.

Soils compacted at a water content less than the optimum water content generally have a flocculated structure, regardless of the method of compaction. Soils compacted at a water content more than the optimum water content usually have a dispersed structure if the compaction induces large shear strains and a flocculated structure if the shear strains are relatively small.

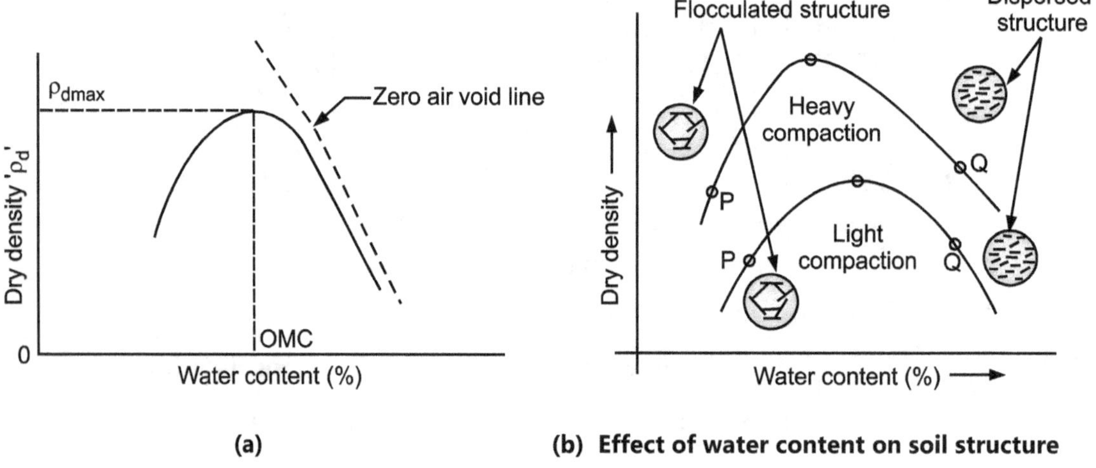

(a)   **(b) Effect of water content on soil structure**

Fig. 5.4

In [Fig. 5.4 (b)] at point P which is on the dry side of the optimum water content, the water content is so low that the attractive forces are more predominant than the repulsive forces. This results in a flocculated structure. As the water content is increased beyond the optimum value, the repulsive forces increase and the particles get oriented into a dispersed structure. If the compactive effort is increased, there is a corresponding increase in the orientation of the particles and higher dry densities are obtained, as shown by the upper curve.

2. Compactive Effort : With increase in the compactive effort, dry density of soil increases and optimum moisture content decreases.

However, it may be mentioned that, maximum dry density does not go on increasing, with increase in the compaction effort. Finally a stage is reached, beyond which there is no further increase in dry density, with an increase in the compaction effort.

3. Type of Soil : The dry density achieved depends upon the type of soil. The maximum dry density and the optimum content for different soils are shown in Fig. 5.5. In general, coarse-grained soils can be compacted to higher dry density than fine grained soils. With the addition of even a small quantity of fines to a coarse-grained soil, the soil attains a much higher dry-density for the same compactive effort. However, if the quantity of fines is increased to a value more than that required to fill the voids of the coarse-grained soils, the maximum dry density decreases. A well graded sand attains a much higher dry density than a poorly graded soil.

Cohesive soils have higher air voids. These soils attain a relatively lower maximum dry density as compared with the cohesionless soils. Such soils require more water than cohesionless soils, and therefore, the optimum water content is high. Heavy clays of very high plasticity have very low dry density and a very high optimum water content.

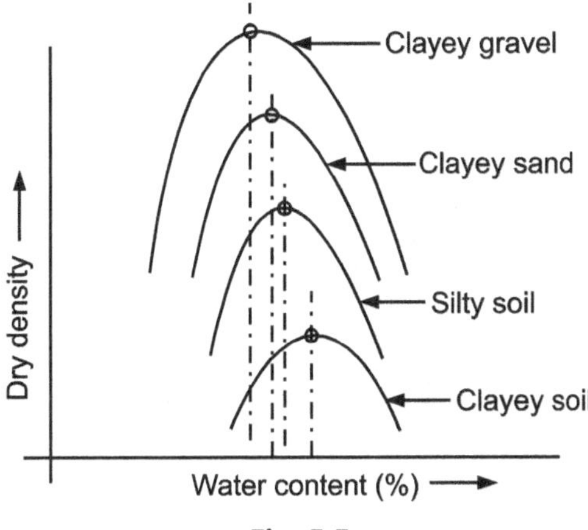

Fig. 5.5

5.5 COMPACTION TESTS (LABORATORY TEST)　　[Nov. 15, May 15]

The laboratory tests that are normally used for determining the optimum moisture content and maximum dry density of a given soil are :

5.5.1 Standard Proctor Compaction Test　　　　　　　(Nov. 15)

I.S. light compaction test specified by Indian Standards is equivalent to Standard Proctor test. This test was first devised by R.R. Proctor. It uses a standard cylindrical mould, 945×10^{-6} m³ in volume $\left(\dfrac{1}{30}\text{ cft}\right)$ and a drop hammer weighing 2.5 kg (5.5 lb), with a drop of 305 mm (12″) (Fig. 5.6). About 3 kg soil, passing 4.75 mm sieve is mixed with water and compacted in the mould in three layers, each layer being given 25 blows of the drop hammer, imparting an effort equivalent to 595 kJ/m³.

Dry density and water content are determined for several trials using more and more water content to obtain the moisture-density curve from which MDD (Maximum Dry Density) and OMC (Optimum Moisture Content) are found out.

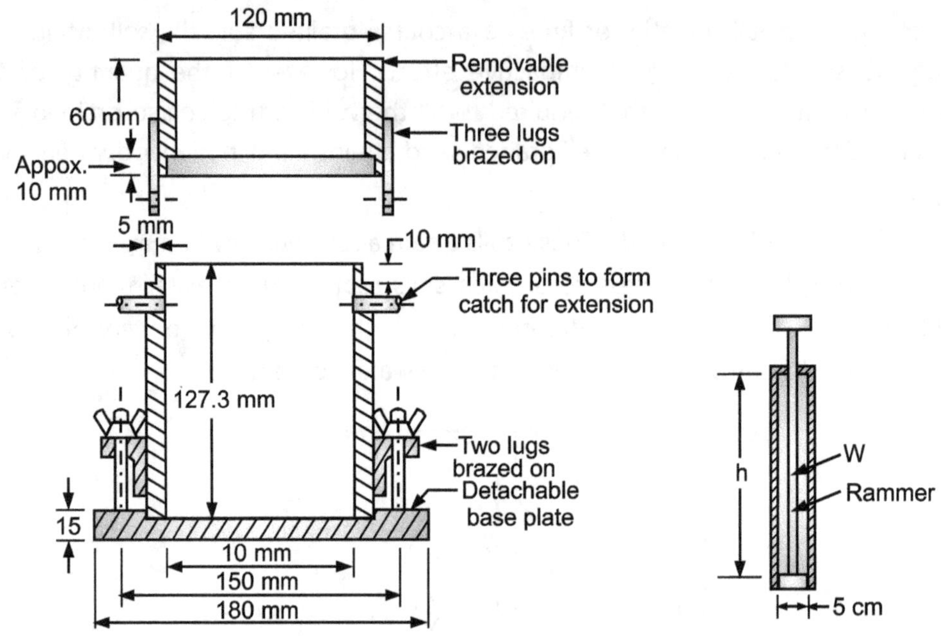

(a) Mould for compaction　　　　**(b) Compaction apparatus**

(Compaction	H (mm)	W (kg)
Light	310 mm	2.6
Heavy	450 mm	4.89

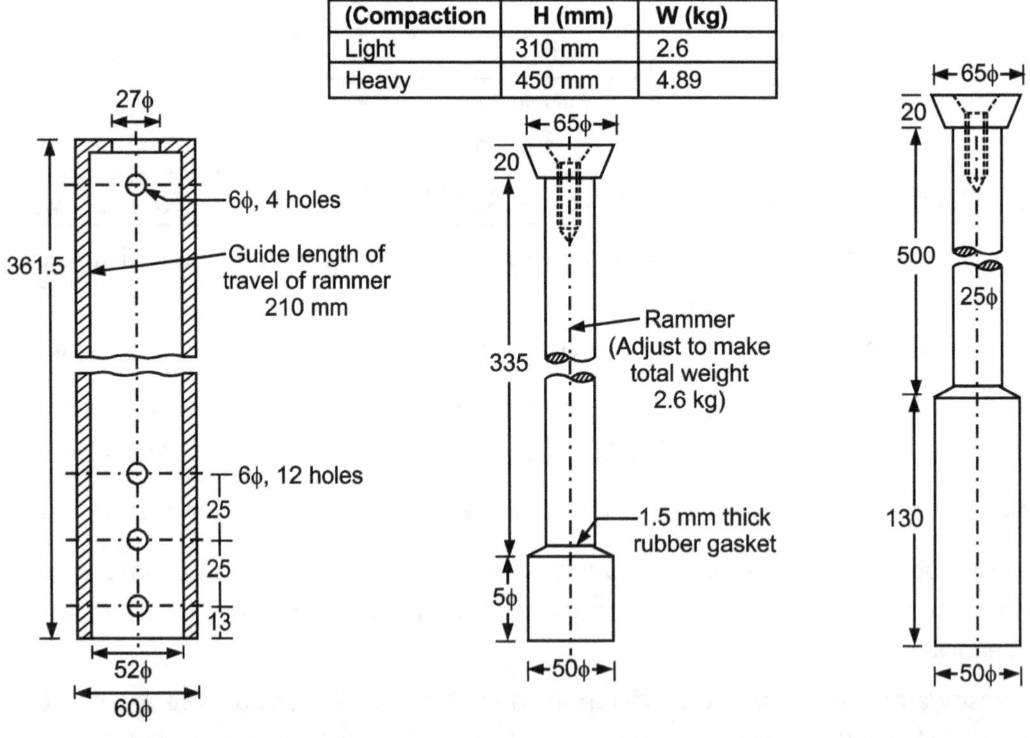

(c) For light compaction　　　　**(d) For heavy compaction**

Fig. 5.6 : Proctor compaction test equipments

5.5.2 Heavy Compaction Test or Modified Proctor Test

This test uses a mould of 1000 ml capacity. The soil is compacted in five layers each taking a 25 blows of a drop hammer dropping through a height of 450 mm. The drop hammer has face diameter of 50 mm and a total mass of 4.89 kg.

Standard Proctor test has been used for field compaction control of road and air field pavements, embankments and fills etc. Higher compaction is needed for heavier transport and military aircrafts. The modified proctor test was developed to give a higher standard of compaction. Results of a lab compaction test are tabulated in the observation table (Table 5.1).

The compactive energy delivered is of the order of 2700 kJ/m³, which is about 4.5 times that of Standard Proctor Test.

5.5.3 Moisture Content – Dry Density Relationship
(Standard Proctor Compaction Test)   (Nov. 16, May 15)

Aim : To determine the relation between the moisture content and the dry density of soil.

Procedure :

- Take about 25 kg of air-dried soil passed through 50 mm IS sieve. Sieve the soil through 20 mm and 4.75 mm sieve and find the fractions passing and retained in each sieve. Reject the fraction retained on 20 mm sieve.

- From the soil passing 20 mm IS sieve, find the ratio of soil fraction retained on 4.75 mm IS sieve to the soil fraction passing 4.75 mm sieve.

- If the fraction retained on 4.75 mm IS sieve is more than 20%, maintain the ratio of such material to the material passing 4.75 mm IS sieve. Take about 20 kg of the material in the calculated proportion, as mentioned above. If the fraction retained on 4.75 mm IS sieve is less than 20% then directly take about 20 kg of soil passing 20 mm IS sieve.

- Add enough water to bring its moisture content to about 7% (for sandy soils) or 10% (for clayey soils) less than the estimated optimum moisture content. Keep the processed soil in an air-tight container for about 18 hours for moisture equilibrium.

- Clean, dry and measure the dimensions of the empty mould. Weigh the empty mould to the nearest one gram (M_m). Fit in the base plate and the extension collar.

- Divide the processed soil - water mix into eight equal parts.

- Take one part $\left(\text{about } 2\frac{1}{2}\,\text{kg}\right)$ of the processed soil and compact it into the mould in three equal layers, each layer being given 25 blows from the rammer, weighing 2.6 kg, dropping from a height of 310 mm. Allow the blow to be distributed uniformly in each layer and score each layer with a spatula before putting the soil for the successive layer.

- Remove the collar and carefully level off the top of the mould by means of a straight edge. Weigh the mould.

- Eject the soil from the mould, cut at the middle and take representative samples for water content determination.
- Repeat steps 7 to 9 for 5 to 6 samples, using a fresh part of the soil specimen each time and adding a higher water content than the proceeding specimen, so that at least two readings each below and above the optimum moisture content are available.

5.5.4 Correction for Oversize Fraction

Correction for oversize fraction may be applied as follows :

If the material retained on 20 mm IS Sieve (or 4.75 mm IS Sieve) has been excluded from the test, a correction has to be applied for getting the values of the maximum dry density and optimum moisture content for the entire soil. For this purpose, the specific gravity of the portion retained and passing the 20 mm IS Sieve or the 4.75 mm IS Sieve, as the case may be, should be determined separately.

$$\text{Corrected maximum dry density } = \frac{\rho_s \, \rho_{d_{max}}}{n_1 \, \rho_{d_{max}} + n_2 \, \rho_s}$$

$$\text{Corrected optimum moisture content} = n_1 \, A_o + n_2 \, W_o$$

where ρ_s = unit mass of oversize gravel particles in g/cm^3 = $G \cdot \gamma_w$ (where G is the specific gravity of gravel particles);

$\rho_{d_{max}}$ = maximum dry density obtained in the test in g/cm^3;

n_1 = fraction by mass of the oversize particles in the total soil expressed as ratio;

n_2 = fraction by mass of the portion passing the 20 mm IS Sieve (or 4.75 mm IS Sieve) expressed as a ratio of the total soil;

A_o = water absorption capacity of oversize material, if any, expressed as percentage of water absorbed, and

W_o = optimum moisture content obtained in the test.

This formula is based on the assumption that the volume of a compacted portion passing a 20 mm sieve (or a 4.75 mm sieve) is sufficient to fill the voids between the oversize particles.

Computations :

Compute the volume, (V_m) of the mould from the height and diameter of the mould. The mass of wet soil in the mould is M,

$$\text{Bulk density,} \qquad \rho \text{ g/cc} = \left(\frac{M}{V_m}\right)$$

$$\text{Dry density,} \qquad \rho_d \text{ g/cc} = \left(\frac{\rho}{1 + w/100}\right)$$

Observation Table 5.1 : (Laboratory Compaction Test)

1. **Sample type**
2. **Mass of empty mould (M_m)**
3. **Volume of mould (V_m)**
4. **Test type**

Trial No.	Mass of mould with soil (kg)	Mass of soil (M) (kg)	Bulk density kg/m³ $\rho = \dfrac{M}{V}$	Water content (w)%	Dry density kg/m³ $\rho_d = \dfrac{\rho}{1 + w}$	MDD	OMC
1.							
2.							
3.							
4.							
5.							

5.5.5 Comparison Between Light Compaction and Heavy Compaction

Table 5.2 : Comparison between Light Compaction and Heavy Compaction

		Light Compaction	Heavy Compaction
1.	Size of the mould	Same mould for both tests (100 mm dia. × 127 mm height)	
2.	Weight of rammer	2.6 kg	4.89 kg
3.	Height of fall of rammer	310 mm	450 mm
4.	No. of layers	3	5
5.	No. of blows per layer	25	25
6.	Compaction energy	60.45 kg m per litre	272.6 kg m per litre

5.5.6 Zero Air Voids or Saturation Curve   (Nov. 16)

A line which shows the water content dry density relation for the compacted soil containing a constant percentage of air voids is known as *air void line* and can be obtained as under :

$$\rho_d = \frac{G \cdot \rho_w (1 - n_a)}{1 + w \cdot G}$$

where,

n_a = % air voids

w = water content of the soil

ρ_d = dry density corresponding to 'w'

When, $n_a = 0$

$$\boxed{\rho_d = \frac{G \cdot \rho_w}{1 + wG}}$$ ... (5.1)

This is the equation of zero air void line or saturation line.

Alternatively, a line showing the relation between water content and dry density for a constant degree of saturation S_r is obtained from :

$$\rho_d = \frac{G \cdot \rho_w}{1 + e} = \frac{G\rho_w}{1 + \dfrac{wG}{S_r}} \quad (S_r \cdot e = w.G.)$$ ... (5.2)

For $S_r = 100\%$, equation (5.2) reduces to equation 5.1.

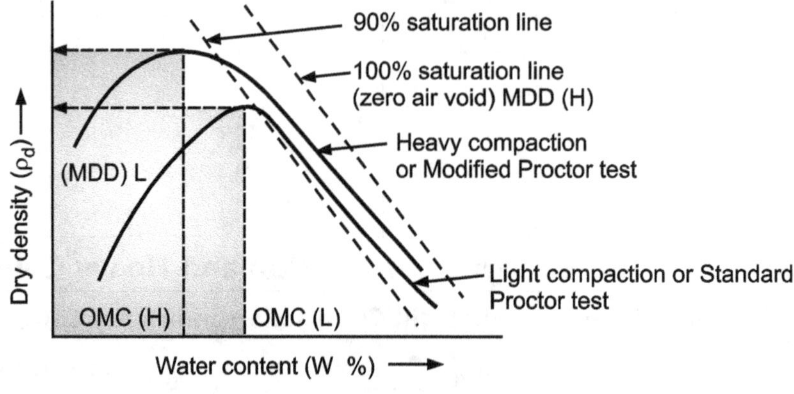

Fig. 5.7

5.5.7 Optimum Moisture Content (OMC)

It is found that a given soil can be compacted to a maximum degree only at a particular moisture content, for a given compactive effort. This water content at which maximum dry density (MDD) is achieved is known as the *optimum moisture content*. It is a characteristic of the finer fraction of the soil. A plot showing the relation of water content with dry density is known as *moisture density curve* Fig. 5.7 which shows maximum dry density at the OMC.

5.6 EFFECT OF COMPACTION ON SOIL PROPERTIES

The main aim of compacting a soil is to improve some desirable properties of the soil, such as reduction of compressibility, water absorption and permeability, increase in soil strength, bearing capacity etc. and change in swelling and shrinkage characteristics. However, the effect of compaction on soil properties very much depends on the structure attained by the soil during compaction.

1. **Change in Structure of Soil :** The structure of a soil during compaction depends upon :
- Type of soil,
- Moulding water content and
- Type and amount of compaction.

For the purposes of discussion, let us divide the soils into three types :

- Coarse grained soils with little or no fines,

- Composite soils, and

- Purely cohesive soils (i.e. clays).

The soils of the first type (i.e. coarse grained soils), maintain a single grained structure at any possible voids ratio or water content. However, the structure of composite soils, after being compacted depend upon the relative proportion of coarse particles and fines and their structure can either be *coarse grained skeleton structure or cohesive matrix structure.*

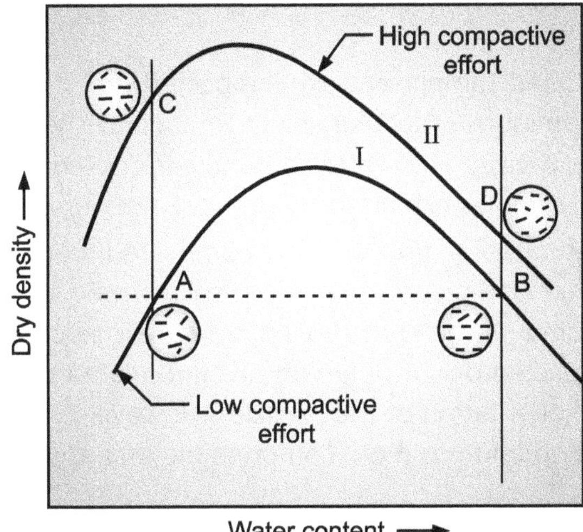

Fig. 5.8 : Effects of compaction on structure of clay (after Lambe, 1958)

In contrast to these, the structure of compacted clay is complicated. At the same compactive effort, the soil structure becomes increasingly oriented (i.e. dispersed with increasing water content. When compacted dry of optimum, the structure of clay is always *flocculated.* Fig. 5.8 shows two compaction curves for a clay - one at lower compactive effort and other at higher compactive effort. At water content higher than optimum, the soil at points B and D of the two curves is more oriented than at point A. However, the structure is more oriented at C than at A.

2. **Permeability :** The following points are noteworthy :

- As the dry density increases due to compaction, the voids go on reducing and hence the permeability goes on decreasing.

- For the same density, fine grained samples compacted dry of optimum are more permeable than those compacted wet of optimum. This is so because these soils have flocculated structure when compacted dry of optimum, and have dispersed structure (i.e. parallel orientation) when compacted wet of optimum.

- For a given voids ratio, greater the size of the individual pores, greater is the permeability.

- As the compactive effort is increased, the permeability of soil decreases because of the increased dry density and better orientation of particles.

3. Shrinkage : For the same density, soil sample compacted dry of optimum shrink appreciably less than the sample compacted wet of optimum. This is so because the soil particles having dispersed structure have nearly parallel orientation and can pack more efficiently.

4. Swelling : A clayey soil sample compacted dry of optimum water content has high water deficiency and more random orientation and hence exert greater swelling pressure and swell to higher water content than the sample of the same density obtained from wet side compaction.

5. Pore pressure : Saturated sample of clay, compacted dry of optimum, tend to develop substantially lower pore pressure at low strains in undrained shear test than the sample of the same soil of the same density and water content, compacted wet of optimum. However, at higher strains, both the samples exhibit the same pore pressure.

6. Compressibility : Saturated sample of clay, compacted wet side of optimum is more compressible than another sample of the same soil, having the same voids ratio, but compacted dry of the optimum, when the applied pressure is in low pressure range. This is so because the sample compacted dry of optimum has flocculated structure and requires extra pressure to cause parallel orientation of the particles. However, in the high pressure range, a sample compacted dry of optimum is more compressible than the one compacted wet of the optimum.

7. Stress-strain Characteristics : For a given soil, a sample compacted dry side of optimum has a steeper stress-strain curve and hence has a higher modulus of elasticity, than the one which is compacted wet of optimum (Fig. 5.9) at the same density. Soil compacted wet of optimum have *brittle failure* while soil compacted wet of optimum, and having dispersed structure, continue to increase in strength even at higher strains.

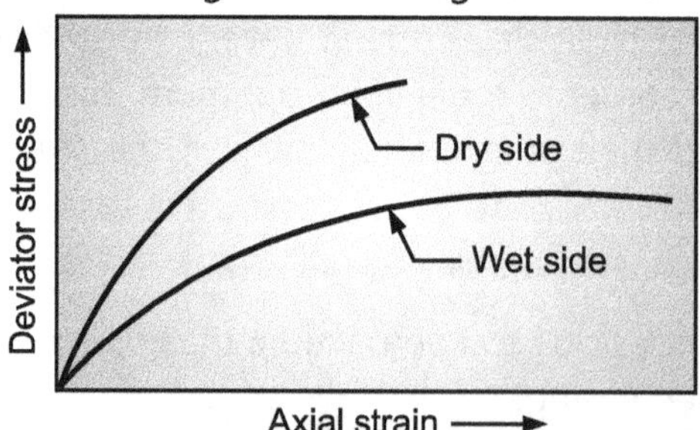

Fig. 5.9 : Stress - strain curves

8. Shear Strength : The shear strength of compacted clays depend upon (i) dry density, (ii) moulding water content, (iii) soil structure, (iv) method of compaction, (v) strain used to define strength, (vi) drainage condition and (vii) type of soil.

In general, at low strains, strength of cohesive soils compacted dry of optimum is higher than those compacted wet of optimum. Fig. 5.10 shows the failure envelope of two samples of the same soil, one compacted dry of optimum and the other compacted wet of the optimum, but both compacted at the same density.

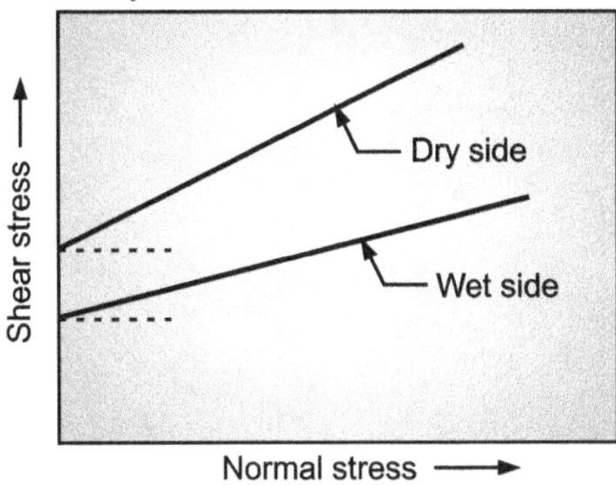

Fig. 5.10 : Failure envelopes

However, at higher strains, the flocculated structure of the same compacted on the dry side is broken, giving rise to ultimate strength for both the samples. The manner of compaction also influences the strength of the soil sample compacted wet of optimum. It is interesting to note that the clay cores in earth dams are usually compacted wet of optimum to tolerate large settlements without cracking.

5.7 FIELD COMPACTION [Dec. 14]

5.7.1 Placement Water Content

The water content used in the field compaction is called the placement water content which may be equal to, lower than or higher than the optimum water content. For a given soil, the laboratory optimum water content and the field optimum water content may differ, depending upon the type of the compaction equipment used and the type of structure to be constructed.

5.7.2 Field Compaction Control

Control of quality of field compaction is necessary to ensure that engineering properties assumed in the design of soil structures are actually accomplished uniformly during construction. Quality control is exercised by controlling the thickness of the compacted layer, dry density and water content, besides involving choice of quarry material, thickness of lifts, number of passes, and choice of rollers (heavy or light; kneading or vibratory). Specifications state that the soil should be compacted to 95% of the maximum dry density, at a water content ± 2% of OMC as obtained in a standard compaction test. Relative compaction (RC) is yet another controlling factor that may be specified. *Relative compaction is the ratio of the field dry density to the laboratory maximum dry density.* The RC values should range from 90 to 105%.

Compaction control is achieved by measuring the dry unit weight and the water content of the soil compacted in the field.

1. Dry Unit Weight : The dry unit weight is measured commonly by using the core-cutter method and sand replacement method.

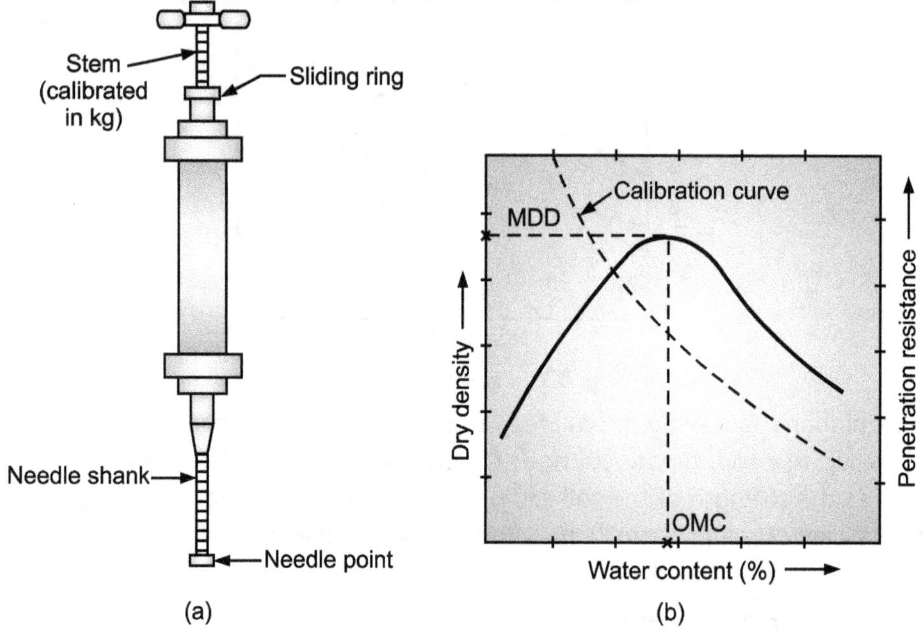

Fig. 5.11 : Field compaction control by proctor needle

2. Water Content :

(a) Oven Drying Method : The oven drying method of determination of water content takes 24 hours. Hence it is not suitable for the field. In the field, the water content is determined by using the sand bath method, alcohol method, calcium carbide method or nuclear method.

(b) Proctor Needle Method : The water content can also be determined directly using a Proctor needle. The Proctor needle consists of a rod attached to a spring loaded plunger [Fig. 5.11 (a)]. The stem of the plunger is marked to read the resistance in kg. The equipment is provided with a series of needle points of different cross-sectional areas (0.25, 0.50, 1.0 and 2.5 cm²). For cohesive soils, needle points of larger cross-sectional areas are required and for cohesionless soil, those of smaller cross-sectional areas are used.

To use the needle in the field, a calibration curve [Fig. 5.11 (b)] is plotted in the laboratory between the penetration resistance as the ordinate and the water content as the abscissa. The laboratory penetration resistance is measured by inserting the Proctor needle in the compacted soil in the Proctor mould. The penetration resistance corresponding to various water contents are thus noted at the end of each Proctor compaction, and a calibration curve is plotted.

This may be used to determine the placement water content. The penetration resistance of the compacted soil in the field is determined with the Proctor's needle and its water content is read from the calibration curve.

5.7.3 Compacting Equipments

Different types of compacting equipments have been used in the earth construction. The equipment may be broadly classified as :

- Pressure type : Smooth wheel rollers, pneumatic rollers.
- Kneading type : Sheep's foot roller, tamping roller.
- Impact type : Rammers and tampers, drop weight.
- Vibration type : Vibratory rollers, vibrating plates.

The choice of equipment depends on the nature of the job, the type of soil, and economy. Vibratory and pressure type equipment suits non-cohesive soils, while kneading type is best suited for cohesive soils.

Rollers : Field compaction by rollers is the most effective method. Rollers are hollow drums, subsequently filled by ballast or kentledge to make them heavy. A vibrator may also be attached on the inside. The rollers pass on the layers to be compacted and densify the soil mainly by the pressure exerted due to their weight. Rollers are of four types :

(i) Smooth Wheel or Iron Tyred Rollers : Smooth wheel rollers are self-propelled and give 100 p.c. coverage below the wheels, with a contact pressure of about 400 kN/m^2. These are particularly suitable for cohesionless soils and are commonly used in road construction. The depth of compacted layer depends on the mass of the roller (5,000 - 15,000 kg) and ranges between 100 mm and 450 mm. Smooth wheel rollers are also used for the finishing operation. Pressure rolling may be combined with flooding and vibration in non-cohesive soils.

(ii) Pneumatic or Rubber Tyred Rollers : Pneumatic rollers are comparatively heavy (25,000 to 2,00,000 kg) and are towed type or propeller type. The tyre pressure ranges from 450 to 1000 kN/m^2. The rollers have a number of wheels, arranged on two axels, so as to give large coverage on a pass. The coverage is about 80 per cent. The rollers are suitable for both cohesive as well as non-cohesive soils. Kneading action is provided by wobbling wheels and tyre grips. The performance depends on the contact area, tyre pressure and number of wheels. Rubber tyred rollers are more popular because they are more economical and more efficient than smooth wheel rollers.

(iii) Sheep-Foot Rollers : Studs or projections known as sheeps-foot are mounted on the cylindrical periphery of the roller drum. Each foot has about 300 to 800 mm^2 area and projects about 200 mm. The tapered or clubfooted steel studs penetrate into the ground under high foot pressure. Large and hard clay lumps are crushed, mixed and compacted under a kneading action. Remoulding of the soil under the foot is caused by bearing capacity failure and causes densification. Several drums are arranged side by side or one following another and are towed together by pneumatic tyred tractors. Sheep-foot rollers are most suitable for cohesive soils but are also used for other soils (except clean sands and gravels). Light rollers have foot pressures of 400 to 2000 kN/m^2 and heavy type have pressures greater than 2000 kN/m^2. Rolling is continued till the roller *walks out* after six to eight passes. Sheep-foot rollers ensure good bond between successive compacted layers.

(iv) Tampers and Rammers : Tampers and rammers are impact type devices, used for field compaction in narrow restricted areas, such as corners of retaining walls and abutments, trenches etc. where the use of rolling equipment is impractical. *Tamper* is a heavy mass which is lifted in the air and dropped onto the ground surface repeatedly. Compaction is achieved by shearing action under the impact. A hand tamper consists of a block of iron, stone or wood weighing about 3 to 10 kg, falling through a drop of 100 to 250 mm. Pneumatic tampers are much faster. Jumping tampers and vibrating plates are similar tamping devices. Compaction wet of optimum yields good results. *Rammers* are pneumatic or internal combustion type devices weighing about 20 to 80 kg. Drop weights are heavy masses dropped through 2 or 3 m on the ground surface, at close spots, over a large area, to achieve compaction of the surface layer. Compaction dry of optimum yields good results.

(v) Vibratory Rollers : Light rollers are attached with vibratory or impact devices for more effective compaction of granular soils. A vibrator consists of two eccentric masses rotating at a speed of 1000 to 2000 rpm and producing repeated impulses. Vibratory rollers are available in both smooth wheel and rubber tyred models. Vibrations combined with weight of the roller break the soil aggregates, bring about collapse of the soil structures and at high acceleration and impact, rearrange particles in optimum packing positions. Layers from 300 to 450 mm thick can be compacted to 100 % of the standard proctor density, in one or two passes of the machine.

Compaction by Vibration : Non-cohesive soils are greatly influenced by vibrations. Light surface vibrator compacts loose sandy soils to a limited shallow depth of less than 0.5 m. With the use of a large number of passes, compaction upto 1.5 m depth may be achieved. The basic principle underlying vibratory compaction is the reduction of frictional resistance due to vibration, causing the particles to slip and occupy closer position. The compactive effort of a roller is amplified by two revolving excentric masses, within the roller drum.

Pile driving is an effective method of compacting non-cohesive soils to great depths. Controlled explosions are also useful in compacting loose cohesionless soils. Vibrations are most effective in sandy soils, when acceleration lies between 1 g and 2.5 g or when frequency is close to resonance but have little effect on cohesive soils. Large drum vibrators (about 15,000 kg) are very effective in compacting broken rock.

Suitability of Rollers : Iron tyred rollers crush the aggregate by shear weight and aid compaction. Pneumatic rollers have a two-fold advantage of crushing and kneading. Sheeps-foot roller provides kneading and mixing action which is particularly useful in cohesive soils. Highly intensive foot pressure is applied to the lift at varying depths, till the roller *walks out*. As such sheeps-foot roller gives a more uniform compaction than a rubber tyred roller. Vibratory rollers are most suitable in non-cohesive soils.

SOLVED EXAMPLES

Example 5.1 : A laboratory compaction test on a soil having specific gravity 2.7 gave a maximum dry density of 1830 kg/m³ at the moisture content of 17%. Find the degree of saturation, air content and percentage air voids at the maximum density.

Solution : We know,

$$\rho_d = \frac{G.\rho_w}{1 + \frac{G.w}{S_r}}$$

(i) Degree of saturation

$$(S_r) = \frac{1830 \times 2.7 \times 0.17}{2.7 \times 1000 \times 1830}$$

$$= 0.96 \text{ or } 96\%$$

(ii) Air content

$$(a_c) = 1 - S_r = 1 - 0.96 = 4\%$$

(iii)

$$\rho_d = \frac{G.\rho_w}{1 + G.w} (1 - n_a)$$

or

$$(1 - n_a) = \frac{\rho_d (1 + G.w)}{G.\rho_w}$$

$$= \frac{1830 (1 + 2.7 \times 0.17)}{2.7 \times 1000} = 0.98$$

$$\therefore \quad n_a = \mathbf{2\%}$$

Example 5.2 : The following observations were noted during Proctor compaction test with a soil :   **[Dec. 13 7 M]**

Water content (%)	9.6	11.0	12.5	14.0	16.0	18.0	19.5
Bulk density (kg/m³)	1800	1900	1960	2045	2100	2050	2010

Specific gravity of soil grains is 2.6. Find out MDD and OMC for the soil. Plot the zero air void curve and 85% saturation curve also.

Solution : First

$$\rho_d = \frac{\rho}{1 + w}$$

Then ρ_d for $S_r = 100\%$ and $S_r = 85\%$ can be calculated by equation,

$$\rho_d = \frac{G.\rho_w}{1 + \frac{G.w}{S_r}}$$

Keeping value of $S_r = 1$ and 0.85 respectively. Now, three curves A, B and C between ρ_d and w have been drawn for (i) S = 100%, (ii) S = 85% and for finding out OMC and MDD as shown in Fig. 5.12.

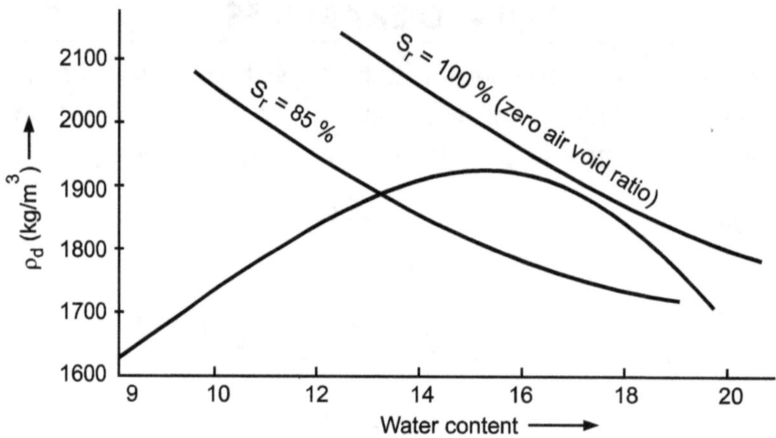

Fig. 5.12

From the graph,

MDD = 1815 kg/m³ and OMC = 15.5%.

Water content (%)	9.6	11.0	12.5	14.0	16.0	18.0	19.5
Dry density (ρ_d) (kg/m³)	1640	1710	1745	1795	1810	1740	1680
ρ_d for S_r = 100%	2080	2020	1960	1905	1838	1775	1730
ρ_d for S_r = 85%	2025	1950	1880	1825	1750	1680	1630

Example 5.3 : Assuming the following data obtained from a compaction test, determine the MDD and OMC.

Water content (%)	10.5	14.0	18.3	20.6	24.0	27.5
Bulk density (kg/m³)	1650	1760	1900	1980	1950	1850

Solution : Calculation is shown in tabular form below :

Water content %	10.5	14.0	18.3	20.6	24.0	27.5
Dry density ρ_d (kg/m³)	1493.2	1543.8	1606.0	1641.8	1572.6	1450.9

where
$$\rho_d = \frac{\rho}{1 + w}$$

Shows the compaction curve.

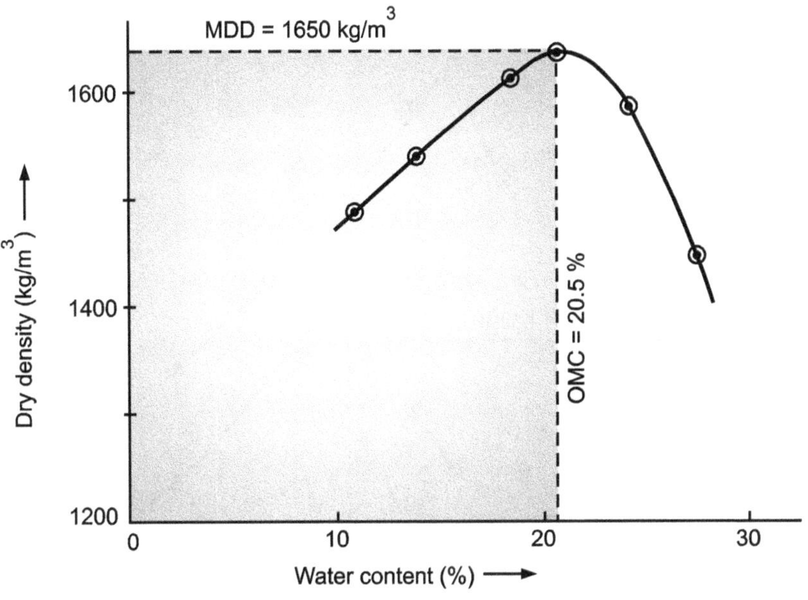

Fig. 5.13

Example 5.4 : In a Modified Proctor test, the following observations were recorded :

Water content (%)	10	13	16.5	20	24.5	29.0
Bulk density (kg/m³)	1650	1780	1950	1980	1850	1800

Plot the moisture density curve and find MDD and OMC. Also plot the ZAV line.

Take G_s = 2.70.

Solution : Calculations are shown in tabular form below :

Water content %	10	13	16.5	20	24.5	29.0
Bulk density kg/m³ (ρ)	1650	1780	1950	1980	1850	1800
Dry density kg/m³ (ρ_d) $\rho_d = \dfrac{\rho}{1 + w}$	1500	1575.2	1673.8	1650	1485.9	1395.3
ρ_d for $S_r = 100\%$ $\rho_d = \dfrac{G.\rho_w}{1 + \dfrac{G.w}{S_r}}$ kg/m³	2125.9	1998.5	1867.8	1735.2	1625.0	1514.3

Value of MDD = 1676 kg/m³ , Value of OMC = 16.4%.

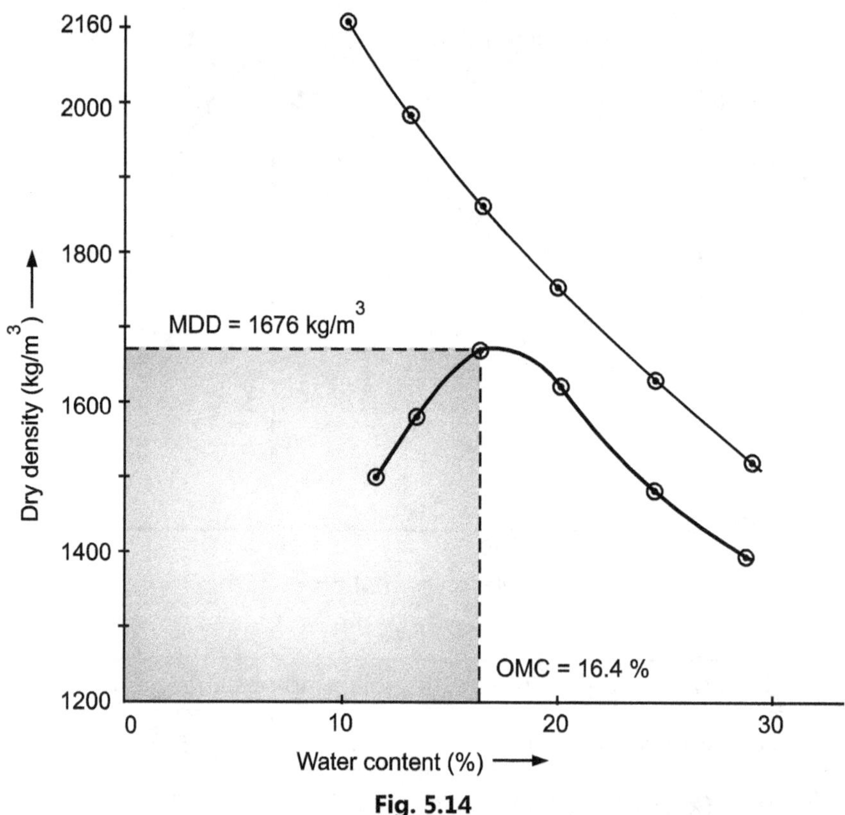

Fig. 5.14

Example 5.5 : 100 cu.m. of embankment is to be constructed with a bulk density of 2 gm/cc at 18% water content using soil from a borrow pit having bulk density of 1.70 gm/cc at 12% water content. Determine the quantity of soil to be excavated from the borrow pit, and also the quantity of water to be added while compacting.

Solution:

Dry mass of soil in the embankment = Dry mass of soil obtained from the borrow pit

i.e.
$$\frac{\text{Bulk mass in embankment}}{1 + \text{water content}} = \frac{\text{Bulk mass from borrow pit}}{1 + \text{water content}}$$

$$\therefore \quad \frac{100 \times 2000 \text{ kg/m}^3}{1 + 0.18} = \frac{200 \text{ tons}}{1.18} = 170 \text{ tons}$$

$$\rho_{bulk} = (1 + w) \, \rho_{dry} = \frac{M}{V}$$

Bulk borrow pit = 1.70 gm/cc = 1.70 tons/cu.m.

$\therefore$ Weight of dry soil in one cu.m. of soil from borrow pit

$$= \frac{1.70}{1 + w} = \frac{1.70}{1.12}$$

$\therefore$ Volume of soil to be excavated from borrow pit to get 170 tons of dry soil

$$= 112 \text{ cu.m.}$$

Quantity of water in 100 cu.m. of soil in embankment,

$$= \text{(Bulk wt.)} - \text{(Dry wt.)}$$

$$= 200 - 170 \;\; = 30 \;\; \text{tons.} \qquad \text{... (i)}$$

Quantity of water in 112 cu.m. of soil from the borrow pit

$$= \text{(Bulk wt. of 112 cu.m. of soil)} - \text{(Dry wt.)}$$

$$= 112 \times 1.70 - 170 = 20.4 \text{ tons}$$

∴ Quantity of water to be added in 112 cu.m. of soil from borrow pit

$$= 30 - 20.4 = 9.6 \text{ tons}$$

∴ Water to be added per cu.m. $= \dfrac{9.6}{112} \times 1000 \;\; \text{kg} = 85.714 \text{ kg.}$

Example 5.6 : Determine the dry density and void ratio of a soil sample having water content of 15% and saturation of 85%. Assume G = 2.65.

Solution :

$$\rho_{dry} = \frac{G.\rho_w}{1 + \dfrac{w.G}{S_r}} = \frac{G.\rho_w}{1 + e}$$

∴

$$e = \frac{wG}{S_r} = \frac{0.15 \times 2.65}{0.85} = 0.47$$

∴

$$\rho_{dry} = \frac{2.65 \times 1}{1 + 0.47} = 1.8 \text{ gm/cc}$$

Example 5.7 : A soil sample has OMC of 15% and bulk density of 1.84 gm/cc. Determine the following : Void ratio, porosity, % of saturation and maximum dry density.

Assume G = 2.70. **[May 16, 6 M]**

Solution :

$$\rho_{dry\,(max)} = \frac{\rho_{bulk}}{1 + w} = \frac{1.84}{1 + 0.15} = 1.60 \text{ gm/cc} = \frac{G.\rho_w}{1 + e}$$

or

$$e = \frac{G - \rho_{dry}}{\rho_{dry}} \quad \frac{2.70 - 1.60}{1.60} = \frac{1.1}{1.6} = 0.6875$$

$$n = \frac{e}{1 + e} = \frac{6875}{1 + 6875} = \frac{G - \rho_{dry}}{G} = \frac{2.7 - 1.7}{2.7}$$

$$= 0.4074$$

$$S_r \cdot e = w.G$$

∴

$$S_r = \frac{0.15 \times 2.7}{6875} \times 100 = 0.5890 = 58.90\%$$

Example 5.8 : Draw zero air void line and 90% saturation line for a soil sample having specific gravity of 2.65. Show calculations of at least 3 points for each curve.

Solution :

$$\rho_{dry} = \frac{G \cdot \rho_w}{1 + \frac{G \cdot w}{S_r}} = \frac{1}{\left(\frac{1}{G} + \frac{w}{S_r}\right)}$$

where ρ_w density of water = 1

$$S_r = \frac{\% \text{ saturation}}{100}$$

$$= \frac{1}{\left(\frac{1}{2.65} + \frac{w}{1}\right)} \qquad (\dots \text{ For 100\% saturation line})$$

$$= \frac{1}{\left(\frac{1}{2.65} + \frac{w}{0.9}\right)} \qquad (\dots \text{ For 90\% saturation line})$$

w	10%	15%	20%	25%	30%
ρ_d **for 100% saturation**	2.095	1.096	1.7320	1.594	1.476
ρ_d **for 90% saturation**	2.047	1.838	1.668	1.526	1.4071

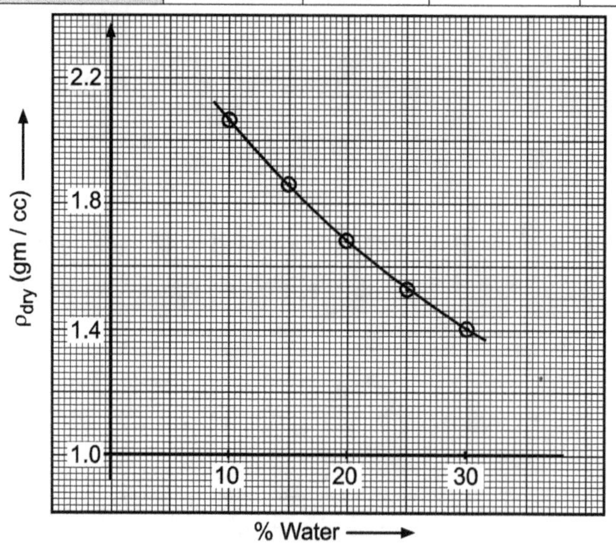

Graph

Example 5.9 : In the light compaction test, the following results were obtained :

	1	2	3	4	5
Water content (%)	13.5	20.2	28.9	36.7	41.5
Mass of soil in 1000 ml mould (kg)	1.63	1.94	1.97	1.82	1.72

Plot the moisture density curve and obtain the value of OMC and MDD.

Solution :

Since the volume of mould is 1000 ml = 1 litre,

$$\rho_{bulk} = \frac{\text{Mass in kg} \times 1000}{1000}$$

$$= \text{gm/cc}$$

$$\rho_{dry} = \frac{\rho_{bulk}}{1 + w}$$

$$\left(w = \frac{\text{water content}}{100} \right)$$

Calculations For ρ_d are as under :

Water Content (%)	13.5%	20.2%	28.9%	36.7%	41.5%
$\rho_{dry} = \dfrac{(\rho_{bulk})}{1 + w}$ $= \dfrac{\textbf{Mass of soil in mould in kg}}{1 + w}$	1.436 gm/cc	1.64	1.528	1.334	1.2155 gm/cc

From graph,

$$\text{OMC} = 20.2\%$$

$$\text{MDD} = 1.64 \text{ gm/cc}$$

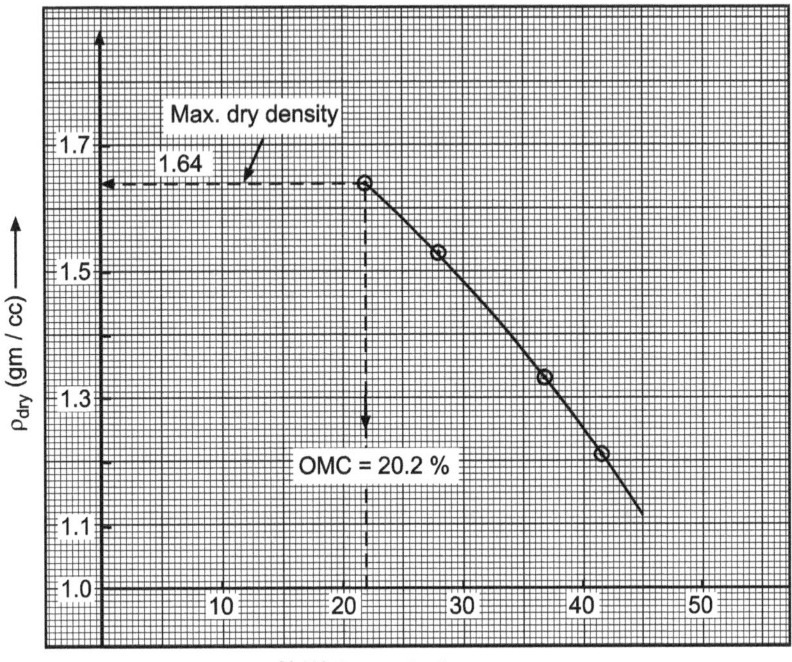

Graph

Example 5.10 : The following observations were recorded in a standard proctor test :

Water Content (%)	Bulk Density (kg/m^2)
16.10	1310
19.50	1515
27.55	1875
33.69	1860
34.77	1775

Find OMC and MDD plotting a graph. If G$_s$ = 2.70, plot ZAV curve on the same graph paper.   **[May 17, 7 M]**

Solution :
$$\rho_{dry} = \frac{\rho_{bulk}}{1 + w} \qquad \qquad \text{... (i)}$$

$$\rho_d = \frac{G \cdot \rho_w}{1 + \dfrac{G \cdot w}{S_r}} \qquad \qquad \text{... (ii)}$$

where,
$$w = \frac{\% \text{ water content}}{100}$$

$$S_r = \frac{\% \text{ of saturation}}{100}$$

$$= 1$$

$$\rho_w = 1 \text{ gm/cc}$$

Calculations are carried out as under :

Water Content (%)	16.1	19.5	27.55	33.69	34.77
Bulk Density (kg/m^3)	1310	1515	1875	1860	1775
ρ_d of the sample (kg/m^3) [Refer eq. (i)]	1128.3	1267.8	1470.01	1391.28	1317.05
ρ_d in gm/cc	1.1283	1.2678	1.470	1.391	1.317
ρ_d for 100% saturation [Refer eq. (ii)]	1.8855	1.7687	1.548	1.4319	1.3926

$$\gamma_{dry} = \frac{2.7 \times 1}{1 + \dfrac{2.7 \times 0.161}{1}} = 1.8855$$

From Graph,   OMC = 28.0%

MDD = 1.48 gm/cc

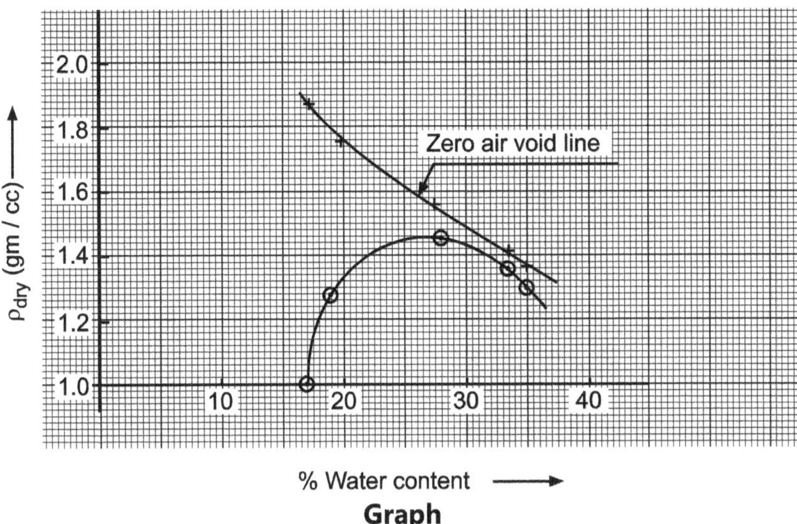

Example 5.11 : The following are the data from a laboratory light weight compaction :

Water Content (%)	Bulk Density (g/cc)
17.5	1.87
19.0	1.95
20.0	1.97
21.0	1.98
22.0	1.99
22.5	1.97
24.0	1.96

Plot the moisture content and dry density curve and find MDD and OMC.

Take G_s = 2.7.

Solution :

$$\rho_d = \frac{G \cdot \rho_w}{1 + G \cdot w}$$

$$= \frac{1}{\left(\dfrac{1}{G} + \cdot w\right)}$$

$$\rho_w = 1$$

$$= \frac{\rho}{(0.3704 + w)}$$

Water content (%)	17.5	19	20	21	22	22.5	24
ρ_{bulk} (gm/cc)	1.87	1.95	1.97	1.98	1.99	1.97	1.96
ρ_{dry} = ρ_{bulk} (1 + w)	1.5915	1.63865	1.6417	1.6363	1.6311	1.608	1.5806
ρ_d for 100% saturation line	1.8375	1.7844	1.75315	1.723	1.694	1.6795	1.638

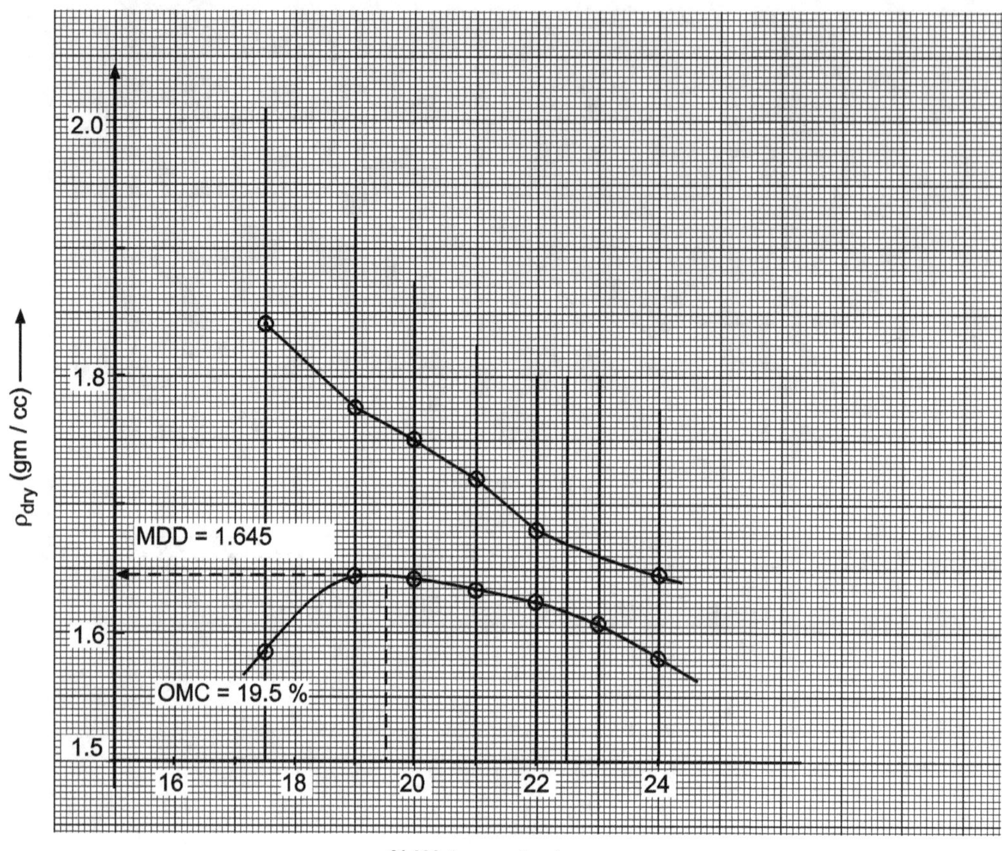

Graph

From Graph,	OMC	=	19.5%
	MDD	=	1.645 gm/cc

Example 5.12 : The following data have been obtained in a standard laboratory proctor compaction test on a glacial till :

Water Content (%)	Weight of Mould and Compacted Soil (kg)
5.02	3.580
8.81	3.730
11.25	3.932
13.05	4.000
14.40	4.007
19.25	3.907

The specific gravity of the soil particles is 2.77. The mould is 944 cm^3 in volume and its weight is 1.978 kg. Plot the compaction curve and determine the OMC and MDD. Also compute the void ratio and degree of saturation at optimum condition.

Solution : The following procedure is adopted :

$$\text{Dry density} = \frac{\text{Bulk density}}{1 + \dfrac{\%\ \text{water content}}{100}}$$

$$\text{Bulk density} = \frac{\left(\begin{array}{c}\text{Mass of soil +}\\ \text{Mass of mould in gm}\end{array}\right) - \left(\begin{array}{c}\text{Mass of mould}\\ \text{in gm}\end{array}\right)}{\text{Volume of mould in cc. (944)}}$$

Sample	1	2	3	4	5	6
(a) wt. of soil + wt. of mould in gm	3580	3730	3932	4000	4007	3907
(b) wt. of mould in gm	1978	1978	1978	1978	1978	1978
(c) wt. of wet soil = (a) − (b) in gm	1602	1752	1954	2022	2029	1929
(d) $\rho_{bulk} = \dfrac{\text{(c) in gms}}{944\ cc}$	1.697	1.856	2.07	2.1420	2.149	2.043
(e) % water content	5.02	8.81	11.25	13.05	14.4	19.25
(f) $\rho_{dry} = \dfrac{\rho_{bulk}}{1 + w}$ gm/cc	1.6159	1.706	1.8606	1.8947	1.879	1.714

$$\rho_{dry} = \frac{G \cdot \rho_w}{1 + e} \qquad \rho_w = 1\ \text{gm/cc}$$

$$\therefore \qquad e = \left(\frac{G}{\rho_{dry}} - 1\right)$$

$$= \frac{2.77}{1.895} - 1 = 0.4617$$

(from graph MDD = 1.895 gm/cc)

$$\text{OMC} = 13\%$$

Also,
$$S_r \cdot e = W.\ G.$$

$$\therefore \qquad S_r = \frac{0.13 \times 2.77}{0.4617}$$

$$= 0.7799 = 78\%$$

$$\therefore \qquad \%\ \text{of saturation at OMC} = 78\%$$

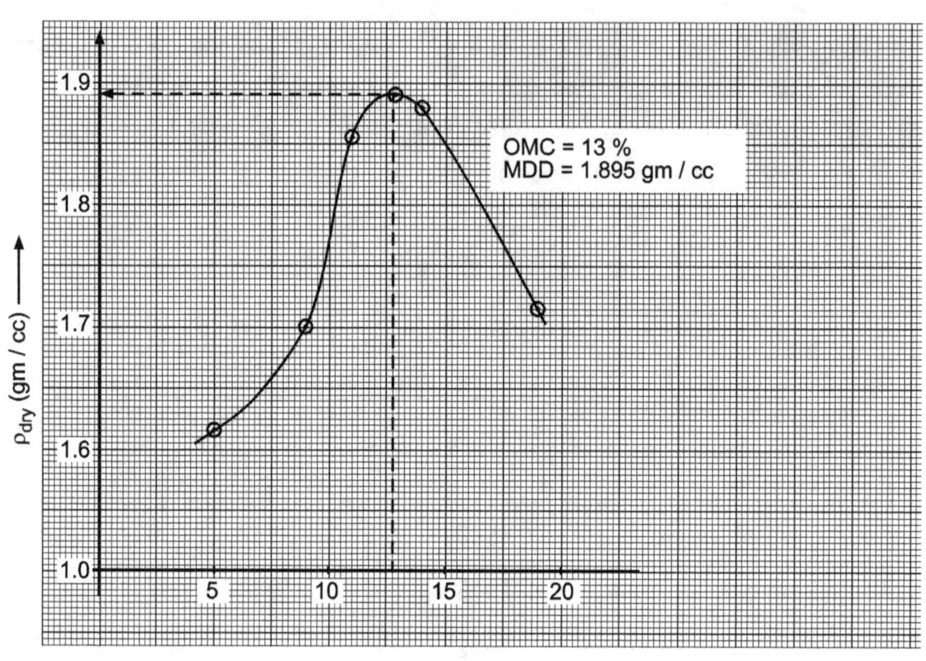

Graph (for ex. 6 and ex. 7)

Example 13 : The following results were obtained from a standard compaction test :

Bulk Density (kg/m³)	Water Content (%)
1978	11.3
2083	12.2
2147	13.0
2208	14.2
2188	15.1
2147	16.4

(i) Draw moisture-density curve and determine MDD and OMC.

(ii) Draw the saturation line on the same graph (G = 2.7).

Calculate total energy imparted in a light compaction test.

Solution :

Sample No.	1	2	3	4	5	6
ρ_{bulk} (kg/m³)	1978	2083	2147	2208	2188	2147

w (%)	11.3	12.2	13.0	14.2	15.1	16.4
$\rho_{dry} = \dfrac{\rho_{bulk}}{1 + \dfrac{w}{100}}$ (kg/m³)	1777	1856	1900	1933	1901	1844

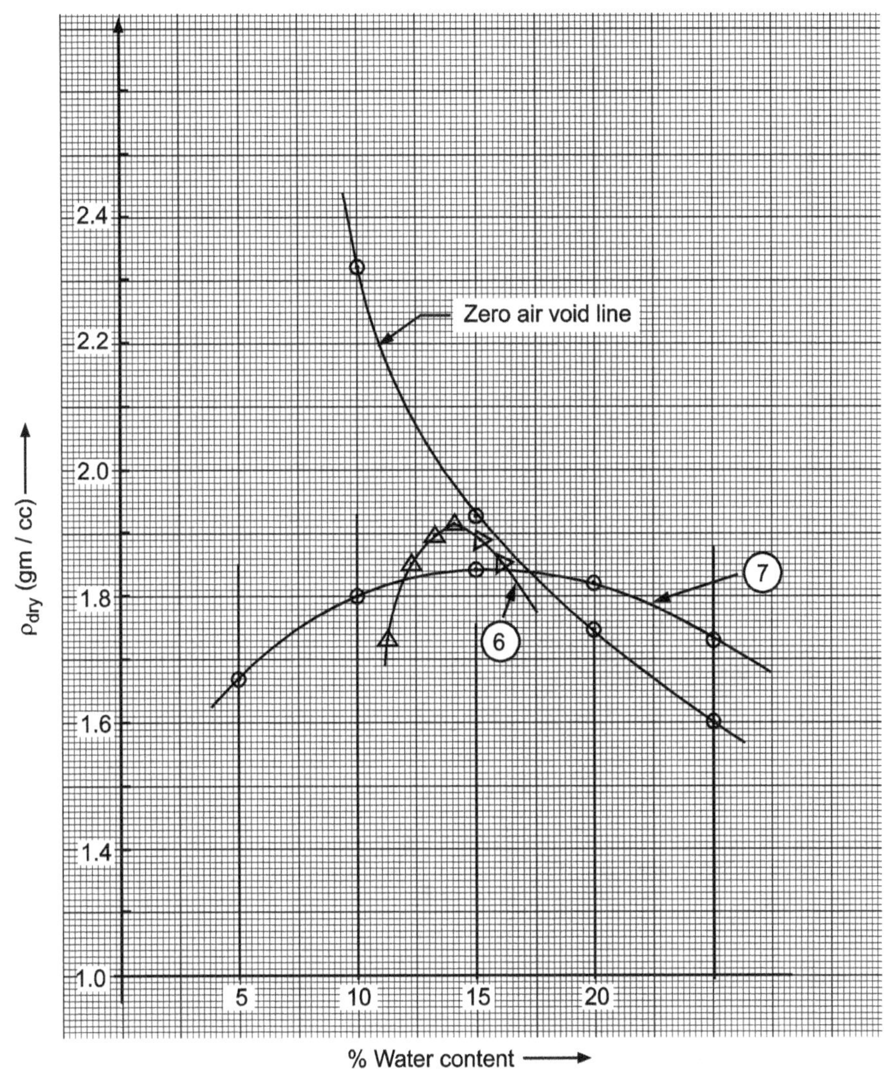

Graph (For ex. 6 and ex. 7)

From graph, it is noticed that,

OMC = 14%

MDD = 1.9 gm/cc

Example 5.14 : The results of standard compaction test on a sample of soil are as follows :

Water Content (%)	Bulk Density (g/cm3)
5	1.77
10	1.98
14	2.1
20	2.18
25	2.16

Plot the compaction curve and obtain the optimum moisture content and maximum dry density. Calculate the water content necessary to completely saturate the sample at its maximum dry density, assuming no change in the volume. Take G = 2.7.

Solution :
$$\rho_{dry} = \frac{\rho_{bulk}}{1 + w} = \frac{G}{1 + \dfrac{G\,w}{S_r}} = \frac{1}{\dfrac{1}{G} + w} \qquad \text{(if } S_r = 1)$$

$$= \left(\frac{1}{0.3704 + w}\right)$$

ρ_{bulk} **(g/cc)**	1.77	1.98	2.10	2.18	2.16
w (%)	5	10	14	20	25
$\rho_{dry} = \dfrac{\rho_{bulk}}{1 + w}$	1.686	1.80	1.842	1.817	1.728
(zero air void curve) $(\rho_{dry})_{max}$	2.371	2.126	1.959	1.753	1.612

Comments : From the graph it will be noticed that, ZAV line is cutting the compaction curve. After moisture of 16%. **This is not possible.** Hence the reading beyond 16%. **Viz, last two readings are incorrect.** The curve (7) has to be below ZAV line.

SUMMARY

1. During compaction, reduction in volume of soil is due to expulsion of air, whereas that during consolidation is due to removal of water.

2. Application of load, during consolidation is natural, whereas that during compaction is sudden.

3. For consolidation, the soil has to be fully saturated.

4. For a given compaction energy.

    For a soil, there exists, a water content at which dry density will be maximum and this water content is called as Optimum Water Content (OMC). However, if compaction energy is increased, dry density will increase, but OMC will be lesser than the previous one.

5. Coarser the soil, higher will be dry density and finer the soil, lesser will be dry density.

6. If a graph of dry density versus water content is plotted, it will be similar to that shown in Fig. 5.4. On increasing compaction energy, the curve will try to shift nearer to zero. Air void line, but will never cross zero air void line.

7. Zero air void line can be plotted using the following equation :

$$\rho_d = \frac{G\rho_w}{1 + \dfrac{wG}{S_r}} \text{, where } S_r \text{ is \% of saturation.}$$

For zero air void line, $S_r = 100\%$.

8. By using correct value of "G", for different values of water content corresponding dry density can be calculated and plotted. No experiment is required to be carried out to plot zero air void line.

9. To carry out light compaction test, proctor mould of 100 mm dia. × 127 mm height, having volume of one litre is used. The soil is computed in 3 layers, for each layer 25 blows of hammer weighing 2.6 kg, with a height of drop of 30 cm are given.

10. To carry heavy compaction test, suitable changes in weight of hammer, height of drop and number of layers are made.

11. In heavy compaction, the compaction energy is 4.25 times than that used in light compaction test.

12. In field, to known, whether water be used for compaction is appropriate or not, proctor needle is used. Before using the needle calibration curve is required to be plotted, by carrying out experiment in laboratory, before actually using the needle at site.

EXERCISE

1. Define compaction? Explain the mechanics of compaction.
2. Differentiate between compaction and consolidation.
3. Explain the factors affecting compaction.
4. What are the effects of compaction on soil proportion?
5. Explain standard proctor compaction test.
6. Write a short note on field compaction.
7. In compaction test a soil having specific gravity 2.7 gave a maximum dry density of 1800 kg/m^3 at the moisture content of 15%. Find the degree of saturation, air content and percentage air voids at the maximum density.
8. A soil sample has OMC of 10% and bulk density of 1.80 gm/cc. Determine the following: Void ratio, porosity, % of saturation and maximum dry density. take G = 2.70.
9. 150 cu.m. of embankment is to be constructed with a bulk density of 2 gm/cc at 15% water content using soil from a borrow pit having bulk density of 1.50 gm/cc at 10% water content. Determine the quantity of soil to be excavated from the borrow pit, and also the quantity of water to be added while compacting.

SOLVED UNIVERSITY QUESTIONS AND NUMERICALS

December 2013

1. The following observations were noted during proctor compaction test with soil.

Water content (%)	9.6	11.0	12.5	14.0	16.0	18	19.5
Bulk density (kg/m^3)	1800	1900	1960	2045	2100	2050	2010

Specific gravity is 2.6, find MDD and OMC for the soil.
Also draw zero air void curve.   **[7]**
[**Ans.:** Refer Example 5.2]

May 2014

1. What is compaction ? How is it different from consolidation ? Explain how compacting effort affects compaction ?   **[6]**
[**Ans.:** Refer Article 5.1, 5.3, 5.4]

May 2015

1. Draw a curve showing the relation between dry density and moisture content for standard Proctor test and indicate the salient features of the curve.   **[6]**
[**Ans.:** Refer Article 5.5.3]

November 2015

1. Explain standard proctor compaction test with neat sketch.   **[6]**
[**Ans.:** Refer Article 5.5.1]

May 2016

1. A soil sample has OMC of 15% and bulk density of 1.84 gm/cc. Determine the following: Void ratio, porosity, % of saturation and maximum dry density. Assume G = 2.70.   **[6]**
[**Ans.:** Refer Example 5.7]

November 2016

1. Discuss the moisture-density relation graph for standard and modified proctor test and also explain the significance of ZAV line in the graph.   **[6]**
[**Ans.:** Refer Article 5.5.3, 5.5.6]

May 2017

1. In a standard proctor test the following observations were recorded :   **[7]**

Sample No.	Bulk Density (kg/m^3)	Water Content (%)
1	1310	16.1
2	1515	19.5
3	1875	27.55
4	1860	33.69
5	1775	34.77

Plot the moisture density curve and find MDD and OMC and also draw ZAV line.
[**Ans.:** Refer Example 5.10]

Chapter 6

STREES DISTRIBUTION IN SOILS

6.1 INTRODUCTION

Stresses are induced in the soil mass due to the overlaying soil and due to the applied loads. These stresses are required for the determination of earth pressures, the settlement analysis of foundation and the stability analysis of soil mass. The stresses induced in soil due to applied loads depends upon its stress-strain characteristics. The stress-strain behaviour of soils is extremely complex and it depends upon a large number of factors such as water content, void ratio, rate of loading, drainage conditions, the load level etc. However, for simplifications, some assumptions are made in the analysis to obtain the stresses. Following are the assumptions made :

- The soil mass is homogeneous and isotropic.
- The stress-strain relationship is linear.
- The theory of elasticity is used to determine the stresses in the soil mass.
- The stresses calculated are approximate.

The stress-strain parameters required for the application of elastic theories are modulus of elasticity (E) and Poisson's ratio (μ). The modulus of elasticity can be determined in the laboratory from triaxial compression test. The stress-strain curve is plotted between the deviator stress ($\sigma_1 - \sigma_3$) and the axial strain (ξ) (Fig. 6.1). An unconsolidated undrained test (UU) or unconfined compression test can be performed for saturated cohesive soils. A Consolidated Drained (CD) test is usually conducted for cohensionless soils. The value of modulus is generally taken as the secant modulus at $\frac{1}{2}$ to $\frac{1}{3}$ of the peak stress. Sometimes, the tangent modulus at $\frac{1}{2}$ to $\frac{1}{3}$ of peak stress is also used.

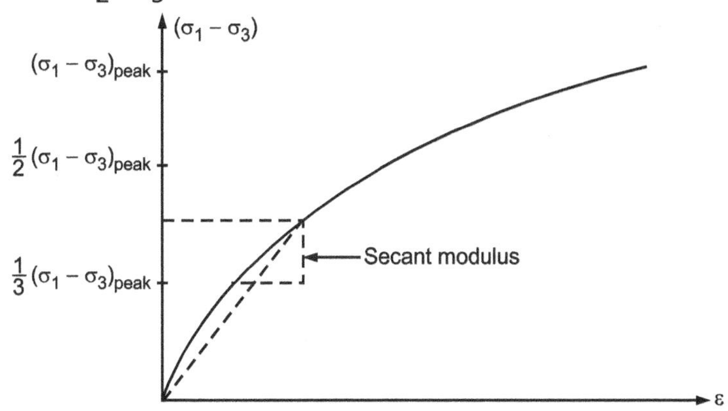

Fig. 6.1 : Stress-strain relationship

The value of Poisson's ratio (μ) for an elastic material varies from zero to 0.50.

For drained conditions, the value of Poisson's ratio is 0.50. For undrained conditions, the Poisson's ratio is less than 0.50. Fortunately, the effect of Poisson's ratio on the computed stresses is not significant and an approximate value can be used without much error.

6.2 GEOSTATIC STRESSES

The stresses due to self weight of soils are generally large in comparison with those induced due to imposed loads. This is unlike many other structures wherein the stresses due to self weight are relatively small. In soil engineering problem the stresses due to self weight are significant.

When ground surface is horizontal and properties of the soil do not change along with the horizontal plane, the *stresses due to self-weight are known as geostatic stresses.* Such condition generally exists in sedimentary deposits. In such a case, the stresses are normal to the horizontal and vertical planes. The shearing stresses on these planes is zero. In short, these planes are principal planes.

The vertical stress on any horizontal plane at depth 'z' due to soil column above is given as,

$$\boxed{\sigma_v = \gamma_z}$$ where γ = Unit weight of soil

The stresses induced due to different loading patterns are normally computed by the following approaches :

- By elastic solutions
- By use of Newmark's chart
- By use of Janbu chart
- By Westergaard's analysis
- By approximate solutions
- By pressure bulb concept
- By contact pressure concept

6.3 ELASTIC SOLUTIONS   [Dec. 14, May 17]

6.3.1 Stresses Due to Point Load   (Dec, 14, May 17)

The analytical solutions for stresses due to concentrated load on the surface is generally computed from Boussinesq's theory. This theory depends upon the following assumptions :

- The soil mass is elastic, homogeneous, isotropic and obeys the Hooke's law.
- The soil is weightless.
- Load acts vertically at a point on the horizontal ground surface.
- The soil mass is semi-infinite, that is, it extends infinitely in all directions below a level surface.

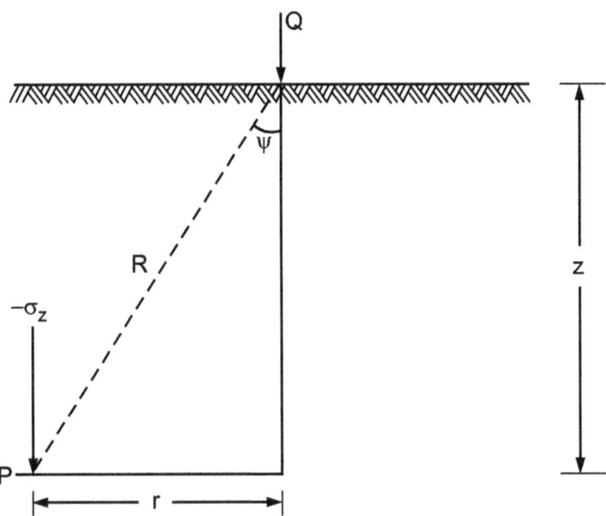

Fig. 6.2 : Vertical pressure due to point load

The vertical normal pressure (σ_z) at a depth (z) and horizontal radial distance (r) from the point of application of concentrated load (Q) is given by

$$\sigma_z = \frac{3}{2} \cdot \frac{Q}{\pi} \cdot \frac{\cos \psi}{R^2}$$

where, R = Polar radial co-ordinate of point p $= \sqrt{r^2 + z^2}$

and $\cos \psi = \dfrac{z}{R}$

Thus $\sigma_z = \dfrac{3Q}{2\pi} \cdot \dfrac{z^3}{\left(r^2 + z^2\right)^{5/2}} = \dfrac{3Q}{2\pi z^2} \left[\dfrac{1}{1 + \left(\dfrac{r}{z}\right)^2}\right]^{5/2}$

Since, both the parameters, elasticity (E) and Poisson's ratio (μ) are absent, it can be said that the pressure is independent of elastic properties.

or , $\sigma_z = \dfrac{Q}{z^2} \dfrac{3}{2\pi \left[1 + \left(\dfrac{r}{z}\right)^2\right]^{5/2}}$

$$\sigma_z = \frac{Q}{z^2} \times I_B$$

where, $I_B = \dfrac{3}{2\pi \left[1 + \left(\dfrac{r}{z}\right)^2\right]^{5/2}}$ is   an   influence   factor,   called

Boussinesq influence factor.

The typical values of I_B are given in Table 6.1.

Table 6.1

$\dfrac{r}{z}$	I_B	$\dfrac{r}{z}$	I_B	$\dfrac{r}{z}$	I_B
0.00	0.4775	0.40	0.3294	0.80	0.1386
0.10	0.4657	0.50	0.2733	0.90	0.1083
0.20	0.4329	0.60	0.2214	1.00	0.0844
0.30	0.3849	0.70	0.1762	2.00	0.0085
				3.00	0.0015

The vertical normal pressure (σ_z) decreases with increase in (z). It also decreases on any horizontal plane with increasing radial distance (r).

The vertical normal pressure directly under the concentrated load (r = 0) decreases with square of the depth.

Thus,

$$\sigma_z = \frac{3Q}{z^2 \cdot 2\pi \left[1 + \left(\dfrac{r}{z}\right)^2\right]^{5/2}}$$

6.3.2 Pressure Distribution Diagrams   (Dec. 14, May 16)

Boussinesq's vertical stress equation may be used to draw three types of pressure distribution diagrams (Fig. 6.3). They are :

- The stress isobar,
- The vertical stress distribution on a horizontal plane at a depth of z below the ground surface, and
- The vertical stress distribution on a vertical plane at a distance of r from the load point.

The stress isobar is a stress contour connecting all points of equal stress below the ground surface. There are many isobars for a given load system. Stress isobar is also referred to as bulb of pressure or pressure bulb of the soil mass bounded within. (See Art. 6.6)

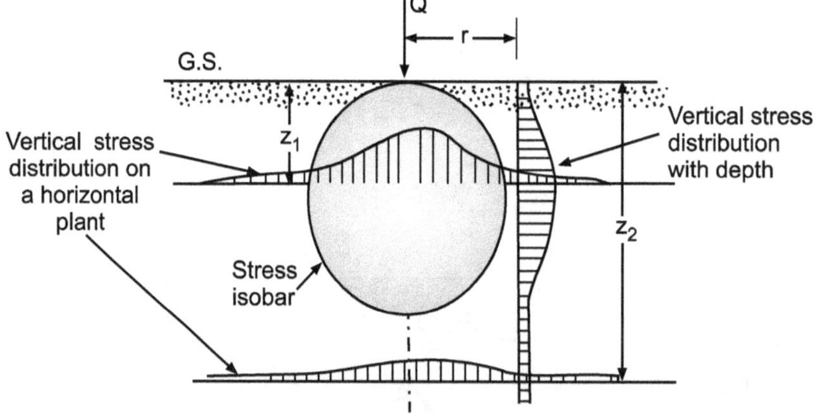

Fig. 6.3 : Vertical stress distribution diagrams

Vertical stress distribution on a horizontal plane at a depth z_1 and z_2 from the ground surface is obtained by varying r. These represents a high value along the load line and decreases with increase in r. The magnitude of vertical stress along the load line decreases with increase in depth (shown by curves of z_1 and z_2).

Vertical stress distribution on a vertical plane at a distance r from the load point is obtained by varying z. The diagrams represents a maximum value at a depth nearer to the ground surface which decreases with depth.

$$\text{At } r = 0,$$

$$\sigma_z = \frac{3Q}{z^2 \times 2\pi \, [1 + 0]^{5/2}} = \frac{3Q}{2\pi z^2}$$

$$\sigma_z = 1.5 \frac{Q}{\pi z^2} = \frac{0.477 \, Q}{z^2}$$

At the surface z = 0, and *the vertical stress just below the load is theoretically infinite. However, realistically, the soil under the load yields due to very high stresses.*

The vertical stress (σ_z) decreases rapidly with an increase in $\dfrac{r}{z}$ ratio. It would be zero only at an infinite distance from the load point, as per equation. But at $\dfrac{r}{z}$ = 5 or more, the vertical stress becomes negligible. The Boussinesq's equation can be applied for upward loads also. If the vertical stress decreases due to an excavation, the negative load would be the weight of the soil removed. The Boussinesq's solution gives conservative values and hence is commonly used in soil engineering problems.

Limitations of Boussinesq's Solution :

- As the soils are far from purely elastic solids, the assumption that the *soils are elastic may be questioned.*
- The application of Boussinesq's solution can be justified when *the stress changes are such that only a stress increase occurs in the soil.*
- In deep sand deposits, the *modulus of elasticity increases* with increase in depth, and therefore *Boussinesq's equation will not give reliable results.* It can be used for homogeneous deposits of clay, man made fills and limited thickness of uniform sand deposits.
- The point loads applied below the ground surface causes somewhat smaller stresses than that caused by surface loads and therefore Boussinesq's equation is not strictly applicable.

6.3.3 Stresses Due to the Load Uniformly Distributed Over a Circular Area

By integrating the Boussinesq's equation, the stresses induced due to this type of loading can be calculated.

Let   a = Radius

q = Pressure intensity

z = Depth below the curve

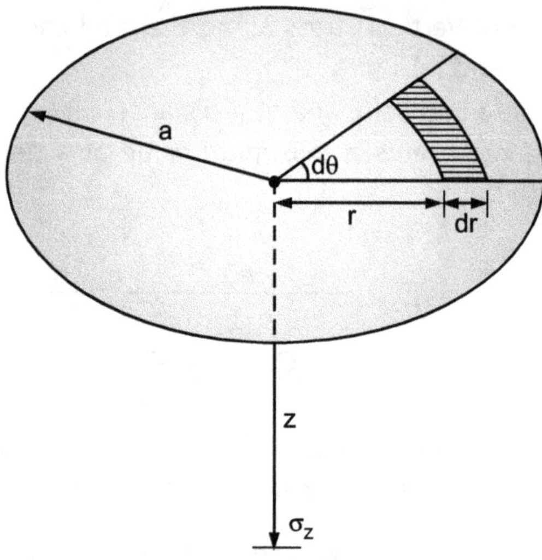

Fig. 6.4 (a)

The vertical stress at a depth 'z' under the centre of a circular area of diameter 2a is (Fig. 6.4).

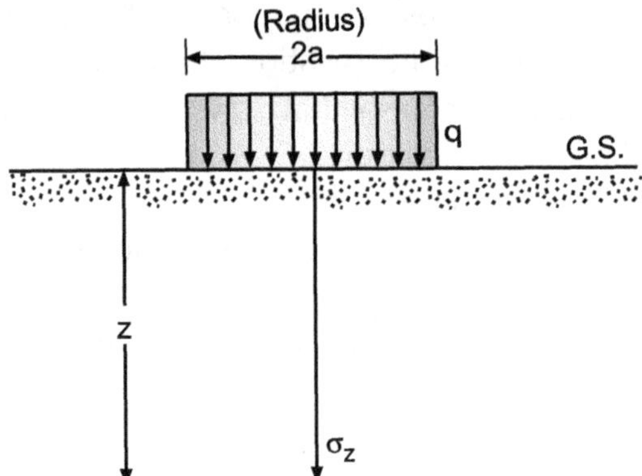

Fig. 6.4 (b) : Vertical stress at the centre of a circular loaded area

$$\sigma_z = q \left[1 - \frac{1}{\left[1 + \left(\dfrac{a}{z} \right)^2 \right]^{3/2}} \right]$$

or

$$\sigma_z = q \cdot I_c$$

where

$$I_c = \text{Influence factor depending upon } \frac{z}{a} \text{ values}$$

$$= 1 - \frac{1}{\left[1 + \left(\dfrac{a}{z} \right)^2 \right]^{3/2}}$$

Table 6.2 : Typical values of I_c, the influence factor

$\dfrac{z}{a}$	I_C	$\dfrac{z}{a}$	I_C	$\dfrac{z}{a}$	I_C
0.0	1.000	0.7	0.818	1.4	0.461
0.1	0.999	0.8	0.756	1.5	0.424
0.2	0.992	0.9	0.701	2.0	0.284
0.3	0.970	1.0	0.646	2.5	0.200
0.4	0.949	1.1	0.595	3.0	0.146
0.5	0.911	1.2	0.547	3.5	0.117
0.6	0.864	1.3	0.502	4.0	0.087

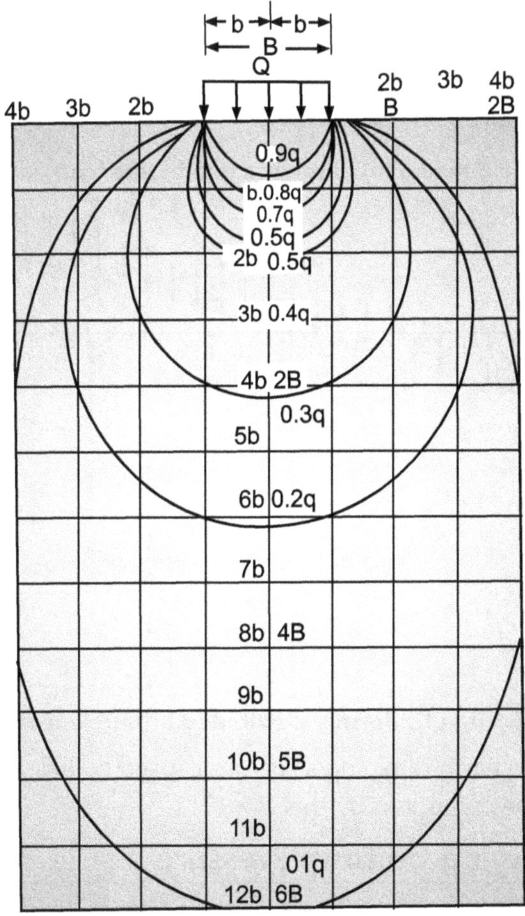

Fig. 6.5 : Isobars of circular loading

6.3.4 Stresses Due to Line Load

The vertical normal pressure due to line load (q) per unit length on the surface at a point 'a' located at depth (z) and distance (r) laterally away is given by : $\sigma_z = \dfrac{2q}{\pi} \dfrac{z^3}{(z^2 + r^2)^2}$.

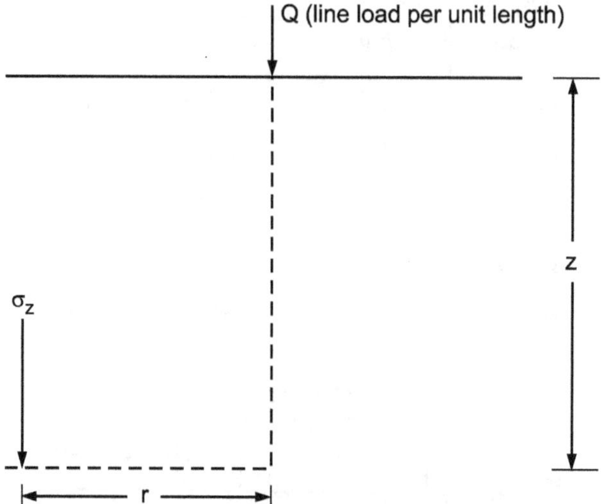

Fig. 6.6 (a) : Pressure due to line load

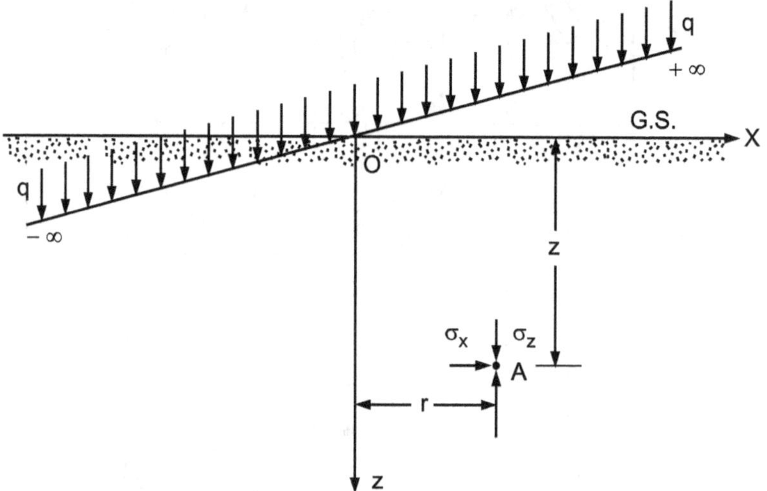

Fig. 6.6 (b) : Uniformly distributed infinite linear load

The lateral pressure on the earth retaining structure caused by line load (e.g. a railway) on the surface of a backfill may be computed by this.

6.3.5 Strip Area Carrying Uniform Pressure

A strip of width B and infinite length, loaded with uniform pressure is shown in Fig. 6.7 (similar to pressure of wall footing). The stresses at point A are given as :

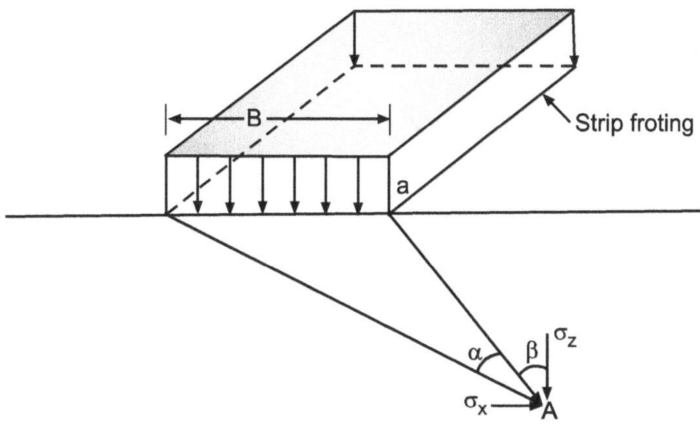

(a) Uniformly distributed infinite strip load

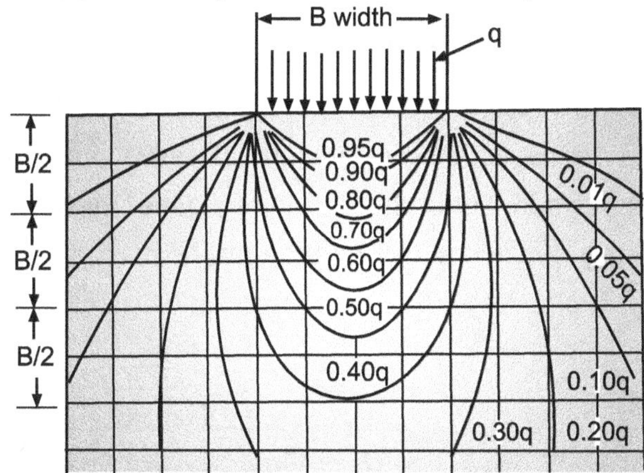

(b) Bulbs of vertical pressure under uniform strip load

Fig. 6.7

$$\sigma_z = \frac{q}{\pi}\{\alpha + \sin \alpha \cos (\alpha + 2\beta)\}$$

and
$$\tau_{xz} = \frac{q}{\pi}\{\sin \alpha \sin \alpha + 2\beta\}$$

A plot of contours of equal vertical stresses is shown in Fig. 6.7 for different stress ratios. As explained earlier, this enables one to fix the depth of stress influence. The distribution of stress beneath a uniform strip load is important in estimating settlements.

6.3.6 Stresses Due to Equivalent Load

The Boussinesq's equation can be used to find the vertical pressure on a point under a uniformly loaded square or rectangular area by dividing the area into similar area units with the load acting as point loads at the centroids of the individual areas. The equation is applied to each unit area in turn and the results are added.

Let (B) be the width of square unit area. When $\dfrac{z}{B}$ for square unit area is 3, the $\dfrac{\sigma_z}{Q}$ ratio by equivalent point load method is about (0.0531) and by the theoretical analysis it is (0.05). Hence if pressures are to be determined at a depth (z), the larger size of unit area should be less than or equal to one third of the depth (z). The Boussinesq's equation is :

$$\sigma_z = \frac{3Q}{2\pi z^2 \left[1 + \left(\dfrac{r}{z}\right)^2\right]^{5/2}}$$

This concept is discussed in detail under the head 6.7 'Approximate solutions' in the same chapter.

6.4 WESTERGUARD'S THEORY

Westerguard (1930) also solved the problem of pressure distribution in soil under a point load, assuming the soil to be an elastic medium of semi-infinite extent but containing numerous, closely spaced, horizontal sheets of negligible thickness of an infinite rigid material which permits only downward deformation on the mass as a whole without allowing it to undergo any lateral strain. Westerguard's expression which closely represents the elastic conditions of a stratified soil mass, is

$$\sigma_z = \frac{Q}{2\pi z^2} = \frac{\sqrt{(1-2\mu)/(2-2\mu)}}{\left[(1-2\mu)/(2-2\mu) + \left(\dfrac{r}{z}\right)^2\right]^{3/2}}$$

In this equation μ = Poisson's ratio. If Poisson's ratio μ is zero, (giving complete lateral restraint),

$$\sigma_z = \frac{Q}{\pi z^2} \cdot \frac{1}{\left[1 + 2\left(\dfrac{r}{z}\right)^2\right]^{3/2}}$$

or

$$\sigma_z = \frac{Q}{z^2} \cdot I_w$$

where,

$$I_w = \frac{1}{\pi \left[1 + 2\left(\dfrac{r}{z}\right)^2\right]^{3/2}}$$

The Westerguard's solution gives smaller values of vertical stresses than the Boussinesq's solution. The typical values of I_w in terms of $\dfrac{r}{z}$ are given in Table 6.3.

Table 6.3 : Influence Stress Coefficient I_w for Point Load, (Westergaard)

$\dfrac{r}{z}$	I_w	$\dfrac{r}{z}$	I_w
0.0	0.318	1.5	0.025
0.1	0.308	2.0	0.008
0.2	0.283	2.5	0.003
0.3	0.248		
0.4	0.210		
0.5	0.173		
0.6	0.141		
1.0	0.084		

6.5 COMPARISON OF BOUSSINESQ'S & WESTERGUARD'S EQUATIONS

For better comparison and estimation of stresses, both the Boussinesq's and Westergaard's formulae may be written in the following form :

Boussinesq's formula :

$$\sigma_z = \frac{Q}{z^2} \cdot \frac{\dfrac{3}{2\pi}}{\left[1 + \left(\dfrac{r}{z}\right)^2\right]^{5/2}} = \frac{Q}{z^2} \cdot I_B \qquad \qquad \dots (6.2)$$

Westerguard's formula :

$$\sigma_z = \frac{Q}{z^2} \cdot \frac{\dfrac{1}{\pi}}{\left[1 + 2\left(\dfrac{r}{z}\right)^2\right]^{3/2}} = \frac{Q}{z^2} \cdot I_w \qquad \qquad \dots (6.3)$$

I_B and I_w are Boussinesq's and Westerguard's stress coefficients respectively. These coefficients are function of $\dfrac{r}{z}$, and their relationship is shown in Fig. 6.8.

Fig. 6.8 (a) illustrates the difference in the distribution of stress as per the Boussinesq and Westerguard's equation. The vertical stress distribution with depth along the vertical plane below the load is shown in Fig. 6.8 (b).

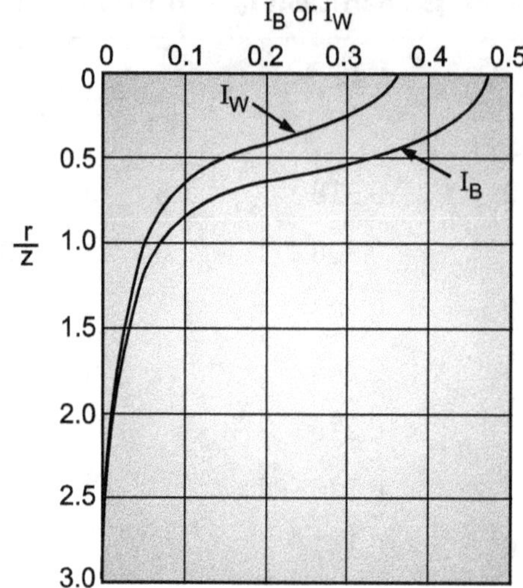

(a) Values of I_B or I_W in Boussinesq or Westerguard's formula

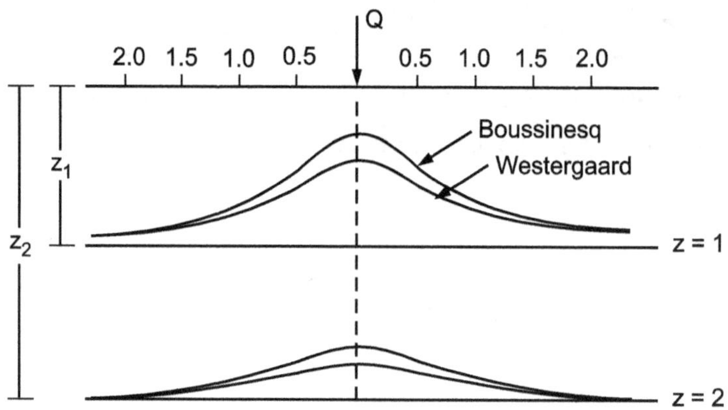

(b) Stress distribution on horizontal planes

Fig. 6.8

It is clear from the curves in Fig. 6.9 that the Westergaard's equation gives consistently less stress than Bousinesq's equation for the same point load upto a ratio of $\frac{r}{z}$ equal to 0.5. When the ratio exceeds 1.5, Westergaard's formula gives a greater stress. For all ratios of $\frac{r}{z}$ less than about 0.8, the vertical stresses as per Westergaard's formula are approximately equal to two thirds of the values given by its Boussinesq's formula.

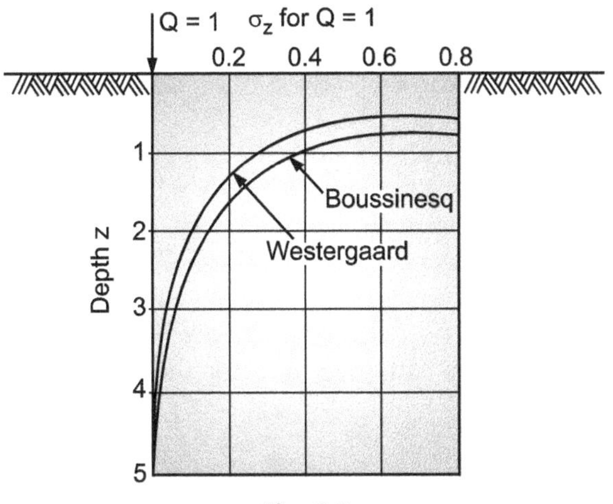

Fig. 6.9

6.6 STRESS ISOBAR OR PRESSURE BULB CONCEPT   [May 14]

An *'isobar'* is a stress contour or a line which connects all points below the ground surface at which the vertical pressure is the same. In fact, an isobar is a spatial curved surface and resembles a bulb in shape; this is because the vertical pressure at all points in a horizontal plane at equal radial distances from the load is the same. Thus, the stress isobar is also called the 'bulb of pressure' or simply the 'pressure bulb'. The vertical pressure at each point on the pressure bulb is the same.

Pressure at points inside the bulb are greater than that at a point on the surface of the bulb; and pressures at points outside the bulb are smaller than that on the surface. Any number of pressure bulbs may be drawn for any applied load, since each one corresponds to an arbitrarily chosen value of stress. A system of isobars indicates the decrease in stress intensity from the inner to the outer ones and reminds one of an 'Onion bulb'. Hence the term 'pressure bulb'. An isobar diagram, consisting of a system of isobars appears somewhat as shown in Fig. 6.10.

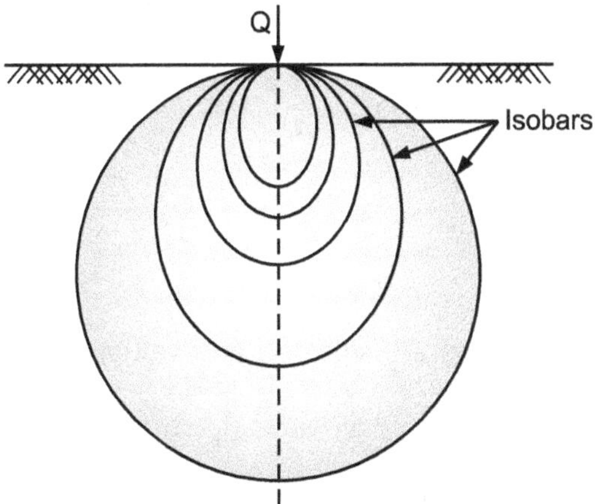

Fig. 6.10 : Isobar diagram (A system of pressure bulbs for a point load - Boussinesq's)

The procedure for plotting an isobar is as follows :

Let it be required to plot an isobar for which σ_z = 0.1 Q per unit area (10% isobar) :

$$\sigma_z = \frac{Q}{z^2} I_B$$

$$I_B = \frac{\sigma_z \cdot z^2}{Q} = \frac{0.1 \, Q \cdot z^2}{Q} = 0.1 \, z^2$$

Assuming various values for z, the corresponding I_B values are computed; for these values of I_B, the corresponding r/z-values are obtained; and for the assumed values of z, r-values are got.

It is obvious that, for the same value of r on any side of the z-axis, or line of action of the point load, the value of σ_z is the same; hence the isobar is symmetrical with respect to this axis.

When r = 0, I_B = 0.4775; the isobar crosses the line of action of the load at a depth of,

$$z = \sqrt{I_B / 0.1} = \sqrt{\frac{0.4775}{0.1}} = \sqrt{4.775} = 2.185 \text{ units}$$

A 'significant depth' or 'significant stressed zone' is the depth below the foundation upto *which pressure increase may be assumed to cause significant deformation of the soil.* For practical purposes, this depth is taken as the level at which the pressure increases due to the foundation loading and is *equal to twenty per cent* of the overburden pressure. Many times the significant stress value is taken to correspond to an isobar of 0.1 Q or 0.2 Q intensity and this defines the depth of the pressure bulb. (Fig. 6.10)

If the 0.2 value is adopted as a significant stress to define the pressure bulb, then :

$$\sigma_z = \text{Vertical pressure due to point load}$$

$$\sigma_z = 0.20 \, Q, \text{ i.e. 20\% of (Q) per unit area}$$

But we know that :

$$\sigma_z = I_B \times \frac{Q}{z^2}$$

$$I_B = \sigma_z \times \frac{z^2}{Q} = \frac{0.2Q \times z^2}{Q}$$

$$I_B = 0.2 \times z^2$$

A number of numerical values of (z) are selected and values of (I_B) are calculated from the above equation. Corrsponding to these values of (I_B), the values of $\frac{r}{z}$ are found from Table 6.1 and thus corresponding values of (r) can be computed. Thus, we get co-ordintates (r, z) of various points where σ_z = 0.2 Q.

6.7 APPROXIMATE METHODS

Methods explained earlier for evaluation of stresses are relatively more accurate, but are time consuming. Hence, following methods which are less accurate but easy to adopt, are used.

(a) Equivalent Point Load Method : The vertical stress at a point under a loaded area of any shape can be determined by dividing the load area into small areas and replacing the distributed load on each small area by an equivalent point load acting at the centroid of the area. The total load is thus converted into a number of point loads. The vertical stress at any point below or outside the loaded area is equal to the sum of the vertical stresses due to these equivalent loads. Refer Fig. 6.11.

We have
$$\sigma_z = I_B \, \frac{Q}{z^2}$$

Let the whole loaded area be divided into n number of small areas.

Then :
$$\sigma_z = \frac{Q_1 \times (I_B)_1 + Q_2 \, (I_B)_2 + Q_3 \, (I_B)_3 \; + \; ... \; + \; Q_n \, (I_B)_n}{z^2}$$

$$\sigma_z = \frac{1}{z^2} \sum_{i=1}^{n} Q_i \, (I_B)_i$$

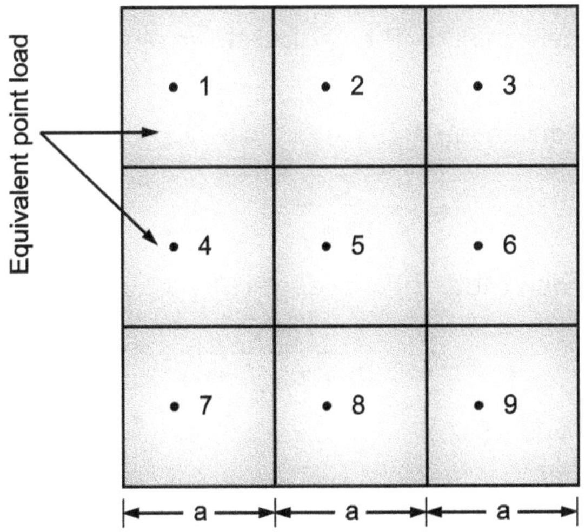

Equivalent point load

• 1	• 2	• 3
• 4	• 5	• 6
• 7	• 8	• 9

|← a →|← a →|← a →|

Fig. 6.11 : Equivalent point load system

(b) Two to One Load Distribution Method : The actual distribution of the load with the depth is complex. However, it can be assumed to spread approximately at slope of two (vertical) to one (horizontal).

The vertical pressure at any depth (z) below the soil surface can be determined approximately by constructing a frustum of pyramid of depth (z) and side slopes (2 : 1). The pressure distribution is assumed to be uniform on a horizontal plane at that depth. Refer Fig. 6.12.

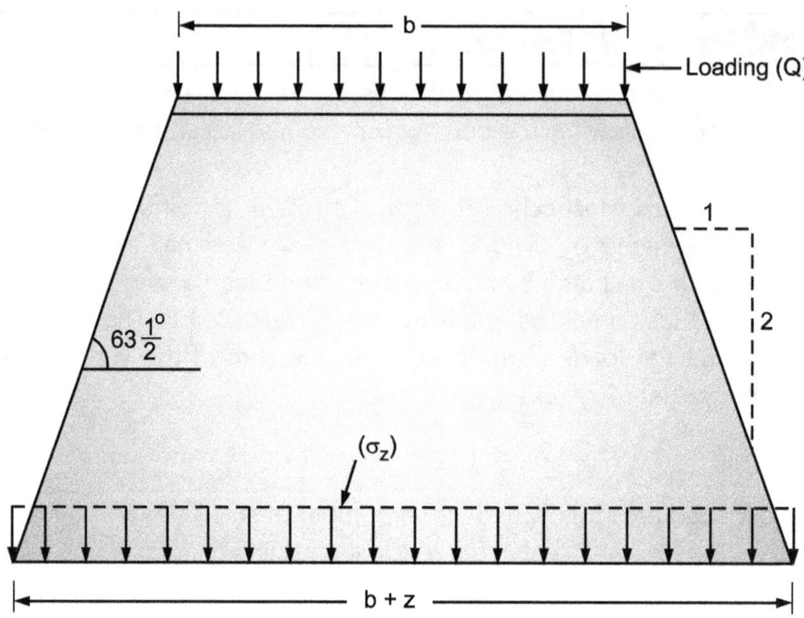

Fig. 6.12 : Two to one distribution system

This method gives fairly accurate values of the average vertical stress if the depth (z) is less than 2.5 times the width of the loaded area. The maximum stress is normally taken as 1.5 times the average stress determined. The vertical stress distribution for various footings is as below :

(i)   Circular area with diameter (D) :

$$\sigma_z = \frac{QD^2}{(D + z)^2}$$

(ii) Rectangular area with width (b) and length (l) :

$$\sigma_z = \frac{Q\,(b \times l)}{(b + z) \times (l + z)}$$

(iii) Square area with side (b) :

$$\sigma_z = \frac{Qb^2}{(b + z)^2}$$

(iv) Strip area with width (b) and unit length :

$$\sigma_z = \frac{Q\,(b \times l)}{(b + z) \times (z + 1)}$$

(c) Sixty Degree Distribution : If the pressure distribution is assumed along lines making an angle of 60° with the horizontal instead of $63\frac{1}{2}^{\circ}$ (2 : 1), then it is termed as 'sixty degree distribution' system. It gives approximately same results.

SOLVED EXAMPLES

Example 6.1 : A concentrated load of 300 kN is applied at the ground surface. Determine the vertical stress at a point Q which is 6 m directly below it. Also compute the vertical stress at a point R which is at depth 6 m but at a horizontal distance of 5 m from the load axis.

(Nov. 15, 6M)

Solution : We have,

$$\sigma_z = \frac{3Q}{2\pi z^2} \times \frac{1}{\left[1 + \left(\dfrac{r}{z}\right)^2\right]^{5/2}}$$

At point (Q), $\dfrac{r}{z} = 0$ since $r = 0$

$$\sigma_z = \frac{3 \times 300}{2\pi \times 6^2}\left[\frac{1}{(1 + 0)^{5/2}}\right] = 3.98 \text{ kN/m}^2$$

At point (R), $r = 5$, $z = 6$, $\dfrac{r}{z} = \dfrac{5}{6}$

$$\sigma_z = \frac{3 \times 300}{2\pi \times 6^2}\left[\frac{1}{\left[1 + \left(\dfrac{5}{6}\right)^2\right]^{5/2}}\right]$$

$$= \mathbf{1.06 \text{ kN/m}^2}$$

Example 6.2 : A line load of 150 kN/m is acting on the ground surface along a vertically downward direction. Determine the vertical stress at P which is 3.6 m deep and 2 m away horizontally.

Solution :

$$\sigma_z = \frac{2Q}{\pi}\,\frac{z^3}{(z^2 + r^2)^2}$$

$$= \frac{2 \times 150}{\pi} \times \frac{(3.6)^3}{(3.6^2 + 2^2)^2}$$

$$= \mathbf{15.49 \text{ kN/m}^2}$$

Example 6.3 : Use Westergaard's solution to determine the vertical stresses at a point (P) which is 4 m below and at a radial distance of 4 m from the vertical load of 200 kN.

Solution :

$$\sigma_z = \frac{Q}{\pi z^2\left[1 + 2\left(\dfrac{r}{z}\right)^2\right]^{3/2}}$$

$$= \frac{200}{\pi \times 4^2\left[1 + 2\left(\dfrac{4}{4}\right)^2\right]^{3/2}} = \mathbf{0.765 \text{ kN/m}^2}$$

Example 6.4 : Calculate the vertical stresses at a point (P) at a depth of 3 m directly under the centre of the circular area of radius 2 m and subjected to a load of 200 kN/m^2.

Also calculate the vertical stress at a point (R) which is at the same depth of 3 m but 3 m away from centre of loaded area.

Solution :

$$\sigma_z = Q\left[1 - \left\{\frac{1}{1 + \left(\frac{a}{z}\right)^2}\right\}^{3/2}\right]$$

At point (P),

$$\sigma_z = 200\left[1 - \left\{\frac{1}{1 + \left(\frac{2}{3}\right)^2}\right\}^{3/2}\right]$$

$$= \textbf{84.80 kN/m}^2$$

To get vertical stresses at (R), it is necessary to refer the isobars of different intensities. For point (R) with z = 3 m and r = 3 m the vertical stress is about 0.23 Q.

At point (R), $\sigma_z = 0.23 \times 200 = \textbf{46 kN/m}^2$

Example 6.5 : Find out the vertical pressures at depths 3 m and 4 m directly below a load of 500 kN when (a) the load acts as point load, (b) the load is spread over circular area of radius 2 m on the surface.

Solution : (a) $\sigma_z = \dfrac{0.477\,Q}{z^2}$ $r = 0 \therefore I_B = 0.477$ (Refer Table 6.1)

At depth 3 m, $\sigma_z = \dfrac{0.477 \times 500}{3^2} = \textbf{26.5 kN/m}^2$

At depth 4 m, $\sigma_z = \dfrac{0.477 \times 500}{4^2} = \textbf{14.9 kN/m}^2$

(b) Here the load (Q) is distributed over circular area of radius 2 m.

Hence load intensity, $Q_1 = \dfrac{Q}{A} = \dfrac{500}{\left(\frac{\pi}{4}\, 4^2\right)} = 39.8$ kN/m^2.

At depth 3 m :

$$\sigma_z = Q_1\left[1 - \frac{1}{\left[1 + \left(\frac{a}{z}\right)^2\right]^{3/2}}\right]$$

$$= 39.8\left[1 - \frac{1}{\left\{1 + \left(\frac{2}{3}\right)^2\right\}^{3/2}}\right] = \textbf{16.9 kN/m}^2$$

At depth 4 m :

$$\sigma_z = 39.8\left[1 - \frac{1}{\left\{1 + \left(\frac{2}{4}\right)^2\right\}^{3/2}}\right] = \textbf{11.32 kN/m}^2$$

Example 6.6 : Four column loads of 1000 kN each are spaced to form a square 4 m × 4 m. Determine the vertical increment in stress at a depth 10 m below the centre of the square using Boussinesq's theory. Assume the column load as a point from the figure.

Solution : Since $R^2 = (2)^2 + (2)^2 = 8$

Boussinesq's equation is $\sigma_T = \dfrac{3Q}{2\pi z^2}\left[\dfrac{1}{1 + \dfrac{R^2}{z^2}}\right]^{3/2}$

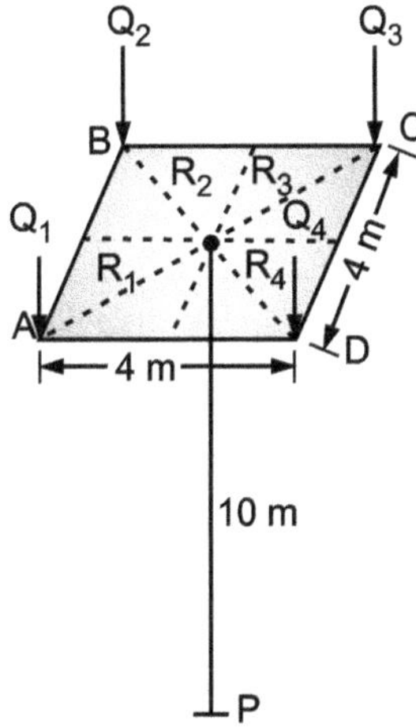

Fig. 6.13

$\therefore$ Stress at P due to Q_1

$$d_{z_1} = \frac{3 \times 1000}{2\pi(10^2)}\left[\frac{1}{1 + \left(\frac{8}{(10)^2}\right)}\right]^{5/2}$$

$$= \mathbf{3.94\ kN/m^2}$$

Since, Q_1, Q_2, Q_3, Q_4 are equal and R_1, R_2, R_3, R_4 are also same.

$\therefore$ By symmetry :

$$\sigma_{Total} = 4 \times 3.94 = 15.76\ kN/m^2$$

Now let P be below Q_1 at depth 10 m :

$\therefore$ $R^2 = 0$

$\therefore$ $$\sigma_{ZQ_1} = \frac{3 \times 1000}{2\pi\ (10)^2}\left[\frac{1}{1}\right]^{5/2}$$

$$= 4.775\ kN/m^2\ \ (\text{due to } Q_1)$$

σ_{ZQ_2} due to Q_2. Here R = 4 m

$$\therefore \qquad \sigma_{ZQ_2} = \frac{3 \times 1000}{2\pi(10)^2}\left[\frac{1}{1 + \dfrac{(4)^2}{(10)^2}}\right]^{5/2}$$

$$= \mathbf{3.29\ kN/m^2}$$

σ_{ZQ_3} due to Q_3. Here $R^2 = (4)^2 + (4)^2 = 32$

$$\therefore \qquad \sigma_{ZQ_3} = \frac{3 \times 1000}{2\pi(10)^2}\left[\frac{1}{1 + \dfrac{32}{(10)^2}}\right]^{5/2}$$

$$= \mathbf{2.385\ kN/m^2}$$

σ_{ZQ_4} due to Q_4. Here $R = 4$

$$\therefore \qquad \sigma_{ZQ_4} = \frac{3 \times 1000}{2\pi(10)^2}\left[\frac{1}{1 + \dfrac{16}{(10)^2}}\right]^{5/2} = \mathbf{3.29\ kN/m^3}$$

$\therefore$ Total σ_z when P is below Q_1 :

$$= 4.755 + 3.29 + 2.385 + 3.29 = 13.74\ kN/m^2$$

$\therefore$ Increase in stress : $= 15.76 - 13.74$

$$= \mathbf{2.02\ kN/m^2}$$

Note : In solved examples 6, 7 and 8 the (R) indicates the horizontal radial distance from the point of application of load (Q).

Example 6.7 : Three point loads act at points A, B, C on the surface of the soil with the point B between A and C. The distances are AB = 4 m, BC = 8 m. The value of point loads are 200 kN at A, 400 kN at B, 800 kN at C. Find the vertical stress at a point 8 m below B.

(Nov. 16 6 M)

Solution :

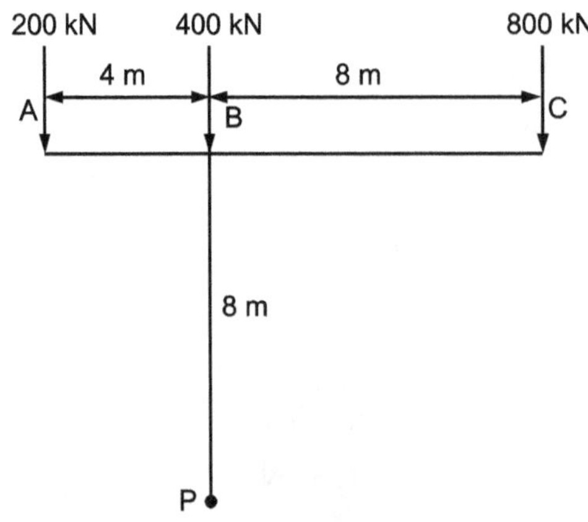

Fig. 6.14

For 200 kN load :

$$R = 4 \text{ m}$$

$$\frac{R}{z} = \frac{4}{8} = 0.5 \text{ m}$$

$$I_B = \frac{3}{2\pi} \left[\frac{1}{1\left(\frac{R}{z}\right)^2} \right]^{5/2}$$

$$= \frac{3}{2\pi} \left[\frac{1}{1 + (0.5)^2} \right]^{5/2} = \mathbf{0.273}$$

$$\sigma_{Z_A} = I_B \frac{Q}{z^2}$$

$$= 0.273 \frac{200}{(8)^2} = 0.854 \text{ kN/m}^2$$

For 400 kN load :

$$\frac{R}{z} = 0$$

$$\therefore \quad I_B = \frac{3}{2\pi} \left[\frac{1}{1 + (0)^2} \right]^{5/2} = 0.477$$

$$\therefore \quad \sigma_{Z_B} = 0.477 \times \frac{400}{(8)^2} = 2.98 \text{ kN/m}^2$$

For 800 kN load :

$$\frac{R}{z} = \frac{8}{8} = 1$$

$$I_B = \frac{3}{2\pi} \left[\frac{1}{1 + 1} \right]^{5/2} = 0.08$$

$$\therefore \quad \sigma_{Z_C} = 0.08 \times \frac{800}{(8)^2} = 1.055 \text{ kN/m}^2$$

$\therefore \quad \sigma_{Z_{Total}}$ at point 8 m below B :

$$= \sigma_{Z_A} + \sigma_{Z_B} + \sigma_{Z_C} = 0.854 + 2.98 + 1.055$$

$$= \mathbf{4.889 \text{ kN/m}^2}$$

Example 6.8 : In a soil mass 'R' the horizontal distance of a point from a point load at the surface is such that the vertical stress at a point at depth z = 1 m is equal to the stress at another point at depth z = 1.2 m and radial distance R = 1 m.

Solution :   For z = 1.2 m :

$$\therefore \quad \sigma_T = \frac{3}{2\pi (1.2)^2} \left[\frac{1}{1 + \left(\frac{1}{1.2}\right)^2} \right]^{5/2}$$

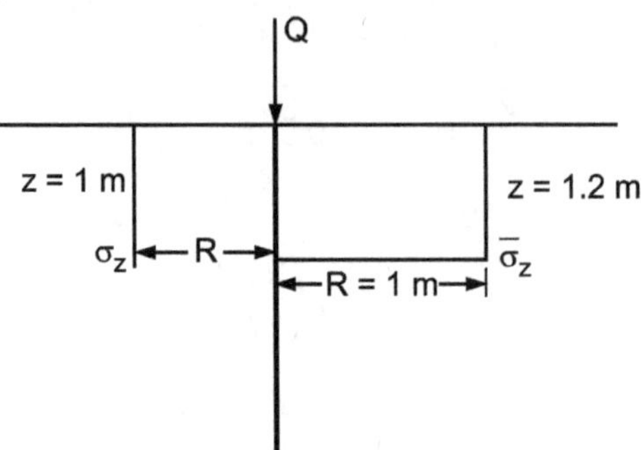

Fig. 6.15

For z = 1.0 m :
$$\sigma_z = \frac{3}{2\pi (1)^2} \left[\frac{1}{1 \times \left(\frac{R}{1}\right)^2} \right]^{5/2}$$

∴ σ_z is same for both the cases.

∴ $$\frac{3}{2\pi (1.2)^2} \left[\frac{1}{1 + \left(\frac{1}{1.2}\right)^2} \right]^{5/2} = \frac{3}{2\pi (1)^2} \left[\frac{1}{1 \times \left(\frac{R}{1}\right)^2} \right]^{5/2} = R = \mathbf{0.98\ m}$$

Example 6.9 : A footing 2 m × 4 m has a udl of 1000 kN/m². Considering the udl on a four equivalent point loads acting at the centre of each quadrant, find the vertical stress below the corner of the loaded area at a depth of 2 m. Use Boussinesq's equation.

Solution : Given : $Q_1 = Q_2 = Q_3 = Q_4 = 1000\ (1 \times 2) = 2000$ kN

Since U.D.L. = 1000 kN/m²

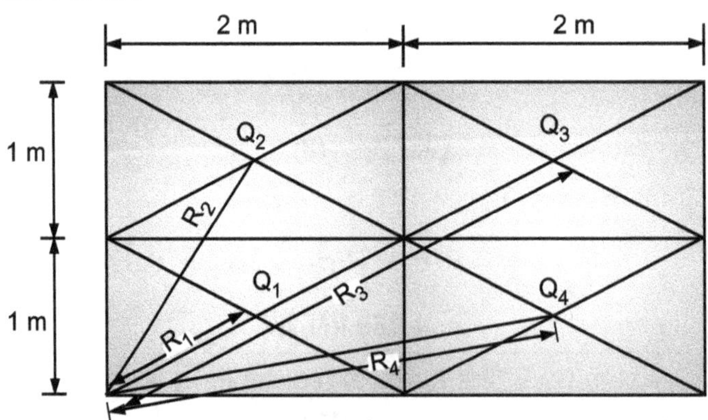

Fig. 6.16

$$R_1^2 = (1)^2 + (0.5)^2 = 1.25\ m^2$$

$$R_2^2 = (1)^2 + (1.5)^2 = 3.25\ m^2$$

$$R_3^2 = (3)^2 + (1.5)^2 = 11.25\ m^2$$

$$R_4^2 = (3)^2 + (0.5)^2 = 9.25 \text{ m}^2$$

$$\sigma_1 = \frac{3 \times 2000}{2\pi(2)^2} \left[\frac{1}{1 + \dfrac{1.25}{4}} \right]^{5/2} = 120.96 \text{ kN/m}^2$$

$$\sigma_2 = \frac{3 \times 2000}{2\pi(2)^2} \left[\frac{1}{1 + \dfrac{3.25}{4}} \right]^{5/2} = 53.98 \text{ kN/m}^2$$

$$\sigma_3 = \frac{3 \times 2000}{2\pi(2)^2} \left[\frac{1}{1 + \dfrac{11.25}{4}} \right]^{5/2} = 8.41 \text{ kN/m}^2$$

$$\sigma_4 = \frac{3 \times 2000}{2\pi(2)^2} \left[\frac{1}{1 + \dfrac{9.25}{4}} \right]^{5/2} = 11.95 \text{ kN/m}^2$$

$$\sigma_{Total} = \sigma_1 + \sigma_2 + \sigma_3 + \sigma_4 = \mathbf{195.308 \text{ kN/m}^2}$$

Example 6.10 : Two railway – wagon lines in a yard are located at 6 m centre to centre. The average load per metre run in the lines is 100 and 80 kN/m. Find the vertical stress induced by this loading at a depth of 2 m beneath each load and half-way between them. If a 100 kN crane is installed exactly mid-way between the lines, what additional stress is caused below the crane at the same depth.

Solution : Consider the railway–wagon load as a line load of infinite extent. The vertical stress is given as

$$\sigma_z = \frac{2qz^3}{\pi \, (z^2 + r^2)^2} \qquad\qquad \text{(Refer Article 6.3.4)}$$

(i)   Stress below 100 kN/m load :

$$= \frac{2 \times 100}{\pi} \left[\frac{2^3}{(0^2 + 2^2)^2} \right] + \frac{2 \times 80}{\pi} \left[\frac{2^3}{(6^2 + 2^2)^2} \right] = \mathbf{32.08 \text{ kN/m}^2}$$

(ii) Stress below 80 kN/m load :

$$= \frac{2 \times 80}{\pi} \left[\frac{2^3}{(0^2 + 2^2)^2} \right] + \frac{2 \times 100}{\pi} \left[\frac{2^3}{(6^2 + 2^2)^2} \right] = \mathbf{25.78 \text{ kN/m}^2}$$

(iii) Stress mid-way between two loadings :

$$= \frac{2 \times 100}{\pi} \left[\frac{2^3}{(3^2 + 2^2)^2} \right] + \frac{2 \times 80}{\pi} \left[\frac{2^3}{(3^2 + 2^2)^2} \right] = \mathbf{5.42 \text{ kN/m}^2}$$

The additional stress below the crane, considering the crane load as vertical concentrated load, is given as

$$\sigma_z = \frac{3Q}{2\pi z^2} \left[\frac{1}{1 + \left(\dfrac{r}{2}\right)^2} \right]^{5/2} = \frac{3 \times 100}{2\pi \, 2^2} \left[\frac{1}{1 + \left(\dfrac{0}{2}\right)^2} \right]^{5/2} = \mathbf{11.94 \text{ kN/m}^2}$$

Example 6.11 : A water tank is supported by a ring foundation having outer diameter of 8 m and inner diameter of 6 m. The uniform load intensity on the foundation is 200 kN/m². Compute the vertical stress caused by the water tank at a depth of 4 m below the centre of the foundation.

Solution : The equation applicable to find vertical stress under a wholly loaded circular area used in above example can be extended to such cases where the entire circular area is not loaded and only a ring portion is loaded between the radius R_o and R_i as shown in Fig. 6.17.

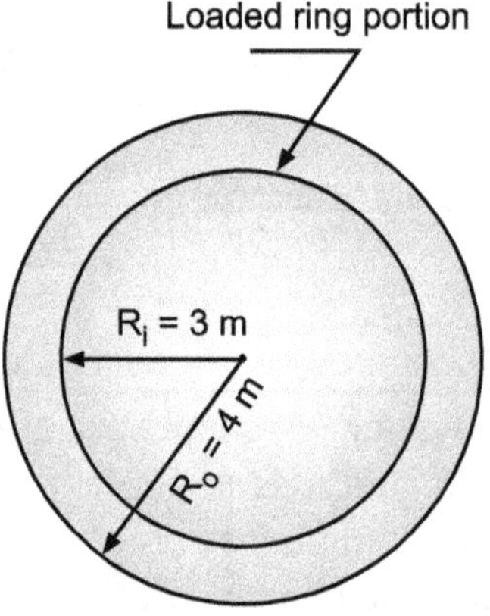

Fig. 6.17

$$\sigma_z = q\left[1 - \left[\frac{1}{1 + \left(\frac{R_o}{z}\right)^2}\right]^{3/2}\right] - q\left[1 - \left[\frac{1}{1 + \left(\frac{R_i}{z}\right)^2}\right]^{3/2}\right]$$

where,

R_o = Outer radius of ring = 4 m

R_i = Inner radius of ring = 3 m

q = 200 kN/m²

z = 4 m

$\therefore$

$$\sigma_z = 200\left[1 - \left[\frac{1}{1 + \left(\frac{4}{4}\right)^2}\right]^{3/2}\right] - 200\left[1 - \left[\frac{1}{1 + \left(\frac{3}{4}\right)^2}\right]^{3/2}\right]$$

$$= 200\left[1 - \left[\frac{1}{2}\right]^{3/2}\right] - 200\left[1 - \left[\frac{1}{1.5625}\right]^{3/2}\right]$$

$$= 200\,[1 - 0.354] - 200\,[1 - 0.512]$$

$$= 129.29 - 97.6$$

$$= \mathbf{31.69\ kN/m^2}$$

Example 6.12 : Prove that, (a) (i) Maximum vertical stress on a plane at a distance 'r' from concerned load Q acting at ground surface will be at a depth $z = 1.225\ r$ and (ii) the value of maximum stress will be,

$$\sigma_{z\ max} = \frac{0.0887\ Q}{r^2}$$

(b) Hence or otherwise find max. vertical pressure on a vertical plane at a distance of 2.5 m from the line of action of 125 kN load.

Solution : (a) From Boussinesq's equation,

$$\sigma_z = \frac{3Q}{2\pi\ z^2} \cdot \frac{1}{\left[\left(1 + \dfrac{2}{3}\right)^2\right]^{5/2}} \qquad \text{...(i)}$$

$$= \frac{3Q}{2\pi} \left\{\frac{z^5}{z^2\ (z^2 + r^2)^{5/2}}\right\}$$

$$= \frac{3Q}{2\pi} \left[\frac{z^3}{(z^2 + r^2)^{5/2}}\right]$$

Differentiating w.r.t. σ_z and equating to zero, we get

$$\frac{d\sigma_z}{dz} = \frac{3Q}{2\pi} \left\{\frac{3z^2\ (z^2 + r^2)^{5/2} - \dfrac{5}{2}\ (r^2 + z^2)^{3/2} \cdot 2z \times z^3}{(z^2 + r^2)^5}\right\} = 0$$

$$\therefore \qquad 3z^2\ (z^2 + r^2) = 5z^4$$

$$\text{i.e. } 2z^4 = 3z^2\ r^2$$

$$\therefore \qquad z^2 = \frac{3}{2}\ r^2$$

$$\text{i.e.} \qquad z = \sqrt{\frac{3}{2}} \cdot r = \mathbf{1.225\ r} \qquad \text{...(ii)}$$

Substituting in equation (i),

$$\sigma_{max} = \frac{0.4775\ Q}{(1.225\ r)^2} \left\{\frac{1}{1 + \left(\dfrac{r}{1.225r}\right)^2}\right\}^{5/2}$$

$$= \frac{\mathbf{0.0887\ Q}}{\mathbf{r^2}} \qquad \text{...(iii)}$$

Hence, the proof.

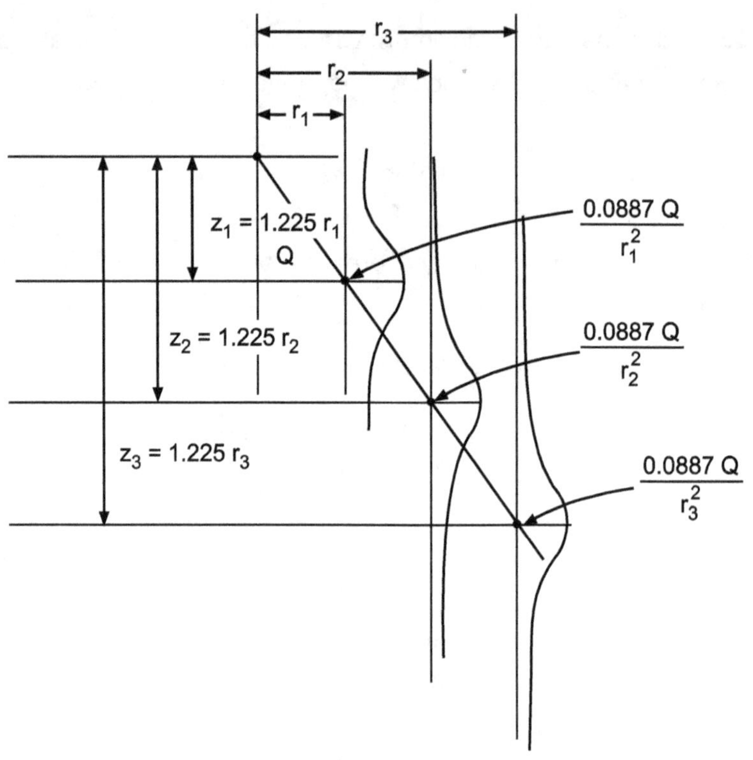

Fig. 6.18

(b)
$$\sigma_{z\,max} = \frac{0.0887\,Q}{r^2}$$

Here
$$Q = 125 \text{ kN} \quad \text{and} \quad r = 2.5 \text{ m}$$

$\therefore$
$$\sigma_{z\,max} = \frac{0.0887 \times 125}{(2.5)^2} = 1.774 \text{ kN/m}^2$$

$\sigma_{z\,max}$ will occur at $z = 1.225$ i.e. $r = 1.225 \times 2.5 = 3.0625$ m

$$\tan\theta = \frac{r}{1.225r} = 0.81632653$$

$\therefore$
$$\theta = \tan^{-1} 0.81632653$$
$$= 31° - 13' - 32.43'' \, (\approx 31.2256°)$$

Example 6.13 : Calculate by using Boussinesq's equation for vertical stress at any point in soil mass due to a point load on the surface along the centre line of the load for the following data : (i) Surface point load 10 kN, (ii) Values z = 1, 2, 3 and 4 m, and also plot its variation.

Solution : Given : $Q_0 = 10$ kN, $r = 0$, $z = 1, 2, 3, 4$ m.

We know :
$$\sigma_z = \frac{3Q_0}{2\pi z^2}\left[\frac{1}{1 + \left(\dfrac{r}{z}\right)^2}\right]^{5/2}$$

Put $r = 0$, $Q_0 = 10$ kN, $\sigma_z = \dfrac{4.77}{z^2}$

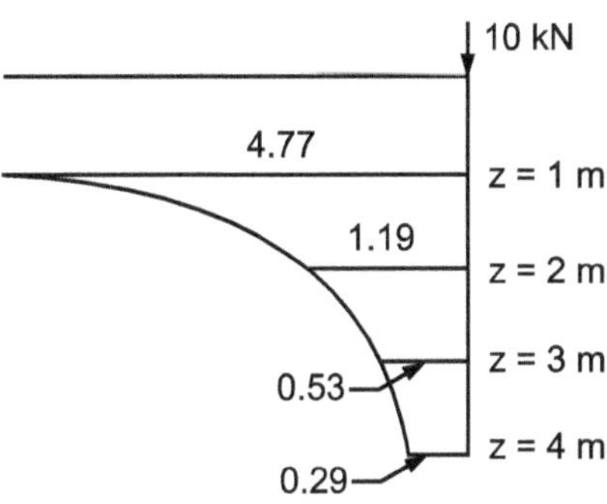

Fig. 6.19

Now when $z = 1$ $\sigma_{z_1} = $ **4.77 kN/m²**

$z = 2$ $\sigma_{z_2} = $ **1.19 kN/m²**

$z = 3$ $\sigma_{z_3} = $ **0.53 kN/m²**

$z = 4$ $\sigma_{z_4} = $ **0.29 kN/m²**

Total vertical stress = Stress due to self weight + Stress due to surface load intensity

1. Stress due to self weight :

$$\sigma_v = \gamma \cdot z$$

$$= 23 \times 6 = 138 \text{ kN/m}^2$$

2. Stress (σ_z) due to surface load intensity :

$$q_0 = \frac{2000}{4 \times 4} = 125 \text{ kN/m}^2$$

Now $\sigma_z = q_0 \cdot I$

where $I = 0.1069$ for $m = \dfrac{B}{z} = n = 0.66$

$\therefore$ $\sigma_z = 125 \times 0.1069$

$$= 13.36 \text{ kN/m}^2$$

$\therefore$ Total vertical stress :

$$\sigma = \sigma_v + \sigma_z$$

$$= 138 + 13.36$$

$$= \textbf{151.36 kN/m}^2$$

Example 6.14 : A concentrated load of 100 kN is applied at the ground surface. Compute the vertical pressure (i) at a depth of 4 m below the load, (ii) at a distance of 3 m at the same depth. Use Boussinesq's equation. Given m = n = 0.66, I = 0.1069.

Solution : We have :

$$\sigma_z = \frac{3Q}{2\pi z^2} \cdot \frac{1}{\left[1 + \left(\dfrac{r}{z}\right)^2\right]^{5/2}}$$

Case 1 : $\dfrac{r}{z}$ = 0; since r = 0, z = 4 m

$$\sigma_z = \frac{3 \times 100}{2\pi \times 4} \left[\frac{1}{\left(1 + (0)^2\right)^{5/2}}\right]$$

$$= \textbf{29.84 kN/m}^2$$

Case 2 : r = 3, z = 4, $\dfrac{r}{z}$ = 0.75

$$\sigma_z = \frac{3 \times 100}{2\pi \times 4} \left[\frac{1}{\left(1 + (0.75)^2\right)^{5/2}}\right]$$

$$= \textbf{3.9 kN/m}^2$$

Example 6.15 : A pit 8 m square and 6 m deep is excavated in a soil of γ = 20 kN/m³. Calculate the relief in the vertical stress produced below the centre point of excavation to a depth of 8 m below the base of excavation. Given for m = n = 0.5, I = 0.082.

Solution : The effect of excavation of the soil is the reverse of an applied uniform load. The stress relief of 6 m depth can thus be calculated as follows :

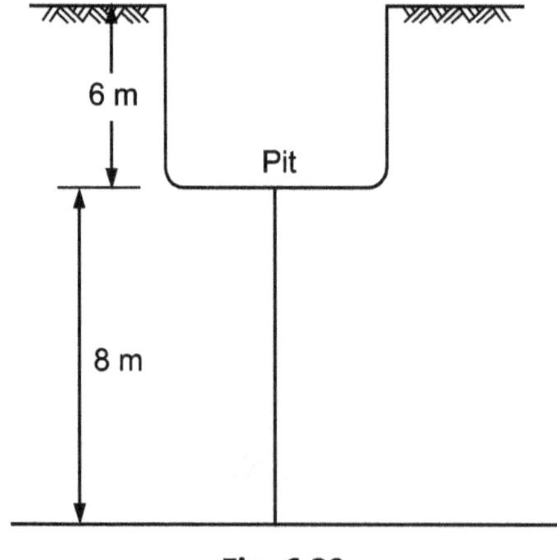

Fig. 6.20

Relief of pressure at base of excavation

$$= \gamma . z = 20 \times 6 \text{ kN/m}^2$$

$$= \textbf{120 kN/m}^2$$

The pit can be divided into four squares 4 m × 4 m each, with a corner at the centre of excavation. Then for each shape m = 0.5 = n and I = 0.082.

The resulting relief pressure is given by

$$\sigma_z = 4 \times q \cdot I$$

$$= 4 \times 120 \times 0.082 = \mathbf{39.369 \ kN/m^2}$$

Example 6.16 : A concentrated load of 40 kN is applied vertically on a horizontal ground surface. Determine the vertical stress intensities at the following points :

(i) At a depth of 3 m below the point of application of the load.

(ii) At a depth of 1 m and at a radial distance of 3 m from the line of action of the load.

Solution : (i) $\quad \sigma_z = 0.4775 \dfrac{Q}{z^2} = 0.4775 \times \dfrac{40}{3^2} = \mathbf{2.1222 \ kN/m^2} \quad [z = 3; \ r = 0]$

(ii) $\quad \sigma_z = 0.4775 \dfrac{Q}{z^2} \left(\dfrac{1}{1 + \left(\dfrac{r}{z}\right)^2} \right)^{5/2} \quad [z = 1; \ r = 3]$

$$= \frac{0.4775 \times 40}{1^2} \left(\frac{1}{[1 + (3)^2]^{5/2}} \right) = \frac{19}{316} = \mathbf{0.0604 \ kN/m^2}$$

Example 6.17 : For a single, concentrated load of 500 kN acting on the ground surface, construct an isobar for $\sigma_z = 20 \ kN/m^2$. Show at least six points on the isobar.

Solution : $\quad \sigma_z = 20 = \dfrac{0.4775 \, Q}{z^2} \left[\dfrac{1}{1 + \left(\dfrac{r}{z}\right)^2} \right]^{5/2}$

$$Q = 500 \ kN$$

(i) When r = 0 $\quad z = \sqrt{\dfrac{0.4775 \times 500}{20}} = 5\sqrt{0.4775} = \mathbf{3.455 \ m}$

(ii) When z = 2 $\quad \left[1 + \left(\dfrac{r}{z}\right)^2 \right] = \left(\dfrac{0.4775 \times 500}{20 \times 2 \times 2} \right)^{0.4} = 1.5486$

$\therefore \quad \left(\dfrac{r}{z}\right)^2 = 1.5486 - 1 = 0.5486$

$\therefore \quad \dfrac{r}{z} = \sqrt{0.5486} = 0.7407$

$\therefore \quad r = z \times 0.7407 = 2 \times 0.7407 = \mathbf{1.4814}$

(iii) When z = 1 $\quad r = \sqrt{\left(\dfrac{0.4775 \times 500}{20 \times 1} \right)^{0.4} - 1} = \mathbf{1.3024}$

(iv) When z = 0.5

$$\left(\frac{r}{z}\right) = \sqrt{\left(\frac{0.4775 \times 500}{20 \times 0.5 \times 0.5}\right)^{0.4} - 1} = \mathbf{1.9221}$$

$$\therefore \qquad r = 0.5 \times 1.9221 = \mathbf{0.961}$$

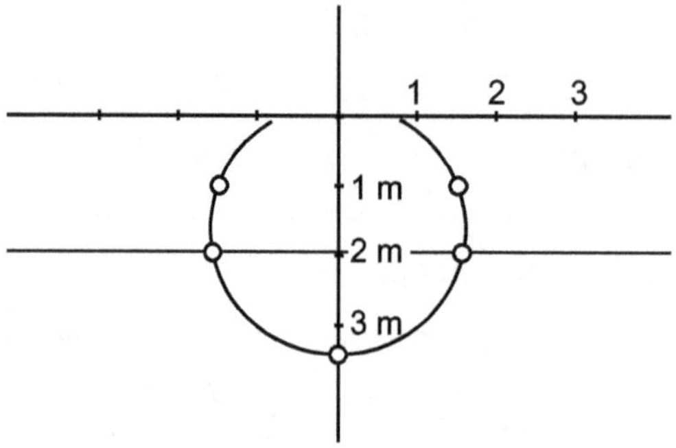

Fig. 6.21

Example 6.18 : A load of 1000 kN acts as a point load at the surface of a soil mass. Estimate the stress at a point 3 m below and 4 m away from the point of action of the load by Boussinesq's formula. Compare the value with the result from Westergaard's theory.

(May 15, 6 M)

Solution : As per Boussinesq's theory,

$$\sigma_z = \frac{0.4775 \times Q}{z^2}\left[\frac{1}{\left(1 + \left(\dfrac{r}{z}\right)^2\right)}\right]^{5/2}$$

$$Q = 1000 \text{ kN}$$
$$z = 3$$
$$r = 4$$

$$\therefore \qquad \sigma_z = \frac{0.4775 \times 1000}{9} \times \frac{1}{\left[1 + \left(\dfrac{4}{3}\right)^2\right]^{5/2}}$$

$$= \frac{53}{12.75} = \mathbf{4.1544 \text{ kN/m}^2}$$

As per Westergaard theory,

$$\sigma_z = \frac{Q}{\pi z^2}\frac{1}{\left[1 + 2\left(\dfrac{r}{z}\right)^2\right]^{3/2}}$$

$$= \frac{1000}{\pi \times 4 \times 4}\left(\frac{1}{\left[1 + 2 \times \left(\dfrac{4}{3}\right)^2\right]^{3/2}}\right) = \frac{35.368}{7.6665}$$

$$= \mathbf{3.6588 \text{ kN/m}^2}$$

Example 6.19 : Four column loads 1000 kN each are spaced to form a square 4 m × 4 m. Determine the vertical stress increment at a depth of 10 m below the centre of the square using Boussinesq's equation.

Solution :

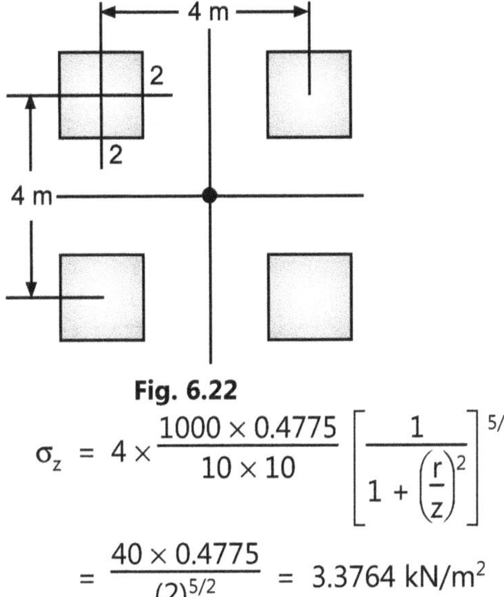

Fig. 6.22

$$\sigma_z = 4 \times \frac{1000 \times 0.4775}{10 \times 10} \left[\frac{1}{1 + \left(\dfrac{r}{z}\right)^2} \right]^{5/2}$$

$$= \frac{40 \times 0.4775}{(2)^{5/2}} = 3.3764 \ \text{kN/m}^2$$

Example 6.20 : (a) Four column loads of 1000 kN each are spaced to form a square of 4 m × 4 m, determine the vertical stress increment at a depth of 10 m below the centre of the square, using Boussinesq's theory.

(b) Prove that stress below the point load as calculated by Wasterguard and Boussinesq's theory are in the ratio of 1 : 1.5 approximately.

Solution : (a) : Refer Q. No. 8 above.

(b)

$$\sigma_z = \frac{Q}{\dfrac{2}{3} \pi z^2} \frac{1}{\left[1 + \left(\dfrac{r}{z}\right)^2 \right]^{5/2}} \qquad \text{... Boussinesq's theory}$$

$$= \frac{1.5 \, Q}{\pi z^2} \left[\text{if } \frac{r}{z} = 0 \right] \qquad \text{...(i)}$$

$$\sigma_z = \frac{Q}{\pi z^2} \frac{1}{\left[1 + 2\left(\dfrac{r}{z}\right)^2 \right]^{3/2}} \qquad \text{... Westergaard's theory}$$

$$= \frac{Q}{\pi z^2} \left[\text{if } \frac{r}{z} = 0 \right] \qquad \text{...(ii)}$$

Dividing equation (ii) by equation (i), we get

$$\frac{\sigma_{W \ (Westergaard)}}{\sigma_{z \ (Boussinesq)}} = \frac{1}{1.5}$$

Example 6.21 : A raft of size 6m × 4m carries a uniformly distributed load of 160 kN/m². Determine the intensity of vertical stress at depth of 2 m below the base of raft, assuming (2 : 1) distribution.

Solution :

$$\sigma_z = \frac{a\,(b \times l)}{(b + z)\,(l + z)}$$

$$\sigma_z' = \frac{6 \times 4 \times 160}{(4 + 2)\,(6 + 2)}$$

$$= \frac{24 \times 160}{6 \times 8}$$

$$= \mathbf{80\ kN/m^2}$$

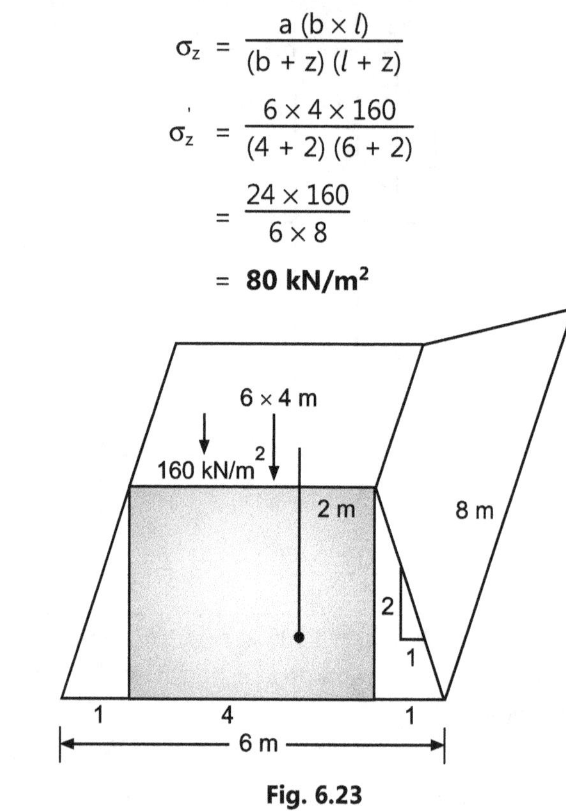

Fig. 6.23

Example 6.22 : A raft of size 3 m × 5 m carries uniformly distributed load of 175 kN/m². Determine the intensity of vertical stress at a depth of 2 m below G.L. (Assume load distribution as 2 vertical : 1 horizontal).

Solution :

$$\sigma_z' = \frac{3 \times 5 \times 175}{(3 + 2)\,(5 + 2)} = \mathbf{75\ kN/m^2}$$

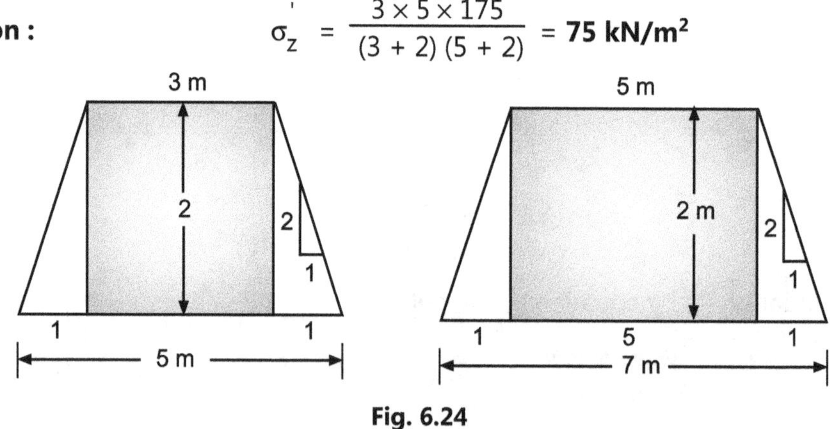

Fig. 6.24

Example 6.23 : A circular foundation rests on the horizontal upper surface of a semi-infinite soil mass, whose properties comply with the usual elasticity requirements and carries a load of 1000 kN. The contact pressure is uniform and the foundation is flexible. The base of the foundation is frictionless. The diameter of the foundation is 3 m. Determine the vertical stress distribution on horizontal planes along the central axis of the foundation to a depth of 10 m below the surface.

Solution : Total load coming through circular foundation in a uniform manner

$$= 1000 \text{ kN}$$

$$\text{Area of foundation } = \frac{\pi D^2}{4} = \frac{\pi \times 3^2}{4} \text{ m}^2 = 7.069 \text{ m}^2$$

$$\therefore \quad \text{Uniform load intensity } = \frac{1000}{7.069} = 141.47 \text{ kN/m}^2$$

The vertical stress caused by uniform load on circular area is

$$\sigma_z = q\left[1 - \left[\frac{1}{1 + \left(\frac{R}{z}\right)^2}\right]^{3/2}\right]$$

Here, $q = 141.47 \text{ kN/m}^2$, R = Radius = 1.5 m, z = 10 m

$$\therefore \quad \sigma_z = 141.47\left[1 - \left[\frac{1}{1 + \left(\frac{1.5}{10}\right)^2}\right]^{3/2}\right]$$

$$= \textbf{4.64 kN/m}^2$$

Example 6.24 : The foundation of water tank is a circular ring type. The pressure distribution on the soil is 70 kN/m². The outer radius of the foundation is 6 metres and the width of the foundation ring is 2 metres. Calculate the intensity of vertical pressure at a point 7.5 m, below its centre.

Solution :

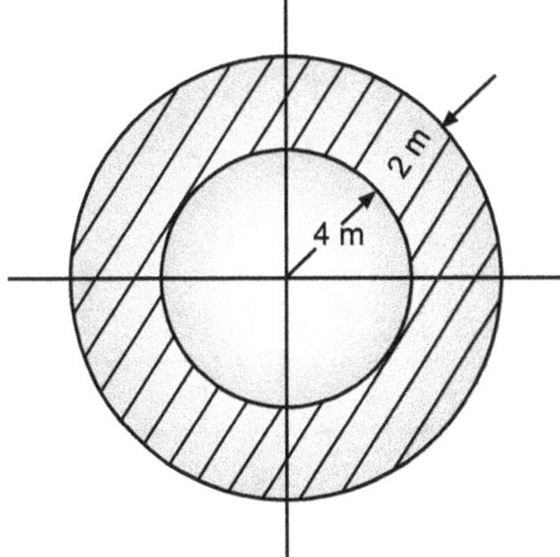

Fig. 6.25

$$\sigma_z = q\left[1-\left[\frac{1}{1+\left(\frac{R_o^2}{z}\right)}\right]^{3/2}\right] - q\left[1-\left[\frac{1}{1+\left(\frac{R_i}{z}\right)^2}\right]^{3/2}\right]$$

$q = 70 \ kN/m^2, \quad R_o = 6 \ m, \quad R_i = 4 \ m, \quad z = 7.5 \ m$

$$\frac{R_o}{z} = \frac{6}{7.5} = 0.8$$

$$\frac{R_i}{z} = \frac{4}{6} = 0.67$$

$$\therefore \quad \sigma_z = 70\left\{\left[1-\left(\frac{1}{1+(0.8)^2}\right)^{3/2}\right]-\left[1-\left(\frac{1}{1+(0.67)^2}\right)^{3/2}\right]\right\}$$

$70\,(-\,0.4761395 + 0.57338) = \quad 70\,(0.09724) = 6.80682 \ kN/m^2$

Example 6.25 : An overhead water tank is supported at a depth of 3 m by four isolated square footings of 2 m side each placed in a square pattern with a centre to centre spacing of 8 m. Compute the vertical stress at the foundation level :

(i) At the centre of the four footings; and (ii) At the centre of one footing.

Adopt Boussinesq's point load approximation. The load on each footing is 700 kN.

Solution :

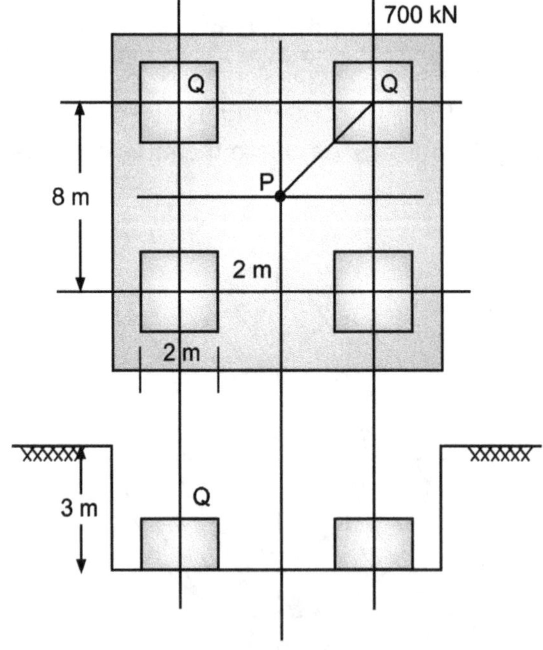

Fig. 6.26

(i) Stress at 3 m below P [which is C.G. of foundation] due to 700 kN at Q by each of point column

$$= \frac{(700 \times 0.4775) \times 4}{z^2 \times \left\{ \dfrac{1}{1 + \left(\dfrac{r}{z}\right)^2} \right\}^{5/2}}$$

Here,

$$z = 3 \text{ m}$$
$$PQ = 4\sqrt{2} = 5.657 \text{ m}$$

$\therefore$

$$\text{Stress} = \frac{2800 \times 0.4775}{9} \left\{ \frac{1}{1 + \left(\dfrac{5.657}{3}\right)^2} \right\}^{5/2}$$

$$= 148.5355 \times \frac{1}{(4.5555)^{5/2}}$$

$$= \frac{148.5555}{44.295} = \mathbf{3.3538 \text{ kN/m}^2}$$

(ii) Point P is at 3 m below point A.

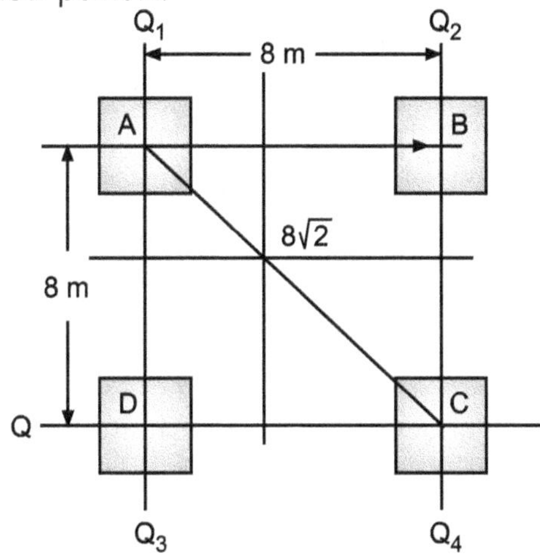

Fig. 6.27

$$\text{Stress at P} = \text{Stress due to Q at A} + \text{Stress due to Q at B}$$
$$+ \text{Stress due to Q at C} + \text{Stress due to Q at D}$$

$$= \frac{0.4775\, Q}{z^2} + \frac{0.4775 Q}{z^2} \left(\frac{1}{1 + \left(\dfrac{r_2}{z}\right)^2} \right)^{5/2}$$

$$+ \frac{0.4775\, Q}{z^2} \left(\frac{1}{1 + \left(\dfrac{r_3}{z}\right)^2} \right)^{5/2} + \frac{0.4775\, Q}{z^2} \left[\frac{1}{1 + \left(\dfrac{r_4}{z}\right)^2} \right]^{5/2}$$

$$= \frac{0.4775\,Q}{z^2}\left\{1 + 2\left[\left(\frac{1}{1+\left(\frac{8}{3}\right)^2}\right)^{5/2}\right] + \left[\frac{1}{1+\left(\frac{8\sqrt{2}}{3}\right)^2}\right]^{5/2}\right\}$$

$$= \frac{0.4775 \times 700}{9}\left\{1 + \frac{2}{(8.1111)^{5/2}} + \frac{1}{(15.2222)^{5/2}}\right\}$$

$$= 37.13888\left(1 + \frac{2}{187.369} + \frac{1}{903.73}\right)$$

$$= 37.13888\,(1 + 0.01067 + 1.10653 \times 10^{-3})$$

$$= \mathbf{37.576\ kN/m^2}$$

SUMMARY

1. The Boussinesq's solution for point load is the most popular and is applicable to a homogeneous, isotropic and elastic semi-infinite medium, which obeys Hooke's law within the range of stresses considered.

2. Stresses in the ground come from two kinds of sources : geostatic stresses are those due to the weight of the ground itself, while induced stresses are due to external loads.

3. Geostatic stresses, i.e. stress due to self weight of soil mass are neglected in the analysis by Boussinesq i.e. it is assumed that soil is weightless.

4. In Westergaard's theory it is assumed that, soil strata consists of (a) Thin layers, (b) Each layer has infinite rigidity, (c) Deformation is in downward direction, (d) Deformation in lateral direction is zero i.e. μ = Poisson's ratio is zero.

5. The locus of a point at which the vertical stress intensity is same is called as isobar or pressure bulb.

   For layered deposits, which show large lateral restraint, the more appropriate theory of stress distribution is considered to be Westergaard's theory .

6. The vertical stress intensity σ_z at a depth z directly beneath a concentrated load Q, according to Boussinesq is $\dfrac{3Q}{2\pi z^2}$, whereas that according to Westergaard is $\dfrac{Q}{\pi z^2}$.

7. Equations for vertical stress σ_z at depth z are :

$$\sigma_z = \frac{Q}{\frac{2}{3}\pi z\left[1+\left(\frac{r}{z}\right)^2\right]^{5/2}} \quad \text{... Boussinesq}$$

$$= \frac{Q}{\pi z^2}\frac{1}{\left[1+2\left(\frac{r}{z}\right)^2\right]^{3/2}} \quad \text{... Westergaard}$$

8. When stresses caused by concentrated load vertically below for depth z by Boussinesq's analysis are compared with that by Westergaadr analysis, former is 1.5 times more than later. In general, stresses determined using Boussinesq's theory are always higher than that due to Westergaadr analysis.

9. Maximum vertical stress on a plane at distance "r" from concentrated load Q will be at depth z = 1.225 r and its value will be

$$\sigma_{max} = \frac{0.0887\ Q}{r^2}$$

10. Only 5% stress intensity $\left[\text{i.e. } \dfrac{Q}{20}\right]$ will occur at depth

$$z = 3.09 \text{ m by Boussinesq theory}$$
$$= 2.53 \text{ m by Westergaard theory}$$

EXERCISE

1. Write the assumptions made in analysis of stresses of soil. Also draw stress-strain relationship.

2. Write a short note on Geostatic stresses.

3. Write limitations of Boussinesq's solutions.

4. State the Westergaard's theory. Write its expression for elastic condition of soil.

5. Explain the concept of pressure bulb or stress isobar.

6. Explain following methods.

    (a) Equivalent point load method

    (b) Two to one load distribution method.

7. Use Westergaard's theory to determine vertical stresses at a point (P) which is 5 m below and at radial distance of 5 m from vertical load of 250 kN.

8. Calculate the vertical stresses at a point (P) at a depth of 2 m directly under the centre of the circular area of radius 2 m and subjected to a load of 150 kN/m^2.

9. Using Boussinesq's equation solve following example a footing 3 m × 6 m has a udl of 1200 kN/m^2. Considering the udl on a four equivalent point loads acting at the centre of each quadrant, find the vertical stress below the corner of the loaded area at a depth of 2 m.

SOLVED UNIVERSITY QUESTIONS AND NUMERICALS

May 2014

1. Explain the term pressure bulb and its significance. **[6]**
   [**Ans.:** Refer Article 6.6]

December 2014

2. State and explain the terms involved in Boussinesq's point load and circular load equation for vertical stress determination. **[6]**
   [**Ans.:** Refer Article 6.3.1, 6.3.2]

May 2015

1. A load 1000 kN acts as a point load at the surface of a soil mass. Estimate the stress at a point 3 m below and 4 m away from the point of action of the load by Boussinesq's formula. Compare the value with the result from Westerguard's theory. **[6]**
   [**Ans.:** Refer Example 6.18]

November 2015

1. A concentrated load of 300 kN is applied at the ground surface. Compute the vertical pressure : **[6]**
   (i) at a depth of 6 m below the load
   (ii) at a distance of 5 m at the same depth.
   [**Ans.:** Refer Example 6.1]

May 2016

1. State the assumptions in Boussinesq's theory and explain the equation for vertical stress determination for point load with the terms involved in it. **[6]**
   [**Ans.:** Refer Article 6.3.2]

November 2016

1. Three point loads act at points A, B, C on the surface of the soil with the point B between A and C. The distances are AB = 4 m, BC = 8 m. The value of point loads are 200 kN at A, 400 kN at B, 800 kN at C. Find the vertical stress at a point 8 m below B. **[6]**
   [**Ans.:** Refer Example 6.7]

May 2017

1. Write any four assumptions made by Boussinesq to evaluate the stress at a point inside the soil mass due to a point load. Also explain in brief stress Isobar. **[7]**
   [**Ans.:** Refer Article 6.3.1]

Chapter 7
STREES DISTRIBUTION IN SOILS

7.1 SHEAR STRESS IN SOIL

The shear stresses develop when the soil is subjected to compression. The shear stresses developed when soil is subjected to direct tension, are not relevant, as the soil in this case fails in tension and does not fail in shear. The shear strength of the soil is its maximum resistance to shear stresses just before the failure. Thus, the shear failure of soil mass occurs when shear stresses induced due to applied compressive loads exceed the shear strength of the soil.

The shearing resistance i.e. *shearing strength of soil basically constitutes* of the following components :

- the *structural resistance* to displacement of the soil because of interlocking of the particles,
- the *frictional resistance* to translocation between the individual soil particles at their contact points and
- *cohesion* or *adhesion* between the surface of the soil particles.

The shear strength in cohesionless soil results from intergranular friction alone, while in all other soils it results from both internal friction as well as cohesion. However, plastic undrained clay does not possess internal friction.

The shear strength is the most important engineering property which governs the bearing capacity of the soil, the stability of slopes in soils, earth pressure and many other problems in soil mechanics. All problems in soil engineering are related in one way or the other with the shear strength of the soil.

7.2 EFFECTIVE STRESS AND PORE WATER PRESSURE [May 15, 17]

Soil differs from other engineering materials in one very important aspect, that it is a particulate three-phase-system. The void spaces enclosed by solid grains, are filled either fully by air (dry soil), fully by water (saturated soil), or partially by both (moist or partially saturated soil). When a soil mass is externally loaded, the network of particles tends to deform. A dry soil under compressive loading deforms instantaneously by compressing or expelling air in the voids. A saturated soil also under a compressive loading has a tendency to compress the pore water or to expel it. Expulsion is easy if the soil is highly pervious. The soil network undergoes compression only when it shares the external load. If the soil is impervious, the tendency to compress the pore water, which is incompressible would lead to development of internal pressure in water, known as *pore water pressure* (u_w). Development of pore water pressure has no effect in compressing the soil mass. Hence, it is also known as *neutral pressure*. No soil, however, can be ideally impervious. Development of pore water pressure within the void spaces creates hydraulic gradient and water starts flowing out of the network of soil grains. The rate of flow of water, as stated by Darcy's law depends on the hydraulic gradient and the coefficient of permeability. For a given hydraulic gradient, a highly pervious soil causes the pore water to flow very fast, giving scope for compression of soil network, under the given external load.

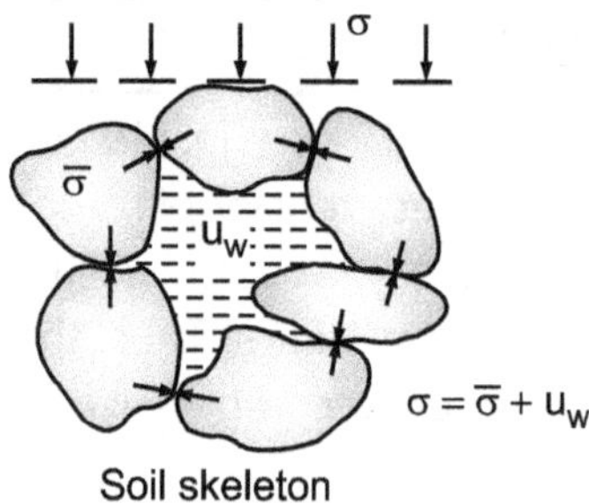

Soil skeleton

Fig. 7.1

In the case of impervious soils, the rate of flow is very small and compression is gradual With the escape of water from the soil network, the pore water pressure dissipates. Dissipation of pore water pressure transfers the load through particle contacts, to the soil skeleton, in the form of intergranular pressure and is effective in causing the soil mass to undergo compressive deformation. Hence, the intergranular pressure is known as *effective* stress $(\sigma')^*$. The externally applied pressure is known as *applied* or *total* stress, (σ). The soil network undergoes compression only after it shares the external load, in the form of effective stress. The time dependent relation,

$$\textbf{Effective stress, } \bar{\sigma} \textbf{ or } \sigma' = \sigma - u_w \qquad \qquad ... (7.1)$$

is known as *effective stress equation* (Fig. 7.1).

7.2.1 Effective Stress Concept

Consider a wavy surface Y - Y through a *saturated* soil (Fig. 7.2) , which pass through the points of contact without cutting across the particles. At the contact points, the stress intensity is so high (even under small finite interparticle forces), that the points of contact yield or crush and develop small areas of contact (Fig. 7.3). The normal and tangential forces at the contact points are therefore distributed on the contact areas. If the wavy surface is projected on a horizontal (or vertical) plane, the total area A, comprises of the contact area, A_m and area of water A_w together taking the vertical component V. It is easy to see that the contact area A_m is very small compared to the total cross-section A.

---

* σ' or $\bar{\sigma}$ are the notations used for effective stress.

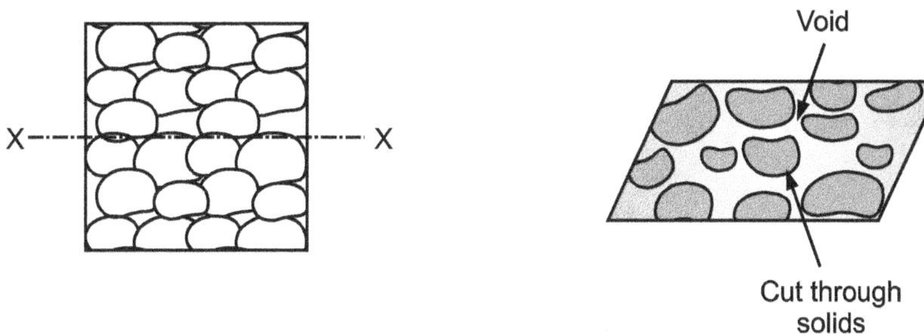

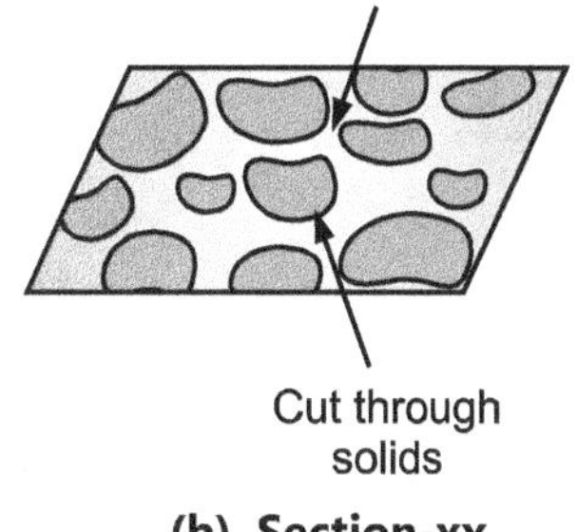

(a)   **(b) Section-xx**

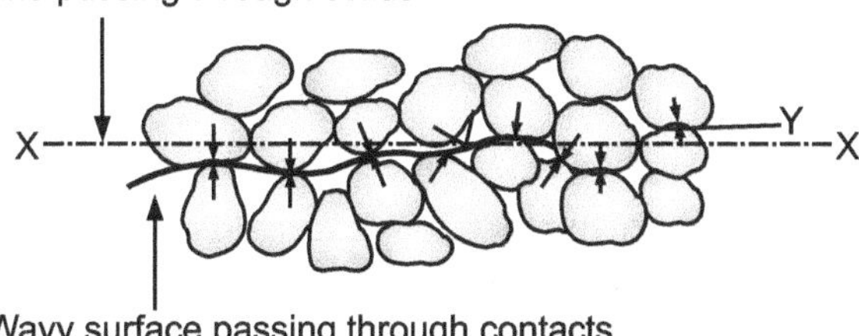

(c) Wavy surface treated as equivalent to a plane

Fig. 7.2

In a saturated soil, on a horizontal plane as shown

$$V \;=\; \sigma A \;=\; N + u \cdot A_w$$

where, σ = Average applied stress or total stress

N = Total force carried by the particles at contact

A_w = The area of plane passing through water

A = Total projected area = $A_m + A_w$

u = Pore water pressure (= u_w, for saturated soil).

$$\therefore \qquad \sigma \;=\; \frac{N}{A} + u \cdot \frac{A_w}{A}$$

But the contact area being very small, $A_m \approx 0$, $A \approx A_w$

$$\sigma \;=\; N/A + u = \sigma' + u \qquad\qquad \text{... (7.2)}$$

where σ' = N/A is the stress carried by particles at the contact and is known as effective stress[*]. It is the stress calculated on the basis of total area A and not on the contact area, A_m.

---

[*]   The stress at particle contacts would be N/A_m = $N/(A - A_w)$, which is very large but has little physical meaning.

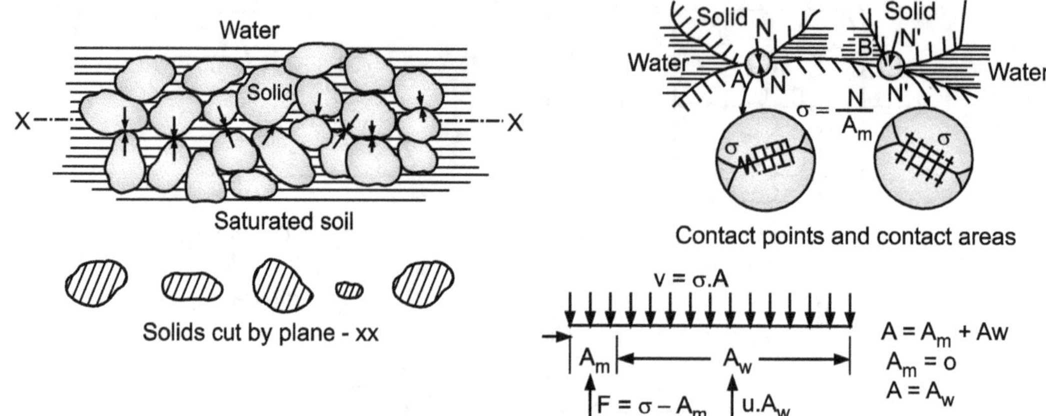

Fig. 7.3 : Effective stress concept

The applied or total stress, σ is known from the external loading (weight of soil, surface load) and pore water pressure can be actually measured or determined.

Effective stress σ' (or $\bar{\sigma}$) is computed as

$$\sigma' = \sigma - u, \; \sigma'_v = \sigma_v - u, \; \sigma'_h = \sigma_h - u \qquad \qquad ... (7.3)$$

The effective stress concept was first introduced by Terzaghi. It is a very important principle in soil mechanics. Many properties such as volume change, shearing strength, permeability, compressibility etc. depend on effective stresses.

To summarize, the principle of effective stress may be stated as :

- Effective stress **equals the total stress minus pore pressure**.
- Effective stress **controls shearing strength of soil**.
- Effective stress **governs volume changes in soils**.

7.2.2 Effective Stress in Dry or Drained Condition

In dry soils, pore water does not exist. Hence, there is no pore water pressure. Naturally, effective stress σ', in dry soils is equal to the total stress σ ($\sigma' = \sigma - u = \sigma$), u being zero.[**]

In saturated sandy and gravelly soils, the permeability is so high (10^{-2} to 10^{-5} m/s) that usual application of load does not develop any pore pressure, because drainage is faster than the rate of loading. Hence effective stress, σ' equals applied stress, σ, ($\sigma' = \sigma$; u = 0).

7.2.3 Importance of Effective Stress Concept

The concept of effective stress has great significance in geotechnical problems. Application of stress cannot produce instantaneous strains in soils, as in the case of steel or concrete. Application of an external load to a saturated soil develops pore pressure, which is dissipated

---

[**] Actually pore pressure consists of pore water pressure and pore air pressure,

$u = u_w + u_a$, in partially saturated soils.

and converted into intergranular or effective pressure, with some time lag. The rate of dissipation depends on the type of soil.

The problems of pore pressure are more severe in the case of clayey soils than in sandy soils. Even in sandy soils, shock loading and vibration can develop pore pressure resulting in problems like *liquefaction*. **Liquefaction means turning of a saturated fine sand or silt into a fluid mass due to loss of particle contacts under an impact loading**. Shear strength and volume changes in soils are functions of effective stress. Equal increase in total stress and pore pressure ($\Delta\sigma = \Delta u$) (keeping effective stress constant) would not cause change in volume. However, increase in effective stress causes soil particles to shift into denser packing. Hence, stability analyses and settlement computations have to make use of effective stresses.

Rate of shearing is an important consideration in development of effective stress. Failures of earth structures are usually *progressive* and may require even several months before failure occurs. In such cases, pore pressures may not play any significant role. On the other hand foundation loading on a soft clay, develops pore pressure under poor drainage.

7.3 STRESS–STRAIN CURVE

Consider an element of soil subjected to a varying shear stress under a constant normal stress. Fig. 7.4 shows a typical shear stress-shear strain curve. Initially, when the shear stress is low, the soil behaves like elastic material depicting a linear shear strain. At a particular stress level, significant plastic shear starts to develop and the point is referred to as "yield". The shearing resistance of the soil increases with the plastic shear strain and material is said to 'work harden' or 'strain harden'. The strain hardening can only increase the resistance to a particular maximum shear stress and that maximum resistance is called the "peak shear strength' or simply the shear strength of the soil (τ_f). The yield level is considered to be unstable and the soil is said to fail. In some soils, the maximum shearing resistance decreases after this point and soil is said to be *strain softening* or *work softening*. After a continued large strain, the shearing resistance attains a constant level and the corresponding shearing resistance is called the *residual shear strength* or simply the residual strength (τ_r).

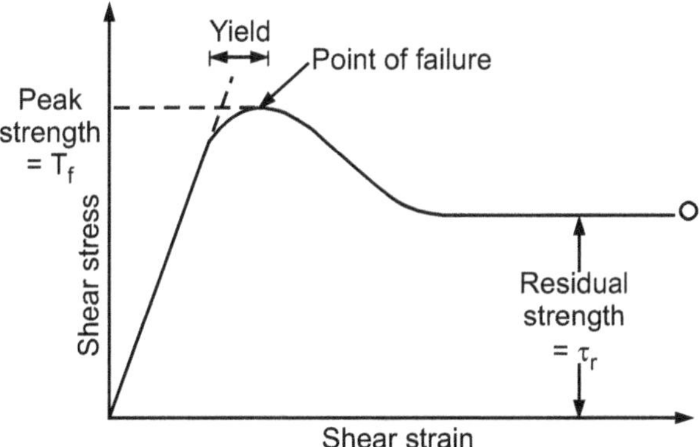

Fig. 7.4 : Principal plane and Principal stresses

7.3.1 Stress-strain Relations in Soils and Rocks

Stress-strain relations for soils and rocks which are inelastic materials are more complex (Fig. 7.5). The stress-strain curves are not linear and the elastic constants E and μ can be defined only arbitrarily. Still, engineering problems need the use of such parameters, because they serve to determine the deformations of a given structure under loading, at least approximately.

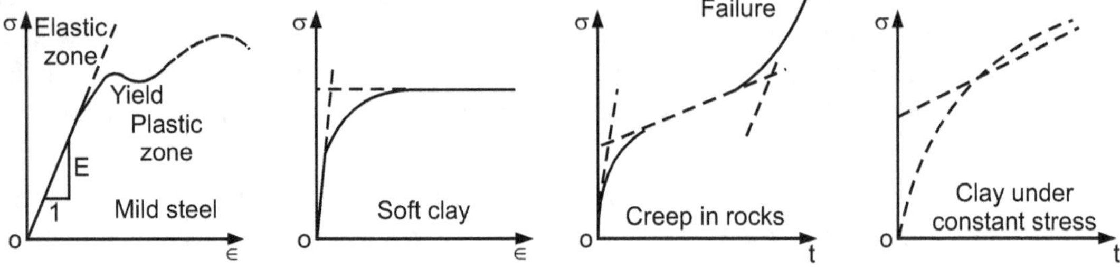

Fig. 7.5 : Actual stress strain time curves

The stress-strain characteristics of cohesive soils are studied by measurements on the unconfined compression or triaxial compression. For cohesionless soils, soil specimens cannot be tested without lateral pressure.

Hence, the soil characteristics are obtained either by triaxial laoding or by confined compression. The concepts of elasticity are applicable to soils only approximately and within a small range of stresses near zero.

7.3.2 Determination of Soil Modulus

The stress-strain diagrams as shown in Fig. 7.5 to 7.7 are used to determine the soil modulus. Let the stress-strain curve give the ultimate stress, σ_u in a load test, (Fig. 7.6).

(i) Tangent Modulus : The slope of the tangent at any point P on the curve, defines the tangent modulus, E_{st}. If the tangent modulus is obtained at the initial point (origin) O, it is known as the initial tangent modulus, E_t.

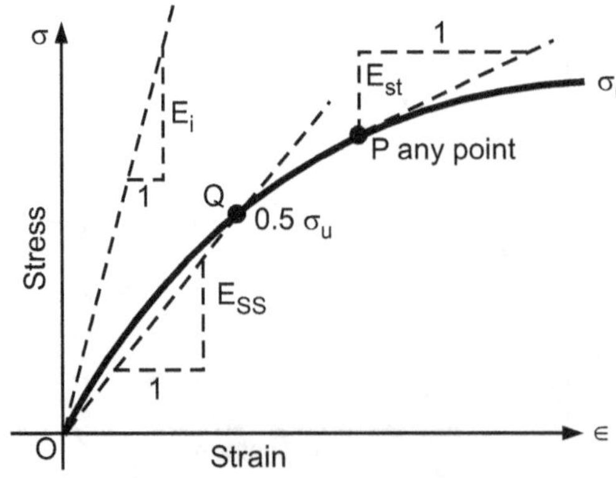

Fig. 7.6 : Stress-strain curve

(ii) Secant Modulus : Let Q be any point on the curve. OQ is the secant of the curve. The slope of the secant OQ is defined as the *secant modulus E_{ss}*. The choice of point Q is only arbitrary and may be taken as 0.5 σ_u, 0.33 σ_u or 0.67 σ_u. This is the range of working stresses in the foundation problems, wherein safety factors from 1.5 to 3 are commonly used. The value of soil modulus is usually the secant modulus obtained as above. It may be noted that the initial tangent modulus is the *limiting* value of the secant modulus. The other elastic constant viz. Poisson's ratio, μ for a soil is determined from the data of sonic testing. The Poisson's ratio μ ranges between 0.15 and 0.35 for sands and between 0.35 and 0.5 for clay and may be taken as 0.3 and 0.4 respectively.

Sandy Soils :

Stress-strain characteristics for triaxial loading of sands depend on the confining pressure σ_c, and for a given confining pressure, it depends on the density index (hence on void ratio) and angularity of grains. The stress-strain curve is essentially non-linear, but for very low stresses the initial tangent modulus, E_i may be used as the elastic modulus. The value for dense sand is several times greater than that for a loose sand and increases with increase in lateral pressure, [Fig. 7.7 (a)]. ***Saturation of sands does not have appreciable influence on E_i but submergence causes reduction in unit weight and consequent decrease in the modulus, E_t, due to loss of confinement.***

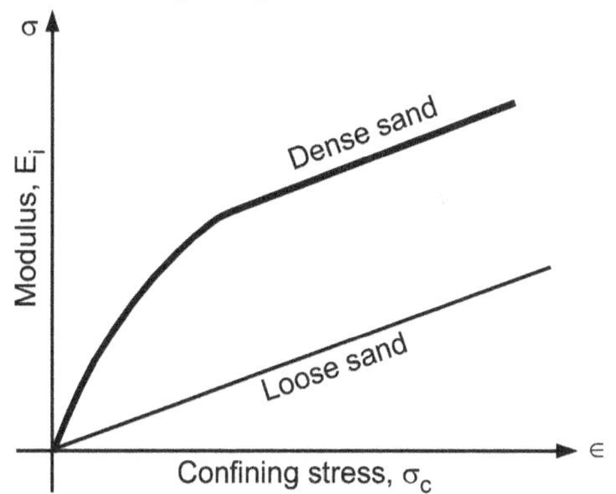

Fig. 7.7 (a) : Modulus of sands

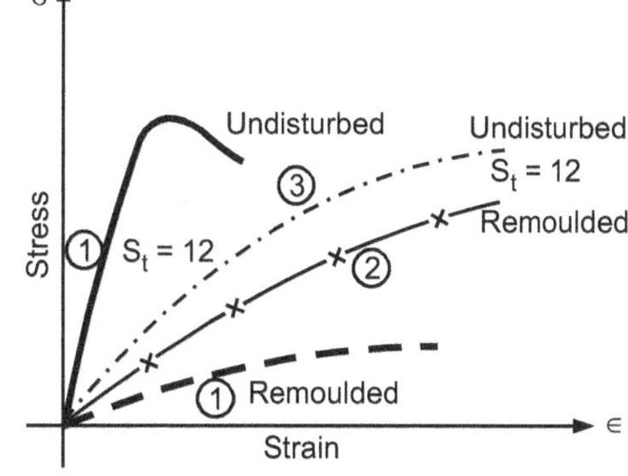

Fig. 7.7 (b) : Typical stress-strain curves for clayey soils

In the standard triaxial test the stress-strain curve may be fitted by a hyperbolic equation given by

$$\sigma_1 - \sigma_3 = \in_1 / (a + b\in_1)$$

where, a and b are constants to be obtained experimentally.

Table 7.1 : Deformation Modulus, E_s and Poisson's Ratio, μ

	Material	E (kN/m²)	μ	k_S (kN/m³)
1.	Very soft clay (CH)	350-2,800	0.4 to 0.5	–
2.	Soft clay (CH, MH)	1,750-4,200	–	15,000-30,000

...Conti.

3.	Medium clay, silt (CH, MH)	4,200-8,400	0.3 to 0.4	30,000-60,000
4.	Stiff/Hard clay (CH, MH)	7,000-17,500	0.1 to 0.3	> 60,000
5.	Sandy clay (CI, MI)	28,000-42,000	0.2 to 0.3	–
6.	Silty sand (SM, SC)	7,000-20,000	0.3 to 0.35	30,000-60,000
7.	Loose sand (SP, SM)	10,000-24,500	–	–
8.	Dense sand (SW)	49,000-84,000	0.2 to 0.25	80,000-160,000
9.	Dense sand, gravel (GW)	100,000-200,000	0.15	–
10.	Rock-Basalt	45 to 100×10^6	0.27 to 0.32	–
11.	Rock-Granite	25 to 45×10^6	0.26 to 0.30	–
12.	Concrete	10 to 30×10^6	0.15	–
13.	Steel	210×10^6	0.25	–

Clayey Soils : Uniaxial compression is the simplest method of measuring stress-strain relationship of clayey soils. The values of E_i depends on the sensitivity of the soil, the soil with high sensitivity giving a large linear range in the undisturbed state. Low sensitivity yields a non-linear curve [Fig. 7.7 (b)]. Remoulding decreases the modulus by a great extent in the case of sensitive clays.

7.4 PRINCIPAL PLANES

A soil mass is subjected to a three-dimensional stress system. But the stresses in the third direction are not relevant. Hence the stress system is simplified as two-dimensional. The plain strain conditions are normally assumed, in which the strain in the third direction becomes zero. Such conditions occur under strip footing.

At every point in a stressed body, there are three planes on which the shear stresses are zero. These planes are known as principal planes. The compressive stresses on the principal planes are maximum or minimum. The plane with maximum compressive stress (σ_1) is known as a major principal plane and that with minimum compressive stress (σ_3) is called as a minor principal plane. The third principal plane is subjected to the stress which is intermediate between (σ_1) and (σ_3) which is of not much relevance. Only the major principal stress (σ_1) and the minor principal stress (σ_3) are important.

Unlike solid mechanics, the compressive stresses are taken as positive and tensile stresses are taken as negative in soil engineering. This is purely to avoid excessive negative signs, since *in soil engineering problems, tensile stresses rarely occur.* Consider an element of a soil. Fig. 7.8 shows a plane which is perpendicular to the intermediate principal plane. A major principal plane is horizontal and the minor principal plane is vertical. Let us consider a plane AB which is inclined at an angle θ to the major principal plane (AC).

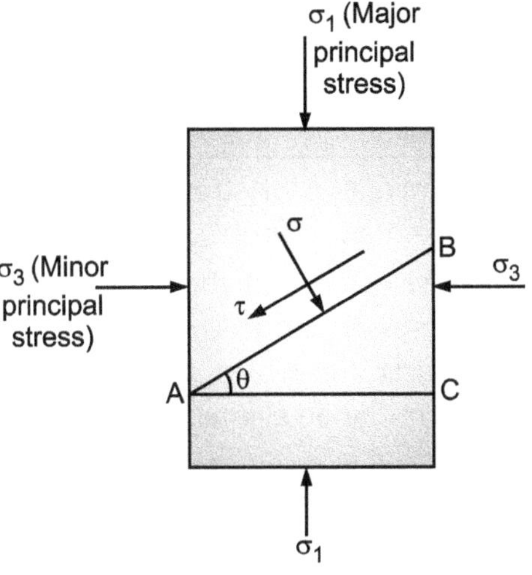

Fig. 7.8

Let σ be the normal stress and τ be the shear stress on AB.

Resolving the forces acting on the wedge ABC in the x direction.

$$\sigma_3 BC = \sigma AB \sin\theta - \tau AB \cos\theta$$

$$\sigma_3 \frac{BC}{AB} = \sigma \sin\theta - \tau \cos\theta$$

But

$$\frac{BC}{AB} = \sin\theta$$

$$\sigma_3 \sin\theta = \sigma \sin\theta - \tau \cos\theta \qquad \text{... (7.4)}$$

Resolving the forces in y direction :

$$\sigma_1 AC = \sigma AB \cos\theta + \tau AB \sin\theta$$

$$\sigma_1 \cos\theta = \sigma \cos\theta + \tau \sin\theta \qquad \text{... (7.5)}$$

Multiplying equation (7.4) by $\cos\theta$ and (7.5) by $\sin\theta$ and subtracting :

$$(\sigma_1 - \sigma_3)\sin\theta\cos\theta = \sigma(\cos\theta \cdot \sin\theta - \cos\theta \cdot \sin\theta) + \tau(\sin^2\theta + \cos^2\theta)$$

$$(\sigma_1 - \sigma_3)\sin\theta \cdot \cos\theta = \tau$$

$$\boxed{\tau = \frac{1}{2}(\sigma_1 - \sigma_3)\, \sin 2\theta} \qquad \text{... (7.6)}$$

Substituting in equation (7.4) :

$$\sigma_3 \sin\theta = \sigma \sin\theta - \frac{\sigma_1 - \sigma_3}{2}\sin 2\theta \cdot \cos\theta$$

$$\sigma_3 = \sigma - (\sigma_1 - \sigma_3)\cos^2\theta$$

$$\sigma = \sigma_3 + (\sigma_1 - \sigma_3)\frac{1 + \cos 2\theta}{2}$$

$$\boxed{\sigma = \frac{\sigma_1 + \sigma_3}{2} + \left(\frac{\sigma_1 - \sigma_3}{2}\right)\cos 2\theta} \qquad \text{... (7.7)}$$

Equations (7.6) and (7.7) give the stresses on an inclined plane AB making an angle (θ) with the major principal plane. The angle is measured in the anticlockwise direction.

7.5 MOHR'S CIRCLE

A graphical method for the determination of stresses on a plane inclined to the principal plane is devised by Otto Mohr, a German scientist.

In this method, an origin (O) is selected and the normal stresses are plotted along the horizontal axis and the shear stresses are on the vertical axis. The compressive stresses are taken as positive and plotted towards the right of the origin. The positive shear stresses are plotted upward from the origin. Consider an element ABC.

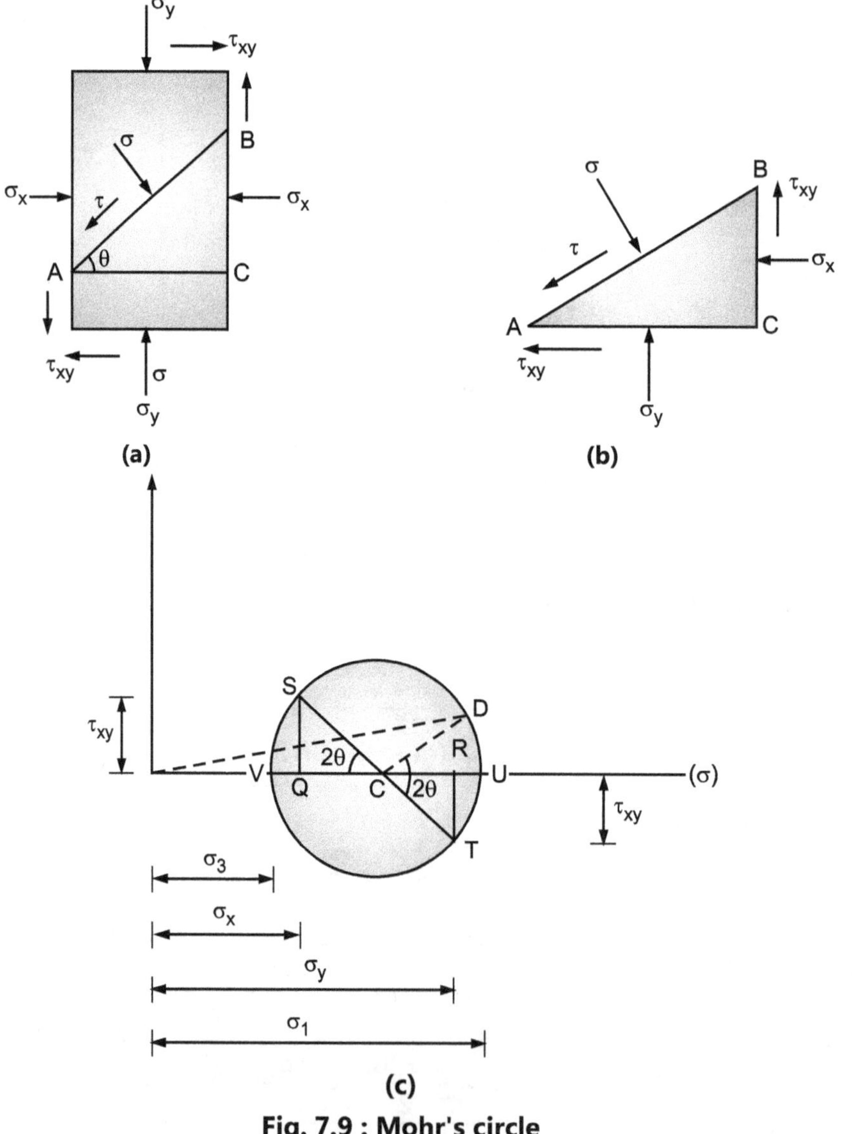

Fig. 7.9 : Mohr's circle

7.5.1 Plotting of Mohr's Circle

Case (I) : When the soil element is subjected to two dimensional stress system of normal stress (σ_x and σ_y) and shear stress (τ_{xy} and τ_{yx}). Fig. 7.9 (a) shows a soil element subjected to two dimensional stress system where σ_x, σ_y = normal stresses in X, Y directions and τ_{xy} = τ_{yx} = shear stresses on these two planes.

To draw a Mohr circle the normal stresses σ_x and σ_y are marked at point Q and R respectively on X axis. At point Q, a perpendicular QS is drawn such that QS = τ_{xy}. Likewise, the distance RT is also equal to τ_{xy}. *The shear stress is positive on plane BC as it causes a counterclockwise moment at a point inside the wedge. While the shear stress on plane AC is negative, because it causes a clockwise moment.* Mohr's circle is drawn with point C midway of QR as the centre.

The co-ordinates of centre of Mohr's circle are $\left[\left(\dfrac{\sigma_x + \sigma_y}{2}\right), 0\right]$. Radius of Mohr's circle is

equal to $\qquad CS = CT = \left[\left(\dfrac{\sigma_y - \sigma_x}{2}\right)^2 + (\tau_{xy})^2\right]^{1/2}$. Fig. 7.9 (c).

The circle passes through point S and T. In short, point (T) represents the stresses on plane (AC) and the point (S) represents the stresses on (BC). A line (CD) drawn at angle of 2θ to the (CT) intersects the Mohr circle at (D). Therefore, the point (D) gives the stresses on inclined plane (AB). The line CU indicates the major principal plane and point U represents the major principal stress (σ_1). The point V gives minor principal stress (σ_3) and line CV represents minor principal plane.

$$\sigma_1 = \frac{\sigma_x + \sigma_y}{2} + \sqrt{\left(\frac{\sigma_y - \sigma_x}{2}\right)^2 + (\tau_{xy})^2}$$

$$\sigma_3 = \frac{\sigma_x + \sigma_y}{2} - \sqrt{\left(\frac{\sigma_y - \sigma_x}{2}\right)^2 + (\tau_{xy})^2}$$

Case (II) : When a soil element is subjected to principal stresses (σ_1 and σ_3). Fig. 7.10 (a) shows a soil element whose sides are the principal planes, i.e. consider the state of stress where only normal stresses are acting on the faces. Fig. 7.10 (b) shows the Mohr circle.

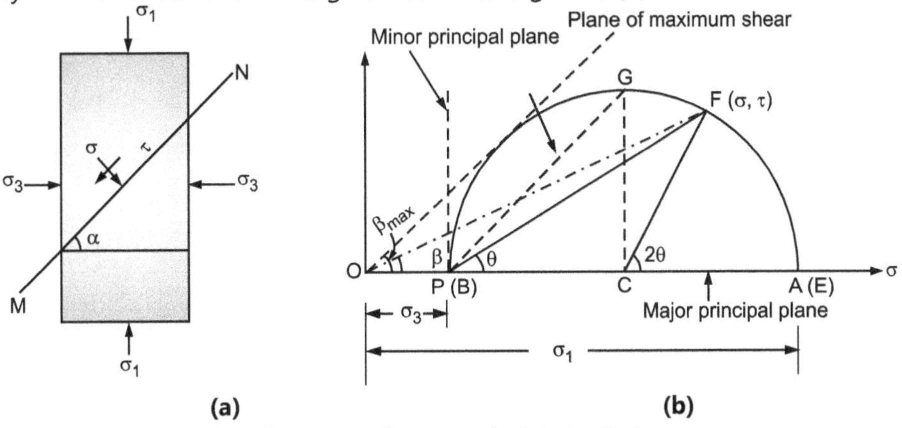

Fig. 7.10 : Plotting of Mohr's circle

Analytically expressions for σ, τ are :

$$\sigma = \frac{\sigma_1 + \sigma_3}{2} + \frac{\sigma_1 - \sigma_3}{2} \cdot \cos 2\theta$$

$$\tau = \frac{\sigma_1 - \sigma_3}{2} \cdot \sin 2\theta$$

The resultant on any plane is $\sqrt{\sigma^2 + \tau^2}$ and its angle of obliquity β is equal to $\tan^{-1}\left(\dfrac{\tau}{\sigma}\right)$.

At the maximum shear stress point (G), τ_{max} is equal to $\dfrac{\sigma_1 - \sigma_3}{2}$ and it occurs on planes with $\theta = 45°$. In Fig. 7.10 (b), PG shows the direction of the plane having maximum shear stress. The normal stress on this plane will be equal to $\dfrac{\sigma_1 + \sigma_3}{2}$.

7.5.2 Location of Pole in Mohr's Circle

A pole is a point in Mohr's circle from where the planes originate. The pole P in Fig. 7.10 (b) has co-ordinates (σ_3, 0) and here the direction of the major principal plane is parallel to x–axis. The principal planes are not horizontal and vertical, but are inclined to Y and X directions. Fig. 7.10 (c) shows an element and Fig. 7.10 (d) shows the corresponding stress circle. Hence to get the position of the plane, a line is drawn through A, parallel to the the major principal plane, to intersect the circle in P. Evidently, PB gives the direction of the minor principal plane. To find the stress components on any plane MN inclined at an angle θ with the major principal, a line PF is drawn through P, at an angle θ with PA, to intersect the circle at F. The co-ordinates (σ, τ) of point F give the stress components on the plane MN.

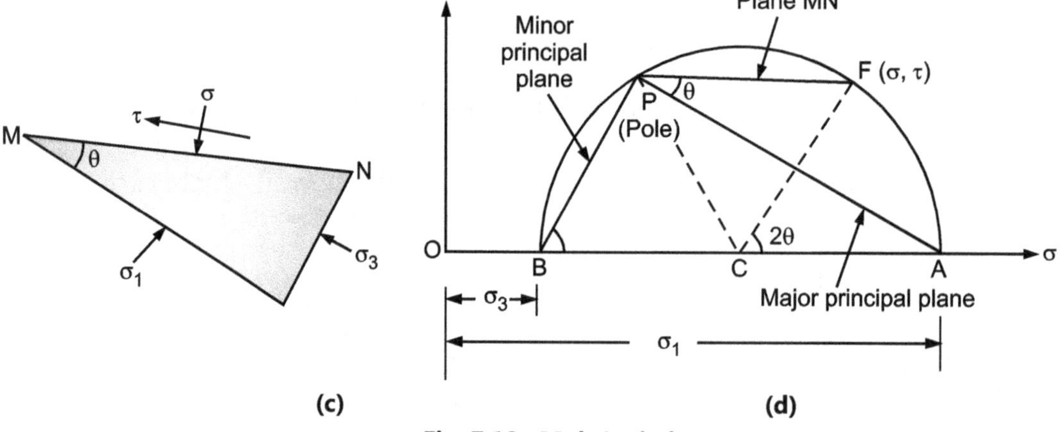

Fig. 7.10 : Mohr's circle

7.5.3 Features of Mohr's Circle

The following are the main characteristics of Mohr's circle :

- The point F on Mohr's circle (Fig. 7.10) represents the stresses (σ, τ) on a plane making an angle (2θ) with the major principal plane.

- The shear stresses on planes at right angles to each other are numerically equal but are of opposite signs.
- As Mohr's circle is symmetrical to σ axis, it is a usual practice to draw the top half for convenience.
- The maximum angle of obliquity (β_{max}) is obtained by drawing a tangent to the circle from the origin (O).

$$\beta_{max} \;=\; \tan^{-1} \frac{(\sigma_1 - \sigma_3)}{\sigma_1 + \sigma_3}$$

- The shear stress (τ_f) on the plane of maximum obliquity is less than maximum shear stress (τ_{max}).

- The maximum shear stress (τ_{max}) is numerically equal to $\dfrac{\sigma_1 - \sigma_3}{2}$ and it occurs on a plane inclined to the principal planes.

7.6 MOHR–COULOMB FAILURE THEORY

Since, soil is a particulate material, the shear failure in soils occurs by slippage of particles due to shear stresses. The shear stresses at failure depends upon the normal stresses on the potential failure plane. According to Mohr, the failure occurs by critical combination of the normal and shear stresses. The soil fails when the shear stress (τ_f) on failure plane is a function of the normal stress (σ) acting on that plane.

$$\tau_f \;=\; f(\sigma)$$

Since, shear stress at failure is defined as shear strength (S), the above equation becomes,

$$\tau_f \;=\; S = f(\sigma) \hspace{3cm} \text{... (7.8)}$$

If normal and shear stress corresponding to failure are plotted, then a curve is obtained. The lot or the curve is called the strength envelope. Fig. 7.11 (a) represents the Mohr's strength envelope which is a curve defined by equation (7.8).

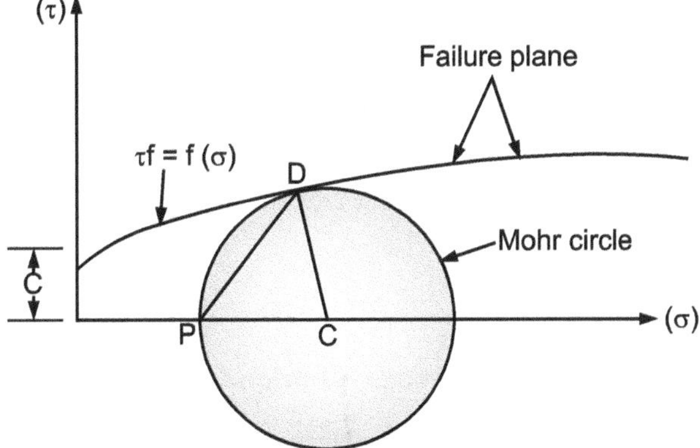

Fig. 7.11 (a) : Mohr's theory

Coulomb has modified Mohr's equation to represent a linear relationship between shearing resistance of soil and σ_f as follows :

$$S = C + \sigma \tan \phi \qquad \qquad \text{... (7.9)}$$

Thus, Mohr's envelope is replaced by a straight line, Fig. 7.11 (b).

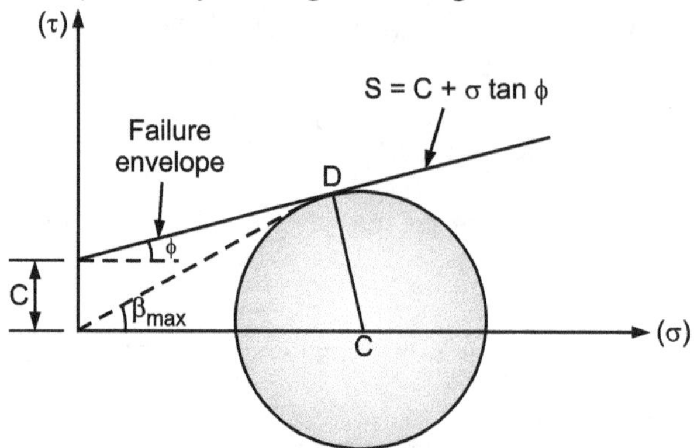

Fig. 7.11 : (b) Mohr's coulomb envelope

Here (C) equals to the intercept on (τ axis) and (φ) is the angle which the envelope makes with (σ axis). The component (C) of the shear strength is known as *cohesion*. Cohesion is independent of normal stress and holds the particles of the soil together. The angle (φ) is called as the angle of internal friction. It represents the frictional resistance between the particles which is directly proportional to the normal stress.

The failure occurs when stresses are such that the Mohr circle touches the failure envelope. Thus, the failure occurs along a plane when a critical combination of the stresses (σ) and (τ) gives the resultant with a maximum obliquity (β_{max}), in which case the resultant just touches the Mohr circle.

For an ideal pure friction material, strength envelope passes through the origin [Fig. 7.11 (c)] and for purely cohesive (plastic) material, the straight line is parallel to the σ axis [Fig. 7.11 (d)].

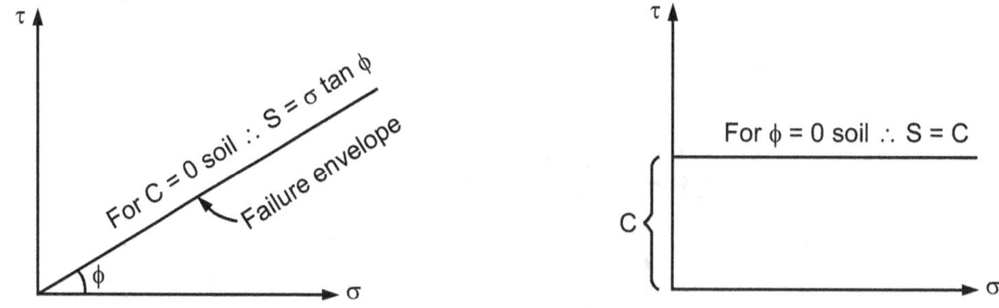

(c) Mohr's coulomb envelope for C = 0 soils (d) Mohr's coulomb envelope for φ = 0 soils

Fig. 7.11

Later research shows that parameters (C) and (φ) depend upon a number of factors such as water content, drainage conditions and conditions of testing.

Terzaghi established that the actual stresses which control the shear strength of a soil are effective stresses and not the total stresses. Thus, the equation 7.9 becomes

$$S = C' + \bar{\sigma} \tan \phi' \qquad \qquad ... (7.10)$$

where,

C' = Effective cohesion intercept

ϕ' = Effective angle of shearing resistance

$\bar{\sigma}$ = Effective stress

The above equation (7.10) is known as the revised Mohr–Coulomb equation for the shear strength of the soil.

7.6.1 Limitations of Mohr–Coulomb Theory

- It neglects the effect of the intermediate principal stress.
- It approximates the curved failure envelope by a straight line, which may not give correct results.
- For some clayey soils, there is no fixed relationship between the normal and shear stresses on the plane of failure. Theory cannot be used for such soils.
- The angle of the failure plane found is not correct.

7.7 ALTERNATE REPRESENTATION OF STRENGTH PARAMETERS

Consider the strength envelope for $C - \phi$ soil :

$$\tau_f = C + \sigma \tan \phi \text{ as shown in Fig. 7.11 (e).}$$

From any point D on the strength envelope draw a perpendicular DC to cut σ axis in C. With C as the centre and CD as the radius, draw Mohr's circle. Then on the Mohr diagram, from triangle CDE :

$$\text{Radius, r} = \frac{\sigma_1 - \sigma_3}{2} = (EO + OC) \sin \phi$$

$$= \left[C \cot \phi + \frac{\sigma_1 + \sigma_3}{2} \right] \sin \phi$$

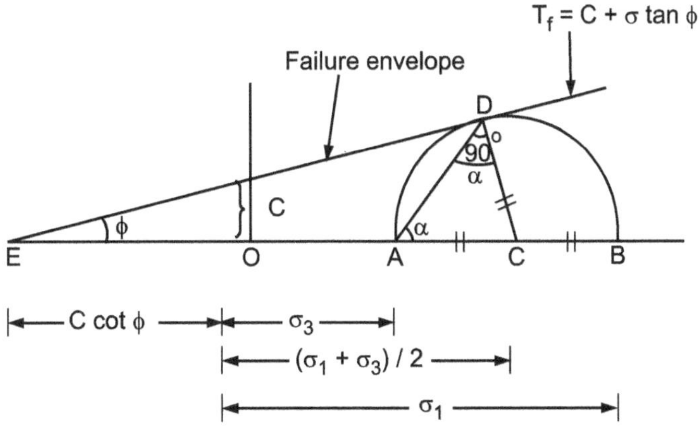

Fig. 7.11 (e)

$$\therefore \qquad \sigma_1 (1 - \sin \phi) = \sigma_3 (1 + \sin \phi) + 2C \cos \phi$$

Or
$$\sigma_1 = \sigma_3 \frac{1 + \sin \phi}{1 - \sin \phi} + 2C \frac{\cos \phi}{1 - \sin \phi}$$

or
$$\sigma_1 = \sigma_3 \frac{1 + \sin \phi}{1 - \sin \phi} + 2C \sqrt{\frac{1 + \sin \phi}{1 - \sin \phi}}$$

or
$$\sigma_1 = \sigma_3 \tan^2 \left(45 + \frac{\phi}{2}\right) + 2C \left(\tan 45 + \frac{\phi}{2}\right)$$

or
$$\sigma_1 = \sigma_3 \tan^2 \alpha + 2C \tan \alpha$$

or
$$\sigma_1 = \sigma_3 N\phi + 2C \sqrt{N\phi}$$

where,
$$N\phi = \tan^2 \alpha = \tan^2 \left(45 + \frac{\phi}{2}\right)$$

This expression is another statement for the law of shearing strength. The equation also holds good for effective stresses as well. Thus,

$$\sigma_1' = \sigma_3' + \tan^2 \alpha' + 2C' \tan \alpha'$$

where,
$$\alpha' = \left(45 + \frac{\phi'}{2}\right)$$

$$C' = \text{Effective cohesion intercept}$$
$$\phi' = \text{Effective angle of shearing resistance}$$

7.7.1 Failure Plane and Plane of Maximum Shear Stress

In Fig. 7.11 (f), JF represents the failure envelope given by the straight line $\tau_f = C + \sigma \tan \phi$. The pole P will be the point with stress co-ordinates as $(\sigma_3, 0)$. The Mohr circle is tangential to the failure envelope (JF) at point F. PF represents the direction of failure plane inclined at θ with the major principal plane.

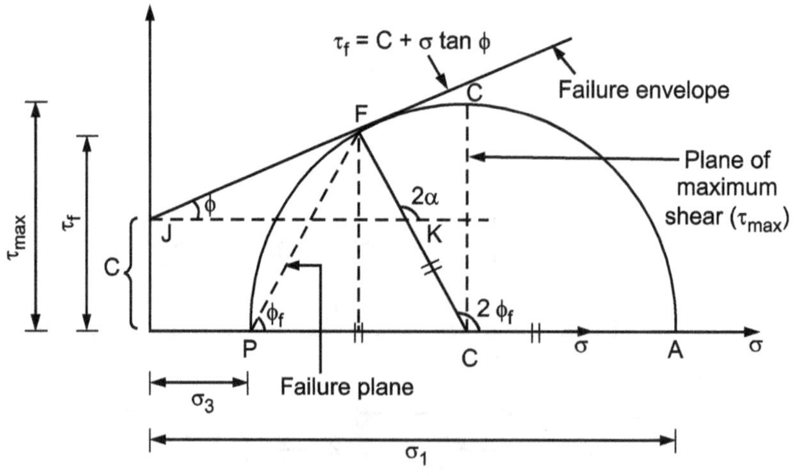

Fig. 7.11 (f)

From geometry of Fig. 7.11 (f), we get from triangle JFK :

$$2\alpha = 90 + \phi$$

or
$$\alpha = 45 + \frac{\phi}{2}$$

In Fig. 7.11 (f) point G represents the point corresponding to maximum shear stress (τ_{max}). Thus, from the figure, it is clear that *failure plane does not carry the maximum shear stress and the plane which has the maximum shear stress is not the failure plane.*

7.8 MEASUREMENT OF SHEAR STRENGTH

In solving geotechnical problems, it is necessary to understand the strength behaviour of a field soil layer under loading. Hence, field testing, if possible, is the most ideal. However, in most cases, it is impractical, elaborate and highly expensive and sample testing in the laboratory is the next alternative. Laboratory testing involves use of samples which need to be procured in the *undisturbed* state. Earth fills for retaining walls, embankments etc. require testing on compacted samples. While clayey soils are resonably manageable, sandy soils pose difficult problems of sampling and handling and their laboratory data are much more unreliable compared to those of clayey soils. In most cases, strength parameters for sandy soils are indirectly obtained by field methods and for clayey soils by sample testing on undisturbed samples. Simulation of field conditions in laboratory testing is naturally a prerequisite.

The most widely used method for evaluation of strength parameters is the *direct shear test*, while the most versatile and accurate method is the *triaxial* test. *Unconfined compression test* is the simplest of all, which is used for soft to medium clays. Laboratory *vane shear* is also used to determine undrained strength in clays. The vane shear test plays an important role in determination of in-situ shearing strength of sensitive clays with the help of a field vane.

The shear strength of a soil is measured by the following tests :

- Direct shear test
- Triaxial compression test
- Unconfined compression test
- Vane shear test

7.8.1 Different Drainage Conditions   (Nov. 15)

Depending upon the drainage conditions, there are three types of tests as explained below :

1. **Unconsolidated – Undrained Conditions :** During this test condition, no drainage is permitted during the consolidation stage. The test can be conducted quickly in a few minutes, and hence is also called as Quick Test or UU Test.

2. **Consolidated – Undrained Conditions :** During this test condition, the specimen is allowed to consolidate in the first stage. The drainage is permitted until the consolidation is complete. In the second stage when the specimen is sheared, no drainage is allowed. This test is also known as 'R' test or CU test.

3. **Consolidated – drained condition :** During this test condition, the drainage is permitted in both the conditions. The specimen is called to consolidate in first stage. When consolidation is complete, it is sheared at a very low rate to ensure that a fully drained condition exists and the excess pore water is zero. This test is also known as CD test.

7.8.2 Mode of Application of Shear Force

The shear force is applied either by increasing the shear displacement at a given rate or by increasing the force at a given rate.

1. **Strain-Controlled Tests :** The test is conducted in such a way that the shearing strain increases at a given rate. Normally, the rate of increasing the shearing strain is kept constant and the specimen is sheared at a uniform rate.

The shear force acting on the specimen is measured indirectly using a proving ring. The rate of shearing strain is controlled manually or by a gear system attached to an electric motor. Most of the shear tests are conducted as strain–controlled.

2. **Stress-Controlled Tests :** The shear force is increased at a given rate. Generally the rate of increase of shear force is kept constant. The shear force is increased such that the shear stresses increase at uniform rate. The resulting shear displacement is obtained by means of a dial gauge.

7.9 DIRECT SHEAR TEST   [Nov. 15, May 14, 16, 17]

This is the most widely used method of shear testing. It consists of forcing a soil specimen to fail along a predetermined shear plane (horizontal) and measuring the resistance to the shearing deformation. A relationship between shear stresses and normal stresses on a horizontal slip plane is used to establish the Mohr–Coulomb law of shearing strength, viz. :

$$\tau_f = C + \sigma_f \tan \phi \qquad \qquad \dots (7.11)$$

(A) Apparatus : A direct shear test is conducted on a soil specimen in a shear box made up of brass or gun metal. Normally, it is a square box of size $60 \times 60 \times 50$ mm. The box is divided horizontally such that the dividing plane passes through the centre. The two halves are held together by locking pins. Suitable spacing screws to separate the two halves are also provided.

The box is provided with grid plates which are toothed and fitted inside it. The gripper plates are plain for undrained tests and perforated for drained tests. The porous stones are placed at the top and bottom of the specimen in drained tests. The normal load is transmitted by a pressure pad at its top. The normal load from the loading yoke is applied on the top of the specimen through a steel ball bearing upon the pressure pad.

The lower half of the box is fixed to the base plate which is rigidly held in position in a large container. The large container is supported on a roller. The container can be pushed forward at a constant rate by a geared jack which works as a strain controlled device. The jack may be operated manually or by an electric motor.

A proving ring is fitted to the upper half of the box to measure the shear force. The proving ring butts against the fixed support. As the box moves, the proving ring records the shear force. The shear displacement is measured with a dial gauge fitted to the container. Another dial gauge is fitted to the top of the pressure pad to measure the change in thickness of the specimen.

The direct shear test is conducted on cohesionless soils. The test can be conducted for any one of the three drainage conditions.

(B) Test : The test is performed in the following manner :

- A soil specimen of size $60 \times 60 \times 25$ is taken. It may be either an undisturbed sample or made from compacted or remoulded soil.
- Depending upon the type of test and drainage conditions, grid plates and porous plates are selected and placed in the shear box. Then the specimen is placed in the box.
- After all other necessary adjustments are made, a known normal load from loading yoke is applied on the top of the specimen.
- The shearing force is applied at a constant rate of strain. The shearing displacement is recorded by a dial gauge.
- The test is repeated with different values of normal load and the corresponding shear load is obtained.
- Dividing normal load and maximum applied shear force by the cross-sectional area of specimen at the shear plane, normal stress (σ) and shearing stress (τ) at failure of the sample can be obtained.

(C) Table of Observations :

The observations are tabulated in Table 7.2.

1. Proving ring constant = 2.Size of sample =
3. Initial density =
4. Water conduct =
5. Shearing data =

Table 7.2

Stress Strain Curve					Shearing Data					
Sr. No.	Elapsed time	Stress dial reading	Shear stress kN/m^2	Strain dial reading	Sr. No.	Normal lead at failure kN	Normal stress at failure kN/m^2	Shear stress at peak kN/m^2	Cohesion kN/m^2	Angle of Shearing resistance (degree)
					1.					
					2.					
					3.					
					4.					
					5.					

(D) Presentation of Results :

1. Failure Envelope : The failure envelope is obtained by plotting the points corresponding to shear stress (τ) as ordinate and normal stress (σ) on the abscissa. The inclination of the failure envelope to the horizontal gives ϕ and its intercept on the vertical axis is equal to the cohesion intercept (See Fig. 7.12).

2. Mohr's Circle : In direct shear test, shear plane is known, but the principal planes are unknown. Draw a circle of stress touching the strength envelope at any point F (σ, τ). To do this, a line FC is drawn perpendicular to the envelope. With C as the centre and CF as the radius, a circle is drawn, which intersects the normal stress axis at points A and B. Locate the pole P by drawing a horizontal line from P. PA and PB are the directions of the major and minor principal planes and β_1 and β_3 their inclination with the horizontal.

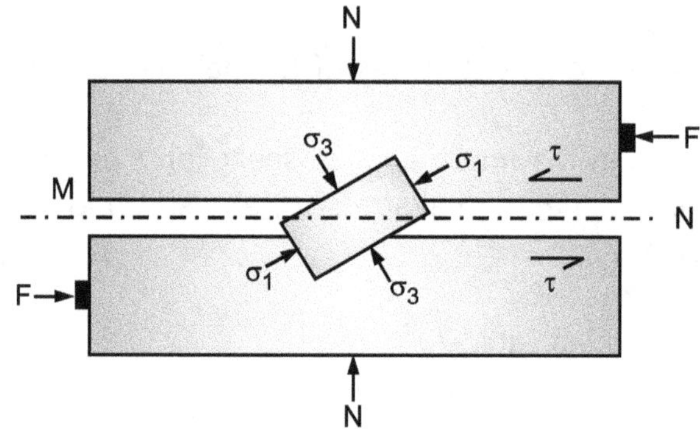

(a) Principle of direct shear box

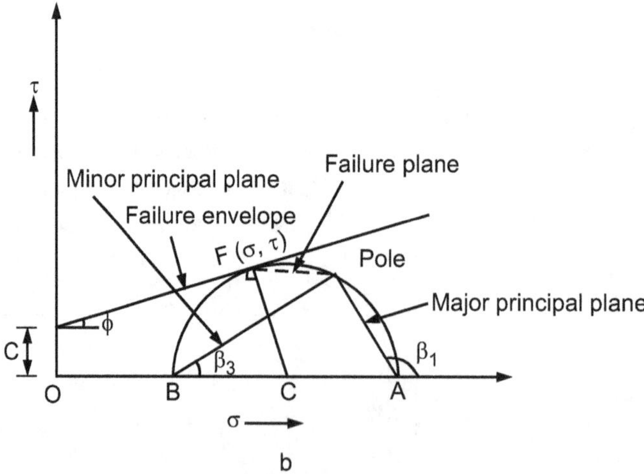

(b) Mohr's envelope and principle stresses during direct shear test

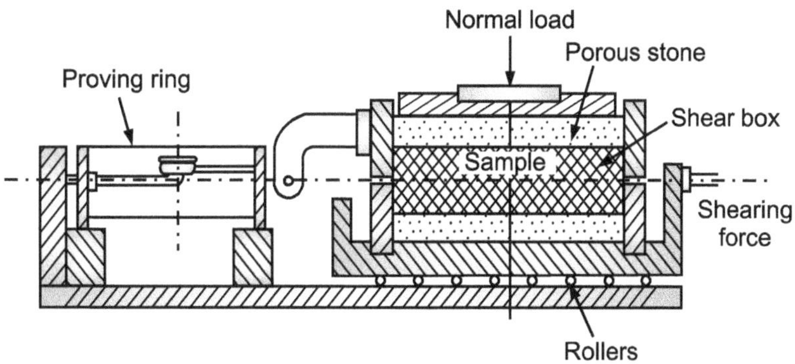

(c) Direct shear test apparatus

Fig. 7.12

(E) Characteristics of Direct Shear Test :

Merits :

- As thickness of the sample is relatively small, the drainage is quick and pore pressure dissipates very rapidly.

- The test is simple and convenient and the sample preparation is easy.

- It is suitable for conducting drained test on a cohesionless soil.

Demerits :

- The stress conditions are known only at failure. The conditions prior to failure are indeterminate.

- The stress distribution on the failure plane is not uniform.

- The area under shear gradually decreases as the test progresses. But the corrected area cannot be determined and hence stresses are computed on basis of original area.

- The orientation of the failure plane is fixed.

- Control on drainage condition is very difficult.

- The measurement of pore water pressure is not possible.

- The side walls of the shear box cause lateral restraint on the specimen and do not allow it to deform laterally.

7.10 TRIAXIAL SHEAR TEST

Loading of soils is more often triaxial than biaxial (as in the direct shear loading). The laboratory test that best simulates the field loading is the triaxial compression test.

(A) Triaxial Test Apparatus : The test apparatus consists of a strain controlled loading frame, a triaxial cell (for 38 mm dia. or 100 mm dia. specimen), pressure chambers, proving ring (or any other read out attachment) sample former, sample trimmer, pore pressure apparatus, volume change measuring device etc. The loading can be done at different rates to simulate fixed conditions. Triaxial cell is a perspex cylinder, attached to the base with rubber seals to make it water tight. The pressure cylinder maintains constant pressure in the triaxial cell. Drainage is controlled through an outlet valve.

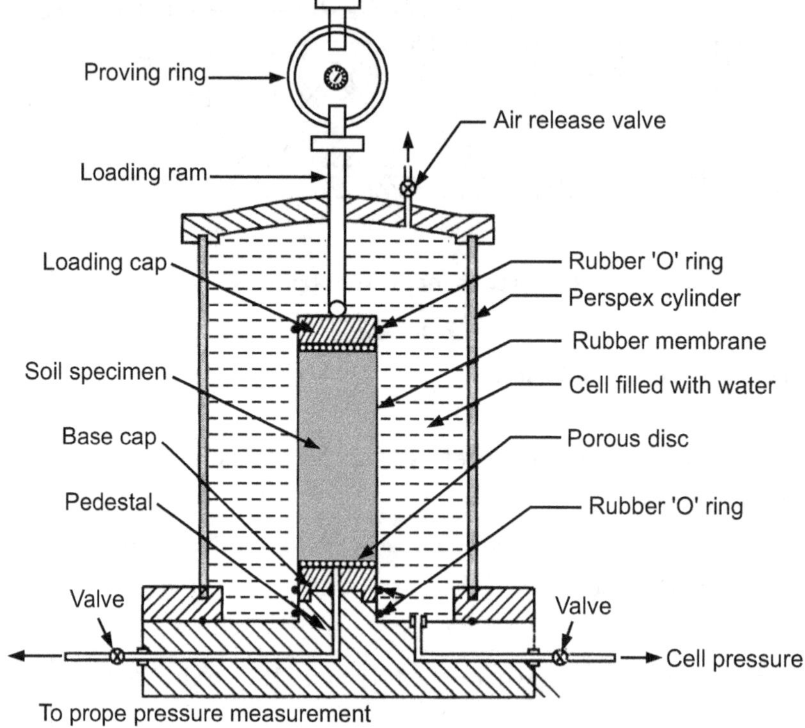

Fig. 7.13

(B) Test Procedure : In the standard triaxial test, a cylindrical sample is fitted between rigid caps and covered with latex membrane. It is then placed in a perpex cell which is filled with water. The sample is subjected to confining pressure (σ_3) by applying pressure to water in the cell. An additional (deviator) stress ($\sigma_d = \sigma_1 - \sigma_3$) is then applied by loading the sample through a ram, and steadily increased until the specimen fails. During triaxial loading, the outlet valve may be kept open to induce drained condition or may be kept closed for an undrained loading. The drainage outlet is connected to the pore pressure apparatus for measuring pore pressure or the volume measuring device to measure change in volume during drained loading.

(C) Test Principle : Mohr diagram has been used to obtain relationship between major and minor principal stresses. For failure condition,

$$\sigma_1 = \sigma_3 \tan^2\left(45 + \frac{\phi}{2}\right) + 2\,c\,\tan\left(45 + \frac{\phi}{2}\right)$$

This equation has two unknowns (c, ϕ). For determining these at least two tests on identical soil specimens need to be done.

(D) Principal Stresses in Triaxial Test : The triaxial test can be considered as conducted in two stages. In the first stage cell water pressure (σ_3) is applied on the specimen and in the second stage, deviator stress $\sigma_d = (\sigma_1 - \sigma_3)$ is applied on the sample till the failure of the specimen. (Fig. 7.14).

Therefore,
$$\sigma_1 = \sigma_d + \sigma_3$$
$$= (\sigma_1 - \sigma_3) + \sigma_3$$

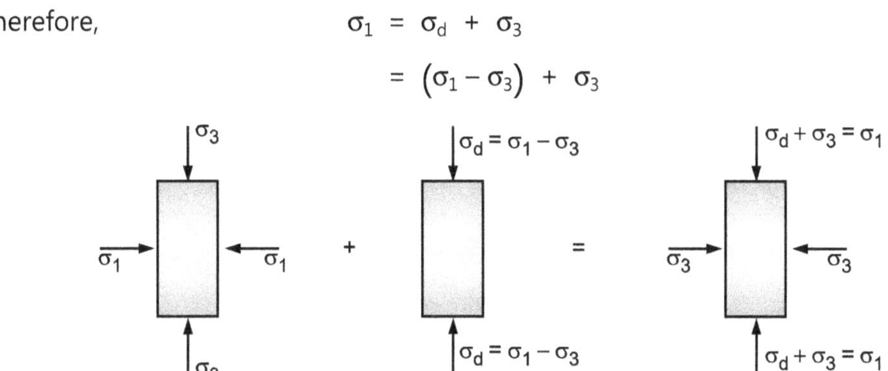

Fig. 7.14

(E) Failure : In triaxial test, failure is defined usually when the deviator stress $\sigma_d = (\sigma_1 - \sigma_3)$ or $\sigma_d' = (\sigma_1' - \sigma_3')$ reaches the maximum (peak) value. When the peak stress is not well defined, stress at 20 p.c. strain may be considered as failure stress.

(F) Failure Envelope : Mohr's circle for each test is plotted. The tangent to the resulting circles gives the Mohr's envelope. The shear strength (c and ϕ) are measured from the plot (Fig. 7.15).

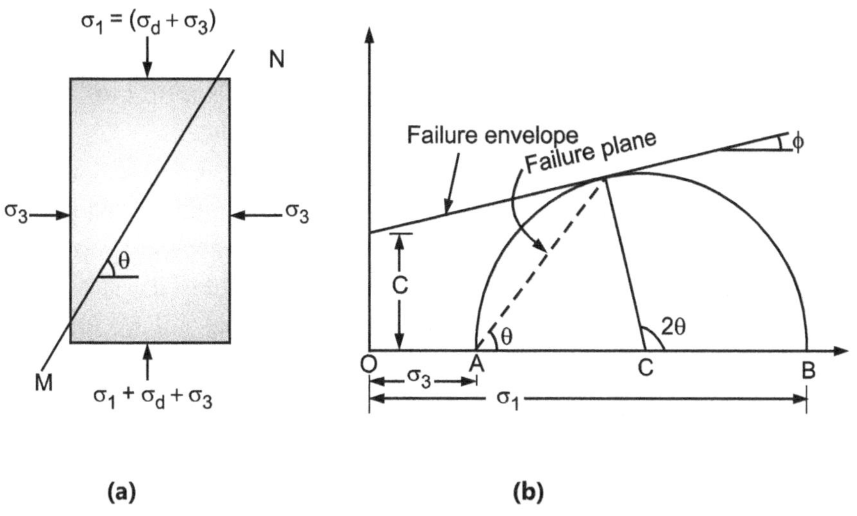

(a)   (b)

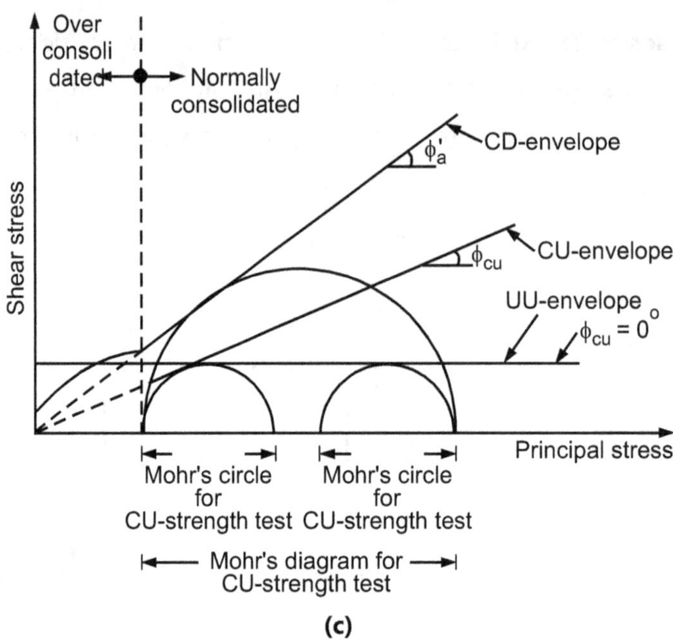

Fig. 7.15 : Typical strength envelopes for CD, CU and UU Tests on clay

(G) Drainage Conditions During Triaxial Test :

1. Consolidated Undrained (CU) Condition : The specimen is fitted between porous discs. When cell pressure is applied, the drainage is allowed and the specimen is allowed to consolidate. On completion of consolidation, the drainage is stopped and the axial stress is increased until failure, without allowing further drainage. The test is repeated on three-four samples, each test is conducted under different cell pressures.

2. Consolidated Drained (CD) Condition : The first state is similar to the CU test. The drainage is also allowed when the axial load is applied and the rate of shear is kept low enough to allow excess pore pressure to dissipate.

The effective stress may be determined by measuring the pore pressure developed within the sample and deducting it from the total stresses. The sample is set up between porous discs which are connected to an apparatus for measuring pore pressure.

3. Unconsolidated Undrained (UU) condition : The specimen is fitted between solid end caps, so that no change in moisture content is possible. The confining cell pressure is raised to confining volume. The axial load is applied without allowing any drainage and consolidation of sample. The axial load is usually applied at a rate of 2% strain per minute.

(H) Correction for Area (For UU condition) : The calculation of deviator stress σ_d must be done on the basis of the changed area of cross-section at failure or during any state of the test. It is calculated by assuming the sample deforms as a cylinder and volume remains unchanged.

$$\therefore \quad A_o L_o = AL = A(L_o - \Delta L)$$

$$A = \frac{A_o\,L_o}{L_o - \Delta L} = \frac{A_1}{1 - \varepsilon}$$

where,

A_o = Original cross-sectional area

L_o = Original length

A = Modified cross-sectional area at any strain

$$\varepsilon = \frac{\Delta L}{L_o} = \text{Strain} = \frac{\text{Change in the length}}{\text{Original length}}$$

The additional (deviator) stress, $\sigma_d = \dfrac{\text{Axial load (P)}}{\text{Modified area (A)}}$

Three samples are tested, each at different values of cell pressure (σ_3). The choice of cell pressure depends on the type of soil.

(I) Table of Observations :

    1.   Proving ring constant

    2.   Size of sample : 38 mm dia. × 76 mm.

    3.   Initial water content and density :

Table 7.3

Stress Strain Curve					Failure load			
Sr. No.	Elapsed time	Stress dial	Devia-tor stress	Strain dia.	Sr. No.	Cell Pressure σ_3	Deviator stress at failure, $\sigma d = (\sigma_1 - \sigma_3)$	Pore pressure 'uf'

(J) Calculations and Results :

- The area 'A' of the specimen at any stage of the test is determined by

$$A = \frac{A_o}{1 - L} = \frac{A_o\,L_o}{L}$$

where,

A_o = Original area of specimen

$$\varepsilon = \frac{L_o - L}{L_o}$$

L_o = Original length of specimen

L = Length of specimen at the stage of the test for which area A is to be determined.

- The deviator stress $(\sigma_1 - \sigma_3)$ is calculated by dividing the axial load by area 'A'.

- For each test, a plot may be made between $(\sigma_1 - \sigma_3)$ and ε.

- The shear parameters are obtained from a plot of Mohr circles for which purpose peak value of deviator stress and cell press are used.

(K) Stress-Strain Curve : The plots of deviator stress and axial strain measured during the triaxial test are typically shown in Fig. 7.16 for undrained, consolidated undrained and drained shear tests. Usually it is non-linear curve, even at very small strains. For dense sand (and over-consolidated clay), the deviator stress reaches a peak value and then it decreases and becomes almost constant, equal to the ultimate stress, at large strains. For loose sand (and normally consolidated clay), the deviator stress increases gradually till the ultimate stress is reached.

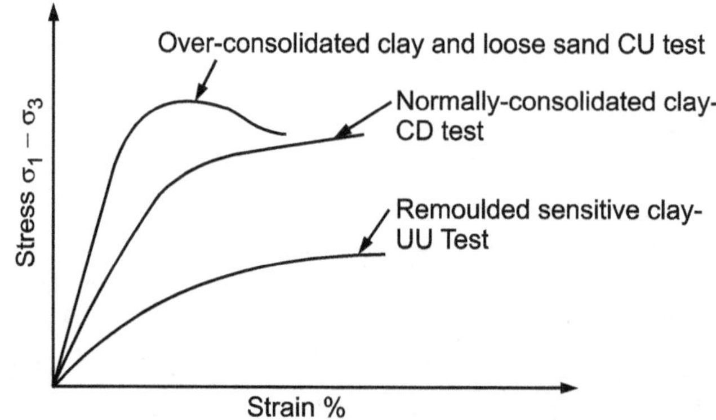

Fig. 7.16 : Typical stress-strain curves from Triaxial shear tests

The volumetric strain is shown in Fig. 7.16. In dense sand (and over-consolidated clay), there is a decrease in the volume at low strains, but at large strains, there is an increase in the volume. In loose sand (and normally consolidated clay) the volume decreases at all strains. (For some loose sands, there is slight tendency to increase the volume at large strains).

(L) Measurement of Pore Water Pressure : Determination of effective stress parameters, C' and ϕ' requires the measurement of the pore water pressures, during undrained loading. In the laboratory, this can be measured only during the triaxial testing. Bishop's pore pressure apparatus (Fig. 7.17) is widely used with triaxial cell.

The apparatus consists of a null indicator connected to the triaxial cell on one side and a pressure gauge on the other. The pressure gauge in the turn is connected to a mercury manometer and adjustable screw controlled plunger. The pore pressure in the triaxial specimen is read on the pressure gauge. Null indicator is brought to zero by operating the screw pump, thus indicating pore pressure on the gauge. Negative pressures are measured using a mercury manometer.

If the specimen is partially saturated, a special fine, porous ceramic disc is placed below the sample in the triaxial cell. The ceramic disc permits only pore water to flow, provided the difference between the pore air pressure and pure water is below a certain value, known as the *air entry value* of the ceramic disc. Under undrained test the ceramic disc will remain fully saturated, provided the air entry value is high.

In modern equipment, sometimes the pore water pressure is measured by means of a transducer and not by a conventional null indicator.

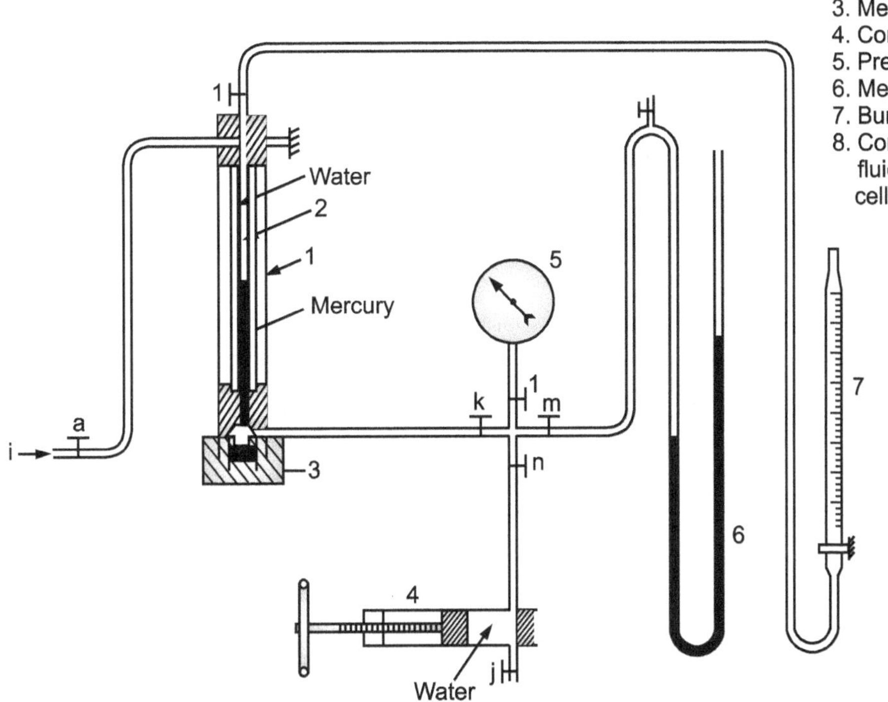

Fig. 7.17

(M) Volume Changes Measurement : Volume changes in a drained test and during consolidation stage of a C – U test are measured by means of a burette connected to the specimen in a triaxial cell. For accurate measurement, the water level in the burette should be approximately at the level of the centre of the specimen (Fig. 7.18).

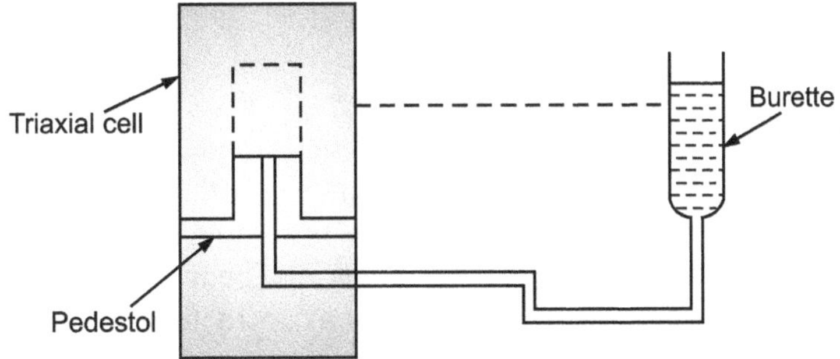

Fig. 7.18 : Volume change measurement

During consolidation stage, the volume of the specimen decreases and the water level in the burette rises. The changes in the volume of the specimen is equal to the volume of water increased in the burette. During shearing of specimens of dense sand when the volume of the sample increases, the water flows from the burette to the specimen. The decrease in volume of the specimen is equal to the volume of water decreased in the burette.

(N) Characteristics of Triaxial Compression Test :

- There is complete control over the drainage conditions.
- The volumetric changes and pore pressure changes can be measured directly.
- The specimen is free to fail on the weakest plane.
- The stress distribution on the failure plane is uniform.
- The Mohr circle can be drawn at any stage of shear because the state of stress at all intermediate levels upto failure is known.
- The test is suitable for research work.
- The drained test takes longer period as compared to the direct shear test.
- The assumption that the specimen remains cylindrical does not hold good.
- In the field, the problem is generally three dimensional, whereas the test stimulates only the axis-symmetrical problem.
- In the field, the consolidation is generally anisotropic, whereas the consolidation in the test is isotropic.
- It is the only reliable test for determination of shear parameters for all types of soils and under all drainage conditions.

7.11 UNCONFINED COMPRESSION TEST   [Dec. 13,14]

(A) Method : This test is a special case of unconsolidated undrained triaxial compression test, with confining cell pressure equal to the atmospheric pressure. It is useful for determining undrained shear strength (S) of saturated cohesive soils ($\phi = 0$). The failure envelope remains horizontal in this case, As $\sigma_3 = 0$ (atmospheric pressure), the Mohr circle passes through the origin and cohesion (C) equals to one half of the axial stress (σ_1) at failure.

$$\text{Shear strength, (S)} = C = \frac{\sigma_1}{2} = \frac{q_u}{2}$$

The test is performed on a cylindrical sample with a height and diameter of 2 : 1. The sample is placed between the plates of mechanical load frames without any lateral support. Axial load is applied to give a rate of strain of about 2% of sample height per minute. Load and deformation readings are taken. Loading is continued until either three or more consecutive reading of the load dial gauge show a decreasing or a constant load. Typical time to failure is about ten to fifteen minutes. The axial stress is calculated on the basis of the deformed area. The peak axial stress is known as *unconfined compressive strength (q_u)*.

(B) Tabulation of Observations :

The test results are tabulated as shown in Table 7.4.

Table 7.4 : Data and Observation Sheet for Determination of Unconfined Compressive Strength

1. Initial diameter of specimen (D_o)
2. Initial length (L_o)
3. Initial area (A_o)
4. Initial density
5. Initial water content.

Sr. No.	Elapsed time in min.	Load (P)	Deforma-tion (mm)	Strain ε (%)	Corrected Area 'A' (mm^2) $A = \dfrac{A_o}{1-\varepsilon}$	Stress $\sigma = \dfrac{P}{A}$

Calculations : (i) From corrected area 'A', the compressive strength is determined by :

$$\sigma = \frac{P}{A}$$

where, P = compressive force

A plot is made between σ and ε. The maximum stress from the curve gives the values of the unconfined compressive strength 'q_u'. When no maximum stress occurs, the 'q_u' is taken as the stress at 20 p.c. of axial strain.

For $\phi = 0$ condition, the shear strength or cohesion of the soil may be taken to be equal to half the unconfined compressive strength.

(C) Undrained shear strength of clays for various consistencies : Following table gives undrained shear strength of clays for various consistencies :

Table 7.5 : Undrained Strength of Clay (C_u)

Consistency	Very stiff	Stiff	Firm to stiff	Firm	Soft to firm	Soft	Very soft
Undrained strength kN/m^2	≥ 150	$100 - 150$	$75 - 100$	$50 - 75$	$40 - 50$	$20 - 40$	≤ 20

To measure the remoulded strength, the failed sample is enclosed in a small polythene bag together with little more of the soil at the same water content and remoulded thoroughly by squeezing and knealing. A test specimen is formed by placing the remoulded soil into 38 mm diameter tube and then extracting it with sample extraction. It is then tested to get the remoulded strength.

(D) Characteristics :

- The test is convenient and quick.
- It is ideally suited for measuring the unconsolidated undrained shear strength of saturated clays.

- The sensitivity of the soil can easily be determined by conducting the test on an undisturbed sample and then on the remoulded sample.

$$\text{Sensitivity, } (S_t) = \frac{(q_u) \text{ undisturbed}}{(q_u) \text{ remoulded}}.$$

- This test cannot be conducted on fissured clays.
- The test may be misleading for soils for which the angle of shearing resistance is not zero. For such soils, the shear strength is not equal to half the compressive strength (q_u).

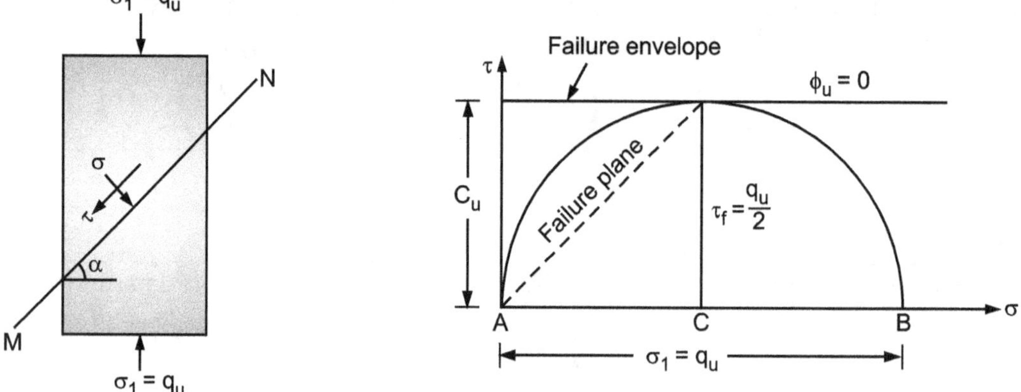

(a) Unconfined compression test

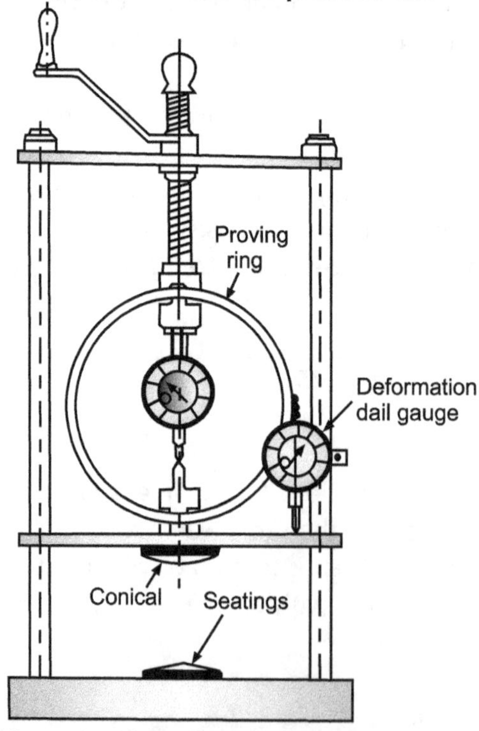

(b) Uncontinued compression test set up

Fig. 7.19

7.12 VANE SHEAR TEST   [Nov. 15, 16, May 15]

The Vane shear test is conducted as per IS : 2720 – XXX – 1980. The test is useful to determine the undrained shear strength (S) of clay and can be conducted in the laboratory as well as in the field.

The apparatus consists of a four bladed vane on the end of a rod. The height of the vane is usually twice its width (diameter). A boring is made to the depth at which the test is to be performed. The vane is inserted into the soil at the bottom of the hole and slowly rotated by a rate of $6°$ per minute using special instrument to measure the torque.

Assuming shear strength (S) is constant over the cylinder of soil sheared by the vane, the torque (T) required to shear the soil is calculated.

The torque (T) is applied till failure equals the sum of the resisting torque at the sides (T_1) and that at the top and bottom (T_2). Thus,

$$T = T_1 + T_2 \qquad \qquad \text{... (7.12)}$$

The resisting torque on the sides equals the resisting force developed on the cylindrical surface multiplied by the radial distance.

$$T_1 = S\pi DH \times \frac{D}{2} = \frac{S\pi D^2 H}{2} \qquad \qquad \text{... (7.13)}$$

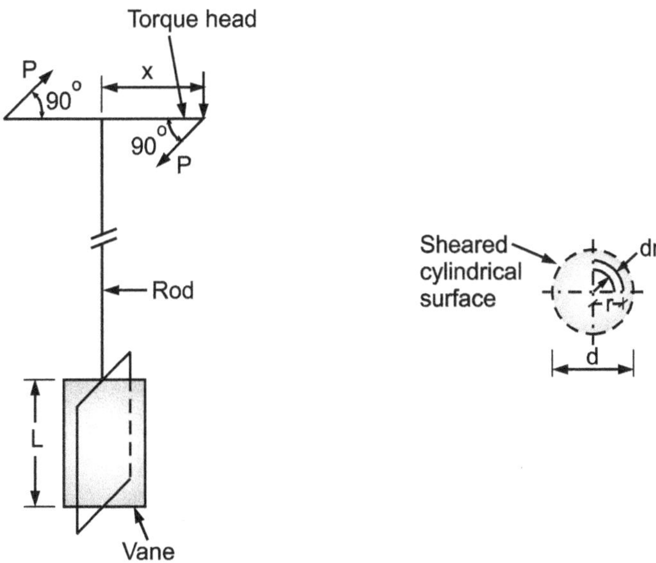

(a) Vane shear test apparatus   **(b)**

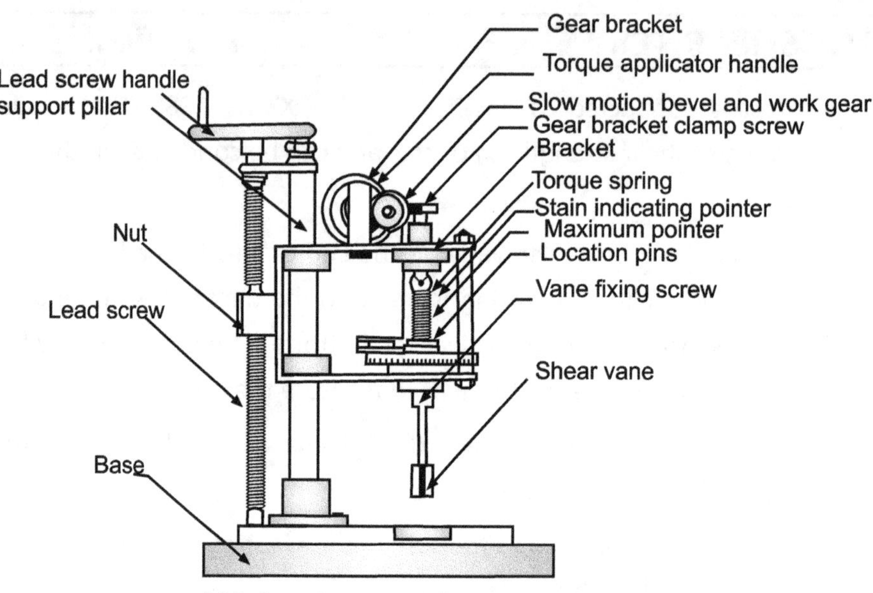

(c) Laboratory vane shear test apparatus

Fig. 7.20

The resisting torque (T_2) due to the resisting forces at the top and bottom of the sheared cylinder can be determined by integration of the torque developed on a circular ring of radius (r) and width (dr).

Thus,
$$T_2 = 2 \int_0^{\frac{D}{2}} [S\,(2\pi r)\,dr]\,r = 4\pi S \left[\frac{r^3}{3}\right]_0^{D/2}$$

$$T_2 = \pi S\,\frac{D^3}{6} \qquad\qquad \dots (7.14)$$

but,
$$T = T_1 + T_2$$

$$T = \frac{S\pi D^2 H}{2} + \pi S\,\frac{D^3}{6} \quad \text{[from equations (7.12), (7.13) and (7.14)]}$$

or
$$\boxed{S = \frac{T}{\pi D^2\left(\dfrac{H}{2} + \dfrac{D}{6}\right)} = \frac{0.2727\,T}{D^3}} \quad \text{If } H = 2D$$

where, S = Shear strength

H = Height of vane

D = Diameter of vane

The typical dimensions of the vane are :

(a) 150 mm × 75 mm for soft clays.

(b) 100 mm × 50 mm for firm clays.

(c) 24 mm × 12 mm laboratory vane for soft clay.

After measuring the maximum torque in the undisturbed state, the remoulded strength may also be determined. The vane is rotated rapidly through a few revolutions so as to remould the soil in the sheared zone. Without further delay, the vane is rotated at 6° per minute to get the remoulded strength.

Then,   Sensitivity, (S_t) $= \dfrac{(S)\ \text{Undisturbed}}{(S)\ \text{Remoulded}}$

If the top of vane is above the soil surface and the depth inside the sample is (H_1), then the shear strength (S) becomes,

$$S = \dfrac{T}{\pi D^2 \left[\dfrac{H_1}{2} + \dfrac{D}{12}\right]}$$

The shear strength of soil under undrained condition equals to the apparent cohesion (C_u).

Characteristics of Vane Shear Test :
- The test is simple and quick.
- It is ideally suited for the determination of the undrained shear strength of non-fissured, fully saturated clay.
- The test can be conveniently used to determine the sensitivity of the soil.
- The test cannot be conducted on the clay containing sand, silt or fissured clay.
- The test does not give accurate results when the failure envelope is not horizontal.

7.13 FACTORS AFFECTING THE SHEAR STRENGTH

(a) Cohesionless soils :
- Shape of particles :   The shearing strength of sand with angular particles and sharp edges is greater than that with rounded particles.
- Gradation : A well graded sand exhibits greater shear strength than a uniform sand.
- Denseness : The shear strength increases with increase in the density.
- Confining pressure : The shear strength increases with the increase in confining pressure.
- Loading : The angle of shearing resistance is independent of loading.
- Capillary moisture : The sand may have apparent cohesion due to capillary moisture. This apparent cohesion is destroyed as soon as the sand becomes saturated.

(b) Cohesive soils :
- Clay content : As clay content increases, cohesion increases and angle of shearing resistance decreases.
- Drainage condition : The soils have very low strength just after the application of the load when undrained condition exists.
- Rate of strain : In the case of normally consolidated clays the effect of rate of strain upon the angle of shearing resistance is very small.

- Confining pressure : The shear strength of clay increases with an increase in confining pressure.
- Plasticity index : *The value of ϕ decreases with an increase in plasticity index of clay.*
- Disturbance : The shear strength of a disturbed sample is less than that of an undisturbed samples.

7.14 SKEMPTONS PORE PRESSURE PARAMETERS

A knowledge of the pore water pressure is essential for the determination of effective stresses from the total stresses. The change in pore pressure due to change in the applied stress during an undrained shear, may be explained in terms of empirical coefficients, called the pore pressures parameters.

If a soil specimen is subjected to triaxial incremental stresses $\Delta\sigma_1$, $\Delta\sigma_2$ and $\Delta\sigma_3$ ($\Delta\sigma_2 = \Delta\sigma_3$) it results in a volume decrease ΔV, and a consequent increase in pore pressure of ΔU. The pore pressure increase may be expressed by Skempton's pore pressure equation as under :

$$\Delta U = B\ [\Delta\sigma_3 + A\ (\Delta\sigma_1 - \Delta\sigma_3)] \qquad \ldots (7.15)$$

where, B and A are known as Skempton's pore pressure parameters.

Factors Affecting A and B : For saturated soils B = 1 and B = 0, for S_r = 0. The 'A' parameter depends on the stress history and strain.

The values of A and B parameters may be used to predict pore pressure in the field.

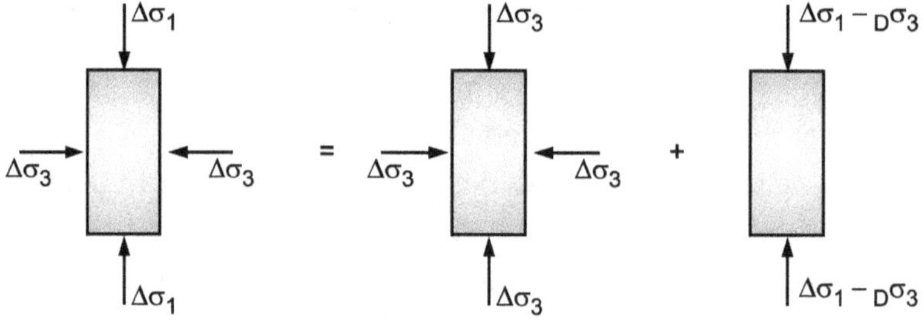

Fig. 7.21

Determination of A and B : In an undrained triaxial test, stress changes are usually made in two stages :

1. an increase in the cell pressure $\Delta\sigma_3$ resulting in an all round change in the stress, and

2. an increase in the axial load resulting in a change in the deviator stress $\Delta\sigma_d = (\Delta\sigma_1 - \Delta\sigma_3)$

Let U_1 be the change in the pore pressure during the first stage and ΔU_2 be the change in pore pressure when deviator stress is applied. Then,

$$\Delta U = \Delta U_1 + \Delta U_2 \qquad \ldots (7.16)$$

Comparing (7.15) and (7.16), we get

$$\Delta U_1 = B\Delta\sigma_3$$

or
$$B = \frac{\Delta U_1}{\Delta \sigma_3}$$

and
$$\Delta U_2 = AB\,(\Delta \sigma_1 - \Delta \sigma_3)$$

$$= \bar{A}\,(\Delta \sigma_1 - \Delta \sigma_3)$$

$$\therefore \quad \bar{A} = \frac{\Delta U_2}{\Delta \sigma_1 - \Delta \sigma_3}$$

The parameter B is determined by measuring ΔU_1 due to change in cell pressure $\Delta \sigma_3$. Then B $= \frac{\Delta U_1}{\Delta \sigma_3}$. The parameter $\bar{A}$ is determined when ΔU_2 measured during, when deviator stress (σ_d) is applied at constant cell pressure. Then $\bar{A} = AB = \frac{\Delta U_2}{\Delta \sigma_1 - \Delta \sigma_3}$. Knowing B and $\bar{A}$, A can be computed.

Table 7.6 : Approximate Values of Pore Pressure Parameters 'A' at Failure

Soil Type	A – Parameter
1. Very loose, fine saturated sand	2 to 3
2. Saturated clays :	
(i) Extra sensitive to quick	1.2 to 2.5
(ii) Normally consolidated	0.7 to 1.3
(iii) Over-consolidated	0.3 to 0.7
(iv) Heavily overconsolidated	-0.5 to 0
3. Compact sand – clays	0.25 to 0.75
4. Compact sand gravels	-0.25 to 0.25

7.15 ULTIMATE STRENGTH AND RESIDUAL STRENGTH

The ultimate shearing resistance after a very large displacement is known as *residual strength*. In Fig. 7.22, the stress strain diagram drops down after a peak and is nearly parallel to the strain axis after a large displacement. This constant value of stress is the residual strength.

The angle of shearing resistance corresponding to residual strength is denoted by ϕ_r', which is less than ϕ' at the peak. The residual strength at a given effective stress is independent of the past history. At the residual strength, volume during shearing remains constant. Hence the angle is also denoted by ϕ_{cv}', meaning constant volume friction angle. As referred to sands, constant volume condition defines the critical void ratio, which is property of the material. The decrease in strength from peak to residual is considered to be due to increase in water content during shear and the reorientation of flaky particles along the shear planes. The difference increases with clay content and OCR, in the case of clays.

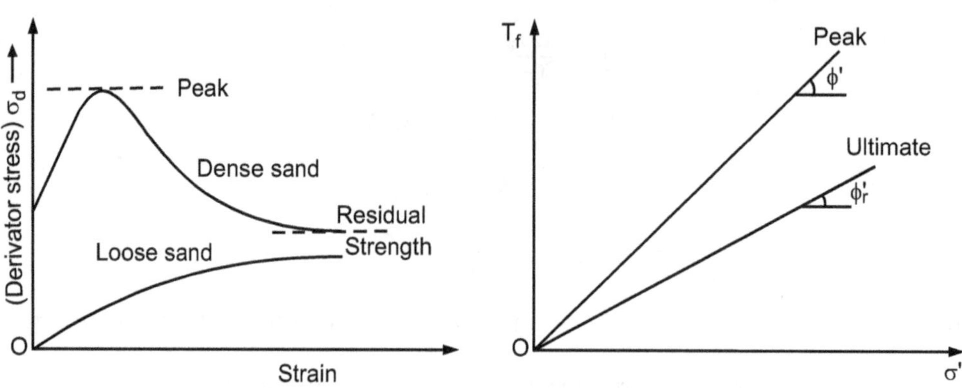

Fig. 7.22 : Residual strength

7.16 THIXOTROPY

The word Thixotropy is derived from two words : thixis meaning touch and tropo, meaning to change. Therefore, thixotropy means any change that occurs by touch.

The loss of strength of a soil due to disturbance is partly due to change in the soil structure and partly due to the disturbance caused by the water molecules in the adsorbed layer. Some of these changes are reversible. If a remoulded soil is allowed to rest, without change in the water content, it gradually regains its lost strength with time. This phenomenon is known as *thixotropy*. It is due to changes or reorientation of the interparticle forces and the adsorbed water.

Thixotropy of soils is of great practical importance in soil engineering. For example, when a pile is driven into the ground, a loss of strength occurs due to the disturbance caused. Thixotropy indicates how much shear strength will be regained after the pile has been driven and left in place for some time.

7.17 SENSITIVITY   [Dec. 14, May 14]

A soil may have a higher strength in the undistributed condition than in the disturbed remoulded condition. This is true for many cohesive soils. The term sensitivity is used to describe this behaviour which is defined, as 'the ratio of the shear strength in the undistributed state to that in the fully remoulded state.

$$S_t = \frac{S_u \text{ (undistributed)}}{S_u \text{ (remoulded)}}$$

The sensitivity may vary from 1 to as high as 100, and thus accordingly they are classified as sensitive, medium sensitive, extra sensitive and quick. Table 7.7 gives the sensitivity classification. Soil deposited in marine environment tends to be highly sensitive. Some quick clays can have sensitivity greater than 100. Over-consolidated soils are found to be insensitive. This is partly due to the low natural water content in the soil deposits.

A part of the disturbance caused due to the remoulding is attributed to the disturbance of adsorbed water in clay layers.

Table 7.7 : Sensitivity Classification

Description	Sensitivity 'S_t'
Insensitive	< 2
Medium sensitive	2 – 4
Sensitive	4 – 8
Very sensitive	8 – 16
Slightly quick	16 – 32
Medium quick	32 – 64
Quick	> 64

Table 7.8 : Typical Effective Angle of Shearing Resistance, ϕ for Coarse Grained Soils

Soil	ϕ' Degrees	
	Loose	Dense
Gravel	34 – 40	40 – 50
Uniform sand	27	33
Well graded sand	33	45
Gravel	35	50
Silty sand	25 – 35	30 – 36

Table 7.9 : Typical Shear Strength Values for Clays

Consistency of clay	Shear strength in N/mm²
Very soft	< 0.120
Soft	0.120 – 0.240
Medium	0.240 – 0.480
Stiff	0.480 – 0.960
Very stiff	0.960 – 1.920
Hard	> 1.920

Table 7.10 : Basic Strength Parameters for Clays

Soil	W_l	I_P	Activity	Water content range %	Drained ϕ_d	Angle of True Internal friction ϕ_r
Undisturbed clay	123	87	1.42	52 – 60	23°	18°
Remoulded clay	98	68	1.11	50 – 60	22°	13.5°
Remoulded Illiteclay	73	45	0.90	37 – 50	22°	16.3°
Remoulded Kaolinite clay	63	25	0.32	46 – 50	21.5°	21°

SOLVED EXAMPLES

Example 7.1 : A soil has an unconfined compressive strength of 120 kN/m². In a triaxial compression test a specimen of same soil when subjected to a cell pressure of 40 kN/m² failed at an additional stress of 160 kN/m².

Determine :

(a) The shear parameters of soil.

(b) The angle made by failure plane with the axial stress (triaxial test).

Solution :   One observation of unconfined compression test and second observation of triaxial compression test is given. Hence two Mohr circles may be drawn. The Mohr circle for unconfined compression test passes through the origin. A common tangent to these circles is the shear envelope.

From Mohr circle :   Cohesion (C) = **43 kN/m²**

and   Angle of internal friction (ϕ) = **19°**

The shear envelope is tangent to the Mohr circle at point (A). Join (A) with centre (C) of the circle. The angle made by (AC) with the horizontal equals to twice the angle between the failure plane and horizontal axis.

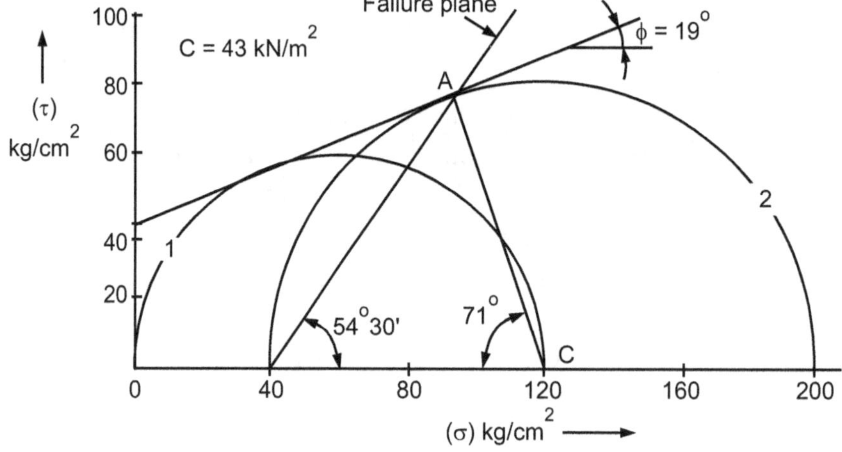

Fig. 7.28

Thus, $2\theta = 71°$

$$\sigma = (180° - 20) \div 2 = (180° - 71)/2 = 54° 30'.$$

∴   The angle made by failure plane with (σ) axis is 54° 30'.

Example 7.2 : Determine the direction of principal planes for the following observations in a direct shear box test :

Normal load (kN)	Shear load (kN)
180	175
360	300
540	400

Solution : Plot a graph between normal load and shear load.

Locate the stress pole and determine the planes of principal stresses.

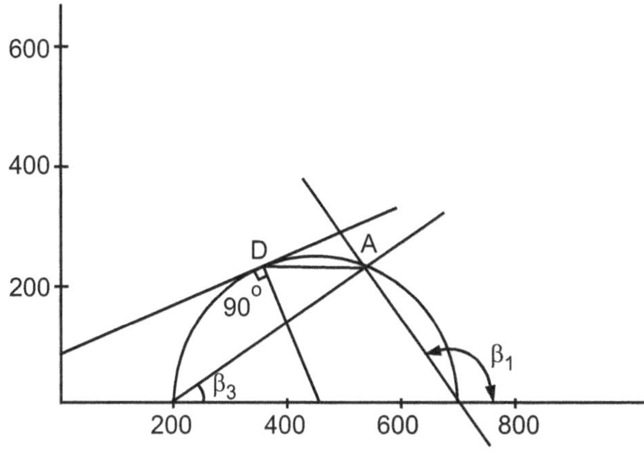

Fig. 7.29

From figure, $\beta_1 = 120°$ and $\beta_3 = 30°$.

Example 7.3 : A soil sample fails under an axial stress of 150 kN/m², when it is laterally unconfined. The failure makes an angle of 55° with the horizontal. Calculate C and ϕ .

Solution : The axial stress is given by

$$\sigma_1 = \sigma_3 \tan^2 \alpha + 2C \tan \alpha$$

$$\alpha = 55° = 45° + \frac{\phi}{2}$$

$$\phi = 2 (55 - 45) = 20°$$

$$\tan \alpha = \tan \left(45° + \frac{\phi}{2}\right) = \tan 55° = 1.43$$

As the sample is laterally unconfined,

$$\sigma_3 = 0$$

$$\sigma_1 = \sigma_3 \tan^2 \alpha + 2C \tan \alpha$$

$$\sigma_1 = 150 = 2C \tan 55 = 2C \times 1.43$$

$$C = \frac{150}{2 \times 1.43} = 52.45 \text{ kN/m}^2$$

Thus, $C = \mathbf{52.45\ kN/m^2}$ and $\phi = \mathbf{20°}$

Example 7.4 : A saturated clay sample of size 5 cm diameter and 10 cm overall height is tested in an unconfined compression tester. Determine the unconfined compressive strength if the specimen fails under an axial load of 50 N. The change in length at failure of specimen is 1 cm.

Solution : Original length of specimen = 10 cm

Initial cross-sectional area, $A_1 = \dfrac{\pi}{4}\, 5^2 = 19.63$ cm²

Change in the length, $\quad \Delta L = 1$ cm

Area at failure, $\quad A = \dfrac{A_1}{1 - \dfrac{\Delta L}{L_1}}$

$\therefore \quad A = \dfrac{19.63}{1 - \dfrac{1}{10}} = 21.81$ cm²

Unconfined compressive strength,

$q_u =$

$\therefore \quad q_u = \dfrac{50}{21.81} = 2.29$ N/cm²

$\therefore \quad q_u = \mathbf{229\ kN/m^2}$

Shear strength, $S = C = \dfrac{q_u}{2} = \dfrac{229}{2}$

$S = C = \mathbf{114.5\ kN/m^2}$

Example 7.5 : Plot the shear stress envelope and find the shear strength parameters with following observations obtained from direct shear test.

Normal stress (kN/m²)	20	40	60
Shear stress (kN/m²)	19.5	28.6	38.0

Solution : From the graph, the shear parameters (C) and (φ) are

$$C = 10 \text{ kN/m}^2, \quad \phi = 35°$$

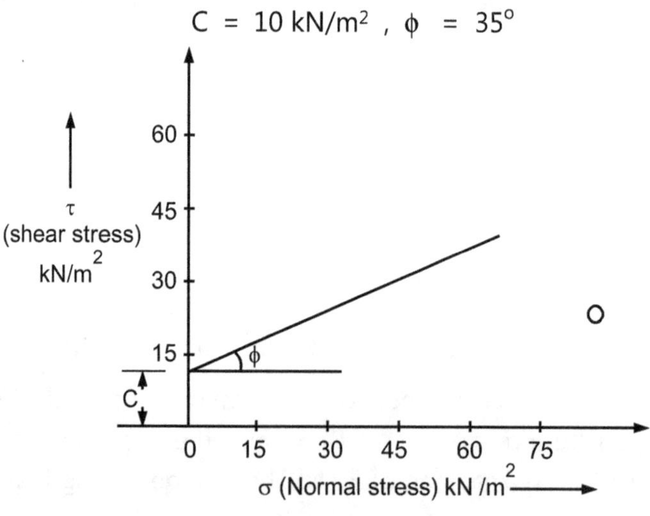

Fig. 7.30

Example 7.6 : A vane, 75 mm in diameter and 150 mm in height was pressed into soft clay in a bore hole. The torque was applied and gradually increased to 50 Nm when failure took place. Determine the undrained shear strength.

Solution : Undrained shear strength = S

$$S = \frac{T}{\pi D^2 \left(\dfrac{H}{2} + \dfrac{D}{6} \right)}$$

$$S = \frac{3T}{11D^3} \text{ (as H = 2D)} = \frac{3 \times 50}{11 \times (0.075)^3}$$

$$S = 3.23 \times 10^4 \ \text{N/m}^2$$

$$S = \textbf{32.3 kN/m}^2$$

Example 7.7 : Following results were obtained from a CU test on a normally consolidated clay. Plot the strength envelope in terms of total stresses and effective stresses and determine the strength parameters.

Specimen No.	Cell pressure	Deviator stress	Pore pressure
1.	250 kN/m²	152 kN/m²	120 kN/m²
2.	500 kN/m²	300 kN/m²	250 kN/m²
3.	750 kN/m²	455 kN/m²	350 kN/m²

Solution : σ_1 = Total stress (Vertical) = Cell pressure + Deviator stress

σ_3 = Cell pressure

The failure envelope for normally consolidated clay passes through the origin. First the Mohr circle of the three tests are drawn in terms of effective stresses corresponding to the failure conditions. Then the best tangent passing through origin is drawn to the three circles. This common tangent is the failure envelope.

$$\bar{\sigma}_3 = \sigma_3 - u$$

$$\bar{\sigma}_1 = \sigma_1 - \bar{\sigma}_3$$

The table shows calculations for total stresses and effective stresses.

Specimen No.	σ_3	σ_1	U	$\bar{\sigma}_3$	$\bar{\sigma}_1$
1.	250	402	120	130	272
2.	500	800	250	250	550
3.	750	1205	350	400	805

(a) Plot in terms of total stresses :

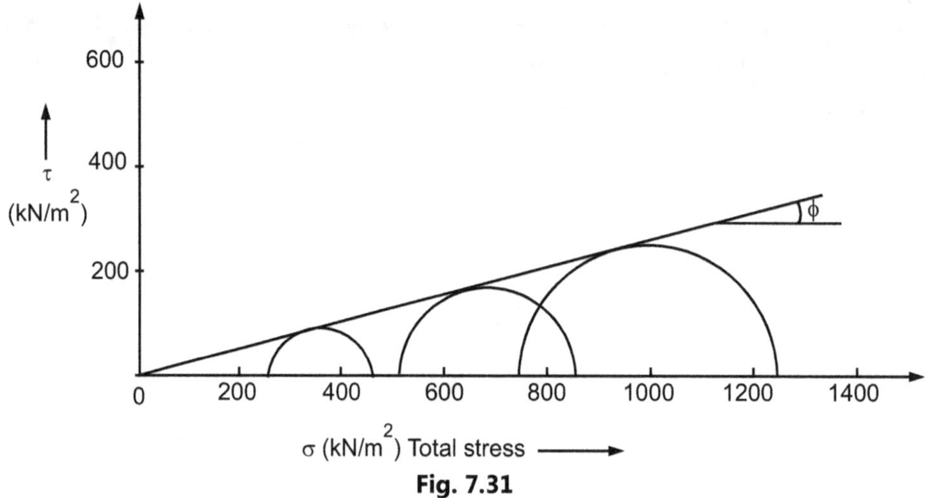

Fig. 7.31

From plot, ϕ = **14°**

(b) Plot in terms of effective stresses :

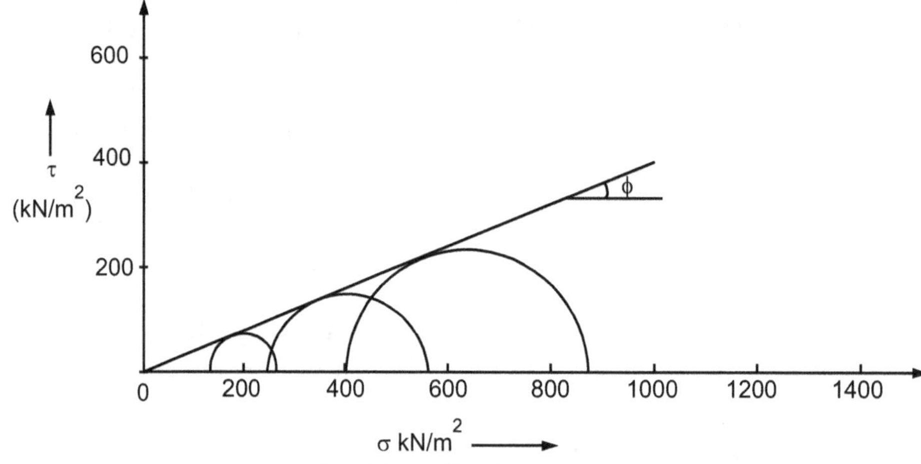

Fig. 7.32 : Effective stresses

From plot, ϕ = 22°

Example 7.8 : A saturated specimen of cohesionless sand was tested in a triaxial compression. The specimen failed at a deviator stress of 150 kN/m², when the cell pressure was 100 kN/m². Find the angle of shearing resistance. What would be the major principal stress at failure if the cell pressure were 200 kN/m² ?

Solution : Given :

$$\sigma_d = 150 \text{ kN/m}^2$$

$$\sigma_3 = 100 \text{ kN/m}^2$$

$$C = 0$$

Using the equation :

$$\sigma_1 = \sigma_3 \tan^2 \alpha + 2C \tan \alpha$$

where,　　　　　　　　　　$\sigma_1 = \sigma_d + \sigma_3 = 100 + 150 = 250$

$\therefore$　　　　　　　　　　$250 = 100 \tan^2 \alpha$

$$\tan^2 \alpha = \frac{250}{100} = 2.5$$

$$\alpha = 45 + \frac{\phi}{2} = 52^\circ\ 41'$$

$\therefore$　　　　　　　　　　$\phi = 15^\circ\ 22'$

If　　　　　　　　　　$\sigma_3 = 200\ \text{kN/m}^2$

　　　　　　　　　　$\sigma_1 = \sigma_3 \tan^2 52^\circ\ 41'$

　　　　　　　　　　$\sigma = 500\ \text{kN/m}^2$

Example 7.9 : A sample of soil failed under the following triaxial stresses : $\sigma_3 = 200$ kN/m², $\sigma_1 = 800$ kN/m². If the soil has an angle of shearing resistance of 22°, what is its unit cohesion ?

Solution :　Given : $\sigma_3 = 200$ kN/m², $\phi = 22^\circ$, $\sigma_1 = 800$ kN/m².

Using equation :

$$\sigma_1 = \sigma_3 \tan^2 \alpha + 2C \tan \alpha$$

$$800 = 200 \tan^2 \left(45 + \frac{22}{2}\right) + 2C \tan \left(45 + \frac{22}{2}\right)$$

$$C = \frac{360.40}{2.96} = \mathbf{121.75\ kN/m^2}$$

Example 7.10 : If a sandy soil is tested in a directed shear box in the saturated condition, what will be the lateral force at failure if $\phi = 35^\circ$ and the normal load is 36 N ?

Solution: Given : $\phi = 35^\circ$, $C = 0$ (sandy soil), $\sigma = 36$ N, $\tau = ?$

Using　　　　　　　　　　$\tau = C + \sigma \tan \theta$

　　　　　　　　　　$\tau = 0 + 36 \tan 35^\circ$

　　　　　　　　　　$\tau = \mathbf{25.20\ N}$

Example 7.11 : A specimen of a stiff saturated clay 37.5 mm in diameter and 75 mm high failed in a unconfined compression, under a load of 120 N, showing a shortening of 15 mm. Determine the law of shear strength if the ruptured plane was found to be 55° inclined to the horizontal.

Solution : Area of specimen at failure :

$$A_f = \frac{A}{1-\zeta} \left[\text{where, } \zeta = \frac{\Delta L}{L}\right]$$

$$= \dfrac{\pi \dfrac{d^2}{4} (37.5)^2}{1 - \left(\dfrac{15}{75}\right)}$$

$$= 1379.88 \ mm^2$$

$$\text{Stress at failure, } \sigma_{uc} = \dfrac{120 \times 10^{-3}}{1379.88 \times 10^{-4}}$$

$$= \mathbf{86.96 \ kN/m^2}$$

The Mohr circle with $\sigma_1 = 86.96$, $\sigma_3 = 0$ is drawn. A plane passing through the origin and at $55°$ to the horizontal is drawn so as to intersect the circle at P. A tangent to P is the strength envelope giving C = 32 kN/m², $\phi = 20°$.

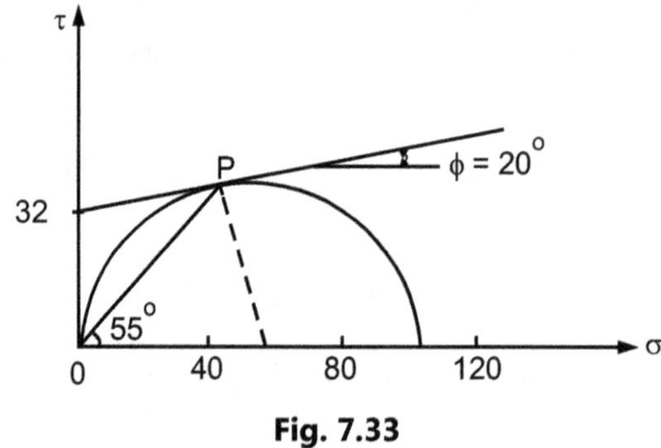

Fig. 7.33

Example 7.12 : Determine the pore pressure parameters from the following data of an undrained triaxial test on a soil specimen :

1. Increase in cell pressure from 100 to 200 kN/m² causes pore pressure to increase by 95 kN/m².

2. Increase in axial stress from 200 to 350 kN/m² at constant cell pressure shows an increase of pore pressure by 120 kN/m² at failure.

Solution : By Skempton's pore pressure equation :

$$\Delta U = B \left[\Delta\sigma_3 + A (\Delta\sigma_1 - \Delta\sigma_3)\right]$$

1. Isotropic loading : $\Delta\sigma_3 = 100$, $\Delta\sigma_1 = \Delta\sigma_3 = 0$

$\therefore$ $\qquad\qquad\qquad \Delta U = B\sigma_3$ or 95 = 100B

$\therefore$ $\qquad\qquad\qquad$ B = **0.95**

2. Deviator stress : $\Delta\sigma_1 - \Delta\sigma_3 = 150$, $\Delta\sigma_3 = 0$

$\therefore$ $\qquad\qquad\qquad \Delta U = BA (\Delta\sigma_1 - \Delta\sigma_3)$ or 120 = 0.95 A (150)

$\therefore$ $\qquad\qquad\qquad$ A = **0.842**

Example 7.13 : The following results were obtained from a direct shear test on a sandy clay sample.

Normal load (kN)	Shear load proving ring reading (Division)
360	13
720	19
1080	26
1440	32

If the shear box is 60 mm square and the proving ring constant is 20 N per division, estimate the shear strength parameters of the soil. Would failure occur on a plane within this soil at a point where the normal stress is 320 kN/m² and the corresponding shear stress is 138 kN/m² ?

Solution :

Normal load (N)	Normal stress (kN/m²)	P.R. dial reading	Shear Stress (kN/m²)
360	$\dfrac{360}{(0.06)^2 \times 1000} = 100$	13	$\dfrac{13 \times 20}{(0.06)^2 \times 1000} = 72.2$
720	200	19	105.6
1080	300	26	144.4
1440	400	32	177.7

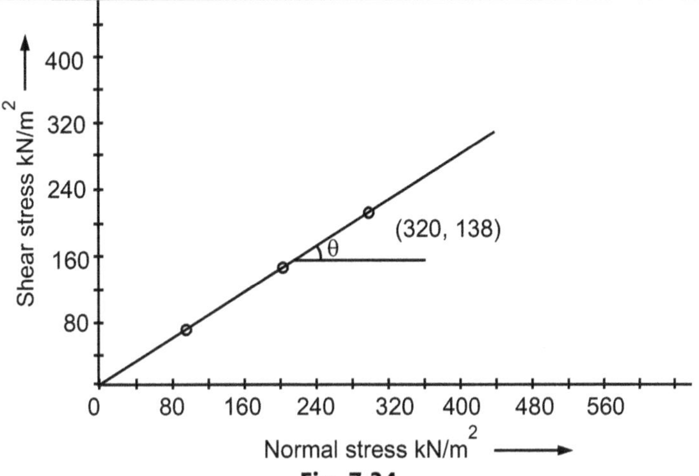

Fig. 7.34

The shear stresses are plotted against the corresponding normal stresses as shown in Fig. 7.34. The straight line having the best fit to the plotted points is drawn. The shear strength parameters taken from the plot are given as :

$$C = \textbf{34 kN/m}^2 \ , \quad \phi = \textbf{20}°$$

The stress state $\tau = 138$ kN/m² and $\sigma = 320$ kN/m² falls below the failure envelope and therefore would not produce failure.

Example 7.14 : A specimen of fine dry sand when subjected to a triaxial compression test, failed at a deviator stress of 400 kN/m². It failed with a pronounced failure plane with an angle of 24° to the axis of the sample. Compute the lateral pressure to which the specimen would have been subjected to.   **(Nov. 16, 6M)**

Solution : The failure angle,

$$\alpha = 45 + \frac{\phi}{2} = 45 + \frac{24}{2}$$

$$= 67°$$

We have $\sigma_1 = \sigma_3 \tan^2 \alpha + 2\,C \tan \alpha$

Since the soil is dry sand, $C = 0$

$\therefore$ $\qquad\qquad \sigma_1 = \sigma_3 \tan^2 \alpha$

Deviator stress, $\sigma_d = \sigma_1 - \sigma_3$

or $\qquad\qquad \sigma_1 = \sigma_d + \sigma_3 = 400 + \sigma_3$

or $\qquad\qquad 400 + \sigma_3 = \sigma_3 \tan^2 (67°)$

or $\qquad\qquad \sigma_3 = \dfrac{400}{\tan^2 (67°) - 1} = \mathbf{87.91\ kN/m^2}$

Example 7.15 : A vane of 80 mm diameter and 160 mm height has been pushed into an in-situ soft clay at the bottom of a bore hole. The torque required to rotate the vane was 76 Nm. Determine the undrained shear strength of the clay. After the test the vane was rotated several times and the ultimate torque was found to be 50 Nm. Estimate the sensitivity of the clay.

Solution : Using equation,

$$S = \frac{T}{\pi \left(\dfrac{D^2 H}{2} + \dfrac{D^3}{6} \right)} = \frac{3T}{11 D^3}$$

(i) For undisturbed sample,

$$S_1 = \frac{76 \times 10^{-3}}{\pi \left[\dfrac{1}{2} \times 0.160 \times (0.08)^2 + \dfrac{1}{6} (0.08)^3 \right]}$$

$$= 40.5\ kN/m^2$$

$\therefore$ The undisturbed undrained strength $= \mathbf{40.5\ kN/m^2}$

(ii) The remoulded undrained strength,

$$S_2 = \frac{50 \times 10^{-3}}{\pi \left[\dfrac{1}{2} \times 0.160 \times (0.08)^2 + \dfrac{1}{6} (0.08)^2 \right]}$$

$$= \mathbf{26.65\ kN/m^2}$$

Alternatively,　　　　　　$S_2 = \dfrac{50}{76} S_1 = \dfrac{50}{76} \times 40.5 = 26.65 \ kN/m^2$

Now,　　　　Sensitivity, $S_t = \dfrac{\text{Undisturbed undrained strength}}{\text{Remoulded undrained strength}}$

$$= \dfrac{40.50}{26.65} = \mathbf{1.52 \ kN/m^2}$$

Example 7.16 : In a direct shear test on the sand, the normal stress was 2.0 kg/cm^2 and shear stress failure was 0.8 kg/cm^2. Determine the orientations of the principal planes at failure.

Solution :

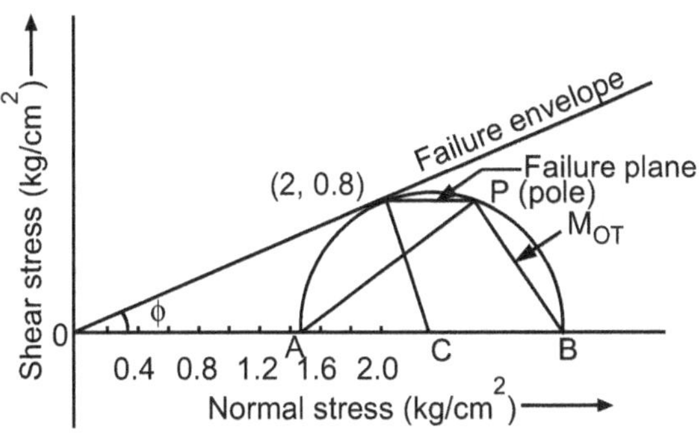

Fig. 7.35

The graphical solution is shown in the Fig. 7.35.

In Fig. 7.30 AP is minor principal plane and BP is major principal plane.

Example 7.17 : Two samples were tested in a triaxial machine. The all found pressure maintained for the first sample was 2 kg/cm^2 and 20 kg/cm^2 and failure occurred at additional axial stress of 7.7 kg./cm^2, while for the second the values were 5.0 kg/cm^2 and 13.7 kg/cm^2 respectively. Find C and φ of the soil.

Solution :

$$\sigma_1 = \sigma_3 \tan^2 \alpha + 2C \tan \alpha \qquad \qquad ...(i)$$

$$\sigma_3 = 2 \ kg/cm^2, \ \sigma_1 = 2 + 7.7 = 9.7 \ kg/cm^2$$

$$\sigma_3' = 5 \ kg/cm^2, \ \sigma_1' = 5 + 13.7 = 18.7 \ kg/cm^2$$

On substituting in Equation (i), we get

$$9.7 = 2 \tan^2 \alpha + 2C \tan \alpha \qquad \qquad ...(ii)$$

$$18.7 = 5 \tan^2 \alpha + 2C \tan \alpha \qquad \qquad ...(iii)$$

We get

$$9.7 - 2 \tan^2 \alpha = 18.7 - 5 \tan^2 \alpha$$

$$3 \tan^2 \alpha = 9, \ \tan \alpha = \sqrt{3}, \ \ \alpha = 60°$$

Now,
$$\alpha = 45° + \frac{\phi}{2}$$

$\therefore$
$$60 = 45° + \frac{\phi}{2} \text{ or } \phi = 30°$$

On substituting for $\tan \alpha$ and $\tan^2 \alpha$ in Equation (ii), we get
$$9.7 = 2 \times 3 + 2C\sqrt{3}$$
$$C = \frac{9.7 - 6}{2.53} = 1.07 \text{ kg/cm}^2$$
$$C = \textbf{1.07 kg/cm}^2$$
$$\phi = \textbf{30°}$$

Example 7.18 : A cylindrical specimen of dry sand was tested in a triaxial test. Failure occurred under a cell pressure of 1.2 kg/cm^2 and at deviator stress of 4.0 kg/mg^2.

(i)   What was the angle of shearing resistance of the soil ?

(ii)   What were the normal and shear stresses on the failure plane ?

(iii) What angle did the failure plane make with the minor principal plane ?

(iv)   What was the maximum shear stress on any plane in the specimen at the instant of failure and how was the plane, in question, oriented with the major principle plane ?

Solution : Here,
$$\sigma_3 = 1.2 \text{ kg/cm}^2$$
$$\sigma_1 - \sigma_3 = 4.0 \text{ kg/cm}^2$$

$\therefore$
$$\sigma_1 = 5.2 \text{ kg/cm}^2$$

Since, the given soil is dry sand, C = 0, i.e., the failure envelop passes through the origin of the Mohr's circle diagram. (Fig. 7.31)

We know,
$$\sigma_1 = \sigma_3 \tan^2 (45° + \phi/2) + 2C \tan (45° + \phi/2)$$
$$= \sigma_3 \tan^2 (45° + \phi/2) \qquad \text{(because C = 0)}$$
$$\frac{5.2}{1.2} = \tan^2 (45° + \phi/2)$$
$$\theta = 45° + \phi/2 = \tan^{-1}\sqrt{4.3333}$$
$$= 64° \ 20'28''$$
$$\phi/2 = 64° \ 20' \ 28'' - 45° = 19° \ 20' \ 28'')$$

$\therefore$ Angle of shearing resistance, $\phi = \textbf{38° 40'56''}$

Stress on failure plane $= \sigma_3 (1 + \sin \phi)$
$$= 1.2 (1 + \sin 38° \ 40'56'')$$
$$= \textbf{1.95 kg/cm}^2$$
$$\textbf{OR}$$

Stress on failure plane $= \dfrac{\sigma_1 - \sigma_3}{2} \sin 2\theta$

$$= \frac{4}{2} \times \sin 128\ 40'56''$$

$$= 1.56\ \text{kg/cm}^2$$

$$\text{Maximum shear-stress} = \frac{\sigma_1 - \sigma_3}{2} = \frac{5.2 - 1.2}{2}$$

$$= \mathbf{2\,kg/cm^2}$$

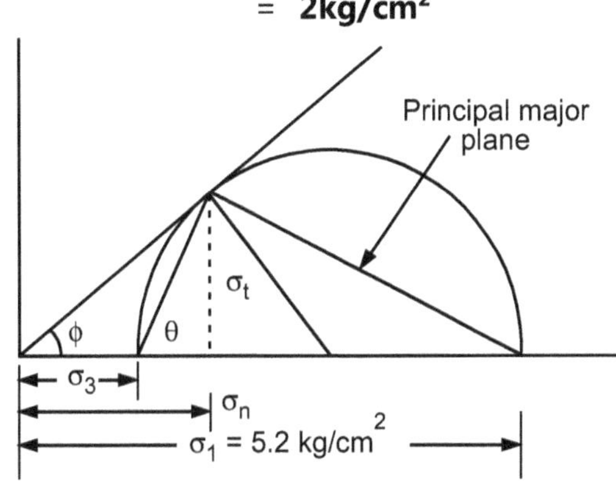

Fig. 7.36 : Mohr's Circle

By measurement, Normal stress, σ_n = **1.95 kg/cm²**; Shear stress, τ = **1.50 kg/cm²**; Angle of shearing resistance, ϕ = **39°**; Inclination of plane, θ = **64° 30'**

Example 7.19 : A cylindrical sample soil, having cohesion of 0.8 kg/cm² and angle of internal friction of 20°, is subjected to a cell pressure of 1.0 kg/cm². Calculate the maximum deviator stress at which the sample will fail and the angle made by the failure plane with the axis of the sample.

Solution : Given : σ_3 = 1.0 kg/cm²; ϕ = 20°, C = 0.8 kg/cm²

Substituting the values in standard equation, we get

$$\sigma_1 = \sigma_3 \tan^2 (45° + \phi/2) + 2C \tan (45° + \phi/2)$$

We get, $\sigma_1 = 1.0 \tan^2 (45° + 10°) + 2 \times 0.8 \tan (45° + 10°)$

$$= 1.0 \tan^2 55° + 1.6 \tan 55° = 2.0396 + 2.2850$$

or σ_1 = 4.3246 kg/cm²

But, deviator stress $\sigma_d = \sigma_1 - \sigma_3$

∴ σ_d = 4.3246 − 1.0 = **3.3246 kg/cm²**

The angle made by the failure plane with major principal plane = (45° + $\phi/2$) = **50°**

The angle made by the failure plane with the axis of sample = $\dfrac{\pi}{4} - \dfrac{\phi}{2}$ = **40°**

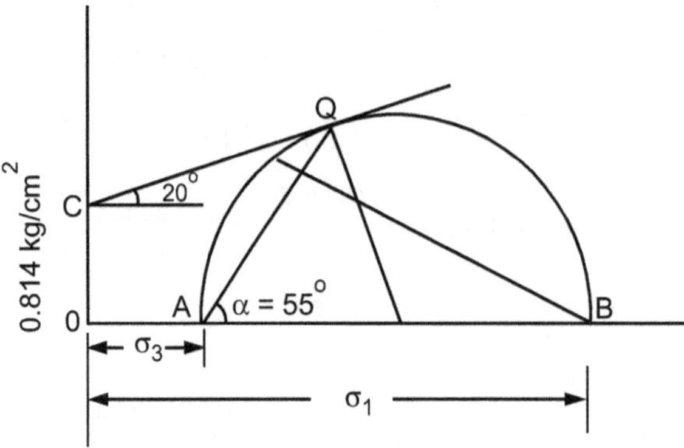

Fig. 7.37

To represent normal direct stressess to represent cohesion.

Let, OA = cell pressure, σ_3 = 1.0 kg/cm^2

OC = Cohesion, C = 0.8 kg/cm^2

Draw $\angle$ Q making an angle 20   with the horizontal.

Draw Mohr's circle with its centre so selected on the x-axis so that it starts from A and touches CQ in Q.

$$OB = \sigma_1 = 4.3 \text{ kg/cm}^2 \text{ and } OA = \sigma_3 = 1 \text{ kg/cm}^2$$

$$\text{Deviator stress, } AB = \sigma_1 - \sigma_3$$

$$= 4.3 - 1.0 = \textbf{3.3 kg/cm}^2$$

$$\angle QAB = \alpha = 55$$

Angle made by failure plane with the axis of the sample

$$= 90 - 55 = \textbf{35}$$

Example 7.20 : An embankment of 5 m height is made of soil whose effective stress parameters are C'= 50 kN/m^2 and ϕ' = 16° and γ = 16.2 kN/m^3. The pore pressure parameters as found from triaxial tests are A = 0.4 and B = 0.92. Find the shear strength of the soil at the base of the embankment just after the soil has been raised from 5 m to 8 m. Assume that the dissipation of pore pressure during the stage of construction is negligible and that the lateral pressure at any point is one half of the vertical pressure.

Solution : Given : γ = 16.2 kN/m^3

$\Delta\sigma_1$ = Increase in vertical stress due to 3 m construction

$$= \gamma \, \Delta H = 16.2 \times 3$$

$$= 48.6 \text{ kN/m}^2$$

$$\Delta\sigma_3 = \frac{1}{2} \Delta\sigma_1$$

$$\Delta\sigma_3 = \frac{1}{2} \times 48.6 = 24.3 \text{ kN/m}^3$$

We know that increase in pore pressure and increase of principal stress are related by the following equation :

$$\Delta u = B [\Delta\sigma_3 + A (\Delta\sigma_1 - \Delta\sigma_3)]$$

$$= 0.92 [24.3 + 0.4 (48.6 - 24.3)]$$

$$= 31.3 \text{ kN/m}^2$$

Original pressure, $\sigma_1 = 5 \times 16.2 = 81.0 \text{ kN/m}^2$

$\therefore$ Effective stress, $\sigma' = \sigma_1 + \Delta\sigma_1 - \Delta u$

$$= 81.0 \times 10^3 + 48.6 \times 10^3 - 31.3 \times 10^3$$

or $\sigma' = 98.3 \text{ kN/m}^2$

$\therefore$ Shear Strength $= C' + \sigma' \tan \phi$

$$= 50 + 98.3 \tan 16$$

$$= \mathbf{78.19 \text{ kN/m}^2}$$

Example 7.21 : Two identical soil specimen were tested in a triaxial apparatus. First specimen failed at a deviator stress of 770 kN/m² when the cell pressure was 200 kN/m². Second specimen failed at a deviator stress of 1370 kN/m² under a cell pressure of 400 kN/m². Determine the value of 'C' and 'ϕ' analytically. If the same soil is tested in a direct shear apparatus with a normal stress of 600 kN/m², estimate the shear stress at failure.

Solution : For the first specimen

Deviator stress, $\sigma_d = 770 \text{ kN/m}^2$, Cell pressure, $\sigma_3 = 200 \text{ kN/m}^2$

We know, $\sigma_1 = \sigma_3 + \sigma_d = 770 + 200 = 970 \text{ kN/m}^2$

Also, $\sigma_1 = \sigma_3 N\phi + 2 C_u \sqrt{N\phi}$

$\therefore$ $970 = 200 N\phi + 2 C_u \sqrt{N\phi}$ ...(i)

For the second specimen :

$$\sigma_d = 1370 \text{ kN.m}^2 \text{ and } \sigma_3 = 400 \text{ kN/m}^2$$

$$\sigma_1 = \sigma_3 + \sigma_d = 1770 \text{ kN/m}^2$$

$\therefore$ $1770 = 400 N\phi + 2 C_u \sqrt{N\phi}$ ...(ii)

From equations (i) and (ii), we have, $800 = 200 N\phi$, or $N\phi = 4$

$\therefore$ $C_u = 42.5 \text{ kN/m}^2$

$\therefore$ From $N_\phi = \tan^2\left(45 + \dfrac{\phi}{2}\right)$

$$4 = \tan^2\left(45 + \dfrac{\phi}{2}\right)$$

$\therefore$ $\phi = 36.869°$

We know, stress at failure, $\qquad \sigma_n = 600$ kN/m^2

Shear stress at failure, $\qquad \tau_f = \sigma_n \tan\phi + C_u$

$$= 600 \tan(36.869) + 42.5$$

$$= \mathbf{492.485 \ kN/m^2}$$

Example 7.22 : A standard specimen of cohesionless sand was tested in triaxial compression and the sample failed at a deviator stress of 482 kN/m^2 when the cell pressure was 100 kN/m^2 under drained conditions. Find the effective angle of shearing resistance of sand. What would be the deviator stress and the major principal stress at failure for another identical specimen of sand if it is tested under a cell pressure of 200 kN/m^2 .

Solution : We know that in the drained tests, the effective stresses are equal to the total stress.

$\therefore \qquad \sigma_3 = 100$ kN/m^2

$$= \frac{100 \times 1000}{100 \times 100} = 10 \ \text{N/cm}^2 = 1 \ \text{kg/cm}^2$$

(i) $\qquad \sigma_1 = \sigma_3 + \sigma_d = 100 + 482$

$$= 582 \ \text{kN/m}^2 = 5.82 \ \text{kg/cm}^2$$

Again, $\qquad \sigma_1' = \sigma_3' \tan^2\left(45° + \dfrac{\phi}{2}\right)$

where $\qquad \sigma_1' = $ Effective major principal stress

$\qquad \sigma_3' = $ Total stress

$\qquad \phi' = $ Effective angle of shearing resistance of sand

$$45° + \frac{\phi'}{2} = \tan^{-1}\left(\sqrt{5.82}\right)$$

$$= 67°.5$$

$$\phi' = 45°$$

(ii) $\qquad \sigma_1' = \sigma_3' \tan^2\left(45° + \dfrac{\phi}{2}\right) \qquad \{\sigma_3 = 2 \ \text{kg/cm}^2\}$

$$= 2 \tan^2\left(45° + \frac{45°}{2}\right)$$

$$= 11.66 \ \text{kg/m}^2$$

$$= 116.6 \ \text{N/cm}^2$$

$$= \mathbf{1166 \ kN/m^2}$$

Deviator stress, $\sigma_d = \sigma_1 - \sigma_3 = 11.66 - 2$

$$= \mathbf{9.66 \ kg/cm^2}$$

Example 7.23 : In a vane shear test on clay, the following observations are made.

Applied Torque = 183 kg cm. Height of Vane = 10 cm. , Diameter of vane = 5 cm. Calculate the strength of the clay.

Solution : T = 183 kg cm, H = 10 cm, d = 5 cm.

$$C_u = \frac{T}{\pi d^2 \left(\dfrac{H}{2} + \dfrac{d}{6}\right)}$$

$$= \frac{183}{\pi \times 5^2 \left(\dfrac{10}{2} + \dfrac{5}{6}\right)}$$

$$C_u = 0.4 \text{ kg/cm}^2$$

Example 7.24 : A vane of 80 mm diameter and 160 mm height has been pushed into an in-situ soft clay at the bottom of a bore hole. The torque required to rotate the vane was 76 Nm. Determine the undrained shear strength of the clay. After the test, the vane was rotated several times and the ultimate torque was found to be 50 Nm. Estimate the sensitivity of the clay.

Solution :

$$C_u = \frac{T}{\pi d^2 \left(\dfrac{H}{2} + \dfrac{d}{6}\right)}$$

$$= \frac{76 \text{ Nm}}{\pi \times 80^2 \left(\dfrac{160}{2} + \dfrac{80}{6}\right)}$$

$$= \frac{76 \times 6 \times 1000}{\pi \times 80^2 \times (480 + 80)}$$

$$= 0.04049 \text{ N/mm}^2 = 40.49 \text{ kN/m}^2$$

$$\text{Sensitivity of clay} = \frac{\text{Torque in undisturbed state}}{\text{Torque in disturbed state}} = \frac{76 \text{ Nm}}{50 \text{ Nm}} = 1.52$$

Example 7.25 : Laboratory results on a soil have shown that its UCC is 1.2 kg/cm^2. In a triaxial compression test a specimen of the soil when subjected to a cell pressure of 0.4 kg/cm^2 failed at an additional stress of 1.6 kg/cm^2. Estimate the shearing strength of the same soil along a horizontal plane at a depth of 4 m in a deposit. The ground water table is at a depth of 2.5 m from the ground level. Take dry unit weight of soil as 1.7 gm/cc and specific gravity as 2.7.

Solution : Given :

$$q_u = 1.2 \text{ kg/cm}^2$$

$$\text{Cohesion} = C_u = \frac{q_u}{2} = \frac{1.2}{2}$$

$$= 0.6 \text{ kg/cm}^2$$

Triaxial test gives,

$$\sigma_3 = 0.4 \text{ kg/cm}^2$$

$$\sigma_d = 1.6 \text{ kg/cm}^2$$

But, $\sigma_1 = \sigma_3 + \sigma_d$

$$= 0.4 + 1.6 = 2.0 \text{ kg/cm}^2$$

Again, $\sigma_1 = \sigma_3 \tan^2 \alpha + 2 C_u \tan \alpha$

or $2 = 0.4 \tan^2 \alpha + 2 \times 0.6 \tan \alpha$

Putting $\tan \alpha = x$, we have

$\therefore$ $0.4 x^2 + 1.2 x - 2 = 0$

or $x = 1.1925$

$\therefore$ $\tan \alpha = 1.1925$

$$\alpha = 50°$$

But, $\alpha = 45° + \dfrac{\phi}{2}$

$\therefore$ $\phi = 10°$

Now, shear strength of soil, $\tau = C + \sigma \tan \phi$

Also, we know $\gamma_d = 1.7 \text{ gm/cc} = 17 \text{ k N/m}^3, G = 2.7$

Now, $\gamma_d = \dfrac{G\gamma_w}{1 + e}$

or $17 = \dfrac{2.7 \times 10}{1 + e}$

or $e = 0.588$

$$\gamma_{sat} = \dfrac{\gamma_w[G + e]}{1 + e} = 20.31$$

$\therefore$ Pressure at 4 m $= 17 \times 2.5 + 20.31 \times 1.5$

$$= 72.16 \text{ kN/m}^2$$

Shear strength, $\tau = 60 + 72.16 \tan 10 = \mathbf{71.58 \text{ kN/m}^2}$

Example 7.26 : In a direct shear box test (60 mm × 60 mm × 25 mm) a soil specimen failed under a shear load of 50 kN/m² and normal load of 90 kN/m². If the soil is non-cohesive, what would be the deviator stress at failure, if the same soil is tested in triaxial compression under a cell pressure of 150 kN/m² ?

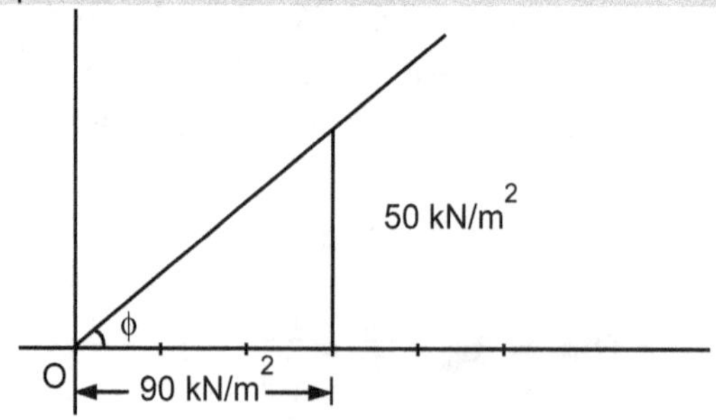

Fig. 7.38

Solution :

$$\tan \phi = \frac{50}{90}$$

$$\therefore \quad \phi = 29.0546°$$

$$\alpha = \frac{\pi}{4} + \frac{\phi}{2}$$

$$= 59.5273°$$

$$\tan \alpha = 1.69995$$

$$\sigma_1 = 2\,C \tan \alpha + \sigma_3 \tan^2 \alpha$$

$C = 0$, $\tan \alpha = 1.7$, $\sigma_3 = 150 \text{ kg/m}^2$

$$= 150 \times (1.6995)^2$$

$$= 433.25 \text{ kN/m}^2$$

$$\therefore \quad \text{Deviator stress} = \sigma_1 - \sigma_3$$

$$= 433.5 - 150$$

$$= \mathbf{283.25 \text{ kN/m}^2}$$

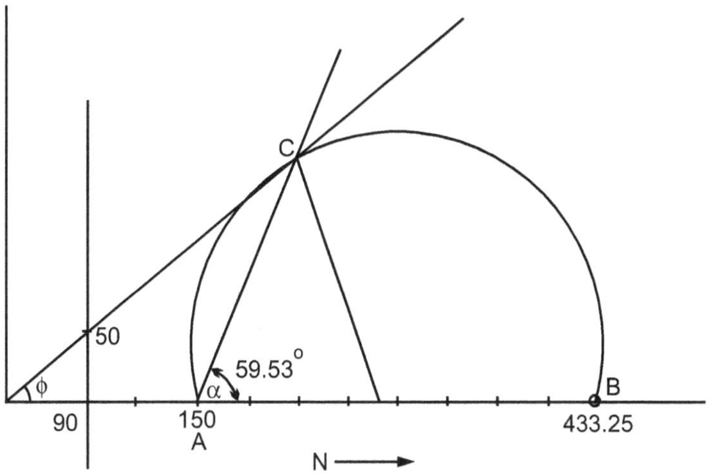

Fig. 7.39

Example 7.27 : The following are the test results (carried out on a soil sample) while performing direct shear test. Determine the shear parameters and indicate the plane of failure.

Normal Stress in kN/m²	Shear Stress in kN/m²
10	15
16	19.5
20	22.5

If the same sample is tested in the triaxial shear test by applying lateral stress of 10 kN/m^2, determine the deviator stress to cause failure. Draw Mohr's envelope and show plane of failure.

Solution :

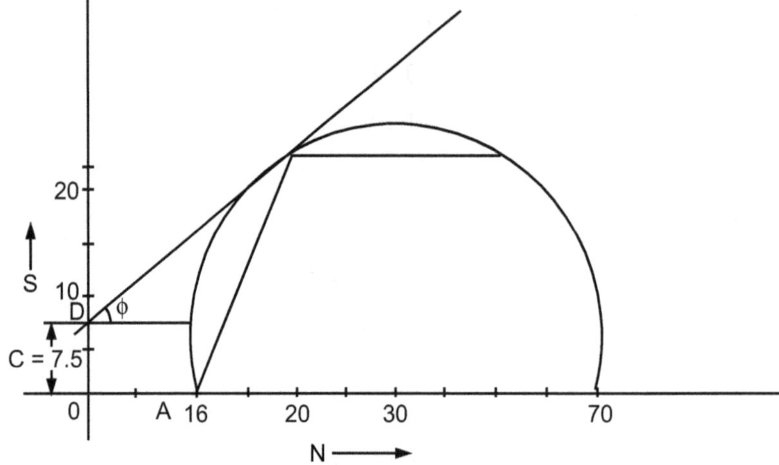

Fig. 7.40

$$\phi = \tan^{-1}\frac{22.5 - 15}{20 - 10} = \tan^{-1} 0.75$$

$$= 36.87°$$

$$= 36° \ 52' \ 11.67''$$

$$S = C + N \tan\phi$$

$$\therefore \quad C = 15 - 10 \times \tan\phi = 7.5 \ \text{kN/m}^2$$

$$\alpha = \frac{\pi}{4} + \frac{\phi}{2} = 63.4349°$$

$$\tan\alpha = 2$$

$$\sigma_1 = 2 \cdot C \tan\alpha + \sigma_3 \tan^2\alpha \qquad [\sigma_3 = 10 \ \text{kN/m}^2]$$

$$= 2 \times 7.5 \times 2 + 10 \times 2^2$$

$$= 30 + 40 = 70 \ \text{kN/m}^2$$

$$\text{Deviator Stress} = \sigma_1 - \sigma_3$$

$$= 70 - 10$$

$$= \mathbf{60 \ kN/m^2}$$

Example 7.28 : Specimens of a silty sand were subjected to the direct shear test in the laboratory, in a shear box of 6 cm × 6 cm size. The normal load and the corresponding shear forces at failure are shown below :

Normal Load (kN)	Shear Force (kN)
0.10	0.089
0.20	0.147
0.30	0.205

Draw the failure envelop and determine the apparent angle of shearing resistance and cohesion of the soil.

Solution : To plot a graph of Shear stress Vs Normal stress in kN/m^2 corresponding to shear force and Normal force will be divided by $\dfrac{6\ cm \times 6\ cm}{100 \times 100}$ and are calculated as under :

Normal		Shear Force	
Load (kN)	Stress kN/m^2	kN	Stress
0.1	27.716	0.089	24.72
0.2	55.555	0.147	49.444
0.3	83.33	0.205	74.1666

$$\phi = \frac{74.1666 - 24.72}{83.33 - 27.716}$$

$$= \frac{49.4466}{55.614} = 0.8091$$

$$\therefore \quad \phi = \mathbf{41.64}$$

$$S = C + N \tan \phi$$

$$\therefore \quad C = S - N \tan \phi = 49.444 - 55.555 \tan 41.64$$

$$= 49.4440 - 49.3939 = 0.05265$$

$$= \mathbf{0.05\ kN/m^2}$$

Example 7.29 : A triaxial test was performed and the following data was obtained :

Test No.	σ_3 (kPa)	σ_1 (kPa)
1.	50	139.5
2.	100	249.5
3.	150	359.4

Determine C and ϕ.

Solution : Analytically, the problem can be solved as under.

$$\sigma_1 = 2 C \tan \alpha + \sigma_3 \tan^2 \alpha$$

$$\therefore \qquad 359.4 \;=\; 2\,C\tan\alpha + 150\tan^2\alpha \qquad \text{...(i)}$$

$$249.5 \;=\; 2\,C\tan\alpha + 100\tan^2\alpha \qquad \text{...(ii)}$$

Deducting equation (ii) from equation (i), we get

$$\tan\alpha \;=\; \sqrt{\dfrac{359.4 - 249.5}{50}}$$

$$= \sqrt{2.198} \;=\; 1.482565$$

$$\therefore \qquad \alpha \;=\; 56^\circ$$

$$= \dfrac{\pi}{4} + \dfrac{\phi}{2}$$

$$\therefore \qquad \phi \;=\; (56 - 45)\times 2 = \mathbf{22^\circ}$$

Substituting for $\tan\alpha$ in equation (ii), we get

$$2\,C\tan\alpha \;=\; 249.5 - 219.8 = 29.7$$

$$\therefore \qquad C \;=\; \mathbf{10\ kN/m^2}$$

Example 7.30 : A specimen of a stiff saturated clay 37.5 mm in diameter and 75 mm high failed in an unconfined compression, under a load of 120 N, showing a shortening of 15 mm. Determine the law of shearing strength if the rupture plane was found to be 55° inclined to the horizontal.

Solution :   Stress of failure $= \sigma_1 = \dfrac{\dfrac{120N}{A_0}}{1-\epsilon}$

where, A_0 = Initial cross-sectional area of sample.

$$= \dfrac{\pi}{4}\times d^2 \qquad\qquad (d = 37.5\ \text{mm})$$

$$\epsilon \;=\; \dfrac{\Delta L}{L}$$

$$= \dfrac{15\ \text{mm}}{75\ \text{mm}} = 0.2$$

$$\therefore \qquad \sigma_1 \;=\; \dfrac{120\ N}{\dfrac{\dfrac{\pi}{4}(37.5)^2}{1-0.2}} \;=\; \dfrac{120\times 0.8}{\dfrac{\pi}{4}(37.5)^2} \;=\; \dfrac{96}{1104.466}$$

$$= 0.08692\ N/mm^2$$

$$= 2\,C\tan\alpha + \sigma_3\tan^2\alpha$$

where, $\qquad \alpha \;=\; \dfrac{\pi}{4} + \dfrac{\phi}{2}$

$$= 55^\circ \qquad\qquad [\therefore\ \phi = (55 - 45)\times 2 = 20^\circ]$$

$$\sigma_3 = 0$$

$\therefore \qquad C = \dfrac{0.08692}{2 \times \tan 55}$

$\qquad\qquad = 0.030431 \text{ N/mm}^2$

$\tan \phi = \tan 20° = 0.364 = 30.431 \text{ kN/m}^2$

Law of shearing resistance, $\qquad S = C + N \tan \phi,$

where, $\qquad\qquad S = $ Shearing resistance in kN/m^2

$\qquad\qquad C = $ Unit cohesion $= 30.43 \text{ kN/m}^2$

and $\qquad\qquad \tan \phi = 0.364$

Example 7.31 : In an unconfined compression test on a saturated clay, the unconfined compressive strength was found to be 175 kPa. In a CU test, the soil showed an angle of shearing resistance of 10. State whether it is safe to use $C_u = q_u/2$ and calculate the % error.

Solution : $\qquad \sigma_1 = 2C \tan \alpha + \sigma_3 \tan^2 \alpha$

where, $\qquad\qquad \alpha = \dfrac{\pi}{4} + \dfrac{\phi}{2}$

$\qquad\qquad \phi = $ Angle of shearing resistance $= 10°$

$\therefore \qquad\qquad \alpha = 45° + \dfrac{10}{2} = 50°$

This being unconfirmed compression test,

$$\sigma_3 = 0,$$

$$\sigma_1 = 175 \text{ kPa} = 2C \tan \alpha$$

$\therefore \qquad$ Actual value of $2C = \dfrac{175}{\tan \alpha} = \dfrac{175}{\tan 50°}$

$\qquad\qquad = 146.84 \text{ kPa}$

$\qquad$ Apparent value of $q_u = 175 \text{ kPa}$

$\qquad$ Apparent value of $C = \dfrac{q_u}{2} = \dfrac{175}{2} = 87.5 \text{ kPa}$

$\qquad$ Actual value of $C = \dfrac{146.84}{2} = 73.42 \text{ kPa}$

Actual value of cohesion is less by

$\qquad 87.5 - 73.42 = 13.08 \text{ kPA}$

$\therefore \quad$ % error when compared to actual value

$\qquad\qquad = \dfrac{13.08}{73.42}$

$\qquad\qquad = \mathbf{17.81\%}$

Example 7.32 : In an unconfined compression test on soft clay , the following data were obtained :

Length of specimen = 10 cm, initial area = 10 cm^2, compression of sample at failure = 2.5 cm.

Determine the unconfined compressive strength parameters with corrected area if the failure load was 0.32 kN.

Solution : A_C = Corrected area $= \dfrac{A_0}{1 - \dfrac{\Delta L}{L}} = \dfrac{A_0}{1 - \dfrac{2.5}{10}}$

$$= \dfrac{A_0}{0.75}$$

$$C = \dfrac{q_u}{2} = \dfrac{1}{2} \times \dfrac{0.32 \text{ kN}}{A_c}$$

$$= \dfrac{0.16 \times 0.75}{A_0}$$

$$= \dfrac{0.12}{\dfrac{\pi}{4}(0.1)^2}$$

$$= \dfrac{12}{100\pi} \times 4 \times 100$$

$$= \mathbf{15.28 \ kN/m^2}$$

Example 7.33 : A sample of 38 mm diameter and 76 mm height was tested using unconfined compression test apparatus. The stress and strain at failure was found to be 0.15 N/mm^2 and 2% respectively. Assuming the sample to be purely cohesive, determine unconfined compressive strength and cohesion.

Solution : A_C = Corrected area $= \dfrac{A_0}{1 - \epsilon} = \dfrac{A_0}{1 - 0.02} = \dfrac{A_0}{0.98}$

$$q_u = \dfrac{(0.15 \text{ N/mm}^2)}{\dfrac{A_0}{0.98}} \times A_0 = 0.98 \times 0.15$$

$$= 0.147 \text{ N/mm}^2$$

$$= \dfrac{0.147}{1000} \times 1000 \times 1000 = 147 \text{ kN/m}^2$$

$$C = \dfrac{q_u}{2} = \dfrac{147}{2} = \mathbf{73.5 \ kN/m^2}$$

Example 7.34 : A triaxial test (CU) was performed and the following data was obtained at failure :

Test	σ_3 kPa	σ_1 kPa
(1)	60	309
(2)	120	640
(3)	180	900

Plot Mohr's circles and find C and ϕ. What type of soil do you think it is ?

Solution : It is similar to Problem No. 29

$$309 = 2\,C\tan\alpha + 60\tan^2\alpha \qquad\qquad \text{...(i)}$$

$$900 = 2\,C\tan\alpha + 180\tan^2\alpha \qquad\qquad \text{...(ii)}$$

$$\therefore \qquad \tan\alpha = \sqrt{\frac{900-309}{120}}$$

$$= 2.219234 = \angle\tan 65.74° = \angle\tan\left(\frac{\pi}{4}+\frac{\phi}{2}\right)$$

$$\therefore \qquad \phi/2 = 64.74 - 45 = 19.74°$$

$$\therefore \qquad \phi = 2\,(19.74) = 39.48°$$

$$C = \frac{900 - 180\cdot\tan^2\alpha}{2\tan\alpha} = \frac{13.5}{2\times 2.21929}$$

$$= \textbf{3.04 kPa}$$

Example 7.35 : In a triaxial test on a saturated sandy specimen, the deviator stress at failure was measured to be 250 kN/m². The angle of friction, $\phi = 35°$. What would be the major principal stress at failure.

Solution :

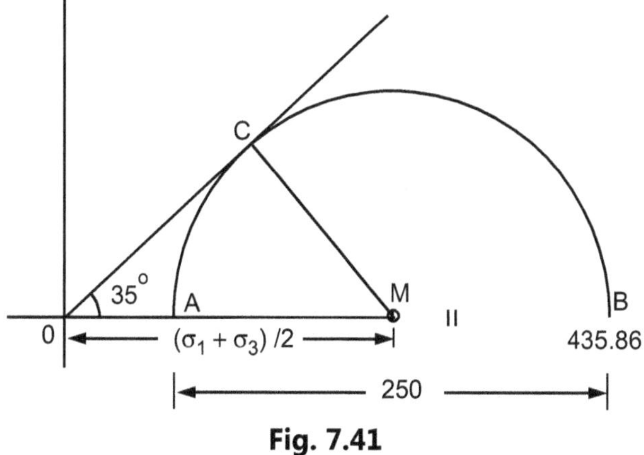

Fig. 7.41

$$\sin \phi \;=\; \sin 35° \;=\; \frac{CM}{OM}$$

$$=\; \frac{\sigma_1 - \sigma_3}{2} \times \frac{2}{\sigma_1 + \sigma_3}$$

$\therefore \qquad 0.5736 \;=\; \dfrac{250}{\sigma_1 + \sigma_3}$

$\therefore \qquad \sigma_1 + \sigma_3 \;=\; 435.86 \qquad\qquad \ldots (i)$

$\qquad\qquad \sigma_1 - \sigma_3 \;=\; 250 \qquad\qquad \ldots (ii)$

Adding equations (i) and (ii), we get

$\therefore \qquad \sigma_1 \;=\; \dfrac{435.86 + 250}{2}$

$$=\; 342.93 \text{ kN/m}^2$$

Substituting in equation (ii), $\quad \sigma_3 \;=\; 342.93 - 250 \;=\; \mathbf{92.93 \text{ kN/m}^2}$

Example 7.36 : A triaxial test gave the following observations. Determine the strength envelope, in terms of effective stresses and in terms of total stresses :

	Sample 1	Sample 2
Cell pressure	100 kN/m^2	200 kN/m^2
Added axial stress	120 kN/m^2	160 kN/m^2
Pore water pressure at failure	40 kN/m^2	70 kN/m^2

Solution : The major and minor principal stresses, considering total stress analysis and effective stress analysis are tabulated below :

Sample	Cell pressure σ_3 in kN/m^2	Deviator stress = σ_d	σ_1 (total) = $\sigma_3 + \sigma_d$	u = pore water pressure	$\sigma_3' = (\sigma_3 - u)$	$\sigma_1' = (\sigma_1 - u)$
1.	100	120	220	40	100 − 40 = 60	220 − 40 = 180
2.	200	160	360	70	200 − 70 = 130	360 − 70 = 290

$$\sigma_1 \;=\; 2\,C \tan \alpha + \sigma_3 \tan^2 \alpha$$

(A) Total Stress Analysis : $\quad 360 \;=\; 2\,C \tan \alpha + 200 \tan^2 \alpha \qquad\qquad \ldots(i)$

$\qquad\qquad\qquad\qquad\quad 220 \;=\; 2\,C \tan \alpha + 100 \tan^2 \alpha \qquad\qquad \ldots(ii)$

$$\therefore \quad \tan \alpha = \sqrt{\frac{360 - 220}{100}} = 1.1832 = 49.797°$$

$$= \frac{\pi}{4} + \frac{\phi}{2}$$

$$\therefore \quad \phi = 2\,(49.797 - 45)$$

$$= 9.5941° = 9°\,35'\,39''$$

Multiplying equation (ii) by 2 and deducting from it equation (i),

$$440 - 360 = 2\,C\,\tan \alpha$$

$$= 2C \times 1.1832 = 80$$

$$\therefore \quad C = \mathbf{33.806\ kN/m^2}$$

(B) Effective Stress Analysis :

$$\sigma_1' = 2C'\,\tan \alpha' + \sigma_3'\,\tan^2 \alpha'$$

$$\therefore \quad 180 = 2\,C'\,\tan \alpha + 60\,\tan^2 \alpha' \qquad \qquad \text{...(iii)}$$

$$290 = 2\,C'\,\tan \alpha + 130\,\tan^2 \alpha' \qquad \qquad \text{...(iv)}$$

Deducting equation (3) from (4), we get

$$\tan^2 \alpha' = \frac{290 - 180}{130 - 60} = \frac{110}{70}$$

$$= 1.9714$$

$$\therefore \quad \tan \alpha' = 1.25366 = \tan 51.4198°$$

$$= \tan\left(\frac{\pi}{4} + \frac{\phi}{2}\right)$$

$$\therefore \quad \phi = 2\,[51.4198° - 45°] = 12.8396°$$

$$= 12°\,50'22.5''$$

Substituting values of $\tan^2 \alpha'$ and $\tan \alpha'$ in equation (iii), we get

$$C' = \frac{1}{2}\left[\frac{180 - 60 \times 1.9714}{1.253566}\right] = \mathbf{34.19\ kN/m^2}$$

It will be noticed that, in effective stress analysis, value of ϕ increases whereas that of cohesion decreases.

Example 7.37 :

(a)   Explain how shear parameters can be determined from the graph of

$$\frac{\sigma_1 - \sigma_3}{2} \quad \text{Vs} \quad \frac{\sigma_1 + \sigma_3}{2}$$

(b)   Explain the advantages of this method.

Solution : **(a)** We know that,

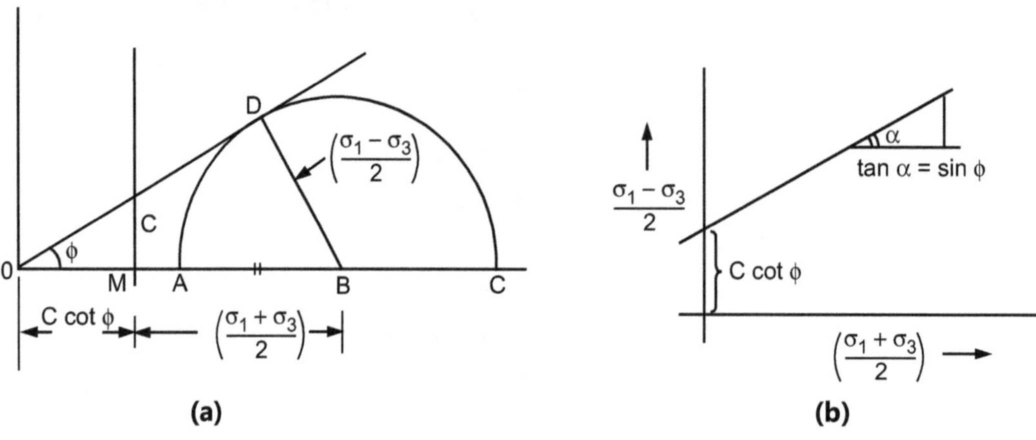

(a)   (b)

Fig. 7.42

$$\sin \phi = \frac{BD}{OB}$$

$$= \frac{BD}{OM + MB}$$

$$= \frac{\dfrac{\sigma_1 - \sigma_3}{2}}{C \cot \phi + \left(\dfrac{\sigma_1 + \sigma_3}{2}\right)}$$

$$\therefore \qquad \frac{\sigma_1 - \sigma_3}{2} = C \cdot \cos \phi + \left(\frac{\sigma_1 + \sigma_3}{2}\right) \cdot \sin \phi \qquad \qquad …(i)$$

from this equation (i), it will be noticed that, if we plot graph of $\left(\dfrac{\sigma_1 - \sigma_3}{2}\right)$ Vs $\left(\dfrac{\sigma_1 + \sigma_3}{2}\right)$

then, intercept on y-axis $= C \cos \phi$

m = Slope of straight line $= \sin \phi$.

knowing value of $\sin \phi$, value of ϕ can be determined, hence value of $\cos \phi$ can be found out.

Intercept on Y axis will give value of $C. \cos \phi$.

Dividing this, by value of $\cos \phi$, value of "C" can be found out.

(b) In this method, we do have not to plot Mohr's circles and plotting of tangent line to

Mohr's circles can also be eliminated. Plotting a straight line from the value of $\left(\dfrac{\sigma_1 - \sigma_3}{2}\right)$ and

$\left(\dfrac{\sigma_1 + \sigma}{2}\right)$ is easier.

Example 7.38 : The following table gives the results of a series of unconsolidated undrained test on a over-consolidated clay, with pore pressure measurements. Plot the graphs of

(a) $\dfrac{\sigma_1 - \sigma_3}{2}$ and $\dfrac{\sigma_1 + \sigma_3}{2}$ (b) $\dfrac{\bar{\sigma}_1 - \bar{\sigma}_3}{2}$ and $\dfrac{\bar{\sigma}_1 + \bar{\sigma}_3}{2}$.

σ_3 kPa	σ_1 kPa	u kp
100	510	– 65
200	720	– 10
400	1120	80
520	1580	100

From this evaluate values of (i) C, ϕ, (ii) $\bar{C}$, $\bar{\phi}$

(iii) Determine maximum and minimum value of Pore Pressure parameters A_f.

Solution : The following table gives the values of σ_1, σ_3, u, $\bar{\sigma}_1$, $\bar{\sigma}_3$, $\dfrac{\sigma_1 + \sigma_3}{2}$, $\dfrac{\sigma_1 - \sigma_3}{2}$, $\dfrac{\bar{\sigma}_1 + \bar{\sigma}_3}{2}$.

σ_3	σ_1	$\dfrac{\sigma_1 - \sigma_3}{2}$	$\dfrac{\sigma_1 + \sigma_3}{2}$	u	$\bar{\sigma}_3 = \sigma_3 - u$	$\bar{\sigma}_1 = (\sigma_1 - u)$	$\dfrac{\bar{\sigma}_1 - \bar{\sigma}_3}{2}$	$\dfrac{\bar{\sigma}_1 + \bar{\sigma}_3}{2}$
(1)	(2)	(3)	(4)	(5)	(6)	(7)	(8)	(9)
100	510	205	305	−65	165	575	205	370
200	720	260	460	−10	210	730	260	470
400	1120	360	760	80	320	1040	360	680
520	1580	530	1050	100	420	1480	530	950

Graphs for total stress and effective stress analysis, are shown in Fig. 7.38.

(i) **From Graph 1** (Fig. 7.43) : $\tan \theta = \dfrac{530 - 205}{1050 - 305} = 0.43624 = \sin \phi$

$\therefore$ $\phi = \mathbf{25.8643°}$

y = intercept on Y-axis = 70 = C · cos ϕ.

$\therefore$ $C = \dfrac{70}{\cos \phi}$

$$= \dfrac{70}{\cos 25.5643°} = \mathbf{77.79 \ kPa}$$

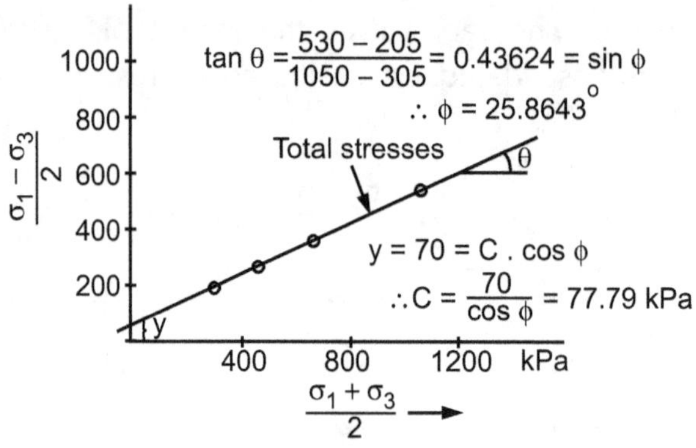

Fig. 7.43

(ii)   **From Graph 2** (Fig. 7.44) **:** (For effective stresses) :

$$\tan \theta = \frac{530 - 205}{950 - 370} = 0.5603 = \sin \phi$$

$\therefore$
$$\bar{\phi} = \sin^{-1} 0.5603 = \textbf{34.08°}$$

$$y' = \text{Intercept on Y-axis} = 20 = \bar{C} \cos \bar{\phi}$$

$\therefore$
$$\bar{C} = \frac{20}{\cos \phi} = \frac{20}{\cos 34.00} = \textbf{24.14 kPa}$$

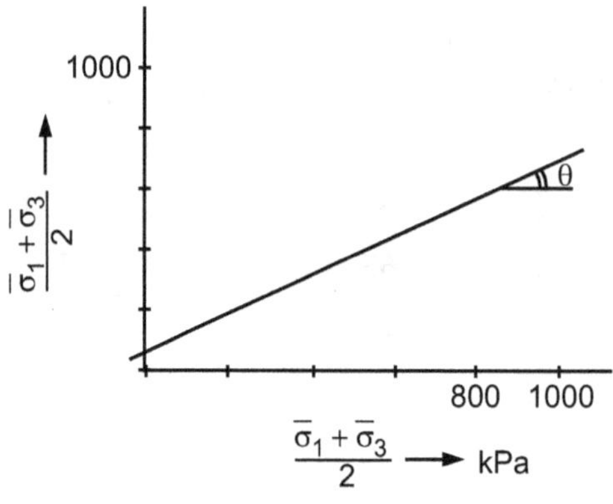

Fig. 7.44

(iii)   Skempton's Pore Pressure equation is

$$\Delta u = B\left[(\Delta\sigma_3 + A(\Delta\sigma_1 - \Delta\sigma_3))\right]$$

But, B = 0

$\therefore$
$$A = \frac{\Delta U}{\Delta\sigma_1 - \Delta\sigma_3} = \frac{\Delta u}{\sigma_1 - \sigma_3}$$

$\therefore$
$$A = \frac{\text{column 5}}{2\,(\text{column 3 or column 8})}$$

Test	Δu	$\Delta \sigma = \left[\dfrac{(\sigma_1 - \sigma_3)}{2}\right] \times 2$	$A = \dfrac{\Delta u}{\Delta \sigma}$	Remarks
1.	-65	$205 \times 2 = 410$	-0.16	Minimum value of A
2.	-10	$260 \times 2 = 520$	-0.02	
3.	80	$360 \times 2 = 720$	$+0.11$	Maximum value of A
4.	100	$530 \times 2 = 1060$	$+0.094$	

Example 7.39 : The following are the results of triaxial test carried on consolidated undermined test with pore pressure measurements. Determine shear parameters and Skempton's Pore Pressure parameters considering (i) total stress, (ii) effective stress.

Sample No.	Cell Pressure (σ_3) (all pressures in kPa)	Deviator stress in kPa ($\sigma_1 - \sigma_3$)	Pore pressure (u)
1.	100	131	18
2.	200	162	42
3.	300	189	86

Solution : The given test results are tabulated as under :

Sr. No.	Cell Pressure σ_3	$(\sigma_1 - \sigma_3)$	σ_1	$\dfrac{s_1 - s_3}{2}$	$\dfrac{s_1 + s_3}{2}$	u	$\bar{s}_1 = (\because -u)$	$\bar{s}_3 = (\sigma_3 - u)$	$\dfrac{\bar{s}_1 + \bar{s}_3}{2}$	$\dfrac{\bar{s}_1 - \bar{s}_3}{2}$
1.	100	131	231	65.5	115.5	18	213	82	147.5	65.5
2.	200	162	362	81	181	42	320	158	239	81
3.	300	189	489	94.5	244.5	86	403	214	308.5	94.5

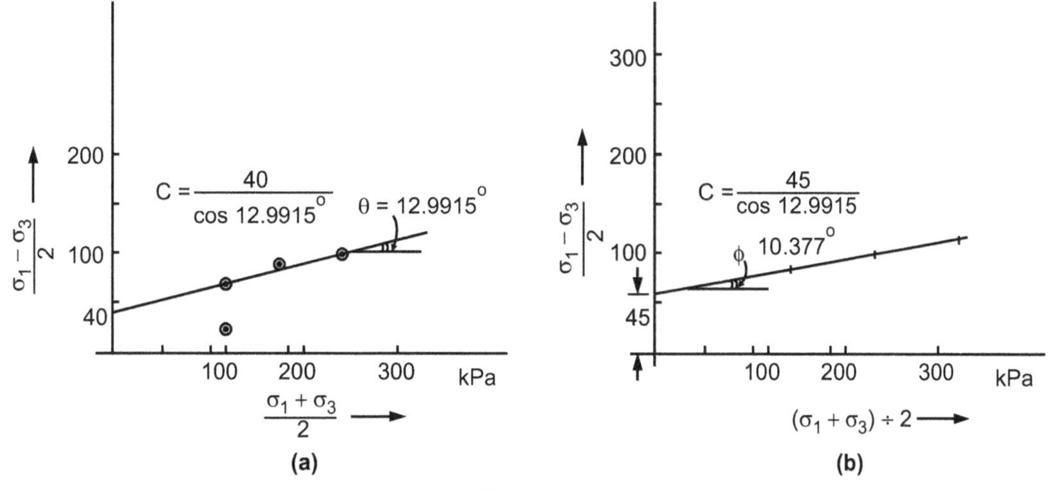

Fig. 7.45

(i) Effective Stress Analysis :

Graph of $\dfrac{\sigma_1 - \sigma_3}{2}$ Vs $\dfrac{\sigma_1 + \sigma_3}{2}$ is as shown in Fig. 7.40 (b).

From graph, $\tan \bar{\theta} = \dfrac{94.5 - 65.5}{308.5 - 147.5} = \sin \phi$

$\therefore \quad \sin \bar{\phi} = 0.180124$

$\therefore \quad \phi = \mathbf{10.377°}$

$y = $ intercept on Y-axis $= 45 = C \cos \bar{\phi}$

$= C \cos 10.377 = 45$

$\therefore \quad \bar{C} = \dfrac{45}{\cos \phi}$

$= \dfrac{45}{\cos (10.377°)} = 45.748 \text{ kPa}$

(ii) Total Stress Analysis : (Refer graph 7.40 (a)).

from graph, $\tan \phi = \dfrac{94.5 - 65.5}{244.5 - 115.5}$

$= 0.2248 = \sin \phi$

$\therefore \quad \phi = 12.9915°$

Intercept on Y-axis $= C \cos \phi$

$= C \cos 12.9915 = 40$

$\therefore \quad C = \dfrac{40}{\cos 12.9915°} = 41.05 \text{ kPa}$

(The example can as well be solved graphically)

Skempton's pore pressure **parameter 'A'**

Parameter B $= 0$

$\therefore \quad A = \dfrac{\Delta u}{\Delta \sigma} = \dfrac{\Delta u}{(\sigma_1 - \sigma_3)}$

Sample	$\Delta \mu$	$\sigma_1 - \sigma_3$	$A = \dfrac{\Delta \mu}{(\sigma_1 - \sigma_3)}$
1.	18	131	0.1374
2.	42	162	0.25925
3.	86	189	0.455

Example 7.40 : The following are the results of drained triaxial tests carried on three identical samples having initial 37.5 mm diameter and 75 mm height. Determine shear parameters.

Sample No.	Cell Pressure kN/m^2 σ_3	Deviator local (kN)	Change in volume (cc) = ΔV	Axial deformation (mm) = ΔL
1.	50	0.045	(–) 1.1	9
2.	100	0.05	(–) 1.5	11.5
3.	200	0.08	(–) 1.7	12.5

$$\text{Corrected Area of C/s} = A_C = \frac{V_o \pm \Delta V}{L_o - \Delta L} \qquad \text{...(i)}$$

$$V_o = \left[\frac{\pi}{4}(3.75)^2\right] \times 7.5 = 82.835 \text{ CC}$$

$$L_o = 7.5 \text{ cm}$$

Using equation (i), corrected area of cross-section is calculated and tabulated below.

$$\text{knowing } A_C, \quad \text{deviator stress} = \frac{\text{Deviator load}}{A_C}$$

$$= \sigma_1 - \sigma_3$$

$$\sigma_1 = \sigma_3 + \text{deviator stress.}$$

Sample	σ_3 kN/m^2	Corrected Area $A_C = \dfrac{V_o - \Delta V}{L - L_o}$	Deviator Load (kN)	Deviator Stress = $(\sigma_1 - \sigma_3)$ = $\dfrac{\text{Deviator Load}}{A_c}$	$\sigma_1 =$ Deviator stress + σ_3	$\dfrac{\sigma_1 - \sigma_3}{2}$	$\dfrac{\sigma_1 + \sigma_3}{2}$
(1)	(2)	(3)	(4)	(5)	(6)	(7)	(8)
1.	50	$\dfrac{82.835 - 1.1}{7.5 - 0.9}$ $= 12.384 \text{ m}^2$	0.045	36.337 kN/m^2	86.337	18.1685	68.1685
2.	100	$\dfrac{82.835 - 1.5}{7.5 - 1.15}$ $= 12.80866$	0.05	39.036 kN/m^3	139.036	19.518	119.58
3.	200	12.9816	0.08	61.625 kN/m^2	261.625	30.8125	230.8125

Plotting graph of $\dfrac{\sigma_1 - \sigma_3}{2}$ Vs $\dfrac{\sigma_1 - \sigma_3}{2}$,

$$\tan \theta = \text{slope of graph} = \frac{30.8125 - 18.1685}{230.8125 - 68.1685}$$

$$= 0.077740$$

$$= \sin \phi$$

$$\therefore \quad \phi = \sin^{-1} 0.077740$$

$$\therefore \quad \phi = 4.4586°$$

$$\text{Intercept on Y-axis} = 16.7 = C \cos \phi$$

$$\therefore \quad C = \frac{16.7}{\cos 4.4586} = \mathbf{16.75 \ kN/m^2}$$

Alternatively knowing, σ_1, σ_3, for each sample, Mohr's circles and hence the envelope can be drawn from which value of C and ϕ can be determined.

However, above method eliminates drawing of Mohr's circles and its envelope.

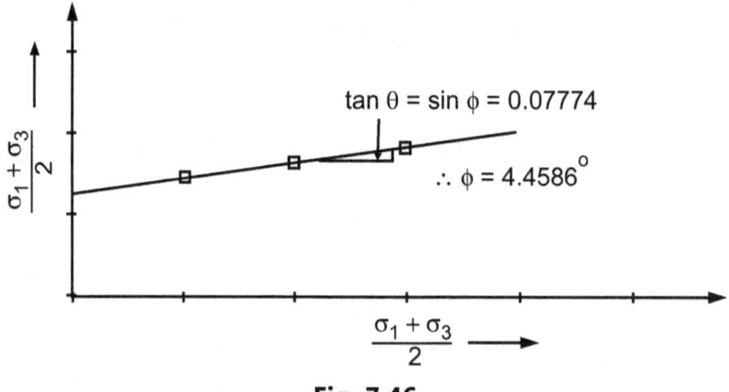

Fig. 7.46

Example 7.41 : In a triaxial test on a saturated sample the pore water pressure at failure was measured as 30 kN/m². Establish the Skepton's Pore water pressure equation, if deviator stress at failure was 110 kN/m², at a constant cell pressure of 100 kN/m².

Solution :

$$\Delta U = \Delta U_1 + \Delta U_2$$

$$= B \left[\Delta \sigma_3 + A (\Delta \sigma_1 - \Delta \sigma_3) \right] \qquad \text{...(i)}$$

$$\Delta U_1 = B \Delta \sigma_3$$

$$\therefore \quad B = \frac{\Delta U_1}{\Delta \sigma_3} = \frac{70}{100}$$

$$= 0.7$$

$$\Delta U_2 = AB (\Delta \sigma_1 - \Delta \sigma_3)$$

$$= \bar{A} \cdot (\Delta \sigma_1 - \Delta \sigma_3)$$

$$\therefore \quad \bar{A} = \frac{\Delta U_2}{(\Delta \sigma_1 - \Delta \sigma_3)} = \frac{100}{110} = \mathbf{0.909}$$

Example 7.42 : A direct shear test was performed on dry sand. Under normal stress of 150 kPa, failure occurred when the shear stress was 65 kPa. Draw the Mohr's envelope and hence determine the magnitude and orientation of maximum and minimum principal stresses.

Solution : Draw OR = 150 kPa, RQ = 65 kPa. Draw OQ.

Draw QC $\perp$ to OQ

With C as centre, draw semicircle AQPB.

OA = 108 kPa = σ_3, OB = σ_1 = 247 kPa,

$\angle$ QOA = 25

Draw line QP parallel to X-axis, meeting the semicircle, on P. P is considered as the pole of the Mohr's circle.

Join PA and PB

$$\angle PAB = 32.5° = \alpha' \qquad (\pi/4 - \phi/2 = 45° - 25°/2)$$
$$\angle PBA = 57.5° = \alpha \qquad (\pi/4 + \phi/2 = 45° + 25°/2)$$

The minor and major principal planes are inclined to horizontal at 32.5° and 52.5° respectively. The orientation of the planes are shown in Fig. 7.47.

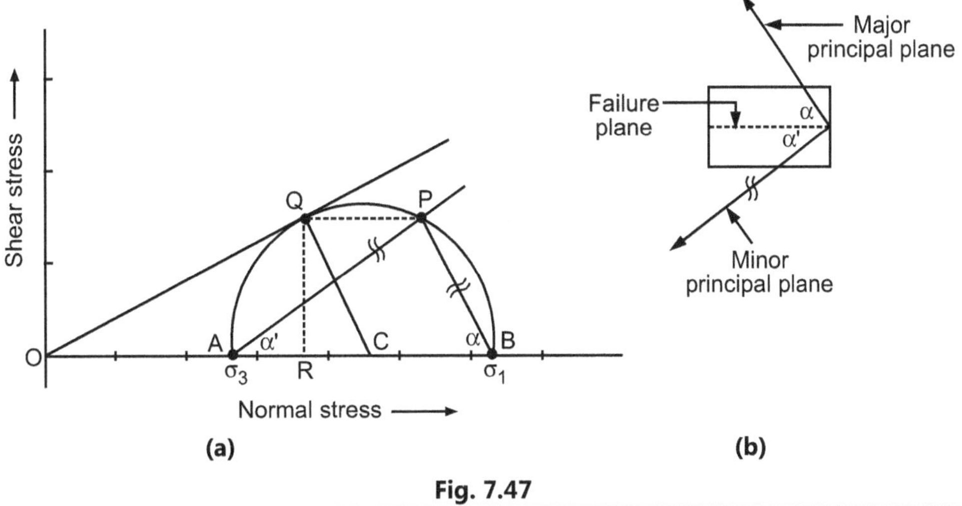

Fig. 7.47

Example 7.43 : A saturated clay is known to have effective strength parameters of C' = 10 kPa and ϕ = 28°. A sample of this clay was brought to failure quickly, so that, no dissipation of pore water could occur. At failure, it was known that $\bar{\sigma}_1$ = 60 kPa and $\bar{\sigma}_3$ = 10 kPa, U_f = 20 kPa.

(a) Estimate values of σ_1 and σ_3 at failure.

(b) What was the effective normal stress on failure plane ?

(c) What was the value of undrained Shear Strength C_u ?

Solution : Given : Effective shear stress parameter C' = 10 kPa

ϕ' = 28 , σ_1' = 60 kPa, σ_3' = 10kPa, U_f = 20 kPa

(a) Values of σ_1 and σ_3 at failure :

Since, Total Stress = Effective stress + Pore water pressure

$\therefore$

$$\sigma_1 = \sigma_1' + U_f$$
$$= 60 + 20 = 80 \text{ kPa}$$

and

$$\sigma_3 = \sigma_3' + U_f$$
$$= 10 + 20 = \mathbf{30 \text{ kPa}}$$

(b) Mohr circles to illustrate the effective stress and total stress :

The effective normal stress on the failure plane will be 30 kPa i.e. σ_n = **30 kPa.**

(c) Value of undrained shear strength (C_u) :

Angle which the failure plane makes with principle plane,

$$\theta = 45° + \frac{\phi'}{2} = 45° + \frac{28}{2} = 59°$$

Effective normal stress, $$\sigma' = \frac{\sigma_1' + \sigma_3'}{2} + \frac{\sigma_1' - \sigma_3'}{2} \cos 2\theta$$

$$= \frac{60 + 10}{2} + \frac{60 - 10}{2} \times \cos 118°$$

$$= \mathbf{23.26 \text{ kPa}}$$

Hence, undrained shear strength,

$$C_u = C' + \sigma' \tan \phi'$$
$$= 10 + 23.26 \tan 28 = \mathbf{22.37 \text{ kPa}}$$

Example 7.44 : The stresses acting on the plane of maximum shearing stress through a given point in sand are as follows : total normal stress = 250 kN/m², pore water pressure = 88.5 kN/m², shearing stress = 85 kN/m². Failure occurs in the region surrounding the point. Determine the major and minor principal effective stresses, the normal effective stress and the shearing stress on the plane of failure and the friction angle of the sand. Define clearly the terms 'plane of maximum shearing stress' and 'plane of failure' in relation to the Mohr's rupture diagram.

Solution :

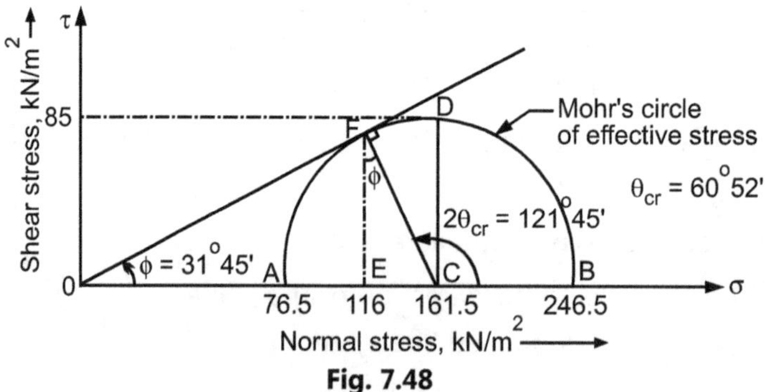

Fig. 7.48

$$\text{Total normal stress} = 250 \text{ kN/m}^2$$
$$\text{Pore water pressure} = 88.5 \text{ kN/m}^2$$
$$\text{Effective normal stress on the plane of maximum shear} = (250 - 88.5) = \mathbf{161.5 \text{ kN/m}^2}$$
$$\text{Maximum shear stress} = \mathbf{85 \text{ kN/m}^2}$$

Analytical Solution :

$$\left(\frac{\bar{\sigma}_1 + \bar{\sigma}_3}{2}\right) = \text{Normal stress on the plane of max. shear}$$

$$= 161.5 \qquad \qquad \text{...(i)}$$

$$\left(\frac{\bar{\sigma}_1 - \bar{\sigma}_3}{2}\right) = \text{Maximum shear stress} = 85 \qquad \qquad \text{...(ii)}$$

$$\text{Solving equations (i) and (ii), } \bar{\sigma}_1 = 246.5 \text{ kN/m}^2 \quad \text{(Major principal effective stress)}$$

$$\bar{\sigma}_3 = 76.5 \text{ kN/m}^2 \quad \text{(Minor principal effective stress)}$$

$$\sin \phi = \frac{(\bar{\sigma}_1 - \bar{\sigma}_3)/2}{(\bar{\sigma}_1 + \bar{\sigma}_3)/2} = \frac{85}{161.5} = \mathbf{0.526}$$

$\therefore$ Angle of internal friction, $\phi = 31° \, 45'$ nearly.

$$\text{Normal stress on the failure plane} = \left(\frac{\bar{\sigma}_1 + \bar{\sigma}_3}{2}\right) - \left(\frac{\bar{\sigma}_1 - \bar{\sigma}_3}{2}\right) \sin \phi$$

$$= 161.5 - 85 \, [\sin 31° \, 45'] = \mathbf{116.76 \text{ kN/m}^2}$$

$$\text{Shear stress on the failure plane} = \left(\frac{\bar{\sigma}_1 - \bar{\sigma}_3}{2}\right) \cdot \cos \phi$$

$$= 85 \times \cos 31° \, 45' = \mathbf{72.27 \text{ kN/m}^2}$$

The answers from a graphical approach compare very well with those from the analytical approach. The planes of maximum shear, i.e. the planes on which the shearing stress is maximum, are inclined at 45° with the principal planes. The failure plane i.e., the plane on which the resultant has maximum obliquity, is inclined at (45° + ϕ/2) or 61° 52' (Counterclockwise) with the major principal plane. These observations are confirmed from the Mohr's circle of stress.

Graphical Solution : The normal stress on the plane of maximum shear stress is plotted as

OC to a suitable scale, CD is plotted perpendicular to $\bar{\sigma}$ axis as the maximum shear stress. With C as centre and CD as radius, the Mohr's circle is established. A tangent drawn to the circle from the origin O establishes the strength envelope. The foot of the perpendicular E from the point of tangency F is located. The principal effective stresses and the stresses on the plane of failure are scaled off. The angle of internal friction is measured with a protractor.

The results are : Major effective principal stress = (OB) = 246.5 kN/m^2

Minor effective principal stress (OA) = 76.5 kN/m^2

Angle of internal friction, ϕ (angle FOB) = 31° 45'

Normal effective stress on plane of failure (OE) = 116 kN/m^2

Shearing stress on the plane of failure (EF) = 72 kN/m^2

Example 7.45 : Triaxial test was carried out on identical clayey samples, with pore pressure measurements. The results are as under :

Sample No.	Lateral Pressure (All in kPa)	Deviator stress of failure (kPa)	Pore water pressure
1.	100	120	40
2.	200	160	70

Determine analytically shear parameters using (i) total stress analysis, (ii) effective stress analysis.

Solution :
$$\sigma_1 = 2 C \tan \alpha + \sigma_3 \tan^2 \alpha$$

$\therefore$ $120 + 100 = 220 = 2 C \tan \alpha + 100 \tan^2 \alpha$ ...(i)

$\therefore$ $160 + 200 = 360 = 2 C \tan \alpha + 200 \tan^2 \alpha$ ...(ii)

Deducting equation (i) from (ii), we get

$$(200 - 100) \tan^2 \alpha = 360 - 220 = 140$$

$\therefore$ $100 \tan^2 \alpha = 140$ ...(iii)

$\therefore$ $\tan^2 \alpha =$

$\therefore$ $\alpha = \tan^{-1} \sqrt{\dfrac{140}{100}} = 49.797° = 49° 47' 49.32" = \dfrac{\pi}{4} + \dfrac{\phi}{2}$

$\therefore$ $\phi = 9° .35' \times 36.4"$

From equations (i) and (iii) $2C \tan \alpha = 220 - 100 \tan^2 \alpha$

$$= 220 - 140 = 80$$

$\therefore$ $C = \dfrac{80}{2 \tan \alpha} = 33.806$ kN/m^2 ...(iv)

$\therefore$ $S = C + N \tan \phi$ $(\phi = 9°.35' / 36.4")$

$$= 33.806 + N \tan \phi$$

$$= \mathbf{33.806 + 0.169\ N}$$ ...(v) Ans.

Considering Effective Stresses : $\sigma_1 = 2 C \tan \alpha' + \sigma_3 \tan^2 \alpha$

$\therefore$ $(120 + 100 - 40) = 2 C \tan \alpha + \sigma_3 \tan^2 \alpha$

$\therefore$ $180 = 2 C \tan \alpha + 100 \tan^2 \alpha$ ... (vi)

$\therefore$ $200 + 160 - 70 = 290 = 2 C \tan \alpha + 200 \tan^2 \alpha$ ...(vii)

From equations (vi) and (vii) ,

$$290 - 180 = 100 \times \tan^2 \alpha$$

$$\therefore \quad 110 = 100 \tan^2 \alpha \qquad \text{...(viii)}$$

$$\therefore \quad \tan \alpha = \sqrt{1.1} = 1.049$$

$$= \tan^{-1} 46.3647$$

$$\phi = 2 [46.3647 - 45] = 2.7294° = 2° 43'46''$$

From equations (vii) and (viii) $290 = 2\,C \tan \alpha + 200 \tan^2 \alpha$

$$\therefore \quad 290 = 2\,C \tan \alpha + 220$$

$$2C \tan \alpha = 70$$

$$\therefore \quad C = \frac{70}{2 \tan \alpha} = \frac{35}{\tan \alpha} = \frac{35}{1.049} = \mathbf{33.365 \ kN/m^2}$$

$$\therefore \quad S = C + N \tan \phi = 33.3651 + N \tan 2° 43' 46''$$

$$= \mathbf{33.3651 + 0.047673\ N} \qquad \text{...(ix)}$$

Example 7.46 : A vane of 75 mm diameter and 150 mm height has been pushed into an in-situ soft clay at the bottom of bore hole. The torque required to rotate the vane was 75 Nm. Determine the undrained shear strength of the clay. After the test, the vane was rotated several times and ultimate torque was found to be 50 m. Estimate sensitivity of clay.

(Dec. 13, 7M)

Solution: Undrained shear strength,

$$S_1 = \frac{T}{\pi D^2 \left(\dfrac{H}{2} + \dfrac{D}{6} \right)}$$

$$S = \frac{3T}{11D^3} \text{ As H = 2D}$$

$$\therefore \quad S = \frac{3 \times 75}{11 \times (0.075)^3} = 48.48 \times 10^3$$

$$\therefore \quad S = \frac{3T}{11D^3}$$

$$\text{Sensitivity } u_g = \frac{\text{Torque in undisturbed state}}{\text{Torque in disturbed state}} = \frac{75}{50} = 1.5$$

Example 7.47 : A Triaxial test was conducted on sand specimen and the sample failed at a deviator stress of 480 kN/m^2, when the cell pressure was 100 kN/m^2 under drained condition. Find the effective angle of shearing resistance of sand.   **(May 14, 4 M)**

Solution:

$$\sigma_d = 480 \text{ kN/m}^2$$

$$\sigma_3 = 100 \text{ kN/m}^2$$

$$c = 0$$

$$\sigma_1 = \sigma_3 \tan^2 \alpha + 2c \tan \alpha$$

$$\therefore \qquad \sigma_1 = \sigma_3 + \sigma_d$$

$$= 100 + 480$$

$$= 580$$

$$580 = 100 \tan^2 \alpha$$

$$\therefore \qquad an^2 \alpha = 5.8$$

$$\therefore \qquad \alpha = 67^\circ\ 22'$$

$$\alpha = 45 + \frac{\phi}{2}$$

$$67^\circ\ 22' = 45 + \frac{\phi}{2}$$

$$\theta = 44^\circ\ 44'$$

If, $$\sigma_3 = 100$$

$$\therefore \qquad \sigma_1 = \sigma_3 \tan^2 67^\circ\ 22'$$

$$\therefore \qquad \sigma_1 = 100 \tan^2 67^\circ\ 22'$$

$$\sigma = 567\ kN/m^2$$

Example 7.48 : Define sensitivity :

A clayey sample when tested in unconfined compression, gave compressive strength of $100\ kN/m^2$. Specimen of same clay, with same initial condition is subjected to undrained, unconsolidated triaxial test under a cell pressure of $100\ kN/m^2$. Determine the axial stress in kN/m^2 of failure. **(Dec. 14, 6 M)**

Solution: Sensitivity: It is defined as the ratio of shear strength of soil in undisturbed state to that in the fully remoulded state.

$$St = \frac{Su\ (undisturbed)}{Su\ (Remoulded)}$$

Sensitivity may very from 1 to 100

Given date :

For unconfined compressive strength test $q_u = 100\ kN/m^2$

For untrained unconsolidated triaxial test

$$\sigma_3 = 100\ kN/m^2$$

$$\sigma_1 = ?$$

For pure clay, $$\phi = 0$$

$$\sigma_1 = \sigma_3 \tan^2\left(45 + \frac{f}{2}\right) + 2c\tan\left(45 + \frac{f}{2}\right)$$

$$\sigma_1 = 100\tan^2(45) + 100$$

$$\boldsymbol{\sigma_1 = 200\ kN/m^2}$$

Example 7.49 : Define total and effective stress.

Determine the shear strength in terms of effective stress on a plane within a saturated soil mass at a point where the total normal stress is 200 kN/m^2 and the pore water pressure is 80 kN/m^2. The effective stress shear strength parameters for the soil are c′ = 16 kN/m^2 and Φ = 39°.   **(May 15, 6 M)**

Solution : Total stress Total : load per unit area.

Total Stress is due to (i) self weight of soil and (ii) over burden on the soil

    Effective stress $\Rightarrow$

It is equal to the total vertical reaction porce transmitted at the points of contact of soil grains divided by total area, including that occupied by water.

Effective stress (σ′) = Total stress (σ) − pore pressure (u)

For Example solution

Given data

$$\sigma_n = 200\ kN/m^2$$
$$u = 80\ kN/m^2$$
$$C' = 16\ kN/m^2$$
$$\phi' = 39°$$
$$\text{Shear strength} = C' + \delta n'\tan\phi'$$
$$= 16 + (200 - 80)\tan 39°$$
$$= 113.17\ kN/m^2$$

Example 7.50 : A dry sand specimen is put through a triaxial test. Cell pressure is 50 kPa and deviator stress is 100 kPa. Determine the angle of internal friction for the sand specimen.
                                          (May 16, 6 M)

Solution :   Given data :

$$\sigma_3 = 50\ kP_a$$
$$\sigma_d = 100\ kP_a$$
$$\sigma_1 = \sigma_3 + \sigma_d$$
$$= 50 + 100$$
$$= 150\ kPa$$
$$\sigma_1 = \sigma_3 \tan^2\alpha_f$$
$$150 = 50\tan^2\alpha_f$$
$$\tan\alpha_f = 1.73$$
$$\alpha_f = 60°$$

Now,
$$45 = \frac{\phi}{2} = \alpha_f$$

$$45 = \frac{\phi}{2} = 60°$$

$$\phi = 30°$$

Example 7.51 : Define total and effective stress. Determine the shear strength in terms of effective stress on a plane within a saturated soil mass at a point where the total normal stress is 200 kN/m^2 and the pore water pressure is 80 kN/m^2. The effective stress shear strength parameters for the soil c' = 16 kN/m^2 and phi = 39°.   **(May 17, 6 M)**

Solution :

$$\text{Total normal stress} = 200 \text{ kN/m}^2$$
$$\text{Pore water pressure} = 80 \text{ kN/m}^2$$

∴ Effective normal stress on the plane of max shear = (200 – 80) = 120 kN/m^2

$$c = 16, \phi = 39°$$

∴   Shear strength = $c + \sigma \tan \phi$

$$= 16 + 120 \times \tan 39° = 113.17 \text{ kpa}$$

SUMMARY

1. Interlocking, friction and cohesion between soil grains are the important phenomena from which a soil derives its shearing strength.

2. Direct shear, triaxial compression and the unconfined compression tests are the more important of laboratory shear strength tests; triaxial compression test is the most versatile test, capable of simulating many field situations. Unconfined compression test is a simple special case of the triaxial compression test. Field vane and penetration tests are commonly used for field tests.

Demerits of Direction Shear Tests :

- The orientation of the failure plane is fixed.

- Control on drainage condition is very difficult.

- The measurement of pore water pressure is not possible.

- The area under shear gradually decreases as the test progresses area cannot be determined and hence stresses are computed on basis of full cross-sectional area.

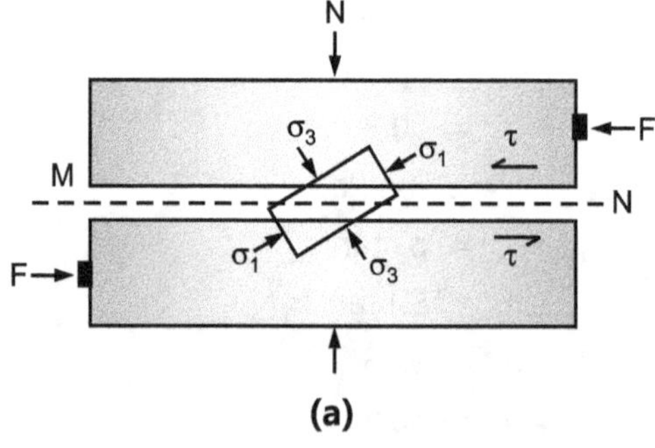

(a)

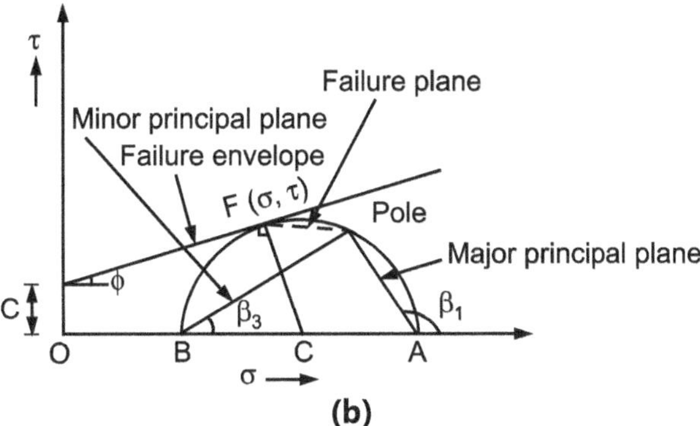

Fig. 7.23 : Mohr's envelope and principle stresses during direct shear test

3. According to the conditions of drainage, shearing strength tests may be classified as the unconsolidated undrained (quick), consolidated undrained (consolidated quick) and drained (slow) tests; these tend to simulate captioned conditions obtaining in field situations.

4. Some soils have ductile stress-strain curves, where failure is defined as 'the peak shear stress'. Other soils have brittle curves, which have two kinds of strength (i) peak strength and (ii) residual strength.

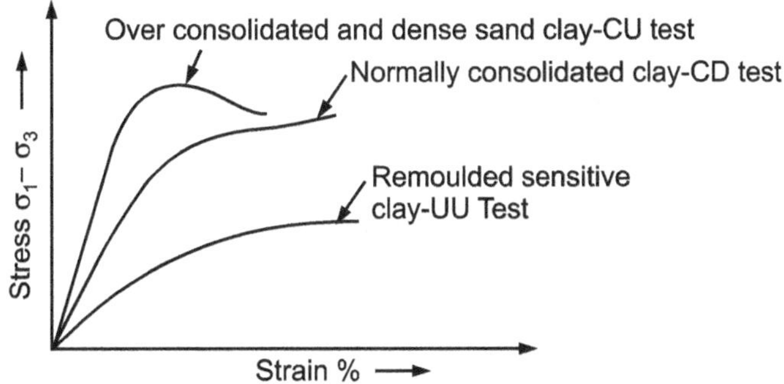

Fig. 7.24 : Typical stress-strain curves from triaxial shear

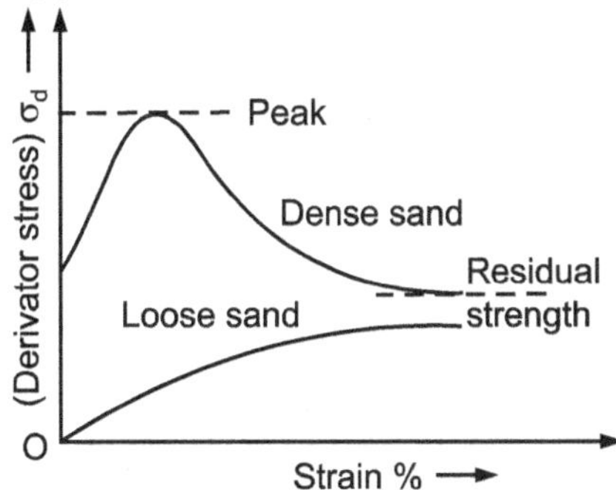

Fig. 7.25 : Residual strength

5. The strength at a large shear displacement is called the *residual strength*. It is useful when evaluating landslide.

6. Unsaturated soils have a higher shear strength due to the presence of apparent cohesion, but this additional strength may be lost if the soil becomes wet in the future.

7. The shear behaviour of over consolidated clay is different from that of normally consolidated clay, the strength envelope for the former will be much flatter than that for the latter.

8. (a) Triaxial shear test

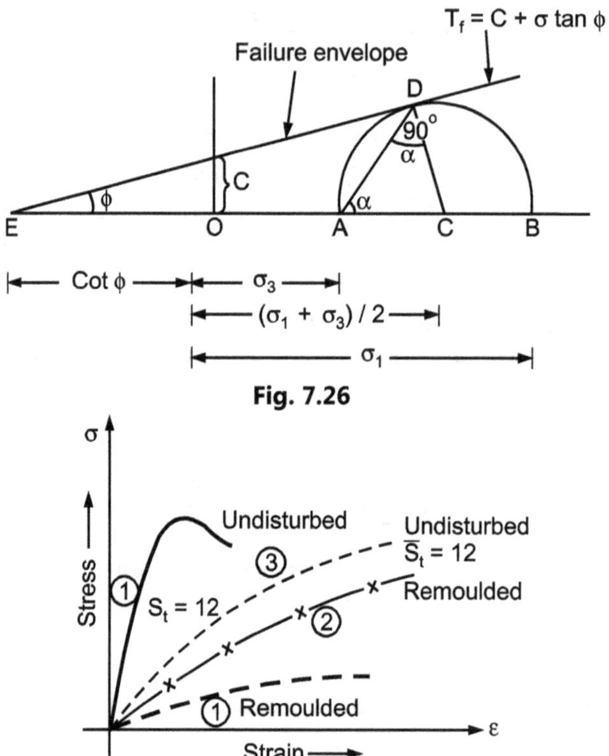

Fig. 7.26

Fig. 7.27 : Typical stress-strain curves for clayey soils

$$\sigma_1 = \sigma_3 \tan^2 \alpha + 2C \tan \alpha$$

$$\sigma_1 = \sigma_3 N\phi + 2C \sqrt{N\phi}$$

$$N\phi = \tan^2 \alpha = \tan^2\left(45 + \frac{\phi}{2}\right)$$

$$\sigma_1 = \sigma_3 \tan^2\left(45 + \frac{\phi}{2}\right) + 2C\left(\tan 45 + \frac{\phi}{2}\right)$$

(b) The change in pore pressure due to change in applied stress is characterised by dimensionless coefficients, called Skempton's pore pressure parameters A and B.

$$\Delta U = B\left(\Delta\sigma_3 + A\left(\Delta\sigma_1 - \Delta\sigma_3\right)\right)$$

where, B and A are known as Skempton's pore pressure parameters.

$$\Delta U_2 = AB\left(\Delta\sigma_1 - \Delta\sigma_3\right) = \overline{A}\left(\Delta\sigma_1 - \Delta\sigma_3\right)$$

$$\bar{A} = \frac{\Delta U_2}{\Delta \sigma_1 - \Delta \sigma_3}, \quad B = \frac{\Delta U_1}{\Delta \sigma_3}$$

9. Unconfined compression test :

$$A_o L_o = AL = A(L_o - \Delta L)$$

$$A = \frac{A_o L_o}{L_o - \Delta L} = \frac{A_1}{1 - \varepsilon}$$

A_o = Original cross-sectional area

L_o = Original length

A = Modified cross-sectional area at any strain

$$\varepsilon = \frac{\Delta L}{L_o} = \text{Strain} = \frac{\text{Change in the length}}{\text{Original length}}$$

10. **Vane shear test :** If the top of vane is below the soil surface and the depth inside the sample is (H_1) and if $H_1 = 2D$, then the shear strength (S) becomes,

$$S = \frac{T}{\pi D^2 \left[\dfrac{H_1}{2} + \dfrac{D}{6} \right]} = \left(\frac{T}{7} \right) \frac{1}{\left(\dfrac{\pi D^3}{6} \right)} = \frac{0.2727\,T}{D^3} = \frac{3}{11D^3}$$

11. **Saturated sands** and gravels are almost always evaluated using effective stress analysis because the excess pore water pressures are minimal.

12. **Saturated clay** and silts can exhibit either drained or undrained conditions, depending on the rate of loading. For normal rates, undrained conditions prevail immediately after the construction.

13. When the **construction increases** the normal stress in **saturated silt or clays**, strength analysis are usually based on the undrained strength and use total stress parameters.

14. When the **construction decreases** the normal stress in **saturated clay and silts**, strength analysis is usually based on the drained strength and use effective stress parameters.

EXERCISE

1. What is shear strength of soils? What are reasons for it?
2. Write a note on effective stress concept? Also state important of it.
3. Explain soil modulus determination with stress strain curve.
4. Explain in detail Mohr-Coulomb failure theory.
5. State the various tests used for measuring shear strength of soil and describe any one in detail.
6. What are the factors affecting the shear strength of soil?
7. Define the following terms.
   (a) Thixotropy   (b) Sensitivity.

8. A sample of soil fluid under following triaxial stresses: $\sigma_3 = 150$ kN/m^2, $\sigma_1 = 700$ kN/m^2. If soil has an angle of shearing resistance of 22°. What is its unit cohesion?

9. Determine orientations of the principal planes at failure if normal stress is 2 kg/cm^2 and shear stress failure is 0.8 kg/cm^2.

10. In triaxial test of saturated sample failure occurs at 30 kN/m^2. Establish skepton's pore water pressure equation if deviator stress at failure is 100 kN/m^2 at constant cell pressure 70 kN/m^2.

11. A saturated clay sample of size 6 cm diameter and 12 cm overall height is tested in an unconfined compression tester. Calculate the unconfined compressive strength if the specimen fails under an axial load of 60 N. The change in length at failure of specimen is 1 cm.

12. In a triaxial machine The all found pressure maintained for the first sample was 2 kg/cm^2 and 20 kg/cm^2 and failure occurred at additional axial stress of 7.5 kg./cm^2, while for the second the values were 5.0 kg/cm^2 and 13.5 kg/cm^2 respectively. Find C and ϕ of the soil.

13. In a vane shear test on clay, following result are obtained Applied Torque = 183 kg cm. Height of Vane = 10 cm. , Diameter of vane = 5 cm. Calculate the strength of the clay.

14. A triaxial test (CU) was performed and the following data was obtained at failure :

Test	σ_3 kPa	σ_1 kPa
(1)	50	300
(2)	100	600
(3)	150	900

Plot Mohr's circles and find C and ϕ. What type of soil do you think it is ?

15. A direct shear test was performed on dry sand. Under normal stress of 100 kPa, failure occurred when the shear stress was 60 kPa. Draw the Mohr's envelope and hence determine the magnitude and orientation of maximum and minimum principal stresses.

SOLVED UNIVERSITY QUESTIONS AND NUMERICALS

December 2013

1. A vane of 75 mm diameter and 150 mm height has been pushed into an in-situ soft clay at the bottom of bore hole. The torque required to rotate the vane was 75 Nm. Determine the undrained shear strength of the clay. After the test, the vane was rotated several times and ultimate torque was found to be 50 m. Estimate sensitivity of clay. **(7)**

[**Ans.:** Refer Example 7.46]

2. Explain the procedure of unconfined compression test with suitable sketch. **(6)**

[**Ans.:** Refer Article 7.11]

May 2014

1. Explain the principle of the direct shear test. What are the advantages of this test ? What are its limitations ? **[4]**

   [**Ans.:** Refer Article 7.9]

2. A Triaxial test was conducted on sand specimen and the sample failed at a deviator stress of 480 kN/m^2, when the cell pressure was 100 kN/m^2 under drained condition. Find the effective angle of shearing resistance of sand. **[4]**

   [**Ans.:** Refer Example 7.47]

3. Write a short note on Sensitivity of soil. **[4]**

   [**Ans.:** Refer Article 7.17]

December 2014

1. Explain the procedure for unconfined compression test with neat sketches. **[6]**

   [**Ans.:** Refer Article 7.11]

2. Define sensitivity :

   A clayey sample when tested in unconfined compression, gave compressive strength of 100 kN/m^2. Specimen of same clay, with same initial condition is subjected to undrained, unconsolidated triaxial test under a cell pressure of 100 kN/m^2. Determine the axial stress in kN/m^2 of failure. **[6]**

   [**Ans.:** Refer Article 7.17 and Example 7.48]

May 2015

1. Write a note on Vane Shear Test with neat sketch and the formulae involved. **[6]**

   [**Ans.:** Refer Article 7.12]

2. Define total and effective stress.

   Determine the shear strength in terms of effective stress on a plane within a saturated soil mass at a point where the total normal stress is 200 kN/m^2 and the pore water pressure is 80 kN/m^2. The effective stress shear strength parameters for the soil are $c' = 16$ kN/m^2 and $\Phi = 39°$. **[6]**

   [**Ans.:** Refer Article 7.2 and Example 7.49]

November 2015

1. Explain how the shear tests are conducted with different drainage conditions and the loading conditions. **[6]**

   [**Ans.:** Refer Article 7.8.1]

2. Describe the vane shear test for measuring in-situ shear strength of soils. Why is it used only in soft sensitive clays ? **[6]**

   [**Ans.:** Refer Article 7.12]

May 2016

1. With the help of neat sketch, explain direct shear test and state the law of shearing strength. **[6]**

   [**Ans.:** Refer Example 7.9]

2. A dry sand specimen is put through a triaxial test. Cell pressure is 50 kPa and deviator stress is 100 kPa. Determine the angle of internal friction for the sand specimen. **[6]**

   [**Ans.:** Refer Example 7.50]

November 2016

1. Which shear test is suitable for shaft saturated clayey soil ? Describe the test with neat sketch. **[6]**

   [**Ans.:** Refer Article 7.12]

2. A specimen of fine dry sand when subjected to a traixial compression test, failed at a deviator stress of 400 kN/m2. It failed with a pronounced failure plane with an angle of 24° to the axis of the sample. Compute the lateral pressure to which the specimen would have been subjected to. **[6]**

   [**Ans.:** Refer Example 7.14]

May 2017

1. Explain direct shear test with respect to the drainage and loading conditions. **[6]**

   [**Ans.:** Refer Article 7.9]

2. Define total and effective stress. Determine the shear strength in terms of effective stress on a plane within a saturated soil mass at a point where the total normal stress is 200 kN/m^2 and the pore water pressure is 80 kN/m^2. The effective stress shear strength parameters for the soil c' = 16 kN/m^2 and phi = 39°. **[6]**

   [**Ans.:** Refer Article 7.2 and Example 7.51]

Chapter 8
LATERAL EARTH PRESSURE

8.1 LATERAL EARTH PRESSURE

Soil in contact with any vertical or inclined face of a structure exerts a force on the structure which is known as *lateral earth pressure*. In the design of retaining walls, sheet piles or other earth retaining structures, it is necessary to compute the lateral pressure exerted by the retained mass of soil. A typical supporting wall for a highway cut is shown in Fig. 8.1.

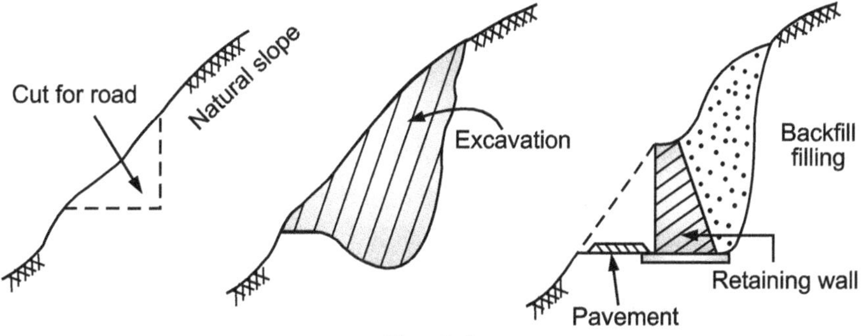

Fig. 8.1

8.2 LIMIT ANALYSIS AND LIMIT EQUILIBRIUM

8.2.1 Definition

The limit analysis method is based on a yield criterion. It is based on the flow rule which considers the stress-strain relationship. It can be used to calculate the lower and upper limits (bounds) of the true collapse load. This analysis may produce the correct results if suitable choice of stress and velocity field is done. All the problems related with earth pressure viz. earth retaining structures, bearing capacity of foundations and stability of slope may be solved by this analysis.

The upper bound theorem states that 'the collapse will occur if for a compatible plastic deformation, the rate at which the external forces do work on the body equals or exceeds the rate of internal dissipation of energy'.

The lower bound theorem states that 'if an equilibrium distribution of stress can be found which balances the applied loads and boundary conditions and nowhere violates the yield criteria, which includes C and ϕ, the soil mass will not fail or will be just at the point of failure'.

8.2.2 Basic Elements

Limit equilibrium analysis method adopts the following basic elements :

- The failure surface is assumed to be of a simple shape (e.g. planar, circular or log-spiral).
- A reasonable assumption about the stress distribution along the failure surface is made.

- An estimation of mobilized shear is made and the mobilized shear strength is assumed to act simultaneously along the failure surface.

  Based on the above basic elements, an overall equilibrium is developed and the problem is solved by simple statics. Thus, the limiting values viz., earth pressure on retaining structures, factor of safety of slopes, bearing capacity of foundation are calculated. Most of the practical problems are statically indeterminate and need assumptions regarding the force systems and directions of their applications.

  e application of limit analysis to practical problems has not been completely made yet because of the difficulties in obtaining a proper stress-strain relationship. The limit equilibrium method has been in wide use because of its simplicity.

8.3 EFFECT OF WALL MOVEMENT ON EARTH PRESSURE

[Dec. 14, May 17]

A retaining wall may generally have any one of the three types of pressures, depending upon the movement of the retaining wall with respect to the backfill.

1. At rest pressure : The lateral earth pressure called as "at rest pressure" is the pressure on the retaining wall when the soil mass is not subjected to any lateral yielding or movement. At rest condition is also known as the elastic equilibrium condition, as no part of the soil mass has failed and attained plastic equilibrium. This generally occurs for no or very less movement of the wall.

2. Active pressure : Pressure exerted on the retaining wall resulting from slight movement of the wall away from the backfill.

3. Passive pressure : A state of passive pressure exists when the movement of the retaining wall is such that the soil tends to compress horizontally. Passive resistance is felt when the wall is forced towards the filling.

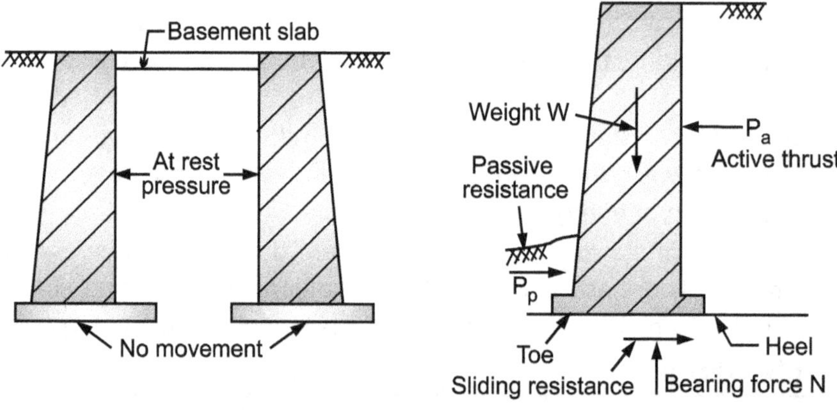

Fig. 8.2   **Fig. 8.3**

Fig. 8.4 : Shows the variation of earth pressure with wall movement.

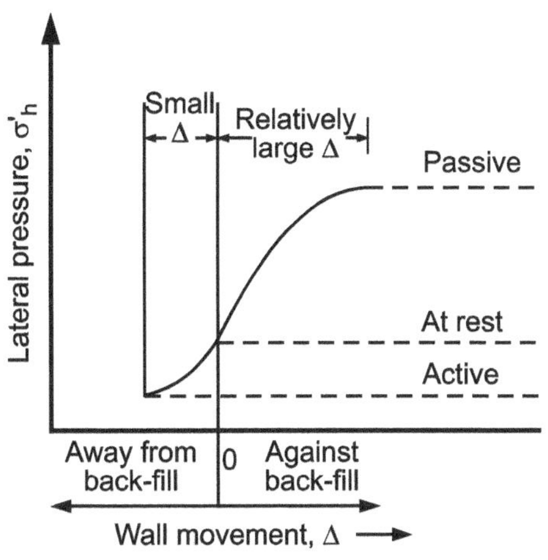

Usual range of earth pressure coefficients	
Cohesionless soils	Cohesive soils
3 - 14	1 - 2
0.4 - 0.6	0.4 - 0.8
0.33 - 0.22	1 - 0.5

Fig. 8.4

8.4 EARTH PRESSURE AT REST [Nov. 15]

The earth pressure at rest, exerted on the back of a rigid retaining wall, can be calculated using theory of elasticity.

For this analysis, soil is assumed to be elastic, homogeneous, isotropic and semi-infinite. The soil can deform vertically under its self weight, but cannot deform laterally because of the infinite extent in that direction. E and μ are modulus of elasticity and Poisson's ratio of soil respectively. For at rest condition, the ratio of horizontal to vertical stress is denoted as coefficient of lateral stress at rest or lateral stress ratio or coefficient of earth pressure at rest 'K_o'.

Fig. 8.5 shows a retaining wall at rest. Consider an element of soil at a depth 'Z' being acted upon by vertical stress σ_v and horizontal stress σ_h.

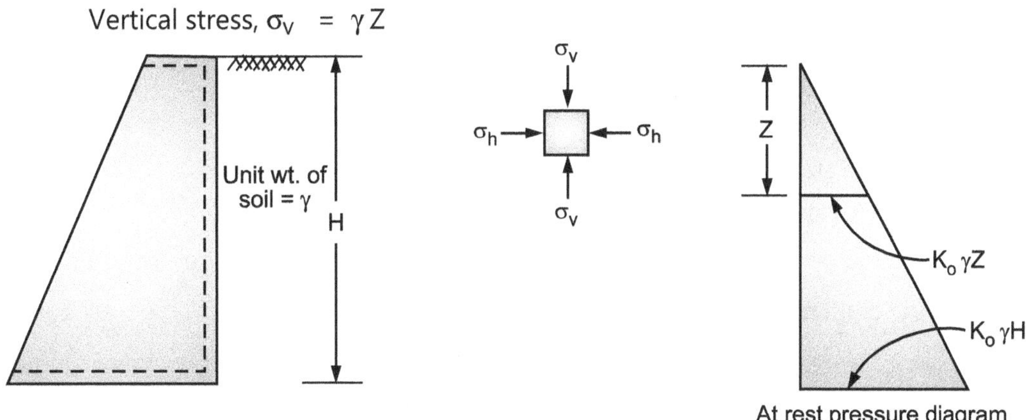

Fig. 8.5

The lateral strain ε_h in the horizontal direction is given by :

$$\varepsilon_h = \frac{1}{E}\left[\sigma_h - \mu\left(\sigma_h + \sigma_v\right)\right]$$

But, ε_h = 0 for "at rest condition".

Hence, σ_h = $\mu [\sigma_h + \sigma_v]$

or, $\sigma_h [1 - \mu]$ = $\mu \cdot \sigma_v$

or, $\dfrac{\sigma_h}{\sigma_v}$ = K_O = $\dfrac{\mu}{1 - \mu}$

where, K_O is the coefficient for earth pressure at rest.

or, σ_h = $K_O \cdot \sigma_v$

Designating σ_h at rest by P_O and substituting $\sigma_v = \gamma \cdot Z$, we have,

$$P_O = K_O \gamma \cdot Z$$

Now, when $Z = 0$, $P_O = 0$ and when $Z = H$, $P_O = K_O \gamma \cdot H$

Hence, pressure distribution diagram is triangular and total pressure P_O per unit length is given by,

$$P_O = \int K_O \gamma \cdot Z \, dZ = \frac{1}{2} K_O \gamma H^2$$

The resultant of P_O will act at the centroid i.e. $\dfrac{H}{3}$ from the bottom of the wall.

8.5 RANKINE'S STATE OF PLASTIC EQUILIBRIUM   [May 14,16,17]

Rankine was the first engineer who used the concepts of plastic equilibrium more rationally to tackle the stability problems. Suppose every part of a semi-infinite soil mass at rest condition is brought on the verge of failure either by stretching or by compressing, then such a state is called a *general state of plastic equilibrium*.

The following assumptions were made by Rankine [1857] for the derivation of earth pressure :

- The soil mass is homogeneous and semi-infinite.
- The soil is dry and cohesionless.
- The ground surface is plane, which may be horizontal or inclined.
- **The back of the retaining wall is smooth and vertical.**
- The soil element is in a state of plastic equilibrium i.e. on the verge of failure.

8.5.1 Active Earth Pressure for Cohesionless Soils   (May 15.17)

The Mohr circle representing the state of stress at failure in a two dimensional element is shown in Fig. 8.6 for cohesionless soil. Shear failure occurs along a plate at an angle of $(45^o + \phi/2)$ to the major principal plane. If the soil mass as a whole is stressed, such that the principal stresses at every point are in the same direction, then, theoretically, there will be a network of failure planes, known as "Slip line field" equally inclined to the principal planes. Plastic equilibrium is developed, only if, sufficient deformation of soil mass takes place.

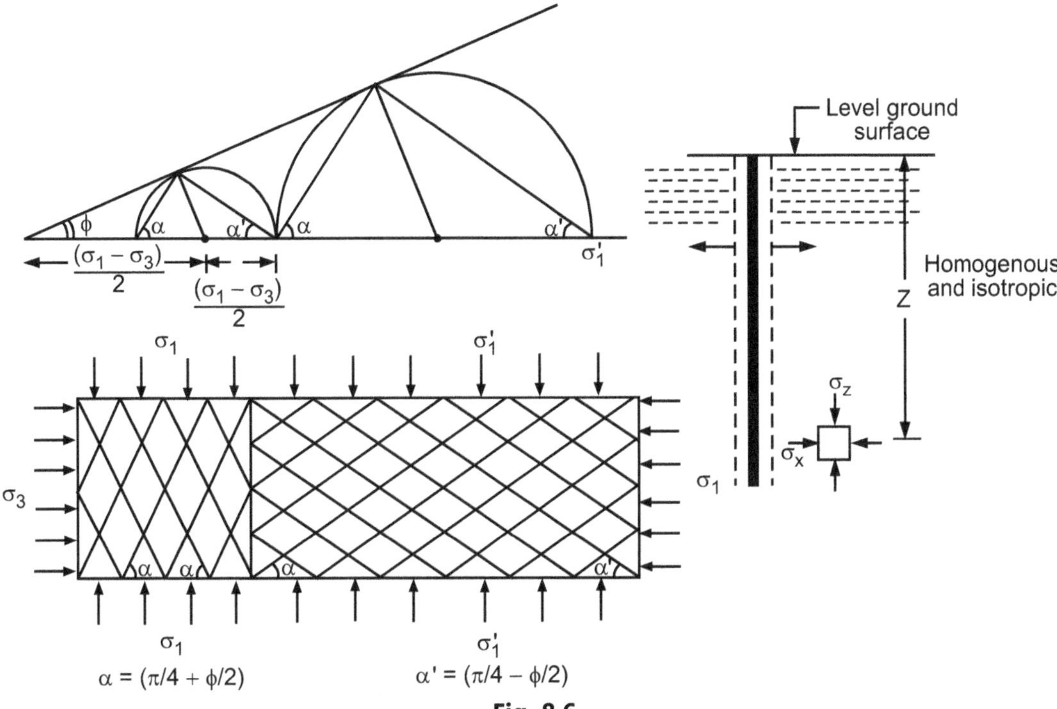

Fig. 8.6

If there is movement of the wall away from the soil, the value of σ_x decreases as the soil dilates or expands outwards. If expansion is large enough, the value of σ_x decreases to a minimum value, such that a state of plastic equilibrium is reached, and horizontal stress σ_x decreases. The vertical stress σ_z is unaltered and becomes the major principal stress [σ_1] and the decreased horizontal stress σ_x becomes the minor principal stress [σ_3].

From the Mohr's circle for cohesionless soil,

$$\sin\phi = \frac{[\sigma_1 - \sigma_3]/2}{[\sigma_1 + \sigma_3]/2} = \left(\frac{\sigma_1 - \sigma_3}{\sigma_1 + \sigma_3}\right)$$

$$\therefore \quad 1 - \sin\phi = 1 - \left(\frac{\sigma_1 - \sigma_3}{\sigma_1 + \sigma_3}\right) = \frac{(\sigma_1 + \sigma_3) - (\sigma_1 - \sigma_3)}{\sigma_1 + \sigma_3}$$

$$= \frac{2\sigma_3}{\sigma_1 + \sigma_3} \qquad \ldots (8.1)$$

Similarly,
$$1 + \sin\phi = \frac{2\sigma_1}{\sigma_1 + \sigma_3} \qquad \ldots (8.2)$$

Dividing Equation (8.1) by (8.2), we get,

$$\frac{1 - \sin\phi}{1 + \sin\phi} = \frac{2\sigma_3}{\sigma_1 + \sigma_3} \times \frac{\sigma_1 + \sigma_3}{2\sigma_1} = \frac{\sigma_3}{\sigma_1}$$

$$\therefore \qquad \sigma_3 = \frac{\sigma_1 \, [1 - \sin \phi]}{[1 + \sin \phi]} \qquad \qquad ...(8.3)$$

As stated, σ_1 is the overburden pressure at depth Z i.e.

$$\sigma_1 = \gamma \cdot Z$$

The horizontal stress for the above condition is defined as active pressure $[p_a]$, due to self weight of the soil.

If $\qquad\qquad K_a$ = coefficient of active earth pressure

$$= \frac{[1 - \sin \phi]}{[1 + \sin \phi]}$$

Then, Equation (8.3) can be written as,

$$\sigma_3 = p_a = K_a \cdot \gamma Z$$

Total active pressure p_a exerted on wall can be found out by integrating above equation.

i.e. $$\qquad p_a = \int_{0}^{H} K_a \, \gamma \, Z \, dZ$$

$$p_a = \frac{K_a \cdot \gamma H^2}{2}$$

This will be acting at height H/3 from the base of the wall.

If the soil is dry, γ i.e. dry unit weight of soil is used, and if the soil is wet, moist unit weight of soil should be used (Fig. 8.7).

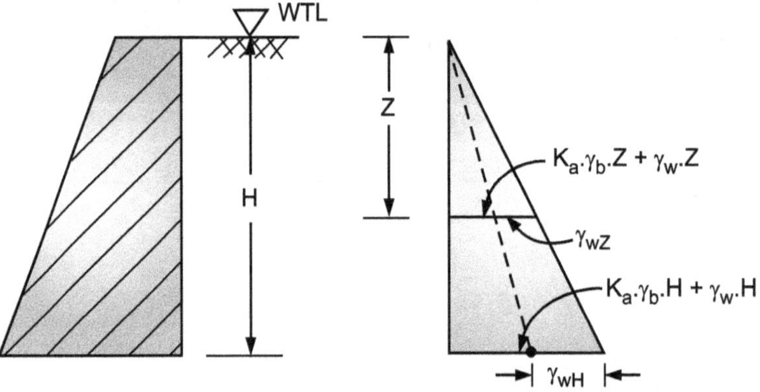

Fig. 8.7

8.5.2 Submerged Backfill   (Nov. 16, Dec. 14)

In this case, backfill behind the retaining wall is submerged with water. The lateral pressure is made up of two components.

1. Lateral pressure due to submerged weight γ_b of the soil, and

2. Lateral pressure due to water.

Thus, at any depth Z below the surface,

$$p_a = K_a \gamma_b Z + \gamma_w \cdot Z$$

When Z = 0, $p_a = 0$

When Z = H, $p_a = K_a \gamma_b H + \gamma_w \cdot H$

If the free water stands on both sides of the wall, the water pressure need not be considered.

If the backfill is partly submerged : Here the backfill is moist to a depth H_1 below the ground level, and then it is submerged [Fig. 8.8 (b)]. The lateral pressure intensity at the base of the wall will be given by :

$$p_a = K_a \cdot \gamma H_1 + K_a [\gamma_{sat} - \gamma_w] H_2 + \gamma_w \cdot H_2$$

The above expression is on the assumption that the value of ϕ is the same for the moist and submerged soil. If it is different, say ϕ_1 and ϕ_2 respectively, the earth pressure coefficient K_{a1} and K_{a2} will be different. The lateral pressure intensity [Fig. 8.8 (c)] at base of wall is given by :

$$p_a = K_{a1} \gamma H_1 + [\gamma_{sat} - \gamma_w] K_{a2} \cdot H_2 + \gamma_w H_2$$

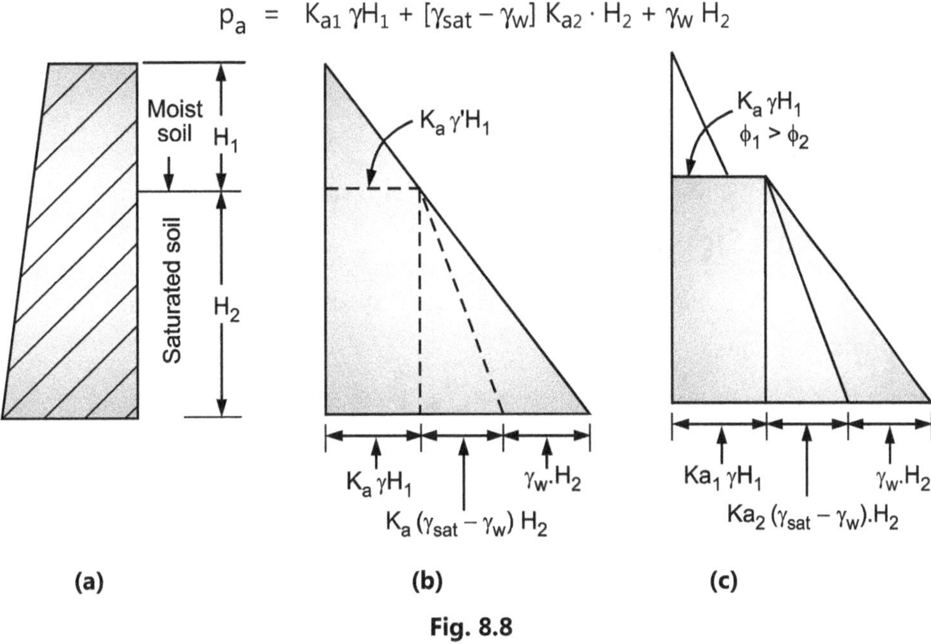

Fig. 8.8

8.5.3 Backfill with Uniform Surcharge   (May 15)

If the backfill is horizontal and carries a surcharge of uniform intensity q per unit area, the vertical pressure increment at any depth Z, will increase by q. The increase in the lateral pressure due to this will be $K_a q$ (Fig. 8.9).

Hence, the lateral pressure at any depth Z is given by

$$p_a = K_a \gamma Z + K_a \cdot q$$

When $Z = 0$, $p_a = K_a \cdot q$ and when $Z = H$, $p_a = K_a \gamma H + K_a \cdot q$

The height of backfill Z_e, equivalent to the uniform surcharge intensity is given by,

$$K_a \gamma Z_e = K_a \cdot q$$

$$Z_e = \frac{q}{\gamma}$$

This means "the effect of surcharge of intensity q is the same as that of a fill of height Z_e above the ground surface".

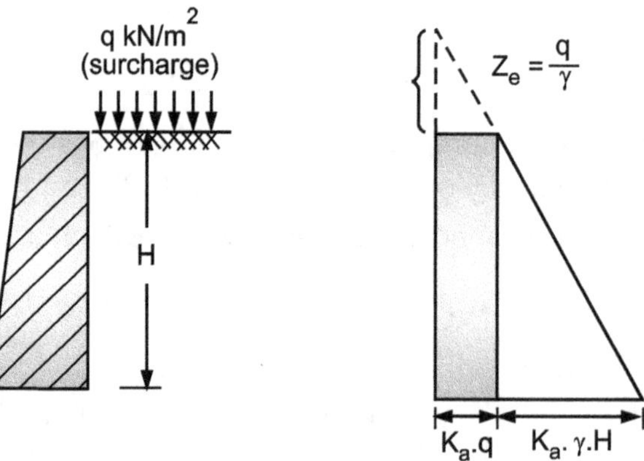

Fig. 8.9 : Backfill with uniform surcharge

8.5.4 Backfill with Sloping Surface

Let the sloping surface behind the wall be inclined at an angle β with the horizontal. β is called the *surcharge angle*.

In finding out the active earth pressure for this case by Rankine's theory, *an additional assumption that the vertical and lateral stresses are conjugate, is made.*

For the present case value of K_a i.e. coefficient of active earth is given by :

$$K_a = \cos \beta \cdot \frac{\cos \beta - \sqrt{\cos^2\beta - \cos^2\phi}}{\cos \beta + \sqrt{\cos^2\beta - \cos^2\phi}} \qquad \text{[For derivation, see Ex. 8.9]}$$

When, $\beta = 0$ [i.e. horizontal ground surface]

$$K_a = \frac{1 - \sin \phi}{1 + \sin \phi}$$

The lateral earth pressure at any depth Z is given by,

$$p_a = K_a \gamma \cdot Z$$

where,
$$K_a = \cos\beta \cdot \frac{\cos\beta - \sqrt{\cos^2\beta - \cos^2\phi}}{\cos\beta + \sqrt{\cos^2\beta - \cos^2\phi}}$$

When $Z = 0$, $p_a = 0$ and when $Z = H$, $p_a = K_a\,\gamma\cdot H$

Total active pressure, $p_a = \dfrac{1}{2}\,K_a\,\gamma H^2$

The resultant acts at $\dfrac{H}{3}$, above the base in a direction parallel to the surface.

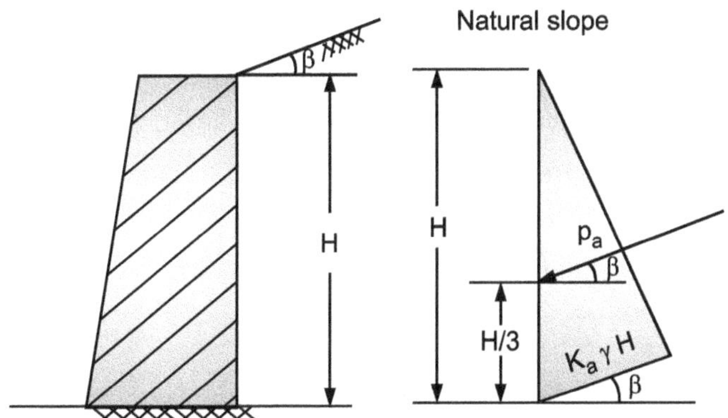

Fig. 8.10 : Lateral pressure distribution for sloping surcharge

8.6 ACTIVE EARTH PRESSURE OF COHESIVE SOILS

[Dec. 13, 14, May 14, 15]

Rankine's original theory was for cohesionless soils. It was extended by Resal and Bell for cohesive soils.

8.6.1 Backfill with No Surcharge   [Nov. 16, May 16]

Consider a smooth vertical retaining wall with a horizontal backfill. At any depth Z, we have,

$$\sigma_1 = \sigma_v = \gamma\cdot Z \quad \text{and} \quad \sigma_3 = \text{lateral pressure, } p_a$$

The principal stress relationship on a failure plane is given by the equation :

$$\sigma_1 = \sigma_3 \tan^2\left(45 + \frac{\phi}{2}\right) + 2C\tan\left(45 + \frac{\phi}{2}\right) \qquad \text{... (8.4)}$$

Substituting σ_1 and σ_3 in equation (8.4), we have,

$$\gamma\cdot Z = p_a \tan^2\alpha + 2C\tan\alpha$$

where,
$$\alpha = 45 + \frac{\phi}{2}$$

or,
$$p_a = \gamma\cdot Z \cot^2\alpha - 2C\cot\alpha \qquad \text{... (8.5)}$$

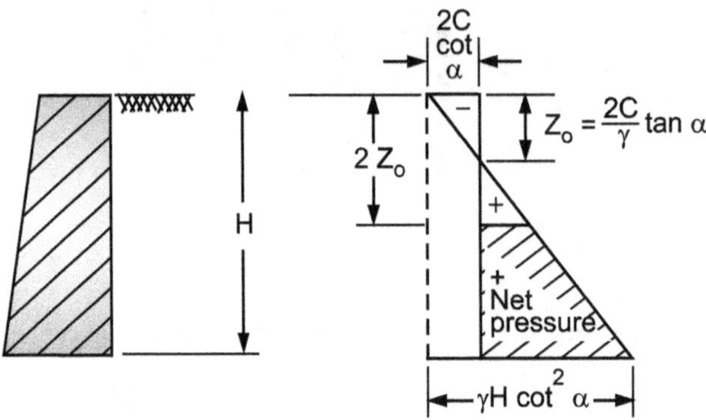

Fig. 8.11

At $Z = 0$, $p_a = -2C \cot \alpha$

This shows that negative pressure [i.e. tension] is developed at the top level of the retaining wall.

At a point where $\quad p_a = 0 \ = \ \gamma Z \cot^2\alpha - 2C \cot \alpha$

$\therefore \qquad\qquad\qquad \gamma Z \ = \ 2C \tan \alpha$

$\therefore \qquad$ When $p_a = 0$, $\quad Z \ = \ Z_o \ = \ \dfrac{2C}{\gamma} \tan \alpha$

Hence tension decreases to zero at a depth,

$$Z_o \ = \ \frac{2C}{\gamma} \tan \alpha \qquad\qquad\qquad \text{... (8.6)}$$

At $Z = H$, $\qquad\qquad p_a \ = \ \gamma H \cot^2\alpha - 2C \cot \alpha$

The total net pressure is given by,

$$P_a \ = \ \int p_a \cdot dZ$$

or $\qquad\qquad\qquad\qquad P_a \ = \ \dfrac{1}{2} H^2 \cot^2\alpha - 2CH \cot \alpha$

Because of negative pressure, a tension crack is usually developed in the soil near the top of the wall upto a depth Z_o. Also, the total net pressure at depth $2Z_o$ is zero. **This means that a cohesive soil should be able to stand with a vertical face, upto a depth of $2Z_o$ without any lateral support.** The lateral height H_c of an unsupported vertical cut in a cohesive soil is thus given by,

$$H_c \ = \ 2Z_o \ = \ \frac{4C}{\gamma} \tan \alpha$$

or $\qquad\qquad\qquad\qquad H_c \ = \ \dfrac{4C}{\gamma} \cdot \dfrac{1}{\sqrt{K_a}}$

where, $\qquad\qquad\qquad K_a \ = \ \cot^2\alpha$

For soft saturated clay, $\phi \ = \ 0$, $K_a \ = \ 1$

$$\therefore \qquad H_c = \frac{4C}{\gamma}$$

As the crack develops in the soil upto depth Z_O, the soil does not remain adhered to the top portion of the wall, upto Z_O. Hence the total lateral thrust is given by integrating equation (8.5) between limits Z_O to H.

$$P_a = \int_{Z_o}^{H} [\gamma Z \cot^2\alpha - 2C \cot\alpha]\, dZ$$

or $\qquad P_a = \frac{1}{2}\gamma[H^2 - Z_o^2]\cot^2\alpha - 2C[H - Z_o]\cot\alpha \qquad\qquad \dots (8.7)$

However, from equation (8.6),

$$Z_o = \frac{2C}{\gamma}\tan\alpha.$$

Substituting for Z_o in equation (8.7), we get,

$$P_a = \frac{1}{2}\gamma H^2 \cot^2\alpha - 2CH \cot^2\alpha + \frac{2C^2}{\gamma}$$

8.6.2 Backfill with Surcharge　　　　　　　　　　　　　　　　　　　(May 15)

If the backfill carries a surcharge of uniform intensity q per unit area, the lateral pressure is increased by $K_a \cdot q$ or $q\cdot\cot^2\alpha$ everywhere. Hence, equation (8.5) for the lateral pressure is modified to

$$p_a = \gamma Z \cot^2\alpha - 2C \cot\alpha + q \cot^2\alpha$$

At $Z = 0$, $\qquad\qquad p_a = q \cot^2\alpha - 2C \cot\alpha$

The depth Z_o at $p_a = 0$ is given by,

$$Z_o = \frac{2C}{\gamma}\tan\alpha - \frac{q}{\gamma}$$

8.6.3 Layered Soils

Lateral pressures in layered soil may be considered in two cases :

(1) Layers with same angle of shearing resistance.

(2) Layers with different angles of shearing resistance.

(a) Non-cohesive soils – c = 0 : In the first case when the ϕ - values for the retained materials are same; the distribution diagrams show the same lateral pressure values at the same depth, (for same σ_v), (Fig. 8.12 (a)) while with different values of ϕ for upper and lower layers, the lateral pressure has a lower value for a higher angle of friction and higher value for a smaller angle of friction. Suppose $\phi_2 > \phi_1$ for the two layers in Fig. 8.12 (b). Since $K_{a_1} > K_{a_2}$, the active pressures are

$$\therefore \quad (\sigma_{a_1})\, z_1 = (\gamma_1\, z_1)\, K_{a_1}$$

$$(\sigma_{a_2})\, z_1 = (\gamma_1 \cdot z_1) \cdot K_{a_2}$$

$$\therefore \quad (\sigma_{a_1})\, z_1 > (\sigma_{a_2})\, z_1$$

i.e. At the same level, lateral pressures are different, although σ_v is same. Similarly, $\phi_3 < \phi_2$ and $K_{a_3} > K_{a_2}$; $(\sigma_{a_3})_{z_2} > (\sigma_{a_2})_{z_2}$.

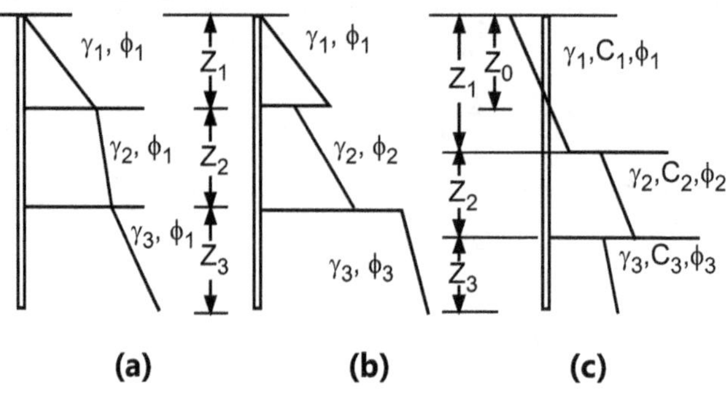

(a)   (b)   (c)

Fig. 8.12 : Layered soils

Lateral pressures for layered cohesive soils may be determined in the same manner. If γ_1, c_1, ϕ_1 and γ_2, c_2, ϕ_2 correspond to the upper and lower layers respectively, then the active pressures at the depth z_1,

$$(\sigma_{a_1})_{z_1} = \gamma_1\, z_1\, K_{a_1} - 2c_1 \sqrt{K_{a_1}}\,, \quad (\sigma_{v_1} = \gamma_1 \cdot z_1)$$

$$(\sigma_{a_2})_{z_1} = \gamma_1\, z_1 \cdot K_{a_2} - 2c_2 \sqrt{K_{a_2}}$$

K_{a_1}, K_{a_2}, c_1 and c_2 being different, the lateral pressures above and below the interface at depth z_1 and z_2 are different as shown in Fig. 8.12 (c).

While determining the lateral pressure distribution within the lower layer, the upper layer may be treated as a simple surcharge of intensity.

$$q_1 = \gamma_1 \cdot z_1$$

Then

$$\sigma_{v_2} = q_1 + \gamma_2 z$$

and

$$\sigma_a = \sigma_v K_a - 2c \sqrt{K_a}$$

for the second layer at the top $(\sigma_a)_{z_1} = (q_1 + 0) \cdot K_{a_2} - 2c_2 \sqrt{K_{a_2}} = q_1 \cdot K_{a_2} - 2c_2 \sqrt{K_{a_2}}$

and for the second layer at the bottom,

$$(\sigma_a)_{z_2} = (q_1 + \gamma_2\, z_2)\, K_{a_2} - 2c_2 \sqrt{K_{a_2}}$$

This procedure can be used for a non-cohesive lower layer also with $c_2 = 0$, γ_2, ϕ_2.

For the third layer, the simple surcharge, q_2 equals

$$q_2 = \gamma_1 z_1 + \gamma_3 z_2$$

and the vertical pressure within the third layer σ_{v_3} for depths, z_2 to z_3 equals.

$$\sigma_{v_3} \;=\; (q_2 + \gamma_3\, z)$$

and active pressure, $\qquad \sigma_a \;=\; \sigma_{v_3} \cdot K_{a_3} \;-\; 2c_3\, \sqrt{K_{a_3}}.$

The procedure can be repeated for any number of layers.

8.7 PASSIVE EARTH PRESSURE   [Dec. 13, May 14, Nov. 15]

Rankine's Theory : In the case of a passive state of plastic equilibrium, the lateral pressure is the major principal stress while the vertical pressure is the minor principal stress. Thus,

$$\sigma_h \;=\; p_p \;=\; \sigma_1$$
$$\sigma_v \;=\; \sigma_3 \;=\; \gamma \cdot Z$$

Substituting this in the principal stress relationship :

$$\sigma_1 \;=\; \sigma_3 \tan^2\alpha \quad [\text{for } C = 0]$$

we get, $\qquad \sigma_h \;=\; \sigma_v \tan^2\alpha$

where, $\qquad p_p \;=\;$ Passive earth pressure intensity,

$\qquad\qquad K_p \;=\;$ Rankine's coefficient of passive earth pressure

or, $\qquad K_p \;=\; \tan^2\alpha \;=\; N\phi \;=\; \dfrac{1 + \sin\phi}{1 - \sin\phi} \;=\; \dfrac{1}{K_a}$

Case A : Retaining wall with vertical back and cohesionless backfill.

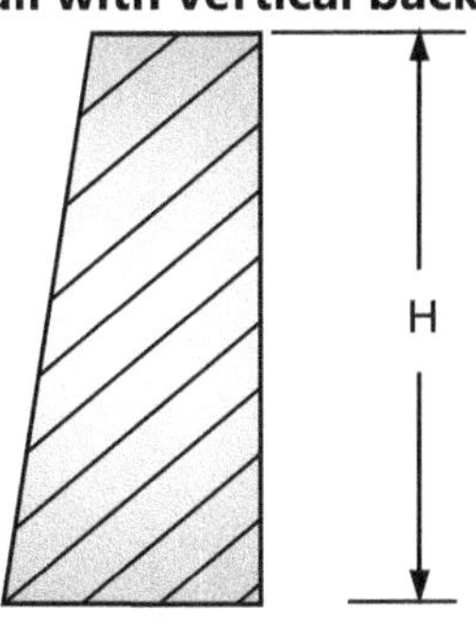
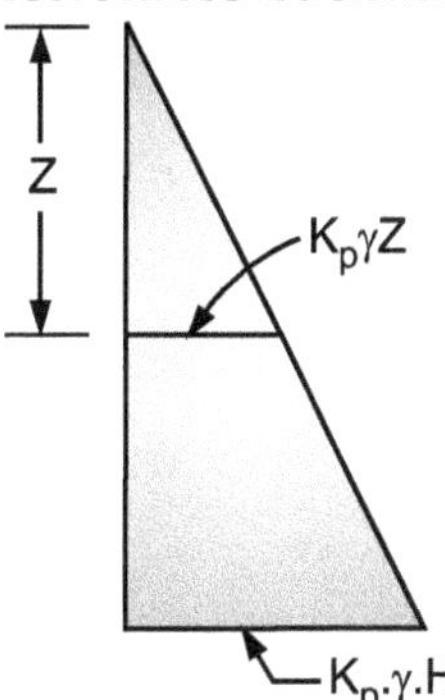

Fig. 8.13

The passive pressure at any depth Z is given by,

$$p_p \;=\; K_p\, \gamma \cdot Z$$

When Z = 0, $\qquad p_p \;=\; 0$

When Z = H, $\qquad p_p \;=\; K_p \cdot \gamma \cdot H$

The total pressure, $\qquad P_p \;=\; \displaystyle\int K_p \cdot \gamma \cdot Z\, dZ$

$$\qquad\qquad\qquad\quad =\; \frac{1}{2}\, K_p \cdot \gamma \cdot H^2$$

Case B : Cohesionless backfill having top surface inclined at an angle β with horizontal.

The passive pressure at any depth Z is :

$$p_p = \gamma Z \cos\beta \cdot \frac{\cos\beta + \sqrt{\cos^2\beta - \cos^2\phi}}{\cos\beta - \sqrt{\cos^2\beta - \cos^2\phi}}$$

or,

$$p_p = K_p \cdot \gamma \cdot Z$$

where,

$$K_p = \cos\beta \cdot \frac{\cos\beta + \sqrt{\cos^2\beta - \cos^2\phi}}{\cos\beta - \sqrt{\cos^2\beta - \cos^2\phi}}$$

Case C : Cohesive backfill with $\beta = 0$.

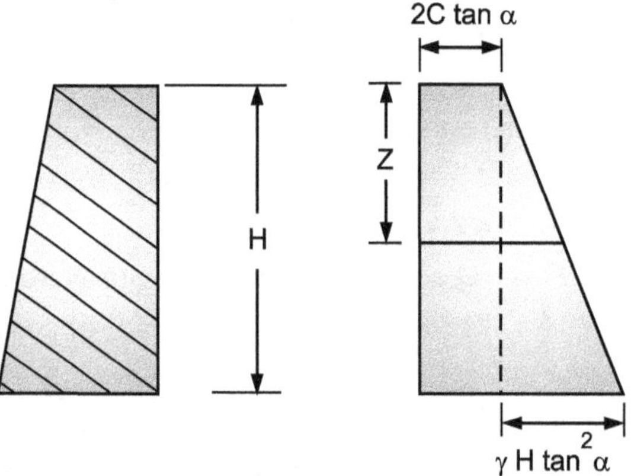

Fig. 8.14

For a cohesive soil, the principal stress relationship at failure is given by :

$$\sigma_1 = \sigma_3 \tan^2\alpha + 2C \tan\alpha \qquad \ldots (8.8)$$

For case of cohesive pressure

$$\sigma_1 = \sigma_h = p_p$$
$$\sigma_3 = \sigma_v = \gamma Z$$

Hence equation (8.8) will be,

$$p_p = \gamma Z \tan^2\alpha + 2C \tan\alpha$$

At Z = 0,

$$p_p = 2C \tan\alpha$$

At Z = H,

$$p_p = \gamma h \tan^2\alpha + 2C \tan\alpha$$

The total pressure,

$$P_p = \int p_p \cdot dZ$$

$$P_p = \frac{1}{2} \gamma H^2 \tan^2\alpha + 2CH \tan\alpha$$

8.8 COULOMB'S WEDGE THEORY   [Dec. 13, Nov. 15, May 14, 17]

Rankine's theory of earth pressure is applicable only to smooth vertical walls. In practice, this is a too ideal condition in most retaining wall problems.

Coulomb in 1776 developed an earth pressure theory which includes the effect of friction between the backfill and the wall. The theory considers a dry non-cohesive inclined back fill, and the lateral pressure required to maintain the equilibrium of a sliding wedge with a plane slip surface is calculated.

Following are the basic assumptions of the Coulomb's wedge theory :

- The backfill is dry, cohesionless, homogeneous, isotropic and elastically undeformable but breakable.
- The slip surface is plane which passes through the heel of the wall.
- The sliding wedge itself acts as a rigid body and the value of earth pressure is obtained by considering the limiting equilibrium of the sliding wedge as a whole.
- The position and direction of the resultant earth pressure is known.
- There is wall friction on pressure surface.
- Failure is two dimensional.

Consider a retaining wall (as shown in Fig. 8.14) with its backface inclined at an angle 'α' with the horizontal, Fig. 8.15 depicts the following details :

- AB is the pressure face.
- The backfill surface AE is plane inclined at an angle i with the horizontal.
- α is the angle made by the pressure face AB with the horizontal.
- H is height of the wall.
- BC is the probable assumed rupture plane, and
- θ is the angle made by the surface BC with the horizontal.

If BC in Fig. 8.15 is the probable rupture plane, the weight of the wedge W per unit length of the wall may be written as

$$W = \gamma A, \text{ where } A = \text{area of wedge ABC}$$

$$\text{Area of wedge ABC} = A = \frac{1}{2} \, BC \cdot AD$$

where AD is drawn perpendicular to BC.

From the law of sines, we have,

$$BC = AB \cdot \frac{\sin [\alpha + i]}{\sin [\theta - i]}$$

$$AD = AB \sin [\alpha + \theta]$$

$$AB = \frac{H}{\sin \alpha}$$

Making the substitution and simplifying, we have,

$$W = \gamma A = \frac{\gamma H^2}{2 \sin^2\alpha} \sin [\alpha + \theta] \frac{\sin [\alpha + i]}{\sin [\theta - i]} \qquad \dots (8.9)$$

The various forces that are acting on the wedge are shown in fig. 8.15 (a). As the pressure face AB moves away from the backfill, there will be sliding of the soil mass along the wall from A towards B. The sliding of the soil mass is resisted by the friction of the surface. The active thrust p_a is inclined at an angle δ to the normal to the wall.

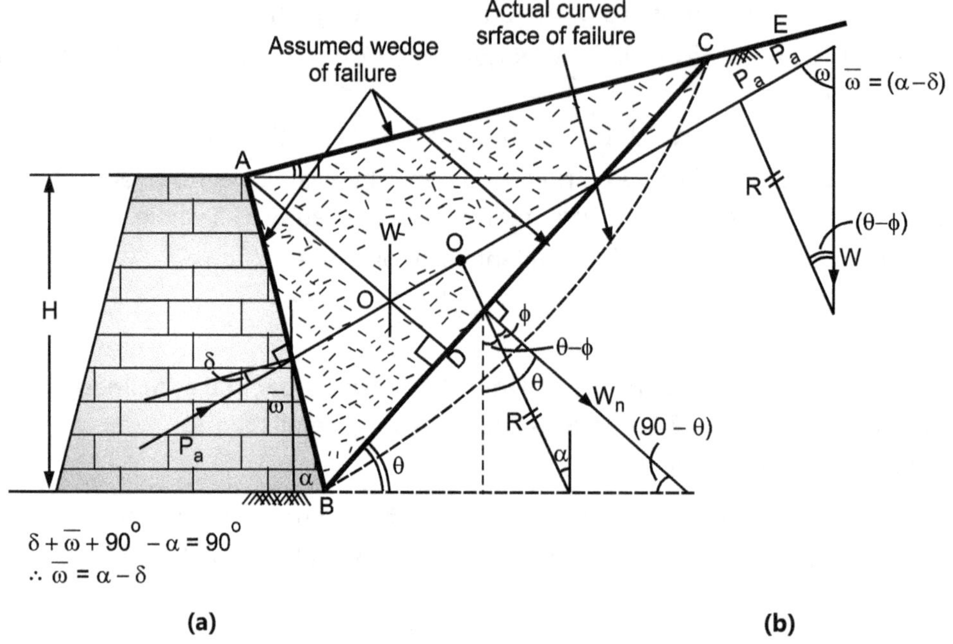

Fig. 8.15 : Conditions for failure under active conditions

The polygon of forces is shown in Fig. 8.15 (b). From the polygon of forces, we may write,

$$\frac{p_a}{\sin [\theta - \phi]} = \frac{W}{\sin [180° - \alpha - \theta + \phi + \delta]}$$

or

$$p_a = \frac{W \sin [\theta - \phi]}{\sin [180° - \alpha - \theta + \phi + \delta]} \qquad \ldots (8.10)$$

In equation (8.10), the only variable is θ and all the other terms for a given case are constant. Substituting for W, we have,

$$p_a = \frac{\gamma H^2}{2 \sin^2\alpha} \frac{\sin [\theta - \phi]}{\sin [180° - \alpha - \theta + \phi + \delta]}$$
$$\times \left[\sin [\alpha + \theta] \frac{\sin [\alpha + i]}{\sin [\theta - i]} \right]$$
$$\ldots (8.11)$$

The maximum value for p_a is obtained by differentiating the equation (8.11) with respect to θ and equating the derivative to zero i.e.,

$$\frac{dp_a}{d\theta} = 0$$

The maximum value of p_a so obtained may be written as

$$p_a = \frac{1}{2}\,\gamma H^2 \frac{K_A}{\sin \alpha \cos \delta} \qquad \qquad \text{... (8.12)}$$

where K_A is called as the active earth pressure coefficient. The value of this is

$$K_A = \frac{\sin^2[\alpha + \phi]\cos\delta}{\sin\alpha \cdot \sin[\alpha - \delta]\left(1 + \sqrt{\dfrac{\sin[\phi + \delta]\sin[\phi - i]}{\sin[\alpha - \delta]\sin[\alpha + i]}}\right)^2} \qquad \text{... (8.13)}$$

The total normal component P_{an} of the earth pressure on the back of the wall is

$$P_{an} = p_a \cos\delta = \frac{1}{2}\,\gamma H^2 \frac{K_A}{\sin\alpha} \qquad \qquad \text{... (8.14)}$$

If the wall is vertical and smooth, and if the backfill is horizontal, we have,

$$i = \delta = 0 \text{ and } \alpha = 90°$$

Substituting these values in equation (8.13), we have,

$$K_A = \frac{1 - \sin\phi}{1 + \sin\phi} = \tan^2[45° - \phi/2] = \frac{1}{\tan^2[45° + \phi/2]} \quad \text{... (8.15)}$$

The coefficient K_A in equation (8.15) is the same as the Rankine's coefficient. The effect of wall friction is frequently neglected where active pressures are concerned. K_A decreases with the increase of δ and the maximum decrease is not more than 10%.

From Fig. 8.16, it will be clear that, the effect of wall friction is more in respect of failure due to passive pressure than due to active pressure. Therefore, determination of active pressure by Rankine's method involves lesser error.

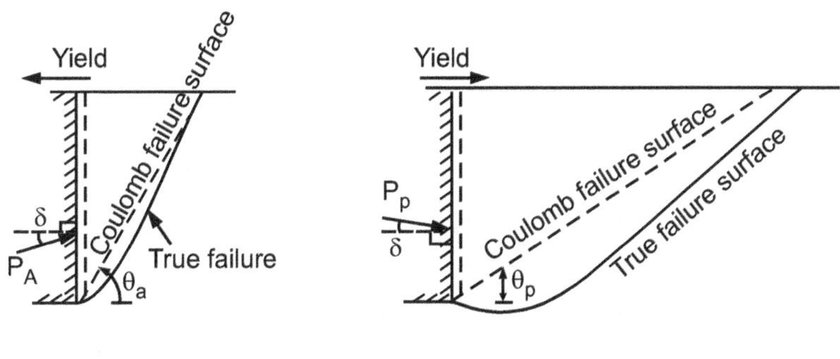

(a) Active case   **(b) Passive case**

Fig. 8.16 : Curvature of failure surface due to wall friction

The polygon of forces for the passive state are shown in Fig. 8.17 (b). Proceeding in the same way as for active earth pressure, we may write the following equations :

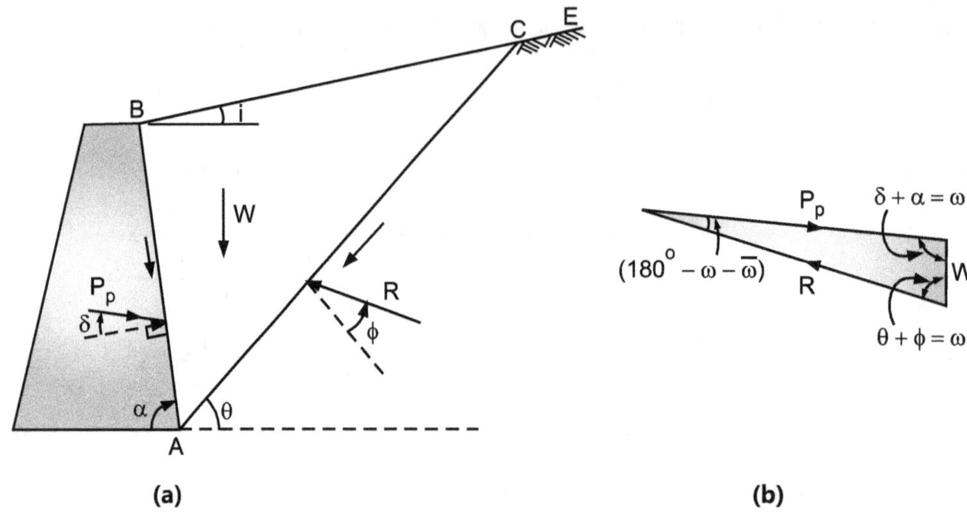

Fig. 8.17 : Conditions for failure under passive state

$$W \;=\; \frac{\gamma H^2}{2\sin^2\alpha}\,\sin[\alpha + \theta]\,\frac{\sin[\alpha + i]}{\sin[\theta - i]} \qquad \ldots (8.16)$$

$$P_p \;=\; \frac{W\sin[\theta + \phi]}{\sin[180 - \theta - \phi - \delta - \alpha]} \qquad \ldots (8.17)$$

Differentiating equation (8.17) with respect to θ and setting the derivative to zero, gives the minimum value of P_p as

$$P_p \;=\; \frac{1}{2}\,\gamma H^2\,K_p \qquad \ldots (8.18)$$

where K_p which is called as the passive earth pressure coefficient is expressed as

$$K_P \;=\; \frac{\sin^2[\alpha - \phi]\cdot\cos\delta}{\sin\alpha\cdot\sin[\alpha + \delta]\left(1 - \sqrt{\dfrac{\sin[\phi + \delta]\,\sin[\phi + i]}{\sin[\alpha + \delta]\,\sin[\alpha + i]}}\right)} \qquad \ldots (8.19)$$

Equation (8.19) is valid for both the positive and negative values of i and δ.

8.9 REHBANN'S CONSTRUCTION OF ACTIVE PRESSURE/ PONCELET METHOD　　　　　　　　　[Dec. 14, May 15]

Rehbann's [1871] gave a graphical method for the determination of total active pressure according to Coulomb's theory on a rough wall for a non-cohesive, homogeneous and inclined back-fill. It is based on Poncelet's solution and is therefore known as Poncelet's method.

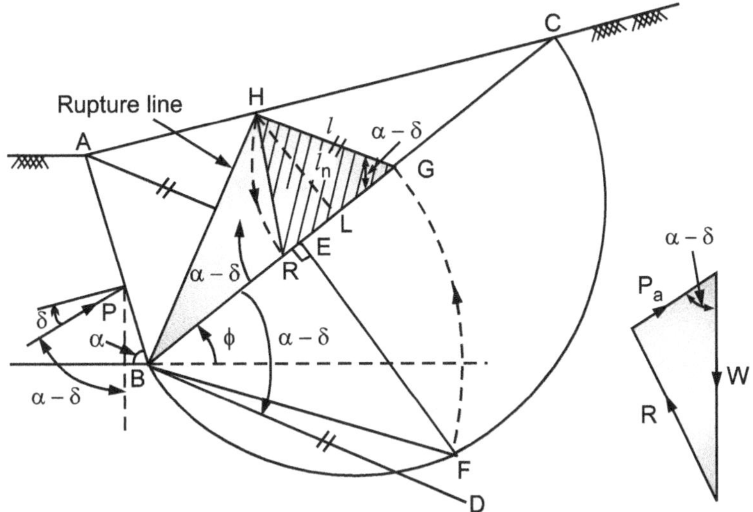

Fig. 8.18 : Active earth pressure by Poncelet construction for cohesionless soils

Procedure :

- Draw the retaining wall to a suitable scale and the backfill surface at the required angle.
- Draw the ϕ-line BC to intersect the surface at C.
- Draw a semi-circle on BC as diameter.
- Draw pressure line BD at an angle $[\alpha - \delta]$ to the ϕ-line.
- Draw AE parallel to BD.
- Erect a perpendicular to BC at E to cut the semi-circle in F.
- With centre B and radius BF, draw an arc to cut BC in G.
- Draw GH parallel to AE.
- BC is now the rupture plane.
- With G as centre and HG as radius draw an arc to cut BC at R.

Now, the area of the triangle HGR in its natural units multiplied by the unit weight of the soil gives the active earth pressure P_a, that is,

$$P_a \;=\; \frac{1}{2}\,\gamma\, l\, l_n$$

where,　　　　l = length of side HG = GR

　　　　　　　l_n = height of perpendicular HL

8.9.1 Special Cases of Poncelet Construction

Two special cases may arise in Poncelet construction. They are :

Case 1 : When the slope of the ground surface i is approximately equal to the angle of friction ϕ of the backfill material.

Case 2 : When the slope of the ground surface i is equal to the angle of friction ϕ of the backfill material.

Case 1 : When i and ϕ are nearly equal :

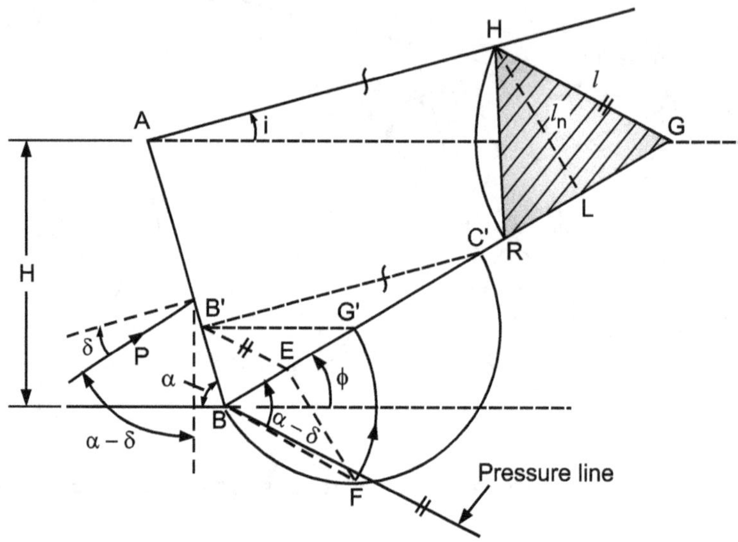

**Fig. 8.19 : Special case of Poncelet construction when the angle
i is approximately equal to ϕ**

In this case, the ϕ-line may not intersect the ground within the limits of the paper. The construction should therefore be modified so as to get the pressure triangle with the limits of the paper. The construction shown in Fig. 8.19 is explained below :

- Choose any arbitrary point C' on ϕ-line and construct a semi-circle with BC' as diameter.
- Draw B'C' parallel to ground surface.
- Draw B'E parallel to the pressure line.
- Draw EF perpendicular to the ϕ-line.
- Make BG' = BF.
- Join B'G'.
- Draw AG parallel to B'G'.
- Draw GH parallel to the pressure line.
- Make GH = GR.

Now,　　　　　　　　P_a = Area of triangle GHR × Unit weight of material

$$= \frac{1}{2}\,\gamma\,l\,l_n$$

where,　　　　　　l = GH = GR

and　　　　　　　l_n = HL

Case 2 : When the ground line and the ϕ-line are parallel to each other :

When the two lines meet at infinity, the pressure triangle may be constructed at any point on the ϕ-line. The construction procedure is [Fig. 8.20].

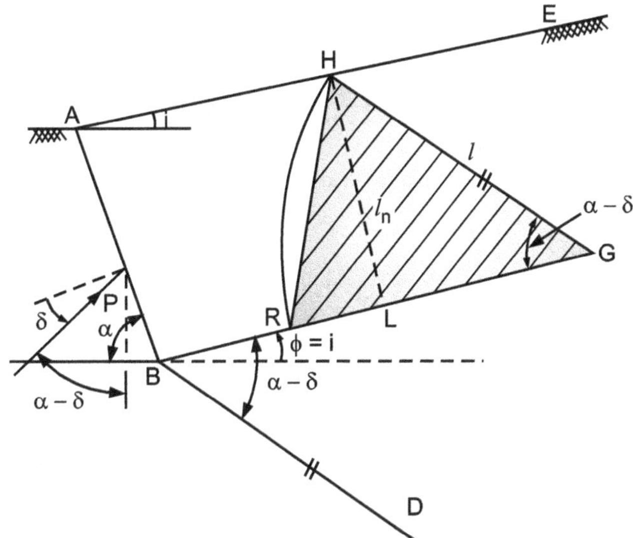

Fig. 8.20 : Special cases of poncelet construction when i = φ for active case

- From any point G on the φ-line, draw line GH parallel to the pressure line BD.
- Make GR = GH. The pressure triangle is GHR.

$$\therefore \qquad P_a \; = \; \frac{1}{2}\, l\, l_n \; = \; HG \; = \; GR$$

and $\qquad\qquad l_n \; = \; HL$

In this case, the φ-line itself is the rupture line.

8.10 CULMANN'S GRAPHICAL METHOD　　　[Dec. 13, May 16, 17]

Culmann developed a method which is more general than Rehbann's method. It can be used to determine Coulomb's earth pressure for ground surface of any configuration, for various types of surcharge loads and layered backfills.

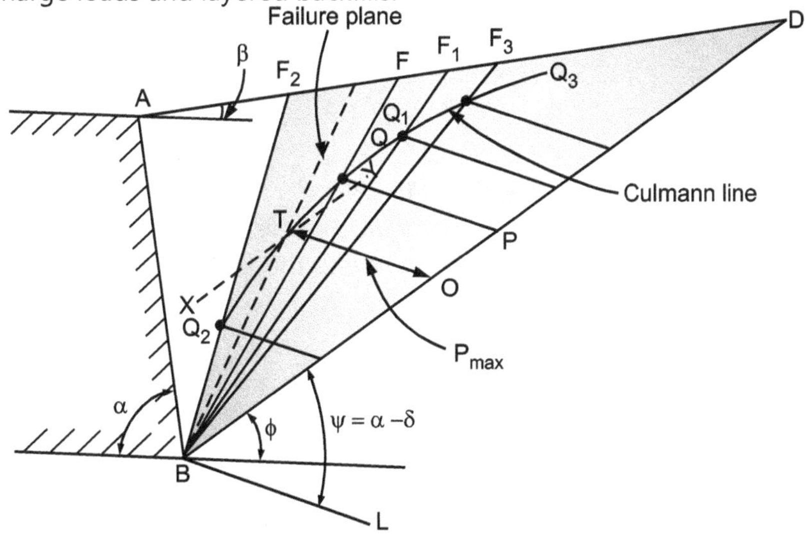

Fig. 8.21 : Culmann's graphical method

The procedure consists of the following steps :

Procedure :

- Draw the retaining wall AB to the scale.
- Draw the ϕ-line BD.
- A line BL is drawn at an angle ψ with line BD, such that $\psi = \alpha - \delta$.
- A failure surface BF is assumed, and the weight [W] of failure wedge ABF [$\gamma \cdot$ABF] is computed.
- The weight [W] is plotted along BD such that BP = W.
- A line PQ is drawn from point P parallel to BL to intersect the failure surface BF and Q.
- The length PQ represents the magnitude of P_a required to maintain equilibrium for the assumed failure plane.
- Several other failure planes BF_2, BF_1, BF_3 etc. are assumed and the procedure is repeated. Thus, the point Q_2, Q_1, Q_3, etc. are obtained.
- A smooth curve is drawn joining points Q_2, Q, Q_1, Q_3 etc. The curve is called Culmann's line.
- A line XY [shown dotted] is drawn tangential to the Culmann line and parallel to BD. Point T is the point of tangency.
- The magnitude of the largest value of P_a is measured by drawing a line TO from T on BD and parallel to BL. It is equal to Coulomb's pressure [P_a].
- The actual failure plane passes through the point T [shown dotted].

SOLVED EXAMPLES

Example 8.1 : Determine the lateral earth pressure at rest per unit length of the wall shown in Fig. 8.22. Also determine the location of the resultant earth pressure. Take $K_o = 1 - \sin \phi$. **(Dec. 13 6 M)**

Solution :

$$K_o = 1 - \sin \phi = 1 - \sin 30 = 0.50$$

At point B :
$$P_o = K_o \times \gamma \times 2$$
$$= 0.5 \times 17 \times 2 = 17 \ kN/m^2$$

At point C :
$$P_o = 2 \times K_o \cdot \gamma + 2K_o \times \gamma_b + 2 \cdot \gamma_w$$
$$= 0.5 \times 2 \times 17 + 0.5 \times 2 [19 - 10] + 2 \times 10$$
$$= 17 + 9 + 20 = \mathbf{46 \ kN/m^2}$$

Fig. 8.22 shows the pressure distribution diagram. The diagram has been divided into four parts. Let P_1, P_2, P_3 and P_4 be the total pressures due to these.

Thus,
$$P_1 = \frac{1}{2} \times 17 \times 2 = 17 \ kN$$

$$P_2 = 2 \times 17 = 34 \ kN$$

$$P_3 = \frac{1}{2} \times 9 \times 2 = 9 \ kN$$

$$P_4 = \frac{1}{2} \times 20 \times 2 = 20 \ kN$$

$$P_o = P_1 + P_2 + P_3 + P_4 = 17 + 34 + 9 + 20 = \mathbf{80\ kN}$$

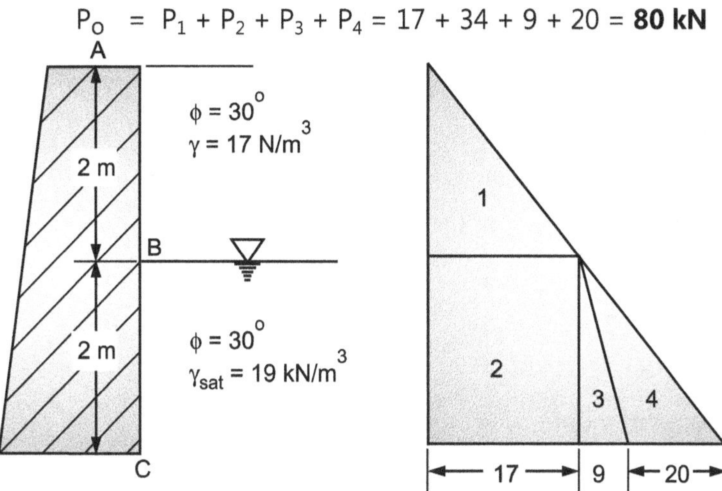

Fig. 8.22

The line of action is determined by taking moment about C.

$$P_o\, Z = 17 \times 2.667 + 34 \times 1.0 + 9.0 \times 0.667 + 20 \times 0.667$$

$$\therefore \qquad Z = \frac{45.3 + 34 + 6 + 13.3}{80} = \mathbf{1.23\ m}$$

Example 8.2 : Determine the active pressure on the retaining wall shown in Fig. 8.23.

Solution : For upper layer,

$$K_{a_1} = \frac{1 - \sin 35^o}{1 + \sin 35^o} = 0.271$$

For lower layer,

$$K_{a_2} = \frac{1 - \sin 38^o}{1 + \sin 38^o} = 0.238$$

At point B,

$$P_a = K_{a_1} \cdot \gamma \cdot H_1$$
$$= 0.271 \times 17 \times 2.5 = 11.5\ kN/m^2$$

At point C,

$$P_a = K_{a_2} \cdot \gamma \cdot H_1 + K_{a_2} \cdot \gamma_b \cdot H_2 + \gamma_w H_2$$
$$= 10.1 + 4.8 + 25 = 39.9\ kN/m^2$$

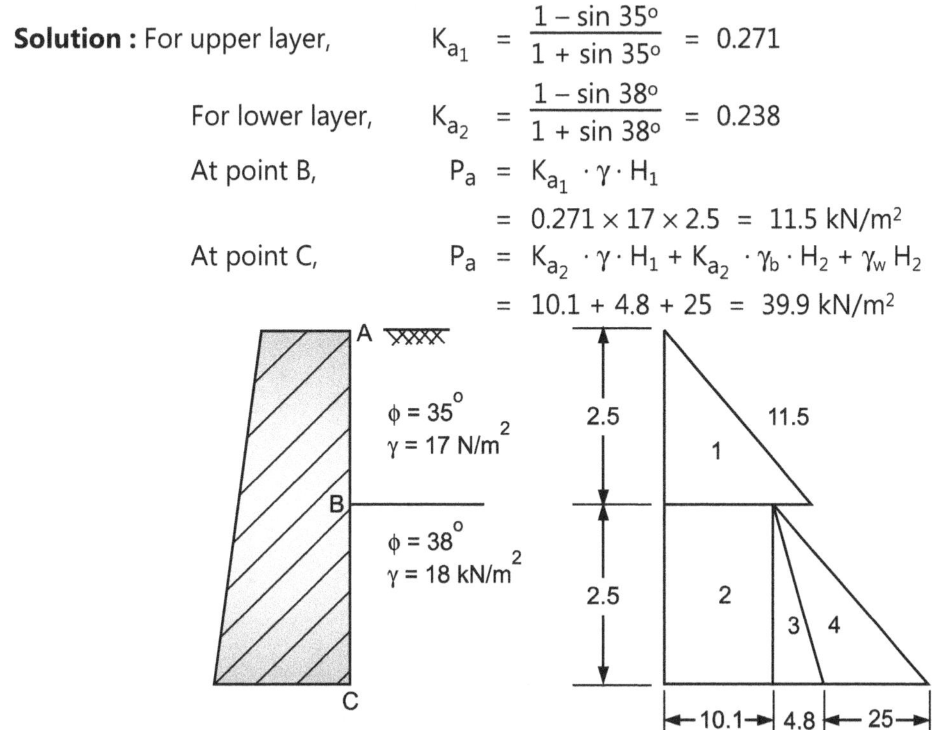

Fig. 8.23

P_1, P_2, P_3, P_4 are determined from the pressure distribution diagram.

$$P_1 = \frac{1}{2} \times 2.5 \times 11.5 = 14.4 \text{ kN}$$

$$P_2 = 2.5 \times 10.1 = 25.3 \text{ kN}$$

$$P_3 = \frac{1}{2} \times 2.5 \times 4.8 = 6 \text{ kN}$$

$$P_4 = \frac{1}{2} \times 2.5 \times 25 = 31.3 \text{ kN}$$

Total $P_a = 77.0$ kN

Taking moment about C,

$$Z = \frac{14.4 \times 3.33 + 25.3 \times 12.5 + 6 \times 0.8333 + 31.3 \times 0.8333}{77} = \mathbf{5.1336 \text{ m}}$$

Example 8.3 : Determine the active pressure on the wall shown in Fig. 8.24 using Rankine's theory.

Solution :

$$K_a = \cos\beta \times \frac{\cos\beta - \sqrt{\cos^2\beta - \cos^2\phi}}{\cos\beta + \sqrt{\cos^2\beta - \cos^2\phi}}$$

where, $\beta = 15°$ and $\phi = 30°$

$\therefore$ $K_a = 0.373$

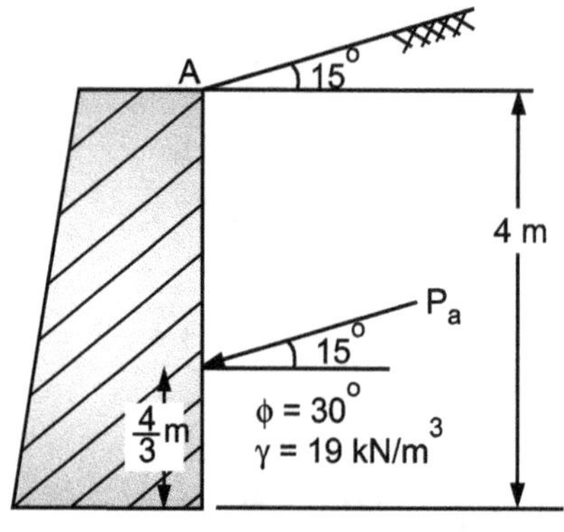

Fig. 8.24

$$P_a \text{ at } B = K_a \cdot \gamma \cdot H$$

$$= 0.373 \cdot 19 \cdot 4$$

$$\text{Total pressure, } P_a = \frac{1}{2} \times 0.373 \times 19 \times [4]^2$$

$$= \mathbf{56.7 \text{ kN}}$$

Pressure acts at a height $\frac{4}{3}$ m and is inclined at 15° with the normal.

Example 8.4 : A vertical excavation was made in a clay deposit having unit weight of 20 kN/m^3. It cracked after the digging reached the depth of 4 metres.

Calculate : [i] Total active earth pressure, [ii] Total passive earth pressure.

Solution : Critical height H_c of an unsupported vertical cut in cohesive soil is given by,

$$H_c = \frac{4C}{\gamma} \tan \alpha$$

As $\phi = 0$,　　　　$\tan \alpha = \tan\left(45 + \frac{\phi}{2}\right) = 1$

$$C = \frac{H_c \cdot \gamma}{4} = \frac{4 \times 20}{4} = 20 \text{ kN/m}^2$$

[i] Total active earth pressure is given by,

$$P_a = \frac{1}{2}\gamma H^2 \cdot \cot^2\alpha - 2CH \cot\alpha$$

$$= \frac{1}{2} \times 20 \times [8]^2 \cdot \cot^2 45 - 2 \times 20 \times 8 \cdot \cot 45$$

$$= 640 - 320 = 320 \text{ kN/m}^2$$

[ii]　Total passive earth pressure is given by,

$$P_p = \frac{1}{2}\gamma H \tan^2\alpha + 2CH \tan\alpha$$

$$= \frac{1}{2} \times 20 \times [8]^2 + 2 \times 20 \times 8$$

$$= 640 + 320 = \textbf{960 kN/m}^2$$

Example 8.5 : For an earth retaining structure shown in Fig. 8.25, construct earth pressure diagram for active state and find the total thrust per unit length of wall.

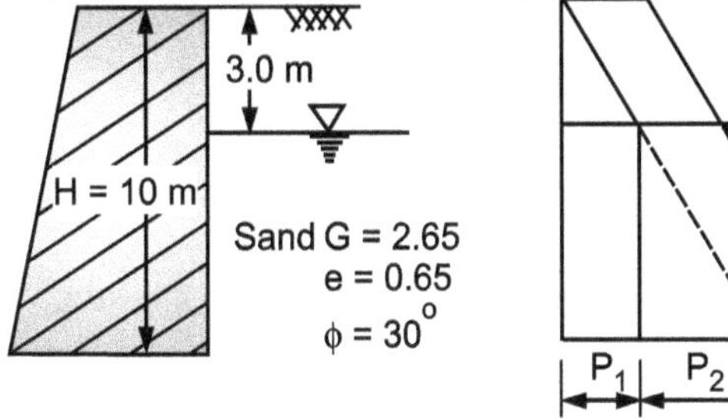

Fig. 8.25

Solution :　　For $\phi = 30°$,　　$K_a = \dfrac{1 - \sin 30}{1 + \sin 30} = 0.333$

Dry unit weight,　　$\gamma_d = \dfrac{G}{1 + e} \cdot \gamma_w$

$$= \frac{2.65}{1 + 0.65} \times 10 = 16 \text{ kN/m}^2$$

Submerged unit weight,

$$\gamma_b = \frac{G-1}{1+e} \cdot \gamma_w$$

$$= \frac{2.65-1}{1+0.65} \times 10 = 10 \text{ kN/m}^2$$

Assuming the soil above the water table as dry,

$$P_1 = K_a\, \gamma\, H_1$$
$$= 0.333 \times 16 \times 3 = 15.984 \text{ kN/m}^2$$
$$P_2 = K_a\, \gamma_b\, H_z$$
$$= 0.333 \times 10 \times 7 = 23.31 \text{ kN/m}^2$$
$$P_3 = K_a \cdot q$$
$$= 0.33 \times 14 = 4.66 \text{ kN/m}^2$$
$$P_4 = \gamma_w\, H_z$$
$$= 10 \times 7 = 70 \text{ kN/m}^2$$

Total thrust = Sum of area of different parts of pressure diagram

$$= \frac{1}{2}\, P_1 H_1 + P_1 H_2 + \frac{1}{2}\, P_2 H_2 + P_3 [H_1 + H_2] + \frac{1}{2}\, P_4 H_2$$

$$= \mathbf{509.3 \text{ kN/m}}$$

Example 8.6 : For a retaining wall system, the following data was available :
1. Height of the wall = 7 m
2. Properties of the backfill, γ_d = 16 kN/m^2, ϕ = 35°
3. Angle of the wall friction, δ = 20°
4. Back of the wall is inclined at 20° to the vertical.
5. Backfill is sloping at 1 : 10.

Determine the magnitude of active earth pressure by Culmann's method.

Solution :

- Retaining wall is drawn to the scale 1 cm = 1 m.

  ϕ-line and pressure line is also drawn as in Fig. 8.26.

- Trial pressure lines BC_1, BC_2, BC_3 etc. are drawn by making $AC_1 = C_1 C_2 = C_2 C_3$ etc. = 2 cm.

- The length of perpendicular from B to the backfill surface = 8.2 cm.

- The area of wedges BAC_1, BAC_2, BAC_3 etc. are equal = $\frac{1}{2}$ [Base length AC_1 or AC_2 or AC_3, etc.] $\times$ 8.2 cm.

- The weight of wedges in [4] above per unit length of wall may be found out by multiplying the area by the unit weight of the soil.

- The weights of wedges BAC_1, BAC_2 etc. are respectively plotted as BD_1, BD_2 etc. on the ϕ-line using the scale 1 cm = 100 kN.

- Lines drawn parallel to the pressure line from points D_1, D_2, D_3 etc. meet the trial rupture lines BC_1, BC_2 etc. at points E_1, E_2, E_3 etc respectively.

- Pressure locus is drawn passing through the points E_1, E_2, E_3 etc.

- Line ZZ is drawn tangential to the pressure locus at a point at which this is parallel to the ϕ-line. This point coincides with point E_3.

- E_3D_3 gives the active earth pressure, P_a = 180 kN/m on the length of the wall.

- BC_3 is the critical rupture line.

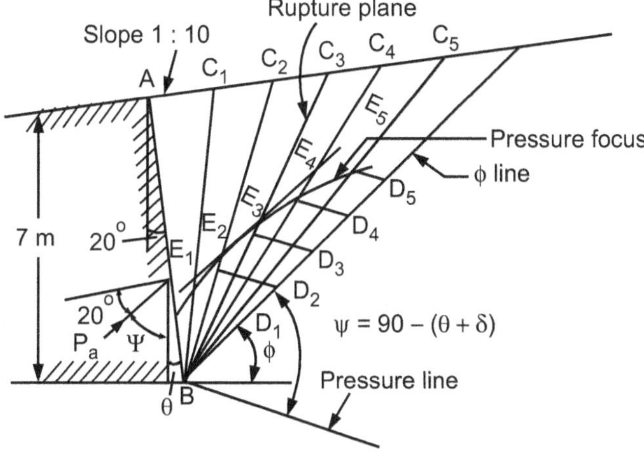

Fig. 8.26

Example 8.7 : Solve Example 6 by Poncelet construction.

Solution : $\theta = 20°$, $\delta = 20°$, $\psi + \theta + \delta = 90°$.

$$\therefore \quad \psi = 90 - \theta - \delta = \psi = 90 - 20 - 20 = 50°$$

1. Draw the wall and backfill as shown in Fig. 8.26.
2. Draw $\phi = 35°$ line and pressure line.
3. With ϕ-line BC as diameter, draw a semicircle BEC.
4. From A draw a line parallel to the pressure line, cutting the ϕ-line in point D. Draw DE perpendicular to the ϕ-line, and with B as the centre and BE as the radius draw EF.
5. From F draw a line parallel to the pressure line and cutting the ground line at G. Then the line BA is the critical failure plane.
6. Measure GF which is equal to 5.42 cm = 0.0542 m
7. Hence active earth pressure,

$$P_a = \frac{1}{2}\, \gamma\, [GF]^2 \cdot \sin \psi$$

$$= \frac{1}{2} \times 16 \times [5.42]^2 \cdot \sin 50°$$

$$= 180 \text{ kN/m length of wall}$$

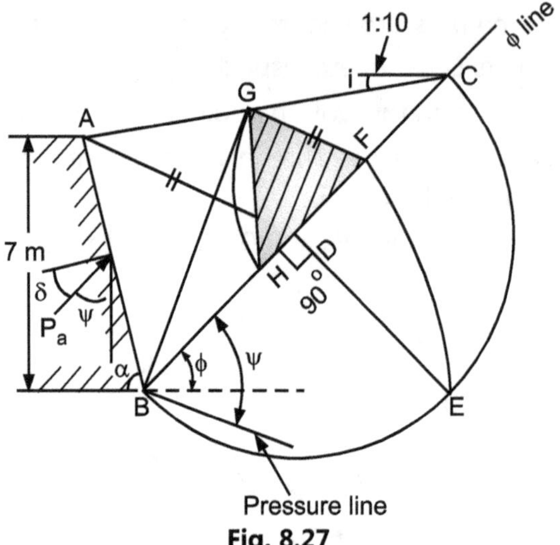

Fig. 8.27

Example 8.8 : A retaining wall 13 metres high is proposed to hold sand in (i) loose state, (ii) dense state. The values of the void ratio and φ in loose state are 0.6 and 30° while in the dense state they are 0.4 and 40°. Assuming the sand to be dry and having G = 2.7, compare the values of active earth pressure in both cases.   **(Nov. 16 [6 M])**

Solution : (i) In loose state :

$$\text{Dry unit weight of sand} = \frac{G \cdot \gamma_w}{1 + e} = \frac{2.7 \times 10}{1 + 0.6} = \textbf{16.9 kN/m}^3$$

(ii) In dense state :

$$\text{Dry unit weight of sand} = \frac{2.7 \times 10}{1 + 0.4} = \textbf{19.3 kN/m}^3$$

Coefficient of active earth pressure, K_a :

- In loose state : $$K_a = \frac{1 - \sin \phi}{1 + \sin \phi} = \frac{1 - 0.5}{1 + 0.5} = \textbf{0.333}$$

- In dense state : $$K_a = \frac{1 - 0.643}{1 + 0.643} = \textbf{0.217}$$

$$\text{Active earth pressure} = \frac{1}{2} K_a \cdot \gamma_d \, h^2$$

- In loose state : $$= \frac{1}{2} \times 0.333 \times 16.9 \times [13]^2$$
  $$= \textbf{475.5 kN/m length}$$

- In dense state : $$= \frac{1}{2} \times 0.217 \times 19.3 \times [13]^2$$
  $$= \textbf{353 kN/m length}$$

It may be noted that the active pressure on wall is more when the soil is in loose state, than that in the dense state.

Example 8.9 : Define conjugate stresses and conjugate ratio for a non-cohesive sloping ground surface of finite slope, extending at an angle β with the horizontal. State the expression for the conjugate ratio for active and passive states of plastic equilibrium.

Solution : Two stresses are called conjugated stresses when the direction of one stress is parallel to the plane on which the other stress acts. The ratio of the smaller stress to the larger stress [conjugate] is known as the conjugate ratio.

Consider a sloping ground surface of infinite extent at an angle β with the horizontal of a non-cohesive soil, $[\gamma, C = 0, \phi]$. Fig. 8.28 (a) shows a soil element at point A at depth Z with backfill. Let σ_v and P be the conjugate stresses, σ_v being vertical and P being parallel to the sloping backfill. The intensity of the vertical stress $[\sigma_v]$ on the element is given by :

$$\sigma_v = \frac{\text{Weight of element width 'b'}}{\text{Area of cross-section}}$$

$$= \frac{\gamma_z\,[b \times 1]}{b \times 1 \sec \beta} = \gamma_z \cos \beta \qquad \ldots \text{(i)}$$

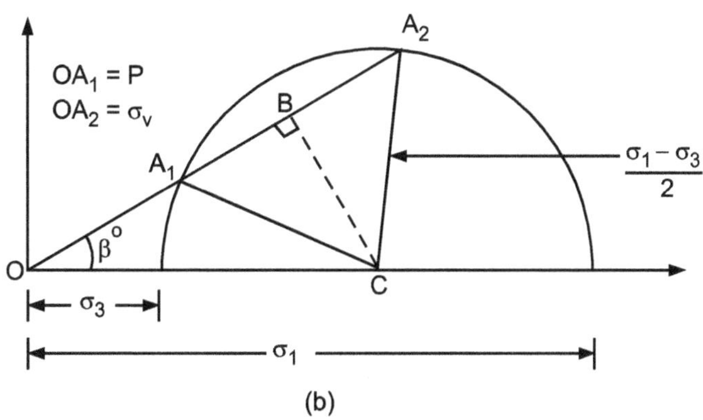

Fig. 8.28

Let σ_1 and σ_3 be the major and minor principal stresses on the soil element at A.

Fig. 8.28 [b] shows Mohr circle for σ_1 and σ_3. The obliquity of σ_v and P is $\beta°$. Hence, draw a line at obliquity $\beta°$ through origin O, to cut the circle at A_1 and A_2. Thus, OA_1 represents resultant stress P and $OA_2 = \sigma_v$. Draw CB perpendicular to A_1A_2.

Now,
$$OB = OC \cos \beta = \frac{\sigma_1 + \sigma_3}{2} \cdot \cos \beta$$

$$BC = OC \sin \beta = \frac{\sigma_1 + \sigma_3}{2} \cdot \sin \beta$$

$$A_1B = BA_2 = \sqrt{A_1C^2 - BC^2}$$

$$= \sqrt{\left(\frac{\sigma_1 - \sigma_3}{2}\right)^2 - \left(\frac{\sigma_1 + \sigma_3}{2}\right)^2} \cdot \sin \beta$$

But,
$$\sigma_1 - \sigma_3 = [\sigma_1 + \sigma_3] \cdot \sin \phi \ \text{ and } \ \sin \phi = \frac{\sigma_1 - \sigma_3}{\sigma_1 + \sigma_3}$$

Hence,
$$A_1B = BA_2 = \frac{\sigma_1 + \sigma_3}{2} \sqrt{\sin^2\phi - \sin^2\beta}$$

Now, stress, $\sigma_v = OB + BA_2$

or,
$$\sigma_v = \frac{\sigma_1 + \sigma_3}{2} \cos \beta + \frac{\sigma_1 + \sigma_3}{2} \sqrt{\sin^2\phi - \sin^2\beta} \qquad \text{... (ii)}$$

and stress, $P = OB - A_1B$

$$= \frac{\sigma_1 + \sigma_3}{2} \cos \beta - \frac{\sigma_1 + \sigma_3}{2} \sqrt{\sin^2\phi - \sin^2\beta} \qquad \text{... (iii)}$$

Dividing (ii) and (iii), we get,

$$\frac{P}{\sigma_v} = K = \frac{\cos \beta - \sqrt{\sin^2\phi - \sin^2\beta}}{\cos \beta + \sqrt{\sin^2\phi - \sin^2\beta}}$$

or,
$$\frac{P}{\sigma_v} = K = \frac{\cos \beta - \sqrt{\cos^2\beta - \cos^2\phi}}{\cos \beta + \sqrt{\cos^2\beta - \cos^2\phi}} \qquad [\text{as } \sin^2\phi = (1 - \cos^2\phi)]$$

where K is called conjugate ratio.

$\therefore \qquad P = K\sigma_v$

Case (I) For active state :

From equation (i),
$$P = \text{lateral earth pressure} = P_a = \gamma_z \cdot K \cdot \cos \beta$$

or,
$$P_a = \gamma_z \cdot \cos \beta \cdot \frac{\cos \beta - \sqrt{\cos^2\beta - \cos^2\phi}}{\cos \beta + \sqrt{\cos^2\beta - \cos^2\phi}}$$

or,
$$P_a = K_a \cdot \gamma_z$$

where,
$$K_a = \cos \beta \cdot \frac{\cos \beta - \sqrt{\cos^2\beta - \cos^2\phi}}{\cos \beta + \sqrt{\cos^2\beta - \cos^2\phi}}$$

When $\beta = 0$ [horizontal ground surface], then $K_a = \dfrac{1 - \sin \phi}{1 + \sin \phi}$

Case II : For passive state :

Similarly,

$$K_p = \cos\beta \cdot \frac{\cos\beta + \sqrt{\cos^2\beta - \cos^2\phi}}{\cos\beta - \sqrt{\cos^2\beta - \cos^2\phi}}$$

where, K_p = coefficient of passive earth pressure

Example 8.10 : A smooth vertical wall retains a level backfill with $\gamma = 18.5$ kN/m³, $\phi = 30°$ and $C = 0$ to a depth of 10 m. Draw the lateral pressure diagram and compute the total thrust on the retaining wall. What will be the active pressure if water stands at a depth of 4 m ?   **(Nov. 16, 6M; May 16, 7 M]**

Solution :

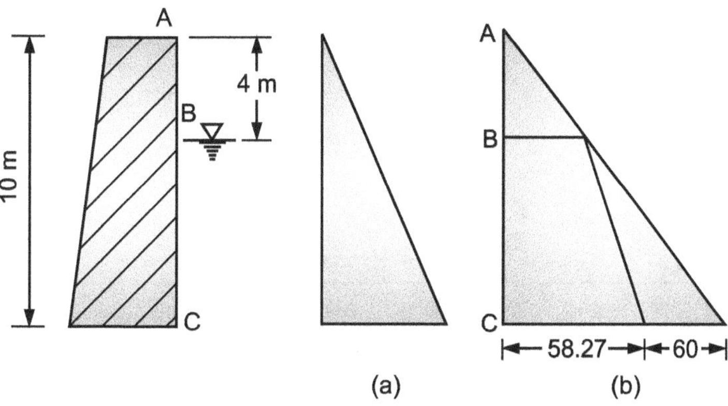

Fig. 8.29

$$K_a = \frac{1 - \sin 30}{1 + \sin 30} = 0.33$$

Case I : Without water table Fig. 8.29 (a) :

$$P_a \text{ at base C} = K_a\,\gamma H = 0.33 \times 18.5 \times 10 = 61.05 \text{ kN/m}^2$$

$$\text{Total pressure, } P_a = \frac{1}{2} \times 61.05 \times 10 = \textbf{305.25 kN/m}^2$$

Case II : With water table at 4 m depth Fig. 8.29 (b) :

At B :

$$P_a = K_a \cdot \gamma H_1$$
$$= 0.33 \times 18.5 \times 4 = \textbf{24.42 kN/m}^2$$

At C :

$$P_a = K_a\,\gamma \cdot H_1 + \gamma_w\,H_2$$
$$= 0.33 \times 18.5 \times 10 + 10 \times 6 = 121.05 \text{ kN/m}^2$$

$$\text{Total } P_a = \frac{1}{2} \times 61.05 \times 10 + \frac{1}{2} \times 6 \times 60$$

$$= 305.25 + 180 = \textbf{485.25 kN/m}^2$$

Taking moment about C :

$$Z = \frac{305.25 \times 3.33 + 180 \times 2}{485.25} = \textbf{2.84}$$

Example 8.11 : A vertical retaining wall retains the level backfill of sand. The water level stands H_1 metres below the top of the backfill. Draw the pressure distribution diagram for the active conditions.

Solution :

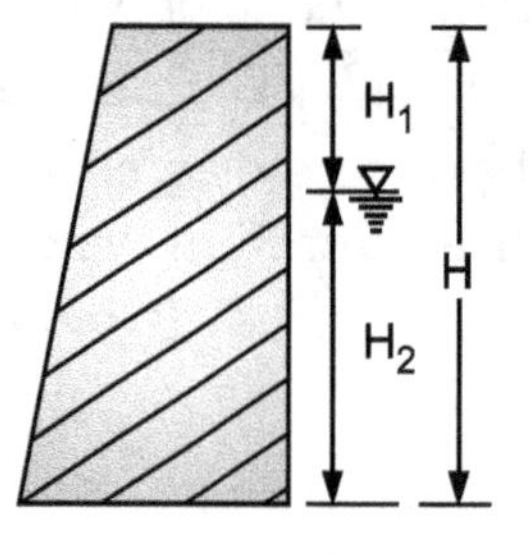
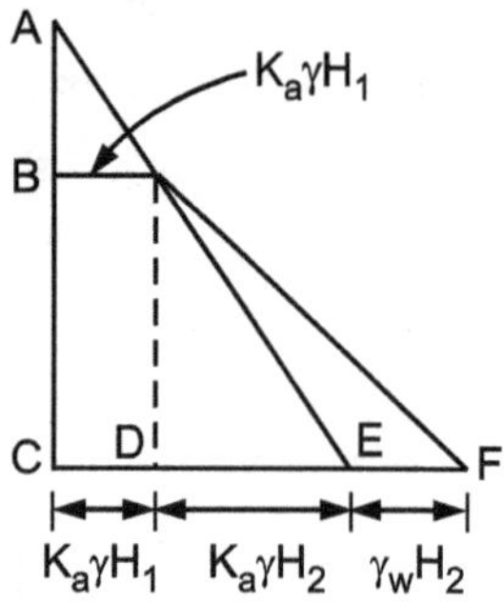

Fig. 8.30

Pressure at A : $P_a = 0$

Pressure at B : $P_a = K_a \gamma H_1$

Pressure at C : $P_a = K_a \gamma H_1 + K_a \gamma H_2 + \gamma_w H_2$

Example 8.12 : A retaining wall 10 m high retains a cohesionless soil having $\phi = 30°$. The surface of the soil is level with the top of the wall. The top 3 m of the fill has a unit weight 18 kN/m^3 and that of the rest is 20 kN/m^3. Determine magnitude and point of application of active pressure per 'm' length of wall. The value of ϕ same for both the soil layers.

[May 14, 6 M]

Solution :

$$K_a = \frac{1 - \sin f}{1 + \sin f} = \frac{1 - \sin 30°}{1 + \sin 30°} = 0.333$$

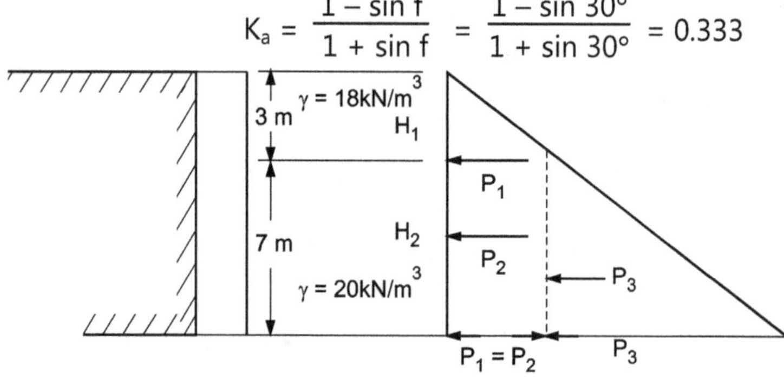

Fig. 3

$$P_1 = \frac{k_a \gamma H^2}{2} = \frac{0.333 \times 18 \times 3^2}{2} = 26.99 \text{ kN/m}$$

acting at $Z_1 = 7 + \dfrac{1}{3}(3) = 8$ m above base

$$P_2 = k_a \times 18 \times 3 \times 7$$
$$= 0.33 \times 18 \times 3 \times 7 = 125.98 \text{ kN/m}$$

acting at $Z_2 = \dfrac{7}{2} = 3.5$ m above base

$$P_3 = k_a\gamma\frac{H^2}{2} = 0.333 \times 20 \times \frac{7^2}{2} = 163.31 \text{ kN/m}$$

Acting at $\qquad \dfrac{7}{3} = 2.333$ above base

Total $\qquad P = 26.99 + 125 + 163.31 = 316.287$ kN/m

Acting at $\Rightarrow$

$$Z = \frac{26.99 \times 8 + 125.98 \times 3.5 + 163.31 \times 2.333}{316.287}$$

Z = 3.28 m above base

Example 8.13 : Define the term lateral earth pressure in passive state. A wall 8 m high with a smooth vertical back retains dry cohesionless sand with $\gamma = 18$ kN/m^3 and $\phi = 30°$. Determine the total lateral pressure per metre length of the wall in passive state.   **(Dec. 14, 7 M)**

Solution : Rankine's Theory : In the case of a passive state of plastic equilibrium, the lateral pressure is the major principal stress while the vertical pressure is the minor principal stress. Thus,

$$\sigma_h = P_p = \sigma_1$$
$$\sigma_v = \sigma_3 = \gamma.Z$$

Substituting this in the principal stress relationship:

$$\sigma_1 = \sigma_3 \tan^2\alpha \qquad\qquad [\text{For } C = 0]$$

We get, $\qquad\qquad \sigma_h = \sigma_v \tan^2\alpha$

Where, $\qquad\qquad P_p = $ Passive earth pressure intensity,

$K_p = $ Rankine's coefficient of passive earth pressure

Or,

$$Kp = \tan2\alpha = N\phi = \frac{1 + \sin\phi}{1 - \sin\phi} - \frac{1}{K_a}$$

$$K_p = \frac{1 + \sin\phi}{1 - \sin\phi} = \frac{1 + 0.5}{1 - 0.5} = \frac{1.5}{0.5} = 3$$

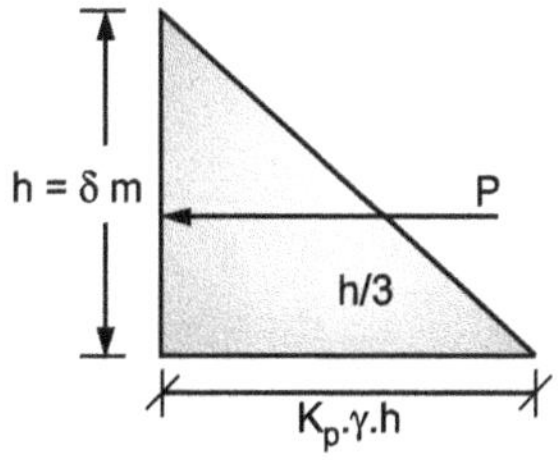

Fig. 8

$$P = (K_p \cdot \gamma \cdot h)\left(\frac{h}{2}\right) = 3 \times 18 \times \frac{8^2}{2}$$

$$= 27 \times 64$$

$$= 1728 \text{ kN/m}$$

It will act horizontally at 8/3 m from bottom.

Example 8.14 : In a cohesionless soil deposit having unit weigth of 15 kN/m^3 and angle of internal friction ϕ of 30°. Determine the active and passive lateral pressure intensities at depth of 10 m.   **(Nov. 15, 7M)**

Solution: Given Data

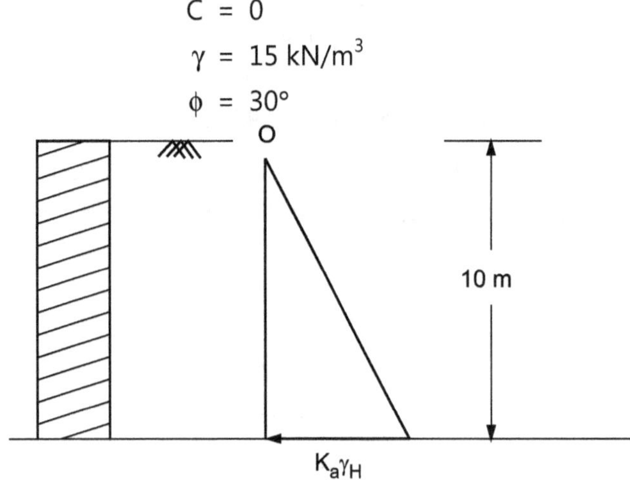

Fig. 2

For active lateral earth pressure intensity

$$K_a = \frac{1 - \sin \phi}{1 + \sin \phi}$$

$$= \frac{1 - \sin 30°}{1 + \sin 30°} = \frac{1}{3}$$

$$p_a = k_a \, \gamma \, H; \quad P_a = \frac{1}{3} \times 15 \times 10$$

$$p_a = 50 \text{ kN/m}^2 \text{ at depth 10 m}$$

For Passive lateral earth pressure

$$K_a = \frac{1 + \sin \phi}{1 - \sin \phi}$$

$$= \frac{1 + \sin 30°}{1 - \sin 30°} = 3$$

$$P_p = k_p \, \gamma H$$

$$= 3 \times 15 \times 10$$

$$P_p = 450 \text{ kN/m}^2 \text{ at depth 10 m}$$

SUMMARY

1. A force of soil in contact with any vertical or inclined face of structure is known as lateral Earth Pressure.

2. Assumption in Rankine theory are as following :

   (a) The soil mass is homogenous

   (b) The soil dry and cohesionless

   (c) The ground surface is plane.

   (d) The back of retaining wall is smooth and vertical.

3. Rankine's theory of Earth Pressure is applicable only smooth vertical walls.

4. Rehbann's construction and Culmann's graphical method used for determination of total active pressure.

5. **Formula :** (i) $K_o = \dfrac{\mu}{1-\mu}$ 　　　　(ii) $P_o = \int K_o \, \gamma \cdot Z \, dZ = \dfrac{1}{2} K_o \, \gamma \, H^2$

   (iii) $p_a = \dfrac{K_a \cdot \gamma H^2}{2}$ 　　　　(iv) $Z_e = \dfrac{q}{\gamma}$

   (v) $H_c = \dfrac{4C}{\gamma}$ 　　　　(vi) $P_a = \dfrac{1}{2} \gamma H^2 \cot^2\alpha - 2CH \cot^2\alpha + \dfrac{2C^2}{\gamma}$

   (vii) $P_p = \dfrac{1}{2} \gamma H^2 \tan^2\alpha + 2CH \tan\alpha$

EXERCISE

1. A retaining wall with a vertical smooth back is 8 m high. It supports a cohesionless soil $[\gamma = 19 \text{ kN/m}^3, \phi = 30°]$. The surface of soil is horizontal. Determine the thrust in the wall.

   (**Ans.** 202.7 kN/m)

2. A retaining wall has a vertical back and is 8 m high. The back of the wall is smooth and the upper surface of the fill is horizontal. Determine the thrust on the wall per unit length. Take $C = 10 \text{ kN/m}^2$, $\gamma = 18 \text{ kN/m}^3$, $\phi = 20°$. Neglect the tension.

   (**Ans.** 181.3 kN)

3. A retaining wall is 7 m high, with its back face smooth and vertical. It retains sand with its surface horizontal. Using Rankine's theory, determine active earth pressure at the

base when the backfill is [a] dry, [b] saturated, [c] submerged, with water table at the surface. Take γ = 18 kN/m³ and ϕ = 30°, γ_{sat} = 21 kN/m³.

(**Ans.** 420 kN/m², 4.9 kN/m², 25.7 kN/m²)

4.   Determine the passive pressure per unit run for a retaining wall 4 m high, with β = 15°, ϕ = 30° and γ = 19 kN/m². The back face of the wall is smooth and vertical.

(**Ans.** 58.3 kN)

5.   A smooth vertical wall retains a level surface with γ = 18 kN/m³, ϕ = 33°, to a depth of 8 m. Water table stands at depth of 4 m. Draw the lateral pressure diagram and compute the total active pressure.

(**Ans.** 151.36 kN)

6.   Determine the active pressure and passive pressure, using Coulomb's theory on the wall as shown in Fig. 8.50.

(**Ans.** 73.0 kN, 413 kN)

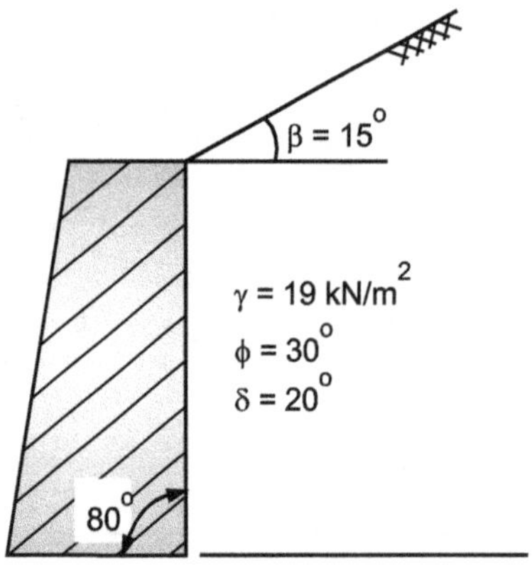

Fig. 8.50

7.   A vertical retaining wall 10 m high supports a cohesionless soil [γ = 18 kN/m³]. The upper surface of backfill rises from the crest of wall at an angle of 15° with the horizontal. Determine the total active pressure by Culmann's method and check the pressure obtained by Rehbann's construction. Take ϕ = 30° and δ = 20°.

(**Ans.** 333.5 kN)

8.   A smooth vertical wall retains a level backfill with γ = 18 kN/m³, ϕ = 33° to a depth of 8 m. Water table stands at a depth of 4 m and it carries a surcharge of 50 kN/m². Determine the total active pressure and its point of application from bottom.

(**Ans.** P_a = 269.36 kN/m, length Z = 3.35 m)

9.   What are the different types of earth pressure ? Give examples.

10.   Define earth pressure at rest. Show the earth pressure distribution on a retaining wall, assuming the soil is dry.

11.   What are the assumptions of Rankine's theory? Derive an expression for active pressure and passive pressure.

12.   What is Coulomb's wedge theory ? Compare Rankine's theory and Coulomb's theory.

13.   Describe Rehbann's construction. What is its use ?

14.   Discuss Culmann's method for the determination of active earth pressure.

15.   Show that the coefficient of lateral earth pressure at rest K_O is given by : $K_O = \dfrac{\mu}{1 - \mu}$

      where μ is the Poisson's ratio.

16.   Derive an expression for the vertical cut that can stand unsupported in a purely cohesive soil.

17.   With the help of neat sketches, differentiate between Rankine's active and passive state of plastic equilibrium.

18.   Find the expression for the active and passive state of pressure at any point in a semifinite, horizontal, homogeneous, isotropic medium possessing both c and ϕ.

19.   State the assumptions in Coulomb's theory of earth pressure.

SOLVED UNIVERSITY QUESTIONS AND NUMERICALS

December 2013

1.   Define active earth pressure, passive earth pressure and earth pressure at rest and explain the same with neat sketch.   **[6]**

     [**Ans.:** Refer Article 8.6, 8.7]

2.   Determine the lateral earth pressure at rest per unit length for the wall of 4 m height retaining wall backfill which has $\phi = 30°$ and unit weight of soil = 17 kN/m^3 for 2 m depth below ground level and 19 kN/m^3 for remaining depth. Assume ground water level at 2 m below ground level. Assume $k_0 = 1$ $\sin\phi$ and $\gamma_w = 10$ kN/m^3. Also determine location of the resultant earth pressure.   **[6]**

     [**Ans.:** Refer Example 8.1]

3.   Explain Culman's graphical method of determination of earth pressure.   **[6]**

     [**Ans.:** Refer Article 8.10]

4.   Discuss points of differentiation between Rankine's and Coulombs theory of earth pressure.   **[6]**

     [**Ans.:** Refer Article 8.6, 8.8]

May 2014

1. State the assumptions made in Rankine's earth pressure theory and distinguish between 'active' and 'passive' earth pressure. **[7]**

   [**Ans.:** Refer Article 8.5, 8.6, 8.7]

2. A retaining wall 10 m high retains a cohesionless soil having $\phi = 30°$. The surface of the soil is level with the top of the wall. The top 3 m of the fill has a unit weight 18 kN/m^3 and that of the rest is 20 kN/m^3. Determine magnitude and point of application of active pressure per 'm' length of wall. The value of ϕ same for both the soil layers. **[6]**

   [**Ans.:** Refer Example 8.12]

3. Explain Coulomb's wedge theory. **[7]**

   [**Ans.:** Refer Article 8..8]

December 2014

1. Determine the relation for lateral earth pressure in active state for submerged cohesionless backfill. **[7]**

   [**Ans.:** Refer Article 8.5.2]

2. Explain step by step procedure for determination of lateral earth pressure graphically by Rehbann's method with neat sketch. **[6]**

   [**Ans.:** Refer Article 8.9]

3. Define the term lateral earth pressure in passive state. A wall 8 m high with a smooth vertical back retains dry cohesionless sand with $\gamma = 18 \ kN/m^3$ and $\phi = 30°$. Determine the total lateral pressure per metre length of the wall in passive state. **[7]**

   [**Ans.:** Refer Example 8.13]

4. Determine the relation for lateral earth pressure in active state for dry and cohesive backfill. **[6]**

   [**Ans.:** Refer Article 8.6]

May 2015

1. Describe Rehbann's construction for determination of earth pressure with neat sketch. **[7]**

   [**Ans.:** Refer Article 8.9]

2. Derive the expression for the active state of pressure at any point for submerged cohesionless backfill along with pressure diagrams. **[6]**

   [**Ans.:** Refer Article 8.5.1]

November 2015

1. In a cohesionless soil deposit having unit weigth of 15 kN/m^3 and angle of internal friction ϕ of 30°. Determine the active and passive lateral pressure intensities at depth of 10 m. **[7]**

   [**Ans.:** Refer Example 8.14]

2. Define earth pressure at rest. Show that the coefficient of lateral earth pressure at rest K_0 is given by : **[6]**

$$K_0 = \frac{\mu}{1 - \mu}$$

   [**Ans.:** Refer Article 8.4]

3. What is Coulaomb's wedge theory ? Compare Rankine's theory and Coulomb's theory. **[6]**

   [**Ans.:** Refer Article 8.7, 8.8]

May 2016

1. Explain Rankine's lateral stress distribution theory for active, passive and at rest state with the assumptions involved. **[6]**

   [**Ans.:** Refer Article 8.5]

2. A smooth vertical wall retains a level backfill with γ = 18.5 kN/m^2, ϕ = 30° and C = 0 to a depth of 10 m. Draw the lateral pressure diagram and compute the total thrust on the retaining wall what will be the active pressure if water stands at s depth of 4 m? **[7]**

   [**Ans.:** Refer Example 8.10]

3. Explain Culmann's graphical method for the determination of earth pressure on retaining wall. **[6]**

   [**Ans.:** Refer Article 8.10]

4. Find the expression for the active state of pressure for cohesive backfill with no surcharge. **[7]**

   [**Ans.:** Refer Article 8.6.1]

November 2016

1. Derive the relation for lateral pressure due to submerged cohesionless backfill with neat sketch. **[7]**

   [**Ans.:** Refer Article 8.5.2]

2. A smooth vertical wall retains a level backfill with γ = 18.5 kN/m^3, ϕ = 30° and c = 0 to a depth of 10 m. Draw the lateral pressure diagram and compute the total thrust on the retaining wall. What will be the active pressure if water stands at a depth of 4m ? **[6]**

   [**Ans.:** Refer Example 8.10]

3. A retaining wall 13 metres high is proposed to hold sand in :

    (i) loose state

    (ii) dense state.

    The values of the void ratio and ϕ in loose state are 0.6 and 30° while in the dense state they are 0.4 and 40°. Assuming the sand to be dry and having G = 2.7, compare the values of active earth pressure in both cases. **[7]**

    (Assume γ_ω = 10 kN/m^3)

    [**Ans.:** Refer Example 8.8]

4. Derive an expression for the vertical cut that can stand unsupported in a purely cohesive soil. **[6]**

    [**Ans.:** Refer Article 8.6.1]

May 2017

1. Differentiate between Rankine's and Coulomb's theories of earth pressure. **[6]**

    [**Ans.:** Refer Article 8.5, 8.8]

2. Explain Active, Passive Earth Pressure with respect to wall movements with sketches. **[6]**

    [**Ans.:** Refer Article 8.3]

3. Derive the expression for the active state of pressure at any point for a submerged cohesionless backfill along with pressure diagrams. **[6]**

    [**Ans.:** Refer Article 8.5.1]

4. Discuss Culmann's graphical method for the determination of active earth pressure. **[6]**

    [**Ans.:** Refer Article 8.10]

◈ ◈ ◈

Chapter 9
STABILITY OF SLOPES

9.1 INTRODUCTION

An earth is an unsupported inclined surface of soil mass. Earth slopes are formed for railway formation, highways, embankments, earth dams, canal banks, and at many other locations. The stability of these embankments or slopes is important because their failure may lead to loss of human life as well as economical loss. Soil or rock masses with sloping surfaces may be the result of natural agencies or they may be man made. Some examples are given below :

Slides may occur in almost every conceivable manner, slowly or suddenly and with or without any apparent provocation. Usually, slides are due to excavation or undercutting the foot of an existing slope. However, in some instances, they are caused by a gradual disintegration of the structure of the soil, starting at hair cracks which subdivide the soil into angular fragments.

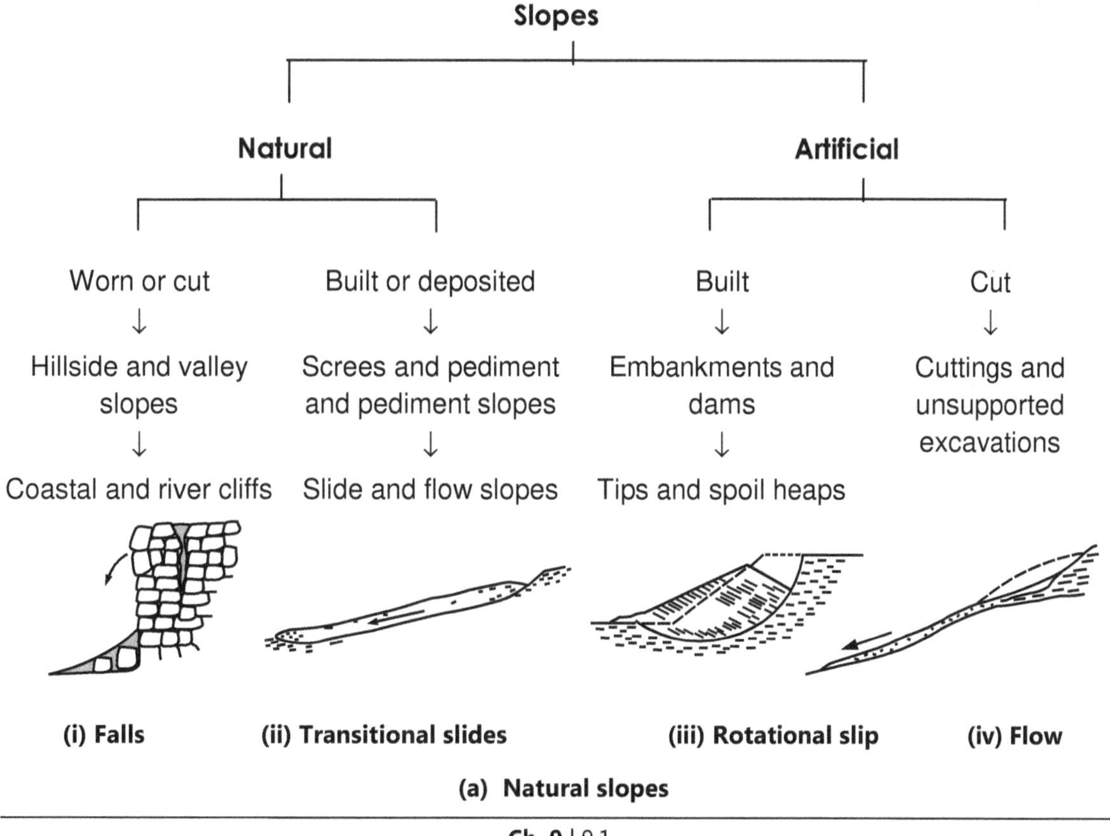

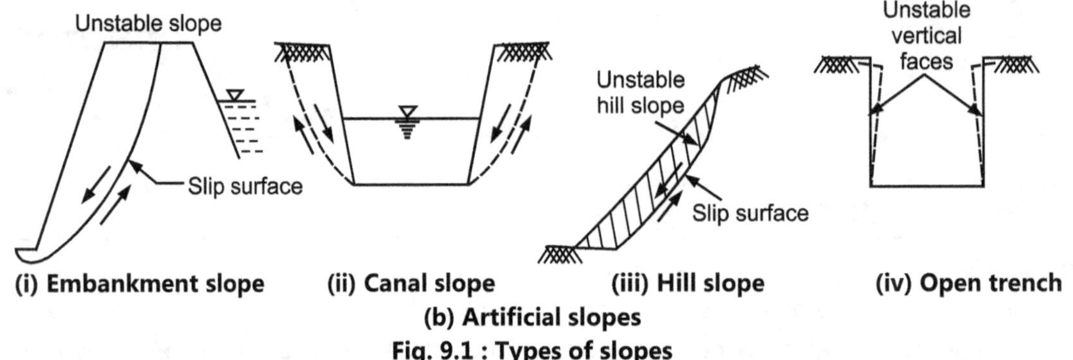

(b) Artificial slopes

Fig. 9.1 : Types of slopes

9.2 FACTORS CAUSING LANDSLIDE AND THEIR EFFECTS ON FACTOR OF SAFETY [Nov. 16, May 15,17]

Large number of factors are responsible to cause instability of a slope. Some of these are : Increase of height or rise of slope, large-scale deformations of earth crust, high frequency vibrations, creep on slope and on foundation material, rains, melting snow, frost, shrinkage, rapid drawdown, change of elevation of water table of distant aquifer and seepage from artificial source of water. These factors and their effects on the factor of safety of a slope was represented by an excellent way by Terzaghi (1950), Fig. 9.2.

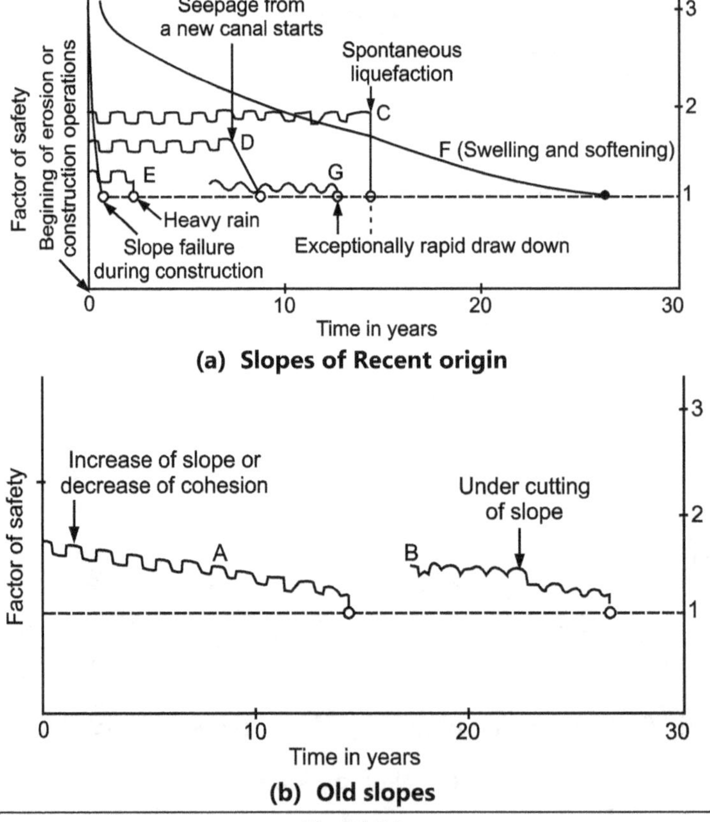

A – Progressive weathering of the slope

B – Heavy rainstorm several years after the foot of the slope undercut

C – Spontaneous liquefaction

D – Seepage through the bottom of a new unlined canal located beyond the upper edge of the slope

E – Heaviest rainfall

F – Gradual softening of stiff, fissured clay

G – Exceptionally rapid drawdown

Fig. 9.2 : Variations of the factor of safety of different slopes prior to a landslide

(Terzaghi, 1950)

9.3 TYPES OF LANDSLIDES ON CLAY SLOPES   [Nov.15]

A systematic classification of landslides in clay and other mass movements was proposed by Skempton and Hutchison (1969).

(a) Falls : Removal of lateral earth support causes bulging at the toe and tension crack at the top. The development of cracks induces additional stresses on the separating mass which ultimately leads to a fall. Clay falls are typically short-term failures in steep slopes. The majority of such slopes are found in overconsolidated fissured clays.

(b) Rotational Slides (Slips, Slumps) : In fairly uniform clays or shales, this type of slides occur. The curved surface of failure, being concave upwards, imparts a back-tilt to the slipping mass resulting in sinking at the rear and heaving at the toe. Such slides are relatively deep seated and may have sliding surfaces which are circular, shallow or non-circular. Circular slips occur typically in uniform, normally or over-consolidated clays (intact and fissured). But non-circular rotational slides usually seem to be associated with slopes of overconsolidated clays in which the degree of non-homogeneity has been produced by weathering. Shallow rotational slips, of both circular and non-circular form, are common on slopes of moderate inclination in weathered or colluvial clays.

(c) Compound Slides and Translation slides : The presence of heterogeneity within the slope predetermines the surface of failure. The heterogeneity usually consists of a weak soil layer or structural feature or a boundary between, for example, clay and rock or between weathered and unweathered material. Such heterogeneity prevents simple rotational slides but introduces translational element in the movement in combination with or without rotational slide. Compound slides are usually in soils with the presence of heterogeneity at moderate depth. Translational slides are planar and most commonly occur in the mantle of weathered or colluvial material, the heterogeneity being at shallow depth. Moreover, such slides occur as block slides or slab slides. Block slides are common in marls and sandstones whereas slab slides are a type of translational failure in weathered clay slopes.

(d) Flows : Flows form a rather neglected and little understood group of movements. Flows are mass movements which may be either of earthflow and mudflow. Earthflows are slow movements of softened weathered debris. Mudflows are glacier like in form which are often well developed below bare slopes in fissured clays.

(e) Multiple and Complex Landslides : Under this division one can distinguish certain more complex landslides on clay slopes which exhibit a multiplication or combination of the basic types of landslides described previously.

(i) Successive slips : Successive rotational slips consist of an assembly of individual shallow rotational slips. Moreover, they are common in over-consolidated fissured clays at the later stages of the free degradation process of the slopes.

(ii) Multiple Retrogressive slides : Multiple slides develop from single failure and are predominantly rotational and sometimes translational. These translational forms of multiple retrogressive slide generally develop from slab slides, and are controlled by similar factors. Moreover, the probable cause for more numerous individual retrogressive failures may be due to less cohesion of sliding mass. Multiple rotational slides occur most frequently on actively eroding slopes in which a thick stratum of overconsolidated fissured clay or clay-shale is overlain by a considerable layer of more competent rock (Fig. 9.3).

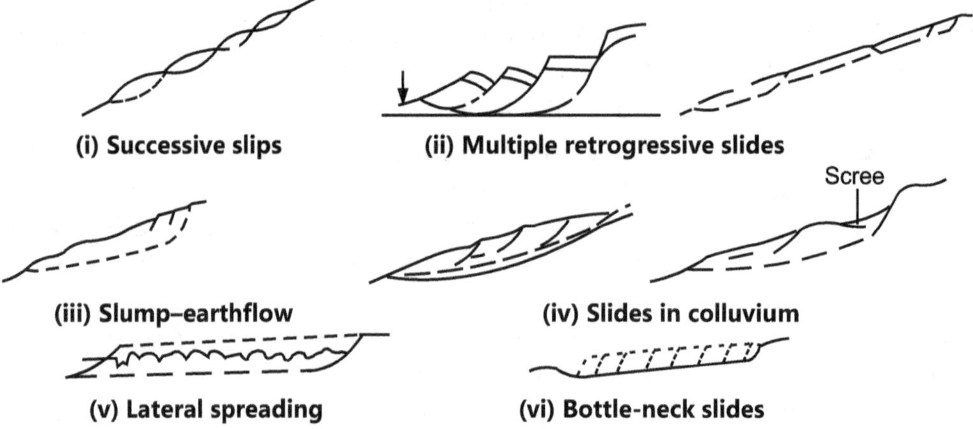

Fig. 9.3 : Multiple and complex landslides (Skempton and Hutchinson)

(iii) Slump-earth flows : These are fairly common type of mass movements which are intermediate between rotational slides and mudflows. They develop typically in a rotational slide of considerable displacement where the toe of the slipping mass which forms into a mudflow in the presence of water softens.

(iv) Slides in colluvium : Colluvium develops typically in the accumulation zones below freely degrading cliffs. The sliding material usually is so shifted and weathered that individual slipped masses are no longer distinguishable.

(v) Spreading features : These are particular type of retrogressive translation slides. The initial rapid movement dies out within a few minutes because of the gentle slopes involved.

(vi) Quick clay slides : Such slides generally being with an initial rotational slip in the bank of stream mass is in part remoulded to the consistency of a liquid which runs out of the cavity, carrying flakes of the stiff, weathered crust. In general, quick clays may fail in any one of the above mentioned forms.

The reduction in the stability of slopes is due to :

- Decrease in shearing resistance brought about by excess pore water pressure
- Leaching of salts
- Softening
- Breakage of cementation bonds and ion exchange.

According to Terzaghi, intermediate between the landslides due to external and internal causes are those due to rapid drawdown, surface erosion and spontaneous liquefaction.

9.4 SLOPE CLASSIFICATION   [May 16]

The slopes may be broadly classified as :

(i) Natural Slopes : Slopes formed by continuous process of erosion and deposition by natural agencies are called natural slopes, e.g. hill sides, river banks.

(ii) Man-made Slopes : The slopes of earth structures which result from the human construction activity are known as man-made slopes, e.g. slopes of embankment of dam, roads, rails, canals, cuts for roads and rails, filling for reclamation trench excavations etc.

The slopes whether natural or man-made may be :

(i)   Infinite slopes
(ii) Finite slopes
(iii) Homogeneous slopes
(iv) Non-homogeneous slopes

(i) Infinite slopes : A slope is infinite [Fig. 9.4 (a)] if its traverse extent is large as compared to the depth of its failure zone.

(ii) Finite slopes : Finite slopes are limited in extent. A slope is finite if its traverse extent is not that large compared to the depth of failure zone. [Fig. 9.4 b)]. The slopes of embankments, earth dams are examples of finite slopes.

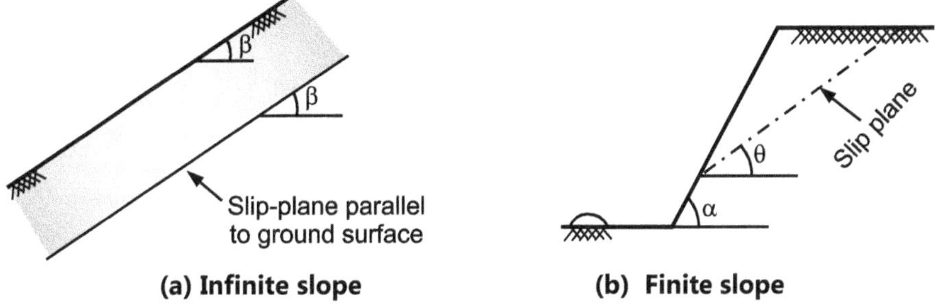

(a) Infinite slope   **(b) Finite slope**

Fig. 9.4

(iii) Homogeneous slopes : A slope is homogeneous if it is made of more or less the same material, within the zone of failure.

(iv) Non-homogeneous : If a slope is made up of more than one earth material or if the failure surface passes through two or more zones of different soil properties, then it is known as non-homogeneous slope.

9.5 BASIS OF ANALYSIS

The soil mass must be safe against slope failure of any conceivable surface across the slope. Although the methods using the theory of elasticity or plasticity are also being increasingly used, the most common methods are based on limiting equilibrium. The methods of limiting equilibrium are statically indeterminate. As the stress-strain relationships along the assumed surface are not known, it is necessary to make assumptions so that the system becomes statically determinate and it can be analysed easily by using the equation of equilibrium. The following assumptions are generally made :

- The stress system is assumed to be two-dimensional. The stresses in the third direction (perpendicular to the section of the soil mass) are taken as zero.
- It is assumed that the Coulomb equation for shear strength is applicable and the strength parameters C and ϕ are known.
- It is further assumed that the seepage conditions and water levels are known, and the corresponding pore water pressure can be estimated.
- The conditions of plastic failure are assumed to be satisfied along the critical surface. In other words, the shearing strains at all points of the critical surface are large enough to mobilise all available shear strength.
- Depending upon the method of analysis, some additional assumptions are made regarding the magnitude and distribution of forces along various planes.

In the analysis, the resultant of all the actuating forces trying to cause the failure is determined. An estimate is also made of the available shear strength. The factor of safety of the slope is determined from the available resisting forces and the actuating forces.

9.6 TYPES OF SLOPE FAILURES (MODES OF FAILURE)

[Dec. 13, May 14,16]

Failure types are different for infinite and finite slopes. The failure may occur either in the form of a plane slide or a rotational slide.

A. For infinite slopes : If a long slope is steep enough, it will fail along a surface parallel to the ground surface. Thus, the sliding surface is a plane (Fig. 9.5).

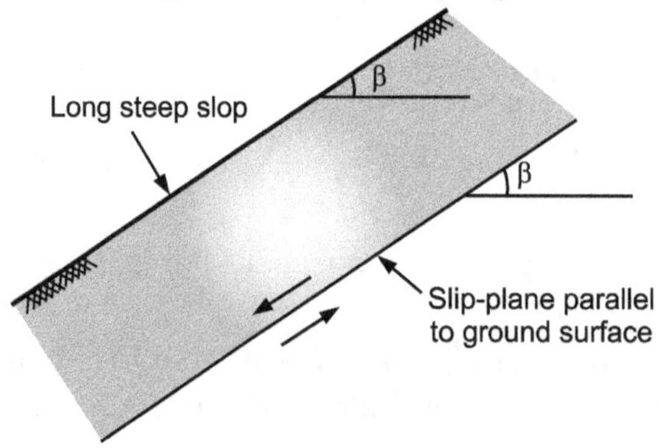

Fig. 9.5 : Plane slide

B. For Finite Slopes : For finite slopes, two basic types of failure may occur,

1.   Slope failure,

2.   Base failure.

1.   Slope failure : If the failure occurs along the sliding surface that intersects the slopes, the slide is known as *slope failure.* The slope failure occurs when the slope material is weaker than the base material. Slope failure may be of two types :

(i)   Face failure

(ii) Toe failure.

(i) Face failure : This is also called as a shallow failure. If the slip surface or the arc of failure intersects the slope above the toe, it is known as *face failure.* For face failure, the slide may be a plane slide or a rotational slide [Fig. 9.6 (a) (b)].

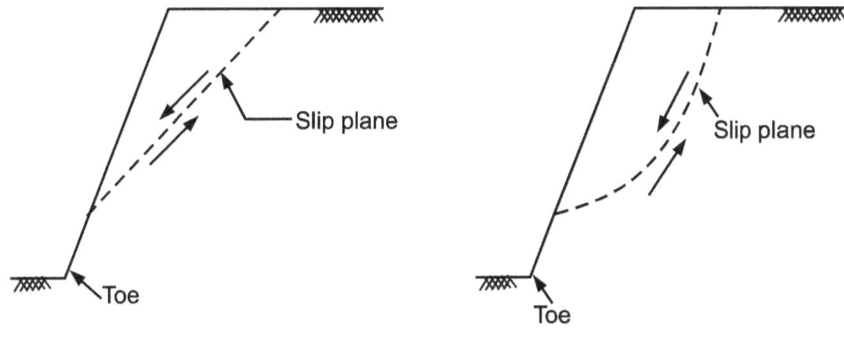

(a) Face failure (plane slide)   (b) Face failure (rotational slide)

Fig. 9.6 : Face failure

(ii) Toe failure : If the arc of the failure passes through the toe, it is known as *toe failure.* For toe failure, the slide may be a plane slide or a rotational slide [Fig. 9.7 (a) (b)].

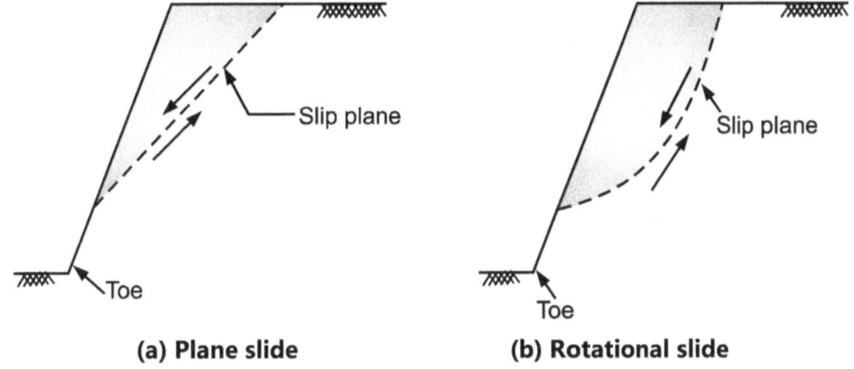

(a) Plane slide   (b) Rotational slide

Fig. 9.7 : Toe failure

2.   Base failure : If the failure occurs along a sliding surface that passes below the toe, i.e. through the base, the slide is known as *base failure.* Base failure occurs when the base material is weaker than the slope material (Fig. 9.8).

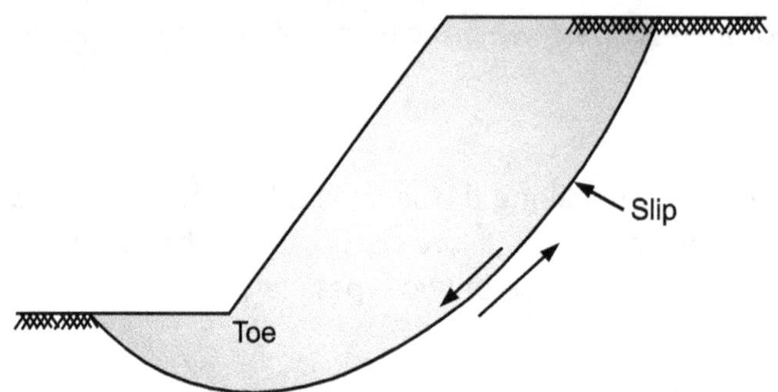

Fig. 9.8 : Base failure – rotational slide

In short the types of failure can be listed as follows :

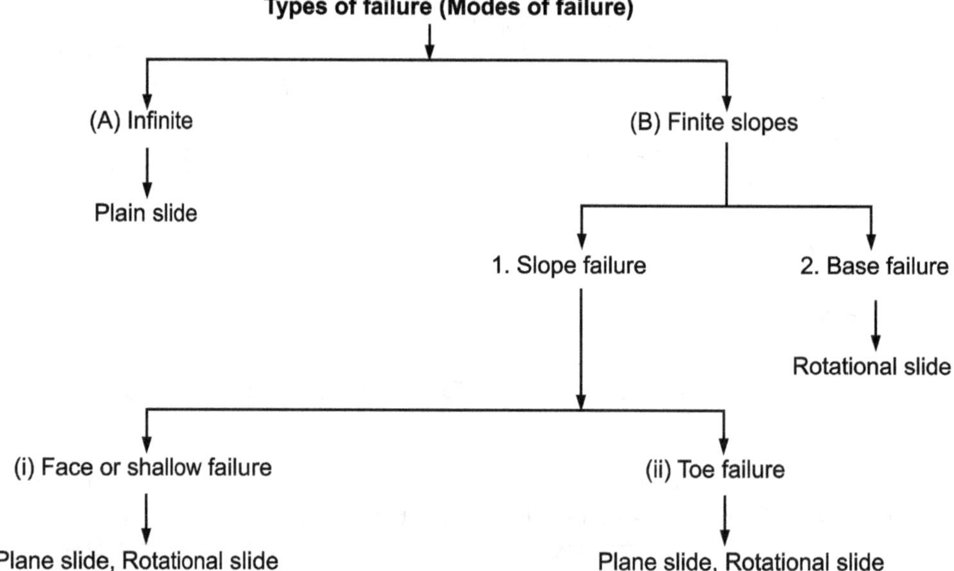

9.7 FACTOR OF SAFETY IN STABILITY PROBLEMS   [May 15, 16]

Following are the different factors of safety, normally used in stability analysis :

(a) Factor of safety with respect to shear strength : In common usage, the factor of safety is defined as 'the ratio of shear strength to the shear stress along the surface of failure'. The factor of safety as defined above is known as the *factor of safety with respect to shear strength.*

Thus,

$$F_s = \frac{S}{\tau_m} \qquad \qquad \dots (9.1)$$

where,

F_s = Factor of safety with respect to shear strength

S = Shear strength

τ_m = Mobilised shear strength (equal to shear stress)

Equation (9.1) can be written in terms of the cohesion intercept and angle of shear resistance as :

$$F_s = \frac{C + \sigma' \tan \phi}{C_m + \sigma' \tan \phi_m} \qquad \dots (9.2)$$

where, C_m = Mobilised cohesion

ϕ_m = Mobilised angle of shear resistance

σ' = Effective pressure

Referring to equation (9.2),

$$\frac{C}{F_s} + \frac{\sigma' \tan \phi}{F_s} = C_m + \sigma' \tan \phi_m$$

Therefore, $C_m = \dfrac{C}{F_s}$ $\qquad \dots (9.3)$

and $\tan \phi_m = \dfrac{\tan \phi}{F_s}$ $\qquad \dots (9.4)$

Equations (9.3) and (9.4) indicate that the factor of safety with respect to the cohesion intercept and that with respect to the angle of shearing resistance are equal to the factor of safety with respect to the shear strength.

(b) Factor of safety with respect to cohesion : The factor of safety with respect to the cohesion (F_c) is the ratio of available cohesion intercept (C) and the mobilised cohesion intercepts, i.e.

$$F_c = \frac{C}{C_m} \qquad \dots (9.5)$$

where, C = Cohesion intercept

C_m = Mobilised cohesion intercept

F_c = Factor of safety with respect to cohesion

(c) Factor of safety with respect to friction : The factor of safety with respect to friction is the ratio of the available frictional strength to the mobilised frictional strength.

Thus, $F_\phi = \dfrac{\sigma' \tan \phi}{\sigma' \tan \phi_m}$ $\qquad \dots (9.6\ a)$

where, F_ϕ = Factor of safety with respect to friction

ϕ = Angle of shearing resistance

ϕ_m = Angle of mobilised shearing resistance

For small angles, equation (9.6 a) can be expressed as :

$$F_\phi = \frac{\phi}{\phi_m} \qquad \dots (9.6\ b)$$

The values of F_c and F_ϕ may range from 1.2 to 2.0. In many problems a combined or overall factor of safety equal to 1.35 to 1.5 may be used.

The minimum factor of safety depends on the hazard or risk involved the method of analysis, reliability of measured strength parameters, and estimated pore pressures. Long term factors of safety are not the same as short term factors of safety.

9.8 FINITE SLOPES – PLANE FAILURE (CULMANN'S METHOD)

[May 14]

Culmann's method is used for the stability analysis of homogeneous slopes, based on the assumption of plane failure. A plane failure surface is not a correct assumption for a homogeneous soil. However, it may be used for very steep slopes and where a definite plane of weakness exists.

Let us consider the equilibrium of triangular wedge ABD formed by the assumed failure surface AB (Fig. 9.9). This is in equilibrium under the three forces :

(1) Weight of the wedge (W).

(2) Cohesive force (C) along surface AB.

(3) Reaction R. The reaction R is inclined at angle ϕ_m to the normal.

The triangle of forces is shown in Fig. 9.9. The magnitude and direction of W and C are known. The direction of R is also known.

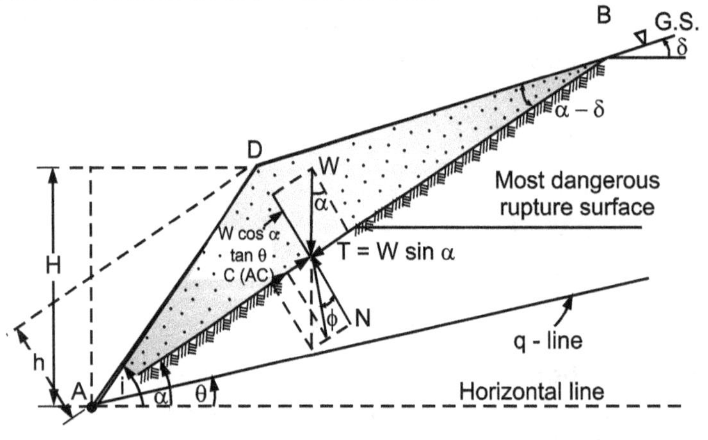

Fig. 9.9 : Plane failure – finite slope

From Fig. 9.9, we have

$$W = \frac{AB \times AD \; \sin(i-\alpha)}{2} \cdot \gamma = \frac{1}{2} L\left(\frac{H}{\sin i}\right) \sin(i-\alpha) \quad \text{... (9.7)}$$

and

$$C = C_m \cdot L \qquad \text{... (9.8)}$$

where,

H = Height of slope

C_m = Mobilised cohesion

ϕ_m = Angle of mobilised friction

L = Length of failure surface AB

From the law of sines :
$$\frac{C}{W} = \frac{\sin (\alpha - \phi_m)}{\sin (\phi_m + 90°)} = \frac{\sin (\alpha - \phi_m)}{\cos \phi_m} \qquad \text{... (9.9)}$$

Substituting the values of W and C from equations (9.7) and (9.8) in equation (9.9) :
$$\frac{C_m \cdot L}{\frac{1}{2} \gamma L \left(\frac{H}{\sin i}\right) \sin (i - \alpha)} = \frac{\sin (\alpha - \phi_m)}{\cos \phi_m} \qquad \text{... (9.10)}$$

or
$$\frac{C_m}{\gamma H} = \frac{1}{2} \operatorname{cosec} i \sin (i - \alpha) \sin (\alpha - \phi_m) \sec \phi_m \qquad \text{... (9.11)}$$

The lefthand side of equation (9.11) is known as the *stability number* (S_n or N). The most dangerous plane is that for which the angle α is such that the stability number becomes maximum, i.e.
$$\frac{d(S_n)}{d\alpha} = 0$$

or $\sin (i - \alpha) \cdot \cos (\alpha - \phi_m) - \sin (\alpha - \phi_m) \cdot \cos (i - \alpha) = 0$

or
$$\tan (i - \alpha) = \tan (\alpha - \phi_m)$$

or
$$(i - \alpha) = \alpha - \phi_m$$

or
$$\alpha_c = \frac{i + \phi_m}{2}$$

where, α_c is the critical slope angle.

Now from equation (9.11) :
$$\left(\frac{C_m}{\gamma H}\right)_{max} = \frac{1}{2} \operatorname{cosec} i \cdot \sec \phi_m \left[\sin \left\{i - \frac{i + \phi_m}{2}\right\}\right] \cdot \left[\sin \left\{\left(\frac{i + \phi_m}{2}\right) - \phi_m\right\}\right]$$

$$= \frac{1}{2} \operatorname{cosec} i \cdot \sec \phi_m \cdot \sin \left(\frac{i - \phi_m}{2}\right) \sin \left(\frac{1 - \phi_m}{2}\right)$$

$$= \frac{1}{2} \operatorname{cosec} i \cdot \sec \phi_m \left[\frac{1 - \cos (i - \phi_m)}{2}\right]$$

or
$$\left(\frac{C_m}{\gamma H}\right)_{max} = \frac{1 - \cos (i - \phi_m)}{4 \sin i \cdot \cos \phi_m} \qquad \text{... (9.12)}$$

or
$$H = \frac{4 C_m \sin i \cdot \cos \phi_m}{\gamma [1 - \cos (i - \phi_m)]}$$

where H is the safe height of the slope.

The Culmann's method gives reasonably accurate results for homogeneous slopes which are vertical or nearly vertical. For flat homogeneous slopes, critical failure surface is rarely plane. Hence, these equations have little practical value.

9.9 CRITICAL HEIGHT OF SLOPE

For any $C - \phi$ soil the Mohr – Coulomb failure envelope is given by
$$\tau_f = C + \sigma_f \tan \phi$$

Line DA represents the strength envelope of any $C - \phi$ soil with angle of shearing resistance as ϕ.

If the slope angle (α) is $\leq \phi$, represented by line OB, no critical state of stress will be reached. In such case, the values of τ and σ will be less than those at failure and the slope will be stable. Hence, line OB (angle $\alpha \leq \phi$) represents a line of stable slope where $F_1\,(\sigma,\,\tau) \leq F\,(\sigma_f\,,\,\tau_f)$.

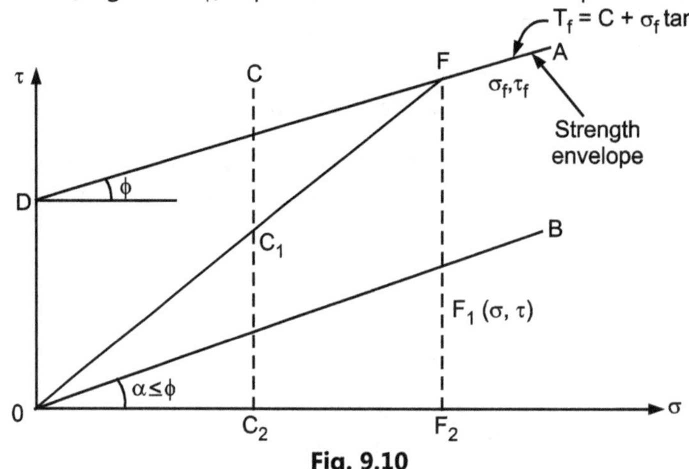

Fig. 9.10

If a line OF is drawn such that angle $\alpha > \phi$, it will cut the strength envelope at point F. At this point F, the shear stress equals the shearing strength τ_F and the slope becomes unstable. Hence point F represents the state of slope failure. Before point F, any depth less than that represented by point F, the shear stress τ is less than the shear strength τ_f and the slope remains stable. For example, at point C_1, corresponding to the same slope $\alpha > \phi$ but the depth is less than that at point F and hence the slope is stable. Hence for a slope $\alpha > \phi$, the slope is stable only upto a limited depth. This limited depth upto which the slope is stable, even if the angle is more than ϕ (angle of shearing resistance of failure) ; is known as *critical depth* or *critical height of slope*.

Hence the factor of safety with respect to cohesion also represents the factor of safety with respect to height.

$$\therefore \quad F_c = \frac{H_c}{H}$$

9.10 STABILITY NUMBER   [Dec. 13, 14, Nov. 16]

The stability of slopes depends on the geometry of slopes expressed in terms of slope angle α, height of slope H, depth of factor D and on soil properties like γ, C_u, ϕ. Thus, factor of safety may be expressed as,

$$F_s = f\,(\alpha,\, H,\, D,\, \gamma,\, C_u,\, \phi)$$

If H is the height of a soil (γ, C_u, ϕ) with slope angle α, a dimensionless number can be defined for homogeneous slopes.

As
$$N = \frac{C_u}{F_s\,\gamma H}$$

where, $F_s H = H_c$ = Critical height of slope

Here F_s = Factor of safety with respect to height/cohesion

This dimensionless quantity $N = \dfrac{C_u}{\gamma H_c}$ is called the *stability number.*

This stability number is used for design purpose to find out the value of the factor of safety F_s. Different charts and tables are prepared giving the value of N corresponding to different values of slopes α and the angle of shearing resistance ϕ. From this value of N and knowing the C and H values, the factor of safety can be found out. Values of N related to the slope angle β, the angle of shearing resistance ϕ_u and the depth factor D_f are given in the charts shown in Fig. 9.11 (a) and (b). For slope angles greater than 53°, the critical circle passes through the toe of the slope and the chart shown in Fig. 9.11 (b) is used. For slope angles less than 53°, the critical circle may pass infront of the toe and the chart shown in Fig. 9.11 (a) is used. When the critical circle will be restricted to passing through the toe, the heavy broken lines on the chart must be used. The value of N, giving the break-out point of the critical circle infront of the toe, can be obtained from the light broken lines.

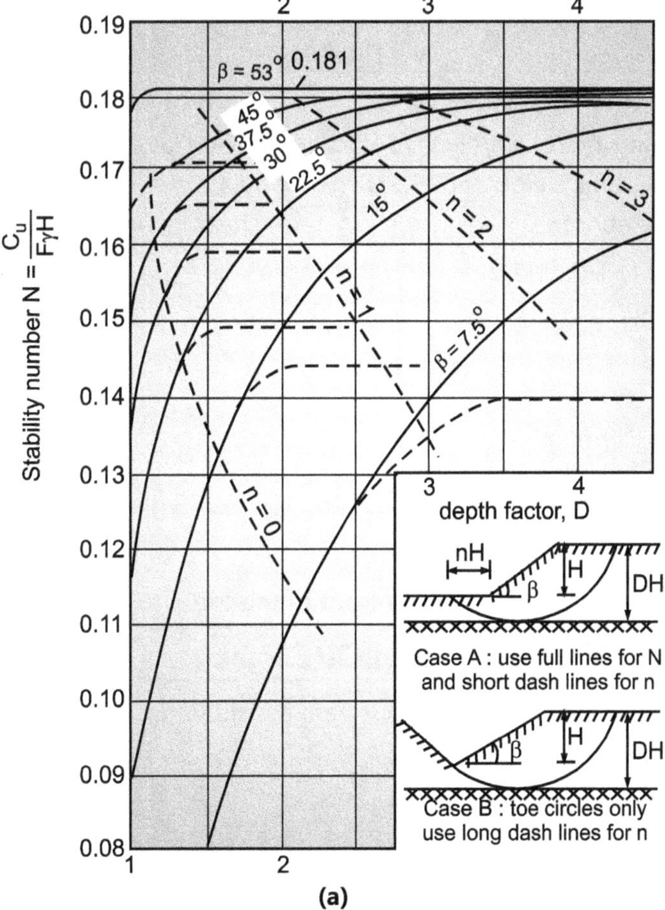

(a)

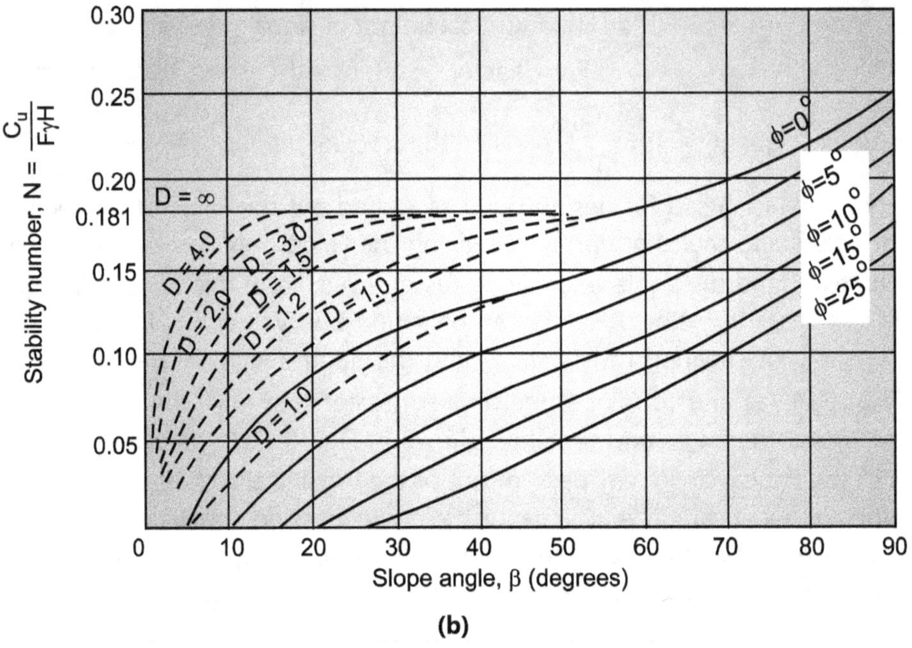

(b)

Fig. 9.11

Example : A cutting in a saturated clay has a depth of 10 m. At a depth of 6 m below the floor of the cutting there is a layer of hard rock. The clay has an undrained cohesion of 34 kN/m² and a bulk unit weight of 19 kN/m³. Calculate the maximum safe slope that will provide a factor of safety of 1.25 against short-term shear failure.

Solution : Refer to Fig. 9.11.

H = 10 m and DH = 16 m

$\therefore$ D = 1.5

$$\text{Required stability number, } \quad N = \frac{C_u}{1.25\,\gamma H} = \frac{34}{1.25 \times 19 \times 10} = 0.143$$

The point on the chart located by D = 1.5 and N = 0.143 gives a slope angle of β = 18°.

Also, from the chart,   n = 0.2

Hence, the circle will break out 2.0 m infront of the toe.

9.11 STABILITY OF INFINITE SLOPES   [May 17]

The following different cases of infinite slopes are considered :

(A) Infinite slopes in sands :

- Dry
- Submerged
- Seepage parallel to slope.

(B) Infinite slopes in clays :

- With seepage
- Without seepage (submerged)
- Undrained condition (total stresses).

1. Dry Infinite Slope : Sandy soil, (c = 0) : AB is the ground surface inclined at an angle β and A' B' is the potential sliding plane, parallel to AB. It may be assumed for an infinite slope, that stresses on the two vertical faces are equal and balance each other. Then stresses on the inclined bottom face and weight of the element enter the equilibrium equation (Fig. 9.12 (i)). Let T' be the tangential resisting force. Then,

$$W = \text{Weight} = \gamma bz$$

$$N = W \cos \beta$$

$$T = W \sin \beta$$

$$T' = W \cos \beta \cdot \tan \phi$$

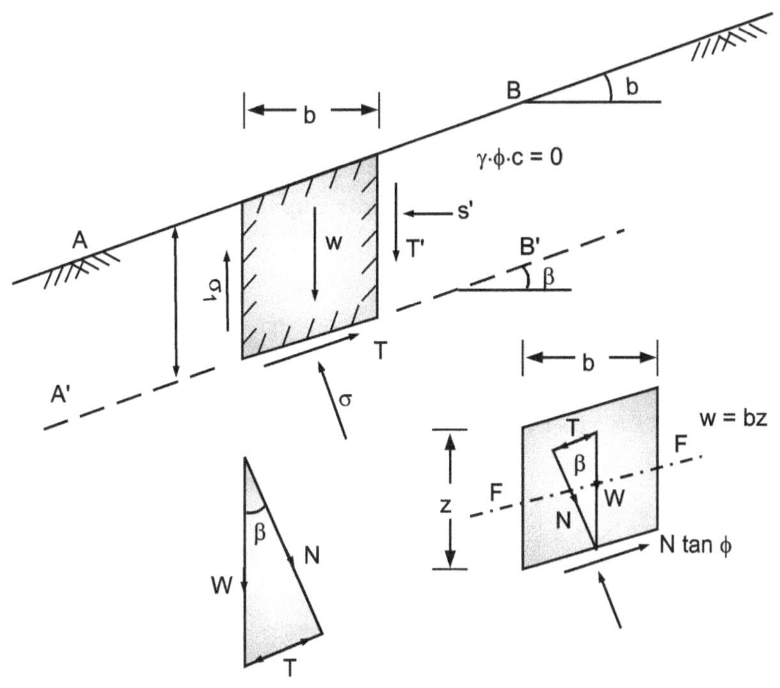

(i) Dry slope

$$W = b \cdot z \cdot \gamma, \quad N = W \cos \beta, \quad T = W \sin \beta, \quad T' = N \tan \phi$$

$$\therefore \quad F_s = \frac{T'}{T} = \frac{AC}{AB} = \frac{W \cos \beta \tan \phi}{W \sin \beta} = \frac{\tan \phi}{\tan \beta} \qquad \ldots (9.13)$$

Thus, for critical condition, the angle of slope equals the angle of shearing resistance. The angle, ϕ here is equal to the angle of repose, ϕ_R for loose dry sands. For a denser packing the slope can be steeper than the angle of repose, ϕ_R.

$$\overline{W} \;=\; \text{Submerged weight}$$

$$\overline{N} \;=\; N - U \;=\; \overline{W}\cos\beta$$

$$T' \;=\; \overline{W}\cos\beta\tan\phi$$

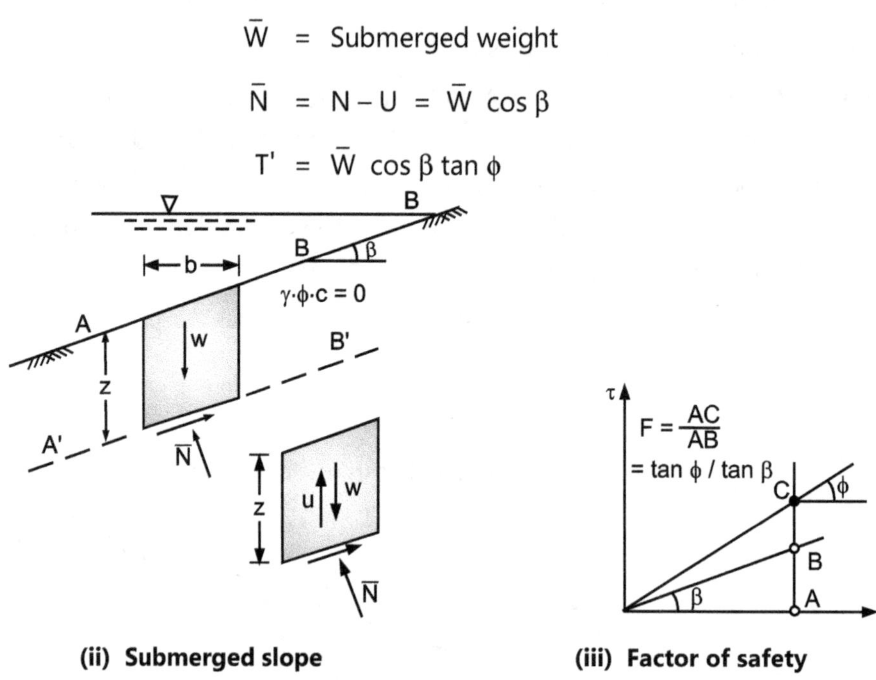

(ii) Submerged slope   **(iii) Factor of safety**

Fig. 9.12 : Stability of infinite slope, Sandy soils

2. Submerged Slope : Sandy soil ($c = 0$) : Water within the sand and above it is in a hydrostatic condition, i.e. there is no flow. Such a condition exists in the submerged slopes in lakes. Consider an element of width b and depth z, [Fig. 9.12 (ii), (iii)]. The forces on its vertical faces balance each other and the resultant $\overline{N}$ acts normally at the bottom. The boundary pore pressure $U = \gamma_w \cdot b \cdot z$ acts normally, opposing the force of weight, $W = \gamma_{sat} \cdot b \cdot z$. Hence,

$$F_s \;=\; \frac{T'}{\overline{W}\sin\beta}$$

$$=\; \frac{\overline{W}\cdot\cos\beta\cdot\tan\phi}{\overline{W}\sin\beta}$$

$$\therefore \qquad F_s \;=\; \frac{\text{Tan }\phi}{\tan\beta} \qquad\qquad \dots (9.14)$$

For the critical condition, $\beta = \phi$. i.e. the slope is stable for $\beta \leq \phi$. This is the same condition as for dry slope, where $\phi = \phi'$.

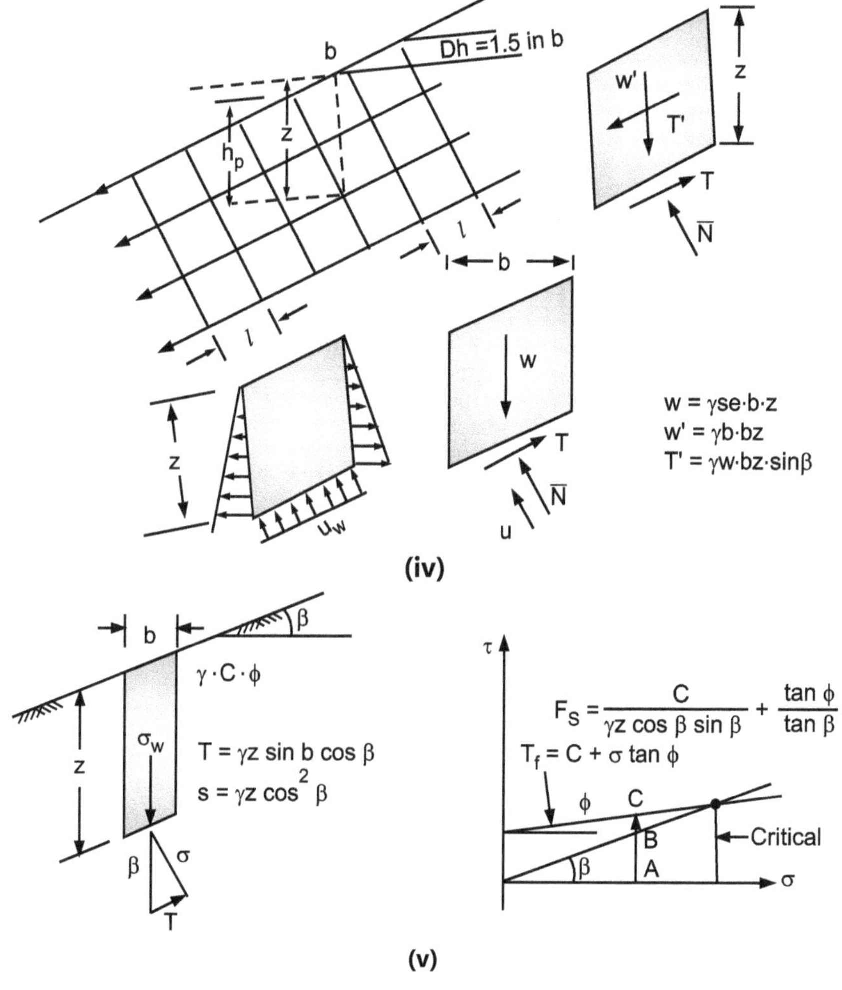

Fig. 9.12 : Infinite slopes

3. Seepage Parallel to Slope : Sandy soil, c = 0 :

Referring to Fig. 9.12 (iv) for slope angle β,

$$\text{Pore pressure} = γ_w \cdot h_p = γ_w \cdot z \cdot \cos^2 \cdot β,$$

$$\text{Resultant, } U = γ_w \cdot z \cdot \cos^2 β \, \frac{b}{\cos β}$$

$$= γ_w \cdot bz \cdot \cos \cdot β$$

$$\text{Saturated weight, } W = γ_{sat} \cdot b \cdot z$$

$$\text{Shear force, } T = γ_{sat} \cdot b \cdot z \cdot \cos β$$

$$\text{Normal force, } N = γ_{sat} \cdot b \cdot z \cdot \cos β$$

$$\text{Effective normal force, } \quad \overline{N}\,' = N - U = (γ_{sat} - γ_w) \, b \cdot z \cdot \cos β = γ_b \cdot b \cdot z \cdot \cos β$$

$$\therefore \quad F_s = \frac{\bar{N} \tan \phi'}{T} = \frac{\gamma_b \cdot b \cdot z \cdot \cos \beta \tan \phi'}{\gamma_{sat} \cdot b \cdot z \cdot \sin \beta}$$

$$= \frac{\gamma_b}{\gamma_{sat}} \cdot \frac{\tan \phi'}{\tan \beta} \qquad \qquad \text{... (9.15)}$$

4. Slopes in clays with seepage parallel to slope : ($\phi > 0$)

$$F_s = \frac{C' + \bar{N} \tan \phi'}{T} \quad , \quad \text{where } C' = c' \frac{b}{\cos \beta} \; ; \; T = W \sin \beta$$

$$F_s = \frac{c'}{\gamma_{sat} \cdot z \cdot \sin \beta \cos \beta} + \frac{\gamma_b \cdot b \cdot z \cdot \cos \beta \cdot \tan \phi'}{\gamma_{sat} \cdot b \cdot z \cdot \sin \beta}$$

$$\text{or} \qquad F_s = \frac{c'}{\gamma_{sat} \cdot z \cdot \sin \beta \cos \beta} + \frac{\gamma_b}{\gamma_{sat}} \cdot \frac{\tan \phi'}{\tan \beta} \qquad \text{... (9.16)}$$

5. Slopes in clays with no seepage. [Fig. 9.12 (v)]

$$F_s = \frac{C' + N' \tan \phi}{W' \sin \beta}$$

(a) Submerged slope ($\gamma = \gamma_b$), $W' = \gamma_b \cdot b \cdot z$

$$F_s = \frac{c' \cdot (b/\cos \beta) + W' \cos \beta \cdot \tan \phi'}{W' \sin \beta}$$

$$= \frac{c'}{\gamma_b \cdot z \cdot \sin \beta \cdot \cos \beta} + \frac{\tan \phi'}{\tan \beta} \qquad \text{... (9.17)}$$

(b) We slope, $\qquad\qquad W' = \gamma \cdot b \cdot z$

$$F_s = \frac{c'}{\gamma \cdot z \cdot \sin \beta \cdot \cos \beta} + \frac{\tan \phi'}{\tan \beta} \qquad \text{... (9.18)}$$

(c) General case, moist slopes : (γ, c, ϕ) : [Fig. 9.12 (v)]

$$F_s = \frac{\text{Resisting force}}{\text{Activating force}} = \frac{\tau_f \cdot A}{\tau \cdot A}$$

$$= \frac{c + \sigma_n \tan \phi}{\tau}$$

$$\sigma_v = \gamma \cdot z \cdot \cos \beta, \quad \sigma_n = \gamma \cdot z \cdot \cos^2 \beta, \quad \tau = \gamma \cdot z \cdot \cos \beta \cdot \sin \beta$$

$$\therefore \quad F_s = \frac{c}{\gamma \cdot z \cdot \cos \beta \cdot \sin \beta} + \frac{\gamma \cdot z \cdot \cos^2 \beta \cdot \tan \phi}{\gamma \cdot z \cdot \cos \beta \cdot \sin \beta}$$

$$= \frac{c}{\gamma \cdot z \cdot \cos \beta \cdot \sin \beta} + \frac{\tan \phi}{\tan \beta} \qquad \text{... (9.19)}$$

9.12 LANDSLIDE REMEDIAL MEASURES   [Dec. 13, Nov. 16, May 15, 17]

Land Slide : Land slides are very rapid soil movements along slopes. Natural slopes are complex in nature and the strength of natural deposits is variable. As such, land slides are very difficult to analyse. Land slides usually give warning of instability by slow movements or by cracks and some triggering event brings about failure. Wetting due to percolating water during heavy rainfall or a tremor may initiate a land slide.

Remedial Measures (Improving stability of slopes) : An earth slope in danger of incipient failure may be stabilised basically by two ways :

(i)   Reducing the causative factors.

(ii)   Increasing the resistive factors.

Following measures have been used :

- Slope fattening reduces the weight of the mass tending to slide.

- When there is a possibility of base failure, by providing berm below the toe of the slope, increases the resistance to movement.

- Growing grass on the slope. This measure reduces percolation into the ground and prevents surface erosion.

- Provision of drainage helps in reducing the seepage forces and hence increases the stability.

- Densification by use of explosives, vibro-floatation helps in increasing the shear strength of cohesionless soils.

- Grouting and injection of cement or other compounds into specific zones helps in increasing the stability of slopes.

- Sheet piles and retaining walls can be installed to provide lateral support and to increase the stability.

- Stabilisation of soil helps in increasing the stability of slopes.

In the interest of economy, relatively inexpensive methods such as flattening and drainage control are generally preferred.

SOLVED EXAMPLES

Example 9.1 : For a slope of 10 m height with stability number equal to 0.055, what is the factor of safety ? Given $\gamma = 20$ kN/m^3, $C = 25$ kN/m^2, $\phi = 0$.

Solution : From equation,

$$S_n = \frac{C}{F_c \cdot \gamma \cdot H}$$

or

$$F_c = \frac{C}{S_n \cdot \gamma \cdot H} = \frac{25}{0.055 \times 20 \times 10} = \textbf{2.27}$$

Example 9.2 : A slope is to be constructed at an inclination of $30°$ with the horizontal. Soil has the following properties :

$C = 18 \ kN/m^2$, $\phi = 20°$ and $\gamma = 20 \ kN/m^3$

The stability number for these conditions is 0.0625. Determine the safe height of slope if the factor of safety is to be 1.5.

Solution : From equation :

$$S_n = \frac{C}{F_c \cdot \gamma \cdot H}$$

$$H = \frac{C}{S_n \cdot F \cdot \gamma}$$

$$= \frac{18}{1.5 \times 0.0625 \times 20} = \textbf{9.6 m}$$

Example 9.3 : Calculate the factor of safety with respect to cohesion of a clay slope laid 1 in 2 to height 10 m if the angle of internal friction $\phi = 10°$, $C = 2.5 \ kN/m^2$ and $y = 19 \ kN/m^3$. What will be the critical height of the slope in this soil ?

Solution : $i = \tan^{-1}\dfrac{1}{2} = 26.5°$

Now for $i = 26.5°$ and $\phi = 10°$, $S_n = 0.064$

But N or $S_n = \dfrac{C}{F_c \cdot \gamma H}$

$\therefore$ $F_c = \dfrac{C}{S_n \cdot \gamma H}$

$$= \frac{25}{0.064 \ \times 19 \times 10} = 2.06$$

The critical height $H_c = F_c \cdot H$

$$= 2.06 \times 10 = \textbf{20.6 m}$$

Example 9.4 : Determine the stability number for a vertical cut in a cohesive soil with the following details : $\gamma = 17.0 \ kN/m^3$, $C = 20 \ kN/m^2$, $\phi = 20°$.

Solution : $H_c = \dfrac{4C}{\gamma} \cdot \dfrac{\sin i \cdot \cos \phi}{1 - \cos (i - \phi)}$

Stability number N or $S_n = \dfrac{C}{\gamma H_c} = \dfrac{1 - \cos \ (i - \phi)}{4 \sin i \cdot \cos \phi}$

                              $i = 90°$

                              $\phi = 20°$

$\therefore$ $S_n = \dfrac{1 - \cos (90 - 20)}{4 \sin 90 \cdot \cos 20} = \textbf{0.1751}$

Example 9.5 : Determine the factor of safety for a cohesive soil ($\phi = 0$) 7 m high, if its stability number is known to be 0.156. The slope material has cohesion = 25 kN/m^2 and unit weight 18.5 kN/m^3.

Solution : From equations,

$$N = S_n = \frac{C}{F_c \cdot \gamma \cdot H}$$

or

$$F_c = \frac{C}{S_n \cdot \gamma \cdot H}$$

$$= \frac{25}{0.156 \times 18.5 \times 7} = \mathbf{1.23}$$

Example 9.6 : Determine the critical height of excavation of a vertical cut in a cohesive soil if $C = 25$ kN/m^2 and $\gamma = 17$ kN/m^3.

Solution : Assume $\phi = 0$ condition

Critical height,
$$H_c = \frac{4C}{\gamma}$$

$$= \frac{4 \times 25}{17} = \mathbf{5.89\ m}$$

Example 9.7 : A slope is to be constructed at an inclination of 30° with the horizontal. Determine the safe height of the slope if the factor of safety should be 1.5. The soil properties are $C = 15$ KP$_a$, $\phi = 22.5°$, $\gamma = 21$ kN/m^3. For $i = 30°$.

Solution :

Critical height, $H_c = \dfrac{4C}{\gamma} \cdot \dfrac{\sin i \cdot \sin \phi}{1 - \cos (1 - \phi)}$

$$= \frac{4 \times 15}{21} \cdot \frac{\sin 30° \times \sin 22.5°}{1 - \cos (30 - 22.5°)}$$

$$= 63.78$$

Safe height $= \dfrac{63.78}{1.5} = \mathbf{42.52\ m}$

Example 9.8 : A smooth vertical wall retain a level surface with $\gamma = 18$ kN/m^3, $\phi = 30°$, to a depth of 8m. Draw the lateral pressure diagram and compute the total active pressure in dry condition and when water table rises to the GL. Assume $\gamma_{set} = 22$ kN/m^3.   **(May 15, 6 M)**

Solution :

$$\gamma = 18 \text{ kN/m}^3$$

$$\gamma_{sat} = 22 \text{ kN/m}^3$$

$$\phi = 30°$$

$$H = 8 \text{ m}$$

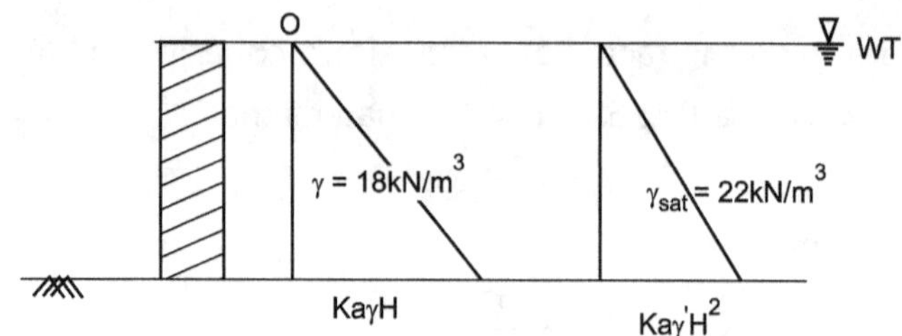

(i) at dry condition (ii) water table at ground level

Fig. 7

(i)   at Dry condition

$$K_a = \frac{1 - \sin \phi}{1 + \sin \phi}$$

$$= \frac{1 - \sin 30°}{1 + \sin 30°} = \frac{1}{3}$$

$$P = \text{Total active pressure}$$

$$= \frac{1}{2} k_a \gamma H^2 = \frac{1}{2} \times \frac{1}{3} \times 18 \times 8^2$$

$$= 192 \text{ kN/m}^2$$

(ii) When water Table at ground level

$$P = \frac{1}{2} k_a \gamma H^2 = \frac{1}{2} \times \frac{1}{3} \times (22 - 9.81) \times 8^2$$

$$= 130 \text{ kN/m}^2$$

SUMMARY

1. Slopes are classifies as

   (a)   Natural slopes   (b)   Man – made slopes.

2. Culmann's methods is used for stability analysis of homogeneous slopes, based on the assumption of plane failure.

3. An Earth slope in danger of incipient failure may be stabilized by two methods.

   (a)   Reducing the causative

   (b)   Increasing the resistive.

4. **Formulae :**

   (i) $F_c = \dfrac{C}{C_m}$

   (ii) $F_\phi = \dfrac{\phi}{\phi_m}$

   (iii) $N = \dfrac{C_u}{\gamma H_c}$ is called the *stability number.*

EXERCISE

1. A simple homogeneous slope has a stability number of 0.16. What would be its safe height to allow a factor of safety of 1.5, if the soil has C = 25 kN/m^2 and γ = 20 kN/m^3 ?

2. A slope having inclination of 30° with the horizontal is to be constructed with soil having following properties :

   C = 15 kN/m^2, γ = 19 kN/m^3 and ϕ = 22°.

   Determine the safe height if the factor of safety is to be 1.50.

3. A long natural slope in an over-consolidated clay (C' = 10 kN/m^2, ϕ = 25°, γ_{sat} = 20 kN/m^3) is inclined at 10° to the horizontal. The water table is at the surface and the seepage is parallel to the slope. If a plane slip has developed at a depth of 5 m below the surface, determine the factor of safety.　　　　　　　**(Ans.** F_s = 1.90)

4. A vertical cut is to be made in clayey soil for which tests gave C = 30 kN/m^2, γ = 16 kN/m^3 and ϕ = 0. Find the maximum height for which the cut may be temporarily unsupported. For ϕ = 0, i = 90°, the value of stability number is 0.261.

   (Ans. 7.18 m)

5. If the stability number for each slope 10 m high is 0.056, determine its factor of safety given ϕ = 20°, C = 30 kN/m^2, γ = 10 kN/m^3.　　　　　　**(Ans.** F_s = 2.68)

6. A 40° slope is excavated to a depth of 8 m in a deep layer of saturated clay. Determine the factor of safety of the slope, if the soil has C = 20 kN/m^2, ϕ = 150° and γ = 20 kN/m^3.

7. What are the assumptions that are generally made in the analysis of the stability of slopes ? Discuss their validity briefly.

8. What are the different types of slope failure ?

9. Differentiate between finite and infinite slopes.

10. What is a stability number ? What is its utility in the analysis of stability of slopes ?

11. Describe Culmann's method for the stability analysis of homogeneous slopes. What are its limitations ?

12. Discuss the various land slides remedial measures.

13. What are the factors that affect the stability of slope ?

14. Draw neat sketches to show :

    (i)　Failure of a finite slope.

    (ii)　Toe failure

    (iii) Base failure.

15. Derive the following expression for the critical depth in the cohesive soil :

$$H_c = \frac{C}{\gamma} \cdot \frac{\sec^2 \cdot i}{\gamma (\tan i - \tan \phi)}$$ with usual notations.

16. Which of the following statements are true

(a) The stability numbers can be used for the analysis of purely cohesionless soil slopes.

(b) The factor of safety of an infinite slope of a cohesive soil depends upon the height H of the slope.

(c) Culmann's method assumes that the failure surface is a plane.

(d) The upstream slope of an earth dam is critical during sudden drawdown conditions.

(e) The total stress analysis can be used for the stability of slopes.

(Ans. True (b), (c), (d), (e))

SOLVED UNIVERSITY QUESTIONS AND NUMERICALS

December 2013

1. Write a short note on Taylors stability number.   **[5]**

   [**Ans. :** Refer Article 9.10]

2. A slope is to be constructed at an inclination of 30° with horizontal. Soil has the following properties :

$$c = 18 \text{ kN/m}^3$$
$$\phi = 20°$$
$$\gamma = 20 \text{ kN/m}^3$$

   Stability number is 0.0625, determine the safe height of slope if factor of safety is to be 1.5.   **[5]**

   [**Ans. :** Refer Example 9.2]

3. Explain with sketch various modes of slope failure in case of finite slope.   **[3]**

   [**Ans. :** Refer Article 9.6]

4. Write short note on land slides.   **[3]**

   [**Ans. :** Refer Article 9.12]

May 2014

1. Write a note on Cullman's graphical method.   **[6]**

    [**Ans. :** Refer Article 9.8]

2. Explain with figure, the modes of failure for finite and infinite slopes.   **[7]**

    [**Ans. :** Refer Article 9.6]

3. Write a note on Taylor's stability number.   **[6]**

    [**Ans. :** Refer Article 9.10]

December 2014

1. Explain Taylor's stability number.

    Determine the factor of safety for a cohesive soil ($\phi = 0$) 7 m high, if its stability number is known to be 0.156. The slope material has cohesion = 25 kN/m^2 and unit weight 18.5 kN/m^3.   **[7]**

    [**Ans. :** Refer Article 9.10, and Example 9.5]

2. Discuss the slope stability measures that can be adopted to avoid the occurrence of landslides.   **[6]**

May 2015

1. A smooth vertical wall retain a level surface with $\gamma = 18$ kN/m^3, $\phi = 30°$, to a depth of 8m. Draw the lateral pressure diagram and compute the total active pressure in dry condition and when water table rises to the GL. Assume $\gamma_{set} = 22$ kN/m^3.   **[6]**

    [**Ans. :** Refer Example 9.8]

2. Write short notes on causes and remedial measures of Landslides.   **[7]**

    [**Ans. :** Refer Article 9.2, 9.12]

3. What is slope stability and how are the different types of factor of safety determined ?   **[7]**

    [**Ans. :** Refer Article 9.7]

November 2015

1. Derive the expression for factor of safety for dry infinite slope and submerged infinite slope in sandy soils.   **[6]**

2. State the assumptions in the analysis of slope stability and also state the different types of landslides on clay slopes.   **[6]**

    [**Ans. :** Refer Article 9.3]

May 2016

1. Explain the factor of safety with respect to shear strength, cohesion and friction.   **[6]**

   [**Ans. :** Refer Article 9.7]

2. Discuss the criteria for slope classification and explain the modes of failure for all these slopes.   **[7]**

   [**Ans. :** Refer Articles 9.4, 9.6]

November 2016

1. Which are the causative and resistive factors resulting into landslides? Discuss the remedial measures to be taken to reduce the effect of these factors.   **[7]**

   [**Ans. :** Refer Article 9.2, 9.12]

2. What is Taylor's stability number ? How can it be used to check the stability of slopes ?   **[6]**

   [**Ans. :** Refer Article 9.10]

May 2017

1. Write short notes on causes and remedial measures of Landslides.   **[7]**

   [**Ans. :** Refer Article 9.2, 9.12]

2. Derive the expression for factor of safety for dry infinite slope and submerged infinite slope in sandy soils.   **[6]**

   [**Ans. :** Refer Article 9.11 (1), (2)]

◈ ◈ ◈

Chapter 10
INTRODUCTION TO
GEOENVIRONMENTAL ENGINEERING

10.1 INTRODUCTION

Any project that deals with the interrelationship among environment, ground surface and subsurface (soil, rock and ground water) falls under the purview of geoenvironmental engineering. Geoenvironmental engineering is more research oriented and new concepts and methodologies are still being developed. Despite a lot of effort, it is very difficult to cut off the harmful effects of pollutants disposed off into the geoenvironment. The damage has already been done to the subsurface and ground water resources, which is precious. An effective waste containment system is one of the solutions to this problem. However, such a project has different socio-economic and technical perspectives. The realization of such projects require the contribution of environmentalist, remote sensing experts, decision makers, common public during its planning stage, hydrologists, geotechnical engineers for its execution stage and several experts for management and monitoring of the project.

A lot of concepts from soil physics, soil chemistry, soil biology, multi-phase flow, material science and mathematical modelling, need to be taken for planning and execution of an efficient remediation strategy. Another important issue is the reuse and recycling of waste materials, which reduces the burden on our environment manifold. Construction of flood protection works such as embankments and levees also comes under the purview of geoenvironmental engineering. Unless a thorough hydraulic study is conducted, any geotechnical measures for flood protection would prove to be futile.

10.2 ROLE OF SOIL IN GEOENVIRONMENTAL APPLICATIONS

[Nov. 16]

Consider the case of waste dumped on ground surface. During precipitation, water interacts with these wastes and flow out as leachate. When the leachate flows down, soil act as buffer in retaining or delaying several harmful contaminants from reaching ground water. Such a buffering action obviously depends on the texture and constituents of soil mass. While designing a waste containment facility, the role of soil in such projects is enormous. A coarse grained soil with filter property is required for leachate collection whereas a fine grained soil is required for minimizing flow of leachate. These are two entirely different functions expected from soil in the same project. The cap provided for waste dumps also necessitate the use of specific type of soils with the required properties. The amount of water that infiltrates into the waste below is minimized by soil used in such caps. Special type of high swelling soils is used as backfills for storing high level radioactive waste in deep geological repositories. Another important geoenvironmental problem, namely, carbon sequestration uses the geological storage capacity for disposal of anthropogenic CO_2 to mitigate the global warming. Therefore, soil plays a very vital role in geoenvironmental projects and the property by which it becomes important is problem-specific.

10.3 SUBSURFACE CONTAMINATION [Dec. 13, 14, May 17]

Solid, liquid and gaseous waste forms contaminates subsurface and ground water due to indiscriminate disposal. Solid wastes come from municipal, domestic and industrial sources. Municipal wastes amounts to around 50 per cent of the total wastes produced. Household, hospital, agricultural wastes forms part of municipal wastes. Returning these wastes to soil is considered to be a low cost option. Abandoned e-waste, batteries, vehicles, furniture, debris from construction industry is considered as solid waste and is produced from both urban and rural areas. Large scale industrial development produces huge quantities of hazardous waste and the sources are iron and steel industries, packaging factories, paints, dyes, chemicals, glass factories, fertilizer and pesticide industries, mine excavation waste etc. Coal mining, radioactive fuel mining, petroleum mining and thermal power plants generate hazardous solid waste that requires effective management.

The main source and type of hazardous liquid waste include industrial waste water contained in surface impoundments, lagoons or pits. It is also produced from municipal solid refuse and sludge that are disposed on land. If not handled properly sewage becomes an important source of liquid waste that has undesirable effect on environment. Petroleum exploration leaves waste brine solution which needs to be managed to prevent ground water pollution. Liquid waste emerges due to mining operation which is hazardous. A typical example is acid mine drainage from dumped mine wastes.

Some of the gaseous waste includes NO_2, CO, SO_2, volatile hydrocarbons etc. Chemical reaction may take place in air producing secondary pollutants. SO_2 combines with oxygen to produce SO_3, which in turn combines with suspended water droplets to produce H_2SO_4 and fall on ground as acid rain. Natural breakdown of uranium in the geoenvironment emits cancer causing radon gas into atmosphere.

10.4 CONTAMINANT TRANSPORT [Nov. 15, 16]

Rate of flow of the leachate as it travels into unsaturated soil is dependent on the hydraulic gradient causing flow, the permeability of the soil, the initial water content of the soil and the infiltration capacity.

Once it reaches the ground water, the process governing contaminant transport in the saturated zone includes:

- The advective process i.e. flow under a hydraulic gradient causing movement in the direction of ground water flow.

- The diffusive process i.e. flow under a concentration gradient causing expansion in other directions.

- The dispersive process i.e. flow under variable velocity causing expansion in various directions.

- Other processes including coupled processes.

The rate of travel of contaminant is very slow i.e. less than a metre to few tens of metres per year.

Not all contaminants are transported in liquid phase. Some of them such as methane, CO_2, gases produced during biodegradation of municipal solid waste (MSW), petrol leaking from underground storage tank can travel in gaseous phase as pore gas in the unsaturated soil zone above ground water table. Gaseous contaminants spread faster than ground water contaminants.

10.5 EFFECTS OF SUBSURFACE CONTAMINATION [Dec. 13, May 14]

In most of the cases, wastes are disposed off indiscriminately in low-lying areas without taking adequate engineering measures to effectively contain it. This results in a highly unhygienic and unhealthy environment leading to breeding of pests, mosquitoes and several harmful microorganisms. Many of the emerging diseases found these days are direct impact of geoenvironmental contamination due to wastes.

During precipitation, or ground water coming in contact with these wastes generates contaminated water called leachate that can travel far field and pollute the surface and ground water resources. Many of the harmful heavy metals can also travel along with the leachate if it is not contained properly.

Some of the solid waste such as excavation and mining waste, fly ash (wet and dry) from thermal power plants requires large area of land for its storage as wastes. This in turn would interact with rain water and can cause contamination. Several harmful heavy metals well above the contamination limit can enter the life cycle of organisms living in close proximity with such disposal sites.

Disruption of drinking water supply due to contamination of ground water acquifer resulting into serious consequences as remediation of ground water quality is extremely costly and time consuming.

Increase in ground water and soil salinity and uptake of contamination by plant roots resulting in loss of soil fertility and agricultural output.

Most of the impacts are realized much later from rigorous studies, and by the time the damage would have been done. Hence, remediation becomes a tedious and cost-intensive affair. This makes geoenvironmental engineering a challenging and much needed subject. There is a need to focus on research that would help to predict and minimize the long term impact of indiscriminate and mismanaged waste contamination.

10.6 CONTROL AND REMEDIATION   [May 14, 15, 17, Nov. 15]

Based on the toxic level of contaminants and the risk it pose to the environment, a suitable remediation method is selected. It must be noted that the remediation does not aim for entire decontamination. The major focus is to bring the contamination level well below the regulatory toxic limit. This is done by removing the toxic contaminants and/or immobilizing the contaminant that prevents its movement through subsurface geoenvironment. The remediation methods are broadly classified as physico-chemical, biological, electrical, thermal and combination of these methods.

(a) Removal and treatment of contaminated soil :

One of the simplest physical methods for remediation is by removing the contaminated soil and replacing it with clean soil. Essentially, it is a dig, dump and replace procedure. Such a method is practically possible only if the spatial extent and depth of the contaminated region is small. The dug out contaminated soil can be either disposed off in an engineered landfill or subjected to simple washing as shown in Fig. 10.1.

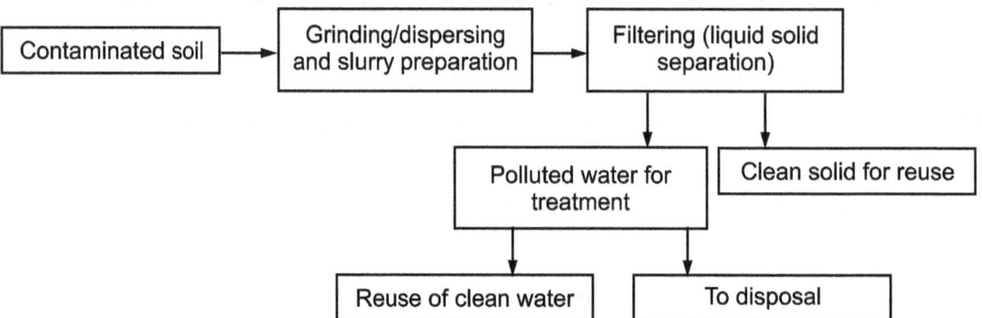

Fig. 10.1 : Soil washing for granular soils contaminated with inorganic pollutant

However, washing procedure is mostly suitable for granular soils with less clay content and contaminated with inorganic pollutants. For clay dominated soils, a chemical dispersion agent need to be added to deflocculate and then chemical washing is employed to break the retention of contaminants with the clay surface. Incineration is suggested for soils contaminated with organic pollutants. In case, it is necessary to remove organic pollutants then certain solvents or surfactants are used as washing agents.

The method is directly applied in-situ where solvent, surfactant solution or water mixed with additives is used to wash the contaminants from the saturated zone by injection and recovery system. The additives are used to enhance contaminant release and mobility resulting in increased recovery and hence decreased soil contamination.

(b) Vacuum extraction :   [Nov. 15,16 May 16]

This method is one of the most widely used in-situ treatment technologies. This method is cost-effective but time consuming and ineffective in water saturated soil. The technique, as depicted in Fig. 10.2, is useful for extracting contaminated ground water and soil vapor from a limited subsurface depth. The contaminated water is then subjected to standard chemical and biological treatment techniques. Vacuum technique is also useful when soil-water is contaminated with volatile organic compound (VOC). The method is then termed as "air sparging". Sometimes biodegradation is clubbed with air sparging for enhanced removal of VOC. Such a technique is then termed as biosparging.

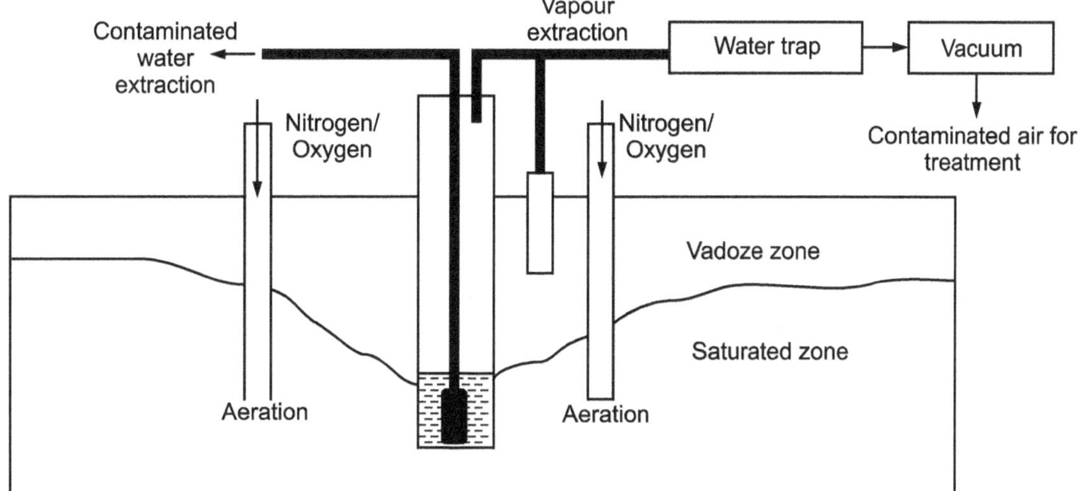

Fig. 10.2 : A schematic diagram for vacuum extraction procedure

An injecting medium is used to extract soil-water and/or soil-air. When oxygen is used instead of nitrogen as the injecting medium, it enhances aerobic biodegradation. Soil structure influences a lot on the passage of extracted water and vapour and hence on the success of vacuum extraction technique. It is not only important that the injecting medium is delivered efficiently but also the extracted product reaches the exit with less hindrance. Granular soils provide better passage whereas the presence of clay and organic matter impedes the transmission of both fluid and vapour. Organic matter provides high retention leading to less volatilization. High density and water content also minimize transmissivity. Apart from soil, the VOC properties such as solubility, sorption, vapour pressure, concentration etc. also influence the extraction process.

(c) Solidification and Stabilization :   (Dec. 14)

This is the process of immobilizing toxic contaminants so that it does not have any effect temporarily and spatially. Stabilization-solidification (SS) is performed in single step or in two steps. In single step, the polluted soil is mixed with a special binder so that polluted soil is fixed and rendered insoluble. In the two step process, the polluted soil is first made insoluble and non-reactive and in the second step it is solidified. SS process is mostly justified for highly toxic pollutants. In-situ SS process is mostly influenced by the transmissivity characteristics of the soil, viscosity and setting time of the binder. Well compacted soil, high clay and organic content do not favour in-situ SS.

In ex-situ methods, polluted soil is first grinded, dispersed, and then mixed with binder material. The resultant SS material need to be disposed in a well contained landfill. It is essential that the resultant SS product does not undergo leaching. The common binders used in practice include cement, lime, fly ash, clays, zeolites, pozzolonic products etc. Organic binders include bitumen, polyethylene, epoxy and resins. These organic binders are used for soil contaminated with organic pollutants.

(d) Chemical Decontamination :   [May 16]

This method is mostly applicable for those soils which have high sorbed concentration of inorganic heavy metals (IHM). The first method is to understand the nature of bonding between the pollutant and the soil surface. A suitable extractant need to be selected for selective sequential extraction (SSE) of IHM from the soil mass. The extractants include electrolytes, weak acids, complexing agents, oxidizing and reducing agents, strong acids etc. The use of these extractants in single or in combination will depend upon the concentration of IHM and nature of the soil mass. In-situ application (as depicted in Fig. 10.3) of extractants would remove IHM from the soil surface and enter into the pore water. The pore water is pumped and treated (pump and treat method) on the ground. While treating the pumped water, both extractants and IHM are removed.

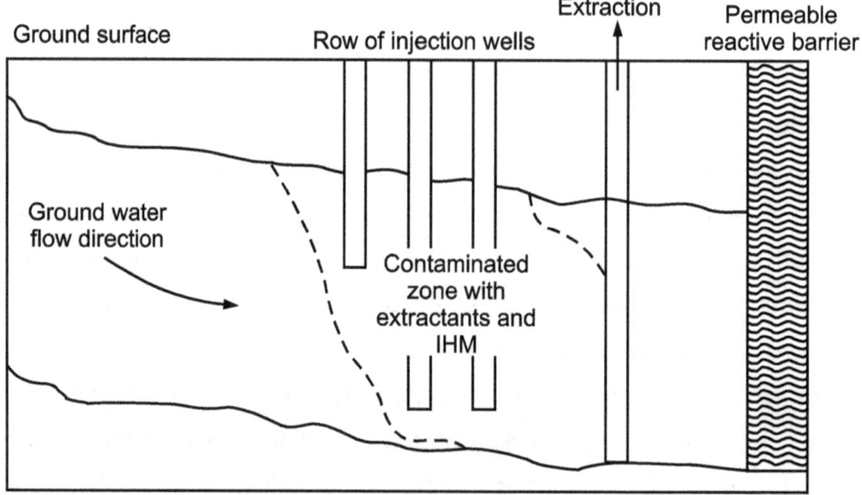

Fig. 10.3 : A schematic diagram for in-situ chemical decontamination

Another method is to allow the contaminated pore water to flow through a permeable reactive barrier (PRB). Hence, the placement of the barrier is determined by the direction of flow of ground water. The material packed in the barrier will retain IHM by exchange (sorption), complexation or precipitation reaction. The transmission and the reaction time determine the thickness of the reactive barrier to be provided. The material to be provided in the barrier is influenced by the knowledge of IHM to be removed. This is mainly due to the fact that the above mentioned reaction occurs differently when IHM is present as single or as multiple species.

The successful use of PRB or treatment wall (TW) depends upon its location such that majority of the contaminated ground water flows through it. It is essential to have a good knowledge on the hydrogeological conditions where such barriers need to be placed. In some cases, sheet pile walls are used to confine the flow towards the permeable barrier. Some of the materials used in such PRBs are exchange resins, activated carbon, zeolites, various biota, ferric oxides, ferrous hydroxide etc. Hydraulic conductivity of the PRB should be greater than or equal to the surrounding soil for proper permeation to occur. Further, reaction kinetics and permeability of the barrier would determine the thickness of the wall to be provided such that enough residence time is achieved for the removal reaction to occur.

Remediation being very expensive and difficult, to control further subsurface contamination following measures can be adopted:

(a) For Solid Wastes : Providing impermeable flexible liners at the base and covers on top of all solid waste disposal facilities to minimize leachate formation.

(b) For Slurry Wastes : Providing storage in ponds and impoundments having incrementally raised embankments and impermeable flexible liners at base.

(c) For Liquids : Providing storage in ponds with impermeable flexible liners

(d) For Underground Liquid Storage Facilities : providing double walled tanks with leakage detection system placed between the walls.

10.7 SOIL-A GEOCHEMICAL TRAP [Dec. 13, 14]

Soil acts as a geochemical filter or 'geochemical trap' as it interacts with contaminants present resulting in immobilization and retardation of some of the contaminants. And the ability of soil to interact and retard contaminants is called the geochemical attenuation capacity of the soil. This attenuation capacity can be determined by laboratory tests and is highest in clays but least in sands and gravel.

When the source of contamination is small or temporary, the influence of attenuation on contaminant transport is important whereas it is limited for large and permanent sources.

The contaminated soil strata beneath the waste dump is made of three zones:

(a) Core Zone : In this zone concentration of contaminants is same as source due to passage of large amount of leachate.

(b) Neutralized Zone : It is the zone away from the core zone and comprises only of non-reactive contaminants which are not affected by soil.

(c) Active Zone : It is the zone in between the above two, where intense interaction between soil and contaminants takes place and immobilization of some reactive contaminants.

10.8 DETECTION OF POLLUTED ZONES

To plan for control measures at a contaminated site, it is necessary to detect and identify the lateral and vertical extent of subsurface contamination which can be done by geophysical methods, drilling and sampling. Of the various geophysical methods, the electromagnetic method helps in measurements of subsurface conductivity down to few tens of meter depth. Changes in conductivity are an indicator of subsurface contamination since presence of inorganic contaminants increases the conductivity of ground water whereas non-polar organic contaminants have the reverse effect.

Drilling and sampling method is time consuming and tedious but more accurate. It is carried out to the required depth at predetermined grid points spaced at regular intervals so as to know the lateral and vertical extent of contaminants. The solid, liquid and gaseous phases of the retrieved samples are separated by vacuum extraction in the laboratory and each fraction is analysed for the presence of contaminants.

Monitoring Effectiveness of Designed Facilities :

Monitoring is required to keep check at sites where waste disposal is carefully organised to ensure early detection of seepage or occurrence of any leakage. Small diameter monitoring wells are placed, such that one is on upstream side and three on downstream side with respect to direction of ground water flow. For thicker acquifer, cluster of wells with screens at different depth for sample collection are provided. With comparison of values of monitored parameters from downstream well with respect to upstream well values, any significant changes with time can be detected.

To detect pore gas in the unsaturated zone, Gas Monitoring Wells are provided having larger diameter than the ground water monitoring wells. Portable gas chromatographs can be directly lowered into them or placed above them to detect presence of gases such as methane etc.

SUMMARY

1. Geoenviromental engineering details with the interrelationship among environment, ground surface and subsurface.
2. Soil plays a very vital role in geoevironmental projects and the property in which it becomes important is problem specific.
3. The remediation methods are brog classified as physico – chemical, biological, electrical, thermal and combination of above methods.
4. Soil acts as a geochemical filter as it interacts with contaminants and retardation.
5. Monitoring is required to keep check at sites where waste disposal in carefully orgnised to ensure detection of seepage.

EXERCISE

1. Explain the importance and scope of geoenvironmental engineering.
2. How soil characteristics are important in geoenvironmental engineering?
3. Write note on : Impact of contamination on geoenvironment.
4. Discuss sources and types of ground contamination.
5. Explain controlling techniques for subsurface contamination.
6. How can the effect of remediation be monitored?
7. How can the horizontal and vertical extent of contamination be determined?
8. Which are the zones in the contaminated soil strata below the waste dump?
9. State the various remediation techniques.
10. Explain pump and treat method of remediation.
11. What is biosparging?
12. How can the control on subsurface contamination be achieved?
13. Explain vacuum extraction technique.
14. How chemical decontamination is carried out?
15. What is Stabilization-solidification, explain?

SOLVED UNIVERSITY QUESTIONS

December 2013

1. What is subsurface contamination ? What are the effects of subsurface contamination.   **[5]**
   [**Ans.**: Refer Article 10.3, 10.5]
2. Write short note on 'geotechnical trap".   **[5]**
   [**Ans.**: Refer Article 10.7]
3. Write a short note on the pressure and significant depth with suitable sketch.   **[6]**

May 2014

1. Write a note on impact of contamination on Geoenvironment.   **[6]**
   [**Ans. :** Refer Article 10.6]

2. What are the effects of sub surface contamination ? Enlist the remedial measures to control the same. **[7]**
[**Ans. :** Refer Article 10.5]

December 2014

1. State and describe the zones in the contaminated soil strata below the waste dump and how is their extent determined ? **[6]**
[**Ans. :** Refer Article 10.7]

2. What is subsurface contamination? Discuss the solidification and stabilization method for control of subsurface contamination. **[6]**
[**Ans. :** Refer Article 10.3, 10.6 (c)]

May 2015

1. Discuss sources and types of ground contamination. **[6]**
[**Ans. :** Refer Article 10.6]

November 2015

1. Explain how the transportation of the contaminant occurs and describe the vacuum extraction process. **[7]**
[**Ans. :** Refer Article 10.6(b)]

May 2016

1. What is biosparging? Also explain vacuum extraction technique with sketch. **[7]**
[**Ans. :** Refer Article 10.6 (b)]

2. How is chemical decontamination carried out? Explain with a neat sketch. **[6]**
[**Ans. :** Refer Article 10.6(d)]

November 2016

1. Discuss the role of soil in geoenvironmental applications and state the process governing contaminant transport. **[6]**
[**Ans. :** Refer Article 10.2, 10.4]

2. Explain the vacuum extraction technique for insitu treatment of soil contamination.**[7]**
[**Ans. :** Refer Article 10.6(b)]

May 2017

1. Discuss sources and types of ground contamination. **[6]**
[**Ans. :** Refer Article 10.3]

2. Explain how soil acts as a geochemical trap an state the various remediation techniques. **[7]**
[**Ans. :** Refer Article 10.6]

Appendix

ORAL QUESTIONS AND ANSWERS

SPECIFIC GRAVITY TEST

Q. 1 Why conical cap is used for a pycnometer ?

Ans. : Due to the conical cap, the area of cross-section reduces and it helps in expelling the air bubbles present.

Q. 2 Whether will you use kerosene or distilled water for determination of specific gravity ? Why ? When you prefer to use kerosene, and why ?

Ans. : Wetting of fine grained soils is relatively difficult than wetting of coarse grained soil. Kerosene is a better *wetting agent* than distilled water. Hence, the use of kerosene is preferred in respect of clayey soils

Q. 3 Define specific gravity and state its units. Give a few values of specific gravity of some substances.

Ans. :

- Specific gravity is a ratio of mass of dry soil to the mass of equal volume of water.
- Since it is a ratio of masses, specific gravity has no units.
- Examples :

Material	Specific gravity
Cement	3.14
Steel	7.8
Mercury	13.4

Aggregate :

Light weight = 2.2 to 2.4 Medium weight = 2.6 to 2.8

Heavy weight = 2.8 to 3.2 Kerosene = 0.8

Q. 4 In what way will the results of a test to find specific gravity of a fine grained soil sample be affected if :

(i) Soil sample used is moist.

(ii) Oven dried.

(iii) Test is carried when temperature is high, say 40°C.

(iv) Kerosene is used, instead of distilled water.

Ans. :

- It is absolutely essential that, the soil sample is oven dried. If moist soil is used, we will get G_{app} i.e. apparent specific gravity, which will be lesser than the true specific gravity G.

$$\text{Moisture content,} \quad m = \left\{ \left(\frac{G_{app}}{G_{app} - 1} \right) \left(\frac{G - 1}{G} \right) - 1 \right\} \times 100$$

- Results will be OK, provided wetting of sample is perfect.
- As the temperature increases, specific gravity of water will decrease, (as compared to specific gravity standardized at 27°C).

$$(G_{soil} @ 27°C) (G_{water} @ 27°C) = (G_{water} @ 40°C) (G_{soil} @ 40°C)$$

- If kerosene is used, better results will be obtained, since wetting of soil with kerosene will be better. However, initially specific gravity of kerosene must be determined accurately.

$$G_{soil} = (G_{kerosene}) \left[\cfrac{\text{Dry mass of soil}}{\left(\begin{array}{c}\text{Pycnometer +}\\\text{Kerosene + Soil}\end{array}\right) - \left(\begin{array}{c}\text{Pycnometer}\\\text{+ Kerosene}\end{array}\right)} \right]$$

Q. 5   During construction of a highway embankment soil having true specific gravity 9 is used. The soil with varying water content is used in compacting the embankment. How will you determine the water content of various samples, without making use of an oven or any heating arrangement.

Ans. : Let G_{ap1}, G_{ap2}, ... be the apparent specific gravities of soil samples with water content m_1, m_2, m_3, ... etc.

Then, $$m_1 = \left\{ \left(\frac{G_{app}}{G_{app} - 1} \right) \times \left(\frac{G - 1}{G} \right) - 1 \right\} \times 100$$

Similarly, knowing G_{ap2}, G_{ap3}, ..., etc., m_1, m_2, m_3, ..., etc. can be found out. Thus, the results can be obtained, without actually heating and drying the soil sample.

Q. 6 A student, while determining the specific gravity of soil sample found it to be 2.3 as against the true specific gravity of 2.7. All weights were taken accurately. What must be the reason for the error ?

Ans. : While taking the soil sample, the sample must be moist. Also, after placing the sample in the specific gravity bottle, the water in the specific gravity bottle should be boiled to expel air. If this precaution is not taken, errors will be introduced.

Q. 7 Find water content of soil in Q. No. 6.

Ans. : $$m \% = \left\{ \left(\frac{G_{app}}{G_{app} - 1} \right) \left(\frac{G_{true} - 1}{G_{true}} \right) - 1 \right\} \times 100$$

$$= \left\{ \left(\frac{2.3}{2.3 - 1} \right) \left(\frac{2.7 - 1}{2.7} \right) - 1 \right\} \times 100$$

$$= \left(\frac{2.3}{1.3} \times \frac{1.7}{2.7} - 1 \right) = \frac{3.91 - 3.51}{3.51} \times 100 = \frac{0.4}{3.51} \times 100 = 11.1\%$$

LIQUID LIMIT, PLASTIC LIMIT, SHRINKAGE LIMIT

Q. 1 What is the use of knowing the liquid limit, plastic limit and shrinkage limit of a soil sample ?

Ans. : At liquid limit, shear strength of the soil is zero and at this moisture content, soil starts behaving like a liquid.

Soil with water content between liquid limit and plastic limit behaves like a plastic material. i.e. if load is applied on such soils, deformation will take place and the same will not be regained like a elastic material.

By knowing shrinkage limit, we know whether the soil has tendency towards low, medium, high shrinkage or swelling property. Swelling soils are problematic.

Q. 2 How will you prepare a soil sample to carry out consistency limit tests ?

Ans. : About 150 to 200 gm of *air dried* soil passing through an IS sieve of 425 μ is taken and thoroughly mixed with distilled water to form a thick paste and is left to stand for 24 hours to ensure uniform distribution of water.

Soil paste so formed is used to carry liquid limit, plastic limit and shrinkage limit tests.

Q. 3 (i) State difference between Casagrande grooving tool and ASTM grooving tool.

(ii) Which tool is used when ? Why ?

(iii) What is similarity between the two tools ?

Ans. : When soil sample consists of sufficient clayey material, a groove can be made in the soil with Casagrande grooving tool. However, if the soil consists of non-plastic clay or silt, and if an effort is made to cut groove with Casagrande grooving tool, the soil goes on tearing and neat groove cannot be made. In such cases, groove can be made by using ASTM tools. The handle of each tool is such that, the thickness of the handle is 1 cm and the same is used as a gauge to adjust the height of drop of cup.

Q. 4 How the height of fall of Casagrande cup to 1 cm adjusted ?

Ans. : Any gauge with thickness of 1 cm is inserted below the Casagrande cup and the screw with which the height of fall of the cup can be adjusted is moved up or down, in such a way, that when the cup drops off the gauge, it should give least sound.

Q. 5 The results of liquid limit test are plotted on a semi-log paper i.e. number of blows to close the groove on log scale and % water content on y-axis. What is the necessity of using semi-log paper when number of blows range between 10 to 50.

Ans. : If instead of using semi-log scale, arithmetic scale is used, and a graph is plotted, it will turn out to be a curve, log spiral curve as shown in Fig. A.1 (a) below. However, when log scale is used, the graph will be as shown in Fig. A.1 (b). tan θ, the slope of graph in Fig. A.1 (b) is defined as the flow index. It is easier to determine the same with the help of the graph in Fig. A.1 (b).

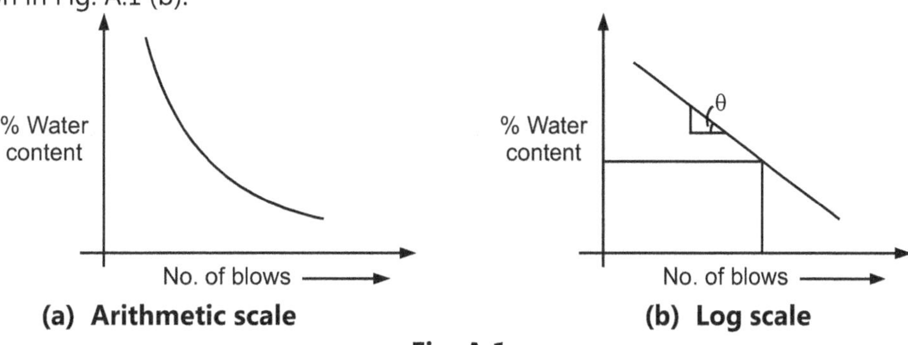

Fig. A.1

Q. 6 While carrying out liquid limit test, if we adjust water content, such that the groove closes, when the number of blows is 25, the problem of determination of limit is solved. Also water content of only one sample is required to be found out and there is no need to draw a graph using semi-log paper. Despite of such advantages, why do we plot a graph by taking at least four readings ?

Ans. : If we just want to know liquid limit, then the method suggested is OK. However, by plotting the graph of water content versus number of blows (by scale), we can also get information about the flow index. With the knowledge of flow index, we can find out the toughness index, which otherwise is not possible.

Q. 7 What is the necessity of finding flow index ?

Ans. : A graph of liquid limit test for three soils A, B, C is shown below. By knowing (I_f) flow index, we can find out toughness index (I_t) of the soils as follows,

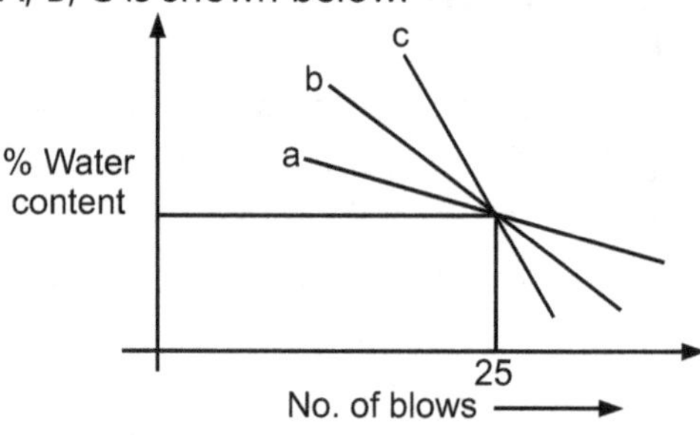

Fig. A.2

$$I_t = \frac{\text{Plasticity index}}{\text{Flow index}} \quad ... (1)$$

It is clear from equation (1) that, lower the flow index, higher will be toughness index. i.e. gentler the slope of the graph, tougher will be the soil.

From the graph, it is noticed that, graph of soil A, B and C meet at a point, when number of blows are 25. Thus, all the three soils have the *same liquid limit at that point.* The possibility of soil A being tougher than soil B and soil B tougher than soil C is very high.

Q. 8 When the plastic limit of soil is to be found out, the thickness of thread (when it is about to reach plastic limit) has to be 3 mm. How do you measure the thickness of thread ?

Ans. : By making use of graph paper, draw two parallel lines 3 mm apart. Over these lines, place a glass plate. Place the thread of the soil, between the two parallel lines and check if the thread is thicker or thinner than 3 mm.

Q. 9 (a) How is I_p i.e. plasticity index determined ?

(b) What does it indicate, if I_p is (i) too less, (ii) medium, (iii) high ?

Ans. : Difference between plastic limit and liquid limit of a soil, gives the value of plasticity index. I_p is an indication of clay content in soil. Higher I_p indicates that the soil has higher clay content, whereas very low plastic index is an indication of low clay content and soil is a non-plastic clay.

Q. 10 In what way information about plastic limit and liquid limit is useful ?

Ans.

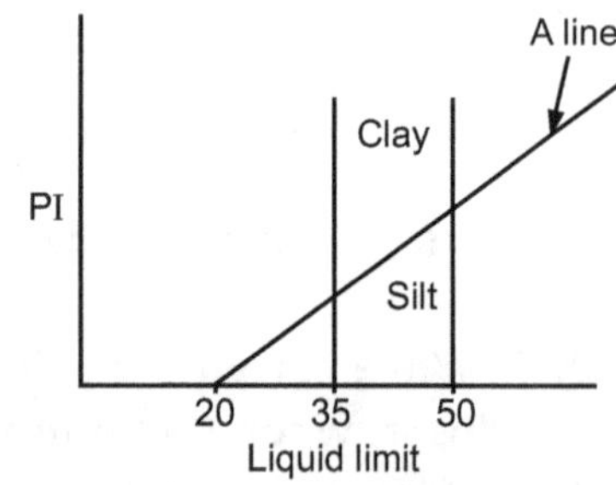

Fig. A.3

- By knowing LL and PL, we can classify the soil, with the help of a plasticity chart.
- We can determine (a) consistency index or liquidity index.
- If water content of soil is at liquid limit, or more than the liquid limit, it indicates that the soil will not have any shearing resistance.
- If water content of soil is between liquid limit and plastic limit, it indicates that soil is in plastic stage.

Q. 11 (a) State the mistakes, which a student has committed in the following graph meant for liquid limit test.

(b) Draw the correct graph.

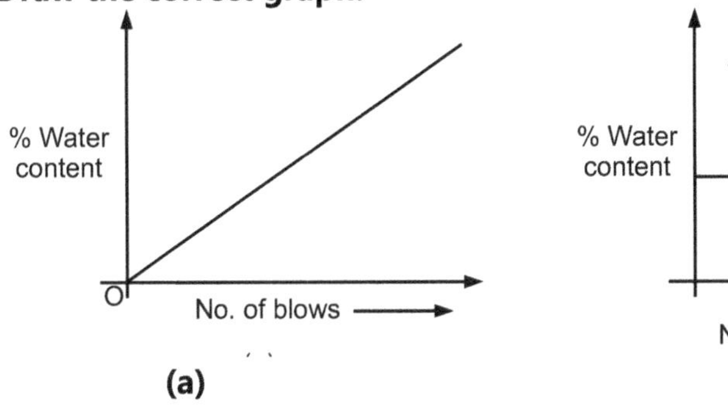

Fig. A.4

- Scale and units on X and Y axis are not given.
- On the log scale, we cannot plot "O". The line is passing through the origin. This is incorrect.
- The flow line slopes down from left to right, whereas it is wrongly sloping up from left to right [Fig. A.4 (a)].

Q. 12 State, whether the following statement is true or false : "As water content of the soil is reduced, volume of the soil continues to decrease".

Ans. : The statement is half true. It should be "As water content of the soil is reduced, volume of soil goes on decreasing till it reaches the shrinkage limit", and any further reduction in water content thereafter does not decrease the volume of soil as shown in the Fig. A.5.

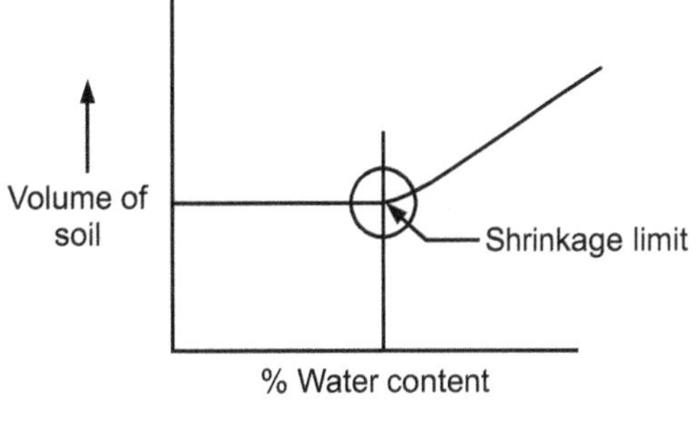

Fig. A.5

SIEVE ANALYSIS

Q. 1 How do you representative soil sample to carry out dry sieve analysis ?

Ans. : A method called "quartering" is adopted for this purpose. It consists of taking about 6 to 8 kg of sample and spreading it on floor uniformly in the form of thin circle. The sample is split into four quadrants. Soil from the opposite two quadrants say 2 and 4 are only taken and mixed thoroughly. Of this homogeneous mix, only half portion weighing about 1.5 to 2 kg is taken for sieve analysis.

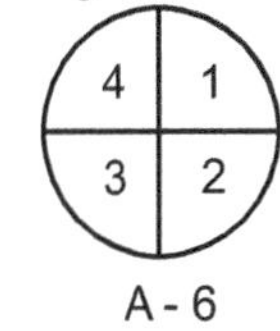

Fig. A.6

Q. 2 Why is the representative sample not directly used to carry out sieve analysis ?

Ans. :

- The representative sample contains any organic matter, then it is air-dried and then pulverized to separate various soil particles.

- If the representative sample does not contain any organic material, then it is oven-dried and then pulverized using wooden or rubber mallet, rubber pestle and mortar. Hence the representative sample does not directly used to carry out sieve analysis.

Q. 3 What will happen, if the sample is not oven dried and pulverized before sieve analysis ?

Ans. : If soil sample contains cohesive fine particles, then, due to moisture, the particles will adhere to coarse particles. For example, in case of black cotton soil, the particles will be in the form of clod and will lead to the wrong conclusion.

Q. 4 If set of sieves of 45 cm diameter and 30 cm diameter are available. Should the quantity of soil sample be the same ?

Ans. : Quantity of soil sample to be taken depends upon

- Maximum size of material present. For example, 20 mm, 4.75 mm.
- Diameter of sieve i.e. 30 cm or 45 cm.

IS sieve	Quantity of material to be taken	
	45 cm diameter sieves	30 cm diameter sieves
20 mm	4 kg	2 kg
4.75 mm	1 kg	0.5 kg

Q. 5 When is the method of dry sieve analysis is used ?

Ans. : Dry sieve analysis is adopted, when less than 10% of the material passes through 75 μ sieve.

Q. 6 (a) What and how the information is obtained to plot the results on a graph paper of sieve analysis ?

(b)   Why is semi-log paper is used ?

(c)   What is plotted on the log scale ?

Ans. : A graph of % finer than versus sieve size in mm on x-axis using log scale is required to be plotted. To get information about "% finer than" following steps are adopted :

- Sieves are arranged in the following sequence : 40 mm, 20 mm, 10 mm, 4.75 mm, 2.36 mm, 1.18 mm, 600 μ, 300 μ, 150 μ, 75 μ and Pan.
- Weight of soil retained on each sieve is determined, say W_1, W_2, W_3, ... etc.
- Cumulative % of weight retained on each sieve is determined.

$$\text{For example, } P_1 = \frac{W_1}{W} \;;\quad P_2 = \frac{W_1 + W_2}{W} \;;\quad P_3 = \frac{W_1 + W_2 + W_3}{W} \;;$$

$$P_n = \frac{W_1 + W_2 + \ldots\ldots + W_n}{W}$$

Corresponding "% finer than" are obtained : $(100 - P_1)$; $(100 - P_2)$; $(100 - P_3)$; ......, $(100 - p_n)$.

These % are plotted on y-axis using arithmetic scale and sieve sizes are plotted on x-axis using log-scale.

(b) and (c) There is vast difference in sieve sizes ranging from 20 mm to 75 μ and the same cannot be accommodated using arithmetic scale. Hence, log scale is used on x-axis to plot sieve sizes.

Q. 7 **(a)** **What is meant by D_{60}, D_{30} and D_{10} size ?**

(b) **In what way these sizes are useful ?**

(c) **Why is D_{10} size called as effective grain size and in what way is it useful ?**

Ans. :

- From the result of sieve analysis plotted, x-co-ordinate i.e. sieve size for the following y-co-ordinates are determined :

  For % finer than 60%   ...   Find sieve size $\rightarrow$ It is called as D_{60} size.

  For % finer than 30%   ...   Find sieve size on x-axis. $\rightarrow$ It is called as D_{30} size.

  For % finer than 10%   ...   Find sieve size on x-axis $\rightarrow$ It is called as D_{10} size.

- For example, if D_{10} size is found to be 0.6 mm, it will indicate that, only 10% of the soil samples are finer than 0.6 mm i.e. 90% of the particles are coarser than 0.6 mm. By knowing D_{60}, D_{30} and D_{10} sizes, we can determine the coefficient of

  uniformity, $C_u = \dfrac{D_{60}}{D_{10}}$ and coefficient of curvature, $C_c = \dfrac{D_{30}^2}{D_{60} \times D_{10}}$.

- D_{10} size is a very important size, because by knowing the same, we can approximately find permeability k of the soil, using Hazen William formula,

  $$k = 100\, D_{10}^2 \text{ in cm/sec } (D_{10} \text{ expressed in mm})$$

  Thus, D_{10} size is very effective in finding the approximate permeability of sand. Hence, it is called as effective grain size.

Q. 8 Suppose, you are not supplied with a semi-log paper and only an ordinary graph paper is available. How can you plot various sieves on log scale ?

Ans. : It will be noticed that, sieve sizes used for sieve analysis get doubled subsequently.

$$2 = \frac{150\,\mu}{75\,\mu} = \frac{300\,\mu}{150\,\mu} = \frac{600\,\mu}{300\,\mu} = \frac{1.18 \text{ mm}}{600\,\mu} = \frac{2.36}{1.18} \approx \frac{4.75}{2.36} \approx \ \dots\dots\dots$$

Taking advantage of this property, if we plot various sieves at a fixed interval of 1 cm or 2 cm or 3 cm, all the sieves will automatically get plotted on the log scale.

x	x	x	x	x				
75 μ	150 μ	300 μ	600 μ	1.18 mm	2.36 mm	4.75 mm	10 mm	20 mm	40 mm

x = 1 cm or 2 cm or any fixed distance

$$(\log 150 - \log 75) = (\log 300 - \log 150)$$
$$= (\log 600 - \log 300) = (\log 1.18 - \log 0.6)$$
$$= (\log 2.36 - \log 1.18) = (\log 4.75 - \log 2.36)$$
$$= (\log 10 - \log 4.75) = (\log 20 - \log 10)$$

Q. 9 Plot the grain size distribution curves for the following :

(i) **Well graded gravel,**

(ii) **Well graded sand,**

(iii) **Standard sand of size 1 mm,**

(iv) **20 mm and 40 mm single sized aggregate for concreting.**

Ans. :

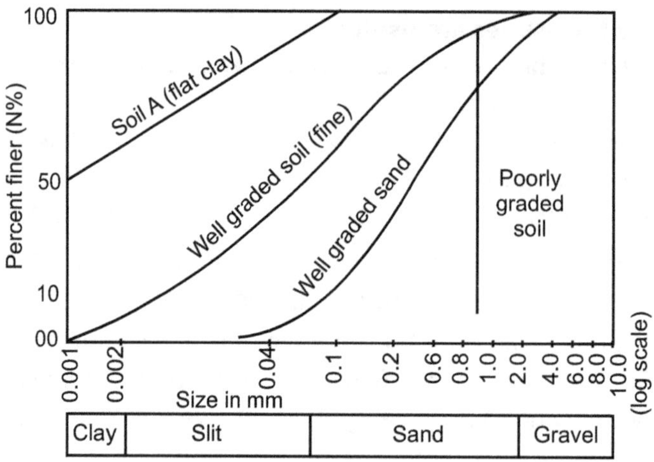

Fig. A.7

Q. 10 Explain with reasons, whether uniformity coefficient can be less or more than unity.

Ans. : $C_u = \dfrac{D_{60}}{D_{10}}$. D_{60} size can never be less than D_{10} size.

Hence C_u cannot be *less than* one.

In case of purely uniformly graded sand, since $D_{60} = D_{30} = D_{10}$, C_u is equal to one.

Q. 11 Two kg of soil sample is given. How and when will you classify a given soil as coarse grained soil and fine grained soil ?

Ans. : Sieve the soil sample through 75 μ sieve. If more than 50% of soil (i.e. more than one kg in this case) is retained on 75 μ sieve, then it is called as coarse grained soil, whereas if more than 50% of the soil passes through 75 μ, then it is called as fine grained soil.

Note : Many students wrongly state that, what is retained on 75 μ sieve is coarse grained and soil that passes 75 μ is fine grained soil. We are considering complete sample of 2 kg and not a part thereof. Many students as well wrongly make mention of 2.36 mm or 4.75 mm sieve. To distinguish between fine grained soil and coarse grained soil, only one sieve viz. 75 μ sieve is required. Complete set of sieves is not required.

Q. 12 2 kg of soil sample is given to you. How you will find, whether the sample is gravelly soil, sandy soil or fine grained soil.

Ans. : As a first step, sieve the sample through 75 μ sieve. If more than 50% of the soil passes through it, then it will be a fine grained soil. If more than 50% of soil is retained on 75 μ, then it is coarse grained soil. Say 1.2 kg is retained. Sieve this 1.2 kg of soil through 4.75 mm sieve.

- If more than 50% of 1.2 kg of soil (i.e. soil retained on 75 μ sieve) is retained on 4.75 mm sieve, then it is gravelly.

- However, if more than $\dfrac{1.2}{2}$ = 0.6 kg passes through 4.75 mm sieve, then it is a sandy soil.

Q. 13 A sample of clayey or silty soil is given to you. Without carrying out any laboratory test, it is required to know, whether the given soil is clayey or silty. How you will proceed ?

Ans. : Make a thick paste of soil sample by adding adequate quantity of water.

- Place the soil sample on the palm of your hand, and shake the palm. If glittering surface is noticed, it indicates that it is a silty soil. The glittering surface will disappear, if sample is slightly pressed by fingers. On shaking once again the glittering surface will reappear. In respect of clayey sample, such phenomenon is not noticed.

- Take a cloth and smear the same with paste of soil. Allow the soil to dry. If soil sample can be removed with little brushing, then it is a silty soil. In case of clayey sample, the soil sticks to cloth firmly and cannot be removed easily.

DETERMINATION OF FIELD DENSITY BY (A) CORE CUTTER METHOD, (B) SAND REPLACEMENT METHOD AND (C) CLOD METHOD.

Determination of Field Density by a Core Cutter Method

Q. 1 Answer the following questions in respect of the core cutter method :

(i)   State the dimensions and volume of core cutter.

(ii)   Why is the height of the core cutter not a rounded figure say 150 mm or 200 mm ?

(iii) What is the necessity of providing a dolly over the core cutter ?

(iv)   Why is the edge of core cutter sharp ?

(v)   What will happen if core cutter is made of 1 cm thick pipe and edges of the core cutter are blunt ?

(vi)   How can you find the void ratio, porosity, % of saturation and dry density from the sample of this test ?

(vii) Can you determine field density by this method, in respect

    (a) Gravelly soil,   **(b) Dry sandy soil,**

    (c) Very soft clay,   **(d) Firm clay,**

    (e) Sand mixed with silt and clay.

Ans. :

- Inside diameter = 10 cm, height of core cutter = 12.75 cm, volume = 1000 cc or one litre.

- With height of 12.75 cm, the volume of core cutters is one litre. As a result, knowing the mass of soil in the core cutter, the bulk density of soil can be easily found out. For example, if the mass of soil in the core is 1.6 kg, then the bulk density will be 1600 kg/cu.m.

- Providing dolly has the following advantages :

    (a) The blows are received on the cutter through the dolly, hence the load is transferred uniformly and cutter is not damaged.

    (b) As the dolly is above the core cutter, the possibility of compressing the soil by a hammer is reduced considerably. In absence of a dolly, soil can get compressed, showing an incorrect increase in density of soil.

- and (v) the sharp edge of the core cutter helps in easy and quick penetration of the cutter in the soil. Thinner the walls of the core cutter, lesser volume of soil is required to be displaced, which results in lesser disturbance to the soil sample. Thicker the wall of the core cutter, larger will be the volume of soil displaced.
- Knowing the weight of the soil sample, water content w and specific gravity G, we can proceed as follows :

$$\gamma_{bulk} = \frac{\text{Mass of soil in kg}}{\text{Volume of soil in litre}} = \ldots\ldots \text{ kg/litre}$$

$$\gamma_{dry} = \frac{\gamma_{bulk}}{1 + w} = \frac{G \cdot \gamma_w}{1 + e}$$

Knowing w, G and assuming γ_w, we can find 'e'. Further

$$S \cdot e = w \cdot G$$

Knowing e, w, G, we can find "S" the % of saturation.

- (a) In case of gravelly soil, it is very difficult to drive a core cutter, hence it is not possible.
  (b) In case of dry sand, due to lack of cohesion, it is not possible to collect the sample. The sample will fall down from the core cutter.
  (c) Same as above.
  (d) and (e) In both these cases, it is possible to collect soil samples and determine the density.

Determination of Field Density by Sand Replacement Method

Q. 1 Answer the following questions in respect of Sand Replacement Method.

(i)   State the dimensions of the calibration cylinder. State its volume.

(ii)   Why is the cylinder named as calibration cylinder ?

(iii) How you can find the volume of the calibration cylinder without measuring its dimensions ?

(iv)   Why is the calibration cylinder and excavated hole filled by using ennore sand ?

(v)   Why is this method called "Sand replacement method" ?

(vi)   How can you find void ratio, porosity, % of saturation and dry density from the sample of this test ?

(vii) Can you determine the field density by this method, in respect of
(a) Gravelly soil,   **(b) Dry sandy soil,**
(c) Very soft clay,   **(d) Sand mixed with silt and clay.**

(viii) The bottom of the sand pouring cylinder, i.e. below the hole through which sand falls, has conical cavity. State the reason for the same.

Ans. :

- 10 cm diameter × 15 cm depth.
- With this cylinder, density of sand is determined/calibrated. Knowing the weight of sand filled in the excavated hole, V, volume of the soil removed is found out by the equation

$$V = \frac{\text{Weight of sand in hole}}{\text{Density of sand (using calibration cylinder)}}$$

- Weigh an empty calibration cylinder. Keep it on a weighing machine. Carefully fill the cylinder completely with water and find out W, weight of water in gm in the cylinder. Volume of cylinder in cc will equal to W.
- If standard sand is used everywhere, density of sand will be same. To have uniformity everywhere, standard sand is used.
- The excavated soil is removed and it is replaced by sand, hence it is called as sand replacement method.
- $$\gamma_{bulk} = \frac{\text{Weight of soil removed from hole}}{\left(\dfrac{\text{Weight of sand filled in the hole}}{\text{Density of sand using calibration cylinder}}\right)}$$

$$\gamma_{dry} = \left(\frac{\gamma_{bulk}}{1 + w}\right) = \frac{G \cdot \gamma_w}{1 + e}$$

$$S_r \cdot e = w \cdot G$$

Various parameters like γ_{dry}, e, S_r can be found out using the above equations assuming a suitable value of G.

- (a) It is difficult to make a hole in gravelly soil. However, if a hole can be made, density of soil can be determined.

  (b) In dry sand a hole cannot be made. The hole will collapse.

  (c)   Same as above.

  (d) and (e) It is possible to carry out the test and determine density.
- If sand is allowed to drop freely from a height, it will form a cone. The shape of the cone is similar to that at the bottom of the sand pouring cylinder.

Determination of Coefficient of Permeability using
(a) Variable Head Method, (b) Constant Head Method

Q. 1 Are different permeameters used to determine the coefficient of permeability by the two methods indicated above.

Ans. : No the same permeameter is used, in both the methods.

Q. 2 (a) Explain the various parts of the permeameter, dimensions and functions of each permeameter.

(b)   What is difference in proctor mould used for compaction test and this test ?

Ans.

- Internal dimensions and volume of proctor compaction mould and permeameter are same viz. 10 cm diameter × 12.7 cm height and volume = 1000 cc.
- The base plate of the mould is such that it houses a porous stone to drain water. Base plate below the porous plate is provided with channels to drain out water.
- An outlet is connected to the base plate so that the water can be allowed to drain out. At the top of the permeameter, two valves are provided : (a) Inlet valve to allow entry of water, (b) Air release valve, to permit the removal of the air bubble.
- A porous plate with filter paper is provided at the top of the sample.

Q. 3 Explain importance of air release valve.

Ans. Before carrying out the experiment, it is essential that any air bubble present in the mould as well as in the plastic tube or in the burette (to which plastic pipe is connected) is removed and discharged from the permeameter steady laminar flow. An air bubble, if any, present anywhere is likely to obstruct the discharge / seepage of water. To release the entrapped air, air release valve is opened.

Q. 4 Why is filter paper provided at the top and bottom of the soil sample ? Is it to obtain filtered water ?

Ans. : When water percolates through the porous stone, it is due to provision of filter paper. In the absence of filter paper, it is likely that, along with the percolating water, soil particles will be carried. Such soil particles can block the pores in the porous stone. This can be prevented by providing filter paper.

Q. 5 Explain step-by-step, how a sample with dry density γ_{dry} and water content w is compacted and placed in the mould.

Ans. :

- Volume of mould = 1000 cc.

$$\gamma_{bulk} \;=\; \gamma_{dry}\,(1 + w) \;\ldots\ldots\; kg/litre$$

  Prepare a soil sample, by taking 1 kg of oven dried sample and thoroughly mixing it with 1000 cc of water.

- The porous stone in the groove of base plate is removed and replaced with a dummy brass base disc whose size and shape is that of the porous stone. The mould is nut bolted to the base plate and the soil sample in layers is compacted exactly. $\gamma_{dry}\,(1 + w)$ gm of soil is compacted in the mould, so as to obtain desired bulk density.

- The mould is detached from the base plate, the brass disc is removed and replaced by the saturated porous stone. On the top of the porous stone, filter paper is provided. Once again the mould is connected to the base plate and nuts and bolts are fully tightened.

- On the top of the sample, wet filter paper, porous stone, and top cover plate is firmly secured with nuts and bolts. Inlet valve is kept open to permit percolation of water. Air release valve is opened, to allow escaping of entrapped air. When steady laminar flow condition is achieved, air release valve is closed.

MODEL QUESTION PAPER

Time : 2 Hrs. (Theory Exam.) **Maximum Marks : 50**

1. (a) The field density of a non-cohesive backfill was found to be 1647 kg/m^3 at water content of 8.4%. If the void ratio in the loosest and densest states were 0.859 and 0.462, determine the density index. **(4)**

(b) Explain the following terms : **(4)**

Plasticity index, liquidity index, consistency index, flow index.

OR

2. (a) Explain the term permeability and explain laboratory method of determining permeability. **(4)**

(b) Explain uses of flow net in detail. **(4)**

3. (a) Explain factors affecting compaction in detail. **(4)**

(b) Differentiate between compaction and consolidation. **(4)**

OR

4. (a) A water tank is supported by ring foundation having outer diameter of 8 m and inner diameter of 6 m. The uniform load intensity of the foundation is 200 kN/m^2. Compute the vertical stress caused by the water tank at the depth of 4 m below the center of the foundation. **(4)**

(b) Write short note on stress isobar. **(4)**

5. (a) Explain in detail vane shear test. **(6)**

(b) Explain in detail the effect of wall movement on earth pressure. **(4)**

(c) A vertical excavation was made in a clay deposit having unit weight of 20 kN/m^3 it cracked after the digging reached the depth of 4 m. Calculate total active earth pressure and total passive earth pressure. **(6)**

OR

6. (a) The following are the test results carried out on a soil sample while performing direct shear test determine the shear parameters and indicate the plain of failure.

Normal stress in kN/m^2	Shear stress in kN/m^2
10	15
16	19.5
20	22.5

If the same sample is tested in triaxial shear test by applying lateral stress of 10 kN/m^2 determine the deviator stress to cause failure. Draw Mohr's envelop and show pain of failure. **(6)**

(M.1)

(b)　Explain in detail Couloms wedge theory.　　**(6)**

　　For the retaining wall system, the following data was available :

　　Height of the wall = 7 m

　　Properties of the backfill, γ_d = 16 kN/m^2, ? = 35

　　Angle of friction = 20

　　Back of the wall is inclined at 20 to vertical

　　Backfill is sloping 1 : 10

　　Determine the magnitude of active earth pressure by Couloms method.

(c)　Explain in detail the rankines state of plastic equilibrium.　　**(4)**

7.　**(a)**　Explain role of soil in geoenvironmental application.　　**(6)**

　　(b)　For a slope of 10 m height with stability number equal to 0.055. What is the factor of safety ? Given : γ = 20 kN/m^3, C = 25 kN/m^2, ? = 0.　　**(6)**

　　(c)　Explain different types of slopes with diagrams.　　**(6)**

OR

8.　**(a)**　Classify slopes in detail and also explain modes of failure of slopes.　　**(6)**

　　(b)　Write short note on stability number.　　**(5)**

　　(c)　What are landslides ? Explain in detail remedial measures for improving stability of slopes.　　**(7)**

◈ ◈ ◈